Three by Ira Levin

Three by Ira Levin

Rosemary's Baby
This Perfect Day
The Stepford Wives

Ira Levin

Random House   New York

Library of Congress Cataloging in Publication Data

Levin, Ira.
Three by Ira Levin.

Contents: Rosemary's baby—This perfect day—
The Stepford wives.
1. Fantastic fiction, American. I. Title.
II. Title: 3 by Ira Levin.
PS3523.E7993A6   1985   813'.54   84-43002
ISBN 0-394-54512-5

Contents

Rosemary's Baby   1

This Perfect Day   163

The Stepford Wives   401

Rosemary's Baby

One

One

Rosemary and Guy Woodhouse had signed a lease on a five-room apartment in a geometric white house on First Avenue when they received word, from a woman named Mrs. Cortez, that a four-room apartment in the Bramford had become available. The Bramford, old, black, and elephantine, is a warren of high-ceilinged apartments prized for their fireplaces and Victorian detail. Rosemary and Guy had been on its waiting list since their marriage but had finally given up.

Guy relayed the news to Rosemary, stopping the phone against his chest. Rosemary groaned "Oh *no!*" and looked as if she would weep.

"It's too late," Guy said to the phone. "We signed a lease yesterday." Rosemary caught his arm. "Couldn't we get out of it?" she asked him. "Tell them something?"

"Hold on a minute, will you, Mrs. Cortez?" Guy stopped the phone again. "Tell them what?" he asked.

Rosemary floundered and raised her hands helplessly. "I don't know, the truth. That we have a chance to get into the Bramford."

"Honey," Guy said, "they're not going to care about that."

"You'll think of *something,* Guy. Let's just look, all right? Tell her we'll look. Please. Before she hangs up."

"We signed a *lease,* Ro; we're stuck."

"Please! She'll hang up!" Whimpering with mock anguish, Rosemary pried the phone from Guy's chest and tried to push it up to his mouth.

Guy laughed and let the phone be pushed. "Mrs. Cortez? It turns out there's a chance we'll be able to get out of it, because we haven't signed the actual lease yet. They were out of the forms so we only signed a letter of agreement. Can we take a look at the apartment?"

Mrs. Cortez gave instructions: they were to go to the Bramford between eleven and eleven-thirty, find Mr. Micklas or Jerome, and tell whichever they found that they were the party she had sent to look at 7E. Then they were to call her. She gave Guy her number.

"You see how you can think of things?" Rosemary said, putting Peds and yellow shoes on her feet. "You're a *marvelous* liar."

Guy, at the mirror, said, "Christ, a pimple."

"Don't squeeze it."

"It's only four rooms, you know. No nursery."

"I'd rather have four rooms in the Bramford," Rosemary said, "than a whole floor in that—that white cellblock."

"Yesterday you loved it."

"I liked it. I never loved it. I'll bet not even the architect loves it. We'll make a dining area in the living room and have a beautiful nursery, when and if."

"Soon," Guy said. He ran an electric razor back and forth across his upper lip, looking into his eyes, which were brown and large. Rosemary stepped into a yellow dress and squirmed the zipper up the back of it.

They were in one room, that had been Guy's bachelor apartment. It had posters of Paris and Verona, a large day bed and a pullman kitchen.

It was Tuesday, the third of August.

Mr. Micklas was small and dapper but had fingers missing from both hands, which made shaking hands an embarrassment, though not apparently for him. "Oh, an actor," he said, ringing for the elevator with a middle finger. "We're very popular with actors." He named four who were living at the Bramford, all of them well known. "Have I seen you in anything?"

"Let's see," Guy said. "I did *Hamlet* a while back, didn't I, Liz? And then we made *The Sandpiper* . . ."

"He's joking," Rosemary said. "He was in *Luther* and *Nobody Loves An Albatross* and a lot of television plays and television commercials."

"That's where the money is, isn't it?" Mr. Micklas said; "the commercials."

"Yes," Rosemary said, and Guy said, "And the artistic thrill, too."

Rosemary gave him a pleading look; he gave back one of stunned innocence and then made a leering vampire face at the top of Mr. Micklas's head.

The elevator—oak-paneled, with a shining brass handrail all around—was run by a uniformed Negro boy with a locked-in-place smile. "Seven," Mr. Micklas told him; to Rosemary and Guy he said, "This apartment has four rooms, two baths, and five closets. Originally the house consisted of very large apartments—the smallest was a nine—but now they've almost all been broken up into fours, fives, and sixes. Seven E is a four that was originally the back part of a ten. It has the original kitchen and master bath, which are enormous, as you'll soon see. It has the original master bedroom for its living room, another bedroom for its bedroom, and two servant's rooms thrown together for its dining room or second bedroom. Do you have children?"

"We plan to," Rosemary said.

"It's an ideal child's room, with a full bathroom and a large closet. The whole set-up is made to order for a young couple like yourselves."

The elevator stopped and the Negro boy, smiling, chivied it down, up, and down again for a closer alignment with the floor rail outside; and still smiling, pulled in the brass inner gate and the outer rolling door. Mr. Micklas stood aside and Rosemary and Guy stepped out—into a dimly lighted hallway walled and carpeted in dark green. A workman at a sculptured green door marked 7B looked at them and turned back to fitting a peepscope into its cut-out hole.

Mr. Micklas led the way to the right and then to the left, through short branches of dark green hallway. Rosemary and Guy, following, saw rubbed-away places in the wallpaper and a seam where it had lifted and was curling inward; saw a dead light bulb in a cut-glass sconce and a patched place of light green tape on the dark green carpet. Guy looked at Rosemary: *Patched carpet?* She looked away and smiled brightly: *I love it; everything's lovely!*

"The previous tenant, Mrs. Gardenia," Mr. Micklas said, not looking back at them, "passed away only a few days ago and nothing has been moved out of the apartment yet. Her son asked me to tell whoever looks at it that the rugs, the air conditioners, and some of the furniture can be had practically for the asking." He turned into another branch of hallway papered in newer-looking green and gold stripes.

"Did she die in the apartment?" Rosemary asked. "Not that it—"

"Oh, no, in a hospital," Mr. Micklas said. "She'd been in a coma for weeks. She was very old and passed away without ever waking. I'll be grateful to go that way myself when the time comes. She was chipper right to the end; cooked her own meals, shopped the departments stores . . . She was one of the first women lawyers in New York State."

They came now to a stairwell that ended the hallway. Adjacent to it, on the left, was the door of apartment 7E, a door without sculptured garlands, narrower than the doors they had passed. Mr. Micklas pressed the pearl bell button—*L. Gardenia* was mounted above it in white letters on black plastic —and turned a key in the lock. Despite lost fingers he worked the knob and threw the door smartly. "After you, please," he said, leaning forward on his toes and holding the door open with the length of an outstretched arm.

The apartment's four rooms were divided two and two on either side of a narrow central hallway that extended in a straight line from the front door.

The first room on the right was the kitchen, and at the sight of it Rosemary couldn't keep from giggling, for it was as large if not larger than the whole apartment in which they were then living. It had a six-burner gas stove with two ovens, a mammoth refrigerator, a monumental sink; it had dozens of cabinets, a window on Seventh Avenue, a high *high* ceiling, and it even had —imagining away Mrs. Gardenia's chrome table and chairs and roped bales of *Fortune* and *Musical America*—the perfect place for something like the blue-and-ivory breakfast nook she had clipped from last month's *House Beautiful.*

Opposite the kitchen was the dining room or second bedroom, which Mrs. Gardenia had apparently used as a combination study and greenhouse. Hundreds of small plants, dying and dead, stood on jerry-built shelves under spirals of unlighted fluorescent tubing; in their midst a rolltop desk spilled over with books and papers. A handsome desk it was, broad and gleaming with age. Rosemary left Guy and Mr. Micklas talking by the door and went to it, stepping over a shelf of withered brown fronds. Desks like this were displayed in antique-store windows; Rosemary wondered, touching it, if it was one of the things that could be had practically for the asking. Graceful blue penmanship on mauve paper said *than merely the intriguing pastime I believed it to be. I can no longer associate myself*—and she caught herself snooping and looked up at Mr. Micklas turning from Guy. "Is this desk one of the things Mrs. Gardenia's son wants to sell?" she asked.

"I don't know," Mr. Micklas said. "I could find out for you, though."

"It's a beauty," Guy said.

Rosemary said "Isn't it?" and smiling, looked about at walls and windows. The room would accommodate almost perfectly the nursery she had imagined. It was a bit dark—the windows faced on a narrow courtyard—but the white-and-yellow wallpaper would brighten it tremendously. The bathroom was small but a bonus, and the closet, filled with potted seedlings that seemed to be doing quite well, was a good one.

They turned to the door, and Guy asked, "What are all these?"

"Herbs, mostly," Rosemary said. "There's mint and basil . . . I don't know what these are."

Farther along the hallway there was a guest closet on the left, and then, on the right, a wide archway opening onto the living room. Large bay windows stood opposite, two of them, with diamond panes and three-sided window seats. There was a small fireplace in the right-hand wall, with a scrolled white marble mantel, and there were high oak bookshelves on the left.

"Oh, Guy," Rosemary said, finding his hand and squeezing it. Guy said "Mm" noncommittally but squeezed back; Mr. Micklas was beside him.

"The fireplace works, of course," Mr. Micklas said.

The bedroom, behind them, was adequate—about twelve by eighteen, with its windows facing on the same narrow courtyard as those of the dining-room-second-bedroom-nursery. The bathroom, beyond the living room, was big, and full of bulbous white brass-knobbed fixtures.

"It's a marvelous apartment!" Rosemary said, back in the living room. She spun about with opened arms, as if to take and embrace it. "I love it!"

"What she's trying to do," Guy said, "is get you to lower the rent."

Mr. Micklas smiled. "We would raise it if we were allowed," he said. "Beyond the fifteen-per-cent increase, I mean. Apartments with this kind of charm and individuality are as rare as hen's teeth today. The new—" He stopped short, looking at a mahogany secretary at the head of the central hallway. "That's odd," he said. "There's a closet behind that secretary. I'm sure there is. There are five: two in the bedroom, one in the second bedroom, and two in the hallway, there and there." He went closer to the secretary.

Guy stood high on tiptoes and said, "You're right. I can see the corners of the door."

"She moved it," Rosemary said. "The secretary; it used to be there." She pointed to a peaked silhouette left ghostlike on the wall near the bedroom door, and the deep prints of four ball feet in the burgundy carpet. Faint scuff-trails curved and crossed from the four prints to the secretary's feet where they stood now against the narrow adjacent wall.

"Give me a hand, will you?" Mr. Micklas said to Guy.

Between them they worked the secretary bit by bit back toward its original place. "I see why she went into a coma," Guy said, pushing.

"She couldn't have moved this by herself," Mr. Micklas said; "she was eighty-nine."

Rosemary looked doubtfully at the closet door they had uncovered. "Should we open it?" she asked. "Maybe her son should."

The secretary lodged neatly in its four footprints. Mr. Micklas massaged his fingers-missing hands. "I'm authorized to show the apartment," he said, and went to the door and opened it. The closet was nearly empty; a vacuum cleaner stood at one side of it and three or four wood boards at the other. The overhead shelf was stacked with blue and green bath towels.

"Whoever she locked in got out," Guy said.

Mr. Micklas said, "She probably didn't need five closets."

"But why would she cover up her vacuum cleaner and her towels?" Rosemary asked.

Mr. Micklas shrugged. "I don't suppose we'll ever know. She may have been getting senile after all." He smiled. "Is there anything else I can show you or tell you?"

"Yes," Rosemary said. "What about the laundry facilities? Are there washing machines downstairs?"

They thanked Mr. Micklas, who saw them out onto the sidewalk, and then they walked slowly uptown along Seventh Avenue.

"It's cheaper than the other," Rosemary said, trying to sound as if practical considerations stood foremost in her mind.

"It's one room less, honey," Guy said.

Rosemary walked in silence for a moment, and then said, "It's better located."

"God, yes," Guy said. "I could walk to all the theaters."

Heartened, Rosemary leaped from practicality. "Oh Guy, let's take it! Please! Please! It's *such* a wonderful apartment! She didn't do *anything* with it, old Mrs. Gardenia! That living room could be—it could be *beautiful,* and *warm,* and—oh please, Guy, let's take it, all right?"

"Well sure," Guy said, smiling. "If we can get out of the other thing."

Rosemary grabbed his elbow happily. "We will!" she said. "You'll think of something, I know you will!"

Guy telephoned Mrs. Cortez from a glass-walled booth while Rosemary, outside, tried to lip-read. Mrs. Cortez said she would give them until three o'clock; if she hadn't heard from them by then she would call the next party on the waiting list.

They went to the Russian Tea Room and ordered Bloody Mary's and chicken salad sandwiches on black bread.

"You could tell them I'm sick and have to go into the hospital," Rosemary said.

But that was neither convincing nor compelling. Instead Guy spun a story about a call to join a company of *Come Blow Your Horn* leaving for a four-month USO tour of Vietnam and the Far East. The actor playing Alan had broken his hip and unless he, Guy, who knew the part from stock, stepped in and replaced him, the tour would have to be postponed for at least two weeks. Which would be a damn shame, the way those kids over there were slugging away against the Commies. His wife would have to stay with her folks in Omaha . . .

He ran it twice and went to find the phone.

Rosemary sipped her drink, keeping her left hand all-fingers-crossed under the table. She thought about the First Avenue apartment she didn't want and made a conscientious mental list of its good points: the shiny new kitchen, the dishwasher, the view of the East River, the central air conditioning . . .

The waitress brought the sandwiches.

A pregnant woman went by in a navy blue dress. Rosemary watched her. She must have been in her sixth or seventh month, talking back happily over her shoulder to an older woman with packages, probably her mother.

Someone waved from the opposite wall—the red-haired girl who had come into CBS a few weeks before Rosemary left. Rosemary waved back. The girl mouthed something and, when Rosemary didn't understand, mouthed it again. A man facing the girl turned to look at Rosemary, a starved-looking waxen-faced man.

And there came Guy, tall and handsome, biting back his grin, with *yes* glowing all over him.

"Yes?" Rosemary asked as he took his seat opposite her.

"Yes," he said. "The lease is void; the deposit will be returned; I'm to keep an eye open for Lieutenant Hartman of the Signal Corps. Mrs. Cortez awaits us at two."

"You called her?"

"I called her."

The red-haired girl was suddenly with them, flushed and bright-eyed. "I said 'Marriage certainly agrees with you, you look marvelous,' " she said.

Rosemary, ransacking for the girl's name, laughed and said, "Thank you! We're celebrating. We just got an apartment in the Bramford!"

"The Bram?" the girl said. "I'm *mad* about it! If you ever want to sub-let, I'm first, and don't you forget it! All those weird gargoyles and creatures climbing up and down between the windows!"

Two

Hutch, surprisingly, tried to talk them out of it, on the grounds that the Bramford was a "danger zone."

When Rosemary had first come to New York in June of 1962 she had joined another Omaha girl and two girls from Atlanta in an apartment on lower Lexington Avenue. Hutch lived next door, and though he declined to be the full-time father-substitute the girls would have made of him—he had raised two daughters of his own and that was quite enough, thank you—he was nonetheless on hand in emergencies, such as The Night Someone Was on The Fire Escape and The Time Jeanne Almost Choked to Death. His name was Edward Hutchins, he was English, he was fifty-four. Under three different pen names he wrote three different series of boys' adventure books.

To Rosemary he gave another sort of emergency assistance. She was the youngest of six children, the other five of whom had married early and made homes close to their parents; behind her in Omaha she had left an angry, suspicious father, a silent mother, and four resenting brothers and sisters. (Only the next-to-the-oldest, Brian, who had a drink problem, had said, "Go on, Rosie, do what you want to do," and had slipped her a plastic handbag with eighty-five dollars in it.) In New York Rosemary felt guilty and selfish, and Hutch bucked her up with strong tea and talks about parents and children and one's duty to oneself. She asked him questions that had been unspeakable in Catholic High; he sent her to a night course in philosophy at NYU. "I'll make a duchess out of this cockney flower girl yet," he said, and Rosemary had had wit enough to say "Garn!"

Now, every month or so, Rosemary and Guy had dinner with Hutch, either in their apartment or, when it was his turn, in a restaurant. Guy found Hutch a bit boring but always treated him cordially; his wife had been a cousin of Terence Rattigan, the playwright, and Rattigan and Hutch corresponded. Connections often proved crucial in the theater, Guy knew, even connections at second hand.

On the Thursday after they saw the apartment, Rosemary and Guy had dinner with Hutch at Klube's, a small German restaurant on Twenty-third Street. They had given his name to Mrs. Cortez on Tuesday afternoon as one of three references she had asked for, and he had already received and answered her letter of inquiry.

"I was tempted to say that you were drug addicts or litterbugs," he said, "or something equally repellent to managers of apartment houses."

They asked why.

"I don't know whether or not you know it," he said, buttering a roll, "but the Bramford had rather an unpleasant reputation early in the century." He looked up, saw that they didn't know and went on. (He had a broad shiny face, blue eyes that darted enthusiastically, and a few strands of wetted-down black hair combed crossways over his scalp.) "Along with the Isadora Duncans and Theodore Dreisers," he said, "the Bramford has housed a considerable number of less attractive personages. It's where the Trench sisters performed their little dietary experiments, and where Keith Kennedy held his parties. Adrian Marcato lived there too; and so did Pearl Ames."

"Who were the Trench sisters?" Guy asked, and Rosemary asked, "Who was Adrian Marcato?"

"The Trench sisters," Hutch said, "were two proper Victorian ladies who were occasional cannibals. They cooked and ate several young children, including a niece."

"Lovely," Guy said.

Hutch turned to Rosemary. "Adrian Marcato practiced witchcraft," he said. "He made quite a splash in the eighteen-nineties by announcing that he had succeeded in conjuring up the living Satan. He showed off a handful of hair and some claw-parings, and apparently people believed him; enough of them, at least, to form a mob that attacked and nearly killed him in the Bramford lobby."

"You're joking," Rosemary said.

"I'm quite serious. A few years later the Keith Kennedy business began, and by the twenties the house was half empty."

Guy said, "I knew about Keith Kennedy and about Pearl Ames, but I didn't know Adrian Marcato lived there."

"And those sisters," Rosemary said with a shudder.

"It was only World War Two and the housing shortage," Hutch said, "that filled the place up again, and now it's acquired a bit of Grand-Old-Apartment-House prestige; but in the twenties it was called Black Bramford and sensible people stayed away. The melon is for the lady, isn't it, Rosemary?"

The waiter placed their appetizers. Rosemary looked questioningly at Guy; he pursed his brow and gave a quick headshake: *It's nothing, don't let him scare you.*

The waiter left. "Over the years," Hutch said, "the Bramford has had far more than its share of ugly and unsavory happenings. Nor have all of them been in the distant past. In 1959 a dead infant was found wrapped in newspaper in the basement."

Rosemary said, "But—awful things probably happen in *every* apartment house now and then."

"Now and then," Hutch said. "The point is, though, that at the Bramford awful things happen a good deal more frequently than 'now and then.' There are less spectacular irregularities too. There've been more suicides there, for instance, than in houses of comparable size and age."

"What's the answer, Hutch?" Guy said, playing serious-and-concerned. "There must be some kind of explanation."

Hutch looked at him for a moment. "I don't know," he said. "Perhaps it's simply that the notoriety of a pair of Trench sisters attracts an Adrian Marcato, and his notoriety attracts a Keith Kennedy, and eventually a house becomes a—a kind of rallying place for people who are more prone than others to certain types of behavior. Or perhaps there are things we don't know yet —about magnetic fields or electrons or whatever—ways in which a place can quite literally be malign. I do know this, though: the Bramford is by no means unique. There was a house in London, on Praed Street, in which five separate brutal murders took place within sixty years. None of the five was in any way connected with any of the others; the murderers weren't related nor were the victims, nor were all the murders committed for the same moonstone or Maltese falcon. Yet five separate brutal murders took place within sixty years. In a small house with a shop on the street and an apartment overhead. It was demolished in 1954—for no especially pressing purpose, since as far as I know the plot was left empty."

Rosemary worked her spoon in melon. "Maybe there are good houses too," she said; "houses where people keep falling in love and getting married and having babies."

"And becoming stars," Guy said.

"Probably there are," Hutch said. "Only one never hears of them. It's the stinkers that get the publicity." He smiled at Rosemary and Guy. "I wish you two would look for a good house instead of the Bramford," he said.

Rosemary's spoon of melon stopped halfway to her mouth. "Are you honestly trying to talk us out of it?" she asked.

"My dear girl," Hutch said, "I had a perfectly good date with a charming woman this evening and broke it solely to see you and say my say. I am honestly trying to talk you out of it."

"Well, Jesus, Hutch—" Guy began.

"I am not saying," Hutch said, "that you will walk into the Bramford and be hit on the head with a piano or eaten by spinsters or turned to stone. I am simply saying that the record is there and ought to be considered along with the reasonable rent and the working fireplace: the house has a high incidence of unpleasant happenings. Why deliberately enter a danger zone? Go to the Dakota or the Osborne if you're dead set on nineteenth-century splendor."

"The Dakota is co-op," Rosemary said, "and the Osborne's going to be torn down."

"Aren't you exaggerating a little bit, Hutch?" Guy said. "Have there been any other 'unpleasant happenings' in the past few years? Besides that baby in the basement?"

"An elevator man was killed last winter," Hutch said. "In a not-at-the-dinner-table kind of accident. I was at the library this afternoon with the *Times Index* and three hours of microfilm; would you care to hear more?"

Rosemary looked at Guy. He put down his fork and wiped his mouth. "It's silly," he said. "All right, a lot of unpleasant things have happened there. That doesn't mean that more of them are going to happen. I don't see why the Bramford is any more of a 'danger zone' than any other house in the city. You can flip a coin and get five heads in a row; that doesn't mean that the next five flips are going to be heads too, and it doesn't mean that the coin is any different from any other coin. It's coincidence, that's all."

"If there were *really* something wrong," Rosemary said, "wouldn't it have been demolished? Like the house in London?"

"The house in London," Hutch said, "was owned by the family of the last chap murdered there. The Bramford is owned by the church next door."

"There you are," Guy said, lighting a cigarette; "we've got divine protection."

"It hasn't been working," Hutch said.

The waiter lifted away their plates.

Rosemary said, "I didn't know it was owned by a church," and Guy said, "The whole city is, honey."

"Have you tried the Wyoming?" Hutch asked. "It's in the same block, I think."

"Hutch," Rosemary said, "we've tried everywhere. There's nothing, absolutely nothing, except the *new* houses, with neat square rooms that are all exactly alike and television cameras in the elevators."

"Is that so terrible?" Hutch asked, smiling

"Yes," Rosemary said, and Guy said, "We were set to go into one, but we backed out to take this."

Hutch looked at them for a moment, then sat back and struck the table with wide-apart palms. "Enough," he said. "I shall mind my own business, as I ought to have done from the outset. Make fires in your working fireplace! I'll give you a bolt for the door and keep my mouth shut from this day forward. I'm an idiot; forgive me."

Rosemary smiled. "The door already has a bolt," she said. "And one of those chain things and a peephole."

"Well, mind you use all three," Hutch said. "And don't go wandering through the halls introducing yourself to all and sundry. You're not in Iowa."

"Omaha."

The waiter brought their main courses.

On the following Monday afternoon Rosemary and Guy signed a two-year lease on apartment 7E at the Bramford. They gave Mrs. Cortez a check for five hundred and eighty-three dollars—a month's rent in advance and a month's rent as security—and were told that if they wished they could take occupancy of the apartment earlier than September first, as it would be cleared by the end of the week and the painters could come in on Wednesday the eighteenth.

Later on Monday they received a telephone call from Martin Gardenia, the son of the apartment's previous tenant. They agreed to meet him at the apartment on Tuesday evening at eight, and, doing so, found him to be a tall man past sixty with a cheerful open manner. He pointed out the things he wanted to sell and named his prices, all of which were attractively low. Rosemary and Guy conferred and examined, and bought two air conditioners, a rosewood vanity with a petit-point bench, the living room's Persian rug, and the andirons, firescreen, and tools. Mrs. Gardenia's rolltop desk, disappointingly, was not for sale. While Guy wrote a check and helped tag the items to be left behind, Rosemary measured the living room and the bedroom with a six-foot folding rule she had bought that morning.

The previous March, Guy had played a role on *Another World*, a daytime television series. The character was back now for three days, so for the rest of the week Guy was busy. Rosemary winnowed a folder of decorating schemes she had collected since high school, found two that seemed appropriate to the apartment, and with those to guide her went looking at furnishings with Joan Jellico, one of the girls from Atlanta she had roomed with on coming to New York. Joan had the card of a decorator, which gave them entrance to wholesale houses and showrooms of every sort. Rosemary looked and made shorthand notes and drew sketches to bring to Guy, and hurried home spilling over with fabric and wallpaper samples in time to catch him on *Another World* and then run out again and shop for dinner. She skipped her sculpture class and canceled, happily, a dental appointment.

On Friday evening the apartment was theirs; an emptiness of high ceilings and unfamiliar dark into which they came with a lamp and a shopping bag, striking echoes from the farthest rooms. They turned on their air conditioners and admired their rug and their fireplace and Rosemary's vanity; admired too their bathtub, doorknobs, hinges, molding, floors, stove, refrigerator, bay windows, and view. They picnicked on the rug, on tuna sandwiches and beer, and made floor plans of all four rooms, Guy measuring and Rosemary drawing. On the rug again, they unplugged the lamp and stripped and made love in the nightglow of shadeless windows. "Shh!" Guy hissed afterwards, wide-eyed with fear. "I hear—the Trench sisters chewing!" Rosemary hit him on the head, hard.

They bought a sofa and a king-size bed, a table for the kitchen and two bentwood chairs. They called Con Ed and the phone company and stores and workmen and the Padded Wagon.

The painters came on Wednesday the eighteenth; patched, spackled, primed, painted, and were gone on Friday the twentieth, leaving colors very much like Rosemary's samples. A solitary paperhanger came in and grumbled and papered the bedroom.

They called stores and workmen and Guy's mother in Montreal. They bought an armoire and a dining table and hi-fi components and new dishes and silverware. They were flush. In 1964 Guy had done a series of Anacin commercials that, shown time and time again, had earned him eighteen thousand dollars and was still producing a sizable income.

They hung window shades and papered shelves, watched carpet go down in the bedroom and white vinyl in the hallway. They got a plug-in phone with three jacks; paid bills and left a forwarding notice at the post office.

On Friday, August 27th, they moved. Joan and Dick Jellico sent a large potted plant and Guy's agent a small one. Hutch sent a telegram: *The Bramford will change from a bad house to a good house when one of its doors is marked R. and G. Woodhouse.*

Three

And then Rosemary was busy and happy. She bought and hung curtains, found a Victorian glass lamp for the living room, hung pots and pans on the kitchen wall. One day she realized that the four boards in the hall closet were shelves, fitting across to sit on wood cleats on the side walls. She covered them with gingham contact paper and, when Guy came home, showed him a neatly filled linen closet. She found a supermarket on Sixth Avenue and a Chinese laundry on Fifty-fifth Street for the sheets and Guy's shirts.

Guy was busy too, away every day like other women's husbands. With Labor Day past, his vocal coach was back in town; Guy worked with him each morning and auditioned for plays and commercials most afternoons. At breakfast he was touchy reading the theatrical page—everyone else was out of town with *Skyscraper* or *Drat! The Cat!* or *The Impossible Years* or *Hot September;* only he was in New York with residuals-from-Anacin—but Rosemary knew that very soon he'd get something good, and quietly she set his coffee before him and quietly took for herself the newspaper's other section.

The nursery was, for the time being, a den, with off-white walls and the furniture from the old apartment. The white-and-yellow wallpaper would come later, clean and fresh. Rosemary had a sample of it lying ready in *Picasso's Picassos,* along with a Saks ad showing the crib and bureau.

She wrote to her brother Brian to share her happiness. No one else in the family would have welcomed it; they were all hostile now—parents, brothers, sisters—not forgiving her for A) marrying a Protestant, B) marrying in only a civil ceremony, and C) having a mother-in-law who had had two divorces and was married now to a Jew up in Canada.

She made Guy chicken Marengo and *vitello tonnato,* baked a mocha layer cake and a jarful of butter cookies.

They heard Minnie Castevet before they met her; heard her through their bedroom wall, shouting in a hoarse midwestern bray. "Roman, come to bed! It's twenty past eleven!" And five minutes later: "Roman? Bring me in some root beer when you come!"

"I didn't know they were still making Ma and Pa Kettle movies," Guy said, and Rosemary laughed uncertainly. She was nine years younger than Guy, and some of his references lacked clear meaning for her.

They met the Goulds in 7F, a pleasant elderly couple, and the German-accented Bruhns and their son Walter in 7C. They smiled and nodded in the hall to the Kelloggs, 7G, Mr. Stein, 7H, and the Messrs. Dubin and DeVore, 7B. (Rosemary learned everyone's name immediately, from doorbells and from face-up mail on doormats, which she had no qualms about reading.) The Kapps in 7D, unseen and with no mail, were apparently still away for the summer; and the Castevets in 7A, heard ("Roman! Where's Terry?") but unseen, were either recluses or comers-and-goers-at-odd-hours. Their door was opposite the elevator, their doormat supremely readable. They got air mail letters from a surprising variety of places: Hawick, Scotland; Langeac, France; Vitória, Brazil; Cessnock, Australia. They subscribed to both *Life* and *Look.*

No sign at all did Rosemary and Guy see of the Trench sisters, Adrian Marcato, Keith Kennedy, Pearl Ames, or their latter-day equivalents. Dubin and DeVore were homosexuals; everyone else seemed entirely commonplace.

Almost every night the midwestern bray could be heard, from the apartment which, Rosemary and Guy came to realize, had originally been the bigger front part of their own. "But it's *impossible* to be a hundred per cent sure!" the woman argued, and, "If you want *my* opinion, we shouldn't tell her at *all;* that's *my* opinion!"

One Saturday night the Castevets had a party, with a dozen or so people talking and singing. Guy fell asleep easily but Rosemary lay awake until after two, hearing flat unmusical singing and a flute or clarinet that piped along beside it.

The only time Rosemary remembered Hutch's misgivings and was made uneasy by them was when she went down to the basement every fourth day or so to do the laundry. The service elevator was in itself unsettling—small, unmanned, and given to sudden creaks and tremors—and the basement was an eerie place of once-whitewashed brick passageways where footfalls whispered distantly and unseen doors thudded closed, where castoff refrigerators faced the wall under glary bulbs in wire cages.

It was here, Rosemary would remember, that a dead baby wrapped in newspaper had not so long ago been found. Whose baby had it been, and how had it died? Who had found it? Had the person who left it been caught and punished? She thought of going to the library and reading the story in old newspapers as Hutch had done; but that would have made it more real, more dreadful than it already was. To know the spot where the baby had lain, to have perhaps to walk past it on the way to the laundry room and again on the way back to the elevator, would have been unbearable. Partial ignorance, she decided, was partial bliss. *Damn Hutch and his good intentions!*

The laundry room would have done nicely in a prison: steamy brick walls, more bulbs in cages, and scores of deep double sinks in iron-mesh cubicles. There were coin-operated washers and dryers and, in most of the padlocked cubicles, privately owned machines. Rosemary came down on weekends or after five; earlier on weekdays a bevy of Negro laundresses ironed and gossiped and had abruptly fallen silent at her one unknowing intrusion. She had smiled all around and tried to be invisible, but they hadn't spoken another word and she had felt self-conscious, clumsy, and Negro-oppressing.

One afternoon, when she and Guy had been in the Bramford a little over two weeks, Rosemary was sitting in the laundry room at 5:15 reading *The New Yorker* and waiting to add softener to the rinse water when a girl her own age came in—a dark-haired cameo-faced girl who, Rosemary realized with a start, was Anna Maria Alberghetti. She was wearing white sandals, black shorts, and an apricot silk blouse, and was carrying a yellow plastic laundry basket. Nodding at Rosemary and then not looking at her, she went to one of the washers, opened it, and began feeding dirty clothes into it.

Anna Maria Alberghetti, as far as Rosemary knew, did not live at the Bramford, but she could well have been visiting someone and helping out with the chores. A closer look, though, told Rosemary that she was mistaken; this girl's nose was too long and sharp and there were other less definable differences of expression and carriage. The resemblance, however, was a remarkable one—and suddenly Rosemary found the girl looking at her with an embarrassed questioning smile, the washer beside her closed and filling.

"I'm sorry," Rosemary said. "I thought you were Anna Maria Alberghetti, so I've been staring at you. I'm sorry."

The girl blushed and smiled and looked at the floor a few feet to her side. "That happens a lot," she said. "You don't have to apologize. People have been thinking I'm Anna Maria since I was, oh, just a kid, when she first started out in *Here Comes The Groom.*" She looked at Rosemary, still blushing but no longer smiling. "I don't see a resemblance at all," she said. "I'm of Italian parentage like she is, but no *physical* resemblance."

"There's a very strong one," Rosemary said.

"I guess there is," the girl said; "everyone's always telling me. I don't see it though. I wish I did, believe me."

"Do you know her?" Rosemary asked.

"No."

"The way you said 'Anna Maria' I thought—"

"Oh no, I just call her that. I guess from talking about her so much with everyone." She wiped her hand on her shorts and stepped forward, holding it out and smiling. "I'm Terry Gionoffrio," she said, "and *I* can't spell it so don't *you* try."

Rosemary smiled and shook hands. "I'm Rosemary Woodhouse," she said. "We're new tenants here. Have you been here long?"

"I'm not a tenant at all," the girl said. "I'm just staying with Mr. and Mrs. Castevet, up on the seventh floor. I'm their guest, sort of, since June. Oh, you know them?"

"No," Rosemary said, smiling, "but our apartment is right behind theirs and used to be the back part of it."

"Oh for goodness' sake," the girl said, "you're the party that took the old lady's apartment! Mrs.—the old lady who died!"

"Gardenia."

"That's right. She was a good *friend* of the Castevets. She used to grow herbs and things and bring them in for Mrs. Castevet to cook with."

Rosemary nodded. "When we first looked at the apartment," she said, "one room was full of plants."

"And now that she's dead," Terry said, "Mrs. Castevet's got a miniature greenhouse in the kitchen and grows things herself."

"Excuse me, I have to put softener in," Rosemary said. She got up and got the bottle from the laundry bag on the washer.

"Do you know who *you* look like?" Terry asked her; and Rosemary, unscrewing the cap, said, "No, who?"

"Piper Laurie."

Rosemary laughed. "Oh, no," she said. "It's funny your saying that, because my husband used to date Piper Laurie before she got married."

"No kidding? In Hollywood?"

"No, here." Rosemary poured a capful of the softener. Terry opened the washer door and Rosemary thanked her and tossed the softener in.

"Is he an actor, your husband?" Terry asked.

Rosemary nodded complacently, capping the bottle.

"No kidding! What's his name?"

"Guy Woodhouse," Rosemary said. "He was in *Luther* and *Nobody Loves An Albatross,* and he does a lot of work in television."

"Gee, I watch TV all day long," Terry said. "I'll bet I've seen him!" Glass crashed somewhere in the basement; a bottle smashing or a windowpane. "Yow," Terry said.

Rosemary hunched her shoulders and looked uneasily toward the laundry room's doorway. "I hate this basement," she said.

"Me too," Terry said. "I'm glad you're here. If I was alone now I'd be scared stiff."

"A delivery boy probably dropped a bottle," Rosemary said.

Terry said, "Listen, we could come down together regular. Your door is by the service elevator, isn't it? I could ring your bell and we could come down together. We could call each other first on the house phone."

"That would be great," Rosemary said. "I hate coming down here alone."

Terry laughed happily, seemed to seek words, and then, still laughing, said, "I've got a good luck charm that'll maybe do for both of us!" She pulled away the collar of her blouse, drew out a silver neckchain, and showed Rosemary on the end of it a silver filigree ball a little less than an inch in diameter.

"Oh, that's *beautiful*," Rosemary said.

"Isn't it?" Terry said. "Mrs. Castevet gave it to me the day before yesterday. It's three hundred years old. She grew the stuff inside it in that little greenhouse. It's good luck, or anyway it's supposed to be."

Rosemary looked more closely at the charm Terry held out between thumb and fingertip. It was filled with a greenish-brown spongy substance that pressed out against the silver openwork. A bitter smell made Rosemary draw back.

Terry laughed again. "I'm not mad about the smell either," she said. "I hope it works!"

"It's a beautiful charm," Rosemary said. "I've never seen anything like it."

"It's European," Terry said. She leaned a hip against a washer and admired the ball, turning it one way and another. "The Castevets are the most wonderful people in the world, bar none," she said. "They picked me up off the sidewalk—and I mean that literally; I conked out on Eighth Avenue—and they brought me here and adopted me like a mother and father. Or like a grandmother and grandfather, I guess."

"You were sick?" Rosemary asked.

"That's putting it mildly," Terry said. "I was starving and on dope and doing a lot of other things that I'm so ashamed of I could throw up just thinking about them. And Mr. and Mrs. Castevet completely rehabilitated me. They got me off the H, the dope, and got food into me and clean clothes on me, and now nothing is too good for me as far as they're concerned. They give me all kinds of health food and vitamins, they even have a doctor come give me regular check-ups! It's because they're childless. I'm like the daughter they never had, you know?"

Rosemary nodded.

"I thought at first that maybe they had some kind of ulterior motive," Terry said. "Maybe some kind of sex thing they would want me to do, or he would want, or she. But they've really been like real grandparents. Nothing like that. They're going to put me through secretarial school in a little while and later on I'm going to pay them back. I only had three years of high school but there's a way of making it up." She dropped the filigree ball back into her blouse.

Rosemary said, "It's nice to know there are people like that, when you hear so much about apathy and people who are afraid of getting involved."

"There aren't many like Mr. and Mrs. Castevet," Terry said. "I would be dead now if it wasn't for them. That's an absolute fact. Dead or in jail."

"You don't have any family that could have helped you?"

"A brother in the Navy. The less said about *him* the better."

Rosemary transferred her finished wash to a dryer and waited with Terry for hers to be done. They spoke of Guy's occasional role on *Another World* ("Sure I remember! You're married to *him?*"), the Bramford's past (of which Terry knew nothing), and the coming visit to New York of Pope Paul. Terry was, like Rosemary, Catholic but no longer observing; she was anxious, though, to get a ticket to the papal mass to be celebrated at Yankee Stadium. When her wash was done and drying the two girls walked together to the service elevator and rode to the seventh floor. Rosemary invited Terry in to see the apartment, but Terry asked if she could take a rain check; the Castevets ate at six and she didn't like to be late. She said she would call Rosemary on the house phone later in the evening so they could go down together to pick up their dry laundry.

Guy was home, eating a bag of Fritos and watching a Grace Kelly movie. "Them sure must be clean clothes," he said.

Rosemary told him about Terry and the Castevets, and that Terry had remembered him from *Another World.* He made light of it, but it pleased him. He was depressed by the likelihood that an actor named Donald Baumgart was going to beat him out for a part in a new comedy for which both had read a second time that afternoon. "Jesus Christ," he said, "what kind of a name is *Donald Baumgart?*" His own name, before he changed it, had been Sherman Peden.

Rosemary and Terry picked up their laundry at eight o'clock, and Terry came in with Rosemary to meet Guy and see the apartment. She blushed and was flustered by Guy, which spurred him to flowery compliments and the bringing of ashtrays and the striking of matches. Terry had never seen the apartment before; Mrs. Gardenia and the Castevets had had a falling-out shortly after her arrival, and soon afterwards Mrs. Gardenia had gone into the coma from which she had never emerged. "It's a lovely apartment," Terry said.

"It will be," Rosemary said. "We're not even halfway furnished yet."

"I've *got* it!" Guy cried with a handclap. He pointed triumphantly at Terry. "Anna Maria Alberghetti!"

Four

A package came from Bonniers, from Hutch; a tall teakwood ice bucket with a bright orange lining. Rosemary called him at once and thanked him. He had seen the apartment after the painters left but not since she and Guy had moved in; she explained about the chairs that were a week late and the sofa that wasn't due for another month. "For God's sake don't even think yet about entertaining," Hutch said. "Tell me how everything is."

Rosemary told him, in happy detail. "And the neighbors certainly don't *seem* abnormal," she said. "Except normal abnormal like homosexuals; there are two of them, and across the hall from us there's a nice old couple named Gould with a place in Pennsylvania where they breed Persian cats. We can have one any time we want."

"They shed," Hutch said.

"And there's another couple that we haven't actually met yet who took in this girl who was hooked on drugs, whom we *have* met, and they completely cured her and are putting her through secretarial school."

"It sounds as if you've moved into Sunnybrook Farm," Hutch said; "I'm delighted."

"The basement is kind of creepy," Rosemary said. "I curse you every time I go down there."

"Why on earth me?"

"Your *stories.*"

"If you mean the ones I write, I curse me too; if you mean the ones I told you, you might with equal justification curse the fire alarm for the fire and the weather bureau for the typhoon."

Rosemary, cowed, said, "It won't be so bad from now on. That girl I mentioned is going down there with me."

Hutch said, "It's obvious you've exerted the healthy influence I predicted and the house is no longer a chamber of horrors. Have fun with the ice bucket and say hello to Guy."

The Kapps in apartment 7D appeared; a stout couple in their middle thirties with an inquisitive two-year-old daughter named Lisa. "What's your name?" Lisa asked, sitting in her stroller. "Did you eat your egg? Did you eat your Captain Crunch?"

"My name is Rosemary," Rosemary said. "I ate my egg but I've never even *heard* of Captain Crunch. Who is he?"

On Friday night, September 17th, Rosemary and Guy went with two other couples to a preview of a play called *Mrs. Dally* and then to a party given by a photographer, Dee Bertillon, in his studio on West Forty-eighth Street. An argument developed between Guy and Bertillon over Actors Equity's policy of blocking the employment of foreign actors—Guy thought it was right, Bertillon thought it was wrong—and though the others present buried the disagreement under a quick tide of jokes and gossip, Guy took Rosemary away soon after, at a few mintues past twelve-thirty.

The night was mild and balmy and they walked; and as they approached the Bramford's blackened mass they saw on the sidewalk before it a group of twenty or so people gathered in a semicircle at the side of a parked car. Two police cars waited double-parked, their roof lights spinning red.

Rosemary and Guy walked faster, hand in hand, their senses sharpening. Cars on the avenue slowed questioningly; windows scraped open in the Bramford and heads looked out beside gargoyles' heads. The night doorman Toby came from the house with a tan blanket that a policeman turned to take from him.

The roof of the car, a Volkswagen, was crumpled to the side; the windshield was crazed with a million fractures. "Dead," someone said, and someone else said, "I look up and I think it's some kind of a big bird zooming down, like an eagle or something."

Rosemary and Guy stood on tiptoes, craned over people's shoulders. "Get back now, will you?" a policeman at the center said. The shoulders separated, a sport-shirted back moved away. On the sidewalk Terry lay, watching the sky with one eye, half of her face gone to red pulp. Tan blanket flipped over her. Settling, it reddened in one place and then another.

Rosemary wheeled, eyes shut, right hand making an automatic cross. She kept her mouth tightly closed, afraid she might vomit.

Guy winced and drew air in under his teeth. "Oh, Jesus," he said, and groaned. "Oh my God."

A policeman said, "Get back, will you?"

"We know her," Guy said.

Another policeman turned and said, "What's her name?"

"Terry."

"Terry what?" He was forty or so and sweating. His eyes were blue and beautiful, with thick black lashes.

Guy said, "Ro? What was her name? Terry what?"

Rosemary opened her eyes and swallowed. "I don't remember," she said. "Italian, with a G. A long name. She made a joke about spelling it. Not being able to."

Guy said to the blue-eyed policeman, "She was staying with people named Castevet, in apartment seven A."

"We've got that already," the policeman said.

Another policeman came up, holding a sheet of pale yellow notepaper. Mr. Micklas was behind him, tight-mouthed, in a raincoat over striped pajamas. "Short and sweet," the policeman said to the blue-eyed one, and handed him the yellow paper. "She stuck it to the window sill with a Band-Aid so it wouldn't blow away."

"Anybody there?"

The other shook his head.

The blue-eyed policeman read what was written on the sheet of paper, sucking thoughtfully at his front teeth. "Theresa Gionoffrio," he said. He pronounced it as an Italian would. Rosemary nodded.

Guy said, "Wednesday night you wouldn't have guessed she had a sad thought in her mind."

"Nothing but sad thoughts," the policeman said, opening his pad holder. He laid the paper inside it and closed the holder with a width of yellow sticking out.

"Did you know her?" Mr. Micklas asked Rosemary.

"Only slightly," she said.

"Oh, of course," Mr. Micklas said; "you're on seven too."

Guy said to Rosemary, "Come on, honey, let's go upstairs."

The policeman said, "Do you have any idea where we can find these people Castevet?"

"No, none at all," Guy said. "We've never even met them."

"They're usually at home now," Rosemary said. "We hear them through the wall. Our bedroom is next to theirs."

Guy put his hand on Rosemary's back. "Come on, hon," he said. They nodded to the policeman and Mr. Micklas, and started toward the house.

"Here they come now," Mr. Micklas said. Rosemary and Guy stopped and turned. Coming from downtown, as they themselves had come, were a tall, broad, white-haired woman and a tall, thin, shuffling man. "The Castevets?" Rosemary asked. Mr. Micklas nodded.

Mrs. Castevet was wrapped in light blue, with snow-white dabs of gloves, purse, shoes, and hat. Nurselike she supported her husband's forearm. He was dazzling, in an every-color seersucker jacket, red slacks, a pink bow tie, and a gray fedora with a pink band. He was seventy-five or older; she was sixty-eight or -nine. They came closer with expressions of young alertness, with friendly quizzical smiles. The policeman stepped forward to meet them and their smiles faltered and fell away. Mrs. Castevet said something worryingly; Mr. Castevet frowned and shook his head. His wide, thin-lipped mouth was rosy-pink, as if lipsticked; his cheeks were chalky, his eyes small and bright in deep sockets. She was big-nosed, with a sullen fleshy underlip. She wore pink-rimmed eyeglasses on a neckchain that dipped down from behind plain pearl earrings.

The policeman said, "Are you folks the Castevets on the seventh floor?"

"We are," Mr. Castevet said in a dry voice that had to be listened for.

"You have a young woman named Theresa Gionoffrio living with you?"

"We do," Mr. Castevet said. "What's wrong? Has there been an accident?"

"You'd better brace yourselves for some bad news," the policeman said. He waited, looking at each of them in turn, and then he said, "She's dead. She killed herself." He raised a hand, the thumb pointing back over his shoulder. "She jumped out of the window."

They looked at him with no change of expression at all, as if he hadn't spoken yet; then Mrs. Castevet leaned sideways, glanced beyond him at the red-stained blanket, and stood straight again and looked him in the eyes. "That's not possible," she said in her loud midwestern Roman-bring-me-some-root-beer voice. "It's a mistake. Somebody else is under there."

The policeman, not turning from her, said, "Artie, would you let these people take a look, please?"

Mrs. Castevet marched past him, her jaw set.

Mr. Castevet stayed where he was. "I knew this would happen," he said. "She got deeply depressed every three weeks or so. I noticed it and told my wife, but she pooh-poohed me. She's an optimist who refuses to admit that everything doesn't always turn out the way she wants it to."

Mrs. Castevet came back. "That doesn't mean that she killed herself," she said. "She was a very happy girl with no *reason* for self-destruction. It must have been an accident. She must have been cleaning the windows and lost her hold. She was always surprising us by cleaning things and doing things for us."

"She wasn't cleaning windows at midnight," Mr. Castevet said.

"Why not?" Mrs. Castevet said angrily. "Maybe she was!"

The policeman held out the pale yellow paper, having taken it from his pad holder.

Mrs. Castevet hesitated, then took it and turned it around and read it. Mr. Castevet tipped his head in over her arm and read it too, his thin vivid lips moving.

"Is that her handwriting?" the policeman asked.

Mrs. Castevet nodded. Mr. Castevet said, "Definitely. Absolutely."

The policeman held out his hand and Mrs. Castevet gave him the paper. He said, "Thank you. I'll see you get it back when we're done with it."

She took off her glasses, dropped them on their neckchain, and covered both her eyes with white-gloved fingertips. "I don't believe it," she said. "I just don't believe it. She was so happy. All her troubles were in the past." Mr. Castevet put his hand on her shoulder and looked at the ground and shook his head.

"Do you know the name of her next-of-kin?" the policeman asked.

"She didn't have any," Mrs. Castevet said. "She was all alone. She didn't have anyone, only us."

"Didn't she have a brother?" Rosemary asked.

Mrs. Castevet put on her glasses and looked at her. Mr. Castevet looked up from the ground, his deep-socketed eyes glinting under his hat brim.

"Did she?" the policeman asked.

"She said she did," Rosemary said. "In the Navy."

The policeman looked to the Castevets.

"It's news to me," Mrs. Castevet said, and Mr. Castevet said, "To both of us."

The policeman asked Rosemary, "Do you know his rank or where he's stationed?"

"No, I don't," she said, and to the Castevets: "She mentioned him to me the other day, in the laundry room. I'm Rosemary Woodhouse."

Guy said, "We're in seven E."

"I feel just the way you do, Mrs. Castevet," Rosemary said. "She seemed so happy and full of—of good feelings about the future. She said *wonderful* things about you and your husband; how grateful she was to both of you for all the help you were giving her."

"Thank you," Mrs. Castevet said, and Mr. Castevet said, "It's nice of you to tell us that. It makes it a little easier."

The policeman said, "You don't know anything else about this brother except that he's in the Navy?"

"That's all," Rosemary said. "I don't think she liked him very much."

"It should be easy to find him," Mr. Castevet said, "with an uncommon name like Gionoffrio."

Guy put his hand on Rosemary's back again and they withdrew toward the house. "I'm so stunned and so sorry," Rosemary said to the Castevets, and Guy said, "It's such a pity. It's—"

Mrs. Castevet said, "Thank you," and Mr. Castevet said something long and sibilant of which only the phrase "her last days" was understandable.

They rode upstairs ("Oh, my!" the night elevator man Diego said; "Oh, my! Oh, my!"), looked ruefully at the now-haunted door of 7A, and walked through the branching hallway to their own apartment. Mr. Kellogg in 7G peered out from behind his chained door and asked what was going on down-stairs. They told him.

They sat on the edge of their bed for a few minutes, speculating about Terry's reason for killing herself. Only if the Castevets told them some day what was in the note, they agreed, would they ever learn for certain what had driven her to the violent death they had nearly witnessed. And even knowing what was in the note, Guy pointed out, they might still not know the full answer, for part of it had probably been beyond Terry's own understanding. Something had led her to drugs and something had led her to death; what that something was, it was too late now for anyone to know.

"Remember what Hutch said?" Rosemary asked. "About there being more suicides here than in other buildings?"

"Ah, Ro," Guy said, "that's crap, honey, that 'danger zone' business."

"Hutch believes it."

"Well, it's *still* crap."

"I can imagine what he's going to say when he hears about this."

"Don't tell him," Guy said. "He sure as hell won't read about it in the papers." A strike against the New York newspapers had begun that morning, and there were rumors that it might continue a month or longer.

They undressed, showered, resumed a stopped game of Scrabble, stopped it, made love, and found milk and a dish of cold spaghetti in the refrigerator. Just before they put the lights out at two-thirty, Guy remembered to check the answering service and found that he had got a part in a radio commercial for Cresta Blanca wines.

Soon he was asleep, but Rosemary lay awake beside him, seeing Terry's pulped face and her one eye watching the sky. After a while, though, she was at Our Lady. Sister Agnes was shaking her fist at her, ousting her from leadership of the second-floor monitors. "Sometimes I wonder how come you're the leader of *anything!*" she said. A bump on the other side of the wall woke Rosemary, and Mrs. Castevet said, "And please don't tell me what Laura-Louise said because I'm not interested!" Rosemary turned over and burrowed into her pillow.

Sister Agnes was furious. Her piggy-eyes were squeezed to slits and her nostrils were bubbling the way they always did at such moments. Thanks to Rosemary it had been necessary to brick up all the windows, and now Our Lady had been taken out of the beautiful-school competition being run by the *World-Herald.* "If you'd listened to *me,* we wouldn't have *had* to do it!" Sister Agnes cried in a hoarse midwestern bray. "We'd have been all set to go now instead of starting all over from scratch!" Uncle Mike tried to hush her. He was the principal of Our Lady, which was connected by passageways to his body shop in South Omaha. "I *told* you not to tell her anything in advance," Sister Agnes continued lower, piggy-eyes glinting hatefully at Rosemary. "I *told* you she wouldn't be open-minded. Time enough *later* to let her in on it." (Rosemary had told Sister Veronica about the windows being bricked up and

Sister Veronica had withdrawn the school from the competition; otherwise no one would have noticed and they would have won. It had been right to tell, though, Sister Agnes notwithstanding. A Catholic school shouldn't win by trickery.) "Anybody! Anybody!" Sister Agnes said. "All she has to be is young, healthy, and not a virgin. She doesn't have to be a no-good drug-addict whore out of the gutter. Didn't I say that in the beginning? Anybody. As long as she's young and healthy and not a virgin." Which didn't make sense at all, not even to Uncle Mike; so Rosemary turned over and it was Saturday afternoon, and she and Brian and Eddie and Jean were at the candy counter in the Orpheum, going in to see Gary Cooper and Patricia Neal in *The Fountainhead,* only it was live, not a movie.

Five

On the following Monday morning Rosemary was putting away the last of a double armload of groceries when the doorbell rang; and the peephole showed Mrs. Castevet, white hair in curlers under a blue-and-white kerchief, looking solemnly straight ahead as if waiting for the click of a passport photographer's camera.

Rosemary opened the door and said, "Hello. How are you?"

Mrs. Castevet smiled bleakly. "Fine," she said. "May I come in for a minute?"

"Yes, of course; please do." Rosemary stood back against the wall and held the door wide open. A faint bitter smell brushed across her as Mrs. Castevet came in, the smell of Terry's silver good luck charm filled with spongy greenish-brown. Mrs. Castevet was wearing toreador pants and shouldn't have been; her hips and thighs were massive, slabbed with wide bands of fat. The pants were lime green under a blue blouse; the blade of a screwdriver poked from her hip pocket. Stopping between the doorways of the den and kitchen, she turned and put on her neckchained glasses and smiled at Rosemary. A dream Rosemary had had a night or two earlier sparked in her mind—something about Sister Agnes bawling her out for bricking up windows—and she shook it away and smiled attentively, ready to hear what Mrs. Castevet was about to say.

"I just came over to thank you," Mrs. Castevet said, "for saying those nice things to us the other night, poor Terry telling you she was grateful to us for what we done. You'll never know how comforting it was to hear something like that in such a shock moment, because in both of our minds was the thought that maybe we had failed her in some way and *drove* her to it, although her note made it crystal clear, of course, that she did it of her own free will; but anyway it was a blessing to hear the words spoken out loud like that by somebody Terry had confided in just before the end."

"Please, there's no reason to thank me," Rosemary said. "All I did was tell you what she said to me."

"A lot of people wouldn't have bothered," Mrs. Castevet said. "They'd have just walked away without wanting to spend the air and the little bit of muscle-power. When you're older you'll come to realize that acts of kindness are few and far between in this world of ours. So I *do* thank you, and Roman does too. Roman is my hubby."

Rosemary ducked her head in concession, smiled, and said, "You're welcome. I'm glad that I helped."

"She was cremated yesterday morning with no ceremony," Mrs. Castevet said. "That's the way she wanted it. Now we have to forget and go on. It certainly won't be easy; we took a lot of pleasure in having her around, not having children of our own. Do you have any?"

"No, we don't," Rosemary said.

Mrs. Castevet looked into the kitchen. "Oh, that's nice," she said, "the pans hanging on the wall that way. And look how you put the table, isn't that interesting."

"It was in a magazine," Rosemary said.

"You certainly got a nice paint job," Mrs. Castevet said, fingering the door jamb appraisingly. "Did the house do it? You must have been mighty open-handed with the painters; they didn't do this kind of work for *us*."

"All we gave them was five dollars each," Rosemary said.

"Oh, is that all?" Mrs. Castevet turned around and looked into the den. "Oh, that's nice," she said, "a TV room."

"It's only temporary," Rosemary said. "At least I hope it is. It's going to be a nursery."

"Are you pregnant?" Mrs. Castevet asked, looking at her.

"Not yet," Rosemary said, "but I hope to be, as soon as we're settled."

"That's wonderful," Mrs. Castevet said. "You're young and healthy; you ought to have lots of children."

"We plan to have three," Rosemary said. "Would you like to see the rest of the apartment?"

"I'd love to," Mrs. Castevet said. "I'm dying to see what you've done to it. I used to be in here almost every day. The woman who had it before you was a dear friend of mine."

"I know," Rosemary said, easing past Mrs. Castevet to lead the way; "Terry told me."

"Oh, did she," Mrs. Castevet said, following along. "It sounds like you two had some long talks together down there in the laundry room."

"Only one," Rosemary said.

The living room startled Mrs. Castevet. "My goodness!" she said. "I can't get over the change! It looks so much *brighter!* Oh and look at that chair. Isn't that handsome?"

"It just came Friday," Rosemary said.

"What did you pay for a chair like that?"

Rosemary, disconcerted, said, "I'm not sure. I think it was about two hundred dollars."

"You don't mind my asking, do you?" Mrs. Castevet said, and tapped her nose. "That's how I got a big nose, by being nosy."

Rosemary laughed and said, "No, no, it's all right. I don't mind."

Mrs. Castevet inspected the living room, the bedroom, and the bathroom, asking how much Mrs. Gardenia's son had charged them for the rug and the vanity, where they had got the night-table lamps, exactly how old Rosemary was, and if an electric toothbrush was really any better than the old kind. Rosemary found herself enjoying this open forthright old woman with her loud voice and her blunt questions. She offered coffee and cake to her.

"What does your hubby do?" Mrs. Castevet asked, sitting at the kitchen table idly checking prices on cans of soup and oysters. Rosemary, folding a Chemex paper, told her. "I knew it!" Mrs. Castevet said. "I said to Roman yesterday, 'He's so good-looking I'll bet he's a movie actor'! There's three-four of them in the building, you know. What movies was he in?"

"No movies," Rosemary said. "He was in two plays called *Luther* and *Nobody Loves An Albatross* and he does a lot of work in television and radio."

They had the coffee and cake in the kitchen, Mrs. Castevet refusing to let Rosemary disturb the living room on her account. "Listen, Rosemary," she said, swallowing cake and coffee at once, "I've got a two-inch-thick sirloin steak sitting defrosting right this minute, and half of it's going to go to waste with just Roman and me there to eat it. Why don't you and Guy come over and have supper with us tonight, what do you say?"

"Oh, no, we couldn't," Rosemary said.

"Sure you could; why not?"

"No, really, I'm sure you don't want to—"

"It would be a big help to us if you would," Mrs. Castevet said. She looked into her lap, then looked up at Rosemary with a hard-to-carry smile. "We had friends with us last night and Saturday," she said, "but this'll be the first night we'll be alone since—the other night."

Rosemary leaned forward feelingly. "If you're *sure* it won't be trouble for you," she said.

"Honey, if it was trouble I wouldn't ask you," Mrs. Castevet said. "Believe me, I'm as selfish as the day is long."

Rosemary smiled. "That isn't what Terry told me," she said.

"Well," Mrs. Castevet said with a pleased smile, "Terry didn't know what she was talking about."

"I'll have to check with Guy," Rosemary said, "but you go ahead and count on us."

Mrs. Castevet said happily, "Listen! You tell him I won't take no for an answer! I want to be able to tell folks I knew him when!"

They ate their cake and coffee, talking of the excitements and hazards of an acting career, the new season's television shows and how bad they were, and the continuing newspaper strike.

"Will six-thirty be too early for you?" Mrs. Castevet asked at the door.

"It'll be perfect," Rosemary said.

"Roman don't like to eat any later than that," Mrs. Castevet said. "He has stomach trouble and if he eats too late he can't get to sleep. You know where we are, don't you? Seven A, at six-thirty. We'll be looking forward. Oh, here's your mail, dear; I'll get it. Ads. Well, it's better than getting nothing, isn't it?"

Guy came home at two-thirty in a bad mood; he had learned from his agent that, as he had feared, the grotesquely named Donald Baumgart had won the part he had come within a hair of getting. Rosemary kissed him and installed him in his new easy chair with a melted cheese sandwich and a glass of beer. She had read the script of the play and not liked it; it would probably close out of town, she told Guy, and Donald Baumgart would never be heard of again.

"Even if it folds," Guy said, "it's the kind of part that gets noticed. You'll see; he'll get something else right after." He opened the corner of his sandwich, looked in bitterly, closed it, and started eating.

"Mrs. Castevet was here this morning," Rosemary said. "To thank me for telling them that Terry was grateful to them. I think she really just wanted to see the apartment. She's absolutely the nosiest person I've ever seen. She actually asked the prices of things."

"No kidding," Guy said.

"She comes right out and *admits* she's nosy, though, so it's kind of funny and forgivable instead of annoying. She even looked into the medicine chest."

"Just like that?"

"Just like that. And guess what she was wearing."

"A Pillsbury sack with three X's on it."

"No, toreador pants."

"*Toreador* pants?"

"Lime-green ones."

"Ye gods."

Kneeling on the floor between the bay windows, Rosemary drew a line on brown paper with crayon and a yardstick and then measured the depth of the window seats. "She invited us to have dinner with them this evening," she said, and looked at Guy. "I told her I'd have to check with you, but that it would probably be okay."

"Ah, Jesus, Ro," Guy said, "we don't want to do that, do we?"

"I think they're lonely," Rosemary said. "Because of Terry."

"Honey," Guy said, "if we get friendly with an old couple like that we're *never* going to get them off our necks. They're right here on the same floor with us, they'll be looking in six times a day. Especially if she's nosy to begin with."

"I told her she could count on us," Rosemary said.

"I thought you told her you had to check first."

"I did, but I told her she could count on us too." Rosemary looked helplessly at Guy. "She was so anxious for us to come."

"Well it's not my night for being kind to Ma and Pa Kettle," Guy said. "I'm sorry, honey, call her up and tell her we can't make it."

"All right, I will," Rosemary said, and drew another line with the crayon and the yardstick.

Guy finished his sandwich. "You don't have to sulk about it," he said.

"I'm not sulking," Rosemary said. "I see exactly what you mean about them being on the same floor. It's a valid point and you're absolutely right. I'm not sulking at all."

"Oh hell," Guy said, "we'll go."

"No, no, what for? We don't have to. I shopped for dinner before she came, so *that's* no problem."

"We'll go," Guy said.

"We don't have to if you don't want to. That sounds so phony but I really mean it, really I do."

"We'll go. It'll be my good deed for the day."

"All right, but only if you want to. And we'll make it very clear to them that it's only this one time and not the beginning of anything. Right?"

"Right."

Six

At a few minutes past six-thirty Rosemary and Guy left their apartment and walked through the branches of dark green hallway to the Castevets' door. As Guy rang the doorbell the elevator behind them clanged open and Mr. Dubin or Mr. DeVore (they didn't know which was which) came out carrying a suit swathed in cleaner's plastic. He smiled and, unlocking the door of 7B next to them, said, "You're in the wrong place, aren't you?" Rosemary and Guy made friendly laughs and he let himself in, calling "Me!" and allowing them a glimpse of a black sideboard and red-and-gold wallpaper.

The Castevets' door opened and Mrs. Castevet was there, powdered and rouged and smiling broadly in light green silk and a frilled pink apron. "Perfect timing!" she said. "Come on in! Roman's making Vodka Blushes in the blender. My, I'm glad you could come, Guy! I'm fixing to tell people I knew you when! 'Had dinner right off that plate, he did—Guy Woodhouse in person!' I'm not going to wash it when you're done; I'm going to leave it just as is!"

Guy and Rosemary laughed and exchanged glances; *Your friend,* his said, and hers said, *What can I do?*

There was a large foyer in which a rectangular table was set for four, with an embroidered white cloth, plates that didn't all match, and bright ranks of ornate silver. To the left the foyer opened on a living room easily twice the size of Rosemary and Guy's but otherwise much like it. It had one large bay window instead of two smaller ones, and a huge pink marble mantel sculptured with lavish scrollwork. The room was oddly furnished; at the fireplace end there were a settee and a lamp table and a few chairs, and at the opposite end an officelike clutter of file cabinets, bridge tables piled with newspapers, overfilled bookshelves, and a typewriter on a metal stand. Between the two ends of the room was a twenty-foot field of brown wall-to-wall carpet, deep and new-looking, marked with the trail of a vacuum cleaner. In the center of it, entirely alone, a small round table stood holding *Life* and *Look* and *Scientific American.*

Mrs. Castevet showed them across the brown carpet and seated them on the settee; and as they sat Mr. Castevet came in, holding in both hands a small tray on which four cocktail glasses ran over with clear pink liquid. Staring at the rims of the glasses he shuffled forward across the carpet, looking as if with every next step he would trip and fall disastrously. "I seem to have overfilled the glasses," he said. "No, no, don't get up. Please. Generally I pour these out as precisely as a bartender, don't I, Minnie?"

Mrs. Castevet said, "Just watch the carpet."

"But this evening," Mr. Castevet continued, coming closer, "I made a little too much, and rather than leave the surplus in the blender, I'm afraid I thought I . . . There we are. Please, sit down. Mrs. Woodhouse?"

Rosemary took a glass, thanked him, and sat. Mrs. Castevet quickly put a paper cocktail napkin in her lap.

"Mr. Woodhouse? A Vodka Blush. Have you ever tasted one?"

"No," Guy said, taking one and sitting.

"Minnie," Mr. Castevet said.

"It looks delicious," Rosemary said, smiling vividly as she wiped the base of her glass.

"They're very popular in Australia," Mr. Castevet said. He took the final glass and raised it to Rosemary and Guy. "To our guests," he said. "Welcome to our home." He drank and cocked his head critically, one eye partway closed, the tray at his side dripping on the carpet.

Mrs. Castevet coughed in mid-swallow. "The carpet!" she choked, pointing.

Mr. Castevet looked down. "Oh dear," he said, and held the tray up uncertainly.

Mrs. Castevet thrust aside her drink, hurried to her knees, and laid a paper napkin carefully over the wetness. "Brand-new carpet," she said. "Brand-new carpet. This man is so clumsy!"

The Vodka Blushes were tart and quite good.

"Do you come from Australia?" Rosemary asked, when the carpet had been blotted, the tray safely kitchened, and the Castevets seated in straight-backed chairs.

"Oh no," Mr. Castevet said, "I'm from right here in New York City. I've been there though. I've been everywhere. Literally." He sipped Vodka Blush, sitting with his legs crossed and a hand on his knee. He was wearing black loafers with tassels, gray slacks, a white blouse, and a blue-and-gold striped ascot. "Every continent, every country," he said. "Every major city. You name a place and I've been there. Go ahead. Name a place."

Guy said, "Fairbanks, Alaska."

"I've been there," Mr. Castevet said. "I've been all over Alaska: Fairbanks, Juneau, Anchorage, Nome, Seward; I spent four months there in 1938 and I've made a lot of one-day stop-overs in Fairbanks and Anchorage on my way to places in the Far East. I've been in small towns in Alaska too: Dillingham and Akulurak."

"Where are *you* folks from?" Mrs. Castevet asked, fixing the folds at the bosom of her dress.

"I'm from Omaha," Rosemary said, "and Guy is from Baltimore."

"Omaha is a good city," Mr. Castevet said. "Baltimore is too."

"Did you travel for business reasons?" Rosemary asked him.

"Business and pleasure both," he said. "I'm seventy-nine years old and I've been going one place or another since I was ten. You name it, I've been there."

"What business were you in?" Guy asked.

"Just about every business," Mr. Castevet said. "Wool, sugar, toys, machine parts, marine insurance, oil . . ."

A bell pinged in the kitchen. "Steak's ready," Mrs. Castevet said, standing up with her glass in her hand. "Don't rush your drinks now; take them along to the table. Roman, take your pill."

"It will end on October third," Mr. Castevet said; "the day before the Pope gets here. No Pope ever visits a city where the newspapers are on strike."

"I heard on TV that he's going to postpone and wait till it's over," Mrs. Castevet said.

Guy smiled. "Well," he said, "that's show biz."

Mr. and Mrs. Castevet laughed, and Guy along with them. Rosemary smiled and cut her steak. It was overdone and juiceless, flanked by peas and mashed potatoes under flour-laden gravy.

Still laughing, Mr. Castevet said, "It *is,* you know! That's *just* what it is; show biz!"

"You can say *that* again," Guy said.

"The costumes, the rituals," Mr. Castevet said; "every religion, not only Catholicism. Pageants for the ignorant."

Mrs. Castevet said, "I think we're offending Rosemary."

"No, no, not at all," Rosemary said.

"You aren't religious, my dear, are you?" Mr. Castevet asked.

"I was brought up to be," Rosemary said, "but now I'm an agnostic. I wasn't offended. Really I wasn't."

"And you, Guy?" Mr. Castevet asked. "Are you an agnostic too?"

"I guess so," Guy said. "I don't see how anyone can be anything else. I mean, there's no absolute proof one way or the other, is there?"

"No, there isn't," Mr. Castevet said.

Mrs. Castevet, studying Rosemary, said, "You looked uncomfortable before, when we were laughing at Guy's little joke about the Pope."

"Well he *is* the Pope," Rosemary said. "I guess I've been conditioned to have respect for him and I still do, even if I don't think he's holy any more."

"If you don't think he's holy," Mr. Castevet said, "you should have no respect for him at *all,* because he's going around deceiving people and pretending he *is* holy."

"Good point," Guy said.

"When I *think* what they spend on robes and jewels," Mrs. Castevet said.

"A good picture of the hypocrisy behind organized religion," Mr. Castevet said, "was given, I thought, in *Luther.* Did you ever get to play the leading part, Guy?"

"Me? No," Guy said.

"Weren't you Albert Finney's understudy?" Mr. Castevet asked.

"No," Guy said, "the fellow who played Weinand was. I just covered two of the smaller parts."

"That's strange," Mr. Castevet said; "I was quite certain that *you* were his understudy. I remember being struck by a gesture you made and checking in the program to see who you were; and I could swear you were listed as Finney's understudy."

"What gesture do you mean?" Guy asked.

"I'm not sure now; a movement of your—"

"I used to do a thing with my arms when Luther had the fit, a sort of involuntary reaching—"

"Exactly," Mr. Castevet said. "That's just what I meant. It had a wonderful authenticity to it. In contrast, may I say, to everything Mr. Finney was doing."

"Oh, come on now," Guy said.

"I thought his performance was considerably overrated," Mr. Castevet said. "I'd be most curious to see what *you* would have done with the part."

Laughing, Guy said, "That makes two of us," and cast a bright-eyed glance at Rosemary. She smiled back, pleased that Guy was pleased; there would be no reproofs from him now for an evening wasted talking with Ma and Pa Settle. No, Kettle.

"My father was a theatrical producer," Mr. Castevet said, "and my early years were spent in the company of such people as Mrs. Fiske and Forbes-Robertson, Otis Skinner and Modjeska. I tend, therefore, to look for something more than mere competence in actors. You have a most interesting inner quality, Guy. It appears in your television work too, and it should carry you very far indeed; provided, of course, that you get those initial 'breaks' upon which even the greatest actors are to some degree dependent. Are you preparing for a show now?"

"I'm up for a couple of parts," Guy said.

"I can't believe that you won't get them," Mr. Castevet said.

"*I* can," Guy said.

Mr. Castevet stared at him. "Are you serious?" he asked.

Dessert was a homemade Boston cream pie that, though better than the steak and vegetables, had for Rosemary a peculiar and unpleasant sweetness. Guy, however, praised it heartily and ate a second helping. Perhaps he was only acting, Rosemary thought; repaying compliments with compliments.

After dinner Rosemary offered to help with the cleaning up. Mrs. Castevet accepted the offer instantly and the two women cleared the table while Guy and Mr. Castevet went into the living room.

The kitchen, opening off the foyer, was small, and made smaller still by the miniature greenhouse Terry had mentioned. Some three feet long, it stood on a large white table near the room's one window. Goosenecked lamps leaned close around it, their bright bulbs reflecting in the glass and making it blinding white rather than transparent. In the remaining space the sink, stove, and refrigerator stood close together with cabinets jutting out above them on all sides. Rosemary wiped dishes at Mrs. Castevet's elbow, working diligently and conscientiously in the pleasing knowledge that her own kitchen was larger and more graciously equipped. "Terry told me about that greenhouse," she said.

"Oh yes," Mrs. Castevet said. "It's a nice hobby. You ought to do it too."

"I'd like to have a spice garden some day," Rosemary said. "Out of the city, of course. If Guy ever gets a movie offer we're going to grab it and go live in Los Angeles. I'm a country girl at heart."

"Do you come from a big family?" Mrs. Castevet asked.

"Yes," Rosemary said. "I have three brothers and two sisters. I'm the baby."

"Are your sisters married?"

"Yes, they are."

Mrs. Castevet pushed a soapy sponge up and down inside a glass. "Do they have children?" she asked.

"One has two and the other has four," Rosemary said. "At least that was the count the last I heard. It could be three and five by now."

"Well that's a good sign for *you*," Mrs. Castevet said, still soaping the glass. She was a slow and thorough washer. "If your sisters have lots of children, chances are you will too. Things like that go in families."

"Oh, we're fertile, all right," Rosemary said, waiting towel in hand for the glass. "My brother Eddie has *eight* already and he's only twenty-six."

"My goodness!" Mrs. Castevet said. She rinsed the glass and gave it to Rosemary.

"All told I've got twenty nieces and nephews," Rosemary said. "I haven't even *seen* half of them."

"Don't you go home every once in a while?" Mrs. Castevet asked.

"No, I don't," Rosemary said. "I'm not on the best of terms with my family, except one brother. They feel I'm the black sheep."

"Oh? How is that?"

"Because Guy isn't Catholic, and we didn't have a church wedding."

"Tsk," Mrs. Castevet said. "Isn't it something the way people fuss about religion? Well, it's *their* loss, not yours; don't you let it bother you any."

"That's more easily said than done," Rosemary said, putting the glass on a shelf. "Would you like me to wash and you wipe for a while?"

"No, this is fine, dear," Mrs. Castevet said.

Rosemary looked outside the door. She could see only the end of the living room that was bridge tables and file cabinets; Guy and Mr. Castevet were at the other end. A plane of blue cigarette smoke lay motionless in the air.

"Rosemary?"

She turned. Mrs. Castevet, smiling, held out a wet plate in a green rubber-gloved hand.

It took almost an hour to do the dishes and pans and silver, although Rosemary felt she could have done them alone in less than half that time. When she and Mrs. Castevet came out of the kitchen and into the living room, Guy and Mr. Castevet were sitting facing each other on the settee, Mr. Castevet driving home point after point with repeated strikings of his forefinger against his palm.

"Now Roman, you stop bending Guy's ear with your Modjeska stories," Mrs. Castevet said. "He's only listening 'cause he's polite."

"No, it's interesting, Mrs. Castevet," Guy said.

"You see?" Mr. Castevet said.

"*Minnie,*" Mrs. Castevet told Guy. "I'm Minnie and he's Roman; okay?" She looked mock-defiantly at Rosemary. "Okay?"

Guy laughed. "Okay, Minnie," he said.

They talked about the Goulds and the Bruhns and Dubin-and-DeVore, about Terry's sailor brother who had turned out to be in a civilian hospital in Saigon; and, because Mr. Castevet was reading a book critical of the Warren Report, about the Kennedy assassination. Rosemary, in one of the straight-backed chairs, felt oddly out of things, as if the Castevets were old friends of Guy's to whom she had just been introduced. "Do *you* think it could have been a plot of some kind?" Mr. Castevet asked her, and she answered awkwardly, aware that a considerate host was drawing a left-out guest into conversation. She excused herself and followed Mrs. Castevet's directions to the bathroom, where there were flowered paper towels inscribed *For Our Guest* and a book called *Jokes for The John* that wasn't especially funny.

They left at ten-thirty, saying "Good-by, Roman" and "Thank you, Minnie" and shaking hands with an enthusiasm and an implied promise of more such evenings together that, on Rosemary's part, was completely false. Rounding the first bend in the hallway and hearing the door close behind them, she blew out a relieved sigh and grinned happily at Guy when she saw him doing exactly the same.

"Naow Roman," he said, working his eyebrows comically, "yew stop bendin' Guy's ee-yurs with them thar Mojesky sto-rees!"

Laughing, Rosemary cringed and hushed him, and they ran hand in hand on ultra-quiet tiptoes to their own door, which they unlocked, opened, slammed, locked, bolted, chained; and Guy nailed it over with imaginary beams, pushed up three imaginary boulders, hoisted an imaginary drawbridge, and mopped his brow and panted while Rosemary bent over double and laughed into both hands.

"About that steak," Guy said.

"Oh my God!" Rosemary said. "The pie! How did you eat two pieces of it? It was *weird!*"

"Dear girl," Guy said, "that was an act of superhuman courage and self-sacrifice. I said to myself, 'Ye gods, I'll bet nobody's ever asked this old bat for seconds on *anything* in her entire life! So I did it." He waved a hand grandly. "Now and again I get these noble urges."

They went into the bedroom. "She raises herbs and spices," Rosemary said, "and when they're full-grown she throws them out the window."

"Shh, the walls have ears," Guy said. "Hey, how about that silverware?"

"Isn't that funny?" Rosemary said, working her feet against the floor to unshoe them; "only three dinner plates that match, and they've got that beautiful, beautiful silver."

"Let's be nice; maybe they'll will it to us."

"Let's be nasty and buy our own. Did you go to the bathroom?"

"There? No."

"Guess what they've got in it."

"A bidet."

"No, *Jokes for The John.*"

"No."

Rosemary shucked off her dress. "A book on a hook," she said. "Right next to the toilet."

Guy smiled and shook his head. He began taking out his cufflinks, standing beside the armoire. "Those stories of Roman's, though," he said, "were pretty damn interesting, actually. I'd never even heard of Forbes-Robertson before, but he was a very big star in his day." He worked at the second link, having trouble with it. "I'm going to go over there again tomorrow night and hear some more," he said.

Rosemary looked at him, disconcerted. "You are?" she asked.

"Yes," he said, "he asked me." He held out his hand to her. "Can you get this off for me?"

She went to him and worked at the link, feeling suddenly lost and uncertain. "I thought we were going to do something with Jimmy and Tiger," she said.

"Was that definite?" he asked. His eyes looked into hers. "I thought we were just going to call and see."

"It wasn't *definite,*" she said.

He shrugged. "We'll see them Wednesday or Thursday."

She got the link out and held it on her palm. He took it. "Thanks," he said. "You don't have to come along if you don't want to; you can stay here."

"I think I will," she said. "Stay here." She went to the bed and sat down.

"He knew Henry Irving too," Guy said. "It's really terrifically interesting."

Rosemary unhooked her stockings. "Why did they take down the pictures?" she said.

"What do you mean?"

"Their pictures; they took them down. In the living room and in the hallway leading back to the bathroom. There are hooks in the wall and clean places. And the one picture that *is* there, over the mantel, doesn't fit. There are two inches of clean at both sides of it."

Guy looked at her. "I didn't notice," he said.

"And why do they have all those files and things in the living room?" she asked.

"*That* he told me," Guy said, taking off his shirt. "He puts out a newsletter for stamp collectors. All over the world. That's why they get so much foreign mail."

"Yes, but why in the living room?" Rosemary said. "They have three or four other rooms, all with the doors closed. Why doesn't he use one of those?"

Guy went to her, shirt in hand, and pressed her nose with a firm fingertip. "You're getting nosier than Minnie," he said, kissed air at her, and went out to the bathroom.

Ten or fifteen minutes later, while in the kitchen putting on water for coffee, Rosemary got the sharp pain in her middle that was the night-before signal of her period. She relaxed with one hand against the corner of the stove, letting the pain have its brief way, and then she got out a Chemex paper and the can of coffee, feeling disappointed and forlorn.

She was twenty-four and they wanted three children two years apart; but Guy "wasn't ready yet"—nor would he ever be ready, she feared, until he was as big as Marlon Brando and Richard Burton put together. Didn't he know how handsome and talented he was, how sure to succeed? So her plan was to get pregnant by "accident"; the pills gave her headaches, she said, and rubber gadgets were repulsive. Guy said that subconsciously she was still a good Catholic, and she protested enough to support the explanation. Indulgently he studied the calendar and avoided the "dangerous days," and she said, "No, it's safe today, darling; I'm sure it is."

And again this month he had won and she had lost, in this undignified contest in which he didn't even know they were engaged. "Damn!" she said, and banged the coffee can down on the stove. Guy, in the den, called, "What happened?"

"I bumped my elbow!" she called back.

At least she knew now why she had become depressed during the evening.

Double damn! If they were living together and not married she would have been pregnant fifty times by now!

Seven

The following evening after dinner Guy went over to the Castevets'. Rosemary straightened up the kitchen and was debating whether to work on the window-seat cushions or get into bed with *Manchild in The Promised Land* when the doorbell rang. It was Mrs. Castevet, and with her another woman, short, plump, and smiling, with a Buckley-for-Mayor button on the shoulder of a green dress.

"Hi, dear, we're not bothering you, are we?" Mrs. Castevet said when Rosemary had opened the door. "This is my dear friend Laura-Louise McBurney, who lives up on twelve. Laura-Louise, this is Guy's wife Rosemary."

"Hello, Rosemary! Welcome to the Bram!"

"Laura-Louise just met Guy over at our place and she wanted to meet you too, so we came on over. Guy said you were staying in not doing anything. Can we come in?"

With resigned good grace Rosemary showed them into the living room.

"Oh, you've got new chairs," Mrs. Castevet said. "Aren't they beautiful!"

"They came this morning," Rosemary said.

"Are you all right, dear? You look worn."

"I'm fine," Rosemary said and smiled. "It's the first day of my period."

"And you're up and around?" Laura-Louise asked, sitting. "On *my* first days I experienced such pain that I couldn't move or eat or *anything*. Dan had to give me gin through a straw to kill the pain and we were one-hundred-per-cent Temperance at the time, with that one exception."

"Girls today take things more in their stride than we did," Mrs. Castevet said, sitting too. "They're healthier than we were, thanks to vitamins and better medical care."

Both women had brought identical green sewing bags and, to Rosemary's surprise, were opening them now and taking out crocheting (Laura-Louise) and darning (Mrs. Castevet); settling down for a long evening of needlework and conversation. "What's that over there?" Mrs. Castevet asked. "Seat covers?"

"Cushions for the window seats," Rosemary said, and thinking *Oh all right, I will,* went over and got the work and brought it back and joined them.

Laura-Louise said, "You've certainly made a tremendous change in the apartment, Rosemary."

"Oh, before I forget," Mrs. Castevet said, "this is for you. From Roman and me." She put a small packet of pink tissue paper into Rosemary's hand, with a hardness inside it.

"For me?" Rosemary asked. "I don't understand."

"It's just a little present is all," Mrs. Castevet said, dismissing Rosemary's puzzlement with quick hand-waves. "For moving in."

"But there's no reason for you to . . ." Rosemary unfolded the leaves of used-before tissue paper. Within the pink was Terry's silver filigree ball-charm and its clustered-together neckchain. The smell of the ball's filling made Rosemary pull her head away.

"It's real old," Mrs. Castevet said. "Over three hundred years."

"It's lovely," Rosemary said, examining the ball and wondering whether she should tell that Terry had shown it to her. The moment for doing so slipped by.

"The green inside is called tannis root," Mrs. Castevet said. "It's good luck."

Not for Terry, Rosemary thought, and said, "It's lovely, but I can't accept such a—"

"You already have," Mrs. Castevet said, darning a brown sock and not looking at Rosemary. "Put it on."

Laura-Louise said, "You'll get used to the smell before you know it."

"Go on," Mrs. Castevet said.

"Well, thank you," Rosemary said; and uncertainly she put the chain over her head and tucked the ball into the collar of her dress. It dropped down between her breasts, cold for a moment and obtrusive. *I'll take it off when they go,* she thought.

Laura-Louise said, "A friend of ours made the chain entirely by hand. He's a retired dentist and his hobby is making jewelry out of silver and gold. You'll meet him at Minnie and Roman's on—on some night soon, I'm sure, because they entertain so much. You'll probably meet all their friends, all *our* friends."

Rosemary looked up from her work and saw Laura-Louise pink with an embarrassment that had hurried and confused her last words. Minnie was busy darning, unaware. Laura-Louise smiled and Rosemary smiled back.

"Do you make your own clothes?" Laura-Louise asked.

"No, I don't," Rosemary said, letting the subject be changed. "I try to every once in a while but nothing ever hangs right."

It turned out to be a fairly pleasant evening. Minnie told some amusing stories about her girlhood in Oklahoma, and Laura-Louise showed Rosemary two useful sewing tricks and explained feelingly how Buckley, the Conservative mayoral candidate, could win the coming election despite the high odds against him.

Guy came back at eleven, quiet and oddly self-contained. He said hello to the women and, by Rosemary's chair, bent and kissed her cheek. Minnie said, "*Eleven?* My land! Come on, Laura-Louise." Laura-Louise said, "Come and visit me any time you want, Rosemary; I'm in twelve F." The two women closed their sewing bags and went quickly away.

"Were his stories as interesting as last night?" Rosemary asked.

"Yes," Guy said. "Did you have a nice time?"

"All right. I got some work done."

"So I see."

"I got a present too."

She showed him the charm. "It was Terry's," she said. "They gave it to her; she showed it to me. The police must have—given it back."

"She probably wasn't even wearing it," Guy said.

"I'll bet she was. She was as proud of it as—as if it was the first gift anyone had ever given her." Rosemary lifted the chain off over her head and held the chain and the charm on her palm, jiggling them and looking at them.

"Aren't you going to wear it?" Guy asked.

"It smells," she said. "There's stuff in it called tannis root." She held out her hand. "From the famous greenhouse."

Guy smelled and shrugged. "It's not bad," he said.

Rosemary went into the bedroom and opened a drawer in the vanity where she had a tin Louis Sherry box full of odds and ends. "Tannis, anybody?" she asked herself in the mirror, and put the charm in the box, closed it, and closed the drawer.

Guy, in the doorway, said, "If you took it, you ought to wear it."

That night Rosemary awoke and found Guy sitting beside her smoking in the dark. She asked him what was the matter. "Nothing," he said. "A little insomnia, that's all."

Roman's stories of old-time stars, Rosemary thought, might have depressed him by reminding him that his own career was lagging behind Henry Irving's and Forbes-Whosit's. His going back for more of the stories might have been a form of masochism.

She touched his arm and told him not to worry.

"About what?"

"About anything."

"All right," he said, "I won't."

"You're the greatest," she said. "You know? You are. And it's all going to come out right. You're going to have to learn karate to get rid of the photographers."

He smiled in the glow of his cigarette.

"Any day now," she said. "Something big. Something worthy of you."

"I know," he said. "Go to sleep, honey."

"Okay. Watch the cigarette."

"I will."

"Wake me if you can't sleep."

"Sure."

"I love you."

"I love *you,* Ro."

A day or two later Guy brought home a pair of tickets for the Saturday night performance of *The Fantasticks,* given to him, he explained, by Dominick, his vocal coach. Guy had seen the show years before when it first opened; Rosemary had always been meaning to see it. "Go with Hutch," Guy said; "it'll give me a chance to work on the *Wait Until Dark* scene."

Hutch had seen it too, though, so Rosemary went with Joan Jellico, who confided during dinner at the Bijou that she and Dick were separating, no longer having anything in common except their address. The news upset Rosemary. For days Guy had been distant and preoccupied, wrapped in something he would neither put aside nor share. Had Joan and Dick's estrangement begun in the same way? She grew angry at Joan, who was wearing too much make-up and applauding too loudly in the small theater. No wonder she and Dick could find nothing in common; she was loud and vulgar, he was reserved, sensitive; they should never have married in the first place.

When Rosemary came home Guy was coming out of the shower, more vivacious and *there* than he had been all week. Rosemary's spirits leaped. The show had been even better than she expected, she told him, and bad news, Joan and Dick were separating. They really were birds of completely different feathers though, weren't they? How had the *Wait Until Dark* scene gone? Great. He had it down cold.

"Damn that tannis root," Rosemary said. The whole bedroom smelled of it. The bitter prickly odor had even found its way into the bathroom. She got a piece of aluminum foil from the kitchen and wound the charm in a tight triple wrapping, twisting the ends to seal them.

"It'll probably lose its strength in a few days," Guy said.

"It better," Rosemary said, spraying the air with a deodorant bomb. "If it doesn't, I'm going to throw it away and tell Minnie I lost it."

They made love—Guy was wild and driving—and later, through the wall, Rosemary heard a party in progress at Minnie and Roman's; the same flat unmusical singing she had heard the last time, almost like religious chanting, and the same flute or clarinet weaving in and around and underneath it.

Guy kept his keyed-up vivacity all through Sunday, building shelves and shoe racks in the bedroom closets and inviting a bunch of *Luther* people over for Moo Goo Gai Woodhouse; and on Monday he painted the shelves and shoe racks and stained a bench Rosemary had found in a thrift shop, canceling his session with Dominick and keeping his ear stretched for the phone, which he caught every time before the first ring was finished. At three in the afternoon it rang again, and Rosemary, trying out a different arrangement of the living room chairs, heard him say, "Oh God, no. Oh, the poor guy."

She went to the bedroom door.

"Oh God," Guy said.

He was sitting on the bed, the phone in one hand and a can of Red Devil paint remover in the other. He didn't look at her. "And they don't have any idea what's causing it?" he said. "My God, that's awful, just awful." He listened, and straightened as he sat. "Yes, I am," he said. And then, "Yes, I would. I'd hate to get it this way, but I—" He listened again. "Well, you'd have to speak to Allan about that end of it," he said—Allan Stone, his agent—"but I'm sure there won't be any problem, Mr. Weiss, not as far as we're concerned."

He had it. The Something Big. Rosemary held her breath, waiting.

"Thank *you*, Mr. Weiss," Guy said. "And will you let me know if there's any news? Thanks."

He hung up and shut his eyes. He sat motionless, his hand staying on the phone. He was pale and dummylike, a Pop Art wax statue with real clothes and props, real phone, real can of paint remover.

"Guy?" Rosemary said.

He opened his eyes and looked at her.

"What is it?" she asked.

He blinked and came alive. "Donald Baumgart," he said. "He's gone blind. He woke up yesterday and—he can't see."

"Oh no," Rosemary said.

"He tried to hang himself this morning. He's in Bellevue now, under sedation."

They looked painfully at each other.

"I've got the part," Guy said. "It's a hell of a way to get it." He looked at the paint remover in his hand and put it on the night table. "Listen," he said, "I've got to get out and walk around." He stood up. "I'm sorry. I've got to get outside and absorb this."

"I understand, go ahead," Rosemary said, standing back from the doorway.

He went as he was, down the hall and out the door, letting it swing closed after him with its own soft slam.

She went into the living room, thinking of poor Donald Baumgart and lucky Guy; lucky she-and-Guy, with the good part that would get attention even if the show folded, would lead to other parts, to movies maybe, to a house in Los Angeles, a spice garden, three children two years apart. Poor Donald Baumgart with his clumsy name that he didn't change. He must have been good, to have won out over Guy, and there he was in Bellevue, blind and wanting to kill himself, under sedation.

Kneeling on a window seat, Rosemary looked out the side of its bay and watched the house's entrance far below, waiting to see Guy come out. When would rehearsals begin? she wondered. She would go out of town with him, of course; what fun it would be! Boston? Philadelphia? Washington would be exciting. She had never been there. While Guy was rehearsing afternoons, she could sightsee; and evenings, after the performance, everyone would meet in a restaurant or club to gossip and exchange rumors . . .

She waited and watched but he didn't come out. He must have used the Fifty-fifth Street door.

Now, when he should have been happy, he was dour and troubled, sitting with nothing moving except his cigarette hand and his eyes. His eyes followed her around the apartment; tensely, as if she were dangerous. "What's *wrong?*" she asked a dozen times.

"Nothing," he said. "Don't you have your sculpture class today?"

"I haven't gone in two months."

"Why don't you go?"

She went; tore away old plasticine, reset the armature, and began anew, doing a new model among new students. "Where've you been?" the instructor asked. He had eyeglasses and an Adam's apple and made miniatures of her torso without watching his hands.

"In Zanzibar," she said.

"Zanzibar is no more," he said, smiling nervously. "It's Tanzania."

One afternoon she went down to Macy's and Gimbels, and when she came home there were roses in the kitchen, roses in the living room, and Guy coming out of the bedroom with one rose and a forgive-me smile, like a reading he had once done for her of Chance Wayne in *Sweet Bird.*

"I've been a living turd," he said. "It's from sitting around hoping that Baumgart won't regain his sight, which is what I've been doing, rat that I am."

"That's natural," she said. "You're bound to feel two ways about—"

"Listen," he said, pushing the rose to her nose, "even if this thing falls through, even if I'm Charley Cresta Blanca for the rest of my days, I'm going to stop giving you the short end of the stick."

"You haven't—"

"Yes I have. I've been so busy tearing my hair out over *my* career that I haven't given Thought One to yours. Let's have a baby, okay? Let's have three, one at a time."

She looked at him.

"A baby," he said. "You know. Goo, goo? Diapers? Waa, waa?"

"Do you mean it?" she asked.

"Sure I mean it," he said. "I even figured out the right time to start. Next Monday and Tuesday. Red circles on the calendar, please."

"You *really* mean it, Guy?" she asked, tears in her eyes.

"No, I'm kidding," he said. "*Sure* I mean it. Look, Rosemary, for God's sake don't cry, all right? Please. It's going to upset me very much if you cry, so stop right now, all right?"

"All right," she said. "I won't cry."

"I really went rose-nutty, didn't I?" he said, looking around brightly. "There's a bunch in the bedroom too."

Eight

She went to upper Broadway for swordfish steaks and across town to Lexington Avenue for cheeses; not because she couldn't get swordfish steaks and cheeses right there in the neighborhood but simply because on that snappy bright-blue morning she wanted to be all over the city, walking briskly with her coat flying, drawing second glances for her prettiness, impressing tough clerks with the precision and know-how of her orders. It was Monday, October 4th, the day of Pope Paul's visit to the city, and the sharing of the event made people more open and communicative than they ordinarily were; *How nice it is,* Rosemary thought, *that the whole city is happy on a day when I'm so happy.*

She followed the Pope's rounds on television during the afternoon, moving the set out from the wall of the den (soon nursery) and turning it so she could watch from the kitchen while readying the fish and vegetables and salad greens. His speech at the UN moved her, and she was sure it would help ease the Vietnam situation. "War never again," he said; wouldn't his words give pause to even the most hard-headed statesman?

At four-thirty, while she was setting the table before the fireplace, the telephone rang.

"Rosemary? How are you?"

"Fine," she said. "How are you?" It was Margaret, the older of her two sisters.

"Fine," Margaret said.

"Where are you?"

"In Omaha."

They had never got on well. Margaret had been a sullen, resentful girl, too often used by their mother as the caretaker of the younger children. To be called by her like this was strange; strange and frightening.

"Is everyone all right?" Rosemary asked. *Someone's dead,* she thought. *Who? Ma? Pa? Brian?*

"Yes, everyone's fine."

"They are?"

"Yes. Are you?"

"Yes; I said I was."

"I've had the funniest feeling all day long, Rosemary. That something happened to you. Like an accident or something. That you were hurt. Maybe in the hospital."

"Well, I'm not," Rosemary said, and laughed. "I'm fine. Really I am."

"It was such a strong feeling," Margaret said. "I was *sure* something had happened. Finally Gene said why don't I call you and find out."

"How is he?"

"Fine."

"And the children?"

"Oh, the usual scrapes and scratches, but they're fine too. I've got another one on the way, you know."

"No, I didn't know. That's wonderful. When is it due?" *We'll have one on the way soon too.*

"The end of March. How's your husband, Rosemary?"

"He's fine. He's got an important part in a new play that's going into rehearsal soon."

"Say, did you get a good look at the Pope?" Margaret asked. "There must be terrific excitement there."

"There is," Rosemary said. "I've been watching it on television. It's in Omaha too, isn't it?"

"Not live? You didn't go out and see him live?"

"No, I didn't."

"Really?"

"Really."

"Honest to goodness, Rosemary," Margaret said. "Do you know Ma and Pa were going to *fly* there to see him but they couldn't because there's going to be a strike vote and Pa's seconding the motion? Lots of people did fly, though; the Donovans, and Dot and Sandy Wallingford; and you're right there, *living* there, and didn't go out and see him?"

"Religion doesn't mean as much to me now as it did back home," Rosemary said.

"Well," Margaret said, "I guess that's inevitable," and Rosemary heard, unspoken, *when you're married to a Protestant.* She said, "It was nice of you to call, Margaret. There's nothing for you to worry about. I've never been healthier or happier."

"It was such a strong feeling," Margaret said. "From the minute I woke up. I'm so used to taking care of you little brats . . ."

"Give my love to everyone, will you? And tell Brian to answer my letter."

"I will. Rosemary—"

"Yes?"

"I still have the feeling. Stay home tonight, will you?"

"That's just what we're planning to do," Rosemary said, looking over at the partially set table.

"Good," Margaret said. "Take care of yourself."

"I will," Rosemary said. "You too, Margaret."

"I will. Good-by."

"Good-by."

She went back to setting the table, feeling pleasantly sad and nostalgic for Margaret and Brian and the other kids, for Omaha and the irretrievable past.

With the table set, she bathed; then powdered and perfumed herself, did her eyes and lips and hair, and put on a pair of burgundy silk lounging pajamas that Guy had given her the previous Christmas.

He came home late, after six. "Mmm," he said, kissing her, "you look good enough to eat. Shall we? Damn!"

"What?"

"I forgot the pie."

He had told her not to make a dessert; he would bring home his absolute all-time favorite, a Horn and Hardart pumpkin pie.

"I could *kick* myself," he said. "I passed *two* of those damn retail stores; not one but two."

"It's all right," Rosemary said. "We can have fruit and cheese. That's the best dessert anyway, really."

"It is not; Horn and Hardart pumpkin pie is."

He went in to wash up and she put a tray of stuffed mushrooms into the oven and mixed the salad dressing.

In a few minutes Guy came to the kitchen door, buttoning the collar of a blue velour shirt. He was bright-eyed and a bit on edge, the way he had been the first time they slept together, when he knew it was going to happen. It pleased Rosemary to see him that way.

"Your pal the Pope really loused up traffic today," he said.

"Did you see any of the television?" she asked. "They've had fantastic coverage."

"I got a glimpse up at Allan's," he said. "Glasses in the freezer?"

"Yes. He made a wonderful speech at the UN. 'War never again,' he told them."

"Rotsa ruck. Hey, *those* look good."

They had Gibsons and the stuffed mushrooms in the living room. Guy put crumpled newspaper and sticks of kindling on the fireplace grate, and two big chunks of cannel coal. "Here goes nothing," he said, and struck a match and lit the paper. It flamed high and caught the kindling. Dark smoke began spilling out over the front of the mantel and up toward the ceiling. "Good grief," Guy said, and groped inside the fireplace. "The paint, the paint!" Rosemary cried.

He got the flue opened; and the air conditioner, set at exhaust, drew out the smoke.

"Nobody, but nobody, has a fire tonight," Guy said.

Rosemary, kneeling with her drink and staring into the spitting flame-wrapped coals, said, "Isn't it gorgeous? I hope we have the coldest winter in eighty years."

Guy put on Ella Fitzgerald singing Cole Porter.

They were halfway through the swordfish when the doorbell rang. "Shit," Guy said. He got up, tossed down his napkin, and went to answer it. Rosemary cocked her head and listened.

The door opened and Minnie said, "Hi, Guy!" and more that was unintelligible. *Oh, no,* Rosemary thought. *Don't let her in, Guy. Not now, not tonight.*

Guy spoke, and then Minnie again: ". . . extra. We don't need them." Guy again and Minnie again. Rosemary eased out held-in breath; it didn't sound as if she was coming in, thank God.

The door closed and was chained *(Good!)* and bolted *(Good!)*. Rosemary watched and waited, and Guy sidled into the archway, smiling smugly, with both hands behind his back. "*Who* says there's nothing to ESP?" he said, and coming toward the table brought forth his hands with two white custard cups sitting one on each palm. "Madame and Monsieur shall have ze dessairt after all," he said, setting one cup by Rosemary's wineglass and the other by his own. "*Mousse au chocolat,*" he said, "or 'chocolate mouse,' as Minnie calls it. Of course with her it could *be* chocolate mouse, so eat with care."

Rosemary laughed happily. "That's wonderful," she said. "It's what *I* was going to make."

"See?" Guy said, sitting. "ESP." He replaced his napkin and poured more wine.

"I was afraid she was going to come charging in and stay all evening," Rosemary said, forking up carrots.

"No," Guy said, "she just wanted us to try her chocolate mouse, seein' as how it's one of her speci-*al*-ities."

"It *looks* good."

"It does, doesn't it."

The cups were filled with peaked swirls of chocolate. Guy's was topped with a sprinkling of chopped nuts, and Rosemary's with a half walnut.

"It's sweet of her, really," Rosemary said. "We shouldn't make fun of her."

"You're right," Guy said, "you're right."

The mousse was excellent, but it had a chalky undertaste that reminded Rosemary of blackboards and grade school. Guy tried but could find no "undertaste" at all, chalky or otherwise. Rosemary put her spoon down after two swallows. Guy said, "Aren't you going to finish it? That's silly, honey; there's no 'undertaste.' "

Rosemary said there was.

"Come on," Guy said, "the old bat slaved all day over a hot stove; eat it."

"But I don't like it," Rosemary said.

"It's delicious."

"You can have mine."

Guy scowled. "All right, don't eat it," he said; "you don't wear the charm she gave you, you might as well not eat her dessert too."

Confused, Rosemary said, "What does one thing have to do with the other?"

"They're both examples of—well, unkindness, that's all." Guy said. "Two minutes ago you said we should stop making fun of her. That's a form of making fun too, accepting something and then not using it."

"Oh—" Rosemary picked up her spoon. "If it's going to turn into a big scene —" She took a full spoonful of the mousse and thrust it into her mouth.

"It isn't going to turn into a big scene," Guy said. "Look, if you really can't stand it, don't eat it."

"Delicious," Rosemary said, full-mouthed and taking another spoonful, "no undertaste at all. Turn the records over."

Guy got up and went to the record player. Rosemary doubled her napkin in her lap and plopped two spoonfuls of the mousse into it, and another half-spoonful for good measure. She folded the napkin closed and then showily scraped clean the inside of the cup and swallowed down the scrapings as Guy came back to the table. "There, Daddy," she said, tilting the cup toward him. "Do I get a gold star on my chart?"

"Two of them," he said. "I'm sorry if I was stuffy."

"You were."

"I'm sorry." He smiled.

Rosemary melted. "You're forgiven," she said. "It's nice that you're considerate of old ladies. It means you'll be considerate of me when *I'm* one."

They had coffee and crème de menthe.

"Margaret called this afternoon," Rosemary said.

"Margaret?"

"My sister."

"Oh. Everything okay?"

"Yes. She was afraid something had happened to me. She had a feeling."

"Oh?"

"We're to stay home tonight."

"Drat. And I made a reservation at Nedick's. In the Orange Room."

"You'll have to cancel it."

"How come you turned out sane when the rest of your family is nutty?"

The first wave of dizziness caught Rosemary at the kitchen sink as she scraped the uneaten mousse from her napkin into the drain. She swayed for a moment, then blinked and frowned. Guy, in the den, said, "He isn't there yet. Christ, what a mob." The Pope at Yankee Stadium.

"I'll be in in a minute," Rosemary said.

Shaking her head to clear it, she rolled the napkins up inside the tablecloth and put the bundle aside for the hamper. She put the stopper in the drain, turned on the hot water, squeezed in some Joy, and began loading in the dishes and pans. She would do them in the morning, let them soak overnight.

The second wave came as she was hanging up the dish towel. It lasted longer, and this time the room turned slowly around and her legs almost slued out from under her. She hung on to the edge of the sink.

When it was over she said "Oh boy," and added up two Gibsons, two glasses of wine (or had it been three?), and one crème de menthe. No wonder.

She made it to the doorway of the den and kept her footing through the next wave by holding on to the knob with one hand and the jamb with the other.

"What is it?" Guy asked, standing up anxiously.

"Dizzy," she said, and smiled.

He snapped off the TV and came to her, took her arm and held her surely around the waist. "No wonder," he said. "All that booze. You probably had an empty stomach, too."

He helped her toward the bedroom and, when her legs buckled, caught her up and carried her. He put her down on the bed and sat beside her, taking her hand and stroking her forehead sympathetically. She closed her eyes. The bed was a raft that floated on gentle ripples, tilting and swaying pleasantly. "Nice," she said.

"Sleep is what you need," Guy said, stroking her forehead. "A good night's sleep."

"We have to make a baby."

"We will. Tomorrow. There's plenty of time."

"Missing the mass."

"Sleep. Get a good night's sleep. Go on . . ."

"Just a nap," she said, and was sitting with a drink in her hand on President Kennedy's yacht. It was sunny and breezy, a perfect day for a cruise. The President, studying a large map, gave terse and knowing instructions to a Negro mate.

Guy had taken off the top of her pajamas. "Why are you taking them off?" she asked.

"To make you more comfortable," he said.

"I'm comfortable."

"Sleep, Ro."

He undid the snaps at her side and slowly drew off the bottoms. Thought she was asleep and didn't know. Now she had nothing on at all except a red bikini, but the other women on the yacht—Jackie Kennedy, Pat Lawford, and Sarah Churchill—were wearing bikinis too, so it was all right, thank goodness. The President was in his Navy uniform. He had completely recovered from the assassination and looked better than ever. Hutch was standing on the dock with armloads of weather-forecasting equipment. "Isn't Hutch coming with us?" Rosemary asked the President.

"Catholics only," he said, smiling. "I wish we weren't bound by these prejudices, but unfortunately we are."

"But what about Sarah Churchill?" Rosemary asked. She turned to point, but Sarah Churchill was gone and the family was there in her place: Ma, Pa, and everybody, with the husbands, wives, and children. Margaret was pregnant, and so were Jean and Dodie and Ernestine.

Guy was taking off her wedding ring. She wondered why, but was too tired to ask. "Sleep," she said, and slept.

It was the first time the Sistine Chapel had been opened to the public and she was inspecting the ceiling on a new elevator that carried the visitor through the chapel horizontally, making it possible to see the frescoes exactly as Michelangelo, painting them, had seen them. How glorious they were! She saw God extending his finger to Adam, giving him the divine spark of life; and the underside of a shelf partly covered with gingham contact paper as she was carried backward through the linen closet. "Easy," Guy said, and another man said, "You've got her too high."

"Typhoon!" Hutch shouted from the dock amid all his weather-forecasting equipment. "Typhoon! It killed fifty-five people in London and it's heading this way!" And Rosemary knew he was right. She must warn the President. The ship was heading for disaster.

But the President was gone. Everyone was gone. The deck was infinite and bare, except for, far away, the Negro mate holding the wheel unremittingly on its course.

Rosemary went to him and saw at once that he hated all white people, hated her. "You'd better go down below, Miss," he said, courteous but hating her, not even waiting to hear the warning she had brought.

Below was a huge ballroom where on one side a church burned fiercely and on the other a black-bearded man stood glaring at her. In the center was a bed. She went to it and lay down, and was suddenly surrounded by naked men and women, ten or a dozen, with Guy among them. They were elderly, the women grotesque and slack-breasted. Minnie and her friend Laura-Louise were there, and Roman in a black miter and a black silk robe. With a thin black wand he was drawing designs on her body, dipping the wand's point in a cup of red held for him by a sun-browned man with a white moustache. The point moved back and forth across her stomach and down ticklingly to the insides of her thighs. The naked people were chanting—flat, unmusical, foreign-tongued syllables—and a flute or clarinet accompanied them. "She's awake, she sees!" Guy whispered to Minnie. He was large-eyed, tense. "She *don't* see," Minnie said. "As long as she ate the mouse she can't see nor hear. She's like dead. Now sing."

Jackie Kennedy came into the ballroom in an exquisite gown of ivory satin embroidered with pearls. "I'm so sorry to hear you aren't feeling well," she said, hurrying to Rosemary's side.

Rosemary explained about the mouse-bite, minimizing it so Jackie wouldn't worry.

"You'd better have your legs tied down," Jackie said, "in case of convulsions."

"Yes, I suppose so," Rosemary said. "There's always a chance it was rabid." She watched with interest as white-smocked interns tied her legs, and her arms too, to the four bedposts.

"If the music bothers you," Jackie said, "let me know and I'll have it stopped."

"Oh, no," Rosemary said. "Please don't change the program on my account. It doesn't bother me at all, really it doesn't."

Jackie smiled warmly at her. "Try to sleep," she said. "We'll be waiting up on deck." She withdrew, her satin gown whispering.

Rosemary slept a while, and then Guy came in and began making love to her. He stroked her with both hands—a long, relishing stroke that began at her bound wrists, slid down over her arms, breasts, and loins, and became a voluptuous tickling between her legs. He repeated the exciting stroke again and again, his hands hot and sharp-nailed, and then, when she was ready-ready-more-than-ready, he slipped a hand in under her buttocks, raised them, lodged his hardness against her, and pushed it powerfully in. Bigger he was than always; painfully, wonderfully big. He lay forward upon her, his other arm sliding under her back to hold her, his broad chest crushing her breasts. (He was wearing, because it was to be a costume party, a suit of coarse leathery armor.) Brutally, rhythmically, he drove his new hugeness. She opened her eyes and looked into yellow furnace-eyes, smelled sulphur and tannis root, felt wet breath on her mouth, heard lust-grunts and the breathing of onlookers.

This is no dream, she thought. *This is real, this is happening.* Protest woke in her eyes and throat, but something covered her face, smothering her in a sweet stench.

The hugeness kept driving in her, the leathery body banging itself against her again and again and again.

The Pope came in with a suitcase in his hand and a coat over his arm. "Jackie tells me you've been bitten by a mouse," he said.

"Yes," Rosemary said. "That's why I didn't come see you." She spoke sadly, so he wouldn't suspect she had just had an orgasm.

"That's all right," he said. "We wouldn't want you to jeopardize your health."

"Am I forgiven, Father?" she asked.

"Absolutely," he said. He held out his hand for her to kiss the ring. Its stone was a silver filigree ball less than an inch in diameter; inside it, very tiny, Anna Maria Alberghetti sat waiting.

Rosemary kissed it and the Pope hurried out to catch his plane.

Nine

"Hey, it's after nine," Guy said, shaking her shoulder.

She pushed his hand away and turned over onto her stomach. "Five minutes," she said, deep in the pillow.

"No," he said, and yanked her hair. "I've got to be at Dominick's at ten."

"Eat out."

"The hell I will." He slapped her behind through the blanket.

Everything came back: the dreams, the drinks, Minnie's chocolate mousse, the Pope, that awful moment of not-dreaming. She turned back over and raised herself on her arms, looking at Guy. He was lighting a cigarette, sleep-rumpled, needing a shave. He had pajamas on. She was nude.

"What time is it?" she asked.

"Ten after nine."

"What time did I go to sleep?" She sat up.

"About eight-thirty," he said. "And you didn't go to sleep, honey; you passed out. From now on you get cocktails *or* wine, not cocktails *and* wine."

"The dreams I had," she said, rubbing her forehead and closing her eyes. "President Kennedy, the Pope, Minnie and Roman . . ." She opened her eyes and saw scratches on her left breast; two parallel hairlines of red running down into the nipple. Her thighs stung; she pushed the blanket from them and saw more scratches, seven or eight going this way and that.

"Don't yell," Guy said. "I already filed them down." He showed short smooth fingernails.

Rosemary looked at him uncomprehendingly.

"I didn't want to miss Baby Night," he said.

"You mean you—"

"And a couple of my nails were ragged."

"While I was—out?"

He nodded and grinned. "It was kind of fun," he said, "in a necrophile sort of way."

She looked away, her hands pulling the blanket back over her thighs. "I dreamed someone was—raping me," she said. "I don't know who. Someone —unhuman."

"Thanks a lot," Guy said.

"You were there, and Minnie and Roman, other people . . . It was some kind of ceremony."

"I tried to wake you," he said, "but you were out like a light."

She turned further away and swung her legs out on the other side of the bed.

"What's the matter?" Guy asked.

"Nothing," she said, sitting there, not looking around at him. "I guess I feel funny about your doing it that way, with me unconscious."

"I didn't want to miss the night," he said.

"We could have done it this morning or tonight. Last night wasn't the only split second in the whole month. And even if it *had* been . . ."

"I thought you would have wanted me to," he said, and ran a finger up her back.

She squirmed away from it. "It's supposed to be shared, not one awake and one asleep," she said. Then: "Oh, I guess I'm being silly." She got up and went to the closet for her housecoat.

"I'm sorry I scratched you," Guy said. "I was a wee bit loaded myself."

She made breakfast and, when Guy had gone, did the sinkful of dishes and put the kitchen to rights. She opened windows in the living room and bedroom —the smell of last night's fire still lingered in the apartment—made the bed, and took a shower; a long one, first hot and then cold. She stood capless and immobile under the downpour, waiting for her head to clear and her thoughts to find an order and conclusion.

Had last night really been, as Guy had put it, Baby Night? Was she now, at this moment, actually pregnant? Oddly enough, she didn't care. She was unhappy—whether or not it was silly to be so. Guy had taken her without her knowledge, had made love to her as a mindless body ("kind of fun in a necrophile sort of way") rather than as the complete mind-and-body person she was; and had done so, moreover, with a savage gusto that had produced scratches, aching soreness, and a nightmare so real and intense that she could almost see on her stomach the designs Roman had drawn with his red-dipped wand. She scrubbed soap on herself vigorously, resentfully. True, he had done it for the best motive in the world, to make a baby, and true too he had drunk as much as she had; but she wished that no motive and no number of drinks could have enabled him to take her that way, taking only her body without her soul or self or she-ness—whatever it was he presumably loved. Now, looking back over the past weeks and months, she felt a disturbing presence of overlooked signals just beyond memory, signals of a shortcoming in his love for her, of a disparity between what he said and what he felt. He was an actor; could anyone know when an actor was true and not acting?

It would take more than a shower to wash away these thoughts. She turned the water off and, between both hands, pressed out her streaming hair.

On the way out to shop she rang the Castevets' doorbell and returned the cups from the mousse. "Did you like it, dear?" Minnie asked. "I think I put a little too much cream de cocoa in it."

"It was delicious," Rosemary said. "You'll have to give me the recipe."

"I'd love to. You going marketing? Would you do me a teeny favor? Six eggs and a small Instant Sanka; I'll pay you later. I hate going out for just one or two things, don't you?"

There was distance now between her and Guy, but he seemed not to be aware of it. His play was going into rehearsal November first—*Don't I Know You From Somewhere?* was the name of it—and he spent a great deal of time studying his part, practicing the use of the crutches and leg-braces it called for, and visiting the Highbridge section of the Bronx, the play's locale. They had dinner with friends more evenings than not; when they didn't, they made natural-sounding conversation about furniture and the ending-any-day-now newspaper strike and the World Series. They went to a preview of a new musical and a screening of a new movie, to parties and the opening of a friend's exhibit of metal constructions. Guy seemed never to be looking at her, always at a script or TV or at someone else. He was in bed and asleep before she was. One evening he went to the Castevets' to hear more of Roman's theater stories, and she stayed in the apartment and watched *Funny Face* on TV.

"Don't you think we ought to talk about it?" she said the next morning at breakfast.

"About what?"

She looked at him; he seemed genuinely unknowing. "The conversations we've been making," she said.

"What do you mean?"

"The way you haven't been looking at me."

"What are you *talking* about? I've been looking at you."

"No you haven't."

"I have *so*. Honey, what is it? What's the matter?"

"Nothing. Never mind."

"No, don't say that. What is it? What's bothering you?"

"Nothing."

"Ah look, honey, I know I've been kind of preoccupied, with the part and the crutches and all; is that it? Well gee whiz, Ro, it's *important,* you know? But it doesn't mean I don't love you, just because I'm not riveting you with a passionate *gaze* all the time. I've got to think about *practical* matters too." It was awkward and charming and sincere, like his playing of the cowboy in *Bus Stop.*

"All right," Rosemary said. "I'm sorry I'm being pesty."

"You? You couldn't be pesty if you tried."

He leaned across the table and kissed her.

Hutch had a cabin near Brewster where he spent occasional weekends. Rosemary called him and asked if she might use it for three or four days, possibly a week. "Guy's getting into his new part," she explained, "and I really think it'll be easier for him with me out of the way."

"It's yours," Hutch said, and Rosemary went down to his apartment on Lexington Avenue and Twenty-fourth Street to pick up the key.

She looked in first at a delicatessen where the clerks were friends from her own days in the neighborhood, and then she went up to Hutch's apartment, which was small and dark and neat as a pin, with an inscribed photo of Winston Churchill and a sofa that had belonged to Madame Pompadour. Hutch was sitting barefoot between two bridge tables, each with its typewriter and piles of paper. His practice was to write two books at once, turning to the second when he struck a snag on the first, and back to the first when he struck a snag on the second.

"I'm really looking forward to it," Rosemary said, sitting on Madame Pompadour's sofa. "I suddenly realized the other day that I've never been alone in my whole life—not for more than a few hours, that is. The idea of three or four days is heaven."

"A chance to sit quietly and find out who you are; where you've been and where you're going."

"Exactly."

"All right, you can stop forcing that smile," Hutch said. "Did he hit you with a lamp?"

"He didn't hit me with anything," Rosemary said. "It's a very difficult part, a crippled boy who *pretends* that he's adjusted to his crippled-ness. He's got to work with crutches and leg-braces, and naturally he's preoccupied and—and, well, preoccupied."

"I see," Hutch said. "We'll change the subject. The *News* had a lovely rundown the other day of all the gore we missed during the strike. Why didn't you tell me you'd had another suicide up there at Happy House?"

"Oh, didn't I tell you?" Rosemary asked.

"No, you didn't," Hutch said.

"It was someone we knew. The girl I told you about; the one who'd been a drug addict and was rehabilitated by the Castevets, these people who live on our floor. I'm *sure* I told you *that.*"

"The girl who was going to the basement with you."

"That's right."

"They didn't rehabilitate her very successfully, it would seem. Was she living with them?"

"Yes," Rosemary said. "We've gotten to know them fairly well since it happened. Guy goes over there once in a while to hear stories about the theater. Mr. Castevet's father was a producer around the turn of the century."

"I shouldn't have thought Guy would be interested," Hutch said. "An elderly couple, I take it?"

"He's seventy-nine; she's seventy or so."

"It's an odd name," Hutch said. "How is it spelled?"

Rosemary spelled it for him.

"I've never heard it before," he said. "French, I suppose."

"The name may be but they aren't," Rosemary said. "He's from right here and she's from a place called—believe it or not—Bushyhead, Oklahoma."

"My God," Hutch said. "I'm going to use that in a book. That one. I know just where to put it. Tell me, how are you planning to get to the cabin? You'll need a car, you know."

"I'm going to rent one."

"Take mine."

"Oh no, Hutch, I couldn't."

"Do, please," Hutch said. "All I do is move it from one side of the street to the other. Please. You'll save me a great deal of bother."

Rosemary smiled. "All right," she said. "I'll do you a favor and take your car."

Hutch gave her the keys to the car and the cabin, a sketch-map of the route, and a typed list of instructions concerning the pump, the refrigerator, and a variety of possible emergencies. Then he put on shoes and a coat and walked her down to where the car, an old light-blue Oldsmobile, was parked. "The registration papers are in the glove compartment," he said. "Please feel free to stay as long as you like. I have no immediate plans for either the car or the cabin."

"I'm sure I won't stay more than a week," Rosemary said. "Guy might not even want me to stay that long."

When she was settled in the car, Hutch leaned in at the window and said, "I have all kinds of good advice to give you but I'm going to mind my own business if it kills me."

Rosemary kissed him. "Thank you," she said. "For that and for this and for everything."

She left on the morning of Saturday, October 16th, and stayed five days at the cabin. The first two days she never once thought about Guy—a fitting revenge for the cheerfulness with which he had agreed to her going. Did she *look* as if she needed a good rest? Very well, she would *have* one, a long one, never once thinking about him. She took walks through dazzling yellow-and-orange woods, went to sleep early and slept late, read *Flight of The Falcon* by Daphne du Maurier, and made glutton's meals on the bottled-gas stove. Never once thinking about him.

On the third day she thought about him. He was vain, self-centered, shallow, and deceitful. He had married her to have an audience, not a mate. (Little Miss Just-out-of-Omaha, what a *goop* she had been! "Oh, I'm *used* to actors; I've been here almost a year now." And she had all but followed him around the studio carrying his newspaper in her mouth.) She would give him a year to shape up and become a good husband; if he didn't make it she would pull out, and with no religious qualms whatever. And meanwhile she would go back to work and get again that sense of independence and self-sufficiency she had been so eager to get rid of. She would be strong and proud and ready to go if he failed to meet her standards.

Those glutton's meals—man-size cans of beef stew and chili con carne—began to disagree with her, and on that third day she was mildly nauseated and could eat only soup and crackers.

On the fourth day she awoke missing him and cried. What was she doing there, alone in that cold crummy cabin? What had he done that was so terrible? He had gotten drunk and had grabbed her without saying may I. Well that was really an earth-shaking offense, now wasn't it? There he was, facing the biggest challenge of his career, and *she*—instead of being there to help him, to cue and encourage him—was off in the middle of nowhere, eating herself sick and feeling sorry for herself. Sure he was vain and self-centered; he was an actor, wasn't he? Laurence *Olivier* was probably vain and self-centered. And yes he might lie now and then; wasn't that exactly what had attracted her and still did?—that freedom and nonchalance so different from her own boxed-in propriety?

She drove into Brewster and called him. Service answered, the Friendly One: "Oh hi, dear, are you back from the country? Oh. Guy is out, dear; can he call you? *You'll* call *him* at five. Right. You've certainly got lovely weather. Are you enjoying yourself? Good."

At five he was still out, her message waiting for him. She ate in a diner and went to the one movie theater. At nine he was still out and Service was someone new and automatic with a message for her: she should call him before eight the next morning or after six in the evening.

That next day she reached what seemed like a sensible and realistic view of things. They were both at fault; he for being thoughtless and self-absorbed, she for failing to express and explain her discontent. He could hardly be expected to change until she showed him that change was called for. She had only to talk—no, *they* had only to talk, for he might be harboring a similar discontent of which she was similarly unaware—and matters couldn't help but improve. Like so many unhappinesses, this one had begun with silence in the place of honest open talk.

She went into Brewster at six and called and he was there. "Hi, darling," he said. "How are you?"

"Fine. How are you?"

"All right. I miss you."

She smiled at the phone. "I miss *you,*" she said. "I'm coming home tomorrow."

"Good, that's great," he said. "All kinds of things have been going on here. Rehearsals have been postponed until January."

"Oh?"

"They haven't been able to cast the little girl. It's a break for me though; I'm going to do a pilot next month. A half-hour comedy series."

"You are?"

"It fell into my lap, Ro. And it really looks good. ABC loves the idea. It's called *Greenwich Village;* it's going to be filmed there, and I'm a way-out writer. It's practically the lead."

"That's marvelous, Guy!"

"Allan says I'm suddenly very hot."

"That's wonderful!"

"Listen, I've got to shower and shave; he's taking me to a screening that Stanley Kubrick is going to be at. When are you going to get in?"

"Around noon, maybe earlier."

"I'll be waiting. Love you."

"Love you!"

She called Hutch, who was out, and left word with his service that she would return the car the following afternoon.

The next morning she cleaned the cabin, closed it up and locked it, and drove back to the city. Traffic on the Saw Mill River Parkway was bottlenecked by a three-car collision, and it was close to one o'clock when she parked the car half-in half-out-of the bus stop in front of the Bramford. With her small suitcase she hurried into the house.

The elevator man hadn't taken Guy down, but he had been off duty from eleven-fifteen to twelve.

He was there, though. The *No Strings* album was playing. She opened her mouth to call and he came out of the bedroom in a fresh shirt and tie, headed for the kitchen with a used coffee cup in his hand.

They kissed, lovingly and fully, he hugging her one-armed because of the cup.

"Have a good time?" he asked.

"Terrible. Awful. I missed you so."

"How are you?"

"Fine. How was Stanley Kubrick?"

"Didn't show, the fink."

They kissed again.

She brought her suitcase into the bedroom and opened it on the bed. He came in with two cups of coffee, gave her one, and sat on the vanity bench while she unpacked. She told him about the yellow-and-orange woods and the still nights; he told her about *Greenwich Village,* who else was in it and who the producers, writers, and director were.

"Are you *really* fine?" he asked when she was zipping closed the empty case. She didn't understand.

"Your period," he said. "It was due on Tuesday."

"It was?"

He nodded.

"Well it's just two days," she said—matter-of-factly, as if her heart weren't racing, leaping. "It's probably the change of water, or the food I ate up there."

"You've never been late before," he said.

"It'll probably come tonight. Or tomorrow."

"You want to bet?"

"Yes."

"A quarter?"

"Okay."

"You're going to lose, Ro."

"Shut up. You're getting me all jumpy. It's only two days. It'll probably come tonight."

Ten

It didn't come that night or the next day. Or the day after that or the day after that. Rosemary moved gently, walked lightly, so as not to dislodge what might possibly have taken hold inside her.

Talk with Guy? No, that could wait.

Everything could wait.

She cleaned, shopped, and cooked, breathing carefully. Laura-Louise came down one morning and asked her to vote for Buckley. She said she would, to get rid of her.

"Give me my quarter," Guy said.

"Shut up," she said, giving his arm a backhand punch.

She made an appointment with an obstetrician and, on Thursday, October 28th, went to see him. His name was Dr. Hill. He had been recommended to her by a friend, Elise Dunstan, who had used him through two pregnancies and swore by him. His office was on West Seventy-second Street.

He was younger than Rosemary had expected—Guy's age or even less—and he looked a little bit like Dr. Kildare on television. She liked him. He asked her questions slowly and with interest, examined her, and sent her to a lab on Sixtieth Street where a nurse drew blood from her right arm.

He called the next afternoon at three-thirty.

"Mrs. Woodhouse?"

"Dr. Hill?"

"Yes. Congratulations."

"Really?"

"Really."

She sat down on the side of the bed, smiling past the phone. *Really, really, really, really, really.*

"Are you there?"

"What happens now?" she asked.

"Very little. You come in and see me again next month. And you get those Natalin pills and start taking them. One a day. And you fill out some forms that I'm going to mail you—for the hospital; it's best to get the reservation in as soon as possible."

"When will it be?" she asked.

"If your last period was September twenty-first," he said, "it works out to June twenty-eighth."

"That sounds so far away."

"It is. Oh, one more thing, Mrs. Woodhouse. The lab would like another blood sample. Could you drop by there tomorrow or Monday and let them have it?"

"Yes, of course," Rosemary said. "What for?"

"The nurse didn't take as much as she should have."

"But—I'm pregnant, aren't I?"

"Yes, they did *that* test," Dr. Hill said, "but I generally have them run a few others besides—blood sugar and so forth—and the nurse didn't know and only took enough for the one. It's nothing to be concerned about. You're pregnant. I give you my word."

"All right," she said. "I'll go back tomorrow morning."

"Do you remember the address?"

"Yes, I still have the card."

"I'll put those forms in the mail, and let's see you again—the last week in November."

They made an appointment for November 29th at one o'clock and Rosemary hung up feeling that something was wrong. The nurse at the lab had seemed to know exactly what she was doing, and Dr. Hill's offhandedness in speaking about her hadn't quite rung true. Were they afraid a mistake had been made?—vials of blood mixed up and wrongly labeled?—and was there still a possibility that she wasn't pregnant? But wouldn't Dr. Hill have told her so frankly and not have been as definite as he had?

She tried to shake it away. Of course she was pregnant; she had to be, with her period so long overdue. She went into the kitchen, where a wall calendar hung, and in the next day's square wrote *Lab;* and in the square for November 29th, *Dr. Hill*—1:00.

When Guy came in she went to him without saying a word and put a quarter in his hand. "What's this for?" he asked, and then caught on. "Oh, that's great, honey!" he said. "Just great!"—and taking her by the shoulders he kissed her twice and then a third time.

"Isn't it?" she said.

"Just great. I'm so happy."

"Father."

"Mother."

"Guy, listen," she said, and looked up at him, suddenly serious. "Let's make this a new beginning, okay? A new openness and talking-to-each-other. Because we haven't been open. You've been so wrapped up in the show and the pilot and the way things have been breaking for you—I'm not saying you shouldn't be; it wouldn't be normal if you weren't. But that's why I went to the cabin, Guy. To settle in my mind what was going wrong between us. And that's what it was, and is: a lack of openness. On my part too. On my part as much as yours."

"It's true," he said, his hands holding her shoulders, his eyes meeting hers earnestly. "It's true. I felt it too. Not as much as you did, I guess. I'm so God-damned self-centered, Ro. That's what the whole trouble is. I guess it's why I'm in this idiot nutty profession to begin with. You know I love you though, don't you? I *do*, Ro. I'll try to make it plainer from now on, I swear to God I will. I'll be as open as—"

"It's my fault as much as—"

"Bull. It's mine. Me and my self-centeredness. Bear with me, will you, Ro? I'll try to do better."

"Oh, Guy," she said in a tide of remorse and love and forgiveness, and met his kisses with fervent kisses of her own.

"Fine way for parents to be carrying on," he said.

She laughed, wet-eyed.

"Gee, honey," he said, "do you know what I'd love to do?"

"What?"

"Tell Minnie and Roman." He raised a hand. "I know, I know; we're supposed to keep it a deep dark secret. But I told them we were trying and they were so pleased, and, well, with people that old"—he spread his hands ruefully—"if we wait too long they might never get to know at all."

"Tell them," she said, loving him.

He kissed her nose. "Back in two minutes," he said, and turned and hurried to the door. Watching him go, she saw that Minnie and Roman had become deeply important to him. It wasn't surprising; his mother was a busy self-involved chatterer and none of his fathers had been truly fatherly. The Castevets were filling a need in him, a need of which he himself was probably unaware. She was grateful to them and would think more kindly of them in the future.

She went into the bathroom and splashed cold water on her eyes and fixed her hair and lips. "You're pregnant," she told herself in the mirror. *(But the lab wants another blood sample. What for?)*

As she came back out they came in at the front door: Minnie in a housedress, Roman holding in both hands a bottle of wine, and Guy behind them flushed and smiling. "Now *that's* what I call good news!" Minnie said. "Con*grat-u-la*-tions!" She bore down on Rosemary, took her by the shoulders, and kissed her cheek hard and loud.

"Our best wishes to you, Rosemary," Roman said, putting his lips to her other cheek. "We're more pleased than we can say. We have no champagne on hand, but this 1961 Saint Julien, I think, will do just as nicely for a toast."

Rosemary thanked them.

"When are you due, dear?" Minnie asked.

"June twenty-eighth."

"It's going to be so exciting," Minnie said, "between now and then."

"We'll do all your shopping for you," Roman said.

"Oh, no," Rosemary said. "Really."

Guy brought glasses and a corkscrew, and Roman turned with him to the opening of the wine. Minnie took Rosemary's elbow and they walked together into the living room. "Listen, dear," Minnie said, "do you have a good doctor?"

"Yes, a very good one," Rosemary said.

"One of the top obstetricians in New York," Minnie said, "is a dear friend of ours. Abe Sapirstein. A Jewish man. He delivers all the Society babies and he would deliver yours too if we asked him. And he'd do it *cheap,* so you'd be saving Guy some of his hard-earned money."

"Abe Sapirstein?" Roman asked from across the room. "He's one of the finest obstetricians in the country, Rosemary. You've heard of him, haven't you?"

"I think so," Rosemary said, recalling the name from an article in a newspaper or magazine.

"*I* have," Guy said. "Wasn't he on *Open End* a couple of years ago?"

"That's right," Roman said. "He's one of the finest obstetricians in the country."

"Ro?" Guy said.

"But what about Dr. Hill?" she asked.

"Don't worry, I'll tell him something," Guy said. "You know me."

Rosemary thought about Dr. Hill, so young, so Kildare, with his lab that wanted more blood because the nurse had goofed or the technician had goofed or *someone* had goofed, causing her needless bother and concern.

Minnie said, "I'm not going to *let* you go to no Dr. Hill that nobody heard of! The *best* is what *you're* going to have, young lady, and the best is Abe Sapirstein!"

Gratefully Rosemary smiled her decision at them. "If you're sure he can take me," she said. "He might be too busy."

"He'll take you," Minnie said. "I'm going to call him right now. Where's the phone?"

"In the bedroom," Guy said.

Minnie went into the bedroom. Roman poured glasses of wine. "He's a brilliant man," he said, "with all the sensitivity of his much-tormented race." He gave glasses to Rosemary and Guy. "Let's wait for Minnie," he said.

They stood motionless, each holding a full wineglass, Roman holding two. Guy said, "Sit down, honey," but Rosemary shook her head and stayed standing.

Minnie in the bedroom said, "Abe? Minnie. Fine. Listen, a dear friend of ours just found out today that she's pregnant. Yes, isn't it? I'm in her apartment now. We told her you'd be glad to take care of her and that you wouldn't charge none of your fancy Society prices neither." She was silent, then said, "Wait a minute," and raised her voice. "Rosemary? Can you go see him tomorrow morning at eleven?"

"Yes, that would be fine," Rosemary called back.

Roman said, "You see?"

"Eleven's fine, Abe," Minnie said. "Yes. You too. No, not at all. Let's hope so. Good-by."

She came back. "There you are," she said. "I'll write down his address for you before we go. He's on Seventy-ninth Street and Park Avenue."

"Thanks a million, Minnie," Guy said, and Rosemary said, "I don't know how to thank you. Both of you."

Minnie took the glass of wine Roman held out to her. "It's easy," she said. "Just do everything Abe tells you and have a fine healthy baby; that's all the thanks we'll ever ask for."

Roman raised his glass. "To a fine healthy baby," he said.

"Hear, hear," Guy said, and they all drank; Guy, Minnie, Rosemary, Roman.

"Mmm," Guy said. "Delicious."

"Isn't it?" Roman said. "And not at all expensive."

"Oh my," Minnie said, "I can't wait to tell the news to Laura-Louise."

Rosemary said, "Oh, please. Don't tell anyone else. Not yet. It's so early."

"She's right," Roman said. "There'll be plenty of time later on for spreading the good tidings."

"Would anyone like some cheese and crackers?" Rosemary asked.

"Sit down, honey," Guy said. "I'll get it."

That night Rosemary was too fired with joy and wonder to fall asleep quickly. Within her, under the hands that lay alertly on her stomach, a tiny egg had been fertilized by a tiny seed. Oh miracle, it would grow to be Andrew or Susan! ("Andrew" she was definite about; "Susan" was open to discussion with Guy.) What was Andrew-or-Susan now, a pinpoint speck? No, surely it was more than that; after all, wasn't she in her second month already? Indeed she was. It had probably reached the early tadpole stage. She would have to find a chart or book that told month by month exactly what was happening. Dr. Sapirstein would know of one.

A fire engine screamed by. Guy shifted and mumbled, and behind the wall Minnie and Roman's bed creaked.

There were so many dangers to worry about in the months ahead; fires, falling objects, cars out of control; dangers that had never been dangers before but were dangers now, now that Andrew-or-Susan was begun and living. (Yes, living!) She would give up her occasional cigarette, of course. And check with Dr. Sapirstein about cocktails.

If only prayer were still possible! How nice it would be to hold a crucifix again and have God's ear: ask Him for safe passage through the eight more months ahead; no German measles, please, no great new drugs with Thalidomide side effects. Eight good months, please, free of accident and illness, full of iron and milk and sunshine.

Suddenly she remembered the good luck charm, the ball of tannis root; and foolish or not, wanted it—no, needed it—around her neck. She slipped out of bed, tiptoed to the vanity, and got it from the Louis Sherry box, freed it from its aluminum-foil wrapping. The smell of the tannis root had changed; it was still strong but no longer repellent. She put the chain over her head.

With the ball tickling between her breasts, she tiptoed back to bed and climbed in. She drew up the blanket and, closing her eyes, settled her head down into the pillow. She lay breathing deeply and was soon asleep, her hands on her stomach shielding the embryo inside her.

Two

One

Now she was alive; was doing, was being, was at last herself and complete. She did what she had done before—cooked, cleaned, ironed, made the bed, shopped, took laundry to the basement, went to her sculpture class—but did everything against a new and serene background of knowing that Andrew-or-Susan (or Melinda) was every day a little bit bigger inside her than the day before, a little bit more clearly defined and closer to readiness.

Dr. Sapirstein was wonderful; a tall sunburned man with white hair and a shaggy white moustache (she had seen him somewhere before but couldn't think where; maybe on *Open End*) who despite the Miës van der Rohe chairs and cool marble tables of his waiting room was reassuringly old-fashioned and direct. "Please don't read books," he said. "Every pregnancy is different, and a book that tells you what you're going to feel in the third week of the third month is only going to make you worry. No pregnancy was ever exactly like the ones described in the books. And don't listen to your friends either. They'll have had experiences very different from yours and they'll be absolutely certain that their pregnancies were the normal ones and that yours is abnormal."

She asked him about the vitamin pills Dr. Hill had prescribed.

"No, no pills," he said. "Minnie Castevet has a herbarium and a blender; I'm going to have her make a daily drink for you that will be fresher, safer, and more vitamin-rich than any pill on the market. And another thing: don't be afraid to satisfy your cravings. The theory today is that pregnant women invent cravings because they feel it's expected of them. I don't hold with that.

I say if you want pickles in the middle of the night, make your poor husband go out and get some, just like in the old jokes. *Whatever* you want, be sure you get it. You'll be surprised at some of the strange things your body will ask for in these next few months. And any questions you have, call me night or day. Call *me,* not your mother or your Aunt Fanny. That's what I'm here for."

She was to come in once a week, which was certainly closer attention than Dr. Hill gave his patients, and he would make a reservation at Doctors Hospital without any bother of filling out forms.

Everything was right and bright and lovely. She got a Vidal Sassoon haircut, finished with the dentist, voted on Election Day (for Lindsay for mayor), and went down to Greenwich Village to watch some of the outdoor shooting of Guy's pilot. Between takes—Guy running with a stolen hot-dog wagon down Sullivan Street—she crouched on her heels to talk to small children and smiled *Me too* at pregnant women.

Salt, she found, even a few grains of it, made food inedible. "That's perfectly normal," Dr. Sapirstein said on her second visit. "When your system needs it, the aversion will disappear. Meanwhile, obviously, no salt. Trust your aversions the same as you do your cravings."

She didn't have any cravings though. Her appetite, in fact, seemed smaller than usual. Coffee and toast was enough for breakfast, a vegetable and a small piece of rare meat for dinner. Each morning at eleven Minnie brought over what looked like a watery pistachio milkshake. It was cold and sour.

"What's in it?" Rosemary asked.

"Snips and snails and puppy-dogs' tails," Minnie said, smiling.

Rosemary laughed. "That's fine," she said, "but what if we want a girl?"

"Do you?"

"Well of course we'll take what we get, but it *would* be nice if the first one were a *boy.*"

"Well there you are," Minnie said.

Finished drinking, Rosemary said, "No, really, what's in it?"

"A raw egg, gelatin, herbs . . ."

"Tannis root?"

"Some of that, some of some other things."

Minnie brought the drink every day in the same glass, a large one with blue and green stripes, and stood waiting while Rosemary drained it.

One day Rosemary got into a conversation by the elevator with Phyllis Kapp, young Lisa's mother. The end of it was a brunch invitation for Guy and her on the following Sunday, but Guy vetoed the idea when Rosemary told him of it. In all likelihood he would be in Sunday's shooting, he explained, and if he weren't he would need the day for rest and study. They were having little social life just then. Guy had broken a dinner-and-theater date they had made a few weeks earlier with Jimmy and Tiger Haenigsen, and he had asked Rosemary if she would mind putting off Hutch for dinner. It was because of the pilot, which was taking longer to shoot than had been intended.

It turned out to be just as well though, for Rosemary began to develop abdominal pains of an alarming sharpness. She called Dr. Sapirstein and he asked her to come in. Examining her, he said that there was nothing to worry about; the pains came from an entirely normal expansion of her pelvis. They would disappear in a day or two, and meanwhile she could fight them with ordinary doses of aspirin.

Rosemary, relieved, said, "I was afraid it might be an ectopic pregnancy."

"Ectopic?" Dr. Sapirstein asked, and looked skeptically at her. She colored. He said, "I thought you weren't going to read books, Rosemary."

"It was staring me right in the face at the drug store," she said.

"And all it did was worry you. Will you go home and throw it away, please?"

"I will. I promise."

"The pains will be gone in two days," he said. " 'Ectopic pregnancy.' " He shook his head.

But the pains weren't gone in two days; they were worse, and grew worse still, as if something inside her were encircled by a wire being drawn tighter and tighter to cut it in two. There would be pain for hour after hour, and then a few minutes of relative painlessness that was only the pain gathering itself for a new assault. Aspirin did little good, and she was afraid of taking too many. Sleep, when it finally came, brought harried dreams in which she fought against huge spiders that had cornered her in the bathroom, or tugged desperately at a small black bush that had taken root in the middle of the living room rug. She woke tired, to even sharper pain.

"This happens sometimes," Dr. Sapirstein said. "It'll stop any day now. Are you sure you haven't been lying about your age? Usually it's the older women with less flexible joints who have this sort of difficulty."

Minnie, bringing in the drink, said, "You poor thing. Don't fret, dear; a niece of mine in Toledo had exactly the same kind of pains and so did two other women I know of. And their deliveries were real easy and they had beautiful healthy babies."

"Thanks," Rosemary said.

Minnie drew back righteously. "What do you mean? That's the gospel truth! I swear to God it is, Rosemary!"

Her face grew pinched and wan and shadowed; she looked awful. But Guy insisted otherwise. "What are you talking about?" he said. "You look great. It's that *haircut* that looks awful, if you want the truth, honey. That's the biggest mistake you ever made in your whole life."

·   ·   ·

The pain settled down to a constant presence, with no respite whatever. She endured it and lived with it, sleeping a few hours a night and taking one aspirin where Dr. Sapirstein allowed two. There was no going out with Joan or Elise, no sculpture class or shopping. She ordered groceries by phone and stayed in the apartment, making nursery curtains and starting, finally, on *The Decline and Fall of The Roman Empire.* Sometimes Minnie or Roman came in of an afternoon, to talk a while and see if there was anything she wanted. Once Laura-Louise brought down a tray of gingerbread. She hadn't been told yet that Rosemary was pregnant. "Oh my, I *do* like that haircut, Rosemary," she said. "You look so pretty and up-to-date." She was surprised to hear she wasn't feeling well.

When the pilot was finally finished Guy stayed home most of the time. He had stopped studying with Dominick, his vocal coach, and no longer spent afternoons auditioning and being seen. He had two good commercials on deck —for Pall Mall and Texaco—and rehearsals of *Don't I Know You From Somewhere?* were definitely scheduled to begin in mid-January. He gave Rosemary a hand with the cleaning, and they played time-limit Scrabble for a dollar a game. He answered the phone and, when it was for Rosemary, made plausible excuses.

She had planned to give a Thanksgiving dinner for some of their friends who, like themselves, had no family nearby; with the constant pain, though, and the constant worry over Andrew-or-Melinda's well-being, she decided not to, and they ended up going to Minnie and Roman's instead.

Two

One afternoon in December, while Guy was doing the Pall Mall commercial, Hutch called. "I'm around the corner at City Center picking up tickets for Marcel Marceau," he said. "Would you and Guy like to come on Friday night?"

"I don't think so, Hutch," Rosemary said. "I haven't been feeling too well lately. And Guy's got two commercials this week."

"What's the matter with you?"

"Nothing, really. I've just been a bit under the weather."

"May I come up for a few minutes?"

"Oh do; I'd love to see you."

She hurried into slacks and a jersey top, put on lipstick and brushed her hair. The pain sharpened—locking her for a moment with shut eyes and clenched teeth—and then it sank back to its usual level and she breathed out gratefully and went on brushing.

Hutch, when he saw her, stared and said, "My God."

"It's Vidal Sassoon and it's very in," she said.

"What's *wrong* with you?" he said. "I don't mean your hair."

"Do I look that bad?" She took his coat and hat and hung them away, smiling a fixed bright smile.

"You look terrible," Hutch said. "You've lost God-knows-how-many pounds and you have circles around your eyes that a panda would envy. You aren't on one of those 'Zen diets,' are you?"

"No."

"Then what is it? Have you seen a doctor?"

"I suppose I might as well tell you," Rosemary said. "I'm pregnant. I'm in my third month."

Hutch looked at her, nonplussed. "That's ridiculous," he said. "Pregnant women *gain* weight, they don't lose it. And they look *healthy,* not—"

"There's a slight complication," Rosemary said, leading the way into the living room. "I have stiff joints or something, so I have pains that keep me awake most of the night. Well, *one* pain, really; it just sort of continues. It's not serious, though. It'll probably stop any day now."

"I never heard of 'stiff joints' being a problem," Hutch said.

"Stiff pelvic joints. It's fairly common."

Hutch sat in Guy's easy chair. "Well, congratulations," he said doubtfully. "You must be very happy."

"I am," Rosemary said. "We both are."

"Who's your obstetrician?"

"His name is Abraham Sapirstein. He's—"

"I know him," Hutch said. "Or *of* him. He delivered two of Doris's babies." Doris was Hutch's elder daughter.

"He's one of the best in the city," Rosemary said.

"When did you see him last?"

"The day before yesterday. And he said just what I told you; it's fairly common and it'll probably stop any day now. Of course he's been saying *that* since it started . . ."

"How much weight have you lost?"

"Only three pounds. It looks—"

"Nonsense! You've lost *far* more than that!"

Rosemary smiled. "You sound like our bathroom scale," she said. "Guy finally threw it out, it was scaring me so. No, I've lost only three pounds and one little space more. And it's perfectly normal to lose a little during the first few months. Later on I'll be gaining."

"I certainly hope so," Hutch said. "You look as if you're being drained by a vampire. Are you sure there aren't any puncture marks?" Rosemary smiled. "Well," Hutch said, leaning back and smiling too, "we'll assume that Dr. Sapirstein knows whereof he speaks. God knows he should; he charges enough. Guy must be doing sensationally."

"He is," Rosemary said. "But we're getting bargain rates. Our neighbors the Castevets are close friends of his; they sent me to him and he's charging us his special non-Society prices."

"Does that mean Doris and Axel are Society?" Hutch said. "They'll be delighted to hear about it."

The doorbell rang. Hutch offered to answer it but Rosemary wouldn't let him. "Hurts less when I move around," she said, going out of the room; and went to the front door trying to recall if there was anything she had ordered that hadn't been delivered yet.

It was Roman, looking slightly winded. Rosemary smiled and said, "I mentioned your name two seconds ago."

"In a favorable context, I hope," he said. "Do you need anything from outside? Minnie is going down in a while and our house phone doesn't seem to be functioning."

"No, nothing," Rosemary said. "Thanks so much for asking. I phoned out for things this morning."

Roman glanced beyond her for an instant, and then, smiling, asked if Guy was home already.

"No, he won't be back until six at the earliest," Rosemary said; and, because Roman's pallid face stayed waiting with its questioning smile, added, "A friend of ours is here." The questioning smile stayed. She said, "Would you like to meet him?"

"Yes, I would," Roman said. "If I won't be intruding."

"Of course you won't." Rosemary showed him in. He was wearing a black-and-white checked jacket over a blue shirt and a wide paisley tie. He passed close to her and she noticed for the first time that his ears were pierced—that the left one was, at any rate.

She followed him to the living-room archway. "This is Edward Hutchins," she said, and to Hutch, who was rising and smiling, "This is Roman Castevet, the neighbor I just mentioned." She explained to Roman: "I was telling Hutch that it was you and Minnie who sent me to Dr. Sapirstein."

The two men shook hands and greeted each other. Hutch said, "One of my daughters used Dr. Sapirstein too. On two occasions."

"He's a brilliant man," Roman said. "We met him only last spring but he's become one of our closest friends."

"Sit down, won't you?" Rosemary said. The men seated themselves and Rosemary sat by Hutch.

Roman said, "So Rosemary has told you the good news, has she?"

"Yes, she has," Hutch said.

"We must see that she gets plenty of rest," Roman said, "and complete freedom from worry and anxiety."

Rosemary said, "That would be heaven."

"I was a bit alarmed by her appearance," Hutch said, looking at Rosemary as he took out a pipe and a striped rep tobacco pouch.

"Were you?" Roman said.

"But now that I know she's in Dr. Sapirstein's care I feel considerably relieved."

"She's only lost two or three pounds," Roman said. "Isn't that so, Rosemary?"

"That's right," Rosemary said.

"And that's quite normal in the early months of pregnancy," Roman said. "Later on she'll gain—probably far too much."

"So I gather," Hutch said, filling his pipe.

Rosemary said, "Mrs. Castevet makes a vitamin drink for me every day, with a raw egg and milk and fresh herbs that she grows."

"All according to Dr. Sapirstein's directions, of course," Roman said. "He's inclined to be suspicious of commercially prepared vitamin pills."

"Is he really?" Hutch asked, pocketing his pouch. "I can't think of anything I'd be less suspicious of; they're surely manufactured under every imaginable safeguard." He struck two matches as one and sucked flame into his pipe, blowing out puffs of aromatic white smoke. Rosemary put an ashtray near him.

"That's true," Roman said, "but commercial pills can sit for months in a warehouse or on a druggist's shelf and lose a great deal of their original potency."

"Yes, I hadn't thought of that," Hutch said; "I suppose they can."

Rosemary said, "I like the *idea* of having everything fresh and natural. I'll bet expectant mothers chewed bits of tannis root hundreds and hundreds of years ago when nobody'd even heard of vitamins."

"Tannis root?" Hutch said.

"It's one of the herbs in the drink," Rosemary said. "Or *is* it an herb?" She looked to Roman. "Can a root be an herb?" But Roman was watching Hutch and didn't hear.

" 'Tannis?' " Hutch said. "I've never heard of it. Are you sure you don't mean 'anise' or 'orris root'?"

Roman said, "Tannis."

"Here," Rosemary said, drawing out her charm. "It's good luck too, theoretically. Brace yourself; the smell takes a little getting-used-to." She held the charm out, leaning forward to bring it closer to Hutch.

He sniffed at it and drew away, grimacing. "I should say it does," he said. He took the chained ball between two fingertips and squinted at it from a distance. "It doesn't look like root matter at all," he said; "it looks like mold or fungus of some kind." He looked at Roman. "Is it ever called by another name?" he asked.

"Not to my knowledge," Roman said.

"I shall look it up in the encyclopedia and find out all about it," Hutch said. "Tannis. What a pretty holder or charm or whatever-it-is. Where did you get it?"

With a quick smile at Roman, Rosemary said, "The Castevets gave it to me." She tucked the charm back inside her top.

Hutch said to Roman, "You and your wife seem to be taking better care of Rosemary than her own parents would."

Roman said, "We're very fond of her, and of Guy too." He pushed against the arms of his chair and raised himself to his feet. "If you'll excuse me, I have to go now," he said. "My wife is waiting for me."

"Of course," Hutch said, rising. "It's a pleasure to have met you."

"We'll meet again, I'm sure," Roman said. "Don't bother, Rosemary."

"It's no bother." She walked along with him to the front door. His right ear was pierced too, she saw, and there were many small scars on his neck like a flight of distant birds. "Thanks again for stopping by," she said.

"Don't mention it," Roman said. "I like your friend Mr. Hutchins; he seems extremely intelligent."

Rosemary, opening the door, said, "He is."

"I'm glad I met him," Roman said. With a smile and a hand-wave he started down the hall.

" 'By," Rosemary said, waving back.

Hutch was standing by the bookshelves. "This room is glorious," he said. "You're doing a beautiful job."

"Thanks," Rosemary said. "I was until my pelvis intervened. Roman has pierced ears. I just noticed it for the first time."

"Pierced ears and piercing eyes," Hutch said. "What was he before he became a Golden Ager?"

"Just about everything. And he's been everywhere in the world. Really everywhere."

"Nonsense; nobody has. Why did he ring your bell?—if I'm not being too inquisitive."

"To see if I needed anything from outside. The house phone isn't working. They're fantastic neighbors. They'd come in and do the cleaning if I let them."

"What's *she* like?"

Rosemary told him. "Guy's gotten very close to them," she said. "I think they've become sort of parent-figures for him."

"And you?"

"I'm not sure. Sometimes I'm so grateful I could kiss them, and sometimes I get a sort of smothery feeling, as if they're being *too* friendly and helpful. Yet how can I complain? You remember the power failure?"

"Shall I ever forget it? I was in an elevator."

"No."

"Yes indeed. Five hours in total darkness with three women and a John Bircher who were all sure that the Bomb had fallen."

"How awful."

"You were saying?"

"We were here, Guy and I, and two minutes after the lights went out Minnie was at the door with a handful of candles." She gestured toward the mantel. "Now how can you find fault with neighbors like that?"

"You can't, obviously," Hutch said, and stood looking at the mantel. "Are those the ones?" he asked. Two pewter candlesticks stood between a bowl of polished stones and a brass microscope; in them were three-inch lengths of black candle ribbed with drippings.

"The last survivors," Rosemary said. "She brought a whole month's worth. What is it?"

"Were they all black?" he asked.

"Yes," she said. "Why?"

"Just curious." He turned from the mantel, smiling at her. "Offer me coffee, will you? And tell me more about Mrs. Castevet. Where does she grow those herbs of hers? In window boxes?"

They were sitting over cups at the kitchen table some ten minutes later when the front door unlocked and Guy hurried in. "Hey, what a surprise," he said, coming over and grabbing Hutch's hand before he could rise. "How are you, Hutch? Good to see you!" He clasped Rosemary's head in his other hand and bent and kissed her cheek and lips. "How you doing, honey?" He still had his make-up on; his face was orange, his eyes black-lashed and large.

"You're the surprise," Rosemary said. "What happened?"

"Ah, they stopped in the middle for a rewrite, the dumb bastards. We start again in the morning. Stay where you are, nobody move; I'll just get rid of my coat." He went out to the closet.

"Would you like some coffee?" Rosemary called.

"Love some!"

She got up and poured a cup, and refilled Hutch's cup and her own. Hutch sucked at his pipe, looking thoughtfully before him.

Guy came back in with his hands full of packs of Pall Mall. "Loot," he said, dumping them on the table. "Hutch?"

"No, thanks."

Guy tore a pack open, jammed cigarettes up, and pulled one out. He winked at Rosemary as she sat down again.

Hutch said, "It seems congratulations are in order."

Guy, lighting up, said, "Rosemary told you? It's wonderful, isn't it? We're delighted. Of course I'm scared stiff that I'll be a lousy father, but Rosemary'll be such a great mother that it won't make much difference."

"When is the baby due?" Hutch asked.

Rosemary told him, and told Guy that Dr. Sapirstein had delivered two of Hutch's grandchildren.

Hutch said, "I met your neighbor, Roman Castevet."

"Oh, did you?" Guy said. "Funny old duck, isn't he? He's got some interesting stories, though, about Otis Skinner and Modjeska. He's quite a theater buff."

Rosemary said, "Did you ever notice that his ears are pierced?"

"You're kidding," Guy said.

"No I'm not; I saw."

They drank their coffee, talking of Guy's quickening career and of a trip Hutch planned to make in the spring to Greece and Turkey.

"It's a shame we haven't seen more of you lately," Guy said, when Hutch had excused himself and risen. "With me so busy and Ro being the way she is, we really haven't seen anyone."

"Perhaps we can have dinner together soon," Hutch said; and Guy, agreeing, went to get his coat.

Rosemary said, "Don't forget to look up tannis root."

"I won't," Hutch said. "And you tell Dr. Sapirstein to check his scale; I still think you've lost more than three pounds."

"Don't be silly," Rosemary said. "Doctors' scales aren't wrong."

Guy, holding open a coat, said, "It's not mine, it must be yours."

"Right you are," Hutch said. Turning, he put his arms back into it. "Have you thought about names yet," he asked Rosemary, "or is it too soon?"

"Andrew or Douglas if it's a boy," she said. "Melinda or Sarah if it's a girl."

" 'Sarah?' " Guy said. "What happened to 'Susan'?" He gave Hutch his hat.

Rosemary offered her cheek for Hutch's kiss.

"I do hope the pain stops soon," he said.

"It will," she said, smiling. "Don't worry."

Guy said, "It's a pretty common condition."

Hutch felt his pockets. "Is there another one of these around?" he asked, and showed them a brown fur-lined glove and felt his pockets again.

Rosemary looked around at the floor and Guy went to the closet and looked down on the floor and up onto the shelf. "I don't see it, Hutch," he said.

"Nuisance," Hutch said. "I probably left it at City Center. I'll stop back there. Let's really have that dinner, shall we?"

"Definitely," Guy said, and Rosemary said, "Next week."

They watched him around the first turn of the hallway and then stepped back inside and closed the door.

"That was a nice surprise," Guy said. "Was he here long?"

"Not very," Rosemary said. "Guess what he said."

"What?"

"I look terrible."

"Good old Hutch," Guy said, "spreading cheer wherever he goes." Rosemary looked at him questioningly. "Well he *is* a professional crepe-hanger, honey," he said. "Remember how he tried to sour us on moving in here?"

"He isn't a professional crepe-hanger," Rosemary said, going into the kitchen to clear the table.

Guy leaned against the door jamb. "Then he sure is one of the top-ranking amateurs," he said.

A few minutes later he put his coat on and went out for a newspaper.

The telephone rang at ten-thirty that evening, when Rosemary was in bed reading and Guy was in the den watching television. He answered the call and a minute later brought the phone into the bedroom. "Hutch wants to speak to you," he said, putting the phone on the bed and crouching to plug it in. "I told him you were resting but he said it couldn't wait."

Rosemary picked up the receiver. "Hutch?" she said.

"Hello, Rosemary," Hutch said. "Tell me, dear, do you go out at all or do you stay in your apartment all day?"

"Well I haven't *been* going out," she said, looking at Guy; "but I could. Why?" Guy looked back at her, frowning, listening.

"There's something I want to speak to you about," Hutch said. "Can you meet me tomorrow morning at eleven in front of the Seagram Building?"

"Yes, if you want me to," she said. "What is it? Can't you tell me now?"

"I'd rather not," he said. "It's nothing terribly important so don't brood about it. We can have a late brunch or early lunch if you'd like."

"That would be nice."

"Good. Eleven o'clock then, in front of the Seagram Building."

"Right. Did you get your glove?"

"No, they didn't have it," he said, "but it's time I got some new ones anyway. Good night, Rosemary. Sleep well."

"You too. Good night."

She hung up.

"What was that?" Guy asked.

"He wants me to meet him tomorrow morning. He has something he wants to talk to me about."

"And he didn't say what?"

"Not a word."

Guy shook his head, smiling. "I think those boys' adventure stories are going to his head," he said. "Where are you meeting him?"

"In front of the Seagram Building at eleven o'clock."

Guy unplugged the phone and went out with it to the den; almost immediately, though, he was back. "You're the pregnant one and I'm the one with yens," he said, plugging the phone back in and putting it on the night table. "I'm going to go out and get an ice cream cone. Do you want one?"

"Okay," Rosemary said.

"Vanilla?"

"Fine."

"I'll be as quick as I can."

He went out, and Rosemary leaned back against her pillows, looking ahead at nothing with her book forgotten in her lap. What was it Hutch wanted to talk about? Nothing terribly important, he had said. But it must be something not *un*important too, or else he wouldn't have summoned her as he had. Was it something about Joan?—or one of the other girls who had shared the apartment?

Far away she heard the Castevets' doorbell give one short ring. Probably it was Guy, asking them if they wanted ice cream or a morning paper. Nice of him.

The pain sharpened inside her.

Three

The following morning Rosemary called Minnie on the house phone and asked her not to bring the drink over at eleven o'clock; she was on her way out and wouldn't be back until one or two.

"Why, that's fine, dear," Minnie said. "Don't you worry about a thing. You don't have to take it at no fixed time; just so you take it *sometime,* that's all. You go on out. It's a nice day and it'll do you good to get some fresh air. Buzz me when you get back and I'll bring the drink in then."

It was indeed a nice day; sunny, cold, clear, and invigorating. Rosemary walked through it slowly, ready to smile, as if she weren't carrying her pain inside her. Salvation Army Santa Clauses were on every corner, shaking their bells in their fool-nobody costumes. Stores all had their Christmas windows; Park Avenue had its center line of trees.

She reached the Seagram Building at a quarter of eleven and, because she was early and there was no sign yet of Hutch, sat for a while on the low wall at the side of the building's forecourt, taking the sun on her face and listening with pleasure to busy footsteps and snatches of conversation, to cars and trucks and a helicopter's racketing. The dress beneath her coat was—for the first satisfying time—snug over her stomach; maybe after lunch she would go to Bloomingdale's and look at maternity dresses. She was glad Hutch had called her out this way (but what did he want to talk about?); pain, even constant pain, was no excuse for staying indoors as much as she had. She would fight it from now on, fight it with air and sunlight and activity, not succumb to it in Bramford gloom under the well-meant pamperings of Minnie and Guy and Roman. *Pain, begone!* she thought; *I will have no more of thee!* The pain stayed, immune to Positive Thinking.

At five of eleven she went and stood by the building's glass doors, at the edge of their heavy flow of traffic. Hutch would probably be coming from inside, she thought, from an earlier appointment; or else why had he chosen here rather than someplace else for their meeting? She scouted the outcoming faces as best she could, saw him but was mistaken, then saw a man she had dated before she met Guy and was mistaken again. She kept looking, stretching now and then on tiptoes; not anxiously, for she knew that even if she failed to see him, Hutch would see her.

He hadn't come by five after eleven, nor by ten after. At a quarter after she went inside to look at the building's directory, thinking she might see a name there that he had mentioned at one time or another and to which she might make a call of inquiry. The directory proved to be far too large and many-named for careful reading, though; she skimmed over its crowded columns and, seeing nothing familiar, went outside again.

She went back to the low wall and sat where she had sat before, this time watching the front of the building and glancing over occasionally at the shallow steps leading up from the sidewalk. Men and women met other men and women, but there was no sign of Hutch, who was rarely if ever late for appointments.

At eleven-forty Rosemary went back into the building and was sent by a maintenance man down to the basement, where at the end of a white institutional corridor there was a pleasant lounge area with black modern chairs, an abstract mural, and a single stainless-steel phone booth. A Negro girl was in the booth, but she finished soon and came out with a friendly smile. Rosemary slipped in and dialed the number at the apartment. After five rings Service answered; there were no messages for Rosemary, and the one message for Guy was from a Rudy Horn, not a Mr. Hutchins. She had another dime and used it to call Hutch's number, thinking that his service might know where he was or have a message from him. On the first ring a woman answered with a worried non-service "Yes?"

"Is this Edward Hutchins' apartment?" Rosemary asked.

"Yes. Who is this, please?" She sounded like a woman neither young nor old—in her forties, perhaps.

Rosemary said, "My name is Rosemary Woodhouse. I had an eleven o'clock appointment with Mr. Hutchins and he hasn't shown up yet. Do you have any idea whether he's coming or not?"

There was silence, and more of it. "Hello?" Rosemary said.

"Hutch has told me about you, Rosemary," the woman said. "My name is Grace Cardiff. I'm a friend of his. He was taken ill last night. Or early this morning, to be exact."

Rosemary's heart dropped. "Taken ill?" she said.

"Yes. He's in a deep coma. The doctors haven't been able to find out yet what's causing it. He's at St. Vincent's Hospital."

"Oh, that's *awful,*" Rosemary said. "I spoke to him last night around ten-thirty and he sounded *fine.*"

"I spoke to him not much later than that," Grace Cardiff said, "and he sounded fine to me too. But his cleaning woman came in this morning and found him unconscious on the bedroom floor."

"And they don't know what from?"

"Not yet. It's early though, and I'm sure they'll find out soon. And when they do, they'll be able to treat him. At the moment he's totally unresponsive."

"How awful," Rosemary said. "And he's never had anything like this before?"

"Never," Grace Cardiff said. "I'm going back to the hospital now, and if you'll give me a number where I can reach you, I'll let you know when there's any change."

"Oh, thank you," Rosemary said. She gave the apartment number and then asked if there was anything she could do to help.

"Not really," Grace Cardiff said. "I just finished calling his daughters, and that seems to be the sum total of what has to be done, at least until he comes to. If there should be anything else I'll let you know."

Rosemary came out of the Seagram Building and walked across the forecourt and down the steps and north to the corner of Fifty-third Street. She crossed Park Avenue and walked slowly toward Madison, wondering whether Hutch would live or die, and if he died, whether she (selfishness!) would ever again have anyone on whom she could so effortlessly and completely depend. She wondered too about Grace Cardiff, who sounded silver-gray and attractive; had she and Hutch been having a quiet middle-aged affair? She hoped so. Maybe this brush with death—that's what it would be, a *brush* with death, not death itself; it couldn't be—maybe this brush with death would nudge them both toward marriage, and turn out in the end to have been a disguised blessing. Maybe. Maybe.

She crossed Madison, and somewhere between Madison and Fifth found herself looking into a window in which a small crèche was spotlighted, with exquisite porcelain figures of Mary and the Infant and Joseph, the Magi and the shepherds and the animals of the stable. She smiled at the tender scene, laden with meaning and emotion that survived her agnosticism; and then saw in the window glass, like a veil hung before the Nativity, her own reflection smiling, with the skeletal cheeks and black-circled eyes that yesterday had alarmed Hutch and now alarmed her.

"Well *this* is what I call the long arm of coincidence!" Minnie exclaimed, and came smiling to her when Rosemary turned, in a white mock-leather coat and a red hat and her neckchained eyeglasses. "I said to myself, 'As long as

Rosemary's out, I might as well go out, and do the last little bit of my Christmas shopping.' And here *you* are and here *I* am! It looks like we're just two of a kind that go the same places and do the same things! Why, what's the matter, dear? You look so sad and downcast."

"I just heard some bad news," Rosemary said. "A friend of mine is very sick. In the hospital."

"Oh, no," Minnie said. "Who?"

"His name is Edward Hutchins," Rosemary said.

"The one Roman met yesterday afternoon? Why, he was going on for an *hour* about what a nice intelligent man he was! Isn't that a pity! What's troubling him?"

Rosemary told her.

"My land," Minnie said, "I hope it doesn't turn out the way it did for poor Lily Gardenia! And the doctors don't even know? Well at least they admit it; usually they cover up what they don't know with a lot of high-flown Latin. If the money spent putting those astronauts up where they are was spent on medical research down here, we'd *all* be a lot better off, if you want *my* opinion. Do you feel all right, Rosemary?"

"The pain is a little worse," Rosemary said.

"You poor thing. You know what I think? I think we ought to be going home now. What do you say?"

"No, no, you have to finish your Christmas shopping."

"Oh shoot," Minnie said, "there's two whole weeks yet. Hold onto your ears." She put her wrist to her mouth and blew stabbing shrillness from a whistle on a gold-chain bracelet. A taxi veered toward them. "How's *that* for service?" she said. "A nice big Checker one too."

Soon after, Rosemary was in the apartment again. She drank the cold sour drink from the blue-and-green-striped glass while Minnie looked on approvingly.

Four

She had been eating her meat rare; now she ate it nearly raw—broiled only long enough to take away the refrigerator's chill and seal in the juices.

The weeks before the holidays and the holiday season itself were dismal. The pain grew worse, grew so grinding that something shut down in Rosemary— some center of resistance and remembered well-being—and she stopped reacting, stopped mentioning pain to Dr. Sapirstein, stopped referring to pain even in her thoughts. Until now it had been inside her; now *she* was inside *it;* pain was the weather around her, was time, was the entire world. Numbed and exhausted, she began to sleep more, and to eat more too—more nearly raw meat.

She did what had to be done: cooked and cleaned, sent Christmas cards to the family—she hadn't the heart for phone calls—and put new money into envelopes for the elevator men, doormen, porters, and Mr. Micklas. She looked at newspapers and tried to be interested in students burning draft cards and the threat of a city-wide transit strike, but she couldn't: this was news from a world of fantasy; nothing was real but her world of pain. Guy bought Christmas presents for Minnie and Roman; for each other they agreed to buy nothing at all. Minnie and Roman gave them coasters.

They went to nearby movies a few times, but most evenings they stayed in or went around the hall to Minnie and Roman's, where they met couples named Fountain and Gilmore and Wees, a woman named Mrs. Sabatini who always brought her cat, and Dr. Shand, the retired dentist who had made the chain for Rosemary's tannis-charm. These were all elderly people who treated Rosemary with kindness and concern, seeing, apparently, that she was less than well. Laura-Louise was there too, and sometimes Dr. Sapirstein joined the group. Roman was an energetic host, filling glasses and launching new topics of conversation. On New Year's Eve he proposed a toast—"To 1966, The Year One"—that puzzled Rosemary, although everyone else seemed to understand and approve of it. She felt as if she had missed a literary or political reference—not that she really cared. She and Guy usually left early, and Guy would see her into bed and go back. He was the favorite of the women, who gathered around him and laughed at his jokes.

Hutch stayed as he was, in his deep and baffling coma. Grace Cardiff called every week or so. "No change, no change at all," she would say. "They still don't know. He could wake up tomorrow morning or he could sink deeper and never wake up at all."

Twice Rosemary went to St. Vincent's Hospital to stand beside Hutch's bed and look down powerlessly at the closed eyes, the scarcely discernible breathing. The second time, early in January, his daughter Doris was there, sitting by the window working a piece of needlepoint. Rosemary had met her a year earlier at Hutch's apartment; she was a short pleasant woman in her thirties, married to a Swedish-born psychoanalyst. She looked, unfortunately, like a younger wigged Hutch.

Doris didn't recognize Rosemary, and when Rosemary had re-introduced herself she made a distressed apology.

"Please don't," Rosemary said, smiling. "I know. I look awful."

"No, you haven't changed at all," Doris said. "I'm terrible with faces. I forget my *children*, really I do."

She put aside her needlepoint and Rosemary drew up another chair and sat with her. They talked about Hutch's condition and watched a nurse come in and replace the hanging bottle that fed into his taped arm.

"We have an obstetrician in common," Rosemary said when the nurse had gone; and then they talked about Rosemary's pregnancy and Dr. Sapirstein's skill and eminence. Doris was surprised to hear that he was seeing Rosemary every week. "He only saw me once a month," she said. "Till near the end, of course. Then it was every two weeks, and *then* every week, but only in the last month. I thought that was fairly standard."

Rosemary could find nothing to say, and Doris suddenly looked distressed again. "But I suppose every pregnancy is a law unto itself," she said, with a smile meant to rectify tactlessness.

"That's what *he* told me," Rosemary said.

That evening she told Guy that Dr. Sapirstein had only seen Doris once a month. "Something is wrong with me," she said. "And he knew it right from the beginning."

"Don't be silly," Guy said. "He would tell you. And even if he wouldn't, he would certainly tell *me.*"

"Has he? Has he said *anything* to you?"

"Absolutely not, Ro. I swear to God."

"Then why do I have to go every week?"

"Maybe that's the way he does it now. Or maybe he's giving you better treatment, because you're Minnie and Roman's friend."

"No."

"Well *I* don't know; ask *him,*" Guy said. "Maybe you're more fun to examine than she was."

She asked Dr. Sapirstein two days later. "Rosemary, Rosemary," he said to her; "what did I tell you about talking to your friends? Didn't I say that every pregnancy is different?"

"Yes, but—"

"And the treatment has to be different too. Doris Allert had had two deliveries before she ever came to me, and there had been no complications whatever. She didn't require the close attention a first-timer does."

"Do you always see first-timers every week?"

"I try to," he said. "Sometimes I can't. There's nothing wrong with you, Rosemary. The pain will stop very soon."

"I've been eating raw meat," she said. "Just warmed a little."

"Anything else out of the ordinary?"

"No," she said, taken aback; wasn't that enough?

"Whatever you want, eat it," he said. "I told you you'd get some strange cravings. I've had women eat paper. And stop worrying. I don't keep things from my patients; it makes life too confusing. I'm telling you the truth. Okay?"

She nodded.

"Say hello to Minnie and Roman for me," he said. "And Guy too."

She began the second volume of *The Decline and Fall,* and began knitting a red-and-orange-striped muffler for Guy to wear to rehearsals. The threatened transit strike had come about but it affected them little since they were both at home most of the time. Late in the afternoon they watched from their bay windows the slow-moving crowds far below. "Walk, you peasants!" Guy said. "Walk! Home, home, and be quick about it!"

Not long after telling Dr. Sapirstein about the nearly raw meat, Rosemary found herself chewing on a raw and dripping chicken heart—in the kitchen one morning at four-fifteen. She looked at herself in the side of the toaster, where her moving reflection had caught her eye, and then looked at her hand, at the part of the heart she hadn't yet eaten held in red-dripping fingers. After a moment she went over and put the heart in the garbage, and turned on the water and rinsed her hand. Then, with the water still running, she bent over the sink and began to vomit.

When she was finished she drank some water, washed her face and hands, and cleaned the inside of the sink with the spray attachment. She turned off the water and dried herself and stood for a while, thinking; and then she got a memo pad and a pencil from one of the drawers and went to the table and sat down and began to write.

Guy came in just before seven in his pajamas. She had the *Life Cookbook* open on the table and was copying a recipe out of it. "What the hell are you doing?" he asked.

She looked at him. "Planning the menu," she said. "For a party. We're giving a party on January twenty-second. A week from next Saturday." She looked among several slips of paper on the table and picked one up. "We're inviting Elise Dunstan and her husband," she said, "Joan and a date, Jimmy and Tiger, Allan and a date, Lou and Claudia, the Chens, the Wendells, Dee Bertillon and a date unless you don't want him, Mike and Pedro, Bob and Thea Goodman, the Kapps"—she pointed in the Kapps' direction—"and Doris and Axel Allert, if they'll come. That's Hutch's daughter."

"I know," Guy said.

She put down the paper. "Minnie and Roman are not invited," she said. "Neither is Laura-Louise. Neither are the Fountains and the Gilmores and the Weeses. Neither is Dr. Sapirstein. This is a very special party. You have to be under sixty to get in."

"Whew," Guy said. "For a minute there I didn't think I was going to make it."

"Oh, you make it," Rosemary said. "You're the bartender."

"Swell," Guy said. "Do you really think this is such a great idea?"

"I think it's the best idea I've had in months."

"Don't you think you ought to check with Sapirstein first?"

"Why? I'm just going to give a party; I'm not going to swim the English Channel or climb Annapurna."

Guy went to the sink and turned on the water. He held a glass under it. "I'll be in rehearsal then, you know," he said. "We start on the seventeenth."

"You won't have to do a thing," Rosemary said. "Just come home and be charming."

"And tend bar." He turned off the water and raised his glass and drank.

"We'll *hire* a bartender," Rosemary said. "The one Joan and Dick used to have. And when you're ready to go to sleep I'll chase everyone out."

Guy turned around and looked at her.

"I want to see them," she said. "Not Minnie and Roman. I'm tired of Minnie and Roman."

He looked away from her, and then at the floor, and then at her eyes again. "What about the pain?" he asked.

She smiled drily. "Haven't you heard?" she said. "It's going to be gone in a day or two. Dr. Sapirstein told me so."

Everyone could come except the Allerts, because of Hutch's condition, and the Chens, who were going to be in London taking pictures of Charlie Chaplin. The bartender wasn't available but knew another one who was. Rosemary took a loose brown velvet hostess gown to the cleaner, made an appointment to have her hair done, and ordered wine and liquor and ice cubes and the ingredients of a Chilean seafood casserole called *chupe*.

On the Thursday morning before the party, Minnie came with the drink while Rosemary was picking apart crabmeat and lobster tails. "That looks interesting," Minnie said, glancing into the kitchen. "What is it?"

Rosemary told her, standing at the front door with the striped glass cold in her hand. "I'm going to freeze it and then bake it Saturday evening," she said. "We're having some people over."

"Oh, you feel up to entertaining?" Minnie asked.

"Yes, I do," Rosemary said. "These are old friends whom we haven't seen in a long time. They don't even know yet that I'm pregnant."

"I'd be glad to give you a hand if you'd like," Minnie said. "I could help you dish things out."

"Thank you, that's sweet of you," Rosemary said, "but I really can manage by myself. It's going to be buffet, and there'll be very little to do."

"I could help you take the coats."

"No, really, Minnie, you do enough for me as it is. Really."

Minnie said, "Well, let me know if you change your mind. Drink your drink now."

Rosemary looked at the glass in her hand. "I'd rather not," she said, and looked up at Minnie. "Not this minute. I'll drink it in a little while and bring the glass back to you."

Minnie said, "It doesn't do to let it stand."

"I won't wait long," Rosemary said. "Go on. You go back and I'll bring the glass to you later on."

"I'll wait and save you the walk."

"You'll do no such thing," Rosemary said. "I get very nervous if anyone watches me while I'm cooking. I'm going out later, so I'll be passing right by your door."

"Going out?"

"Shopping. Scoot now, go on. You're too nice to me, really you are."

Minnie backed away. "Don't wait too long," she said. "It's going to lose its vitamins."

Rosemary closed the door. She went into the kitchen and stood for a moment with the glass in her hand, and then went to the sink and tipped out the drink in a pale green spire drilling straight down into the drain.

She finished the *chupe,* humming and feeling pleased with herself. When it was covered and stowed away in the freezer compartment she made her own drink out of milk, cream, an egg, sugar, and sherry. Shaken in a covered jar, it poured out tawny and delicious-looking. "Hang on, David-or-Amanda," she said, and tasted it and found it great.

Five

For a little while around half past nine it looked as if no one was going to come. Guy put another chunk of cannel coal on the fire, then racked the tongs and brushed his hands with his handkerchief; Rosemary came from the kitchen and stood motionless in her pain and her just-right hair and her brown velvet; and the bartender, by the bedroom door, found things to do with lemon peel and napkins and glasses and bottles. He was a prosperous-looking Italian named Renato who gave the impression that he tended bar only as a pastime and would leave if he got more bored than he already was.

Then the Wendells came—Ted and Carole—and a minute later Elise Dunstan and her husband Hugh, who limped. And then Allan Stone, Guy's agent, with a beautiful Negro model named Rain Morgan, and Jimmy and Tiger, and Lou and Claudia Comfort and Claudia's brother Scott.

Guy put the coats on the bed; Renato mixed drinks quickly, looking less bored. Rosemary pointed and gave names: "Jimmy, Tiger, Rain, Allan, Elise, Hugh, Carole, Ted—Claudia and Lou and Scott."

Bob and Thea Goodman brought another couple, Peggy and Stan Keeler. "Of *course* it's all right," Rosemary said; "don't be silly, the more the merrier!" The Kapps came without coats. "What a trip!" Mr. Kapp ("It's Bernard") said. "A bus, three trains, and a ferry! We left five hours ago!"

"Can I look around?" Claudia asked. "If the rest of it's as nice as this I'm going to cut my throat."

Mike and Pedro brought bouquets of bright red roses. Pedro, with his cheek against Rosemary's, murmured, "Make him feed you, baby; you look like a bottle of iodine."

Rosemary said, "Phyllis, Bernard, Peggy, Stan, Thea, Bob, Lou, Scott, Carole . . ."

She took the roses into the kitchen. Elise came in with a drink and a fake cigarette for breaking the habit. "You're so lucky," she said; "it's the greatest apartment I've ever seen. Will you look at this kitchen? Are you all right, Rosie? You look a little tired."

"Thanks for the understatement," Rosemary said. "I'm not all right but I will be. I'm pregnant."

"You aren't! How *great!* When?"

"June twenty-eighth. I go into my fifth month on Friday."

"That's *great!*" Elise said. "How do you like C. C. Hill? Isn't he the dreamboy of the western world?"

"Yes, but I'm not using him," Rosemary said.

"No!"

"I've got a doctor named Sapirstein, an older man."

"What *for?* He can't be better than Hill!"

"He's fairly well known and he's a friend of some friends of ours," Rosemary said.

Guy looked in.

Elise said, "Well congratulations, Dad."

"Thanks," Guy said. "Weren't nothin' to it. Do you want me to bring in the dip, Ro?"

"Oh, yes, would you? Look at these roses! Mike and Pedro brought them."

Guy took a tray of crackers and a bowl of pale pink dip from the table. "Would you get the other one?" he asked Elise.

"Sure," she said, and took a second bowl and followed after him.

"I'll be out in a minute," Rosemary called.

Dee Bertillon brought Portia Haynes, an actress, and Joan called to say that she and her date had got stuck at another party and would be there in half an hour.

Tiger said, "You dirty stinking secret-keeper!" She grabbed Rosemary and kissed her.

"Who's pregnant?" someone asked, and someone else said, "Rosemary is."

She put one vase of roses on the mantel—"Congratulations," Rain Morgan said, "I understand you're pregnant"—and the other in the bedroom on the dressing table. When she came out Renato made a Scotch and water for her. "I make the first ones strong," he said, "to get them happy. Then I go light and conserve."

Mike wig-wagged over heads and mouthed *Congratulations.* She smiled and mouthed *Thanks.*

"The Trench sisters lived here," someone said; and Bernard Kapp said, "Adrian Marcato too, and Keith Kennedy."

"And Pearl Ames," Phyllis Kapp said.

"The Trent sisters?" Jimmy asked.

"Trench," Phyllis said. "They ate little children."

"And she doesn't mean just ate them," Pedro said; "she means *ate them!*"

Rosemary shut her eyes and held her breath as the pain wound tighter. Maybe because of the drink; she put it aside.

"Are you all right?" Claudia asked her.

"Yes, fine," she said, and smiled. "I had a cramp for a moment."

Guy was talking with Tiger and Portia Haynes and Dee. "It's too soon to say," he said; "we've only been in rehearsal six days. It plays much better than it reads, though."

"It couldn't play much worse," Tiger said. "Hey, what ever happened to the other guy? Is he still blind?"

"I don't know," Guy said.

Portia said, "Donald Baumgart? You know who *he* is, Tiger; he's the boy Zöe Piper lives with."

"Oh, is *he* the one?" Tiger said. "Gee, I didn't know he was someone I knew."

"He's writing a great play," Portia said. "At least the first two scenes are great. Really burning anger, like Osborne before he made it."

Rosemary said, "Is he still blind?"

"Oh, yes," Portia said. "They've pretty much given up hope. He's going through hell trying to make the adjustment. But this great play is coming out of it. He dictates and Zöe writes."

Joan came. Her date was over fifty. She took Rosemary's arm and pulled her aside, looking frightened. "What's the *matter* with you?" she asked. "What's *wrong?*"

"Nothing's wrong," Rosemary said. "I'm pregnant, that's all."

She was in the kitchen with Tiger, tossing the salad, when Joan and Elise came in and closed the door behind them.

Elise said, "What did you say your doctor's name was?"

"Sapirstein," Rosemary said.

Joan said, "And he's satisfied with your condition?"

Rosemary nodded.

"Claudia said you had a cramp a while ago."

"I have a pain," she said. "But it's going to stop soon; it's not abnormal."

Tiger said, "What kind of a pain?"

"A—a *pain*. A sharp pain, that's all. It's because my pelvis is expanding and my joints are a little stiff."

Elise said, "Rosie, I've had that—two times—and all it ever meant was a few days of like a Charley horse, an ache through the whole area."

"Well, everyone is different," Rosemary said, lifting salad between two wooden spoons and letting it drop back into the bowl again. "Every pregnancy is different."

"Not *that* different," Joan said. "You look like Miss Concentration Camp of 1966. Are you sure this doctor knows what he's doing?"

Rosemary began to sob, quietly and defeatedly, holding the spoons in the salad. Tears ran from her cheeks.

"Oh, God," Joan said, and looked for help to Tiger, who touched Rosemary's shoulder and said, "Shh, ah, shh, don't cry, Rosemary. Shh."

"It's good," Elise said. "It's the best thing. Let her. She's been wound up all night like—like I-don't-*know*-what."

Rosemary wept, black streaks smearing down her cheeks. Elise put her into a chair; Tiger took the spoons from her hands and moved the salad bowl to the far side of the table.

The door started to open and Joan ran to it and stopped and blocked it. It was Guy. "Hey, let me in," he said.

"Sorry," Joan said. "Girls only."

"Let me speak to Rosemary."

"Can't; she's busy."

"Look," he said, "I've got to wash glasses."

"Use the bathroom." She shouldered the door click-closed and leaned against it.

"Damn it, open the door," he said outside.

Rosemary went on crying, her head bowed, her shoulders heaving, her hands limp in her lap. Elise, crouching, wiped at her cheeks every few moments with the end of a towel; Tiger smoothed her hair and tried to still her shoulders.

The tears slowed.

"It hurts so much," she said. She raised her face to them. "And I'm so afraid the baby is going to die."

"Is he doing anything for you?" Elise asked. "Giving you any medicine, any treatment?"

"Nothing, nothing."

Tiger said, "When did it start?"

She sobbed.

Elise asked, "When did the pain start, Rosie?"

"Before Thanksgiving," she said. "November."

Elise said, "*In November?*" and Joan at the door said, "*What?*" Tiger said, "*You've been in pain since November and he isn't doing anything for you?*"

"He says it'll stop."

Joan said, "Has he brought in another doctor to look at you?"

Rosemary shook her head. "He's a very good doctor," she said with Elise wiping at her cheeks. "He's well known. He was on *Open End.*"

Tiger said, "He sounds like a sadistic *nut,* Rosemary."

Elise said, "Pain like that is a warning that something's not right. I'm sorry to scare you, Rosie, but you go see Dr. Hill. See *somebody* besides that—"

"That nut," Tiger said.

Elise said, "He *can't* be right, letting you just go on suffering."

"I won't have an abortion," Rosemary said.

Joan leaned forward from the door and whispered, "Nobody's *telling* you to have an abortion! Just go see another doctor, that's all."

Rosemary took the towel from Elise and pressed it to each eye in turn. "He said this would happen," she said, looking at mascara on the towel. "That my friends would think their pregnancies were normal and mine wasn't."

"What do you mean?" Tiger asked.

Rosemary looked at her. "He told me not to listen to what my friends might say," she said.

Tiger said, "Well you *do* listen! What kind of sneaky advice is *that* for a doctor to give?"

Elise said, "All we're telling you to do is check with another doctor. I don't think any reputable doctor would object to that, if it would help his patient's peace of mind."

"You do it," Joan said. "First thing Monday morning."

"I will," Rosemary said.

"You promise?" Elise asked.

Rosemary nodded. "I promise." She smiled at Elise, and at Tiger and Joan. "I feel a lot better," she said. "Thank you."

"Well you look a lot worse," Tiger said, opening her purse. "Fix your eyes. Fix everything." She put large and small compacts on the table before Rosemary, and two long tubes and a short one.

"Look at my dress," Rosemary said.

"A damp cloth," Elise said, taking the towel and going to the sink with it.

"The garlic bread!" Rosemary cried.

"In or out?" Joan asked.

"In." Rosemary pointed with a mascara brush at two foil-wrapped loaves on top of the refrigerator.

Tiger began tossing the salad and Elise wiped at the lap of Rosemary's gown. "Next time you're planning to cry," she said, "don't wear velvet."

Guy came in and looked at them.

Tiger said, "We're trading beauty secrets. You want some?"

"Are you all right?" he asked Rosemary.

"Yes, fine," she said with a smile.

"A little spilled salad dressing," Elise said.

Joan said, "Could the kitchen staff get a round of drinks, do you think?"

The *chupe* was a success and so was the salad. (Tiger said under her breath to Rosemary, "It's the tears that give it the extra zing.")

Renato approved of the wine, opened it with a flourish, and served it solemnly.

Claudia's brother Scott, in the den with a plate on his knee, said, "His name is Altizer and he's down in—Atlanta, I think; and what he says is that the death of God is a specific historic event that happened right now, in our time. That God literally died." The Kapps and Rain Morgan and Bob Goodman sat listening and eating.

Jimmy, at one of the living-room windows, said, "Hey, it's beginning to snow!"

Stan Keeler told a string of wicked Polish-jokes and Rosemary laughed out loud at them. "Careful of the booze," Guy murmured at her shoulder. She turned and showed him her glass, and said, still laughing, "It's only ginger ale!"

Joan's over-fifty date sat on the floor by her chair, talking up to her earnestly and fondling her feet and ankles. Elise talked to Pedro; he nodded, watching Mike and Allan across the room. Claudia began reading palms.

They were low on Scotch but everything else was holding up fine.

She served coffee, emptied ashtrays, and rinsed out glasses. Tiger and Carole Wendell helped her.

Later she sat in a bay with Hugh Dunstan, sipping coffee and watching fat wet snowflakes shear down, an endless army of them, with now and then an outrider striking one of the diamond panes and sliding and melting.

"Year after year I swear I'm going to leave the city," Hugh Dunstan said; "get away from the crime and the noise and all the rest of it. And every year it snows or the New Yorker has a Bogart Festival and I'm still here."

Rosemary smiled and watched the snow. "This is why I wanted this apartment," she said; "to sit here and watch the snow, with the fire going."

Hugh looked at her and said, "I'll bet you still read Dickens."

"Of course I do," she said. "Nobody stops reading Dickens."

Guy came looking for her. "Bob and Thea are leaving," he said.

By two o'clock everyone had gone and they were alone in the living room, with dirty glasses and used napkins and spilling-over ashtrays all around. ("Don't forget," Elise had whispered, leaving. Not very likely.)

"The thing to do now," Guy said, "is move."

"Guy."

"Yes?"

"I'm going to Dr. Hill. Monday morning."

He said nothing, looking at her.

"I want him to examine me," she said. "Dr. Sapirstein is either lying or else he's—I don't know, out of his mind. Pain like this is a warning that something is wrong."

"Rosemary," Guy said.

"And I'm not drinking Minnie's drink any more," she said. "I want vitamins in pills, like everybody else. I haven't drunk it for three days now. I've made her leave it here and I've thrown it away."

"You've—"

"I've made my own drink instead," she said.

He drew together all his surprise and anger and, pointing back over his shoulder toward the kitchen, cried it at her. "Is *that* what those bitches were giving you in there? Is *that* their hint for today? Change doctors?"

"They're my friends," she said; "don't call them bitches."

"They're a bunch of not-very-bright *bitches* who ought to mind their own God-damned business."

"All they said was get a second opinion."

"You've got the best doctor in New York, Rosemary. Do you know what Dr. Hill is? *Charley Nobody,* that's what he is."

"I'm tired of hearing how great Dr. Sapirstein is," she said, starting to cry, "when I've got this *pain* inside me since before Thanksgiving and all he does is tell me it's going to stop!"

"You're not changing doctors," Guy said. "We'll have to pay Sapirstein and pay Hill too. It's out of the question."

"I'm not going to *change,*" Rosemary said; "I'm just going to let Hill examine me and give his opinion."

"I won't let you," Guy said. "It's—it's not fair to Sapirstein."

"Not fair to—*What are you talking about?* What about what's fair to *me?*"

"You want another opinion? All right. *Tell* Sapirstein; let *him* be the one who decides who gives it. At least have *that* much courtesy to the top man in his field."

"I want Dr. *Hill,*" she said. "If you won't pay I'll pay my—" She stopped short and stood motionless, paralyzed, no part of her moving. A tear slid on a curved path toward the corner of her mouth.

"Ro?" Guy said.

The pain had stopped. It was gone. Like a stuck auto horn finally put right. Like anything that stops and is gone and is gone for good and won't ever be back again, thank merciful heaven. Gone and finished and oh, how good she might possibly feel as soon as she caught her breath!

"Ro?" Guy said, and took a step forward, worried.

"It stopped," she said. "The pain."

"Stopped?" he said.

"Just now." She managed to smile at him. "It stopped. Just like that." She closed her eyes and took a deep breath, and deeper still, deeper than she had been allowed to breathe for ages and ages. Since before Thanksgiving.

When she opened her eyes Guy was still looking at her, still looking worried.

"What was in the drink you made?" he asked.

Her heart dropped out of her. She had killed the baby. With the sherry. Or a bad egg. Or the combination. The baby had died, the pain had stopped. The pain was the baby and she had killed it with her arrogance.

"An egg," she said. "Milk. Cream. Sugar." She blinked, wiped at her cheek, looked at him. "Sherry," she said, trying to make it sound non-toxic.

"How *much* sherry?" he asked.

Something moved in her.

"A lot?"

Again, where nothing had ever moved before. A rippling little pressure. She giggled.

"Rosemary, for Christ's sake, how much?"

"It's alive," she said, and giggled again. "It's moving. It's all right; it isn't dead. It's moving." She looked down at her brown-velvet stomach and put her hands on it and pressed in lightly. Now two things were moving, two hands or feet; one here, one there.

She reached for Guy, not looking at him; snapped her fingers quickly for his hand. He came closer and gave it. She put it to the side of her stomach and held it there. Obligingly the movement came. "You feel it?" she asked, looking at him. "There, again; you feel it?"

He jerked his hand away, pale. "Yes," he said. "Yes. I felt it."

"It's nothing to be afraid of," she said, laughing. "It won't bite you."

"It's wonderful," he said.

"Isn't it?" She held her stomach again, looking down at it. "It's alive. It's kicking. It's in there."

"I'll clean up some of this mess," Guy said, and picked up an ashtray and a glass and another glass.

"All right now, David-or-Amanda," Rosemary said, "you've made your presence known, so kindly settle down and let Mommy attend to the cleaning up." She laughed. "My God," she said, "it's so active! That means a boy, doesn't it?"

She said, "All right, you, just take it easy. You've got five more months yet, so save your energy."

And laughing, "Talk to it, Guy; you're its father. Tell it not to be so impatient."

And she laughed and laughed and was crying too, holding her stomach with both hands.

Six

As bad as it had been before, that was how good it was now. With the stopping of the pain came sleep, great dreamless ten-hour spans of it; and with the sleep came hunger, for meat that was cooked, not raw, for eggs and vegetables and cheese and fruit and milk. Within days Rosemary's skullface had lost its edges and sunk back behind filling-in flesh; within weeks she looked the way pregnant women are supposed to look: lustrous, healthy, proud, prettier than ever.

She drank Minnie's drink as soon as it was given to her, and drank it to the last chill drop, driving away as by a ritual the remembered guilt of *I-killed-the-baby.* With the drink now came a cake of white gritty sweet stuff like marzipan; this too she ate at once, as much from enjoyment of its candylike taste as from a resolve to be the most conscientious expectant mother in all the world.

Dr. Sapirstein might have been smug about the pain's stopping, but he wasn't, bless him. He simply said "It's about time" and put his stethoscope to Rosemary's really-showing-now belly. Listening to the stirring baby, he betrayed an excitement that was unexpected in a man who had guided hundreds upon hundreds of pregnancies. It was this undimmed first-time excitement, Rosemary thought, that probably marked the difference between a great obstetrician and a merely good one.

She bought maternity clothes; a two-piece black dress, a beige suit, a red dress with white polka dots. Two weeks after their own party, she and Guy went to one given by Lou and Claudia Comfort. "I can't get over the *change* in you!" Claudia said, holding onto both Rosemary's hands. "You look a hundred per cent better, Rosemary! A *thousand* per cent!"

And Mrs. Gould across the hall said, "You know, we were quite concerned about you a few weeks ago; you looked so drawn and uncomfortable. But now you look like an entirely different person, really you do. Arthur remarked on the change just last evening."

"I feel much better now," Rosemary said. "Some pregnancies start out bad and turn good, and some go the other way around. I'm glad I've had the bad first and have gotten it out of the way."

She was aware now of minor pains that had been overshadowed by the major one—aches in her spinal muscles and her swollen breasts—but these discomforts had been mentioned as typical in the paperback book Dr. Sapirstein had made her throw away; they *felt* typical too, and they increased rather than lessened her sense of well-being. Salt was still nauseating, but what, after all, was salt?

Guy's show, with its director changed twice and its title changed three times, opened in Philadelphia in mid-February. Dr. Sapirstein didn't allow Rosemary to go along on the try-out tour, and so on the afternoon of the opening, she and Minnie and Roman drove to Philadelphia with Jimmy and Tiger, in Jimmy's antique Packard. The drive was a less than joyous one. Rosemary and Jimmy and Tiger had seen a bare-stage run-through of the play before the company left New York and they were doubtful of its chances. The best they hoped for was that Guy would be singled out for praise by one or more of the critics, a hope Roman encouraged by citing instances of great actors who had come to notice in plays of little or no distinction.

With sets and costumes and lighting the play was still tedious and verbose; the party afterwards was broken up into small separate enclaves of silent gloom. Guy's mother, having flown down from Montreal, insisted to their group that Guy was superb and the play was superb. Small, blonde, and vivacious, she chirped her confidence to Rosemary and Allan Stone and Jimmy and Tiger and Guy himself and Minnie and Roman. Minnie and Roman smiled serenely; the others sat and worried. Rosemary thought that Guy had been even better than superb, but she had thought so too on seeing him in *Luther* and *Nobody Loves An Albatross,* in neither of which he had attracted critical attention.

Two reviews came in after midnight; both panned the play and lavished Guy with enthusiastic praise, in one case two solid paragraphs of it. A third review, which appeared the next morning, was headed *Dazzling Performance Sparks New Comedy-Drama* and spoke of Guy as "a virtually unknown young actor of slashing authority" who was "sure to go on to bigger and better productions."

The ride back to New York was far happier than the ride out.

Rosemary found much to keep her busy while Guy was away. There was the white-and-yellow nursery wallpaper finally to be ordered, and the crib and the bureau and the bathinette. There were long-postponed letters to be written, telling the family all the news; there were baby clothes and more maternity clothes to be shopped for; there were assorted decisions to be made, about birth announcements and breast-or-bottle and the name, the name, the name. Andrew or Douglas or David; Amanda or Jenny or Hope.

And there were exercises to be done, morning and evening, for she was having the baby by natural childbirth. She had strong feelings on the subject and Dr. Sapirstein concurred with them wholeheartedly. He would give her an anesthetic only if at the very last moment she asked for one. Lying on the floor, she raised her legs straight up in the air and held them there for a count of ten; she practiced shallow breathing and panting, imagining the sweaty triumphant moment when she would see whatever-its-name-was coming inch by inch out of her effectively helping body.

She spent evenings at Minnie and Roman's, one at the Kapps', and another at Hugh and Elise Dunstan's. ("You don't have a nurse yet?" Elise asked. "You should have arranged for one long ago; they'll all be booked by now." But Dr. Sapirstein, when she called him about it the next day, told her that he had lined up a fine nurse who would stay with her for as long as she wanted after the delivery. Hadn't he mentioned it before? Miss Fitzpatrick; one of the best.)

Guy called every second or third night after the show. He told Rosemary of the changes that were being made and of the rave he had got in *Variety;* she told him about Miss Fitzpatrick and the wallpaper and the shaped-all-wrong bootees that Laura-Louise was knitting.

The show folded after fifteen performances and Guy was home again, only to leave two days later for California and a Warner Brothers screen test. And then he was home for good, with two great next-season parts to choose from and thirteen half-hour *Greenwich Village's* to do. Warner Brothers made an offer and Allan turned it down.

The baby kicked like a demon. Rosemary told it to stop or she would start kicking back.

Her sister Margaret's husband called to tell of the birth of an eight-pound boy, Kevin Michael, and later a too-cute announcement came—an impossibly rosy baby megaphoning his name, birth date, weight, and length. (Guy said, "What, no blood type?") Rosemary decided on simple engraved announcements, with nothing but the baby's name, their name, and the date. And it would be Andrew John or Jennifer Susan. Definitely. Breast-fed, not bottle-fed.

They moved the television set into the living room and gave the rest of the den furniture to friends who could use it. The wallpaper came, was perfect, and was hung; the crib and bureau and bathinette came and were placed first one way and then another. Into the bureau Rosemary put receiving blankets, waterproof pants, and shirts so tiny that, holding one up, she couldn't keep from laughing.

"Andrew John Woodhouse," she said, "*stop* it! You've got two whole months yet!"

They celebrated their second anniversary and Guy's thirty-third birthday;

they gave another party—a sit-down dinner for the Dunstans, the Chens, and Jimmy and Tiger; they saw *Morgan!* and a preview of *Mame.*

Bigger and bigger Rosemary grew, her breasts lifting higher atop her ballooning belly that was drum-solid with its navel flattened away, that rippled and jutted with the movements of the baby inside it. She did her exercises morning and evening, lifting her legs, sitting on her heels, shallow-breathing, panting.

At the end of May, when she went into her ninth month, she packed a small suitcase with the things she would need at the hospital—nightgowns, nursing brassieres, a new quilted housecoat, and so on—and set it ready by the bedroom door.

On Friday, June 3rd, Hutch died in his bed at St. Vincent's Hospital. Axel Allert, his son-in-law, called Rosemary on Saturday morning and told her the news. There would be a memorial service on Tuesday morning at eleven, he said, at the Ethical Culture Center on West Sixty-fourth Street.

Rosemary wept, partly because Hutch was dead and partly because she had all but forgotten him in the past few months and felt now as if she had hastened his dying. Once or twice Grace Cardiff had called and once Rosemary had called Doris Allert; but she hadn't gone to see Hutch; there had seemed no point in it when he was still frozen in coma, and having been restored to health herself, she had been averse to being near someone sick, as if she and the baby might somehow have been endangered by the nearness.

Guy, when he heard the news, turned bloodless gray and was silent and self-enclosed for several hours. Rosemary was surprised by the depth of his reaction.

She went alone to the memorial service; Guy was filming and couldn't get free and Joan begged off with a virus. Some fifty people were there, in a handsome paneled auditorium. The service began soon after eleven and was quite short. Axel Allert spoke, and then another man who apparently had known Hutch for many years. Afterwards Rosemary followed the general movement toward the front of the auditorium and said a word of sympathy to the Allerts and to Hutch's other daughter, Edna, and her husband. A woman touched her arm and said, "Excuse me, you're Rosemary, aren't you?" —a stylishly dressed woman in her early fifties, with gray hair and an exceptionally fine complexion. "I'm Grace Cardiff."

Rosemary took her hand and greeted her and thanked her for the phone calls she had made.

"I was going to mail this last evening," Grace Cardiff said, holding a book-size brown-paper package, "and then I realized that I'd probably be seeing you this morning." She gave Rosemary the package; Rosemary saw her own name and address printed on it, and Grace Cardiff's return address.

"What is it?" she asked.

"It's a book Hutch wanted you to have; he was very emphatic about it."
Rosemary didn't understand.

"He was conscious at the end for a few minutes," Grace Cardiff said. "I
wasn't there, but he told a nurse to tell me to give you the book on his desk.
Apparently he was reading it the night he was stricken. He was very insistent,
told the nurse two or three times and made her promise not to forget. And
I'm to tell you that 'the name is an anagram.' "

"The name of the book?"

"Apparently. He was delirious, so it's hard to be sure. He seemed to fight
his way out of the coma and then die of the effort. First he thought it was the
next morning, the morning after the coma began, and he spoke about having
to meet you at eleven o'clock—"

"Yes, we had an appointment," Rosemary said.

"And then he seemed to realize what had happened and he began telling the
nurse that I was to give you the book. He repeated himself a few times and
that was the end." Grace Cardiff smiled as if she were making pleasant conversation. "It's an English book about witchcraft," she said.

Rosemary, looking doubtfully at the package, said, "I can't imagine why he
wanted me to have it."

"He did though, so there you are. And the name is an anagram. Sweet
Hutch. He made everything sound like a boy's adventure, didn't he?"

They walked together out of the auditorium and out of the building onto
the sidewalk.

"I'm going uptown; can I drop you anywhere?" Grace Cardiff asked.

"No, thank you," Rosemary said. "I'm going down and across."

They went to the corner. Other people who had been at the service were
hailing taxis; one pulled up, and the two men who had got it offered it to
Rosemary. She tried to decline and, when the men insisted, offered it to Grace
Cardiff, who wouldn't have it either. "Certainly not," she said. "Take full
advantage of your lovely condition. When is the baby due?"

"June twenty-eighth," Rosemary said. Thanking the men, she got into the
cab. It was a small one and getting into it wasn't easy.

"Good luck," Grace Cardiff said, closing the door.

"Thank you," Rosemary said, "and thank you for the book." To the driver
she said, "The Bramford, please." She smiled through the open window at
Grace Cardiff as the cab pulled away.

Seven

She thought of unwrapping the book there in the cab, but it was a cab that had been fitted out by its driver with extra ashtrays and mirrors and hand-lettered pleas for cleanliness and consideration, and the string and the paper would have been too much of a nuisance. So she went home first and got out of her shoes, dress, and girdle, and into slippers and a new gigantic peppermint-striped smock.

The doorbell rang and she went to answer it holding the still-unopened package; it was Minnie with the drink and the little white cake. "I heard you come in," she said. "It certainly wasn't very long."

"It was nice," Rosemary said, taking the glass. "His son-in-law and another man talked a little about what he was like and why he'll be missed, and that was it." She drank some of the thin pale-green.

"That sounds like a sensible way of doing it," Minnie said. "You got mail already?"

"No, someone gave it to me," Rosemary said, and drank again, deciding not to go into *who* and *why* and the whole story of Hutch's return to consciousness.

"Here, I'll hold it," Minnie said, and took the package—"Oh, thanks," Rosemary said—so that Rosemary could take the white cake.

Rosemary ate and drank.

"A book?" Minnie asked, weighing the package.

"Mm-hmm. She was going to mail it and then she realized she'd be seeing me."

Minnie read the return address. "Oh, I know that house," she said. "The Gilmores used to live there before they moved over to where they are now."

"Oh?"

"I've been there lots of times. 'Grace.' That's one of my favorite names. One of your girl friends?"

"Yes," Rosemary said; it was easier than explaining and it made no difference really.

She finished the cake and the drink, and took the package from Minnie and gave her the glass. "Thanks," she said, smiling.

"Say listen," Minnie said, "Roman's going down to the cleaner in a while; do you have anything to go or pick up?"

"No, nothing, thanks. Will we see you later?"

"Sure. Take a nap, why don't you?"

"I'm going to. 'By."

She closed the door and went into the kitchen. With a paring knife she cut the string of the package and undid its brown paper. The book within was *All Of Them Witches* by J. R. Hanslet. It was a black book, not new, its gold lettering all but worn away. On the flyleaf was Hutch's signature, with the inscription *Torquay, 1934* beneath it. At the bottom of the inside cover was a small blue sticker imprinted *J. Waghorn & Son, Booksellers.*

Rosemary took the book into the living room, riffling its pages as she went. There were occasional photographs of respectable-looking Victorians, and, in the text, several of Hutch's underlinings and marginal checkmarks that she recognized from books he had lent her in the Higgins-Eliza period of their friendship. One underlined phrase was "the fungus they call 'Devil's Pepper.' "

She sat in one of the window bays and looked at the table of contents. The name Adrian Marcato jumped to her eye; it was the title of the fourth chapter. Other chapters dealt with other people—all of them, it was to be presumed from the book's title, witches: Gilles de Rais, Jane Wenham, Aleister Crowley, Thomas Weir. The final chapters were *Witch Practices* and *Witchcraft and Satanism.*

Turning to the fourth chapter, Rosemary glanced over its twenty-odd pages; Marcato was born in Glasgow in 1846, he was brought soon after to New York (underlined), and he died on the island of Corfu in 1922. There were accounts of the 1896 tumult when he claimed to have called forth Satan and was attacked by a mob outside the Bramford (not in the lobby as Hutch had said), and of similar happenings in Stockholm in 1898 and Paris in 1899. He was a hypnotic-eyed black-bearded man who, in a standing portrait, looked fleetingly familiar to Rosemary. Overleaf there was a less formal photograph of him sitting at a Paris café table with his wife Hessia and his son Steven (underlined).

Was this why Hutch had wanted her to have the book; so that she could read in detail about Adrian Marcato? But why? Hadn't he issued his warnings long ago, and acknowledged later on that they were unjustified? She flipped through the rest of the book, pausing near the end to read other underlinings.

"The stubborn fact remains," one read, "that whether or not *we* believe, *they* most assuredly do." And a few pages later: "the universally held belief in the power of fresh blood." And "surrounded by candles, which needless to say are also black."

The black candles Minnie had brought over on the night of the power failure. Hutch had been struck by them and had begun asking questions about Minnie and Roman. Was this the book's meaning; that they were *witches?* Minnie with her herbs and tannis-charms, Roman with his piercing eyes? But there *were* no witches, were there? Not *really.*

She remembered then the other part of Hutch's message, that the name of the book was an anagram. *All Of Them Witches.* She tried to juggle the letters in her head, to transpose them into something meaningful, revealing. She couldn't; there were too many of them to keep track of. She needed a pencil and paper. Or better yet, the Scrabble set.

She got it from the bedroom and, sitting in the bay again, put the unopened board on her knees and picked out from the box beside her the letters to spell *All Of Them Witches.* The baby, which had been still all morning, began moving inside her. *You're going to be a born Scrabble-player,* she thought, smiling. It kicked. "Hey, easy," she said.

With *All Of Them Witches* laid out on the board, she jumbled the letters and mixed them around, then looked to see what else could be made of them. She found *comes with the fall* and, after a few minutes of rearranging the flat wood tiles, *how is hell fact met.* Neither of which seemed to mean anything. Nor was there revelation in *who shall meet it, we that chose ill,* and *if he shall come,* all of which weren't real anagrams anyway, since they used less than the full complement of letters. It was foolishness. How could the title of a book have a hidden anagram message for her and her alone? Hutch had been delirious; hadn't Grace Cardiff said so? Time-wasting. *Elf shot lame witch. Tell me which fatso.*

But maybe it was the name of the author, not the book, that was the anagram. Maybe J. R. Hanslet was a pen name; it didn't sound like a real one, when you stopped to think about it.

She took new letters.

The baby kicked.

J. R. Hanslet was *Jan Shrelt.* Or *J. H. Snartle.*

Now that *really* made sense.

Poor Hutch.

She took up the board and tilted it, spilling the letters back into the box.

The book, which lay open on the window seat beyond the box, had turned its pages to the picture of Adrian Marcato and his wife and son. Perhaps Hutch had pressed hard there, holding it open while he underlined "Steven."

The baby lay quiet in her, not moving.

She put the board on her knees again and took from the box the letters of *Steven Marcato.* When the name lay spelled before her, she looked at it for a moment and then began transposing the letters. With no false moves and no wasted motion she made them into *Roman Castevet.*

And then again into *Steven Marcato.*

And then again into *Roman Castevet.*

The baby stirred ever so slightly.

She read the chapter on Adrian Marcato and the one called *Witch Practices,* and then she went into the kitchen and ate some tuna salad and lettuce and tomatoes, thinking about what she had read.

She was just beginning the chapter called *Witchcraft and Satanism* when the front door unlocked and was pushed against the chain. The doorbell rang as she went to see who it was. It was Guy.

"What's with the chain?" he asked when she had let him in.

She said nothing, closing the door and rechaining it.

"What's the matter?" He had a bunch of daisies and a box from Bronzini.

"I'll tell you inside," she said as he gave her the daisies and a kiss.

"Are you all right?" he asked.

"Yes," she said. She went into the kitchen.

"How was the memorial?"

"Very nice. Very short."

"I got the shirt that was in *The New Yorker,*" he said, going to the bedroom. "Hey," he called, "*On A Clear Day* and *Skyscraper* are both closing."

She put the daisies in a blue pitcher and brought them into the living room. Guy came in and showed her the shirt. She admired it.

Then she said, "Do you know who Roman really is?"

Guy looked at her, blinked, and frowned. "What do you mean, honey?" he said. "He's Roman."

"He's Adrian Marcato's son," she said. "The man who said he conjured up Satan and was attacked downstairs by a mob. Roman is his son Steven. 'Roman Castevet' is 'Steven Marcato' rearranged—an anagram."

Guy said, "Who told you?"

"Hutch," Rosemary said. She told Guy about *All Of Them Witches* and Hutch's message. She showed him the book, and he put aside his shirt and took it and looked at it, looked at the title page and the table of contents and then sprung the pages out slowly from under his thumb, looking at all of them.

"There he is when he was thirteen," Rosemary said. "See the eyes?"

"It might just *possibly* be a coincidence," Guy said.

"And another coincidence that he's living here? In the same house Steven Marcato was brought up in?" Rosemary shook her head. "The ages match too," she said. "Steven Marcato was born in August, 1886, which would make him seventy-nine now. Which is what Roman is. It's no coincidence."

"No, I guess it's not," Guy said, springing out more pages. "I guess he's

Steven Marcato, all right. The poor old geezer. No wonder he switched his name around, with a crazy father like that."

Rosemary looked at Guy uncertainly and said, "You don't think he's—the same as his father?"

"What do you mean?" Guy said, and smiled at her. "A witch? A devil worshiper?"

She nodded.

"*Ro,*" he said. "Are you *kidding?* Do you *really*—" He laughed and gave the book back to her. "Ah, Ro, *honey,*" he said.

"It's a religion," she said. "It's an early religion that got—pushed into the corner."

"All right," he said, "but *today?*"

"His father was a *martyr* to it," she said. "That's how it must look to him. Do you know where Adrian Marcato died? In a stable. On Corfu. Wherever *that* is. Because they wouldn't let him into the hotel. Really. 'No room at the inn.' So he died in the stable. And *he* was with him. Roman. Do you think he's given it up after *that?*"

"Honey, it's 1966," Guy said.

"This book was published in 1933," Rosemary said; "there were covens in Europe—that's what they're called, the groups, the congregations; covens—in Europe, in North and South America, in Australia; do you think they've all died out in just thirty-three years? They've got a coven *here,* Minnie and Roman, with Laura-Louise and the Fountains and the Gilmores and the Weeses; those parties with the flute and the chanting, those are *sabbaths* or *esbats* or whatever-they-are!"

"Honey," Guy said, "don't get excited. Let's—"

"Read what they do, Guy," she said, holding the book open at him and jabbing a page with her forefinger. "They use *blood* in their rituals, because blood has *power,* and the blood that has the *most* power is a *baby's* blood, a baby that hasn't been baptized; and they use *more* than the blood, they use the *flesh* too!"

"For God's sake, Rosemary!"

"Why have they been so friendly to us?" she demanded.

"Because they're friendly people! What do you think they are, maniacs?"

"Yes! Yes. Maniacs who think they have magic power, who think they're real storybook witches, *who perform all sorts of crazy rituals and practices* because they're—sick and crazy maniacs!"

"Honey—"

"Those black candles Minnie brought us were from the black mass! That's how Hutch caught on. And their living room is clear in the middle so that they have *room.*"

"Honey," Guy said, "they're old people and they have a bunch of old friends, and Dr. Shand happens to play the recorder. You can get black candles right down in the hardware store, and red ones and green ones and blue ones.

And their living room is clear because Minnie is a lousy decorator. Roman's father was a nut, okay; but that's no reason to think that Roman is too."

"They're not setting foot in this apartment ever again," Rosemary said. "Either one of them. Or Laura-Louise or any of the others. And they're not coming within fifty feet of the baby."

"The fact that Roman changed his name *proves* that he's not like his father," Guy said. "If he were he'd be proud of the name and would have kept it."

"He did keep it," Rosemary said. "He switched it around, but he didn't really change it for something else. And this way he can get into hotels." She went away from Guy, to the window where the Scrabble set lay. "I won't let them in again," she said. "And as soon as the baby is old enough I want to sub-let and move. I don't want them near us. Hutch was right; we never should have moved in here." She looked out the window, holding the book clamped in both hands, trembling.

Guy watched her for a moment. "What about Dr. Sapirstein?" he said. "Is he in the coven too?"

She turned and looked at him.

"After all," he said, "there've been maniac doctors, haven't there? His big ambition is probably to make house calls on a broomstick."

She turned to the window again, her face sober. "No, I don't think he's one of them," she said. "He's—too intelligent."

"And besides, he's Jewish," Guy said and laughed. "Well, I'm glad you've exempted *somebody* from your McCarthy-type smear campaign. Talk about witch-hunting, wow! And guilt by association."

"I'm not saying they're really witches," Rosemary said. "I know they haven't got *real* power. But there are people who *do* believe, even if we don't; just the way my family believes that God hears their prayers and that the wafer is the actual body of Jesus. Minnie and Roman believe *their* religion, believe it and practice it, I know they do; and I'm not going to take any chances with the baby's safety."

"We're not going to sub-let and move," Guy said.

"Yes we are," Rosemary said, turning to him.

He picked up his new shirt. "We'll talk about it later," he said.

"He lied to you," she said. "His father wasn't a producer. He didn't have anything to do with the theater at all."

"All right, so he's a bullthrower," Guy said; "who the hell isn't?" He went into the bedroom.

Rosemary sat down next to the Scrabble set. She closed it and, after a moment, opened the book and began again to read the final chapter, *Witchcraft and Satanism.*

Guy came back in without the shirt. "I don't think you ought to read any more of that," he said.

Rosemary said, "I just want to read this last chapter."

"Not today, honey," Guy said, coming to her; "you've got yourself worked up enough as it is. It's not good for you *or* the baby." He put his hand out and waited for her to give him the book.

"I'm not worked up," she said.

"You're shaking," he said. "You've *been* shaking for five minutes now. Come on, give it to me. You'll read it tomorrow."

"Guy—"

"No," he said. "I mean it. Come on, give it to me."

She said "Ohh" and gave it to him. He went over to the bookshelves, stretched up, and put it as high as he could reach, across the tops of the two Kinsey Reports.

"You'll read it tomorrow," he said. "You've had too much stirring-up today already, with the memorial and all."

Eight

Dr. Sapirstein was amazed. "Fantastic," he said. "Absolutely fantastic. What did you say the name was, 'Machado'?"

"Marcato," Rosemary said.

"Fantastic," Dr. Sapirstein said. "I had no idea whatsoever. I think he told me once that his father was a coffee importer. Yes, I remember him going on about different grades and different ways of grinding the beans."

"He told Guy that he was a producer."

Dr. Sapirstein shook his head. "It's no wonder he's ashamed of the truth," he said. "And it's no wonder that *you're* upset at having discovered it. I'm as sure as I am of anything on earth that Roman doesn't hold any of his father's weird beliefs, but I can understand completely how disturbed you must be to have him for a close neighbor."

"I don't want anything more to do with him or Minnie," Rosemary said. "Maybe I'm being unfair, but I don't want to take even the slightest chance where the baby's safety is concerned."

"Absolutely," Dr. Sapirstein said. "Any mother would feel the same way."

Rosemary leaned forward. "Is there any chance at all," she said, "that Minnie put something harmful in the drink or in those little cakes?"

Dr. Sapirstein laughed. "I'm sorry, dear," he said; "I don't mean to laugh, but really, she's such a kind old woman and so concerned for the baby's well-being . . . No, there's no chance at all that she gave you anything harmful. I would have seen evidence of it long ago, in you or in the baby."

"I called her on the house phone and told her I wasn't feeling well. I won't take anything else from her."

"You won't have to," Dr. Sapirstein said. "I can give you some pills that will be more than adequate in these last few weeks. In a way this may be the answer to Minnie and Roman's problem too."

"What do you mean?" Rosemary said.

"They want to go away," Dr. Sapirstein said, "and rather soon. Roman isn't well, you know. In fact, and in the strictest of confidence, he hasn't got more than a month or two left to him. He wants to pay a last visit to a few of his favorite cities and they were afraid you might take offense at their leaving on the eve of the baby's birth, so to speak. They broached the subject to me the night before last, wanted to know how I thought you would take it. They don't want to upset you by telling you the real reason for the trip."

"I'm sorry to hear that Roman isn't well," Rosemary said.

"But glad at the prospect of his leaving?" Dr. Sapirstein smiled. "A perfectly reasonable reaction," he said, "all things considered. Suppose we do this, Rosemary: I'll tell them that I've sounded you out and you aren't at all offended by the idea of their going; and until they do go—they mentioned Sunday as a possibility—you continue as before, not letting Roman know that you've learned his true identity. I'm sure he would be embarrassed and unhappy if he knew, and it seems a shame to upset him when it's only a matter of three or four more days."

Rosemary was silent for a moment, and then she said, "Are you sure they'll be leaving on Sunday?"

"I know they'd like to," Dr. Sapirstein said.

Rosemary considered. "All right," she said; "I'll go on as before, but only until Sunday."

"If you'd like," Dr. Sapirstein said, "I can have those pills sent over to you tomorrow morning; you can get Minnie to leave the drink and the cake with you and throw them away and take a pill instead."

"That would be wonderful," Rosemary said. "I'd be much happier that way."

"That's the main thing at this stage," Dr. Sapirstein said, "keeping you happy."

Rosemary smiled. "If it's a boy," she said, "I may just name him Abraham Sapirstein Woodhouse."

"God forbid," Dr. Sapirstein said.

Guy, when he heard the news, was as pleased as Rosemary. "I'm sorry Roman is on his last lap," he said, "but I'm glad for your sake that they're going away. I'm sure you'll feel more relaxed now."

"Oh, I will," Rosemary said. "I feel better already, just knowing about it."

Apparently Dr. Sapirstein didn't waste any time in telling Roman about Rosemary's supposed feelings, for that same evening Minnie and Roman stopped by and broke the news that they were going to Europe. "Sunday morning at ten," Roman said. "We fly directly to Paris, where we'll stay for a week or so, and then we'll go on to Zürich, Venice, and the loveliest city in all the world, Dubrovnik, in Yugoslavia."

"I'm green with envy," Guy said.

Roman said to Rosemary, "I gather this doesn't come as a complete bolt from the blue, does it, my dear?" A conspirator's gleam winked from his deep-socketed eyes.

"Dr. Sapirstein mentioned you were thinking of going," Rosemary said.

Minnie said, "We'd have loved to stay till the baby came—"

"You'd be foolish to," Rosemary said, "now that the hot weather is here."

"We'll send you all kinds of pictures," Guy said.

"But when Roman gets the wanderlust," Minnie said, "there's just no holding him."

"It's true, it's true," Roman said. "After a lifetime of traveling I find it all but impossible to stay in one city for more than a year; and it's been fourteen months now since we came back from Japan and the Philippines."

He told them about Dubrovnik's special charms, and Madrid's, and the Isle of Skye's. Rosemary watched him, wondering which he really was, an amiable old talker or the mad son of a mad father.

The next day Minnie made no fuss at all about leaving the drink and the cake; she was on her way out with a long list of going-away jobs to do. Rosemary offered to pick up a dress at the cleaner's for her and buy toothpaste and Dramamine®. When she threw away the drink and the cake and took one of the large white capsules Dr. Sapirstein had sent, she felt just the slightest bit ridiculous.

On Saturday morning Minnie said, "You know, don't you, about who Roman's father was."

Rosemary nodded, surprised.

"I could tell by the way you turned sort of cool to us," Minnie said. "Oh, don't apologize, dear; you're not the first and you won't be the last. I can't say that I really blame you. Oh, I could *kill* that crazy old man if he wasn't dead already! He's been the bane in poor Roman's existence! That's why he likes to travel so much; he always wants to leave a place before people can find out who he is. Don't let on to him that you know, will you? He's so fond of you and Guy, it would near about break his heart. I want him to have a real happy trip with no sorrows, because there aren't likely to be many more. Trips, I mean. Would you like the perishables in my icebox? Send Guy over later on and I'll load him up."

Laura-Louise gave a bon voyage party Saturday night in her small dark tannis-smelling apartment on the twelfth floor. The Weeses and the Gilmores came, and Mrs. Sabatini with her cat Flash, and Dr. Shand. (How had Guy known that it was Dr. Shand who played the recorder? Rosemary wondered.

And that it was a recorder, not a flute or a clarinet? She would have to ask him.) Roman told of his and Minnie's planned itinerary, surprising Mrs. Sabatini, who couldn't believe they were bypassing Rome and Florence. Laura-Louise served home-made cookies and a mildly alcoholic fruit punch. Conversation turned to tornadoes and civil rights. Rosemary, watching and listening to these people who were much like her aunts and uncles in Omaha, found it hard to maintain her belief that they were in fact a coven of witches. Little Mr. Wees, listening to Guy talking about Martin Luther King; could such a feeble old man, even in his dreams, imagine himself a caster of spells, a maker of charms? And dowdy old women like Laura-Louise and Minnie and Helen Wees; could they really bring themselves to cavort naked in mock-religious orgies? (Yet hadn't she seen them that way, seen all of them naked? No, no, that was a dream, a wild dream that she'd had a long, long time ago.)

The Fountains phoned a good-by to Minnie and Roman, and so did Dr. Sapirstein and two or three other people whose names Rosemary didn't know. Laura-Louise brought out a gift that everyone had chipped in for, a transistor radio in a pigskin carrying case, and Roman accepted it with an eloquent thank-you speech, his voice breaking. *He knows he's going to die,* Rosemary thought, and was genuinely sorry for him.

Guy insisted on lending a hand the next morning despite Roman's protests; he set the alarm clock for eight-thirty and, when it went off, hopped into chinos and a T shirt and went around to Minnie and Roman's door. Rosemary went with him in her peppermint-striped smock. There was little to carry; two suitcases and a hatbox. Minnie wore a camera and Roman his new radio. "Anyone who needs more than one suitcase," he said as he double-locked their door, "is a tourist, not a traveler."

On the sidewalk, while the doorman blew his whistle at oncoming cars, Roman checked through tickets, passport, traveler's checks, and French currency. Minnie took Rosemary by the shoulders. "No matter where we are," she said, "our thoughts are going to be with you every minute, darling, till you're all happy and thin again with your sweet little boy or girl lying safe in your arms."

"Thank you," Rosemary said, and kissed Minnie's cheek. "Thank you for everything."

"You make Guy send us lots of pictures, you hear?" Minnie said, kissing Rosemary back.

"I will. I will," Rosemary said.

Minnie turned to Guy. Roman took Rosemary's hand. "I won't wish you luck," he said, "because you won't need it. You're going to have a happy, happy life."

She kissed him. "Have a wonderful trip," she said, "and come back safely."

"Perhaps," he said, smiling. "But I may stay on in Dubrovnik, or Pescara or maybe Mallorca. We shall see, we shall see . . ."

"Come back," Rosemary said, and found herself meaning it. She kissed him again.

A taxi came. Guy and the doorman stowed the suitcases beside the driver. Minnie shouldered and grunted her way in, sweating under the arms of her white dress. Roman folded himself in beside her. "Kennedy Airport," he said; "the TWA Building."

There were more good-by's and kisses through open windows, and then Rosemary and Guy stood waving at the taxi that sped away with hands ungloved and white-gloved waving from either side of it.

Rosemary felt less happy than she had expected.

That afternoon she looked for *All Of Them Witches,* to reread parts of it and perhaps find it foolish and laughable. The book was gone. It wasn't atop the Kinsey Reports or anywhere else that she could see. She asked Guy and he told her he had put it in the garbage Thursday morning.

"I'm sorry, honey," he said, "but I just didn't want you reading any more of that stuff and upsetting yourself."

She was surprised and annoyed. "Guy," she said, "Hutch *gave* me that book. He *left* it to me."

"I didn't think about that part of it," Guy said. "I just didn't want you upsetting yourself. I'm sorry."

"That's a *terrible* thing to do."

"I'm sorry. I wasn't thinking about Hutch."

"Even if he *hadn't* given it to me, you don't throw away another person's books. If I want to read something, I want to read it."

"I'm sorry," he said.

It bothered her all day long. And she had forgotten something that she meant to ask him; that bothered her too.

She remembered it in the evening, while they were walking back from La Scala, a restaurant not far from the house. "How did you know Dr. Shand plays the recorder?" she said.

He didn't understand.

"The other day," she said, "when I read the book and we argued about it; you said that Dr. Shand just happened to play the recorder. How did you know?"

"Oh," Guy said. "He told me. A long time ago. And I said we'd heard a flute or something through the wall once or twice, and he said that was him. How did you think I knew?"

"I didn't think," Rosemary said. "I just wondered, that's all."

She couldn't sleep. She lay awake on her back and frowned at the ceiling. The baby inside her was sleeping fine, but she couldn't; she felt unsettled and worried, without knowing what she was worried about.

Well the *baby* of course, and whether everything would go the way it should. She had cheated on her exercises lately. No more of *that;* solemn promise.

It was really Monday already, the thirteenth. Fifteen more days. Two weeks. Probably all women felt edgy and unsettled two weeks before. And couldn't sleep from being sick and tired of sleeping on their backs! The first thing she was going to do after it was all over was sleep twenty-four solid hours on her stomach, hugging a pillow, with her face snuggled deep down into it.

She heard a sound in Minnie and Roman's apartment, but it must have been from the floor above or the floor below. Sounds were masked and confused with the air conditioner going.

They were in Paris already. Lucky them. Some day she and Guy would go, with their three lovely children.

The baby woke up and began moving.

Nine

She bought cotton balls and cotton swabs and talcum powder and baby lotion; engaged a diaper service and rearranged the baby's clothing in the bureau drawers. She ordered the announcements—Guy would phone in the name and date later—and addressed and stamped a boxful of small ivory envelopes. She read a book called *Summerhill* that presented a seemingly irrefutable case for permissive child-rearing, and discussed it at Sardi's East with Elise and Joan, their treat.

She began to feel contractions; one one day, one the next, then none, then two.

A postcard came from Paris, with a picture of the Arc de Triomphe and a neatly written message: *Thinking of you both. Lovely weather, excellent food. The flight over was perfect. Love, Minnie.*

The baby dropped low inside her, ready to be born.

Early in the afternoon of Friday, June 24th, at the stationery counter at Tiffany's where she had gone for twenty-five more envelopes, Rosemary met Dominick Pozzo, who in the past had been Guy's vocal coach. A short, swarthy, hump-backed man with a voice that was rasping and unpleasant, he seized Rosemary's hand and congratulated her on her appearance and on Guy's recent good fortune, for which he disavowed all credit. Rosemary told him of the play Guy was signing for and of the latest offer Warner Brothers had made. Dominick was delighted; now, he said, was when Guy could truly benefit from intensive coaching. He explained why, made Rosemary promise to have Guy call him, and, with final good wishes, turned toward the elevators. Rosemary caught his arm. "I never thanked you for the tickets to *The Fantasticks,*" she said. "I just loved it. It's going to go on and on forever, like that Agatha Christie play in London."

"*The Fantasticks?*" Dominick said.

"You gave Guy a pair of tickets. Oh, long ago. In the fall. I went with a friend. Guy had seen it already."

"I never gave Guy tickets for *The Fantasticks,*" Dominick said.

"You did. Last fall."

"No, my dear. I never gave *anybody* tickets to *The Fantasticks;* I never had any to give. You're mistaken."

"I'm sure he said he got them from you," Rosemary said.

"Then *he* was mistaken," Dominick said. "You'll tell him to call me, yes?"

"Yes. Yes, I will."

It was strange, Rosemary thought when she was waiting to cross Fifth Avenue. Guy *had* said that Dominick had given him the tickets, she was certain of it. She remembered wondering whether or not to send Dominick a thank-you note and deciding finally that it wasn't necessary. She *couldn't* be mistaken.

Walk, the light said, and she crossed the avenue.

But *Guy* couldn't have been mistaken either. He didn't get free tickets every day of the week; he *must* have remembered who gave them to him. Had he deliberately lied to her? Perhaps he hadn't been given the tickets at all, but had found and kept them. No, there might have been a scene at the theater; he wouldn't have exposed her to that.

She walked west on Fifty-seventh Street, walked very slowly with the bigness of the baby hanging before her and her back aching from withstanding its forward-pulling weight. The day was hot and humid; ninety-two already and still rising. She walked very slowly.

Had he wanted to get her out of the apartment that night for some reason? Had he gone down and bought the tickets himself? To be free to study the scene he was working on? But there wouldn't have been any need for trickery if that had been the case; more than once in the old one-room apartment he had asked her to go out for a couple of hours and she had gone gladly. Most of the time, though, he wanted her to stay, to be his line-feeder, his audience.

Was it a girl? One of his old flames for whom a couple of hours hadn't been enough, and whose perfume he had been washing off in the shower when she got home? No, it was tannis root not perfume that the apartment had smelled of that night; she had had to wrap the charm in foil because of it. And Guy had been far too energetic and amorous to have spent the earlier part of the night with someone else. He had made unusually violent love to her, she remembered; later, while he slept, she had heard the flute and the chanting at Minnie and Roman's.

No, not the flute. Dr. Shand's recorder.

Was that how Guy knew about it? Had he been there that evening? At a sabbath . . .

She stopped and looked in Henri Bendel's windows, because she didn't want to think any more about witches and covens and baby's blood and Guy being over there. Why had she met that stupid Dominick? She should never have gone out today at all. It was too hot and sticky.

There was a great raspberry crepe dress that looked like a Rudi Gernreich. After Tuesday, after she was her own real shape again, maybe she would go in and price it. And a pair of lemon-yellow hip-huggers and a raspberry blouse . . .

Eventually, though, she had to go on. Go on walking, go on thinking, with the baby squirming inside her.

The book (*which Guy had thrown away*) had told of initiation ceremonies, of covens inducting novice members with vows and baptism, with anointing and the infliction of a "witch mark." Was it possible (the shower to wash away the smell of a tannis anointing) that Guy had joined the coven? That he (no, he couldn't be!) was one of them, with a secret mark of membership somewhere on his body?

There had been a flesh-colored Band-Aid on his shoulder. It had been there in his dressing room in Philadelphia ("That damn pimple," he had said when she had asked him) and it had been there a few months before ("Not the same one!" she had said). Was it still there now?

She didn't know. He didn't sleep naked any more. He had in the past, especially in hot weather. But not any more, not for months and months. Now he wore pajamas every night. When had she last seen him naked?

A car honked at her; she was crossing Sixth Avenue. "For God's sake, lady," a man behind her said.

But why, *why?* He was *Guy,* he wasn't a crazy old man with nothing better to do, with no other way to find purpose and self-esteem! He had a *career,* a busy, exciting, every-day-getting-better career! What did he need with wands and witch knives and censers and—and *junk;* with the Weeses and the Gilmores and Minnie and Roman? What could they give him that he couldn't get elsewhere?

She had known the answer before she asked herself the question. Formulating the question had been a way to put off facing the answer.

The blindness of Donald Baumgart.

If you believed.

But she didn't. She didn't.

Yet there Donald Baumgart was, blind, only a day or two after that Saturday. With Guy staying home to grab the phone every time it rang. Expecting the news.

The blindness of Donald Baumgart.

Out of which had come everything; the play, the reviews, the new play, the movie offer . . . Maybe Guy's part in *Greenwich Village,* too, would have been Donald Baumgart's if he hadn't gone inexplicably blind a day or two after Guy had joined (maybe) a coven (maybe) of witches (maybe).

There were spells to take an enemy's sight or hearing, the book had said. *All Of Them Witches.* (Not Guy!) The united mental force of the whole coven, a concentrated battery of malevolent wills, could blind, deafen, paralyze, and ultimately kill the chosen victim.

Paralyze and ultimately kill.

"Hutch?" she asked aloud, standing motionless in front of Carnegie Hall. A girl looked up at her, clinging to her mother's hand.

He had been reading the book that night and had asked her to meet him the next morning. To tell her that Roman was Steven Marcato. And Guy knew of the appointment, and knowing, went out for—what, ice cream?—and rang Minnie and Roman's bell. Was a hasty meeting called? The united mental force . . . But how had they known what Hutch would be telling her? She hadn't known herself; only he had known.

Suppose, though, that "tannis root" wasn't "tannis root" at all. Hutch hadn't heard of it, had he? Suppose it was—that other stuff he underlined in the book, Devil's Fungus or whatever it was. He had told Roman he was going to look into it; wouldn't that have been enough to make Roman wary of him? *And right then and there Roman had taken one of Hutch's gloves,* because the spells can't be cast without one of the victim's belongings! And then, when Guy told them about the appointment for the next morning, they took no chances and went to work.

But no, Roman couldn't have taken Hutch's glove; she had shown him in and shown him out, walking along with him both times.

Guy had taken the glove. He had rushed home with his make-up still on— which he *never* did—and had gone by himself to the closet. Roman must have called him, must have said, "This man Hutch is getting suspicious about 'tannis root'; go home and get one of his belongings, just in case!" And Guy had obeyed. To keep Donald Baumgart blind.

Waiting for the light at Fifty-fifth Street, she tucked her handbag and the envelopes under her arm, unhooked the chain at the back of her neck, drew the chain and the tannis-charm out of her dress and dropped them together down through the sewer grating.

So much for "tannis root." Devil's Fungus.

She was so frightened she wanted to cry.

Because she knew what Guy was giving them in exchange for his success. The baby. To use in their rituals.

He had never *wanted* a baby until after Donald Baumgart was blind. He didn't like to feel it moving; he didn't like to talk about it; he kept himself as distant and busy as if it weren't his baby at all.

Because he knew what they were planning to do to it as soon as he gave it to them.

In the apartment, in the blessedly-cool shaded apartment, she tried to tell herself that she was mad. *You're going to have your baby in four days, Idiot Girl. Maybe even less. So you're all tense and nutty and you've built up a whole lunatic persecution thing out of a bunch of completely unrelated coincidences. There are no real witches. There are no real spells. Hutch died a natural death, even if the doctors couldn't give a name to it. Ditto for Donald Baumgart's blindness. And how, pray tell, did Guy get one of Donald Baumgart's belongings for the big spell-casting? See, Idiot Girl? It all falls apart when you pick at it.*

But why had he lied about the tickets?

She undressed and took a long cool shower, turned clumsily around and around and then pushed her face up into the spray, trying to think sensibly, rationally.

There *must* be another reason why he had lied. Maybe he'd spent the day hanging around Downey's, yes, and had gotten the tickets from one of the gang there; wouldn't he then have said Dominick had given them to him, so as not to let her know he'd been goofing off?

Of course he would have.

There, you see, Idiot Girl?

But why hadn't he shown himself naked in so many months and months?

She was glad, anyway, that she had thrown away that damned charm. She should have done it long ago. She never should have taken it from Minnie in the first place. What a pleasure it was to be rid of its revolting smell! She dried herself and splashed on cologne, lots and lots of it.

He hadn't shown himself naked because he had a little rash of some kind and was embarrassed about it. Actors are vain, aren't they? Elementary.

But why had he thrown out the book? And spent so much time at Minnie and Roman's? And waited for the news of Donald Baumgart's blindness? And rushed home wearing his make-up just before Hutch missed his glove?

She brushed her hair and tied it, and put on a brassiere and panties. She went into the kitchen and drank two glasses of cold milk.

She didn't know.

She went into the nursery, moved the bathinette away from the wall, and thumbtacked a sheet of plastic over the wallpaper to protect it when the baby splashed in its bath.

She didn't know.

She didn't know if she was going mad or going sane, if witches had only the longing for power or power that was real and strong, if Guy was her loving husband or the treacherous enemy of the baby and herself.

It was almost four. He would be home in an hour or so.

. . .

She called Actors Equity and got Donald Baumgart's telephone number.

The phone was answered on the first ring with a quick impatient "Yeh?"

"Is this Donald Baumgart?"

"That's right."

"This is Rosemary Woodhouse," she said. "Guy Woodhouse's wife."

"Oh?"

"I wanted—"

"My God," he said, "you must be a happy little lady these days! I hear you're living in baronial splendor in the 'Bram,' sipping vintage wine from crystal goblets, with scores of uniformed lackeys in attendance."

She said, "I wanted to know how you are; if there's been any improvement."

He laughed. "Why bless your heart, Guy Woodhouse's wife," he said, "I'm fine! I'm splendid! There's been enormous improvement! I only broke six glasses today, only fell down three flights of stairs, and only went tap-a-tap-tapping in front of two speeding fire engines! Every day in every way I'm getting better and better and better and better."

Rosemary said, "Guy and I are both very unhappy that he got his break because of your misfortune."

Donald Baumgart was silent for a moment, and then said, "Oh, what the hell. That's the way it goes. Somebody's up, somebody's down. He would've made out all right anyway. To tell you the truth, after that second audition we did for *Two Hours of Solid Crap,* I was dead certain he was going to get the part. He was terrific."

"He thought *you* were going to get it," Rosemary said. "And he was right."

"Briefly."

"I'm sorry I didn't come along that day he came to visit you," Rosemary said. "He asked me to, but I couldn't."

"Visit me? You mean the day we met for drinks?"

"Yes," she said. "That's what I meant."

"It's good you *didn't* come," he said; "they don't allow women, do they? No, after four they *do,* that's right; and it was after four. That was awfully good-natured of Guy. Most people wouldn't have had the—well, *class,* I guess. *I* wouldn't have had it, I can tell you that."

"The loser buying the winner a drink," Rosemary said.

"And little did we know that a week later—less than a week, in fact—"

"That's right," Rosemary said. "It was only a few days before you—"

"Went blind. Yes. It was a Wednesday or Thursday, because I'd been to a matinee—Wednesday, I think—and the following Sunday was when it happened. Hey"—he laughed—"Guy didn't put anything *in* that drink, did he?"

"No, he didn't," Rosemary said. Her voice was shaking. "By the way," she said, "he has something of yours, you know."

"What do you mean?"

"Don't you know?"

"No," he said.

"Didn't you miss anything that day?"

"No. Not that I remember."

"You're sure?"

"You don't mean my tie, do you?"

"Yes," she said.

"Well he's got mine and I've got his. Does he want his back? He can have it; it doesn't matter to *me* what tie I'm wearing, or if I'm wearing one at all."

"No, he doesn't want it back," Rosemary said. "I didn't understand. I thought he had only borrowed it."

"No, it was a trade. It sounded as if you thought he had *stolen* it."

"I have to hang up now," Rosemary said. "I just wanted to know if there was any improvement."

"No, there isn't. It was nice of you to call."

She hung up.

It was nine minutes after four.

She put on her girdle and a dress and sandals. She took the emergency money Guy kept under his underwear—a not very thick fold of bills—and put it into her handbag, put in her address book too and the bottle of vitamin capsules. A contraction came and went, the second of the day. She took the suitcase that stood by the bedroom door and went down the hallway and out of the apartment.

Halfway to the elevator, she turned and doubled back.

She rode down in the service elevator with two delivery boys.

On Fifty-fifth Street she got a taxi.

Miss Lark, Dr. Sapirstein's receptionist, glanced at the suitcase and said, smiling, "You aren't in labor, are you?"

"No," Rosemary said, "but I have to see the doctor. It's very important."

Miss Lark glanced at her watch. "He has to leave at five," she said, "and there's Mrs. Byron . . ."—she looked over at a woman who sat reading and then smiled at Rosemary—"but I'm sure he'll see you. Sit down. I'll let him know you're here as soon as he's free."

"Thank you," Rosemary said.

She put the suitcase by the nearest chair and sat down. The handbag's white patent was damp in her hands. She opened it, took out a tissue, and wiped her palms and then her upper lip and temples. Her heart was racing.

"How is it out there?" Miss Lark asked.

"Terrible," Rosemary said. "Ninety-four."

Miss Lark made a pained sound.

A woman came out of Dr. Sapirstein's office, a woman in her fifth or sixth month whom Rosemary had seen before. They nodded at each other. Miss Lark went in.

"You're due any day now, aren't you?" the woman said, waiting by the desk.

"Tuesday," Rosemary said.

"Good luck," the woman said. "You're smart to get it over with before July and August."

Miss Lark came out again. "Mrs. Byron," she said, and to Rosemary, "He'll see you right after."

"Thank you," Rosemary said.

Mrs. Byron went into Dr. Sapirstein's office and closed the door. The woman by the desk conferred with Miss Lark about another appointment and then went out, saying good-by to Rosemary and wishing her luck again.

Miss Lark wrote. Rosemary took up a copy of *Time* that lay at her elbow. *Is God Dead?* it asked in red letters on a black background. She found the index and turned to Show Business. There was a piece on Barbra Streisand. She tried to read it.

"That smells nice," Miss Lark said, sniffing in Rosemary's direction. "What is it?"

"It's called 'Detchema,' " Rosemary said.

"It's a big improvement over your regular, if you don't mind my saying."

"That wasn't a cologne," Rosemary said. "It was a good luck charm. I threw it away."

"Good," Miss Lark said. "Maybe the doctor will follow your example."

Rosemary, after a moment, said, "Dr. Sapirstein?"

Miss Lark said, "Mm-hmm. He has the after-shave. But it isn't, is it? Then he has a good luck charm. Only he isn't superstitious. I don't *think* he is. *Anyway*, he has the same *smell* once in a while, *whatever* it is, and when he does, I can't come within five feet of him. Much stronger than yours was. Haven't you ever noticed?"

"No," Rosemary said.

"I guess you haven't been here on the right days," Miss Lark said. "Or maybe you thought it was your own you were smelling. What is it, a chemical thing?"

Rosemary stood up and put down *Time* and picked up her suitcase. "My husband is outside; I have to tell him something," she said. "I'll be back in a minute."

"You can leave your suitcase," Miss Lark said.

Rosemary took it with her though.

Ten

She walked up Park to Eighty-first Street, where she found a glass-walled phone booth. She called Dr. Hill. It was very hot in the booth.

A service answered. Rosemary gave her name and the phone number. "Please ask him to call me back right away," she said. "It's an emergency and I'm in a phone booth."

"All right," the woman said and clicked to silence.

Rosemary hung up and then lifted the receiver again but kept a hidden finger on the hook. She held the receiver to her ear as if listening, so that no one should come along and ask her to give up the phone. The baby kicked and twisted in her. She was sweating. *Quickly, please, Dr. Hill. Call me. Rescue me.*

All of them. All of them. They were all in it together. Guy, Dr. Sapirstein, Minnie, and Roman. All of them witches. *All Of Them Witches.* Using her to produce a baby for them, so that they could take it and—*Don't you worry, Andy-or-Jenny, I'll kill them before I let them touch you!*

The phone rang. She jumped her finger from the hook. "Yes?"

"Is this Mrs. Woodhouse?" It was the service again.

"Where's Dr. *Hill?*" she said.

"Did I get the name right?" the woman asked. "Is it 'Rosemary Wood-house'?"

"Yes!"

"And you're Dr. Hill's patient?"

She explained about the one visit back in the fall. "Please, please," she said, "he *has* to speak to me! It's important! It's—*please. Please tell him to call me.*"

"All right," the woman said.

Holding the hook again, Rosemary wiped her forehead with the back of her hand. *Please, Dr. Hill.* She cracked open the door for air and then pushed it closed again as a woman came near and waited. "Oh, I didn't know that," Rosemary said to the mouthpiece, her finger on the hook. "Really? What else did he say?" Sweat trickled down her back and from under her arms. The baby turned and rolled.

It had been a mistake to use a phone so near Dr. Sapirstein's office. She should have gone to Madison or Lexington. "That's wonderful," she said. "Did he say anything else?" At this very moment he might be out of the door and looking for her, and wouldn't the nearest phone booth be the first place he'd look? She should have gotten right into a taxi, gotten far away. She put her back as much as she could in the direction he would come from if he came. The woman outside was walking away, thank God.

And now, too, Guy would be coming home. He would see the suitcase gone and call Dr. Sapirstein, thinking she was in the hospital. Soon the two of them would be looking for her. And all the others too; the Weeses, the—

"Yes?"—stopping the ring in its middle.

"Mrs. Woodhouse?"

It was Dr. Hill, Dr. Savior-Rescuer-Kildare-Wonderful-Hill. "Thank you," she said. "Thank you for calling me."

"I thought you were in California," he said.

"No," she said. "I went to another doctor, one some friends sent me to, and he isn't good, Dr. Hill; he's been lying to me and giving me unusual kinds of —drinks and capsules. The baby is due on Tuesday—remember, you told me, June twenty-eighth?—and I want *you* to deliver it. I'll pay you whatever you want, the same as if I'd been coming to you all along."

"Mrs. Woodhouse—"

"Please, let me talk to you," she said, hearing refusal. "Let me come and explain what's been going on. I can't stay too long where I am right now. My husband and this doctor and the people who sent me to him, they've all been involved in—well, in a plot; I know that sounds crazy, Doctor, and you're probably thinking, 'My God, this poor girl has completely flipped,' but I *haven't* flipped, Doctor, I swear by all the saints I haven't. Now and then there *are* plots against people, aren't there?"

"Yes, I suppose there are," he said.

"There's one against me and my baby," she said, "and if you'll let me come talk to you I'll tell you about it. And I'm not going to ask you to do anything unusual or wrong or anything; all I want you to do is get me into a hospital and deliver my baby for me."

He said, "Come to my office tomorrow after—"

"Now," she said. "Now. Right now. They're going to be looking for me."

"Mrs. Woodhouse," he said, "I'm not at my office now, I'm home. I've been up since yesterday morning and—"

"I beg you," she said. "I beg you."

He was silent.

She said, "I'll come there and explain to you. I can't stay here."

"My office at eight o'clock," he said. "Will that be all right?"

"Yes," she said. "Yes. Thank you. Dr. Hill?"

"Yes?"

"My husband may call you and ask if I called."

"I'm not going to speak to *anyone,*" he said. "I'm going to take a nap."

"Would you tell your service? Not to say that I called? Doctor?"

"All right, I will," he said.

"Thank you," she said.

"Eight o'clock."

"Yes. Thank you."

A man with his back to the booth turned as she came out; he wasn't Dr. Sapirstein though, he was somebody else.

She walked to Lexington Avenue and uptown to Eighty-sixth Street, where she went into the theater there, used the ladies' room, and then sat numbly in the safe cool darkness facing a loud color movie. After a while she got up and went with her suitcase to a phone booth, where she placed a person-to-person collect call to her brother Brian. There was no answer. She went back with her suitcase and sat in a different seat. The baby was quiet, sleeping. The movie changed to something with Keenan Wynn.

At twenty of eight she left the theater and took a taxi to Dr. Hill's office on West Seventy-second Street. It would be safe to go in, she thought; they would be watching Joan's place and Hugh and Elise's, but not Dr. Hill's office at eight o'clock, not if his service had said she hadn't called. To be sure, though, she asked the driver to wait and watch until she was inside the door.

Nobody stopped her. Dr. Hill opened the door himself, more pleasantly than she had expected after his reluctance on the telephone. He had grown a moustache, blond and hardly noticeable, but he still looked like Dr. Kildare. He was wearing a blue-and-yellow-plaid sport shirt.

They went into his consulting room, which was a quarter the size of Dr. Sapirstein's, and there Rosemary told him her story. She sat with her hands on the chair arms and her ankles crossed and spoke quietly and calmly, knowing that any suggestion of hysteria would make him disbelieve her and think her mad. She told him about Adrian Marcato and Minnie and Roman; about the months of pain she had suffered and the herbal drinks and the little white cakes; about Hutch and *All Of Them Witches* and the *Fantasticks* tickets and black candles and Donald Baumgart's necktie. She tried to keep everything coherent and in sequence but she couldn't. She got it all out without getting hysterical though; Dr. Shand's recorder and Guy throwing away the book and Miss Lark's final unwitting revelation.

"Maybe the coma and the blindness were only coincidences," she said, "or maybe they *do* have some kind of ESP way of hurting people. But that's not important. The important thing is that they want the baby. I'm sure they do."

"It certainly seems that way," Dr. Hill said, "especially in light of the interest they've taken in it right from the beginning."

Rosemary shut her eyes and could have cried. He believed her. He didn't think she was mad. She opened her eyes and looked at him, staying calm and composed. He was writing. Did all his patients love him? Her palms were wet; she slid them from the chair arms and pressed them against her dress.

"The doctor's name is Shand, you say," Dr. Hill said.

"No, Dr. Shand is just one of the group," Rosemary said. "One of the coven. The doctor is Dr. Sapirstein."

"Abraham Sapirstein?"

"Yes," Rosemary said uneasily. "Do you know him?"

"I've met him once or twice," Dr. Hill said, writing more.

"Looking at him," Rosemary said, "or even talking to him, you would never think he—"

"Never in a million years," Dr. Hill said, putting down his pen, "which is why we're told not to judge books by their covers. Would you like to go into Mount Sinai right now, this evening?"

Rosemary smiled. "I would *love* to," she said. "Is it possible?"

"It'll take some wire-pulling and arguing," Dr. Hill said. He rose and went to the open door of his examining room. "I want you to lie down and get some rest," he said, reaching into the darkened room behind him. It blinked into ice-blue fluorescent light. "I'll see what I can do and then I'll check you over."

Rosemary hefted herself up and went with her handbag into the examining room. "Anything they've got," she said. "Even a broom closet."

"I'm sure we can do better than that," Dr. Hill said. He came in after her and turned on an air conditioner in the room's blue-curtained window. It was a noisy one.

"Shall I undress?" Rosemary asked.

"No, not yet," Dr. Hill said. "This is going to take a good half-hour of high-powered telephoning. Just lie down and rest." He went out and closed the door.

Rosemary went to the day bed at the far end of the room and sat down heavily on its blue-covered softness. She put her handbag on a chair.

God bless Dr. Hill.

She would make a sampler to that effect some day.

She shook off her sandals and lay back gratefully. The air conditioner sent a small stream of coolness to her; the baby turned over slowly and lazily, as if feeling it.

Everything's okay now, Andy-or-Jenny. We're going to be in a nice clean bed at Mount Sinai Hospital, with no visitors and—

Money. She sat up, opened her handbag, and found Guy's money that she had taken. There was a hundred and eighty dollars. Plus sixteen-and-change of her own. It would be enough, certainly, for any advance payments that had to be made, and if more were needed Brian would wire it or Hugh and Elise would lend it to her. Or Joan. Or Grace Cardiff. She had plenty of people she could turn to.

She took the capsules out, put the money back in, and closed the handbag; and then she lay back again on the day bed, with the handbag and the bottle of capsules on the chair beside her. She would give the capsules to Dr. Hill; he would analyze them and make sure there was nothing harmful in them. There *couldn't* be. They would want the baby to be healthy, wouldn't they, for their insane rituals?

She shivered.

The—monsters.

And Guy.

Unspeakable, unspeakable.

Her middle hardened in a straining contraction, the strongest one yet. She breathed shallowly until it ended.

Making three that day.

She would tell Dr. Hill.

She was living with Brian and Dodie in a large contemporary house in Los Angeles, and Andy had just started talking (though only four months old) when Dr. Hill looked in and she was in his examining room again, lying on the day bed in the coolness of the air conditioner. She shielded her eyes with her hand and smiled at him. "I've been sleeping," she said.

He pushed the door all the way open and withdrew. Dr. Sapirstein and Guy came in.

Rosemary sat up, lowering her hand from her eyes.

They came and stood close to her. Guy's face was stony and blank. He looked at the walls, only at the walls, not at her. Dr. Sapirstein said, "Come with us quietly, Rosemary. Don't argue or make a scene, because if you say anything more about witches or witchcraft we're going to be forced to take you to a mental hospital. The facilities there for delivering the baby will be less than the best. You don't want that, do you? So put your shoes on."

"We're just going to take you home," Guy said, finally looking at her. "No one's going to hurt you."

"Or the baby," Dr. Sapirstein said. "Put your shoes on." He picked up the bottle of capsules, looked at it, and put it in his pocket.

She put her sandals on and he gave her her handbag.

They went out, Dr. Sapirstein holding her arm, Guy touching her other elbow.

Dr. Hill had her suitcase. He gave it to Guy.

"She's fine now," Dr. Sapirstein said. "We're going to go home and rest."

Dr. Hill smiled at her. "That's all it takes, nine times out of ten," he said. She looked at him and said nothing.

"Thank you for your trouble, Doctor," Dr. Sapirstein said, and Guy said, "It's a shame you had to come in here and—"

"I'm glad I could be of help, sir," Dr. Hill said to Dr. Sapirstein, opening the front door.

They had a car. Mr. Gilmore was driving it. Rosemary sat between Guy and Dr. Sapirstein in back.

Nobody spoke.

They drove to the Bramford.

The elevator man smiled at her as they crossed the lobby toward him. Diego. Smiled because he liked her, favored her over some of the other tenants.

The smile, reminding her of her individuality, wakened something in her, revived something.

She snicked open her handbag at her side, worked a finger through her key ring, and, near the elevator door, turned the handbag all the way over, spilling out everything except the keys. Rolling lipstick, coins, Guy's tens and twenties fluttering, everything. She looked down stupidly.

They picked things up, Guy and Dr. Sapirstein, while she stood mute, pregnant-helpless. Diego came out of the elevator, making tongue-teeth sounds of concern. He bent and helped. She backed in to get out of the way and, watching them, toed the big round floor button. The rolling door rolled. She pulled closed the inner gate.

Diego grabbed for the door but saved his fingers; smacked on the outside of it. "Hey, Mrs. Woodhouse!"

Sorry, Diego.

She pushed the handle and the car lurched upward.

She would call Brian. Or Joan or Elise or Grace Cardiff. Someone.

We're not through yet, Andy!

She stopped the car at nine, then at six, then halfway past seven, and then close enough to seven to open the gate and the door and step four inches down.

She walked through the turns of hallway as quickly as she could. A contraction came but she marched right through it, paying no heed.

The service elevator's indicator blinked from four to five and she knew it was Guy and Dr. Sapirstein coming up to intercept her.

So of course the key wouldn't go into the lock.

But finally did, and she was inside, slamming the door as the elevator door opened, hooking in the chain as Guy's key went into the lock. She turned the bolt and the key turned it right back again. The door opened and pushed in against the chain.

"Open up, Ro," Guy said.

"Go to hell," she said.

"I'm not going to hurt you, honey."

"You promised them the baby. Get away."

"I didn't promise them anything," he said. "What are you talking about? Promised who?"

"Rosemary," Dr. Sapirstein said.

"You too. Get away."

"You seem to have imagined some sort of conspiracy against you."

"Get away," she said, and pushed the door shut and bolted it.

It stayed bolted.

She backed away, watching it, and then went into the bedroom.

It was nine-thirty.

She wasn't sure of Brian's number and her address book was in the lobby or Guy's pocket, so the operator had to get Omaha Information. When the call was finally put through there was still no answer. "Do you want me to try again in twenty minutes?" the operator asked.

"Yes, please," Rosemary said; "in *five* minutes."

"I can't try again in five minutes," the operator said, "but I'll try in twenty minutes if you want me to."

"Yes, please," Rosemary said and hung up.

She called Joan, and Joan was out too.

Elise and Hugh's number was—she didn't know. Information took forever to answer but, having answered, supplied it quickly. She dialed it and got an answering service. They were away for the weekend. "Are they anywhere where I can reach them? This is an emergency."

"Is this Mr. Dunstan's secretary?"

"No, I'm a close friend. It's very important that I speak to them."

"They're on Fire Island," the woman said. "I can give you a number."

"Please."

She memorized it, hung up, and was about to dial it when she heard whispers outside the doorway and footsteps on the vinyl floor. She stood up.

Guy and Mr. Fountain came into the room—"Honey, we're *not* going to hurt you," Guy said—and behind them Dr. Sapirstein with a loaded hypodermic, the needle up and dripping, his thumb at the plunger. And Dr. Shand and Mrs. Fountain and Mrs. Gilmore. "We're your friends," Mrs. Gilmore said, and Mrs. Fountain said, "There's nothing to be afraid of, Rosemary; honest and truly there isn't."

"This is nothing but a mild sedative," Dr. Sapirstein said. "To calm you down so that you can get a good night's sleep."

She was between the bed and the wall, and too gross to climb over the bed and evade them.

They came toward her—"You know I wouldn't let anyone hurt you, Ro" —and she picked up the phone and struck with the receiver at Guy's head.

He caught her wrist and Mr. Fountain caught her other arm and the phone fell as he pulled her around with startling strength. *"Help me, somebod—"* she screamed, and a handkerchief or something was jammed into her mouth and held there by a small strong hand.

They dragged her away from the bed so Dr. Sapirstein could come in front of her with the hypodermic and a dab of cotton, and a contraction far more grueling than any of the others clamped her middle and clenched shut her eyes. She held her breath, then sucked air in through her nostrils in quick little pulls. A hand felt her belly, deft all-over finger-tipping, and Dr. Sapirstein said, "Wait a minute, wait a minute now; we happen to be in labor here."

Silence; and someone outside the room whispered the news: "She's in labor!"

She opened her eyes and stared at Dr. Sapirstein, dragging air through her nostrils, her middle relaxing. He nodded to her, and suddenly took her arm that Mr. Fountain was holding, touched it with cotton, and stabbed it with the needle.

She took the injection without trying to move, too afraid, too stunned.

He withdrew the needle and rubbed the spot with his thumb and then with the cotton.

The women, she saw, were turning down the bed.

Here?

Here?

It was supposed to be Doctors Hospital! Doctors Hospital, with equipment and nurses and everything clean and sterile!

They held her while she struggled, Guy saying in her ear, "You'll be all right, honey, I swear to God you will! I swear to God you're going to be perfectly all right! Don't go on fighting like this, Ro, please don't! I give you my absolute word of honor you're going to be perfectly all right!"

And then there was another contraction.

And then she was on the bed, with Dr. Sapirstein giving her another injection.

And Mrs. Gilmore wiped her forehead.

And the phone rang.

And Guy said, "No, just cancel it, operator."

And there was another contraction, faint and disconnected from her floating eggshell head.

All the exercises had been for nothing. All wasted energy. This wasn't natural childbirth at all; she wasn't helping, she wasn't seeing.

Oh, Andy, Andy-or-Jenny! I'm sorry, my little darling! Forgive me!

Three

One

Light.

The ceiling.

And pain between her legs.

And Guy. Sitting beside the bed, watching her with an anxious, uncertain smile.

"Hi," he said.

"Hi," she said back.

The pain was terrible.

And then she remembered. It was over. It was over. The baby was born.

"Is it all right?" she asked.

"Yes, fine," he said.

"What is it?"

"A boy."

"Really? A boy?"

He nodded.

"And it's all right?"

"Yes."

She let her eyes close, then managed to open them again.

"Did you call Tiffany's?" she asked.

"Yes," he said.

She let her eyes close and slept.

. . .

Later she remembered more. Laura-Louise was sitting by the bed reading the *Reader's Digest* with a magnifying glass.

"Where is it?" she asked.

Laura-Louise jumped. "My goodness, dear," she said, the magnifying glass at her bosom showing red ropes interwoven, "what a *start* you gave me, waking up so suddenly! My goodness!" She closed her eyes and breathed deeply.

"The baby; where is it?" she asked.

"You just wait here a minute," Laura-Louise said, getting up with the *Digest* closed on a finger. "I'll get Guy and Doctor Abe. They're right in the kitchen."

"Where's the baby?" she asked, but Laura-Louise went out the door without answering.

She tried to get up but fell back, her arms boneless. And there was pain between her legs like a bundle of knife points. She lay and waited, remembering, remembering.

It was night. Five after nine, the clock said.

They came in, Guy and Dr. Sapirstein, looking grave and resolute.

"Where's the baby?" she asked them.

Guy came around to the side of the bed and crouched down and took her hand. "Honey," he said.

"Where is it?"

"Honey . . ." He tried to say more and couldn't. He looked across the bed for help.

Dr. Sapirstein stood looking down at her. A shred of coconut was caught in his moustache. "There were complications, Rosemary," he said, "but nothing that will affect future births."

"It's—"

"Dead," he said.

She stared at him.

He nodded.

She turned to Guy.

He nodded too.

"It was in the wrong position," Dr. Sapirstein said. "In the hospital I might have been able to do something, but there simply wasn't time to get you there. Trying anything here would have been—too dangerous for you."

Guy said, "We can have others, honey, and we will, just as soon as you're better. I promise you."

Dr. Sapirstein said, "Absolutely. You can start on another in a very few months and the odds are thousands to one against anything similar happening. It was a tragic one-in-ten-thousand mishap; the baby itself was perfectly healthy and normal."

Guy squeezed her hand and smiled encouragingly at her. "As soon as you're better," he said.

She looked at them, at Guy, at Dr. Sapirstein with the shred of coconut in his moustache. "You're lying," she said. "I don't believe you. You're both lying."

"Honey," Guy said.

"It didn't die," she said. "You took it. You're lying. You're witches. You're lying. You're lying! You're lying! *You're lying! You're lying! You're lying!*"

Guy held her shoulders to the bed and Dr. Sapirstein gave her an injection.

She ate soup and triangles of buttered white bread. Guy sat on the side of the bed, nibbling at one of the triangles. "You were crazy," he said. "You were really ka-pow out of your mind. It happens sometimes in the last couple of weeks. That's what Abe says. He has a name for it. Prepartum I-don't-know, some kind of hysteria. You had it, honey, and with a vengeance."

She said nothing. She took a spoonful of soup.

"Listen," he said, "I know where you got the idea that Minnie and *Roman* were witches, but what made you think Abe and I had joined the party?"

She said nothing.

"That's stupid of me, though," he said. "I guess prepartum whatever-it-is doesn't *need* reasons." He took another of the triangles and bit off first one point and then another.

She said, "Why did you trade ties with Donald Baumgart?"

"Why did I—well what has *that* got to do with anything?"

"You needed one of his personal belongings," she said, "so they could cast the spell and make him blind."

He stared at her. "Honey," he said, "for God's sake what are you *talking* about?"

"You know."

"Holy mackerel," he said. "I traded ties with him because I liked his and didn't like mine, and *he* liked mine and didn't like his. I didn't tell you about it because afterwards it seemed like a slightly faggy thing to have done and I was a little embarrassed about it."

"Where did you get the tickets for *The Fantasticks?*" she asked him.

"*What?*"

"You said you got them from Dominick," she said; "you didn't."

"Boy oh *boy,*" he said. "And that makes me a witch? I got them from a girl named Norma-something that I met at an audition and had a couple of drinks with. What did Abe do? Tie his shoelaces the wrong way?"

"He uses tannis root," she said. "It's a witch thing. His receptionist told me she smelled it on him."

"Maybe Minnie gave him a good luck charm, just the way she gave you one. You mean only witches use it? That doesn't sound very likely."

Rosemary was silent.

"Let's face it, darling," Guy said, "you had the prepartum crazies. And now you're going to rest and get over them." He leaned closer to her and took her hand. "I know this has been the worst thing that ever happened to you," he said, "but from now on everything's going to be roses. Warners is within an inch of where we want them, and suddenly Universal is interested too. I'm going to get some more good reviews and then we're going to blow this town and be in the beautiful hills of Beverly, with the pool and the spice garden and the whole schmeer. And the kids too, Ro. Scout's honor. You heard what Abe said." He kissed her hand. "Got to run now and get famous."

He got up and started for the door.

"Let me see your shoulder," she said.

He stopped and turned.

"Let me see your shoulder," she said.

"Are you kidding?"

"No," she said. "Let me see it. Your left shoulder."

He looked at her and said, "All right, whatever you say, honey."

He undid the collar of his shirt, a short-sleeved blue knit, and peeled the bottom of it up and over his head. He had a white T shirt on underneath. "I generally prefer doing this to music," he said, and took off the T shirt too. He went close to the bed and, leaning, showed Rosemary his left shoulder. It was unmarked. There was only the faint scar of a boil or pimple. He showed her his other shoulder and his chest and his back.

"This is as far as I go without a blue light," he said.

"All right," she said.

He grinned. "The question now," he said, "is do I put my shirt back on or do I go out and give Laura-Louise the thrill of a lifetime."

Her breasts filled with milk and it was necessary to relieve them, so Dr. Sapirstein showed her how to use a rubber-bulbed breast pump, like a glass auto horn; and several times a day Laura-Louise or Helen Wees or whoever was there brought it in to her with a Pyrex measuring cup. She drew from each breast an ounce or two of thin faintly-green fluid that smelled ever so slightly of tannis root—in a process that was a final irrefutable demonstration of the baby's absence. When the cup and the pump had been carried from the room she would lie against her pillows broken and lonely beyond tears.

Joan and Elise and Tiger came to see her, and she spoke with Brian for twenty minutes on the phone. Flowers came—roses and carnations and a yellow azalea plant—from Allan, and Mike and Pedro, and Lou and Claudia. Guy bought a new remote-control television set and put it at the foot of the bed. She watched and ate and took pills that were given to her.

A letter of sympathy came from Minnie and Roman, a page from each of them. They were in Dubrovnik.

The stitches gradually stopped hurting.

. . .

One morning, when two or three weeks had gone by, she thought she heard a baby crying. She rayed off the television and listened. There was a frail faraway wailing. Or was there? She slipped out of bed and turned off the air conditioner.

Florence Gilmore came in with the pump and the cup.

"Do you hear a baby crying?" Rosemary asked her.

Both of them listened.

Yes, there it was. A baby crying.

"No, dear, I don't," Florence said. "Get back into bed now; you know you're not supposed to be walking around. Did you turn off the air conditioner? You mustn't do that; it's a *terrible* day. People are actually dying, it's so hot."

She heard it again that afternoon, and mysteriously her breasts began to leak . . .

"Some new people moved in," Guy said out of nowhere that evening. "Up on eight."

"And they have a baby," she said.

"Yes. How did you know?"

She looked at him for a moment. "I heard it crying," she said.

She heard it the next day. And the next.

She stopped watching television and held a book in front of her, pretending to read but only listening, listening . . .

It wasn't up on eight; it was right there on seven.

And more often than not, the pump and the cup were brought to her a few minutes after the crying began; and the crying stopped a few minutes after her milk was taken away.

"What do you do with it?" she asked Laura-Louise one morning, giving her back the pump and the cup and six ounces of milk.

"Why, throw it away, of course," Laura-Louise said, and went out.

That afternoon, as she gave Laura-Louise the cup, she said, "Wait a minute," and started to put a used coffee spoon into it.

Laura-Louise jerked the cup away. "Don't do that," she said, and caught the spoon in a finger of the hand holding the pump.

"What difference does it make?" Rosemary asked.

"It's just messy, that's all," Laura-Louise said.

Two

It was alive.

It was in Minnie and Roman's apartment.

They were keeping it there, feeding it her milk and please God taking care of it, because, as well as she remembered from Hutch's book, August first was one of their special days, Lammas or Leamas, with special maniacal rituals. Or maybe they were keeping it until Minnie and Roman came back from Europe. For their share.

But it was still alive.

She stopped taking the pills they gave her. She tucked them down into the fold between her thumb and her palm and faked the swallowing, and later pushed the pills as far as she could between the mattress and the box spring beneath it.

She felt stronger and more wide-awake.

Hang on, Andy! I'm coming!

She had learned her lesson with Dr. Hill. This time she would turn to no one, would expect no one to believe her and be her savior. Not the police, not Joan or the Dunstans or Grace Cardiff, not even Brian. Guy was too good an actor, Dr. Sapirstein too famous a doctor; between the two of them they'd have even him, even Brian, thinking she had some kind of post-losing-the-baby madness. This time she would do it alone, would go in there and get him herself, with her longest sharpest kitchen knife to fend away those maniacs.

And she was one up on them. Because she knew—and they didn't *know* she knew—that there was a secret way from the one apartment to the other. The door had been chained that night—she knew that as she knew the hand she was looking at was a hand, not a bird or a battleship—and still they had all come pouring in. So there had to be another way.

Which could only be the linen closet, barricaded by dead Mrs. Gardenia, who surely had died of the same witchery that had frozen and killed poor Hutch. The closet had been put there to break the one big apartment into two smaller ones, and if Mrs. Gardenia had belonged to the coven—she'd given Minnie her herbs; hadn't Terry said so?—then what was more logical than to open the back of the closet in some way and go to and fro with so many steps saved and the Bruhns and Dubin-and-DeVore never knowing of the traffic?

It *was* the linen closet.

In a dream long ago she had been carried through it. That had been no dream; it had been a sign from heaven, a divine message to be stored away and remembered now for assurance in a time of trial.

Oh Father in heaven, forgive me for doubting! Forgive me for turning from you, Merciful Father, and help me, help me in my hour of need! Oh Jesus, dear Jesus, help me save my innocent baby!

The pills, of course, were the answer. She squirmed her arm in under the mattress and caught them out one by one. Eight of them, all alike; small white tablets scored across the middle for breaking in half. Whatever they were, three a day had kept her limp and docile; eight at once, surely, would send Laura-Louise or Helen Wees into sound sleep. She brushed the pills clean, folded them up in a piece of magazine cover, and tucked them away at the bottom of her box of tissues.

She pretended still to be limp and docile; ate her meals and looked at magazines and pumped out her milk.

It was Leah Fountain who was there when everything was right. She came in after Helen Wees had gone out with the milk and said, "Hi, Rosemary! I've been letting the other girls have the fun of visiting with you, but now *I'm* going to take a turn. You're in a regular movie theater here! Is there anything good on tonight?"

Nobody else was in the apartment. Guy had gone to meet Allan and have some contracts explained to him.

They watched a Fred Astaire-Ginger Rogers picture, and during a break Leah went into the kitchen and brought back two cups of coffee. "I'm a little hungry too," Rosemary said when Leah had put the cups on the night table. "Would you mind very much fixing me a cheese sandwich?"

"Of course I wouldn't mind, dear," Leah said. "How do you like it, with lettuce and mayonnaise?"

She went out again and Rosemary got the fold of magazine cover from her tissue box. There were eleven pills in it now. She slid them all into Leah's cup

and stirred the coffee with her own spoon, which she then wiped off with a
tissue. She picked up her own coffee, but it shook so much that she had to put
it down again.

She was sitting and sipping calmly though when Leah came in with the
sandwich. "Thanks, Leah," she said, "that looks great. The coffee's a little
bitter; I guess it was sitting too long."

"Shall I make fresh?" Leah asked.

"No, it's not that bad," Rosemary said.

Leah sat down beside the bed, took her cup, and stirred it and tasted. "Mm,"
she said and wrinkled her nose; she nodded, agreeing with Rosemary.

"It's drinkable though," Rosemary said.

They watched the movie, and after two more breaks Leah's head drooped
and snapped up sharply. She put down her cup and saucer, the cup two-thirds
empty. Rosemary ate the last piece of her sandwich and watched Fred Astaire
and two other people dancing on turntables in a glossy unreal fun house.

During the next section of the movie Leah fell asleep.

"Leah?" Rosemary said.

The elderly woman sat snoring, her chin to her chest, her hands palm-
upward in her lap. Her lavender-tinted hair, a wig, had slipped forward; sparse
white hairs stuck out at the back of her neck.

Rosemary got out of bed, slid her feet into slippers, and put on the blue-and-
white quilted housecoat she had bought for the hospital. Going quietly out of
the bedroom, she closed the door almost all the way and went to the front door
of the apartment and quietly chained and bolted it.

She then went into the kitchen and, from her knife rack, took the longest
sharpest knife—a nearly new carving knife with a curved and pointed steel
blade and a heavy bone handle with a brass butt. Holding it point-down at her
side, she left the kitchen and went down the hallway to the linen-closet door.

As soon as she opened it she knew she was right. The shelves looked neat
and orderly enough, but the contents of two of them had been interchanged;
the bath towels and hand towels were where the winter blankets ought to have
been and vice versa.

She laid the knife on the bathroom threshold and took everything out of
the closet except what was on the fixed top shelf. She put towels and linens
on the floor, and large and small boxes, and then lifted out the four ging-
ham-covered shelves she had decorated and placed there a thousand thousand years ago.

The back of the closet, below the top shelf, was a single large white-painted
panel framed with narrow white molding. Standing close and leaning aside for
better light, Rosemary saw that where the panel and the molding met, the paint
was broken in a continuous line. She pressed at one side of the panel and then
at the other; pressed harder, and it swung inward on scraping hinges. Within
was darkness; another closet, with a wire hanger glinting on the floor and one
bright spot of light, a keyhole. Pushing the panel all the way open, Rosemary

stepped into the second closet and ducked down. Through the keyhole she saw, at a distance of about twenty feet, a small curio cabinet that stood at a jog in the hallway of Minnie and Roman's apartment.

She tried the door. It opened.

She closed it and backed out through her own closet and got the knife; then went in and through again, looked out again through the keyhole, and opened the door just the least bit.

Then opened it wide, holding the knife shoulder-high, point forward.

The hallway was empty, but there were distant voices from the living room. The bathroom was on her right, its door open, dark. Minnie and Roman's bedroom was on the left, with a bedside lamp burning. There was no crib, no baby.

She went cautiously down the hallway. A door on the right was locked; another, on the left, was a linen closet.

Over the curio cabinet hung a small but vivid oil painting of a church in flames. Before, there had been only a clean space and a hook; now there was this shocking painting. St. Patrick's, it looked like, with yellow and orange flames bursting from its windows and soaring through its gutted roof.

Where had she seen it? A church burning . . .

In the dream. The one where they had carried her through the linen closet. Guy and somebody else. "You've got her too high." To a ballroom where a church was burning. Where *that* church was burning.

But how could it be?

Had she *really* been carried through the closet, seen the painting as they carried her past it?

Find Andy. Find Andy. Find Andy.

Knife high, she followed the jog to the left and the right. Other doors were locked. There was another painting; nude men and women dancing in a circle. Ahead were the foyer and the front door, the archway on the right to the living room. The voices were louder. "Not if he's still waiting for a plane, he isn't!" Mr. Fountain said, and there was laughter and then hushing.

In the dream ballroom Jackie Kennedy had spoken kindly to her and gone away, and then all of *them* had been there, the whole coven, naked and singing in a circle around her. Had it been a real thing that had really happened? Roman in a black robe had drawn designs on her. Dr. Sapirstein had held a cup of red paint for him. Red paint? Blood?

"Oh hell now, Hayato," Minnie said, "you're just making fun of me! 'Pulling my leg' is what we say over here."

Minnie? Back from Europe? And Roman too? But only yesterday there had been a card from Dubrovnik saying they were staying on!

Had they ever really been away?

She was at the archway now, could see the bookshelves and file cabinets and bridge tables laden with newspapers and stacked envelopes. The coven was at the other end, laughing, talking softly. Ice cubes clinked.

She bettered her grip on the knife and moved a step forward. She stopped, staring.

Across the room, in the one large window bay, stood a black bassinet. Black and only black it was; skirted with black taffeta, hooded and flounced with black organza. A silver ornament turned on a black ribbon pinned to its black hood.

Dead? But no, even as she feared it, the stiff organza trembled, the silver ornament quivered.

He was in there. In that monstrous perverted witches' bassinet.

The silver ornament was a crucifix hanging upside down, with the black ribbon wound and knotted around Jesus' ankles.

The thought of her baby lying helpless amid sacrilege and horror brought tears to Rosemary's eyes, and suddenly a longing dragged at her to do nothing but collapse and weep, to surrender completely before such elaborate and unspeakable evil. She withstood it though; she shut her eyes tight to stop the tears, said a quick Hail Mary, and drew together all her resolve and all her hatred too; hatred of Minnie, Roman, Guy, Dr. Sapirstein—of all of them who had conspired to steal Andy away from her and make their loathsome uses of him. She wiped her hands on her housecoat, threw back her hair, found a fresh grip on the knife's thick handle, and stepped out where they could every one of them see her and know she had come.

Insanely, they didn't. They went right on talking, listening, sipping, pleasantly partying, as if she were a ghost, or back in her bed dreaming; Minnie, Roman, Guy (contracts!), Mr. Fountain, the Weeses, Laura-Louise, and a studious-looking young Japanese with eyeglasses—all gathered under an over-the-mantel portrait of Adrian Marcato. He alone saw her. He stood glaring at her, motionless, powerful; but powerless, a painting.

Then Roman saw her too; put down his drink and touched Minnie's arm. Silence sprang up, and those who sat with their backs toward her turned around questioningly. Guy started to rise but sat down again. Laura-Louise clapped her hands to her mouth and began squealing. Helen Wees said, "Get back in bed, Rosemary; you know you aren't supposed to be up and around." Either mad or trying psychology.

"Is the mother?" the Japanese asked, and when Roman nodded, said "Ah, sssssssssssss," and looked at Rosemary with interest.

"She killed Leah," Mr. Fountain said, standing up. "She killed my Leah. Did you? Where is she? Did you kill my Leah?"

Rosemary stared at them, at Guy. He looked down, red-faced.

She gripped the knife tighter. "Yes," she said, "I killed her. I stabbed her to death. And I cleaned my knife and I'll stab to death whoever comes near me. Tell them how sharp it is, Guy!"

He said nothing. Mr. Fountain sat down, a hand to his heart. Laura-Louise squealed.

Watching them, she started across the room toward the bassinet.

"Rosemary," Roman said.

"Shut up," she said.

"Before you look at—"

"Shut up," she said. "You're in Dubrovnik. I don't hear you."

"Let her," Minnie said.

She watched them until she was by the bassinet, which was angled in their direction. With her free hand she caught the black-covered handle at the foot of it and swung the bassinet slowly, gently, around to face her. Taffeta rustled; the back wheels squeaked.

Asleep and sweet, so small and rosy-faced, Andy lay wrapped in a snug black blanket with little black mitts ribbon-tied around his wrists. Orange-red hair he had, a surprising amount of it, silky-clean and brushed. *Andy! Oh, Andy!* She reached out to him, her knife turning away; his lips pouted and he opened his eyes and looked at her. His eyes were golden-yellow, all golden-yellow, with neither whites nor irises; all golden-yellow, with vertical black-slit pupils.

She looked at him.

He looked at her, golden-yellowly, and then at the swaying upside-down crucifix.

She looked at them watching her and knife-in-hand screamed at them, *"What have you done to his eyes?"*

They stirred and looked to Roman.

"He has His Father's eyes," he said.

She looked at him, looked at Guy—whose eyes were hidden behind a hand —looked at Roman again. "What are you *talking* about?" she said. "Guy's eyes are *brown,* they're *normal!* What have you *done* to him, you maniacs?" She moved from the bassinet, ready to kill them.

"Satan is His Father, not Guy," Roman said. "*Satan* is His Father, who came up from Hell and begat a Son of mortal woman! To avenge the iniquities visited by the God worshipers upon His never-doubting followers!"

"Hail Satan," Mr. Wees said.

"*Satan* is His Father and His name is Adrian!" Roman cried, his voice growing louder and prouder, his bearing more strong and forceful. "He shall overthrow the mighty and lay waste their temples! He shall redeem the despised and wreak vengeance in the name of the burned and the tortured!"

"Hail Adrian," they said. "Hail Adrian." "Hail Adrian." And "Hail Satan." "Hail Satan." "Hail Adrian." "Hail Satan."

She shook her head. "No," she said.

Minnie said, "He chose *you* out of all the world, Rosemary. Out of all the women in the whole world, He chose *you.* He brought you and Guy to your apartment there, He made that foolish what's-her-name, Terry, made her get all scared and silly so we had to change our plans, He arranged everything that *had* to be arranged, 'cause He wanted *you* to be the mother of His only living Son."

"His power is stronger than stronger," Roman said.

"Hail Satan," Helen Wees said.

"His might will last longer than longer."

"Hair Satan," the Japanese said.

Laura-Louise uncovered her mouth. Guy looked out at Rosemary from under his hand.

"No," she said, "no," the knife hanging at her side. "No. It can't *be.* No."

"Go look at His hands," Minnie said. "And His feet."

"And His tail," Laura-Louise said.

"And the buds of His horns," Minnie said.

"Oh God," Rosemary said.

"God's dead," Roman said.

She turned to the bassinet, let fall the knife, turned back to the watching coven. "Oh God!" she said and covered her face. "Oh God!" And raised her fists and screamed to the ceiling: *"Oh God! Oh God! Oh God! Oh God! Oh God!"*

"God is DEAD!" Roman thundered. *"God is dead and Satan lives! The year is One, the first year of our Lord! The year is One, God is done! The year is One, Adrian's begun!"*

"Hail Satan!" they cried. "Hail Adrian!" "Hail Adrian!" "Hail Satan!"

She backed away—"No, no"—backed farther and farther away until she was between two bridge tables. A chair was behind her; she sat down on it and stared at them. "No."

Mr. Fountain hurried out and down the hallway. Guy and Mr. Wees hurried after him.

Minnie went over and, grunting as she stooped, picked up the knife. She took it out to the kitchen.

Laura-Louise went to the bassinet and rocked it possessively, making faces into it. The black taffeta rustled; the wheels squeaked.

She sat there and stared. "No," she said.

The dream. The dream. It had been true. The yellow eyes she had looked up into. "Oh God," she said.

Roman came over to her. "Clare is just putting on," he said, "holding his heart that way over Leah. He's not that sorry. Nobody really liked her; she was stingy, emotionally as well as financially. Why don't you help us out, Rosemary, be a real mother to Adrian; and we'll fix it so you don't get punished for killing her. So that nobody ever even finds out about it. You don't have to *join* if you don't want to; just be a mother to your baby." He bent over and whispered: "Minnie and Laura-Louise are too old. It's not right."

She looked at him.

He stood straight again. "Think about it, Rosemary," he said.

"I didn't kill her," she said.

"Oh?"

"I just gave her pills," she said. "She's asleep."

"Oh," he said.

The doorbell rang.

"Excuse me," he said, and went to answer it. "Think about it anyway," he said over his shoulder.

"Oh *God,*" she said.

"Shut up with your 'Oh God's' or we'll kill you," Laura-Louise said, rocking the bassinet. "Milk or no milk."

"*You* shut up," Helen Wees said, coming to Rosemary and putting a dampened handkerchief in her hand. "Rosemary is His mother, no matter how she behaves," she said. "You remember that, and show some respect."

Laura-Louise said something under her breath.

Rosemary wiped her forehead and cheeks with the cool handkerchief. The Japanese, sitting across the room on a hassock, caught her eye and grinned and ducked his head. He held up an opened camera into which he was putting film, and moved it back and forth in the direction of the bassinet, grinning and nodding. She looked down and started to cry. She wiped at her eyes.

Roman came in holding the arm of a robust, handsome, dark-skinned man in a snow-white suit and white shoes. He carried a large box wrapped in light blue paper patterned with Teddy bears and candy canes. Musical sounds came from it. Everyone gathered to meet him and shake his hand. "Worried," they said, and "pleasure," and "airport," and "Stavropoulos," and "occasion." Laura-Louise brought the box to the bassinet. She held it up for the baby to see, shook it for him to hear, and put it on the window seat with many other boxes similarly wrapped and a few that were wrapped in black with black ribbon.

"Just after midnight on June twenty-fifth," Roman said. "Exactly half the year 'round from you-know. Isn't it perfect?"

"But why are you surprised?" the newcomer asked with both his hands outstretched. "Didn't Edmond Lautréamont predict June twenty-fifth three hundred years ago?"

"Indeed he did," Roman said, smiling, "but it's such a novelty for one of his predictions to prove accurate!" Everyone laughed. "Come, my friend," Roman said, drawing the newcomer forward, "come see Him. Come see the Child."

They went to the bassinet, where Laura-Louise waited with a shopkeeper's smile, and they closed around it and looked into it silently. After a few moments the newcomer lowered himself to his knees.

Guy and Mr. Wees came in.

They waited in the archway until the newcomer had risen, and then Guy came over to Rosemary. "She'll be all right," he said; "Abe is in there with her." He stood looking down at her, his hands rubbing at his sides. "They promised me you wouldn't be hurt," he said. "And you haven't been, really.

I mean, suppose you'd had a baby and lost it; wouldn't it be the same? And we're getting so much in return, Ro."

She put the handkerchief on the table and looked at him. As hard as she could she spat at him.

He flushed and turned away, wiping at the front of his jacket. Roman caught him and introduced him to the newcomer, Argyron Stavropoulos.

"How proud you must be," Stavropoulos said, clasping Guy's hand in both his own. "But surely that isn't the mother there? Why in the name of—" Roman drew him away and spoke in his ear.

"Here," Minnie said, and offered Rosemary a mug of steaming tea. "Drink this and you'll feel a little better."

Rosemary looked at it, and looked up at Minnie. "What's in it?" she said; "tannis root?"

"*Nothing* is in it," Minnie said. "Except sugar and lemon. It's plain ordinary Lipton tea. You drink it." She put it down by the handkerchief.

The thing to do was kill it. Obviously. Wait till they were all sitting at the other end, then run over, push away Laura-Louise, and grab it and throw it out the window. And jump out after it. *Mother Slays Baby and Self at Bramford.*

Save the world from God-knows-what. From Satan-knows-what.

A tail! The buds of his horns!

She wanted to scream, to die.

She would do it, throw it out and jump.

They were all milling around now. Pleasant cocktail party. The Japanese was taking pictures; of Guy, of Stavropoulos, of Laura-Louise holding the baby.

She turned away, not wanting to see.

Those eyes! Like an animal's, a tiger's, not like a human being's!

He *wasn't* a human being, of course. He was—some kind of a half-breed.

And how dear and sweet he had looked before he had opened those yellow eyes! The tiny chin, a bit like Brian's; the sweet mouth; all that lovely orange-red hair . . . It would be nice to look at him again, if only he wouldn't open those yellow animal-eyes.

She tasted the tea. It was tea.

No, she *couldn't* throw him out the window. He was her baby, no matter who the father was. What she had to do was go to someone who would understand. Like a priest. Yes, that was the answer; a priest. It was a problem for the Church to handle. For the Pope and all the cardinals to deal with, not stupid Rosemary Reilly from Omaha.

Killing was wrong, no matter what.

She drank more tea.

He began whimpering because Laura-Louise was rocking the bassinet too fast, so of course the idiot began rocking it faster.

She stood it as long as she could and then got up and went over.

"Get away from here," Laura-Louise said. "Don't you come near Him. Roman!"

"You're rocking him too fast," she said.

"Sit down!" Laura-Louise said, and to Roman, "Get her out of here. Put her back where she belongs."

Rosemary said, "She's rocking him too fast; that's why he's whimpering."

"Mind your own business!" Laura-Louise said.

"Let Rosemary rock Him," Roman said.

Laura-Louise stared at him.

"Go on," he said, standing behind the bassinet's hood. "Sit down with the others. Let Rosemary rock Him."

"She's liable—"

"Sit down with the others, Laura-Louise."

She huffed, and marched away.

"Rock Him," Roman said to Rosemary, smiling. He moved the bassinet back and forth toward her, holding it by the hood.

She stood still and looked at him. "You're trying to—get me to be his mother," she said.

"Aren't you His mother?" Roman said. "Go on. Just rock Him till He stops complaining."

She let the black-covered handle come into her hand, and closed her fingers around it. For a few moments they rocked the bassinet between them, then Roman let go and she rocked it alone, nice and slowly. She glanced at the baby, saw his yellow eyes, and looked to the window. "You should oil the wheels," she said. "That could bother him too."

"I will," Roman said. "You see? He's stopped complaining. He knows who you are."

"Don't be silly," Rosemary said, and looked at the baby again. He was watching her. His eyes weren't that bad really, now that she was prepared for them. It was the surprise that had upset her. They were pretty in a way. "What are his hands like?" she asked, rocking him.

"They're very nice," Roman said. "He has claws, but they're very tiny and pearly. The mitts are only so He doesn't scratch Himself, not because His hands aren't attractive."

"He looks worried," she said.

Dr. Sapirstein came over. "A night of surprises," he said.

"Go away," she said, "or I'm going to spit in your face."

"Go away, Abe," Roman said, and Dr. Sapirstein nodded and went away.

"Not you," Rosemary said to the baby. "It's not *your* fault. I'm angry at *them,* because they tricked me and lied to me. Don't look so worried; I'm not going to hurt you."

"He knows that," Roman said.

"Then what does he look so worried for?" Rosemary said. "The poor little thing. Look at him."

"In a minute," Roman said. "I have to attend to my guests. I'll be right back." He backed away, leaving her alone.

"Word of honor I'm not going to hurt you," she said to the baby. She bent over and untied the neck of his gown. "Laura-Louise made this too tight, didn't she. I'll make it a little looser and then you'll be more comfortable. You have a very cute chin; are you aware of that fact? You have strange yellow eyes, but you have a very cute chin."

She tied the gown more comfortably for him.

Poor little creature.

He couldn't be *all* bad, he just *couldn't.* Even if he was half Satan, wasn't he half *her* as well, half decent, ordinary, sensible, human being? If she worked *against* them, exerted a good influence to counteract their bad one . . .

"You have a room of your own, do you know that?" she said, undoing the blanket around him, which was also too tight. "It has white-and-yellow wallpaper and a white crib with yellow bumpers, and there isn't one drop of witchy old black in the whole place. We'll show it to you when you're ready for your next feeding. In case you're curious, *I* happen to be the lady who's been supplying all that milk you've been drinking. I'll bet you thought it comes in bottles, didn't you. Well it doesn't; it comes in *mothers,* and I'm yours. That's right, Mr. Worry-face. You seem to greet the idea with no enthusiasm whatsoever."

Silence made her look up. They were gathering around to watch her, stopping at a respectful distance.

She felt herself blushing and turned back to tucking the blanket around the baby. "*Let* them watch," she said; "we don't care, do we? We just want to be all cozy and comfortable, like so. There. Better?"

"Hail Rosemary," Helen Wees said.

The others took it up. "Hail Rosemary." "Hail Rosemary." Minnie and Stavropoulos and Dr. Sapirstein. "Hail Rosemary." Guy said it too. "Hail Rosemary." Laura-Louise moved her lips but made no sound.

"Hail Rosemary, mother of Adrian!" Roman said.

She looked up from the bassinet. "It's Andrew," she said. "Andrew John Woodhouse."

"Adrian Steven," Roman said.

Guy said, "Roman, look," and Stavropoulos, at Roman's other side, touched his arm and said, "Is the name of so great an importance?"

"It is. Yes. It is," Roman said. "His name is Adrian Steven."

Rosemary said, "I understand why you'd like to call him that, but I'm sorry; you can't. His name is Andrew John. He's my child, not yours, and this is one point that I'm not even going to argue about. This and the clothes. He can't wear black all the time."

Roman opened his mouth but Minnie said "Hail Andrew" in a loud voice, looking right at him.

Everyone else said "Hail Andrew" and "Hail Rosemary, mother of Andrew" and "Hail Satan."

Rosemary tickled the baby's tummy. "You didn't like 'Adrian,' did you?" she asked him. "I should think not. 'Adrian Steven'! Will you *please* stop looking so worried?" She poked the tip of his nose. "Do you know how to smile yet, Andy? Do you? Come on, little funny-eyes Andy, can you smile? Can you smile for Mommy?" She tapped the silver ornament and set it swinging. "Come on, Andy," she said. "One little smile. Come on, Andy-candy."

The Japanese slipped forward with his camera, crouched, and took two three four pictures in quick succession.

Completed in August, 1966,
in Wilton, Connecticut,
and Dedicated to Gabrielle

This Perfect Day

Christ, Marx, Wood, and Wei
Led us to this perfect day.
Marx, Wood, Wei, and Christ;
All but Wei were sacrificed.
Wood, Wei, Christ, and Marx
Gave us lovely schools and parks.
Wei, Christ, Marx, and Wood
Made us humble, made us good.

—CHILD'S RHYME FOR
BOUNCING A BALL

I
Growing
Up

One

A city's blank white concrete slabs, the giant ones ringed by the less giant, gave space in their midst to a broad pink-floored plaza, a playground in which some two hundred young children played and exercised under the care of a dozen supervisors in white coveralls. Most of the children, bare, tan, and black-haired, were crawling through red and yellow cylinders, swinging on swings, or doing group calisthenics; but in a shadowed corner where a hopscotch grid was inlaid, five of them sat in a close, quiet circle, four of them listening and one speaking.

"They catch animals and eat them and wear their skins," the speaker, a boy of about eight, said. "And they—they do a thing called 'fighting.' That means they hurt each other, on purpose, with their hands or with rocks and things. They don't love and help each other at all."

The listeners sat wide-eyed. A girl younger than the boy said, "But you *can't* take off your bracelet. It's impossible." She pulled at her own bracelet with one finger, to show how safely-strong the links were.

"You can if you've got the right tools," the boy said. "It's taken off on your linkday, isn't it?"

"Only for a second."

"But it's taken off, isn't it?"

"Where do they live?" another girl asked.

"On mountaintops," the boy said. "In deep caves. In all kinds of places where we can't find them."

The first girl said, "They must be sick."

"Of course they are," the boy said, laughing. "That's what 'incurable' *means,* sick. That's why they're *called* incurables, because they're very, very sick."

The youngest child, a boy of about six, said, "Don't they get their treatments?"

The older boy looked at him scornfully. "Without their bracelets?" he said. "Living in caves?"

"But how do they *get* sick?" the six-year-old asked. "They get their treatments *until* they run away, don't they?"

"Treatments," the older boy said, "don't always work."

The six-year-old stared at him. "They do," he said.

"No they don't."

"My goodness," a supervisor said, coming to the group with volleyballs tucked one under each arm, "aren't you sitting too close together? What are you playing, Who's Got the Rabbit?"

The children quickly hitched away from one another, separating into a larger circle—except the six-year-old boy, who stayed where he was, not moving at all. The supervisor looked at him curiously.

A two-note chime sounded on loudspeakers. "Shower and dress," the supervisor said, and the children hopped to their feet and raced away.

"Shower and dress!" the supervisor called to a group of children playing passball nearby.

The six-year-old boy stood up, looking troubled and unhappy. The supervisor crouched before him and looked into his face with concern. "What's wrong?" she asked.

The boy, whose right eye was green instead of brown, looked at her and blinked.

The supervisor let drop her volleyballs, turned the boy's wrist to look at his bracelet, and took him gently by the shoulders. "What is it, Li?" she asked. "Did you lose the game? Losing's the same as winning; you know that, don't you?"

The boy nodded.

"What's important is having fun and getting exercise, right?"

The boy nodded again and tried to smile.

"Well, that's better," the supervisor said. "That's a little better. Now you don't look like such a sad old sad-monkey."

The boy smiled.

"Shower and dress," the supervisor said with relief. She turned the boy around and gave him a pat on his bottom. "Go on," she said, "skedaddle."

The boy, who was sometimes called Chip but more often Li—his nameber was Li RM35M4419—said scarcely a word while eating, but his sister Peace kept up a continuous jabbering and neither of his parents noticed his silence. It wasn't until all four had seated themselves in the TV chairs that his mother took a good look at him and said, "Are you feeling all right, Chip?"

"Yes, I feel fine," he said.

His mother turned to his father and said, "He hasn't said a word all evening."

Chip said, "I feel fine."

"Then why are you so quiet?" his mother asked.

"Shh," his father said. The screen had flicked on and was finding its right colors.

When the first hour was over and the children were getting ready for bed, Chip's mother went into the bathroom and watched him finish cleaning his teeth and pull his mouthpiece from the tube. "What is it?" she said. "Did somebody say something about your eye?"

"No," he said, reddening.

"Rinse it," she said.

"I did."

"*Rinse it.*"

He rinsed his mouthpiece and, stretching, hung it in its place on the rack. "Jesus was talking," he said. "Jesus DV. During play."

"About what? Your eye?"

"No, not my *eye*. Nobody says anything about my *eye*."

"Then what?"

He shrugged. "Members who—get sick and—leave the Family. Run away and take off their bracelets."

His mother looked at him nervously. "Incurables," she said.

He nodded, her manner and her knowing the name making him more uneasy. "It's true?" he said.

"No," she said. "No, it isn't. No. I'm going to call Bob. He'll explain it to you." She turned and hurried from the room, slipping past Peace, who was coming in closing her pajamas.

In the living room Chip's father said, "Two more minutes. Are they in bed?"

Chip's mother said, "One of the children told Chip about the incurables."

"Hate," his father said.

"I'm calling Bob," his mother said, going to the phone.

"It's after eight."

"He'll come," she said. She touched her bracelet to the phone's plate and read out the nameber red-printed on a card tucked under the screen rim: "Bob NE20G3018." She waited, rubbing the heels of her palms tightly together. "I knew something was bothering him," she said. "He didn't say a single word all evening."

Chip's father got up from his chair. "I'll go talk to him," he said, going.

"Let Bob do it!" Chip's mother called. "Get Peace into bed; she's still in the bathroom!"

. . .

Bob came twenty minutes later.

"He's in his room," Chip's mother said.

"You two watch the program," Bob said. "Go on, sit down and watch." He smiled at them. "There's nothing to worry about," he said. "Really. It happens every day."

"*Still?*" Chip's father said.

"Of course," Bob said. "And it'll happen a hundred years from now. Kids are kids."

He was the youngest adviser they had ever had—twenty-one, and barely a year out of the Academy. There was nothing diffident or unsure about him though; on the contrary, he was more relaxed and confident than advisers of fifty or fifty-five. They were pleased with him.

He went to Chip's room and looked in. Chip was in bed, lying on an elbow with his head in his hand, a comic book spread open before him.

"Hi, Li," Bob said.

Chip said, "Hi, Bob."

Bob went in and sat down on the side of the bed. He put his telecomp on the floor between his feet, felt Chip's forehead and ruffled his hair. "Whatcha readin'?" he said.

"*Wood's Struggle,*" Chip said, showing Bob the cover of the comic book. He let it drop closed on the bed and, with his forefinger, began tracing the wide yellow *W* of "Wood's."

Bob said, "I hear somebody's been giving you some cloth about incurables."

"Is that what it is?" Chip asked, not looking up from his moving finger.

"That's what it is, Li," Bob said. "It used to be true, a long, long time ago, but not anymore; now it's just cloth."

Chip was silent, retracing the *W*.

"We didn't always know as much about medicine and chemistry as we do today," Bob said, watching him, "and until fifty years or so after the Unification, members used to get sick sometimes, a very few of them, and feel that they *weren't* members. Some of them ran away and lived by themselves in places the Family wasn't using, barren islands and mountain peaks and so forth."

"And they took off their bracelets?"

"I suppose they did," Bob said. "Bracelets wouldn't have been much use to them in places like that, would they, with no scanners to put them to?"

"Jesus said they did something called 'fighting.' "

Bob looked away and then back again. " 'Acting aggressively' is a nicer way of putting it," he said. "Yes, they did that."

Chip looked up at him. "But they're dead now?" he said.

"Yes, all dead," Bob said. "Every last one of them." He smoothed Chip's hair. "It was a long, long time ago," he said. "Nobody gets that way today."

Chip said, "We know more about medicine and chemistry today. Treatments *work.*"

"Right you are," Bob said. "And don't forget there were five separate computers in those days. Once one of those sick members had left his home continent, he was completely unconnected."

"My grandfather helped build UniComp."

"I know he did, Li. So next time anyone tells you about the incurables, you remember two things: one, treatments are much more effective today than they were a long time ago; and two, we've got UniComp looking out for us everywhere on Earth. Okay?"

"Okay," Chip said, and smiled.

"Let's see what it says about *you,*" Bob said, picking up his telecomp and opening it on his knees.

Chip sat up and moved close, pushing his pajama sleeve clear of his bracelet. "Do you think I'll get an extra treatment?" he asked.

"If you need one," Bob said. "Do you want to turn it on?"

"Me?" Chip said. "May I?"

"Sure," Bob said.

Chip put his thumb and forefinger cautiously to the telecomp's on-off switch. He clicked it over, and small lights came on—blue, amber, amber. He smiled at them.

Bob, watching him, smiled and said, "Touch."

Chip touched his bracelet to the scanner plate, and the blue light beside it turned red.

Bob tapped the input keys. Chip watched his quickly moving fingers. Bob kept tapping and then pressed the answer button; a line of green symbols glowed on the screen, and then a second line beneath the first. Bob studied the symbols. Chip watched him.

Bob looked at Chip from the corners of his eyes, smiling. "Tomorrow at 12:25," he said.

"Good!" Chip said. "Thank you!"

"Thank Uni," Bob said, switching off the telecomp and closing its cover. "Who told you about the incurables?" he asked. "Jesus who?"

"DV33-something," Chip said. "He lives on the twenty-fourth floor."

Bob snapped the telecomp's catches. "He's probably as worried as you were," he said.

"Can he have an extra treatment too?"

"If he needs one; I'll alert his adviser. Now to *sleep,* brother; you've got school tomorrow." Bob took Chip's comic book and put it on the night table.

Chip lay down and snuggled smilingly into his pillow, and Bob stood up, tapped off the lamp, ruffled Chip's hair again, and bent and kissed the back of his head.

"See you Friday," Chip said.

"Right," Bob said. "Good night."

" 'Night, Bob."

Chip's parents stood up anxiously when Bob came into the living room.

"He's fine," Bob said. "Practically asleep already. He's getting an extra treatment during his lunch hour tomorrow, probably a bit of tranquilizer."

"Oh, what a relief," Chip's mother said, and his father said, "Thanks, Bob."

"Thank Uni," Bob said. He went to the phone. "I want to get some help to the other boy," he said, "the one who told him"—and touched his bracelet to the phone's plate.

The next day, after lunch, Chip rode the escalators down from his school to the medicenter three floors below. His bracelet, touched to the scanner at the medicenter's entrance, produced a winking green *yes* on the indicator; and another winking green *yes* at the door of the therapy section; and another winking green *yes* at the door of the treatment room.

Four of the fifteen units were being serviced, so the line was fairly long. Soon enough, though, he was mounting children's steps and thrusting his arm, with the sleeve pushed high, through a rubber-rimmed opening. He held his arm grown-uply still while the scanner inside found and fastened on his bracelet and the infusion disc nuzzled warm and smooth against his upper arm's softness. Motors burred inside the unit, liquids trickled. The blue light overhead turned red and the infusion disc tickled-buzzed-stung his arm; and then the light turned blue again.

Later that day, in the playground, Jesus DV, the boy who had told him about the incurables, sought Chip out and thanked him for helping him.

"Thank Uni," Chip said. "I got an extra treatment; did you?"

"Yes," Jesus said. "So did the other kids and Bob UT. He's the one who told *me.*"

"It scared me a little," Chip said, "thinking about members getting sick and running away."

"Me too a little," Jesus said. "But it doesn't happen anymore; it was a long, long time ago."

"Treatments are better now than they used to be," Chip said.

Jesus said, "And we've got UniComp watching out for us everywhere on Earth."

"Right you are," Chip said.

A supervisor came and shooed them into a passball circle, an enormous one of fifty or sixty boys and girls spaced out at fingertip distance, taking up more than a quarter of the busy playground.

Two

Chip's grandfather was the one who had given him the name Chip. He had given all of them extra names that were different from their real ones: Chip's mother, who was his daughter, he called "Suzu" instead of Anna; Chip's father was "Mike" not Jesus (and thought the idea foolish); and Peace was "Willow," which she refused to have anything at all to do with. "No! Don't call me that! I'm Peace! I'm Peace KD37T5002!"

Papa Jan was odd. Odd-*looking,* naturally; all grandparents had their marked peculiarities—a few centimeters too much or too little of height, skin that was too light or too dark, big ears, a bent nose. Papa Jan was both taller and darker than normal, his eyes were big and bulging, and there were two reddish patches in his graying hair. But he wasn't only odd-*looking,* he was odd-*talking;* that was the real oddness about him. He was always saying things vigorously and with enthusiasm and yet giving Chip the feeling that he didn't mean them at all, that he meant in fact their exact opposites. On that subject of names, for instance: "Marvelous! Wonderful!" he said. "Four names for boys, four names for girls! What could be more friction-free, more everyone-the-same? Everybody would name boys after Christ, Marx, Wood, or Wei anyway, wouldn't they?"

"Yes," Chip said.

"Of course!" Papa Jan said. "And if Uni gives out four names for boys it has to give out four names for girls too, right? Obviously! Listen." He stopped Chip and, crouching down, spoke face to face with him, his bulging eyes dancing as if he was about to laugh. It was a holiday and they were on their way to the parade, Unification Day or Wei's Birthday or whatever; Chip was seven. "Listen, Li RM35M26J449988WXYZ," Papa Jan said. "Listen, I'm going to tell you something fantastic, incredible. In my day—are you listening? —in my day there were *over twenty different names for boys alone!* Would you believe it? Love of Family, it's the truth. There was 'Jan,' and 'John,' and 'Amu,' and 'Lev.' 'Higa' and 'Mike'! 'Tonio'! And in my father's time there were even more, maybe forty or fifty! Isn't that ridiculous? All those different names when members themselves are exactly the same and interchangeable? Isn't that the silliest thing you ever heard of?"

And Chip nodded, confused, feeling that Papa Jan meant the opposite, that somehow it *wasn't* silly and ridiculous to have forty or fifty different names for boys alone.

"Look at them!" Papa Jan said, taking Chip's hand and walking on with him —through Unity Park to the Wei's Birthday parade. "Exactly the same! Isn't it marvelous? Hair the same, eyes the same, skin the same, shape the same; boys, girls, all the same. Like peas in a pod. Isn't it fine? Isn't it top speed?"

Chip, flushing (not his green eye, not the same as *anybody's*), said, "What does 'peezinapod' mean?"

"I don't know," Papa Jan said. "Things members used to eat before total-cakes. Sharya used to say it."

He was a construction supervisor in EUR55131, twenty kilometers from '55128, where Chip and his family lived. On Sundays and holidays he rode over and visited them. His wife, Sharya, had drowned in a sightseeing-boat disaster in 135, the same year Chip was born; he hadn't remarried.

Chip's other grandparents, his father's mother and father, lived in MEX10405, and the only time he saw them was when they phoned on birthdays. They were odd, but not nearly as odd as Papa Jan.

School was pleasant and play was pleasant. The Pre-U Museum was pleasant although some of the exhibits were a bit scary—the "spears" and "guns," for instance, and the "prison cell" with its striped-suited "convict" sitting on the cot and clutching his head in motionless month-after-month woe. Chip always looked at him—he would slip away from the rest of the class if he had to— and having looked, he always walked quickly away.

Ice cream and toys and comic books were pleasant too. Once when Chip put his bracelet and a toy's sticker to a supply-center scanner, its indicator red-winked *no* and he had to put the toy, a construction set, in the turnback bin. He couldn't understand why Uni had refused him; it was the right day and the toy was in the right category. "There *must* be a reason, dear," the member behind him said. "You go call your adviser and find out."

He did, and it turned out that the toy was only being withheld for a few days, not denied completely; he had been teasing a scanner somewhere, putting his bracelet to it again and again, and he was being taught not to. That winking red *no* was the first in his life for a claim that mattered to him, not just for starting into the wrong classroom or coming to the medicenter on the wrong day; it hurt him and saddened him.

Birthdays were pleasant, and Christmas and Marxmas and Unification Day and Wood's and Wei's Birthdays. Even more pleasant, because they came less frequently, were his linkdays. The new link would be shinier than the others, and would stay shiny for days and days and days; and then one day he would remember and look and there would be only old links, all of them the same and indistinguishable. Like peezinapod.

In the spring of 145, when Chip was ten, he and his parents and Peace were granted the trip to EUR00001 to see UniComp. It was over an hour's ride from carport to carport and the longest trip Chip remembered making, although according to his parents he had flown from Mex to Eur when he was one and a half, and from EUR20140 to '55128 a few months later. They made the UniComp trip on a Sunday in April, riding with a couple in their fifties (someone's odd-looking grandparents, both of them lighter than normal, she with her hair unevenly clipped) and another family, the boy and girl of which were a year older than Chip and Peace. The other father drove the car from the EUR00001 turnoff to the carport near UniComp. Chip watched with interest as the man worked the car's lever and buttons. It felt funny to be riding slowly on wheels again after shooting along on air.

They took snapshots outside UniComp's white marble dome—whiter and more beautiful than it was in pictures or on TV, as the snow-tipped mountains beyond it were more stately, the Lake of Universal Brotherhood more blue and far-reaching—and then they joined the line at the entrance, touched the admission scanner, and went into the blue-white curving lobby. A smiling member in pale blue showed them toward the elevator line. They joined it, and Papa Jan came up to them, grinning with delight at their astonishment.

"What are *you* doing here?" Chip's father asked as Papa Jan kissed Chip's mother. They had told him they had been granted the trip and he had said nothing at all about claiming it himself.

Papa Jan kissed Chip's father. "Oh, I just decided to surprise you, that's all," he said. "I wanted to tell my friend here"—he laid a large hand across Chip's shoulder—"a little more about Uni than the earpiece will. Hello, Chip." He bent and kissed Chip's cheek, and Chip, surprised to be the reason for Papa Jan's being there, kissed him in return and said, "Hello, Papa Jan."

"Hello, Peace KD37T5002," Papa Jan said gravely, and kissed Peace. She kissed him and said hello.

"When did you claim the trip?" Chip's father asked.

"A few days after you did," Papa Jan said, keeping his hand on Chip's shoulder. The line moved up a few meters and they all moved with it.

Chip's mother said, "But you were here only five or six years ago, weren't you?"

"Uni knows who put it together," Papa Jan said, smiling. "We get special favors."

"That's not so," Chip's father said. "No one gets special favors."

"Well, here I am, anyway," Papa Jan said, and turned his smile down toward Chip. "Right?"

"Right," Chip said, and smiled back up at him.

Papa Jan had helped build UniComp when he was a young man. It had been his first assignment.

The elevator held about thirty members, and instead of music it had a man's voice—"Good day, brothers and sisters; welcome to the site of UniComp"— a warm, friendly voice that Chip recognized from TV. "As you can tell, we've started to move," it said, "and now we're descending at a speed of twenty-two meters per second. It will take us just over three and a half minutes to reach Uni's five-kilometer depth. This shaft down which we're traveling . . ." The voice gave statistics about the size of UniComp's housing and the thickness of its walls, and told of its safety from all natural and man-made disturbances. Chip had heard this information before, in school and on TV, but hearing it now, while entering that housing and passing through those walls, while on the very verge of *seeing* UniComp, made it seem new and exciting. He listened attentively, watching the speaker disc over the elevator door. Papa Jan's hand still held his shoulder, as if to restrain him. "We're slowing now," the voice said. "Enjoy your visit, won't you?"—and the elevator sank to a cushiony stop and the door divided and slid to both sides.

There was another lobby, smaller than the one at ground level, another smiling member in pale blue, and another line, this one extending two by two to double doors that opened on a dimly lit hallway.

"Here we are!" Chip called, and Papa Jan said to him, "We don't all have to be together." They had become separated from Chip's parents and Peace, who were farther ahead in the line and looking back at them questioningly— Chip's parents; Peace was too short to be seen. The member in front of Chip turned and offered to let them move up, but Papa Jan said, "No, this is all right. Thank you, brother." He waved a hand at Chip's parents and smiled, and Chip did the same. Chip's parents smiled back, then turned around and moved forward.

Papa Jan looked about, his bulging eyes bright, his mouth keeping its smile. His nostrils flared and fell with his breathing. "So," he said, "you're finally going to see UniComp. Excited?"

"Yes, very," Chip said.

They followed the line forward.

"I don't blame you," Papa Jan said. "Wonderful! Once-in-a-lifetime experience, to see the machine that's going to classify you and give you your assignments, that's going to decide where you'll live and whether or not you'll marry the girl you want to marry; and if you do, whether or not you'll have children and what they'll be named if you have them—of course you're excited; who wouldn't be?"

Chip looked at Papa Jan, disturbed.

Papa Jan, still smiling, clapped him on the back as they passed in their turn into the hallway. "Go look!" he said. "Look at the displays, look at Uni, look at everything! It's all here for you; look at it!"

There was a rack of earpieces, the same as in a museum; Chip took one and put it in. Papa Jan's strange manner made him nervous, and he was sorry not to be up ahead with his parents and Peace. Papa Jan put in an earpiece too. "I wonder what interesting new facts I'm going to hear!" he said, and laughed to himself. Chip turned away from him.

His nervousness and feeling of disturbance fell away as he faced a wall that glittered and skittered with a thousand sparkling minilights. The voice of the elevator spoke in his ear, telling him, while the lights showed him, how UniComp received from its round-the-world relay belt the microwave impulses of all the uncountable scanners and telecomps and telecontrolled devices; how it evaluated the impulses and sent back its answering impulses to the relay belt and the sources of inquiry.

Yes, he was excited. Was anything quicker, more clever, more everywhere than Uni?

The next span of wall showed how the memory banks worked; a beam of light flicked over a crisscrossed metal square, making parts of it glow and leaving parts of it dark. The voice spoke of electron beams and superconductive grids, of charged and uncharged areas becoming the yes-or-no carriers of different bits of information. When a question was put to UniComp, the voice said, it scanned the relevant bits . . .

He didn't understand it, but that made it *more* wonderful, that Uni could know all there was to know so magically, so *un*-understandably!

And the next span was glass not wall, and there it was, UniComp: a twin row of different-colored metal bulks, like treatment units only lower and smaller, some of them pink, some brown, some orange; and among them in the large, rosily lit room, ten or a dozen members in pale blue coveralls, smiling and chatting with one another as they read meters and dials on the thirty-or-so units and marked what they read on handsome pale blue plastic clipboards. There was a gold cross and sickle on the far wall, and a clock that said *11:08 Sun 12 Apr 145 Y.U.* Music crept into Chip's ear and grew louder: "Outward, Outward," played by an enormous orchestra, so movingly, so majestically, that tears of pride and happiness came to his eyes.

He could have stayed there for hours, watching those busy cheerful members and those impressively gleaming memory banks, listening to "Outward, Outward" and then "One Mighty Family"; but the music thinned away (as

11:10 became *11:11*) and the voice, gently, aware of his feelings, reminded him of other members waiting and asked him to move on please to the next display farther down the hallway. Reluctantly he turned himself from UniComp's glass wall, with other members who were wiping at the corners of their eyes and smiling and nodding. He smiled at them, and they at him.

Papa Jan caught his arm and drew him across the hallway to a scanner-posted door. "Well, did you like it?" he asked.

Chip nodded.

"That's not Uni," Papa Jan said.

Chip looked at him.

Papa Jan pulled the earpiece out of Chip's ear. "That's not UniComp!" he said in a fierce whisper. "Those aren't real, those pink and orange boxes in there! Those are *toys,* for the Family to come look at and feel cozy and warm with!" His eyes bulged close to Chip's; specks of his spit hit Chip's nose and cheeks. "It's down below!" he said. "There are three levels under this one, and that's where it is! Do you want to see it? Do you want to see the *real* Uni-Comp?"

Chip could only stare at him.

"Do you, Chip?" Papa Jan said. "Do you want to see it? I can show it to you!"

Chip nodded.

Papa Jan let go of his arm and stood up straight. He looked around and smiled. "All right," he said, "let's go this way," and taking Chip's shoulder he steered him back the way they had come, past the glass wall thronged with members looking in, and the flicking light-beam of the memory banks, and the skittering wall of minilights, and—"Excuse us, please"—through the line of incoming members and down to another part of the hallway that was darker and empty, where a monster telecomp lolled broken away from its wall display and two blue stretchers lay side by side with pillows and folded blankets on them.

There was a door in the corner with a scanner beside it, but as they got near it Papa Jan pushed down Chip's arm.

"The scanner," Chip said.

"No," Papa Jan said.

"Isn't this where we're—"

"Yes."

Chip looked at Papa Jan, and Papa Jan pushed him past the scanner, pulled open the door, thrust him inside, and came in after him, dragging the door shut against its hissing slow-closer.

Chip stared at him, quivering.

"It's all right," Papa Jan said sharply; and then, not sharply, kindly, he took Chip's head in both his hands and said, "It's all right, Chip. Nothing will happen to you. I've done it lots of times."

"We didn't *ask,*" Chip said, still quivering.

"It's all *right,*" Papa Jan said. "Look: who does UniComp belong to?"

"Belong to?"

"Whose is it? Whose computer?"

"It's—it's the whole Family's."

"And you're a member of the Family, aren't you?"

"Yes . . ."

"Well then, it's partly your computer, isn't it? *It* belongs to *you,* not the other way around; *you* don't belong to *it.* "

"No, we're supposed to *ask* for things!" Chip said.

"Chip, please, trust me," Papa Jan said. "We're not going to take anything, we're not even going to touch anything. We're only going to look. That's the reason I came here today, to show you the real UniComp. You want to see it, don't you?"

Chip, after a moment, said, "Yes."

"Then don't worry; it's all right." Papa Jan looked reassuringly into his eyes, and then let go of his head and took his hand.

They were on a landing, with stairs going down. They went down four or five of them—into coolness—and Papa Jan stopped, and stopped Chip. "Stay right here," he said. "I'll be back in two seconds. Don't move."

Chip watched anxiously as Papa Jan went back up to the landing, opened the door to look, and then went quickly out. The door swung back toward closing.

Chip began to quiver again. He had passed a scanner without touching it, and now he was alone on a chilly silent stairway—and Uni didn't know where he was!

The door opened again and Papa Jan came back in with blue blankets over his arm. "It's very cold," he said.

They walked together, wrapped in blankets, down the just-wide-enough aisle between two steel walls that stretched ahead of them convergingly to a faraway cross-wall and reared up above their heads to within half a meter of a glowing white ceiling—not walls, really, but rows of mammoth steel blocks set each against the next and hazed with cold, numbered on their fronts in eye-level black stencil-figures: *H46, H48* on this side of the aisle; *H49, H51* on that. The aisle was one of twenty or more; narrow parallel crevasses between back-to-back rows of steel blocks, the rows broken evenly by the intersecting crevasses of four slightly wider cross-aisles.

They came up the aisle, their breath clouding from their nostrils, blurs of near-shadow staying beneath their feet. The sounds they made—the paplon rustle of their coveralls, the slapping of their sandals—were the only sounds there were, edged with echoes.

"Well?" Papa Jan said, looking at Chip.

Chip hugged his blanket more tightly around him. "It's not as nice as upstairs," he said.

"No," Papa Jan said. "No pretty young members with pens and clipboards down here. No warm lights and friendly pink machines. It's empty down here from one year to the next. Empty and cold and lifeless. Ugly."

They stood at the intersection of two aisles, crevasses of steel stretching away in one direction and another, in a third direction and a fourth. Papa Jan shook his head and scowled. "It's wrong," he said. "I don't know why or how, but it's wrong. Dead plans of dead members. Dead ideas, dead decisions."

"Why is it so cold?" Chip asked, watching his breath.

"Because it's dead," Papa Jan said, then shook his head. "No, I don't know," he said. "They don't work if they're not freezing cold; I don't know; all I knew was getting the things where they were supposed to be without smashing them."

They walked side by side along another aisle: *R20, R22, R24.* "How many are there?" Chip asked.

"Twelve hundred and forty on this level, twelve hundred and forty on the level below. And that's only for *now;* there's twice as much space cut out and waiting behind that east wall, for when the Family gets bigger. Other shafts, another ventilating system already in place . . ."

They went down to the next lower level. It was the same as the one above except that there were steel pillars at two of the intersections and red figures on the memory banks instead of black ones. They walked past *J65, J63, J61.* "The biggest excavation there ever was," Papa Jan said. "The biggest *job* there ever was, making one computer to obsolete the old five. There was news about it every night when I was your age. I figured out that it wouldn't be too late to help when I was twenty, provided I got the right classification. So I asked for it."

"You asked for it?"

"That's what I said," Papa Jan said, smiling and nodding. "It wasn't unheard of in those days. I asked my adviser to ask Uni—well, it wasn't Uni, it was EuroComp—anyway I asked her to ask, and she did, and Christ, Marx, Wood, and Wei, I got it—042C; construction worker, third class. First assignment, here." He looked about, still smiling, his eyes vivid. "They were going to lower these hulks down the shafts one at a time," he said, and laughed. "I sat up all one night and figured out that the job could be done eight months earlier if we tunneled in from the other side of Mount Love"—he thumbed over his shoulder—"and rolled them in on wheels. EuroComp hadn't thought of that simple idea. Or maybe it was in no big rush to have its memory siphoned away!" He laughed again.

He stopped laughing; and Chip, watching him, noticed for the first time that his hair was all gray now. The reddish patches that he'd had a few years earlier were completely gone.

"And here they are," he said, "all in their places, rolled down my tunnel and working eight months longer than they would have been otherwise." He looked at the banks he was passing as if he disliked them.

Chip said, "Don't you—like UniComp?"

Papa Jan was silent for a moment. "No, I don't," he said, and cleared his throat. "You can't argue with it, you can't explain things to it . . ."

"But it knows *everything,*" Chip said. "What's there to explain or argue about?"

They separated to pass a square steel pillar and came together again. "I don't know," Papa Jan said. "I don't know." He walked along, his head lowered, frowning, his blanket wrapped around him. "Listen," he said, "is there any classification that *you* want more than any other? Any assignment that *you're* especially hoping for?"

Chip looked uncertainly at Papa Jan and shrugged. "No," he said. "I want the classification I'll get, the one I'm right for. And the assignments I'll get, the ones that the Family needs me to do. There's only one assignment anyway, helping to spread the—"

" 'Helping to spread the Family through the universe,' " Papa Jan said. "I know. Through the unified UniComp universe. Come on," he said, "let's go back up above. I can't take this brother-fighting cold much longer."

Embarrassed, Chip said, "Isn't there another level? You said there—"

"We can't," Papa Jan said. "There are scanners there, and members around who'd see us not touching them and rush to 'help' us. There's nothing special to see there anyway; the receiving and transmitting equipment and the refrigerating plants."

They went to the stairs. Chip felt let down. Papa Jan was disappointed with him for some reason; and worse, he wasn't well, wanting to argue with Uni and not touching scanners and using bad language. "You ought to tell your adviser," he said as they started up the stairs. "About wanting to argue with Uni."

"I don't want to argue with Uni," Papa Jan said. "I just want to be able to argue *if* I want to argue."

Chip couldn't follow that at all. "You ought to tell him anyway," he said. "Maybe you'll get an extra treatment."

"Probably I would," Papa Jan said; and after a moment, "All right, I'll tell him."

"Uni knows everything about everything," Chip said.

They went up the second flight of stairs, and on the landing outside the display hallway, stopped and folded the blankets. Papa Jan finished first. He watched Chip finish folding his.

"There," Chip said, patting the blue bundle against his chest.

"Do you know why I gave you the name 'Chip'?" Papa Jan asked him.

"No," Chip said.

"There's an old saying, 'a chip off the old block.' It means that a child is like his parents or his grandparents."

"Oh."

"I didn't mean you were like your father or even like me," Papa Jan said.

"I meant you were like *my* grandfather. Because of your eye. He had a green eye too."

Chip shifted, wanting Papa Jan to be done talking so they could go outside where they belonged.

"I know you don't like to talk about it," Papa Jan said, "but it's nothing to be ashamed of. Being a little different from everyone else isn't such a terrible thing. Members used to be so different from each other, you can't imagine. Your great-great-grandfather was a very brave and capable man. His name was Hanno Rybeck—names and numbers were separate then—and he was a cosmonaut who helped build the first Mars colony. So don't be ashamed that you've got his eye. They fight around with the genes today, excuse my language, but maybe they missed a few of yours; maybe you've got more than a green eye, maybe you've got some of my grandfather's bravery and ability too." He started to open the door but turned to look at Chip again. "Try wanting something, Chip," he said. "Try a day or two before your next treatment. That's when it's easiest; to want things, to worry about things . . ."

When they came out of the elevator into the ground-level lobby, Chip's parents and Peace were waiting for them. "Where have you been?" Chip's father asked, and Peace, holding a miniature orange memory bank (not really), said, "We've been waiting so long!"

"We were looking at Uni," Papa Jan said.

Chip's father said, "All this time?"

"That's right."

"You were supposed to move on and let other members have their turn."

"*You* were, Mike," Papa Jan said, smiling. "*My* earpiece said 'Jan old friend, it's good to see you! You and your grandson can stay and look as long as you like!' "

Chip's father turned away, not smiling.

They went to the canteen, claimed cakes and cokes—except Papa Jan, who wasn't hungry—and took them out to the picnic area behind the dome. Papa Jan pointed out Mount Love to Chip and told him more about the drilling of the tunnel, which Chip's father was surprised to hear about—a tunnel to bring in thirty-six not-so-big memory banks. Papa Jan told him that there were more banks on a lower level, but he didn't say how many or how big they were, or how cold and how lifeless. Chip didn't either. It gave him an odd feeling, knowing there was something that he and Papa Jan knew and weren't telling the others; it made the two of them *different* from the others, and the same as each other, at least a little . . .

When they had eaten, they walked to the carport and got on the claim line. Papa Jan stayed with them until they were near the scanners; then he left, explaining that he would wait and go home with two friends from Riverbend who were visiting Uni later in the day. "Riverbend" was his name for '55131, where he lived.

The next time Chip saw Bob NE, his adviser, he told him about Papa Jan; that he didn't like Uni and wanted to argue with it and explain things to it.

Bob, smiling, said, "That happens sometimes with members your grandfather's age, Li. It's nothing to worry about."

"But can't you tell Uni?" Chip said. "Maybe he can have an extra treatment, or a stronger one."

"Li," Bob said, leaning forward across his desk, "the different chemicals we get in our treatments are very precious and hard to make. If older members got as much as they sometimes need, there might not be enough for the younger members, who are really more important to the Family. And to make enough chemicals to satisfy everyone, we might have to neglect the more important jobs. Uni knows what has to be done, how much of everything there is, and how much of everything everyone needs. Your grandfather isn't really unhappy, I promise you. He's just a bit crotchety, and we will be too when we're in our fifties."

"He uses that word," Chip said; "F-blank-blank-blank-T."

"Old members sometimes do that too," Bob said. "They don't really mean anything by it. Words aren't in themselves 'dirty'; it's the actions that the so-called dirty words represent that are offensive. Members like your grandfather use only the words, not the actions. It's not very nice, but it's no real sickness. How about you? Any friction? Let's leave your grandfather to his own adviser for a while."

"No, no friction," Chip said, thinking about having passed a scanner without touching it and having been where Uni hadn't said he could go and now suddenly not wanting to tell Bob about it. "No friction at all," he said. "Everything is top speed."

"Okay," Bob said. "Touch. I'll see you next Friday, right?"

A week or so later Papa Jan was transferred to USA60607. Chip and his parents and Peace drove to the airport at EUR55130 to see him off.

In the waiting room, while Chip's parents and Peace watched through glass the members boarding the plane, Papa Jan drew Chip aside and stood looking at him, smiling fondly. "Chip green-eye," he said—Chip frowned and tried to undo the frown—"you asked for an extra treatment for me, didn't you?"

"Yes," Chip said. "How did you know?"

"Oh, I guessed, that's all," Papa Jan said. "Take good care of yourself, Chip. Remember who you're a chip off of, and remember what I said about trying to want something."

"I will," Chip said.

"The last ones are going," Chip's father said.

Papa Jan kissed them all good-by and joined the members going out. Chip went to the glass and watched; and saw Papa Jan walking through the growing dark toward the plane, an unusually tall member, his take-along kit swinging at the end of a gangling arm. At the escalator he turned and waved—Chip waved back, hoping Papa Jan could see him—then turned again and put his kit-hand wrist to the scanner. Answering green sparked through dusk and distance, and he stepped onto the escalator and was taken smoothly upward.

In the car going back Chip sat silently, thinking that he would miss Papa Jan and his Sunday-and-holiday visits. It was strange, because he was such an odd and different old member. Yet that was exactly why he *would* miss him, Chip suddenly realized; because he was odd and different, and nobody else would fill his place.

"What's the matter, Chip?" his mother asked.

"I'm going to miss Papa Jan," he said.

"So am I," she said, "but we'll see him on the phone once in a while."

"It's a good thing he's going," Chip's father said.

"I want him not to go," Chip said. "I want him to be transferred back here."

"He's not very likely to be," his father said, "and it's a good thing. He was a bad influence on you."

"Mike," Chip's mother said.

"Don't *you* start that cloth," Chip's father said. "My name is Jesus, and his is Li."

"And mine is Peace," Peace said.

Three

Chip remembered what Papa Jan had told him, and in the weeks and months that followed, thought often about wanting something, wanting *to do* something, as Papa Jan at ten had wanted to help build Uni. He lay awake for an hour or so every few nights, considering all the different assignments there were, all the different classifications he knew of—construction supervisor like Papa Jan, lab technician like his father, plasmaphysicist like his mother, photographer like a friend's father; doctor, adviser, dentist, cosmonaut, actor, musician. They all seemed pretty much the same, but before he could really want one he had to pick one. It was a strange thought to think about—to pick, to choose, to decide. It made him feel small, yet it made him feel big too, both at the same time.

One night he thought it might be interesting to plan big buildings, like the little ones he had built with a construction set he had had a long time before (winking red *no* from Uni). That was the night before a treatment, which Papa Jan had said was a good time for wanting things. The next night big-building planner didn't seem any different from any other classification. In fact, the whole idea of wanting one particular classification seemed silly and pre-U that night, and he went straight to sleep.

The night before his next treatment he thought about planning buildings again—buildings of all different shapes, not just the three usual ones—and he wondered why the interestingness of the idea had disappeared the month before. Treatments were to prevent diseases and to relax members who were tense and to keep women from having too many babies and men from having hair on their faces; why should they make an interesting idea seem not interesting? But that was what they did, one month, and the next month, and the next.

Thinking such thoughts might be a form of selfishness, he suspected; but if it was, it was such a minor form—involving only an hour or two of sleep time, never of school or TV time—that he didn't bother to mention it to Bob NE, just as he wouldn't have mentioned a moment's nervousness or an occasional dream. Each week when Bob asked if everything was okay, he said yes it was: top speed, no friction. He took care not to "think wanting" too often or too long, so that he always got all the sleep he needed, and mornings, while washing, he checked his face in the mirror to make sure he still looked right. He did—except of course for his eye.

In 146 Chip and his family, along with most of the members in their building, were transferred to AFR71680. The building they were housed in was a brand-new one, with green carpet instead of gray in the hallways, larger TV screens, and furniture that was upholstered though nonadjustable.

There was much to get used to in '71680. The climate was somewhat warmer, and the coveralls lighter in weight and color; the monorail was old and slow and had frequent breakdowns; and the totalcakes were wrapped in greenish foil and tasted salty and not quite right.

Chip's and his family's new adviser was Mary CZ14L8584. She was a year older than Chip's mother, though she looked a few years younger.

Once Chip had grown accustomed to life in '71680—school, at least, was no different—he resumed his pastime of "thinking wanting." He saw now that there were considerable differences between classifications, and began to wonder which one Uni would give him when the time came. Uni, with its two levels of cold steel blocks, its empty echoing hardnesses . . . He wished Papa Jan had taken him down to the bottom level, where members were. It would be pleasanter to think of being classified by Uni and some members instead of by Uni alone; if he were to be given a classification he didn't like, and members were involved, maybe it would be possible to explain to them . . .

Papa Jan called twice a year; he claimed more, he said, but that was all he was granted. He looked older, smiled tiredly. A section of USA60607 was being rebuilt and he was in charge. Chip would have liked to tell him that he was trying to want something, but he couldn't with the others standing in front of the screen with him. Once, when a call was nearly over, he said, "I'm trying," and Papa Jan smiled like his old self and said, "That's the boy!"

When the call was over, Chip's father said, "What are you trying?"

"Nothing," Chip said.

"You must have meant *something*," his father said.

Chip shrugged.

Mary CZ asked him too, the next time Chip saw her. "What did you mean when you told your grandfather you were trying?" she said.

"Nothing," Chip said.

"Li," Mary said, and looked at him reproachfully. "You said you were trying. Trying what?"

"Trying not to miss him," he said. "When he was transferred to Usa I told him I would miss him, and he said I should try not to, that members were all the same and anyway he would call whenever he could."

"Oh," Mary said, and went on looking at Chip, now uncertainly. "Why didn't you say so in the first place?" she asked.

Chip shrugged.

"And *do* you miss him?"

"Just a little," Chip said. "I'm trying not to."

Sex began, and that was even better to think about than wanting something. Though he'd been taught that orgasms were extremely pleasurable, he had had no idea whatsoever of the all-but-unbearable deliciousness of the gathering sensations, the ecstasy of the coming, and the drained and boneless satisfaction of the moments afterward. *Nobody* had had any idea, none of his classmates; they talked about nothing else and would gladly have devoted themselves to nothing else as well. Chip could hardly think about mathematics and electronics and astronomy, let alone the differences between classifications.

After a few months, though, everyone calmed down, and accustomed to the new pleasure, gave it its proper Saturday-night place in the week's pattern.

One Saturday evening when Chip was fourteen, he bicycled with a group of his friends to a fine white beach a few kilometers north of AFR71680. There they swam—jumped and pushed and splashed in waves made pink-foamed by the foundering sun—and built a fire on the sand and sat around it on blankets and ate their cakes and cokes and crisp sweet pieces of a bashed-open coconut. A boy played songs on a recorder, not very well, and then, the fire crumbling to embers, the group separated into five couples, each on its own blanket.

The girl Chip was with was Anna VF, and after their orgasm—the best one Chip had ever had, or so it seemed—he was filled with a feeling of tenderness toward her, and wished there were something he could give her as a conveyor of it, like the beautiful shell that Karl GG had given Yin AP, or Li OS's recorder-song, softly cooing now for whichever girl he was lying with. Chip had nothing for Anna, no shell, no song; nothing at all, except, maybe, his thoughts.

"Would you like something interesting to think about?" he asked, lying on his back with his arm about her.

"Mm," she said, and squirmed closer against his side. Her head was on his shoulder, her arm across his chest.

He kissed her forehead. "Think of all the different classifications there are—" he said.

"Mm?"

"And try to decide which one you would pick if you had to pick one."

"To pick one?" she said.

"That's right."

"What do you mean?"

"To pick one. To *have*. To *be in*. Which classification would you like best? Doctor, engineer, adviser . . ."

She propped her head up on her hand and squinted at him. "What do you mean?" she said.

He gave a little sigh and said, "We're going to be classified, right?"

"Right."

"Suppose we *weren't* going to be. Suppose we had to classify ourselves."

"That's silly," she said, finger-drawing on his chest.

"It's interesting to think about."

"Let's fuck again," she said.

"Wait a minute," he said. "Just think about all the different classifications. Suppose it were up to us to—"

"I don't want to," she said, stopping drawing. "That's silly. And sick. We *get* classified; there's nothing to think about. Uni know's what we're—"

"Oh, fight Uni," Chip said. "Just pretend for a minute that we're living in—"

Anna flipped away from him and lay on her stomach, stiff and unmoving, the back of her head to him.

"I'm sorry," he said.

"*I'm* sorry," she said. "For you. You're sick."

"No I'm not," he said.

She was silent.

He sat up and looked despairingly at her rigid back. "It just slipped out," he said. "I'm sorry."

She stayed silent.

"It's just a *word,* Anna," he said.

"You're sick," she said.

"Oh, hate," he said.

"You see what I mean?"

"Anna," he said, "look. Forget it. Forget the whole thing, all right? Just forget it." He tickled between her thighs, but she locked them, barring his hand.

"Ah, Anna," he said. "Ah, come on. I said I was sorry, didn't I? Come on, let's fuck again. I'll suck you first if you want."

After a while she relaxed her thighs and let him tickle her.

Then she turned over and sat up and looked at him. "*Are* you sick, Li?" she asked.

"No," he said, and managed to laugh. "Of course I'm not," he said.

"I never heard of such a thing," she said. " 'Classify ourselves.' How could we do it? How could we possibly know enough?"

"It's just something I think about once in a while," he said. "Not very often. In fact, hardly ever."

"It's such a—a funny idea," she said. "It sounds—I don't know—pre-U."

"I won't think about it any more," he said, and raised his right hand, the bracelet slipping back. "Love of Family," he said. "Come on, lie down and I'll suck you."

She lay back on the blanket, looking worried.

The next morning at five of ten Mary CZ called Chip and asked him to come see her.

"When?" he asked.

"Now," she said.

"All right," he said. "I'll be right down."

His mother said, "What does she want to see you on a Sunday for?"

"I don't know," Chip said.

But he knew. Anna VF had called her adviser.

He rode the escalators down, down, down, wondering how much Anna had told, and what he should say; and wanting suddenly to cry and tell Mary that he was sick and selfish and a liar. The members on the upgoing escalators were relaxed, smiling, content, in harmony with the cheerful music of the speakers; no one but he was guilty and unhappy.

The advisory offices were strangely still. Members and advisers conferred in a few of the cubicles, but most of them were empty, the desks in order, the chairs waiting. In one cubicle a green-coveralled member leaned over the phone working a screwdriver at it.

Mary was standing on her chair, laying a strip of Christmas bunting along the top of *Wei Addressing the Chemotherapists.* More bunting was on the desk, a roll of red and a roll of green, and Mary's open telecomp with a container of tea beside it. "Li?" she said, not turning. "That was quick. Sit down."

Chip sat down. Lines of green symbols glowed on the telecomp's screen. The answer button was held down by a souvenir paperweight from RUS81655.

"Stay," Mary said to the bunting and, watching it, backed down off her chair. It stayed.

She swung her chair around and smiled at Chip as she drew it in to her and sat. She looked at the telecomp's screen, and while she looked, picked up the container of tea and sipped from it. She put it down and looked at Chip and smiled.

"A member says you need help," she said. "The girl you fucked last night, Anna"—she glanced at the screen—"VF35H6143."

Chip nodded. "I said a dirty word," he said.

"Two," Mary said, "but that's hardly important. At least not relatively. What *is* important are some of the other things you said, things about deciding which classification you would pick if we didn't have UniComp to do the job."

Chip looked away from Mary, at the rolls of red and green Christmas bunting.

"Is that something you think about often, Li?" Mary asked.

"Just sometimes," Chip said. "In the free hour or at night; never in school or during TV."

"Nighttime counts too," Mary said. "That's when you're supposed to be sleeping."

Chip looked at her and said nothing.

"When did it start?" she asked.

"I don't know," he said, "a few years ago. In Eur."

"Your grandfather," she said.

He nodded.

She looked at the screen, and looked at Chip again, ruefully. "Didn't it ever dawn on you," she said, "that 'deciding' and 'picking' are manifestations of selfishness? *Acts* of selfishness?"

"I thought, maybe," Chip said, looking at the edge of the desktop, rubbing a fingertip along it.

"Oh, Li," Mary said. "What am I here for? What are *advisers* here for? To help us, isn't that so?"

He nodded.

"Why didn't you tell me? Or your adviser in Eur? Why did you wait, and lose sleep, and worry this Anna?"

Chip shrugged, watching his fingertip rubbing the desktop, the nail dark. "It was—interesting, sort of," he said.

" 'Interesting, sort of,' " Mary said. "It might also have been interesting, sort of, to think about the kind of pre-U chaos we'd have if we actually *did* pick our own classifications. Did you think about that?"

"No," Chip said.

"Well, do. Think about a hundred million members deciding to be TV actors and not a single one deciding to work in a crematorium."

Chip looked up at her. "Am I very sick?" he asked.

"No," Mary said, "but you might have ended up that way if not for Anna's helpfulness." She took the paperweight from the telecomp's answer button and the green symbols disappeared from the screen. "Touch," she said.

Chip touched his bracelet to the scanner plate, and Mary began tapping the input keys. "You've been given hundreds of tests since your first day of school," she said, "and UniComp's been fed the results of every last one of them." Her fingers darted over the dozen black keys. "You've had hundreds of adviser meetings," she said, "and UniComp knows about those too. It knows what jobs have to be done and who there is to do them. It knows *everything*. Now who's going to make the better, more efficient classification, you or UniComp?"

"UniComp, Mary," Chip said. "I know that. I didn't really want to do it myself; I was just—just thinking *what if,* that's all."

Mary finished tapping and pressed the answer button. Green symbols appeared on the screen. Mary said, "Go to the treatment room."

Chip jumped to his feet. "Thank you," he said.

"Thank Uni," Mary said, switching off the telecomp. She closed its cover and snapped the catches.

Chip hesitated. "I'll be all right?" he asked.

"Perfect," Mary said. She smiled reassuringly.

"I'm sorry I made you come in on a Sunday," Chip said.

"Don't be," Mary said. "For once in my life I'm going to have my Christmas decorations up before December twenty-fourth."

Chip went out of the advisory offices and into the treatment room. Only one unit was working, but there were only three members in line. When his turn came, he plunged his arm as deep as he could into the rubber-rimmed opening, and gratefully felt the scanner's contact and the infusion disc's warm nuzzle. He wanted the tickle-buzz-sting to last a long time, curing him completely and forever, but it was even shorter than usual, and he worried that there might have been a break in communication between the unit and Uni or a shortage of chemicals inside the unit itself. On a quiet Sunday morning mightn't it be carelessly serviced?

He stopped worrying, though, and riding up the escalators he felt a lot better about everything—himself, Uni, the Family, the world, the universe.

The first thing he did when he got into the apartment was call Anna VF and thank her.

At fifteen he was classified 663D—genetic taxonomist, fourth class—and was transferred to RUS41500 and the Academy of the Genetic Sciences. He learned elementary genetics and lab techniques and modulation and transplant theory; he skated and played soccer and went to the Pre-U Museum and the Museum of the Family's Achievements; he had a girlfriend named Anna from Jap and then another named Peace from Aus. On Thursday, 18 October 151, he and everyone else in the Academy sat up until four in the morning watching the launching of the *Altaira,* then slept and loafed through a half-day holiday.

One night his parents called unexpectedly. "We have bad news," his mother said. "Papa Jan died this morning."

A sadness gripped him and must have shown on his face.

"He was sixty-two, Chip," his mother said. "He had his life."

"Nobody lives forever," Chip's father said.

"Yes," Chip said. "I'd forgot how old he was. How are you? Has Peace been classified yet?"

When they were done talking he went out for a walk, even though it was a rain night and almost ten. He went into the park. Everyone was coming out. "Six minutes," a member said, smiling at him.

He didn't care. He wanted to be rained on, to be drenched. He didn't know why but he wanted to.

He sat on a bench and waited. The park was empty; everyone else was gone. He thought of Papa Jan saying things that were the opposite of what he meant, and then saying what he really meant down in the inside of Uni, with a blue blanket wrapped around him.

On the back of the bench across the walk someone had red-chalked a jagged *FIGHT UNI*. Someone else—or maybe the same sick member, ashamed—had crossed it out with white. The rain began, and started washing it away; white chalk, red chalk, smearing pinkly down the bench back.

Chip turned his face to the sky and held it steady under the rain, trying to feel as if he were so sad he was crying.

Four

Early in his third and final year at the Academy, Chip took part in a complicated exchange of dormitory cubicles worked out to put everyone involved
closer to his or her girlfriend or boyfriend. In his new location he was two
cubicles away from one Yin DW; and across the aisle from him was a shorter-
than-normal member named Karl WL, who frequently carried a green-covered
sketch pad and who, though he replied to comments readily enough, rarely
started a conversation on his own.

This Karl WL had a look of unusual concentration in his eyes, as if he were
close on the track of answers to difficult questions. Once Chip noticed him slip
out of the lounge after the beginning of the first TV hour and not slip in again
till before the end of the second; and one night in the dorm, after the lights
had gone out, he saw a dim glow filtering through the blanket of Karl's bed.

One Saturday night—early Sunday morning, really—as Chip was coming
back quietly from Yin DW's cubicle to his own, he saw Karl sitting in his. He
was on the side of the bed in pajamas, holding his pad tilted toward a flashlight
on the corner of the desk and working at it with brisk chopping hand movements. The flashlight's lens was masked in some way so that only a small beam
of light shone out.

Chip went closer and said, "No girl this week?"

Karl started, and closed the pad. A stick of charcoal was in his hand.

"I'm sorry I surprised you," Chip said.

"That's all right," Karl said, his face only faint glints at chin and cheekbones. "I finished early. Peace KG. Aren't you staying all night with Yin?"

"She's snoring," Chip said.

Karl made an amused sound. "I'm turning in now," he said.

"What are you doing?"

"Just some gene diagrams," Karl said. He turned back the cover of the pad and showed the top page. Chip went close and bent and looked—at cross sections of genes in the B3 locus, carefully drawn and shaded, done with a pen. "I was trying some with charcoal," Karl said, "but it's no good." He closed the pad and put the charcoal on the desk and switched off the flashlight. "Sleep well," he said.

"Thanks," Chip said. "You too."

He went into his own cubicle and groped his way into bed, wondering whether Karl had in fact been drawing gene diagrams, for which charcoal hardly even seemed worth a trial. Probably he should speak to his adviser, Li YB, about Karl's secretiveness and occasional unmemberlike behavior, but he decided to wait awhile, until he was sure that Karl needed help and that he wouldn't be wasting Li YB's time and Karl's and his own. There was no point in being an alarmist.

Wei's Birthday came a few weeks later, and after the parade Chip and a dozen or so other students railed out to the Amusement Gardens for the afternoon. They rowed boats for a while and then strolled through the zoo. While they were gathered at a water fountain, Chip saw Karl WL sitting on the railing in front of the horse compound, holding his pad on his knees and drawing. Chip excused himself from the group and went over.

Karl saw him coming and smiled at him, closing his pad. "Wasn't that a great parade?" he said.

"It was really top speed," Chip said. "Are you drawing the horses?"

"Trying to."

"May I see?"

Karl looked him in the eye for a moment and then said, "Sure, why not?" He riffled the bottom of the pad and, opening it partway through, turned back the upper section and let Chip look at a rearing stallion that crammed the page, charcoaled darkly and vigorously. Muscles bulked under its gleaming hide; its eye was wild and rolling; its forelegs quivered. The drawing surprised Chip with its vitality and power. He had never seen a picture of a horse that came anywhere near it. He sought words, and could only come up with, "This is— great, Karl! Top speed!"

"It's not accurate," Karl said.

"It is!"

"No it isn't," Karl said. "If it were accurate I'd be at the Academy of Art."

Chip looked at the real horses in the compound and at Karl's drawing again; at the horses again, and saw the greater thickness of their legs, the lesser width of their chests.

"You're right," he said, looking at the drawing again. "It's not accurate. But it's—it's somehow *better* than accurate."

"Thanks," Karl said. "That's what I'd like it to be. I'm not finished yet."

Looking at him, Chip said, "Have you done others?"

Karl turned down the preceding page and showed him a seated lion, proud and watchful. In the lower right-hand corner of the page there was an *A* with a circle around it. "Marvelous!" Chip said. Karl turned down other pages; there were two deer, a monkey, a soaring eagle, two dogs sniffing each other, a crouching leopard.

Chip laughed. "You've got the whole fighting zoo!" he said.

"No I haven't," Karl said.

All the drawings had the *A* with the circle around it in the corner. "What's that for?" Chip asked.

"Artists used to sign their pictures. To show whose work it was."

"I know," Chip said, "but why an *A*?"

"Oh," Karl said, and turned the pages back one by one. "It stands for Ashi," he said. "That's what my sister calls me." He came to the horse, added a line of charcoal to its stomach, and looked at the horses in the compound with his look of concentration, which now had an object and a reason.

"I have an extra name too," Chip said. "Chip. My grandfather gave it to me."

"Chip?"

"It means 'chip off the old block.' I'm supposed to be like my grandfather's grandfather." Chip watched Karl sharpen the lines of the horse's rear legs, and then moved from his side. "I'd better get back to the group I'm with," he said. "Those are top speed. It's a shame you weren't classified an artist."

Karl looked at him. "I wasn't, though," he said, "so I only draw on Sundays and holidays and during the free hour. I never let it interfere with my work or whatever else I'm supposed to be doing."

"Right," Chip said. "See you at the dorm."

That evening, after TV, Chip came back to his cubicle and found on his desk the drawing of the horse. Karl, in his cubicle, said, "Do you want it?"

"Yes," Chip said. "Thanks. It's great!" The drawing had even more vitality and power than before. An *A*-in-a-circle was in a corner of it.

Chip tabbed the drawing to the bulletin board behind the desk, and as he finished, Yin DW came in, bringing back a copy of *Universe* she had borrowed. "Where'd you get that?" she asked.

"Karl WL did it," Chip said.

"That's very nice, Karl," Yin said. "You draw well."

Karl, getting into pajamas, said, "Thanks. I'm glad you like it."

To Chip, Yin whispered, "It's all out of proportion. Keep it there, though. It was kind of you to put it up."

· · ·

Once in a while, during the free hour, Chip and Karl went to the Pre-U together. Karl made sketches of the mastodon and the bison, the cavemen in their animal hides, the soldiers and sailors in their countless different uniforms. Chip wandered among the early automobiles and dictypes, the safes and handcuffs and TV "sets." He studied the models and pictures of the old buildings: the spired and buttressed churches, the turreted castles, the large and small houses with their windows and lock-fitted doors. Windows, he thought, must have had their good points. It would be pleasant, would make one feel bigger, to look out at the world from one's room or working place; and at night, from outside, a house with rows of lighted windows must have been attractive, even beautiful.

One afternoon Karl came into Chip's cubicle and stood beside the desk with his hands fisted at his sides. Chip, looking up at him, thought he had been stricken by a fever or worse; his face was flushed and his eyes were narrowed in a strange stare. But no, it was anger that held him, anger such as Chip had never seen before, anger so intense that, trying to speak, Karl seemed unable to work his lips.

Anxiously Chip said, "What is it?"

"Li," Karl said. "Listen. Will you do me a favor?"

"Sure! Of course!"

Karl leaned close to him and whispered, "Claim a pad for me, will you? I just claimed one and was denied. Five fighting hundred of them, a pile this high, and I had to turn it back in!"

Chip stared at him.

"Claim one, will you?" Karl said. "Anyone can try a little sketching in his spare time, right? Go on down, okay?"

Painfully Chip said, "Karl—"

Karl looked at him, his anger retreated, and he stood up straight. "No," he said. "No, I—I just lost my temper, that's all. I'm sorry. I'm sorry, brother. Forget it." He clapped Chip's shoulder. "I'm okay now," he said. "I'll claim again in a week or so. Been doing too much drawing anyway, I suppose. Uni knows best." He went off down the aisle toward the bathroom.

Chip turned back to the desk and leaned on his elbows and held his head, shaking.

That was Tuesday. Chip's weekly adviser meetings were on Woodsday mornings at 10:40, and this time he would tell Li YB about Karl's sickness. There was no longer any question of being an alarmist; there was faulted responsibility, in fact, in having waited as long as he had. He ought to have said something at the first clear sign, Karl's slipping out of TV (to draw, of course), or even when he had noticed the unusual look in Karl's eyes. Why in hate had he waited? He could hear Li YB gently reproaching him: "You haven't been a very good brother's keeper, Li."

Early on Woodsday morning, though, he decided to pick up some coveralls and the new *Geneticist*. He went down to the supply center and walked through the aisles. He took a *Geneticist* and a pack of coveralls and walked some more and came to the art-supplies section. He saw the pile of green-covered sketch pads; there weren't five hundred of them, but there were seventy or eighty and no one seemed in a rush to claim them.

He walked away, thinking that he must be going out of his mind. Yet if Karl were to promise not to draw when he wasn't supposed to . . .

He walked back again—"*Anyone can try a little sketching in his spare time, right?*"—and took a pad and a packet of charcoal. He went to the shortest check-out line, his heart pounding in his chest, his arms trembling. He drew a deep-as-possible breath; another, and another.

He put his bracelet to the scanner, and the stickers of the coveralls, the *Geneticist,* the pad, and the charcoal. Everything was *yes.* He gave way to the next member.

He went back up to the dorm. Karl's cubicle was empty, the bed unmade. He went into his own cubicle and put the coveralls on the shelf and the *Geneticist* on the desk. On the top page of the pad he wrote, his hand still trembling, *Free time only. I want your promise.* Then he put the pad and the charcoal on his bed and sat at the desk and looked at the *Geneticist.*

Karl came, and went into his cubicle and began making his bed. "Are those yours?" Chip asked.

Karl looked at the pad and charcoal on Chip's bed. Chip said, "They're not mine."

"Oh, yes. Thanks," Karl said, and came over and took them. "Thanks a lot," he said.

"You ought to put your nameber on the first page," Chip said, "if you're going to leave it all over like that."

Karl went into his cubicle, opened the pad, and looked at the first page. He looked at Chip, nodded, raised his right hand, and mouthed, "Love of Family."

They rode down to the classrooms together. "What did you have to waste a page for?" Karl said.

Chip smiled.

"I'm not joking," Karl said. "Didn't you ever hear of writing a note on a piece of scrap paper?"

"Christ, Marx, Wood, and Wei," Chip said.

In December of that year, 152, came the appalling news of the Gray Death, sweeping through all the Mars colonies except one and completely wiping them out in nine short days. In the Academy of the Genetic Sciences, as in all the Family's establishments, there was helpless silence, then mourning, and then a massive determination to help the Family overcome the staggering setback it had suffered. Everyone worked harder and longer. Free time was halved; there were classes on Sundays and only a half-day Christmas holiday.

Genetics alone could breed new strengths in the coming generations; everyone was in a hurry to finish his training and get on to his first real assignment. On every wall were the white-on-black posters: *MARS AGAIN!*

The new spirit lasted several months. Not until Marxmas was there a full day's holiday, and then no one quite knew what to do with it. Chip and Karl and their girlfriends rowed out to one of the islands in the Amusement Gardens lake and sunbathed on a large flat rock. Karl drew his girlfriend's picture. It was the first time, as far as Chip knew, that he had drawn a living human being.

In June, Chip claimed another pad for Karl.

Their training ended, five weeks early, and they received their assignments: Chip to a viral genetics research laboratory in USA90058; Karl to the Institute of Enzymology in JAP50319.

On the evening before they were to leave the Academy they packed their take-along kits. Karl pulled green-covered pads from his desk drawers—a dozen from one drawer, half a dozen from another, more pads from other drawers; he threw them into a pile on his bed. "You're never going to get those all into your kit," Chip said.

"I'm not planning to," Karl said. "They're done; I don't need them." He sat on the bed and leafed through one of the pads, tore out one drawing and another.

"May I have some?" Chip asked.

"Sure," Karl said, and tossed a pad over to him.

It was mostly Pre-U Museum sketches. Chip took out one of a man in chain mail holding a crossbow to his shoulder, and another of an ape scratching himself.

Karl gathered most of the pads and went off down the aisle toward the chute. Chip put the pad on Karl's bed and picked up another one.

In it were a nude man and woman standing in parkland outside a blank-slabbed city. They were taller than normal, beautiful and strangely dignified. The woman was quite different from the man, not only genitally but also in her longer hair, protrusive breasts, and overall softer convexity. It was a great drawing, but something about it disturbed Chip, he didn't know what.

He turned to other pages, other men and women; the pictures grew surer and stronger, done with fewer and bolder lines. They were the best drawings Karl had ever made, but in each there was that disturbing something, a lack, an imbalance that Chip was at a loss to define.

It hit him with a chill.

They had no bracelets.

He looked through to check, his stomach knotting sick-tight. No bracelets. No bracelets on any of them. And there was no chance of the drawings being unfinished; in the corner of each of them was an *A* with a circle around it.

He put down the pad and went and sat on his bed; watched as Karl came back and gathered the rest of the pads and, with a smile, carried them off.

There was a dance in the lounge but it was brief and subdued because of Mars. Later Chip went with his girlfriend into her cubicle. "What's the matter?" she asked.

"Nothing," he said.

Karl asked him too, in the morning while they were folding their blankets. "What's the matter, Li?"

"Nothing."

"Sorry to be leaving?"

"A little."

"Me too. Here, give me your sheets and I'll chute them."

"What's his nameber?" Li YB asked.

"Karl WL35S7497," Chip said.

Li YB jotted it down. "And what specifically seems to be the trouble?" he asked.

Chip wiped his palms on his thighs. "He's drawn some pictures of members," he said.

"Acting aggressively?"

"No, no," Chip said. "Just standing and sitting, fucking, playing with children."

"Well?"

Chip looked at the desktop. "They don't have bracelets," he said.

Li YB didn't speak. Chip looked at him; he was looking at Chip. After a moment Li YB said, "Several pictures?"

"A whole padful."

"And no bracelets at all."

"None."

Li YB breathed in, and then pushed out the breath between his teeth in a series of rapid hisses. He looked at his note pad. "KWL35S7497," he said.

Chip nodded.

He tore up the picture of the man with the crossbow, which was aggressive, and tore up the one of the ape too. He took the pieces to the chute and dropped them down.

He put the last few things into his take-along kit—his clippers and mouthpiece and a framed snapshot of his parents and Papa Jan—and pressed it closed.

Karl's girlfriend came by with her kit slung on her shoulder. "Where's Karl?" she asked.

"At the medicenter."

"Oh," she said. "Tell him I said good-by, will you?"

"Sure."

They kissed cheeks. "Good-by," she said.

"Good-by."

She went away down the aisle. Some other students, no longer students, went past. They smiled at Chip and said good-by to him.

He looked around the barren cubicle. The picture of the horse was still on the bulletin board. He went to it and looked at it; saw again the rearing stallion, so alive and wild. Why hadn't Karl stayed with the animals in the zoo? Why had he begun to draw living humans?

A feeling formed in Chip, formed and grew; a feeling that he had been wrong to tell Li YB about Karl's drawings, although he knew of course that he had been right. How could it be wrong to help a sick brother? *Not* to tell would have been wrong, to keep quiet as he had done before, letting Karl go on drawing members without bracelets and getting sicker and sicker. Eventually he might even have been drawing members acting aggressively. Fighting.

Of course he had been right.

Yet the feeling that he had been wrong stayed and kept growing, grew into guilt, irrationally.

Someone came near, and he whirled, thinking it was Karl coming to thank him. It wasn't; it was someone passing the cubicle, leaving.

But that was what was going to happen: Karl was going to come back from the medicenter and say, "Thanks for helping me, Li. I was really sick but I'm a whole lot better now," and *he* was going to say, "Don't thank *me,* brother; thank Uni," and Karl was going to say, "No, no," and insist and shake his hand.

Suddenly he wanted not to be there, not to get Karl's thanks for having helped him; he grabbed his kit and hurried to the aisle—stopped short, uncertainly, and hurried back. He took the picture of the horse from the board, opened his kit on the desk, pushed the drawing in among the pages of a notebook, closed the kit, and went.

He jogged down the downgoing escalators, excusing himself past other members, afraid that Karl might come after him; jogged all the way down to the lowest level, where the rail station was, and got on the long airport line. He stood with his head held still, not looking back.

Finally he came to the scanner. He faced it for a moment, and touched it with his bracelet. *Yes,* it green-winked.

He hurried through the gate.

II
Coming Alive

One

Between July of 153 and Marx of 162, Chip had four assignments: two at research laboratories in Usa; a brief one at the Institute of Genetic Engineering in Ind, where he attended a series of lectures on recent advances in mutation induction; and a five-year assignment at a chemo-synthetics plant in Chi. He was upgraded twice in his classification and by 162 was a genetic taxonomist, second class.

During those years he was outwardly a normal and contented member of the Family. He did his work well, took part in house athletic and recreational programs, had weekly sexual activity, made monthly phone calls and bi-yearly visits to his parents, was in place and on time for TV and treatments and adviser meetings. He had no discomfort to report, either physical or mental.

Inwardly, however, he was far from normal. The feeling of guilt with which he had left the Academy had led him to withhold himself from his next adviser, for he wanted to retain that feeling, which, though unpleasant, was the strongest feeling he had ever had and an enlargement, strangely, of his sense of being; and withholding himself from his adviser—reporting no discomfort, playing the part of a relaxed, contented member—had led over the years to a withholding of himself from everyone around him, a general attitude of guarded watchfulness. Everything came to seem questionable to him: totalcakes, coveralls, the sameness of members' rooms and thoughts, and especially the work he was doing, whose end, he saw, would only be to solidify the universal sameness. There were no alternatives, of course, no imaginable alternatives to anything, but still he withheld himself, and questioned. Only in the first few days after treatments was he really the member he pretended to be.

One thing alone in the world was indisputably right: Karl's drawing of the horse. He framed it—not in a supply-center frame but in one he made himself, out of wood strips ripped from the back of a drawer and scraped smooth—and hung it in his rooms in Usa, his room in Ind, his room in Chi. It was a lot better to look at than *Wei Addressing the Chemotherapists* or *Marx Writing* or *Christ Expelling the Money Changers*.

In Chi he thought of getting married, but he was told that he wasn't to reproduce and so there didn't seem much point in it.

In mid-Marx of 162, shortly before his twenty-seventh birthday, he was transferred back to the Institute of Genetic Engineering in IND26110 and assigned to a newly established Genic Subclassification Center. New microscopes had found distinctions between genes that until then had appeared identical, and he was one of forty 663B's and C's put to defining subclassifications. His room was four buildings away from the Center, giving him a short walk twice a day, and he soon found a girlfriend whose room was on the floor below his. His adviser was a year younger than he, Bob RO. Life apparently was going to continue as before.

One night in April, though, as he made ready to clean his teeth before going to bed, he found a small white something lodged in his mouthpiece. Perplexed, he picked it out. It was a triple bend of tightly rolled paper. He put down the mouthpiece and unrolled a thin rectangle filled with typing. *You seem to be a fairly unusual member,* it said. *Wondering about which classification you would choose, for instance. Would you like to meet some other unusual members? Think about it. You are only partly alive. We can help you more than you can imagine.*

The note surprised him with its knowledge of his past and disturbed him with its secrecy and its "You are only partly alive." What did it mean—that strange statement and the whole strange message? And who had put it in his mouthpiece, of all places? But there was no better place, it struck him, for making certain that he and he alone should find it. Who then, not so foolishly, had put it there? Anyone at all could have come into the room earlier in the evening or during the day. At least two other members had done so; there had been notes on his desk from Peace SK, his girlfriend, and from the secretary of the house photography club.

He cleaned his teeth and got into bed and reread the note. Its writer or one of the other "unusual members" must have had access to UniComp's memory of his boyhood self-classification thoughts, and that seemed to be enough to make the group think he might be sympathetic to them. Was he? They were abnormal; that was certain. Yet what was *he?* Wasn't he abnormal too? *We can help you more than you can imagine.* What did *that* mean? Help him how?

Help him do what? And what if he decided he wanted to meet them; what was he supposed to do? Wait, apparently, for another note, for a contact of some kind. *Think about it,* the note said.

The last chime sounded, and he rolled the piece of paper back up and tucked it down into the spine of his night-table *Wei's Living Wisdom.* He tapped off the light and lay and thought about it. It was disturbing, but it was different too, and interesting. *Would you like to meet some other unusual members?*

He didn't say anything about it to Bob RO. He looked for another note in his mouthpiece each time he came back to his room, but didn't find one. Walking to and from work, taking a seat in the lounge for TV, standing on line in the dining hall or the supply center, he searched the eyes of the members around him, alert for a meaningful remark or perhaps only a look and a head movement inviting him to follow. None came.

Four days went by and he began to think that the note had been a sick member's joke, or worse, a test of some kind. Had Bob RO himself written it, to see if he would mention it? No, that was ridiculous; he was *really* getting sick.

He had been interested—excited even, and hopeful, though he hadn't known of what—but now, as more days went by with no note, no contact, he became disappointed and irritable.

And then, a week after the first note, it was there: the same triple bend of rolled paper in the mouthpiece. He picked it out, excitement and hope coming back instantaneously. He unrolled the paper and read it: *If you want to meet us and hear how we can help you, be between buildings J16 and J18 on Lower Christ Plaza tomorrow night at 11:15. Do not touch any scanners on the way. If members are in sight of one you have to pass, take another route. I'll wait until 11:30.* Beneath was typed, as a signature, *Snowflake.*

Few members were on the walkways, and those were hurrying to their beds with their eyes set straight ahead of them. He had to change his course only once, walked faster, and reached Lower Christ Plaza exactly at 11:15. He crossed the moonlit white expanse, with its turned-off fountain mirroring the moon, and found J16 and the dark channel that divided it from J18.

No one was there—but then, meters back in shadow, he saw white coveralls marked with what looked like a medicenter red cross. He went into the darkness and approached the member, who stood by J16's wall and stayed silent.

"Snowflake?" he said.

"Yes." The voice was a woman's. "Did you touch any scanners?"

"No."

"Funny feeling, isn't it?" She was wearing a pale mask of some kind, thin and close-fitting.

"I've done it before," he said.

"Good for you."

"Only once, and somebody pushed me," he said. She seemed older than he, how much he couldn't tell.

"We're going to a place that's a five-minute walk from here," she said. "It's where we get together regularly, six of us, four women and two men—a terrible ratio that I'm counting on you to improve. We're going to make a certain suggestion to you; if you decide to follow it you might eventually become one of us; if you don't, you won't, and tonight will be our last contact. In that case, though, we can't have you knowing what we look like or where we meet." Her hand came out of her pocket with whiteness in it. "I'll have to bandage your eyes," she said. "That's why I'm wearing these medicenter cuvs, so it'll look all right for me to be leading you."

"At this hour?"

"We've done it before and had no trouble," she said. "You don't mind?"

He shrugged. "I guess not," he said.

"Hold these over your eyes." She gave him two wads of cotton. He closed his eyes and put the wads in place, holding them with a finger each. She began winding bandage around his head and over the wads; he withdrew his fingers, bent his head to help her. She kept winding bandage, around and around, up onto his forehead, down onto his cheeks.

"Are you sure you're really not medicenter?" he said.

She chuckled and said, "Positive." She pressed the end of the bandage, sticking it tight; pressed all over it and over his eyes, then took his arm. She turned him—toward the plaza, he knew—and started him walking.

"Don't forget your mask," he said.

She stopped short. "Thanks for reminding me," she said. Her hand left his arm, and after a moment, came back. They walked on.

Their footsteps changed, became muted by space, and a breeze cooled his face below the bandage; they were in the plaza. "Snowflake's" hand on his arm drew him in a diagonal leftward course, away from the direction of the Institute.

"When we get where we're going," she said, "I'm going to put a piece of tape over your bracelet; over mine too. We avoid knowing one another's namebers as much as possible. I know yours—I'm the one who spotted you —but the others don't; all they know is that I'm bringing a promising member. Later on, one or two of them may have to know it."

"Do you check the history of everyone who's assigned here?"

"No. Why?"

"Isn't that how you 'spotted' me, by finding out that I used to think about classifying myself?"

"Three steps down here," she said. "No, that was only confirmation. And two and three. What I spotted was a look you have, the look of a member who isn't one-hundred-per-cent in the bosom of the Family. You'll learn to recognize it too, if you join us. I found out who you were, and then I went to your room and saw that picture on the wall."

"The horse?"

"No, *Marx Writing,*" she said. "Of course the horse. You draw the way no normal member would even think of drawing. I checked your history *then,* after I'd seen the picture."

They had left the plaza and were on one of the walkways west of it—K or L, he wasn't sure which.

"You've made a mistake," he said. "Someone else drew that picture."

"You drew it," she said; "you've claimed charcoal and sketch pads."

"For the member who drew it. A friend of mine at academy."

"Well *that's* interesting," she said. "Cheating on claims is a better sign than anything. Anyway, you liked the picture well enough to keep it and frame it. Or did your friend make the frame too?"

He smiled. "No, I did," he said. "You didn't miss a thing."

"We turn here, to the right."

"Are you an adviser?"

"Me? Hate, no."

"But you can pull histories?"

"Sometimes."

"Are you at the Institute?"

"Don't ask so many questions," she said. "Listen, what do you want us to call you? Instead of Li RM."

"Oh," he said. "Chip."

" 'Chip'? No," she said, "don't just say the first thing that comes into your mind. You ought to be something like 'Pirate' or 'Tiger.' The others are King and Lilac and Leopard and Hush and Sparrow."

"Chip's what I was called when I was a boy," he said. "I'm used to it."

"All right," she said, "but it's not what *I* would have chosen. Do you know where we are?"

"No."

"Fine. Left now."

They went through a door, up steps, through another door, and into an echoing hall of some kind, where they walked and turned, walked and turned, as if by-passing a number of irregularly placed objects. They walked up a stopped escalator and along a corridor that curved toward the right.

She stopped him and asked for his bracelet. He raised his wrist, and his bracelet was pressed tight and rubbed. He touched it; there was smoothness instead of his nameber. That and his sightlessness made him suddenly feel disembodied; as if he were about to drift from the floor, drift right out through whatever walls were around him and up into space, dissolve there and become nothing.

She took his arm again. They walked farther and stopped. He heard a knock and two more knocks, a door opening, voices stilling. "Hi," she said, leading him forward. "This is Chip. He insists on it."

Chairs scuffed against the floor, voices gave greetings. A hand took his and shook it. "I'm King," a member said, a man. "I'm glad you decided to come."

"Thanks," he said.

Another hand gripped his harder. "Snowflake says you're quite an artist" —an older man than King. "I'm Leopard."

Other hands came quickly, women: "Hello, Chip; I'm Lilac." "And I'm Sparrow. I hope you'll become a regular." "I'm Hush, Leopard's wife. Hello." The last one's hand and voice were old; the other two were young.

He was led to a chair and sat in it. His hands found tabletop before him, smooth and bare, its edge slightly curving; an oval table or a large round one. The others were sitting down; Snowflake on his right, talking; someone else on his left. He smelled something burning, sniffed to make sure. None of the others seemed aware of it. "Something's burning," he said.

"Tobacco," the old woman, Hush, said on his left.

"Tobacco?" he said.

"We smoke it," Snowflake said. "Would you like to try some?"

"No," he said.

Some of them laughed. "It's not really deadly," King said, farther away on his left. "In fact, I suspect it may have some beneficial effects."

"It's very pleasing," one of the young women said, across the table from him.

"No, thanks," he said.

They laughed again, made comments to one another, and one by one grew silent. His right hand on the tabletop was covered by Snowflake's hand; he wanted to draw it away but restrained himself. He had been stupid to come. What was he doing, sitting there sightless among those sick false-named members? His own abnormality was nothing next to theirs. Tobacco! The stuff had been extincted a hundred years ago; where the hate had they got it?

"We're sorry about the bandage, Chip," King said. "I assume Snowflake's explained why it's necessary."

"She has," Chip said, and Snowflake said, "I did." Her hand left Chip's; he drew his from the tabletop and took hold of his other in his lap.

"We're abnormal members, which is fairly obvious," King said. "We do a great many things that are generally considered sick. We think they're not. We *know* they're not." His voice was strong and deep and authoritative; Chip visualized him as large and powerful, about forty. "I'm not going to go into too many details," he said, "because in your present condition you would be shocked and upset, just as you're obviously shocked and upset by the fact that we smoke tobacco. You'll learn the details for yourself in the future, if there *is* a future as far as you and we are concerned."

"What do you mean," Chip said, " 'in my present condition'?"

There was silence for a moment. A woman coughed. "While you're dulled and normalized by your most recent treatment," King said.

Chip sat still, facing in King's direction, stopped by the irrationality of what he had said. He went over the words and answered them: "I'm not dulled and normalized."

"But you are," King said.

"The whole Family is," Snowflake said, and from beyond her came "Everyone, not just you"—in the old man's voice of Leopard.

"What do you think a treatment consists of?" King asked.

Chip said, "Vaccines, enzymes, the contraceptive, sometimes a tranquilizer—"

"*Always* a tranquilizer," King said. "And LPK, which minimizes aggressiveness and also minimizes joy and perception and every other fighting thing the brain is capable of."

"And a sexual depressant," Snowflake said.

"That too," King said. "Ten minutes of automatic sex once a week is barely a fraction of what's possible."

"I don't believe it," Chip said. "Any of it."

They told him it was true. "It's true, Chip." "Really, it's the truth." "It's true!"

"You're in genetics," King said; "isn't that what genetic engineering is working toward?—removing aggressiveness, controlling the sex drive, building in helpfulness and docility and gratitude? Treatments are doing the job in the meantime, while genetic engineering gets past size and skin color."

"Treatments help us," Chip said.

"They help Uni," the woman across the table said.

"And the Wei-worshippers who programmed Uni," King said. "But they don't help *us,* at least not as much as they hurt us. They make us into machines."

Chip shook his head, and shook it again.

"Snowflake told us"—it was Hush, speaking in a dry quiet voice that accounted for her name—"that you have abnormal tendencies. Haven't you ever noticed that they're stronger just before a treatment and weaker just after one?"

Snowflake said, "I'll bet you made that picture frame a day or two *before* a treatment, not a day or two after one."

He thought for a moment. "I don't remember," he said, "but when I was a boy and thought about classifying myself, after treatments it seemed stupid and pre-U, and before treatments it was—exciting."

"There you are," King said.

"But it was *sick* excitement!"

"It was healthy," King said, and the woman across the table said, "You were alive, you were feeling something. *Any* feeling is healthier than no feeling at all."

He thought about the guilt he had kept secret from his advisers since Karl and the Academy. He nodded. "Yes," he said, "yes, that could be." He turned his face toward King, toward the woman, toward Leopard and Snowflake, wishing he could open his eyes and see them. "But I don't understand this," he said. "*You* get treatments, don't you? Then aren't *you*—"

"Reduced ones," Snowflake said.

"Yes, we get treatments," King said, "but we've managed to have them reduced, to have certain components of them reduced, so that we're a little more than the machines Uni thinks we are."

"And that's what we're offering *you,*" Snowflake said; "a way to see more and feel more and do more and enjoy more."

"And to be more unhappy; tell him that too." It was a new voice, soft but clear, the other young woman. She was across the table and to Chip's left, close to where King was.

"That isn't so," Snowflake said.

"Yes it is," the clear voice said—a girl's voice almost; she was no more than twenty, Chip guessed. "There'll be days when you'll *hate* Christ, Marx, Wood, and Wei," she said, "and want to take a torch to Uni. There'll be days when you'll want to tear off your bracelet and run to a mountaintop like the old incurables, just to be able to do what you want to do and make your own choices and live your own life."

"Lilac," Snowflake said.

"There'll be days when you'll hate *us,*" she said, "for waking you up and making you *not* a machine. Machines are at home in the universe; people are aliens."

"Lilac," Snowflake said, "we're trying to get Chip to join us; we're not trying to scare him away." To Chip she said, "Lilac is *really* abnormal."

"There's truth in what Lilac says," King said. "I think we all have moments when we wish there were someplace we could go, some settlement or colony where we could be our own masters—"

"Not me," Snowflake said.

"And since there isn't such a place," King said, "yes, we're sometimes unhappy. Not you, Snowflake; I know. With rare exceptions like Snowflake, being able to feel happiness seems to mean being able to feel *un*happiness as well. But as Sparrow said, any feeling is better and healthier than none at all; and the unhappy moments aren't that frequent, really."

"They are," Lilac said.

"Oh, cloth," Snowflake said. "Let's *stop* all this talk about unhappiness."

"Don't worry, Snowflake," the woman across the table, Sparrow, said; "if he gets up and runs you can trip him."

"Ha, ha, hate, hate," Snowflake said.

"Snowflake, Sparrow," King said. "Well, Chip, what's your answer? Do you want to get your treatments reduced? It's done by steps; the first one is easy, and if you don't like the way you feel a month from now, you can go to your adviser and tell him you were infected by a group of very sick members whom you unfortunately can't identify."

After a moment Chip said, "All right. What do I do?" His arm was squeezed by Snowflake. "Good," Hush whispered.

"Just a moment, I'm lighting my pipe," King said.

"Are you all smoking?" Chip asked. The burning smell was intense, drying and stinging his nostrils.

"Not right now," Hush said. "Only King, Lilac, and Leopard."

"We've all *been* doing it though," Snowflake said. "It's not a continuous thing; you do it awhile and then stop awhile."

"Where do you get the tobacco?"

"We grow it," Leopard said, sounding pleased. "Hush and I. In parkland."

"In *parkland?*"

"That's right," Leopard said.

"We have two patches," Hush said, "and last Sunday we found a place for a third."

"Chip?" King said, and Chip turned toward him and listened. "Basically, step one is just a matter of acting as if you're being *over*treated," King said; "slowing down at work, at games, at everything—slowing down *slightly,* not conspicuously. Make a small mistake at your work, and another one a few days later. And don't do well at sex. The thing to do there is masturbate before you meet your girlfriend; that way you'll be able to fail convincingly."

"Masturbate?"

"Oh, fully treated, fully satisfied member," Snowflake said.

"Bring yourself to an orgasm with your hand," King said. "And then don't be too concerned when you don't have one later. Let your girlfriend tell *her* adviser; don't you tell yours. Don't be too concerned about anything, the mistakes you make, lateness for appointments or whatever; let others do the noticing and reporting."

"Pretend to doze off during TV," Sparrow said.

"You're ten days from your next treatment," King said. "At your next week's adviser meeting, if you've done what I've told you, your adviser will sound you out about your general torpor. Again, no concern on your part. Apathy. If you do the whole thing well, the depressants in your treatment will be slightly reduced, enough so that a month from now you'll be anxious to hear about step two."

"It sounds easy enough," Chip said.

"It is," Snowflake said, and Leopard said, "We've all done it; you can too."

"There's one danger," King said. "Even though your treatment may be slightly weaker than usual, its effects in the first few days will still be strong. You'll feel a revulsion against what you've done and an urge to confess to your adviser and get stronger treatments than ever. There's no way of telling whether or not you'll be able to resist the urge. We did, but others haven't. In the past year we've given this talk to two other members; they did the slowdown but then confessed within a day or two after being treated."

"Then won't my adviser be suspicious when I do the slowdown? He must have heard about those others."

"Yes," King said, "but there are legitimate slowdowns, when a member's need for depressants has lessened, so if you do the job convincingly you'll get away with it. It's the urge to confess that you have to worry about."

"Keep telling yourself"—it was Lilac speaking—"that it's a chemical that's making you think you're sick and in need of help, a chemical that was infused into you without your consent."

"My consent?" Chip said.

"Yes," she said. "Your body is yours, not Uni's."

"Whether you'll confess or hold out," King said, "depends on how strong your mind's resistance is to chemical alteration, and there's not much you can do about it one way or the other. On the basis of what we know of you, I'd say you have a good chance."

They gave him some more pointers on slowdown technique—to skip his midday cake once or twice, to go to bed before the last chime—and then King suggested that Snowflake take him back to where they had met. "I hope we'll be seeing you again, Chip," he said. "Without the bandage."

"I hope so," Chip said. He stood and pushed back his chair. "Good luck," Hush said; Sparrow and Leopard said it too. Lilac said it last: "Good luck, Chip."

"What happens," he asked, "if I resist the urge to confess?"

"We'll know," King said, "and one of us will get in touch with you about ten days after the treatment."

"How will you know?"

"We'll know."

His arm was taken by Snowflake's hand. "All right," he said. "Thank you, all of you."

They said "Don't mention it," and "You're welcome, Chip," and "Glad to be of help." Something sounded strange, and then—as Snowflake led him from the room—he realized what it was: the not-being-said of "Thank Uni."

They walked slowly, Snowflake holding his arm not like a nurse but like a girl walking with her first boyfriend.

"It's hard to believe," he said, "that what I can feel now and see now—isn't all there is."

"It isn't," she said. "Not even half. You'll find out."

"I hope so."

"You will. I'm sure of it."

He smiled and said, "Were you sure about those two who tried and didn't make it?"

"No," she said. Then, "Yes, I was sure of one, but not of the other."

"What's step two?" he asked.

"First get through step one."

"Are there more than two?"

"No. Two, if it works, gets you a major reduction. That's when you *really* come alive. And speaking of steps, there are three right ahead of us, going up."

They went up the three steps and walked on. They were back in the plaza. It was perfectly silent, with even the breeze gone.

"The fucking's the best part," Snowflake said. "It gets much better, much more intense and exciting, and you'll be able to do it almost every night."

"It's incredible."

"And please remember," she said, "that I'm the one who found you. If I catch you even *looking* at Sparrow I'll kill you."

Chip started, and told himself not to be foolish.

"Excuse me," she said; "I'll act aggressively toward you. Maxi-aggressively."

"It's all right," he said. "I'm not shocked."

"Not much."

"What about Lilac?" he said. "May I look at her?"

"All you want; she loves King."

"Oh?"

"With a pre-U passion. He's the one who started the group; first her, then Leopard and Hush, then me, then Sparrow."

Their footsteps became louder and resonant. She stopped him. "We're here," she said. He felt her fingers picking at the side of the bandage; he lowered his head. She began unwinding, peeling bandage from margins of skin that turned instantly cool. She unwound more and more and finally took the cotton from his eyes. He blinked them and stretched them wide.

She was close to him and moonlit, looking at him in a way that seemed challenging while she thrust bandage into her medicenter coveralls. Somehow she had got her pale mask back on—but it wasn't a mask, he saw with a shock; it was her face. She was light. Lighter than any member he had ever seen, except a few near-sixty ones. She was almost white. Almost as white as snow.

"Mask neatly in place," she said.

"I'm sorry," he said.

"That's all right," she said, and smiled. "We're all odd in one way or another. Look at that eye." She was thirty-five or so, sharp-featured and intelligent-looking, her hair freshly clipped.

"I'm sorry," he said again.

"I said it's all right."

"Are you supposed to let me see what you look like?"

"I'll tell you something," she said. "If you don't come through I don't give a fight if the whole bunch of us get normalized. In fact, I think I'd prefer it." She took his head in both hands and kissed him, her tongue prying at his lips. It slid in and flickered in his mouth. She held his head tight, pushed her groin against his, and rubbed circularly. He felt a responsive stiffening and put his hands to her back. He worked his tongue tentatively against hers.

She withdrew her mouth. "Considering that it's the middle of the week," she said, "I'm encouraged."

"Christ, Marx, Wood, and Wei," he said. "Is that how you *all* kiss?"

"Only me, brother," she said, "only me."

They did it again.

"Go on home now," she said. "Don't touch scanners."

He backed away from her. "I'll see you next month," he said.

"You fighting well better had," she said. "Good luck."

He went out into the plaza and headed toward the Institute. He looked back once. There was only empty passageway between the blank moon-white buildings.

Two

Bob RO, seated behind his desk, looked up and smiled. "You're late," he said.

"I'm sorry," Chip said. He sat down.

Bob closed a white folder with a red file tab on it. "How are you?" he asked.

"Fine," Chip said.

"Have a good week?"

"Mm-hmm."

Bob studied him for a moment, his elbow on his chair arm, his fingers rubbing the side of his nose. "Anything in particular you want to talk about?" he asked.

Chip was silent, and then shook his head. "No," he said.

"I hear you spent half of yesterday afternoon doing somebody else's work."

Chip nodded. "I took a sample from the wrong section of the IC box," he said.

"I see," Bob said, and smiled and grunted.

Chip looked questioningly at him.

"Joke," Bob said. "IC, I see."

"Oh," Chip said, and smiled.

Bob propped his jaw on his hand, the side of a finger lying against his lips. "What happened Friday?" he asked.

"Friday?"

"Something about using the wrong microscope."

Chip looked puzzled for a moment. "Oh," he said. "Yes. I didn't really use it. I just went into the chamber. I didn't change any of the settings."

Bob said, "It looks like it *wasn't* such a good week."

"No, I guess it wasn't," Chip said.

"Peace SK says you had trouble Saturday night."

"Trouble?"

"Sexually."

Chip shook his head. "I didn't have any trouble," he said. "I just wasn't in the mood, that's all."

"She says you tried and couldn't erect."

"Well I felt I *ought* to do it, for *her* sake, but I just wasn't in the mood."

Bob watched him, not saying anything.

"I was tired," Chip said.

"It seems you've been tired a lot lately. Is that why you weren't at your photography club meeting Friday night?"

"Yes," he said. "I turned in early."

"How do you feel now? Are you tired now?"

"No. I feel fine."

Bob looked at him, then straightened in his chair and smiled. "Okay, brother," he said, "touch and go."

Chip put his bracelet to the scanner of Bob's telecomp and stood up.

"See you next week," Bob said.

"Yes."

"On time."

Chip, having turned away, turned back and said, "Beg pardon?"

"On time next week," Bob said.

"Oh," Chip said. "Yes." He turned and went out of the cubicle.

He thought he had done it well but there was no way of knowing, and as his treatment came nearer he grew increasingly anxious. The thought of a significant rise in sensation became more intriguing by the hour, and Snowflake, King, Lilac, and the others became more attractive and admirable. So what if they smoked tobacco? They were happy and healthy members—no, *people,* not members!—who had found an escape from sterility and sameness and universal mechanical efficiency. He wanted to see them and be with them. He wanted to kiss and embrace Snowflake's unique lightness; to talk with King as an equal, friend to friend; to hear more of Lilac's strange but provocative ideas. "Your body is yours, not Uni's"—what a disturbing pre-U thing to say! If there were any basis for it, it could have implications that might lead him to—he couldn't think what; a jolting change of some sort in his attitude toward everything!

That was the night before his treatment. He lay awake for hours, then climbed with bandaged hands up a snow-covered mountaintop, smoked to-bacco pleasurably under the guidance of a friendly smiling King, opened

Snowflake's coveralls and found her snow-white with a throat-to-groin red cross, drove an early wheel-steered car through the hallways of a huge Genetic Suffocation Center, and had a new bracelet inscribed *Chip* and a window in his room through which he watched a lovely nude girl watering a lilac bush. She beckoned impatiently and he went to her—and woke feeling fresh and energetic and cheerful, despite those dreams, more vivid and convincing than any of the five or six he had had in the past.

That morning, a Friday, he had his treatment. The tickle-buzz-sting seemed to last a fraction of a second less than usual, and when he left the unit, pushing down his sleeve, he still felt good and himself, a dreamer of vivid dreams, a cohort of unusual people, an outwitter of Family and Uni. He walked falsely-slowly to the Center. It struck him that this of all times was when he should go on with the slowdown, to justify the even greater reduction that step two, whatever it was and whenever he took it, would be aimed at achieving. He was pleased with himself for having realized this, and wondered why King and the others hadn't suggested it. Perhaps they had thought he wouldn't be able to do anything after his treatment. Those other two members had apparently fallen apart completely, unlucky brothers.

He made a good small mistake that afternoon, started to type a report with the mike held wrong-side up while another 663B was looking. He felt a bit guilty about doing it, but he did it anyway.

That evening, to his surprise, he really dozed off during TV, although it was something fairly interesting, a tour of a new radio telescope in Isr. And later, during the house photography club meeting, he could hardly keep his eyes open. He excused himself early and went to his room. He undressed without bothering to chute his used coveralls, got into bed without putting on pajamas, and tapped out the light. He wondered what dreams he would have.

He woke feeling frightened, suspecting that he was sick and in need of help. What was wrong? Had he done something he shouldn't have?

It came to him, and he shook his head, scarcely able to believe it. Was it real? Was it possible? Had he been so—so contaminated by that group of pitiably sick members that he had purposely made mistakes, had tried to deceive Bob RO (and maybe succeeded!), had thought thoughts hostile to his entire loving Family? Oh, Christ, Marx, Wood, and Wei!

He thought of what the young one, "Lilac," had told him: to remember that it was a chemical that was making him think he was sick, a chemical that had been infused into him without his consent. His consent! As if *consent* had anything to do with a treatment given to preserve one's health and well-being, an integral part of the health and well-being of the entire Family! Even before the Unification, even in the chaos and madness of the twentieth century, a member's consent wasn't asked before he was treated against typhic or typho or whatever it was. Consent! And he had listened without challenging her!

The first chime sounded and he jumped from his bed, anxious to make up for his unthinkable wrongs. He chuted the day-before's coveralls, urined, washed, cleaned his teeth, evened up his hair, put on fresh coveralls, made his bed. He went to the dining hall and claimed his cake and tea, sat among other members and wanted to help them, to give them something, to demonstrate that he was loyal and loving, not the sick offender he had been the day before. The member on his left ate the last of his cake. "Would you like some of mine?" Chip asked.

The member looked embarrassed. "No, of course not," he said. "But thanks, you're very kind."

"No I'm not," Chip said, but he was glad the member had said he was.

He hurried to the Center and got there eight minutes early. He drew a sample from his own section of the IC box, not somebody else's, and took it into his own microscope; put on his glasses the right way and followed the OMP to the letter. He drew data from Uni respectfully *(Forgive my offenses, Uni who knows everything)* and fed it new data humbly *(Here is exact and truthful information about gene sample NF5049).*

The section head looked in. "How's it going?" he asked.

"Very well, Bob."

"Good."

At midday he felt worse, though. What about *them,* those sick ones? Was he to leave them to their sickness, their tobacco, their reduced treatments, their pre-U thoughts? He had no choice. They had bandaged his eyes. There was no way of finding them.

But that wasn't so; there *was* a way. Snowflake had shown him her face. How many almost-white members, women of her age, could there be in the city? Three? Four? Five? Uni, if Bob RO asked it, could output their namebers in an instant. And when she was found and properly treated, she would give the namebers of some of the others; and they, the namebers of the ones remaining. The whole group could be found and helped within a day or two.

The way he had helped Karl.

That stopped him. He had helped Karl and felt guilt—guilt he had clung to for years and years, and now it persisted, a part of him. Oh Jesus Christ and Wei Li Chun, how sick beyond imagining he was!

"Are you all right, brother?"

It was the member across the table, an elderly woman. "Yes," he said, "I'm fine," and smiled and put his cake to his lips.

"You looked so *troubled* for a second," she said.

"I'm fine," he said. "I thought of something I forgot to do."

"Ah," she said.

To help them or not to help them? Which was wrong, which was right? He *knew* which was wrong: not to help them, to abandon them as if he weren't his brother's keeper at all.

But he wasn't sure that helping them wasn't wrong too, and how could both be wrong?

He worked less zealously in the afternoon, but well and without mistakes, everything done properly. At the end of the day he went back to his room and lay on his back on his bed, the heels of his hands pressing into his shut eyes and making pulsing auroras there. He heard the voices of the sick ones, saw himself taking the sample from the wrong section of the box and cheating the Family of time and energy and equipment. The supper chime sounded but he stayed as he was, too tangled in himself for eating.

Later Peace SK called. "I'm in the lounge," she said. "It's ten of eight. I've been waiting twenty minutes."

"I'm sorry," he said. "I'll be right down."

They went to a concert and then to her room.

"What's the *matter?*" she said.

"I don't know," he said. "I've been—upset the last few days."

She shook her head and plied his slack penis more briskly. "It doesn't make sense," she said. "Didn't you tell your adviser? I told mine."

"Yes, I did. Look"—he took her hand away—"a whole group of new members came in on sixteen the other day. Why don't you go to the lounge and find somebody else?"

She looked unhappy. "Well I think I ought to," she said.

"I do too," he said. "Go ahead."

"It just doesn't make any sense," she said, getting up from the bed.

He dressed and went back to his room and undressed again. He thought he would have trouble falling asleep but he didn't.

On Sunday he felt even worse. He began to hope that Bob would call, would see that he wasn't well and draw the truth out of him. That way there would be no guilt or responsibility, only relief. He stayed in his room, watching the phone screen. Someone on the soccer team called; he said he wasn't feeling well.

At noon he went to the dining hall, ate a cake quickly, and returned to his room. Someone from the Center called, to find out if he knew someone else's nameber.

Hadn't Bob been told by now that he wasn't acting normally? Hadn't Peace said anything? Or the caller from the soccer team? And that member across the table at lunch yesterday, hadn't she been smart enough to see through his excuse and get his nameber? (Look at him, expecting others to help *him;* who in the Family was he helping?) Where *was* Bob? What kind of adviser was he?

There were no more calls, not in the afternoon, not in the evening. The music stopped once for a starship bulletin.

Monday morning, after breakfast, he went down to the medicenter. The scanner said *no,* but he told the attendant that he wanted to see his adviser; the attendant telecomped, and then the scanners said *yes, yes, yes,* all the way into the advisory offices, which were half empty. It was only 7:50.

He went into Bob's empty cubicle and sat down and waited for him, his hands on his knees. He went over in his mind the order in which he would tell: first about the intentional slowdown; then about the group, what they said and did and the way they could all be found through Snowflake's lightness; and finally about the sick and irrational guilt-feeling he had concealed all the years since he had helped Karl. One, two, three. He would get an extra treatment to make up for anything he mightn't have got on Friday, and he would leave the medicenter sound in mind and sound in body, a healthy contented member.

Your body is yours, not Uni's.

Sick, pre-U. Uni was the will and wisdom of the entire Family. It had *made* him; had granted him his food, his clothing, his housing, his training. It had granted even the permission for his very conception. Yes, it had made him, and from now on he would be—

Bob came in swinging his telecomp and stopped short. "Li," he said. "Hello. Is anything wrong?"

He looked at Bob. The *name* was wrong. He was Chip, not Li. He looked down at his bracelet: *Li RM35M4419.* He had expected it to say *Chip.* When had he had one that said *Chip?* In a dream, a strange happy dream, a girl beckoning . . .

"Li?" Bob said, putting his telecomp on the floor.

Uni had made him *Li.* For Wei. But he was Chip, chip off the old block. Which one was he? Li? Chip? Li?

"What is it, brother?" Bob asked, leaning close, taking his shoulder.

"I wanted to see you," he said.

"About what?"

He didn't know what to say. "You said I shouldn't be late," he said. He looked at Bob anxiously. "Am I on time?"

"On time?" Bob stepped back and squinted at him. "Brother, you're a day early," he said. "Tuesday's your day, not Monday."

He stood up. "I'm sorry," he said. "I'd better get over to the Center"—and started to go.

Bob caught his arm. "Hold on," he said, his telecomp falling on its side, slamming the floor.

"I'm all right," Chip said. "I got mixed up. I'll come tomorrow." He went from Bob's hand, out of the cubicle.

"Li," Bob called.

He kept going.

He watched TV attentively that evening—a track meet in Arg, a relay from Venus, the news, a dance program, and *Wei's Living Wisdom*—and then he went to his room. He tapped the light button but something was covering it and it didn't work. The door closed sharply, had been closed by someone who was near him in the dark, breathing. "Who is it?" he asked.

"King and Lilac," King said.

"What happened this morning?" Lilac asked, somewhere over by the desk. "Why did you go to your adviser?"

"To tell," he said.

"But you didn't."

"I should have," he said. "Get out of here, please."

"You see?" King said.

"We have to try," Lilac said.

"Please go," Chip said. "I don't want to get involved with you again, with any of you. I don't know what's right or wrong anymore. I don't even know who I am."

"You've got about ten hours to find out," King said. "Your adviser's coming here in the morning to take you to Medicenter Main. You're going to be examined there. It wasn't supposed to happen for three weeks or so, after some more slowing down. It would have been step two. But it's happening tomorrow, and it'll probably be step minus-one."

"It doesn't have to be, though," Lilac said. "You can still make it step two if you do what we tell you."

"I don't want to hear," he said. "Just go, please."

They didn't say anything. He heard King make a movement.

"Don't you understand?" Lilac said. "If you do what we tell you, your treatments will be reduced as much as ours are. If you don't, they'll be put back to where they were. In fact, they'll probably be increased beyond that, won't they, King?"

"Yes," King said.

"To 'protect' you," Lilac said. "So that you'll never again even *try* to get out from under. Don't you see, Chip?" Her voice came closer. "It's the only chance you'll ever have. For the rest of your life you'll be a machine."

"No, not a machine, a member," he said. "A healthy member doing his assignment; *helping* the Family, not cheating it."

"You're wasting your breath, Lilac," King said. "If it were a few days later you might be able to get through, but it's too soon."

"Why didn't you tell this morning?" Lilac asked him. "You went to your adviser; why didn't you tell? Others have."

"I was going to," he said.

"Why didn't you?"

He turned away from her voice. "He called me Li," he said. "And I thought I was Chip. Everything got—unsettled."

"But you *are* Chip," she said, coming still closer. "Someone with a name different from the nameber Uni gave him. Someone who thought of picking his own classification instead of letting Uni do it."

He moved away, perturbed, then turned and faced their dim coverall shapes —Lilac, small, opposite him and a couple of meters away; King to his right against the light-outlined door. *How can you speak against Uni?* he asked. "It's granted us everything!"

"Only what we've given it to grant us," Lilac said. "It's denied us a hundred times more."

"It let us be born!"

"How many," she said, "will it *not* let be born? Like your children. Like mine."

"What do you mean?" he said. "That anyone who *wants* children—should be allowed to have them?"

"Yes," she said. "That's what I mean."

Shaking his head, he backed to his bed and sat down. She came to him; crouched and put her hands on his knees. "Please, Chip," she said, "I shouldn't say such things when you're still the way you are, but please, please, believe me. Believe *us*. We are *not sick,* we are *healthy*. It's the world that's sick—with chemistry, and efficiency, and humility, and helpfulness. Do what we tell you. Become healthy. Please, Chip."

Her earnestness held him. He tried to see her face. "Why do you care so much?" he asked. Her hands on his knees were small and warm, and he felt an impulse to touch them, to cover them with his own. Faintly he found her eyes, large and less slanted than normal, unusual and lovely.

"There are so few of us," she said, "and I think that maybe, if there were more, we could do something; get away somehow and make a place for ourselves."

"Like the incurables," he said.

"That's what we learn to call them," she said. "Maybe they were really the unbeatables, the undruggables."

He looked at her, trying to see more of her face.

"We have some capsules," she said, "that will slow down your reflexes and lower your blood pressure, put things in your blood that will make it look as if your treatments are too strong. If you take them tomorrow morning, before your adviser comes, and if you behave at the medicenter as we tell you and answer certain questions as we tell you—then tomorrow will be step two, and you'll take it and be healthy."

"And unhappy," he said.

"Yes," she said, a smile coming into her voice, "unhappy too, though not as much as I said. I sometimes get carried away."

"About every five minutes," King said.

She took her hands from Chip's knees and stood up. "Will you?" she asked.

He wanted to say yes to her, but he wanted to say no too. He said, "Let me see the capsules."

King, coming forward, said, "You'll see them after we leave. They're in here." He put into Chip's hand a small smooth box. "The red one has to be taken tonight and the other two as soon as you get up."

"Where did you get them?"

"One of the group works in a medicenter."

"Decide," Lilac said. "Do you want to hear what to say and do?"

He shook the box but it made no sound. He looked at the two dim figures waiting before him. He nodded. "All right," he said.

They sat and spoke to him, Lilac on the bed beside him, King on the drawn-over desk chair. They told him about a trick of tensing his muscles before the metabolic examination and one of looking above the objective during the depth-perception test. They told him what to say to the doctor who had charge of him and the senior adviser who interviewed him. They told him about tricks that might be played on him: sudden sounds behind his back; being left all alone, but not really, with the doctor's report form conveniently at hand. Lilac did most of the talking. Twice she touched him, once on his leg and once on his forearm; and once, when her hand lay by his side, he brushed it with his own. Hers moved away in a movement that might have begun before the contact.

"That's terrifically important," King said.

"I'm sorry, what was that?"

"Don't ignore it completely," King said. "The report form."

"Notice it," Lilac said. "Glance at it and then act as if it really isn't worth the bother of picking up and reading. As if you don't care much one way or the other."

It was late when they finished; the last chime had sounded half an hour before. "We'd better go separately," King said. "You go first. Wait by the side of the building."

Lilac stood up and Chip stood too. Her hand found his. "I know you're going to make it, Chip," she said.

"I'll try," he said. "Thanks for coming."

"You're welcome," she said, and went to the door. He thought he would see her by the light in the hallway as she went out, but King got up and was in the way and the door closed.

They stood silently for a moment, he and King, facing each other.

"Don't forget," King said. "The red capsule now and the other two when you get up."

"Right," Chip said, feeling for the box in his pocket.

"You shouldn't have any trouble."

"I don't know; there's so much to remember."

They were silent again.

"Thank you very much, King," Chip said, holding out his hand in the darkness.

"You're a lucky man," King said. "Snowflake is a very passionate woman. You and she are going to have a lot of good times together."

Chip didn't understand why he had said that. "I hope so," he said. "It's hard to believe it's possible to have more than one orgasm a week."

"What we have to do now," King said, "is find a man for Sparrow. Then everyone will have someone. It's better that way. Four couples. No friction."

Chip lowered his hand. He suddenly felt that King was telling him to stay away from Lilac, was defining who belonged with whom and telling him to obey the definition. Had King somehow seen him touching Lilac's hand?

"I'm going now," King said. "Turn around, please."

Chip turned around and heard King moving away. The room appeared dimly as the door was opened, a shadow swept across it, and it disappeared again with the door's closing.

Chip turned. How strange it was to think of someone loving one member in particular so much as to want no one else to touch her! Would he be that way too if his treatments were reduced? It was—like so many other things—hard to believe.

He went to the light button and felt what was covering it: tape, with something square and flat underneath. He picked at the tape, peeled it away, and tapped the button. He shut his eyes against the ceiling's glare.

When he could see he looked at the tape; it was skin-colored, with a square of blue cardboard stuck to it. He dropped it down the chute and took the box from his pocket. It was white plastic with a hinged lid. He opened it. A red capsule, a white one, and one that was half white and half yellow lay bedded on a cotton filling.

He took the box into the bathroom and tapped on the light. Setting the open box on the edge of the sink, he turned on the water and pulled a cup from the slot and filled it. He turned the water off.

He started to think, but before he could think too much he picked up the red capsule, put it far back on his tongue, and drank the water.

Two doctors, not one, had charge of him. They led him in a pale blue smock from examination room to examination room, conferred with the examining doctors, conferred with each other, and made checks and notations on a clipboarded report form that they handed back and forth between them. One was a woman in her forties, the other a man in his thirties. The woman sometimes walked with her arm around Chip's shoulders, smiling and calling him "young brother." The man watched him impassively, with eyes that were smaller and set closer together than normal. He had a fresh scar on his cheek, running from the temple to the corner of his mouth, and dark bruises on his cheek and forehead. He never took his eyes off Chip except to look at the report form. Even when conferring with doctors he kept watching him. When the three of them walked to the next examination room he usually dropped behind Chip and the smiling woman doctor. Chip expected him to make a sudden sound, but he didn't.

The interview with the senior adviser, a young woman, went well, Chip thought, but nothing else did. He was afraid to tense his muscles before the metabolic examination because of the doctor watching him, and he forgot about looking above the objective in the depth-perception test until it was too late.

"Too bad you're missing a day's work," the watching doctor said.

"I'll make it up," he said, and realized as he said it that it was a mistake.

He should have said *It's all for the best* or *Will I be here all day?* or simply a dull overtreated *Yes*.

At midday he was given a glass of bitter white liquid to drink instead of a totalcake and then there were more tests and examinations. The woman doctor went away for half an hour but not the man.

Around three o'clock they seemed to be finished and went into a small office. The man sat down behind the desk and Chip sat opposite him. The woman said, "Excuse me, I'll be back in two seconds." She smiled at Chip and went out.

The man studied the report form for a minute or two, running a fingertip back and forth along his scar, and then he looked at the clock and put down the clipboard. "I'll go get her," he said, and got up and went out, closing the door partway.

Chip sat still and sniffed and looked at the clipboard. He leaned over, twisted his head, read on the report form the words *cholinesterase absorption factor, unamplified,* and sat back in his chair again. Had he looked too long?—he wasn't sure. He rubbed his thumb and examined it, then looked at the room's pictures, *Marx Writing* and *Wood Presenting the Unification Treaty.*

They came back in. The woman doctor sat down behind the desk and the man sat in a chair near her side. The woman looked at Chip. She wasn't smiling. She looked worried.

"Young brother," she said, "I'm worried about you. I think you've been trying to fool us."

Chip looked at her. "Fool you?" he said.

"There are sick members in this town," she said; "do you know that?"

He shook his head.

"Yes," she said. "As sick as can be. They cover members' eyes and take them someplace, and tell them to slow down and make mistakes and pretend they've lost their interest in sex. They try to make other members as sick as they are. Do you know any such members?"

"No," Chip said.

"Anna," the man said, "I've *watched* him. There's no reason to think there's anything wrong beyond what showed on the tests." He turned to Chip and said, "Very easily corrected; nothing for you to think about."

The woman shook her head. "No," she said. "No, it doesn't *feel* right. Please, young brother, you want us to help you, don't you?"

"Nobody told me to make mistakes," Chip said. "Why? Why should I?"

The man tapped the report form. "Look at the enzymological rundown," he said to the woman.

"I've looked at it, I've looked at it."

"He's been badly OT'ed there, there, there, and there. Let's give the data to Uni and get him fixed up again."

"I want Jesus HL to see him."

"Why?"

"Because I'm *worried.*"

"I don't know any sick members," Chip said. "If I did I would tell my adviser."

"Yes," the woman said, "and why did you want to see him yesterday morning?"

"Yesterday?" Chip said. "I thought it was my day. I got mixed up."

"Please, let's go," the woman said, standing up holding the clipboard.

They left the office and walked down the hallway outside it. The woman put her arm around Chip's shoulders but she didn't smile. The man dropped behind.

They came to the end of the hallway, where there was a door marked *600A* with a brown white-lettered plaque on it: *Chief, Chemotherapeutics Division.* They went in, to an anteroom where a member sat behind a desk. The woman doctor told her that they wanted to consult Jesus HL about a diagnostic problem, and the member got up and went out through another door.

"A waste of time all around," the man said.

The woman said, "Believe me, I hope so."

There were two chairs in the anteroom, a bare low table, and *Wei Addressing the Chemotherapists.* Chip decided that if they made him tell he would try not to mention Snowflake's light skin and Lilac's less-slanted-than-normal eyes.

The member came back and held the door open.

They went into a large office. A gaunt gray-haired member in his fifties— Jesus HL—was seated behind a large untidy desk. He nodded to the doctors as they approached, and looked absently at Chip. He waved a hand toward a chair facing the desk. Chip sat down in it.

The woman doctor handed Jesus HL the clipboard. "This doesn't feel right to me," she said. "I'm afraid he's malingering."

"Contrary to the enzymological evidence," the other doctor said.

Jesus HL leaned back in his chair and studied the report form. The doctors stood by the side of the desk, watching him. Chip tried to look curious but not concerned. He watched Jesus HL for a moment, and then looked at the desk. Papers of all sorts were piled and scattered on it and lay drifted over an old-style telecomp in a scuffed case. A drink container jammed with pens and rulers stood beside a framed snapshot of Jesus HL, younger, smiling in front of Uni's dome. There were two souvenir paperweights, an unusual square one from CHI61332 and a round one from ARG20400, neither of them on paper.

Jesus HL turned the clipboard end for end and peeled the form down and read the back of it.

"What I would like to do, Jesus," the woman doctor said, "is keep him here overnight and run some of the tests again tomorrow."

"Wasting—" the man said.

"Or better still," the woman said, louder, "question him now under TP."

"Wasting time and supplies," the man said.

"What are we, doctors or efficiency analyzers?" the woman asked him sharply.

Jesus HL put down the clipboard and looked at Chip. He got up from his chair and came around the side of the desk, the doctors stepping back quickly to let him pass. He came and stood directly in front of Chip's chair, tall and thin, his red-crossed coveralls stained with yellow spots.

He took Chip's hands from the chair arms, turned them over, and looked at the palms, which glistened with sweat.

He let one hand go and held the wrist of the other, his fingers at the pulse. Chip made himself look up, unconcernedly. Jesus HL looked quizzically at him for a moment and then suspected—no, *knew*—and smiled his knowledge contemptuously. Chip felt hollow, beaten.

Jesus HL took hold of Chip's chin, bent over, and looked closely at his eyes. "Open your eyes as wide as you can," he said. His voice was King's. Chip stared at him.

"That's right," he said. "Stare at me as if I've said something shocking." It was *King's voice,* unmistakable. Chip's mouth opened. "Don't speak, please," King-Jesus HL said, squeezing Chip's jaw painfully. He stared into Chip's eyes, turned his head to one side and then the other, and then released it and stepped back. He went back around the desk and sat down again. He picked up the clipboard, glanced at it, and handed it to the woman doctor, smiling. "You're mistaken, Anna," he said. "You can put your mind at rest. I've seen many members who were malingering; this one isn't. I commend you on your concern, though." To the man he said, "She's right, you know, Jesus; we mustn't be efficiency analyzers. The Family can afford a little waste where a member's health is involved. What *is* the Family, after all, except the sum of its members?"

"Thank you, Jesus," the woman said, smiling. "I'm glad I was wrong."

"Give that data to Uni," King said, turning and looking at Chip, "so our brother here can be properly treated from now on."

"Yes, right away." The woman beckoned to Chip. He got up from the chair. They left the office. In the doorway Chip turned. "Thank you," he said.

King looked at him from behind his littered desk—only looked, with no smile, no glimmer of friendship. "Thank Uni," he said.

Less than a minute after he got back to his room Bob called. "I just got a report from Medicenter Main," he said. "Your treatments have been slightly out of line but from now on they're going to be exactly right."

"Good," Chip said.

"This confusion and tiredness you've been feeling will gradually pass away during the next week or so, and then you'll be your old self."

"I hope so."

"You will. Listen, do you want me to squeeze you in tomorrow, Li, or shall we just let it go till next Tuesday?"

"Next Tuesday's all right."

"Fine," Bob said. He grinned. "You know what?" he said. "You look better already."

"I feel a little better," Chip said.

Three

He felt a little better every day, a little more awake and alert, a little more sure that sickness was what he had had and health was what he was growing toward. By Friday—three days after the examination—he felt the way he usually felt on the day before a treatment. But his last treatment was only a week behind him; three weeks and more lay ahead, spacious and unexplored, before the next one. The slowdown had worked; Bob had been fooled and the treatment reduced. And the next one, on the basis of the examination, would be reduced even further. What wonders of feeling would he be feeling in five, in six weeks' time?

That Friday night, a few minutes after the last chime, Snowflake came into his room. "Don't mind me," she said, taking off her coveralls. "I'm just putting a note in your mouthpiece."

She got into bed with him and helped him off with his pajamas. Her body to his hands and lips was smooth, pliant, and more arousing than Peace SK's or anyone else's; and his own, as she stroked and kissed and licked it, was more shudderingly reactive than ever before, more strainingly in want. He eased himself into her—deeply, snugly in—and would have driven them both to immediate orgasm, but she slowed him, stopped him, made him draw out and come in again, putting herself into one strange but effective position and then another. For twenty minutes or more they worked and contrived together, keeping as noiseless as they could because of the members beyond the wall and on the floor below.

When they were done and apart she said, "Well?"

"Well it was top speed, of course," he said, "but frankly, from what you said, I expected even more."

"Patience, brother," she said. "You're still an invalid. The time will come when you'll look back on this as the night we shook hands."

He laughed.

"Shh."

He held her and kissed her. "What does it say?" he asked. "The note in my mouthpiece."

"Sunday night at eleven, the same place as last time."

"But no bandage."

"No bandage," she said.

He would see them all, Lilac and all the others. "I've been wondering when the next meeting would be," he said.

"I hear you whooshed through step two like a rocket."

"Stumbled through it, you mean. I wouldn't have made it at all if not for—" Did she know who King really was? Was it all right to speak of it?

"If not for what?"

"If not for King and Lilac," he said. "They came here the night before and prepped me."

"Well of course," she said. "*None* of us would have made it if not for the capsules and all."

"I wonder where they get them."

"I think one of them works in a medicenter."

"Mm, that would explain it," he said. She didn't know. Or she knew but didn't know that *he* knew. Suddenly he was annoyed by the need for carefulness that had come between them.

She sat up. "Listen," she said, "it pains me to say this, but don't forget to carry on as usual with your girlfriend. Tomorrow night, I mean."

"She's got someone new," he said. "You're my girlfriend."

"No I'm not," she said. "Not on Saturday nights anyway. Our advisers would wonder why we took someone from a different house. I've got a nice normal Bob down the hall from me, and you find a nice normal Yin or Mary. But if you give her more than a little quick one I'll break your neck."

"Tomorrow night I won't even be able to give her that."

"That's all right," she said, "you're still supposed to be recovering." She looked sternly at him. "Really," she said, "you have to remember not to get too passionate, except with me. And to keep a contented smile in place between the first chime and the last. And to work hard at your assignment but not *too* hard. It's just as tricky to *stay* undertreated as it is to get that way." She lay back down beside him and drew his arm around her. "Hate," she said, "I'd give anything for a smoke now."

"Is it really so enjoyable?"

"Mm-hmm. Especially at times like this."

"I'll have to try it."

They lay talking and caressing each other for a while, and then Snowflake tried to rouse him again—"Nothing ventured, nothing gained," she said—but everything she did proved unavailing. She left around twelve or so. "Sunday at eleven," she said by the door. "Congratulations."

Saturday evening in the lounge Chip met a member named Mary KK whose boyfriend had been transferred to Can earlier in the week. The birth-year part of her nameber was 38, making her twenty-four.

They went to a pre-Marxmas sing in Equality Park. As they sat waiting for the amphitheater to fill, Chip looked at Mary closely. Her chin was sharp but otherwise she was normal: tan skin, upslanted brown eyes, clipped black hair, yellow coveralls on her slim spare frame. One of her toenails, half covered by a sandal strap, was discolored a bluish purple. She sat smiling, watching the opposite side of the amphitheater.

"Where are you from?" he asked her.

"Rus," she said.

"What's your classification?"

"One-forty B."

"What's that?"

"Ophthalmologic technician."

"What do you do?"

She turned to him. "I attach lenses," she said. "In the children's section."

"Do you enjoy it?"

"Of course." She looked uncertainly at him. "Why are you asking me so many questions?" she asked. "And why are you looking at me so—as if you've never seen a member before?"

"I've never seen *you* before," he said. "I want to know you."

"I'm no different from any other member," she said. "There's nothing unusual about me."

"Your chin is a little sharper than normal."

She drew back, looking hurt and confused.

"I didn't mean to hurt you," he said. "I just meant to point out that there *is* something unusual about you, even if it isn't something important."

She looked searchingly at him, then looked away, at the opposite side of the amphitheater again. She shook her head. "I don't understand you," she said.

"I'm sorry," he said. "I was sick until last Tuesday. But my adviser took me to Medicenter Main and they fixed me up fine. I'm getting better now. Don't worry."

"Well *that's* good," she said. After a moment she turned and smiled cheerfully at him. "I forgive you," she said.

"Thank you," he said, suddenly feeling sad for her.

She looked away again. "I hope we sing 'The Freeing of the Masses,'" she said.

"We will," he said.

"I love it," she said, and smiling, began to hum it.

He kept looking at her, trying to do so in a normal-seeming way. What she had said was true: she was no different from any other member. What did a sharp chin or a discolored toenail signify? She was exactly the same as every Mary and Anna and Peace and Yin who had ever been his girlfriend: humble and good, helpful and hard-working. Yet she made him feel sad. Why? And could all the others have done so, had he looked at them as closely as he was looking at her, had he listened as closely to what they said?

He looked at the members on the other side of him, at the scores in the tiers below, the scores in the tiers above. They were all like Mary KK, all smiling and ready to sing their favorite Marxmas songs, and all saddening; everyone in the amphitheater, the hundreds, the thousands, the tens of thousands. Their faces lined the mammoth bowl like tan beads strung away in immeasurable close-laid ovals.

Spotlights struck the gold cross and red sickle at the bowl's center. Four familiar trumpet notes blasted, and everybody sang:

> One mighty Family,
> A single perfect breed,
> Free of all selfishness,
> Aggressiveness and greed;
> Each member giv-ing all he has to give
> And get-ting all he needs to live!

But they weren't a mighty Family, he thought. They were a weak Family, a saddening and pitiable one, dulled by chemicals and dehumanized by bracelets. It was Uni that was mighty.

> One mighty Family,
> A single noble race,
> Sending its sons and daughters
> Bravely into space . . .

He sang the words automatically, thinking that Lilac had been right: reduced treatments brought new unhappiness.

Sunday night at eleven he met Snowflake between the buildings on Lower Christ Plaza. He held her and kissed her gratefully, glad of her sexuality and humor and pale skin and bitter tobacco taste—all the things that were she and nobody else. "Christ and Wei, I'm glad to see you," he said.

She gave him a tighter hug and smiled happily at him. "It gets to be a shut-off being with normals, doesn't it?" she said.

"And how," he said. "I wanted to kick the soccer team instead of the ball this morning."

She laughed.

He had been depressed since the sing; now he felt released and happy and taller. "I found a girlfriend," he said, "and guess what; I fucked her without the least bit of trouble."

"Hate."

"Not as extensively or as satisfyingly as we did, but with no trouble at all, not twenty-four hours later."

"I can live without the details."

He grinned and ran his hands down her sides and clasped her hipbones. "I think I might even manage to do it again tonight," he said, teasing her with his thumbs.

"Your ego is growing by leaps and bounds."

"My everything is."

"Come on, brother," she said, prying his hands away and holding onto one, "we'd better get you indoors before you start singing."

They went into the plaza and crossed it diagonally. Flags and sagging Marxmas bunting hung motionless above it, dim in the glow of distant walkways. "Where are we going anyway?" he asked, walking happily. "Where's the secret meeting place of the diseased corrupters of healthy young members?"

"The Pre-U," she said.

"The *Museum?*"

"That's right. Can you think of a better place for a group of Uni-cheating abnormals? It's exactly where we belong. Easy," she said, tugging at his hand; "don't walk so energetically."

A member was coming into the plaza from the walkway they were going toward. A briefcase or telecomp was in his hand.

Chip walked more normally alongside Snowflake. The member, coming closer—it was a telecomp he had—smiled and nodded. They smiled and nodded in return as they passed him.

They went down steps and out of the plaza.

"Besides," Snowflake said, "it's empty from eight to eight and it's an endless source of pipes and funny costumes and unusual beds."

"You take things?"

"We leave the beds," she said. "But we make use of them now and again. Meeting solemnly in the staff conference room was just for your benefit."

"What else do you do?"

"Oh, sit around and complain a little. That's Lilac and Leopard's department mostly. Sex and smoking is enough for me. King does funny versions of some of the TV programs; wait till you find out how much you can laugh."

"The making use of the beds," Chip said; "is it done on a group basis?"

"Only by twos, dear; we're not *that* pre-U."

"Who did *you* use them with?"

"Sparrow, obviously. Necessity is the mother of et cetera. Poor girl, I feel sorry for her now."

"Of course you do."

"I do! Oh well, there's an artificial penis in Nineteenth Century Artifacts. She'll survive."

"King says we should find a man for her."

"We should. It would be a much better situation, having four couples."

"That's what King said."

As they were crossing the ground floor of the museum—lighting their way through the strange-figured dark with a flashlight that Snowflake had produced—another light struck them from the side and a voice nearby said, "Hello there!" They started. "I'm sorry," the voice said. "It's me, Leopard."

Snowflake swung her light onto the twentieth-century car, and a flashlight inside it went off. They went over to the glinting metal vehicle. Leopard, sitting behind the steering wheel, was an old round-faced member wearing a hat with an orange plume. There were several dark brown spots on his nose and cheeks. He put his hand, also spotted, through the car's window frame. "Congratulations, Chip," he said. "I'm glad you came through."

Chip shook his hand and thanked him.

"Going for a ride?" Snowflake asked.

"I've been for one," he said. "To Jap and back. Volvo's out of fuel now. And thoroughly wet too, come to think of it."

They smiled at him and at each other.

"Fantastic, isn't it?" he said, turning the wheel and working a lever that projected from its shaft. "The driver was in complete control from start to finish, using both hands and both feet."

"It must have been awfully bumpy," Chip said, and Snowflake said, "Not to mention dangerous."

"But fun too," Leopard said. "It must have been an adventure, really; choosing your destination, figuring out which roads to take to get there, gauging your movements in relation to the movements of other cars—"

"Gauging wrong and dying," Snowflake said.

"I don't think that really happened as often as we're told it did," Leopard said. "If it had, they would have made the front parts of the cars much thicker."

Chip said, "But that would have made them heavier and they would have gone even slower."

"Where's Hush?" Snowflake asked.

"Upstairs with Sparrow," Leopard said. He opened the car's door, and coming out of it with a flashlight in his hand, said, "They're setting things up. Some more stuff was put in the room." He cranked the window of the door halfway up and closed the door firmly. A wide brown belt decorated with metal studs was fastened about his coveralls.

"King and Lilac?" Snowflake asked.

"They're around someplace."

Chip thought, *Making use of one of the beds*—as the three of them went on through the museum.

He had thought about King and Lilac a good deal since seeing King and seeing how old he was—fifty-two or -three or even more. He had thought about the difference between the ages of the two—thirty years, surely, at the very least—and about the way King had told him to stay away from Lilac; and about Lilac's large less-slanted-than-normal eyes and her hands that had rested small and warm on his knees as she crouched before him urging him toward greater life and awareness.

They went up the steps of the unmoving central escalator and across the museum's second floor. The two flashlights, Snowflake's and Leopard's, danced over the guns and daggers, the bulbed and wired lamps, the bleeding boxers, the kings and queens in their jewels and fur-trimmed robes, and the three beggars, filthy and crippled, parading their disfigurements and thrusting out their cups. The partition behind the beggars had been slid aside, opening a narrow passageway that extended farther into the building, its first few meters lit by light from a doorway in the left-hand wall. A woman's voice spoke softly. Leopard went on ahead and through the doorway, while Snowflake, standing beside the beggars, sprung pieces of tape from a first-aid-kit cartridge. "Snowflake's here with Chip," Leopard said inside the room. Chip laid a piece of tape over his bracelet plaque and rubbed it down firmly.

They went to the doorway and into a tobacco-smelling stuffiness where an old woman and a young one sat close together on pre-U chairs with two knives and a heap of brown leaves on a table before them. Hush and Sparrow; they shook Chip's hand and congratulated him. Hush was crinkle-eyed and smiling; Sparrow, large-limbed and embarrassed-looking, her hand hot and moist. Leopard stood by Hush, holding a heat coil in the bowl of a curved black pipe and blowing out smoke around the sides of its stem.

The room, a fairly large one, was a storeroom, its farther reaches filled with a ceiling-high mass of pre-U relics, late and early: machines and furniture and paintings and bundles of clothing; swords and wood-handled implements; a statue of a member with wings, an "angel"; half a dozen crates, opened, unopened, stenciled IND26110 and pasted at their corners with square yellow stickers. Looking around, Chip said, "There are enough things here for another museum."

"All genuine too," Leopard said. "Some of the things on display aren't you know."

"I didn't."

A varied lot of chairs and benches had been set about the forward part of the room. Paintings leaned against the walls, and there were cartons of smaller relics and piles of moldering books. A painting of an enormous boulder caught Chip's eye. He moved a chair to get a full view of it. The boulder, a mountain almost, floated above the earth in blue sky, meticulously painted and jarring to the senses. "What an odd picture," he said.

"A lot of them are odd," Leopard said.

"The ones of Christ," Hush said, "show him with a light around his head, and he doesn't look human at all."

"I've seen those," Chip said, looking at the boulder, "but I've never seen anything like this. It's fascinating; real and unreal at the same time."

"You can't take it," Snowflake said. "We can't take anything that might be missed."

Chip said, "There's no place I could put it anyway."

"How do you like being undertreated?" Sparrow asked.

Chip turned. Sparrow looked away, at her hands holding a roll of leaves and a knife. Hush was at the same task, chopping rapidly at a roll of leaves, cutting it into thin shreds that piled before her knife. Snowflake was sitting with a pipe in her mouth; Leopard was holding the heat coil in the bowl of it. "It's wonderful," Chip said. "Literally. Full of wonders. More of them every day. I'm grateful to all of you."

"We only did what we're told to," Leopard said, smiling. "We helped a brother."

"Not exactly in the approved way," Chip said.

Snowflake offered him her pipe. "Are you ready to try a puff?" she asked.

He went to her and took it. The bowl of it was warm, the tobacco in it gray and smoking. He hesitated for a moment, smiled at them watching him, and put the stem to his lips. He sucked briefly at it and blew out smoke. The taste was strong but pleasant, surprisingly so. "Not bad," he said. He did it again with more assurance. Some of the smoke went into his throat and he coughed.

Leopard, going smiling to the doorway, said, "I'll get you one of your own," and went out.

Chip returned the pipe to Snowflake and, clearing his throat, sat down on a bench of dark worn wood. He watched Hush and Sparrow cutting the tobacco. Hush smiled at him. He said, "Where do you get the seeds?"

"From the plants themselves," she said.

"Where did you get the ones you started with?"

"King had them."

"What did I have?" King asked, coming in, tall and lean and bright-eyed, a gold medallion chain-hung on his coveralled chest. He had Lilac behind him, his hand holding hers. Chip stood up. She looked at him, unusual, dark, beautiful, young.

"The tobacco seeds," Hush said.

King offered his hand to Chip, smiling warmly. "It's good to see you here," he said. Chip shook his hand; its grip was firm and hearty. "Really good to see a new face in the group," King said. "Especially a male one, to help me keep these pre-U women in their proper place!"

"Huh," Snowflake said.

"It's good to be here," Chip said, pleased by King's friendliness. His coldness when Chip left his office must have been only a pretense, for the sake, of course, of the onlooking doctors. "Thank you," Chip said. "For everything. Both of you."

Lilac said, "I'm very glad, Chip." Her hand was still held by King's. She was darker than normal, a lovely near-brown touched with rose. Her eyes were large and almost level, her lips pink and soft-looking. She turned away and said, "Hello, Snowflake." She drew her hand from King's and went to Snowflake and kissed her cheek.

She was twenty or twenty-one, no more. The upper pockets of her coveralls had something in them, giving her the breasted look of the women Karl had drawn. It was a strange, mysteriously alluring look.

"Are you beginning to feel different now, Chip?" King asked. He was at the table, bending and putting tobacco into the bowl of a pipe.

"Yes, enormously," Chip said. "It's everything you said it would be."

Leopard came in and said, "Here you are, Chip." He gave him a yellow thick-bowled pipe with an amber stem. Chip thanked him and tried the feel of it; it was comfortable in his hand and comfortable to his lips. He took it to the table, and King, his gold medallion swinging, showed him the right way to fill it.

Leopard took him through the staff section of the museum, showing him other storerooms, the conference room, and various offices and workrooms. "It's a good idea," he said, "for someone to keep rough track of who goes where during these get-togethers, and then check around later and make sure nothing is conspicuously out of place. The girls could be a little more careful than they are. I generally do it, and when I'm gone perhaps you'll take over the job. Normals aren't quite as unobservant as we'd like them to be."

"Are you being transferred?" Chip asked.

"Oh no," Leopard said. "I'll be dying soon. I'm over sixty-two now, by almost three months. So is Hush."

"I'm sorry," Chip said.

"So are we," Leopard said, "but nobody lives forever. Tobacco ashes are a danger, of course, but everyone's good about that. You don't have to worry about the smell; the air conditioning goes on at seven-forty and whips it right out; I stayed one morning and made sure. Sparrow's going to take over the tobacco growing. We dry the leaves right here, in back of the hot-water tank; I'll show you."

When they got back to the storeroom, King and Snowflake were sitting opposite each other astride a bench, playing intently at a mechanical game of some kind that lay between them. Hush was dozing in her chair and Lilac was crouched at the verge of the mass of relics, taking books one at a time from a carton, looking at them, and putting them in a pile on the floor. Sparrow wasn't there.

"What's that?" Leopard asked.

"New game that came in," Snowflake said, not looking up.

There were levers that they pressed and released, one for each hand, making little paddles hit a rusted ball back and forth on a rimmed metal board. The paddles, some of them broken, squeaked as they swung. The ball bounded this way and that and came to a stop in a depression at King's end of the board. "Five!" Snowflake cried. "There you are, brother!"

Hush opened her eyes, looked at them, and closed them again.

"Losing's the same as winning," King said, lighting his pipe with a metal lighter.

"Like hate it is," Snowflake said. "Chip? Come on, you're next."

"No, I'll watch," he said, smiling.

Leopard declined to play too, and King and Snowflake began another match. At a break in the play, when King had scored a point against Snowflake, Chip said, "May I see the lighter?" and King gave it to him. A bird in flight was painted on the side of it; a duck, Chip thought. He had seen lighters in museums but had never worked one. He opened the hinged top and pushed his thumb against the ridged wheel. On the second try the wick flamed. He closed the lighter, looked at it all over, and at the next break handed it back to King.

He watched them play for another few moments and then moved away. He went over to the mass of relics and looked at it, and then moved nearer to Lilac. She looked up at him and smiled, putting a book on one of several piles beside her. "I keep hoping to find one in the language," she said, "but they're always in the old ones."

He crouched and picked up the book she had just put down. On the spine of it were small letters: *Bädda för död.* "Hmm," he said, shaking his head. He glanced through the old brown pages, at strange words and phrases: *allvarlig, lögnerska, dök ner på brickorna.* The double dots and little circles were over many of the letters.

"Some of them are enough like the language so that you can understand a word or two," she said, "but some of them are—well look at this one." She showed him a book on which backward *N*'s and rectangular open-bottomed characters were mixed in with ordinary *P*'s and *E*'s and *O*'s. "Now what does *that* mean?" she said, putting it down.

"It would be interesting to find one we could read," he said, looking at her cheek's rose-brown smoothness.

"Yes, it would," she said, "but I think they were screened before they were sent here and that's why we can't."

"You think they were screened?"

"There ought to be lots of them in the language," she said. "How could it have *become* the language if it wasn't the one most widely used?"

"Yes, of course," he said. "You're right."

"I keep hoping, though," she said, "that there was a slip in the screening." She frowned at a book and put it on a pile.

Her filled pockets stirred with her movements, and suddenly they looked to Chip like empty pockets lying against round breasts, breasts like the ones Karl had drawn; the breasts, almost, of a pre-U woman. It was possible, considering her abnormal darkness and the various physical abnormalities of the lot of them. He looked at her face again, so as not to embarrass her if she really had them.

"I thought I was double-checking this carton," she said, "but I have a funny feeling I'm triple-checking it."

"But *why* should the books have been screened?" he asked her.

She paused, with her dark hands hanging empty and her elbows on her knees, looking at him gravely with her large, level eyes. "I think we've been taught things that aren't true," she said. "About the way life was before the Unification. In the *late* pre-U, I mean, not the early."

"What things?"

"The violence, the aggressiveness, the greed, the hostility. There was some of it, I suppose, but I can't believe there was nothing else, and that's what we're taught, really. And the 'bosses' punishing the 'workers,' and all the sickness and alcohol-drinking and starvation and self-destruction. Do *you* believe it?"

He looked at her. "I don't know," he said. "I haven't thought much about it."

"I'll tell you what *I* don't believe," Snowflake said. She had risen from the bench, the game with King evidently finished. "*I* don't believe that they cut off the baby boys' foreskins," she said. "In the early pre-U, maybe—in the early, *early* pre-U—but not in the late; it's just too incredible. I mean, they had *some* kind of intelligence, didn't they?"

"It's incredible, all right," King said, hitting his pipe against his palm, "but I've seen photographs. Alleged photographs, anyway."

Chip shifted around and sat on the floor. "What do you mean?" he said. "Can photographs be—not genuine?"

"Of course they can," Lilac said. "Take a close look at some of the ones inside. Parts of them have been drawn in. And parts have been drawn out." She began putting books back into the carton.

"I had no idea that was possible," Chip said.

"It is with the flat ones," King said.

"What we're probably given," Leopard said—he was sitting in a gilded chair, toying with the orange plume of the hat he had worn—"is a mixture of truth and untruth. It's anybody's guess as to which part is which and how much there is of each."

"Couldn't we study these books and learn the languages?" Chip asked. "One would be all we'd really need."

"For what?" Snowflake asked.

"To find out," he said. "What's true and what isn't."

"I tried it," Lilac said.

"She certainly did," King said to Chip, smiling. "A while back she wasted more nights than I care to remember beating her pretty head against one of those nonsensical jumbles. Don't *you* do it, Chip; I beg you."

"Why not?" Chip asked. "Maybe I'll have better luck."

"And suppose you do?" King said. "Suppose you decipher a language and read a few books in it and find out that we *are* taught things that are untrue. Maybe *everything's* untrue. Maybe life in 2000 A.D. was one endless orgasm, with everyone choosing the right classification and helping his brothers and loaded to the ears with love and health and life's necessities. So what? You'll still be right here, in 162 Y.U., with a bracelet and an adviser and a monthly treatment. You'll only be unhappier. We'll *all* be unhappier."

Chip frowned and looked at Lilac. She was packing books into the carton, not looking at him. He looked back at King and sought words. "It would still be worth knowing," he said. "Being happy or unhappy—is that really the most important thing? Knowing the truth would be a different kind of happiness— a more satisfying kind, I think, even if it turned out to be a sad kind."

"A sad kind of happiness?" King said, smiling. "I don't see that at all." Leopard looked thoughtful.

Snowflake, gesturing to Chip to get up, said, "Come on, there's something I want to show you."

He climbed to his feet. "But we'd probably only find that things have been exaggerated," he said; "that there was hunger but not so *much* hunger, aggressiveness but not so *much* aggressiveness. Maybe some of the minor things have been made up, like the foreskin-cutting and the flag-worship."

"If you feel that way, then there's *certainly* no point in bothering," King said. "Do you have any idea what a job it would be? It would be staggering."

Chip shrugged. "It would be good to *know,* that's all," he said. He looked at Lilac; she was putting the last few books into the carton.

"Come on," Snowflake said, and took his arm. "Save us some tobacco, you mems."

They went out and into the dark of the exhibit hall. Snowflake's flashlight lit their way. "What is it?" Chip asked. "What do you want to show me?"

"What do you think?" she said. "A bed. Certainly not more books."

They generally met two nights a week, Sundays and Woodsdays or Thursdays. They smoked and talked and idled with relics and exhibits. Sometimes Sparrow sang songs that she wrote, accompanying herself on a lap-held instrument whose strings at her fingers made pleasing antique music. The songs were short and sad, about children who lived and died on starships, lovers who were transferred, the eternal sea. Sometimes King reenacted the evening's TV, comically mocking a lecturer on climate control or a fifty-member chorus singing "My Bracelet." Chip and Snowflake made use of the seventeenth-century bed and the nineteenth-century sofa, the early pre-U farm wagon and the late pre-U plastic rug. On nights between meetings they sometimes went to one or the other's room. The nameber on Snowflake's door was Anna PY24A9155; the 24, which Chip couldn't resist working out, made her thirty-eight, older than he had thought her to be.

Day by day his senses sharpened and his mind grew more alert and restless. His treatment caught him back and dulled him, but only for a week or so; then he was awake again, alive again. He went to work on the language Lilac had tried to decipher. She showed him the books she had worked from and the lists she had made. *Momento* was moment; *silenzio,* silence. She had several pages of easily recognized translations; but there were words in the books' every sentence that could only be guessed at and the guesses tried elsewhere. Was *allora* "then" or "already"? What were *quale* and *sporse* and *rimanesse?* He worked with the books for an hour or so at every meeting. Sometimes she leaned over his shoulder and looked at what he was doing—said "Oh, of course!" or "Couldn't that be one of the days of the week?"—but most of the time she stayed near King, filling his pipe for him and listening while he talked. King watched Chip working and, reflected in glass panes of pre-U furniture, smiled at the others and raised his eyebrows.

Chip saw Mary KK on Saturday nights and Sunday afternoons. He acted normal with her, smiled through the Amusement Gardens and fucked her simply and without passion. He acted normal at his assignment, slowly following the established procedures. Acting normal began to irritate him, more and more as week followed week.

In July, Hush died. Sparrow wrote a song about her, and when Chip returned to his room after the meeting at which she had sung it, she and Karl (Why hadn't he thought of him sooner?) suddenly came together in his mind. Sparrow was large and awkward but lovely when she sang, twenty-five or so and lonely. Karl presumably had been "cured" when Chip "helped" him, but might he not have had the strength or the genetic capacity or the whatever-it-was to resist the cure, at least to a degree? Like Chip he was a 663; there was a chance that he was right there at the Institute somewhere, an ideal prospect for being led into the group and an ideal match for Sparrow. It was certainly worth a try. What a pleasure it would be to *really* help Karl! Undertreated, he would draw—well what *wouldn't* he draw?—pictures such as no one had ever imagined! As soon as he got up the next morning he got his last nameber book out of his take-along kit, touched the phone, and read out Karl's nameber. But the screen stayed blank and the phone voice apologized; the member he had called was out of reach.

Bob RO asked him about it a few days later, just as he was getting up from the chair. "Oh, say," Bob said, "I meant to ask you; how come you wanted to call this Karl WL?"

"Oh," Chip said, standing by the chair. "I wanted to see how he was. Now that *I'm* all right, I guess I want to be sure that everyone else is."

"Of course he is," Bob said. "It's an odd thing to do, after so many years."

"I just happened to think of him," Chip said.

He acted normal from the first chime to the last and met with the group twice a week. He kept working at the language—Italiano, it was called—although he suspected that King was right and there was no point in it. It was something to do, though, and seemed more worthwhile than playing with mechanical toys. And once in a while it brought Lilac to him, leaning over to look, with one hand on the leather-topped table he worked at and the other on the back of his chair. He could smell her—it wasn't his imagination; she actually smelled of flowers—and he could look at her dark cheek and neck and the chest of her coveralls pushed taut by two mobile round protrusions. They were breasts. They were definitely breasts.

Four

One night late in August, while looking for more books in Italiano, he found one in a different language whose title, *Vers l'avenir,* was similar to the Italiano words *verso* and *avvenire* and apparently meant *Toward the Future.* He opened the book and thumbed its pages, and *Wei Li Chun* caught his eye, printed at the tops of twenty or thirty of them. Other names were at the tops of other clusters of pages, *Mario Sofik, A. F. Liebman.* The book, he realized, was a collection of short pieces by various writers, and two of the pieces were indeed by Wei. The title of one of them, *Le pas prochain en avant,* he recognized (*pas* would be *passo; avant, avanti*) as "The Next Step Forward," in Part One of *Wei's Living Wisdom.*

The value of what he had found, as he began to perceive it, held him motionless. Here in this small brown book, its cover clinging by threads, were twelve or fifteen pre-U-language pages of which he had an exact translation waiting in his night-table drawer. Thousands of words, of verbs in their bafflingly changing forms; instead of guessing and groping as he had done for his near-useless fragments of Italiano, he could gain a solid footing in this second language in a matter of hours!

He said nothing to the others; slipped the book into his pocket and joined them; filled his pipe as if nothing were out of the ordinary. *Le pas-*whatever-it-was-*avant* might not be "The Next Step Forward" after all. But it *was,* it had to be.

It was; he saw it as soon as he compared the first few sentences. He sat up in his room all that night, carefully reading and comparing, with one finger at the lines in the pre-U language and another at the lines translated. He worked his way two times through the fourteen-page essay, and then began making alphabetical word lists.

The next night he was tired and slept, but the following night, after a visit from Snowflake, he stayed up and worked again.

He began going to the museum on nights between meetings. There he could smoke while he worked, could look for other Français books—Français was the language's name; the hook below the *C* was a mystery—and could roam the halls by flashlight. On the third floor he found a map from 1951, artfully patched in several places, where Eur was "Europe," with the division called "France" where Français had been used, and all its strangely and appealingly named cities: "Paris" and "Nantes" and "Lyon" and "Marseille."

Still he said nothing to the others. He wanted to confound King with a language fully mastered, and delight Lilac. At meetings he no longer worked at Italiano. One night Lilac asked him about it, and he said, truthfully, that he had given up trying to unravel it. She turned away, looking disappointed, and he was happy, knowing the surprise he was preparing for her.

Saturday nights were wasted, lying by Mary KK, and meeting nights were wasted too; although now, with Hush dead, Leopard sometimes didn't come, and when he didn't, Chip stayed on at the museum to straighten up and stayed still later to work.

In three weeks he could read Français rapidly, with only a word here and there that was indecipherable. He found several Français books. He read one whose title, translated, was *The Purple Sickle Murders;* and another, *The Pygmies of the Equatorial Forest;* and another, *Father Goriot.*

He waited until a night when Leopard wasn't there, and then he told them. King looked as if he had heard bad news. His eyes measured Chip and his face was still and controlled, suddenly older and more gaunt. Lilac looked as if she had been given a longed-for gift. "You've read *books* in it?" she said. Her eyes were wide and shining and her lips stayed parted. But neither one's reaction could give Chip the pleasure he had looked forward to. He was grave with the weight of what he now knew.

"Three of them," he said to Lilac. "And I'm halfway through a fourth."

"That's marvelous, Chip!" Snowflake said. "What did you keep it a secret for?" And Sparrow said, "I didn't think it was possible."

"Congratulations, Chip," King said, taking out his pipe. "It's an achievement, even with the help of the essay. You've really put me in my place." He looked at his pipe, working the stem of it to get it straight. "What have you found out so far?" he asked. "Anything interesting?"

Chip looked at him. "Yes," he said. "A lot of what we're told is true. There was crime and violence and stupidity and hunger. There was a lock on every door. Flags were important, and the borders of territories. Children waited for their parents to die so they could inherit their money. The waste of labor and material was fantastic."

He looked at Lilac and smiled consolingly at her; her longed-for gift was breaking. "But with it all," he said, "members seem to have felt stronger and happier than we do. Going where they wanted, doing what they wanted, 'earning' things, 'owning' things, choosing, always choosing—it made them somehow more *alive* than members today."

King reached for tobacco. "Well that's pretty much what you expected to find, isn't it?" he said.

"Yes, pretty much," Chip said. "And there's one thing more."

"What's that?" Snowflake asked.

Looking at King, Chip said, "Hush didn't have to die."

King looked at him. The others did too. "What are you talking about?" King said, his fingers stopped in pipe-filling.

"Don't you know?" Chip asked him.

"No," he said. "I don't understand."

"What do you mean?" Lilac asked.

"Don't you know, King?" Chip said.

"*No,*" King said. "What are—I haven't the faintest idea of what you're getting at. How could pre-U books tell you anything about *Hush?* And why should I be expected to know what it is if they could?"

"Living to the age of sixty-two," Chip said, "is no marvel of chemistry and breeding and totalcakes. Pygmies of the equatorial forests, whose life was hard even by pre-U standards, lived to be fifty-five and sixty. A member named Goriot lived to seventy-three and nobody thought it was terribly unusual, and that was in the early nineteenth century. Members lived to their eighties, even to their nineties!"

"That's impossible," King said. "The body wouldn't last that long; the heart, the lungs—"

"The book I'm reading now," Chip said, "is about some members who lived in 1991. One of them has an artificial heart. He gave money to doctors and they put it into him in place of his own."

"Oh for—" King said. "Are you sure you really understand that Frandaze?"

"Fran*cais,*" Chip said. "Yes, I'm positive. Sixty-two isn't a long life; it's a relatively short one."

"But that's when we *die,*" Sparrow said. "Why *do* we, if it isn't—when we have to?"

"We *don't* die . . ." Lilac said, and looked from Chip to King.

"That's right," Chip said. "We're *made* to die. By Uni. It's programmed for efficiency, for efficiency first, last, and always. It's scanned all the data in its memory banks—which aren't the pretty pink toys you've seen if you've made the visit; they're ugly steel monsters—and it's decided that sixty-two is the optimum dying time, better than sixty-one or sixty-three and better than bothering with artificial hearts. If sixty-two isn't a new high in longevity that we're lucky to have reached—and it *isn't,* I *know* it isn't—then that's the only answer. Our replacements are trained and waiting, and off we go, a few months early or late so that everything isn't too suspiciously tidy. Just in case anyone is sick enough to be able to *feel* suspicion."

"Christ, Marx, Wood, and Wei," Snowflake said.

"Yes," Chip said. "Especially Wood and Wei."

"King?" Lilac said.

"I'm staggered," King said. "I see now, Chip, why you thought I'd know." To Snowflake and Sparrow he said, "Chip knows that I'm in chemotherapy."

"And don't you know?" Chip said.

"I don't."

"Is there or is there not a poison in the treatment units?" Chip asked. "You *must* know *that.*"

"Gently, brother, I'm an old member," King said. "There's no poison as such, no; but almost any compound in the setup *could* cause death if too much of it were infused."

"And you don't know how much of the compounds are infused when a member hits sixty-two?"

"No," King said. "Treatments are formulated by impulses that go directly from Uni to the units, and there's no way of monitoring them. I can *ask* Uni, of course, what any particular treatment consisted of or is going to consist of, but if what you're saying is true"—he smiled—"it's going to lie to me, isn't it?"

Chip drew a breath, and let it go. "Yes," he said.

"And when a member dies," Lilac said, "the symptoms are the ones of old age?"

"They're the ones I was *taught* are of old age," King said. "They could very well be the ones of something entirely different." He looked at Chip. "Have you found any medical books in that language?" he asked.

"No," Chip said.

King took out his lighter and thumbed it open. "It's possible," he said. "It's very possible. It never even crossed my mind. Members live to sixty-two; it used to be less, some day it'll be more; we have two eyes, two ears, one nose. Established facts." He lit the lighter and put the flame to his pipe.

"It *must* be true," Lilac said. "It's the final logical end of Wood's and Wei's thinking. Control everyone's life and you eventually get around to controlling everyone's death."

"It's awful," Sparrow said. "I'm glad Leopard's not here. Can you imagine how he'd feel? Not only Hush, but he himself any day now. We mustn't say anything to him; let him think it's going to happen naturally."

Snowflake looked bleakly at Chip. "What did you have to tell *us* for?" she said.

King said, "So that we can experience a happy kind of sadness. Or was it a sad kind of happiness, Chip?"

"I thought you would want to know," he said.

"Why?" Snowflake said. "What can we do about it? Complain to our advisers?"

"I'll tell you one thing we can do," Chip said. "Start getting more members into this group."

"Yes!" Lilac said.

"And where do we find them?" King said. "We can't just grab any Karl or Mary off the walkways, you know."

Chip said, "Do you mean to say that in your assignment you can't pull a print-out on local members with abnormal tendencies?"

"Not without giving Uni a good reason, I can't," King said. "One fuzzy move, brother, and the doctors will be examining *me.* Which would also mean, incidentally, that they'd be *re*examining *you.*"

"Other abnormals are around," Sparrow said. "*Somebody* writes 'Fight Uni' on the backs of buildings."

"We've got to figure out a way to get *them* to find *us,*" Chip said. "A signal of some kind."

"And then what?" King said. "What do we do when we're twenty or thirty strong? Claim a group visit and blow Uni to pieces?"

"The idea has occurred to me," Chip said.

"Chip!" Snowflake said. Lilac stared at him.

"First of all," King said, smiling, "It's impregnable. And second of all, most of us have already been there, so we wouldn't be granted another visit. Or would we *walk* from here to Eur? And what would we do with the world once everything was uncontrolled—once the factories were clogged and the cars had crashed and the chimes had all stopped chiming—get really pre-U and say a prayer for it?"

"If we could find members who know computer and microwave theory," Chip said, "members who know *Uni,* maybe we could work out a way to change its programming."

"*If* we could find those members," King said. "*If* we could get them with us. *If* we could get to EUR-zip-one. Don't you see what you're asking for? The impossible, that's all. *This* is why I told you not to waste time with those books. There's nothing we can do about *anything.* This is *Uni's world,* will you get that through your head? It was handed over to it fifty years ago, and it's going to do its assignment—spread the fighting Family through the fighting universe —and *we're* going to do *our* assignments, including dying at sixty-two and not missing TV. This is it right here, brother: all the freedom we can hope for— a pipe and a few jokes and some extra fucking. Let's not lose what we've got, all right?"

"But if we get other—"

"Sing a song, Sparrow," King said.

"I don't want to," she said.

"Sing a song!"

"All right, I will."

Chip glared at King and got up and strode from the room. He strode into the dark exhibit hall, banged his hip against hardness, and strode on, cursing. He went far from the passageway and the storeroom; stood rubbing his forehead and rocking on the balls of his feet before the jewel-glinting kings and queens, mute darker-than-darkness watchers. "King," he said. "Thinks he really *is*, the brother-fighting . . ."

Sparrow's singing came faintly, and the string-tinkle of her pre-U instrument. And footsteps, coming closer. "Chip?" It was Snowflake. He didn't turn. His arm was touched. "Come on back," she said.

"Leave me alone, will you?" he said. "Just leave me alone for a couple of minutes."

"Come on," she said. "You're being childish."

"Look," he said, turning to her. "Go listen to Sparrow, will you? Go smoke your pipe."

She was silent, and then said, "All right," and went away.

He turned back to the kings and queens, breathing deeply. His hip hurt and he rubbed it. It was infuriating the way King cut off his every idea, made everyone do exactly as he—

She was coming back. He started to tell her to get the hate away but checked himself. He took a clenched-teeth breath and turned around.

It was King coming toward him, his gray hair and coveralls catching the dim glow from the passageway. He came close and stopped. They looked at each other, and King said, "I didn't intend to speak quite that sharply."

"How come you haven't taken one of these crowns?" Chip asked. "And a robe. Just that medallion—hate, that's not enough for a real pre-U king."

King stayed silent for a moment, and then said, "My apologies."

Chip drew a breath and held it, then let it go. "Every member we can get to join us," he said, "would mean new ideas, new information we can draw on, possibilities that maybe we haven't thought of."

"New risks too," King said. "Try to see it from my viewpoint."

"I can't," Chip said. "I'd rather go back to full treatments than settle for just this."

" 'Just this' seems very nice to a member my age."

"You're twenty or thirty years closer to sixty-two than I am; *you* should be the one who wants to change things."

"If change were possible, maybe I would be," King said. "But chemotherapy plus computerization equals no change."

"Not necessarily," Chip said.

"It does," King said, "and I don't want to see 'just this' go down the drain. Even your coming here on off nights is an added risk. But don't take offense" —he raised a hand—"I'm not telling you to stay away."

"I'm not going to," Chip said; and then, "Don't worry, I'm careful."

"Good," King said. "And we'll go on carefully looking for abnormals. Without signals." He held out his hand.

After a moment Chip shook it.

"Come on back in now," King said. "The girls are upset."

Chip went with him toward the passageway.

"What was that you said before, about the memory banks being 'steel monsters'?" King asked.

"That's what they are," Chip said. "Enormous frozen blocks, thousands of them. My grandfather showed them to me when I was a boy. He helped build Uni."

"The brother-fighter."

"No, he was sorry. He wished he hadn't. Christ and Wei, if he were alive he'd be a marvelous member to have with us."

The following night Chip was sitting in the storeroom reading and smoking when "Hello, Chip," Lilac said, and was standing in the doorway with a flashlight at her side.

Chip stood up, looking at her.

"Do you mind my interrupting you?" she asked.

"Of course not, I'm glad to see you," he said. "Is King here?"

"No," she said.

"Come on in," he said.

She stayed in the doorway. "I want you to teach me that language," she said.

"I'd like to," he said. "I was going to ask you if you wanted the lists. Come on in."

He watched her come in, then found his pipe in his hand, put it down, and went to the mass of relics. Catching the legs of one of the chairs they used, he tossed it right side up and brought it back to the table. She had pocketed her flashlight and was looking at the open pages of the book he had been reading. He put the chair down, moved his chair to the side, and put the second chair next to it.

She turned up the front part of the book and looked at its cover.

"It means *A Motive for Passion*," he said. "Which is fairly obvious. Most of it isn't."

She looked at the open pages again. "Some of it looks like Italiano," she said.

"That's how I got onto it," he said. He held the back of the chair he had brought for her.

"I've been sitting all day," she said. "You sit down. Go ahead."

He sat and got his folded lists out from under the stacked Français books. "You can keep these as long as you want," he said, opening them and spreading them out on the table. "I know it all pretty well by heart now."

He showed her the way the verbs fell into groups, following different patterns of change to express time and subject, and the way the adjectives took one form or another depending on the nouns they were applied to. "It's complicated," he said, "but once you get the hang of it, translation's fairly easy." He translated a page of *A Motive for Passion* for her. Victor, a trader in shares of various industrial companies—the member who had had the artificial heart put into him—was rebuking his wife, Caroline, for having been unfriendly to an influential lawmaker.

"It's fascinating," Lilac said.

"What amazes me," Chip said, "is how many non-productive members there were. These share-traders and lawmakers; the soldiers and policemen, bankers, tax-gatherers . . ."

"They weren't non-productive," she said. "They didn't produce *things* but they made it possible for members to live the way they did. They produced the *freedom,* or at least they maintained it."

"Yes," he said. "I suppose you're right."

"I am," she said, and moved restlessly from the table.

He thought for a moment. "Pre-U members," he said, "gave up efficiency —in exchange for freedom. And we've done the reverse."

"*We* haven't done it," Lilac said. "It was done *for* us." She turned and faced him, and said, "Do you think it's possible that the incurables are still alive?"

He looked at her.

"That their descendants have survived somehow," she said, "and have a— a society somewhere? On an island or in some area that the Family isn't using?"

"Wow," he said, and rubbed his forehead. "Sure it's possible," he said. "Members survived on islands *before* the Unification; why not after?"

"That's what *I* think," she said, coming back to him. "There have been five generations since the last ones—"

"Battered by disease and hardship—"

"But reproducing at will!"

"I don't know about a *society,*" he said, "but there might be a colony—"

"A city," she said. "They were the smart ones, the strong ones."

"What an idea," he said.

"It's possible, isn't it?" She was leaning toward him, hands on the table, her large eyes questioning, her cheeks flushed to a rosier darkness.

He looked at her. "What does King think?" he asked. She drew back a bit and he said, "As if I can't guess."

She was angry suddenly, fierce-eyed. "You were *terrible* to him last night!" she said.

"Terrible? *I* was? To *him?*"

"Yes!" She whirled from the table. "You questioned him as if you were— How could you even *think* he would know about Uni killing us and not tell us?"

"I still think he knew."

She faced him angrily. "He didn't!" she said. "He doesn't keep secrets from me!"

"What are you, his adviser?"

"Yes!" she said. "That's *exactly* what I am, in case you want to know."

"You're not," he said.

"I am."

"Christ and Wei," he said. "You really are? You're an adviser? That's the *last classification* I would have thought of. How *old* are you?"

"Twenty-four."

"And you're *his?*"

She nodded.

He laughed. "I decided that you worked in the gardens," he said. "You smell of flowers, do you know that? You really do."

"I wear perfume," she said.

"You *wear* it?"

"The perfume of flowers, in a liquid. King made it for me."

He stared at her. "Parfum!" he said, slapping the open book before him. "I thought it was some kind of germicide; she put it in her bath. Of course!" He groped among the lists, took up his pen, crossed out and wrote. "Stupid," he said. "*Parfum* equals *perfume*. Flowers in a liquid. How did he do *that?*"

"Don't accuse him of deceiving us."

"All right, I won't." He put the pen down.

"Everything we've got," she said, "we owe to him."

"What is it though?" he said. "Nothing—unless we use it to try for more. And he doesn't seem to want us to."

"He's more sensible than we are."

He looked at her, standing a few meters away from him before the mass of relics. "What would you do," he asked, "if we somehow found that there *is* a city of incurables?"

Her eyes stayed on his. "Get to it," she said.

"And live on plants and animals?"

"If necessary." She glanced at the book, moved her head toward it. "Victor and Caroline seem to have enjoyed their dinner."

He smiled and said, "You really are a pre-U woman, aren't you?"

She said nothing.

"Would you let me see your breasts?" he asked.

"What for?" she said.

"I'm curious, that's all."

She pulled open the top of her coveralls and held the two sides apart. Her breasts were rose-brown soft-looking cones that stirred with her breathing, taut on their upper surfaces and rounded below. Their tips, blunt and pink, seemed to contract and grow darker as he looked at them. He felt oddly aroused, as if he were being caressed.

"They're nice," he said.

"I know they are," she said, closing her coveralls and pressing the closure. "That's something else I owe King. I used to think I was the ugliest member in the entire Family."

"You?"

"Until he convinced me I wasn't."

"All right," he said, "you owe King very much. We all do. What have you come to *me* for?"

"I *told* you," she said. "To learn that language."

"Cloth," he said, getting up. "You want me to start looking for places the Family isn't using, for signs that your 'city' exists. Because I'll do it and he won't; because *I'm* not 'sensible,' or old, or content to make fun of TV."

She started for the door but he caught her by the shoulder and pushed her around. "Stay here!" he said. She looked frightenedly at him and he took hold of her jaw and kissed her mouth; clamped her head in both his hands and pushed his tongue against her shut teeth. She pressed at his chest and wrenched her head. He thought she would stop, give in and take the kiss, but she didn't; she kept struggling with increasing vigor, and finally he let go and she pushed away from him.

"That's—that's *terrible!*" she said. "Forcing me! That's—I've never been *held* that way!"

"I love you," he said.

"Look at me, I'm shaking," she said. "Wei Li Chun, is *that* how you love, by becoming an animal? That's *awful!*"

"A human," he said, "like you."

"No," she said. "I wouldn't hurt anyone, hold anyone that way!" She held her jaw and moved it.

"How do you think incurables kiss?" he said.

"Like humans, not like animals."

"I'm sorry," he said. "I love you."

"Good," she said. "I love you too—the way I love Leopard and Snowflake and Sparrow."

"That's not what I mean," he said.

"But it's what *I* mean," she said, looking at him. She went sideways to the doorway and said, "Don't do that again. That's terrible!"

"Do you want the lists?" he asked.

She looked as if she was going to say no, hesitated, and then said, "Yes. That's what I came for."

He turned and gathered the lists on the table, folded them together, and took *Père Goriot* from the stack of books. She came over and he gave them to her.

"I didn't mean to hurt you," he said.

"All right," she said. "Just don't do it again."

"I'll look for places the Family isn't using," he said. "I'll go over the maps at the MFA and see if—"

"I've done that," she said.

"Carefully?"

"As carefully as I could."

"I'll do it again," he said. "It's the only way to begin. Millimeter by millimeter."

"All right," she said.

"Wait a second, I'm going now too."

She waited while he put away his smoking things and got the room back the way it belonged, and then they went out together through the exhibit hall and down the escalator.

"A city of incurables," he said.

"It's possible," she said.

"It's worth looking for anyway," he said.

They went out onto the walkway.

"Which way do you go?" he asked.

"West," she said.

"I'll go a few blocks with you."

"No," she said. "Really, the longer you're out, the more chances there are for someone to see you not touching."

"I touch the rim of the scanner and block it with my body. Very tricky."

"No," she said. "Please, go your own way."

"All right," he said. "Good night."

"Good night."

He put his hand on her shoulder and kissed her cheek.

She didn't move away; she was tense and waiting under his hand.

He kissed her lips. They were warm and soft, slightly parted, and she turned and walked away.

"Lilac," he said, and went after her.

She turned and said, "No. Please, Chip, go," and turned and walked away again.

He stood uncertainly. Another member was in the distance, coming toward them.

He watched her go, hating her, loving her.

Five

Evening after evening he ate quickly (but not *too* quickly), then railed to the Museum of the Family's Achievements and studied its maze of ceiling-high illuminated maps until the ten-of-TV closing. One night he went there after the last chime—an hour-and-a-half walk—but found that the maps were unreadable by flashlight, their markings lost in glare; and he hesitated to put on their internal lights, which, tied in as they seemed to be with the lighting of the entire hall, might have produced a Uni-alerting overdraft of power. One Sunday he took Mary KK there, sent her off to see the Universe of Tomorrow exhibit, and studied the maps for three hours straight.

He found nothing: no island without its city or industrial installation; no mountaintop that wasn't a spacewatch or climatonomy center; no square kilometer of land—or of ocean floor, for that matter—that wasn't being mined or harvested or used for factories or houses or airports or parkland by the Family's eight billion. The gold-lettered legend suspended at the entrance of the map area—*The Earth Is Our Heritage; We Use It Wisely and Without Waste*—seemed true, so true that there was no place left for even the smallest non-Family community.

Leopard died and Sparrow sang. King sat silently, picking at the gears of a pre-U gadget, and Snowflake wanted more sex.

Chip said to Lilac, "Nothing. Nothing at all."

"There must have been hundreds of little colonies to begin with," she said. "One of them *must* have survived."

"Then it's half a dozen members in a cave somewhere," he said.

"Please, keep looking," she said. "You can't have checked *every* island."

He thought about it, sitting in the dark in the twentieth-century car, holding its steering wheel, moving its different knobs and levers; and the more he thought about it, the less possible a city or even a colony of incurables came to seem. Even if he had overlooked an unused area on the maps, could a community exist without Uni learning of it? People made marks on their environment; a thousand people, even a hundred, would raise an area's temperature, soil its streams with their wastes, and its air perhaps with their primitive fires. The land or sea for kilometers around would be affected by their presence in a dozen detectable ways.

So Uni would have long since known of the theoretical city's existence, and having known, would have—done what? Dispatched doctors and advisers and portable treatment units; would have "cured" the incurables and made them into "healthy" members.

Unless, of course, they had defended themselves . . . Their ancestors had fled the Family soon after the Unification, when treatments were optional, or later, when they were compulsory but not yet at present-day effectiveness; surely some of *those* incurables must have defended their retreats by force, with deadly weapons. Wouldn't they have handed on the practice, and the weapons too, to succeeding generations? What would Uni do today, in 162, facing an armed, defensive community with an unarmed, unaggressive Family? What would it have done five or twenty-five years ago, detecting the signs of it? Let it be? Leave its inhabitants to their "sickness" and their few square kilometers of the world? Spray the city with LPK? But what if the city's weapons could bring down planes? Would Uni decide in its cold steel blocks that the cost of the "cure" outweighed its usefulness?

He was two days from a treatment, his mind as active as it ever got. He wished it could get still more active. He felt that there was something he wasn't thinking of, just beyond the rim of his awareness.

If Uni let the city be, rather than sacrifice members and time and technology to the "helping" of it—then *what?* There was *something else,* a next idea to be picked and pried out of that one.

He called the medicenter on Thursday, the day before his treatment, and complained of a toothache. He was offered a Friday-morning appointment, but he said that he was coming in on Saturday morning for his treatment and couldn't he catch two birds with one net? It wasn't a severe toothache, just a slight throb.

He was given an appointment for Saturday morning at 8:15.

Then he called Bob RO and told him that he had a dental appointment at 8:15 on Saturday. Did he think it would be a good idea if he got his treatment then too? Catch two birds with one net.

"I guess you might as well," Bob said. "Hold on"—and switched on his telecomp. "You're Li RM—"

"Thirty-five M4419."

"Right," Bob said, tapping keys.

Chip sat and watched unconcernedly.

"Saturday morning at 8:05," Bob said.

"Fine," Chip said. "Thanks."

"Thank Uni," Bob said.

Which gave him a day longer between treatments than he'd had before.

That night, Thursday, was a rain night, and he stayed in his room. He sat at his desk with his forehead on his fists, thinking, wishing he were in the museum and able to smoke.

If a city of incurables existed, and Uni knew about it and was leaving it to its armed defenders—then—then—

Then Uni wasn't letting the Family know—and be troubled or in some instances tempted—*and it was feeding concealing data to the mapmaking equipment.*

Of course! How could supposedly unused areas be shown on beautiful Family maps? "But look at that place there, Daddy!" a child visiting the MFA exclaims. "Why aren't we Using Our Heritage Wisely and Without Waste?" And Daddy replies, "Yes, that *is* odd . . ." So the city would be labeled IND99999 or Enormous Desk Lamp Factory, and no one would ever be passed within five kilometers of it. If it were an island it wouldn't be shown at all; blue ocean would replace it.

And looking at maps was therefore useless. There could be cities of incurables here, there, everywhere. Or—there could be none at all. The maps proved or disproved nothing.

Was this the great revelation he had racked his brain for—that his map-examining had been stupidity from the beginning? That there was no way at all of finding the city, except possibly by walking everywhere on Earth?

Fight Lilac, with her maddening ideas!

No, not really.

Fight *Uni.*

For half an hour he drove his mind against the problem—how do you find a theoretical city in an untravelable world?—and finally he gave up and went to bed.

He thought then of Lilac, of the kiss she had resisted and the kiss she had allowed, and of the strange arousal he had felt when she showed him her soft-looking conical breasts . . .

On Friday he was tense and on edge. Acting normal was unendurable; he held his breath all day long at the Center, and through dinner, TV, and Photography Club. After the last chime he walked to Snowflake's building— "Ow," she said, "I'm not going to be able to *move* tomorrow!"—and then to the Pre-U. He circled the halls by flashlight, unable to put the idea aside. The city might exist, it might even be somewhere near. He looked at the money display and the prisoner in his cell *(The two of us, brother)* and the locks and the flat-picture cameras.

There was *one* answer that he could see, but it involved getting dozens of members into the group. Each could then check out the maps according to his own limited knowledge. He himself, for instance, could verify the genetics labs and research centers and the cities he had seen or heard spoken of by other members. Lilac could verify the advisory establishments and other cities . . . But it would take forever, and an army of undertreated accomplices. He could hear King raging.

He looked at the 1951 map, and marveled as he always did at the strange names and the intricate networks of borders. Yet members then could go where they wanted, more or less! Thin shadows moved in response to his light at the edges of the map's neat patches, cut to fit precisely into the crosslines of the grid. If not for the moving flashlight the blue rectangles would have been com—

Blue rectangles . . .

If the city were an island it wouldn't be shown; blue ocean would replace it.

And would have to replace it on pre-U maps as well.

He didn't let himself get excited. He moved the flashlight slowly back and forth over the glass-covered map and counted the shadow-moving patches. There were eight of them, all blue. All in the oceans, evenly distributed. Five of them covered single rectangles of the grid, and three covered pairs of rectangles. One of the one-rectangle patches was right there off Ind, in "Bay of Bengal"—Stability Bay.

He put the flashlight on a display case and took hold of the wide map by both sides of its frame. He lifted it free of its hook, lowered it to the floor, leaned its glassed face against his knee, and took up the flashlight again.

The frame was old, but its gray-paper backing looked relatively new. The letters *EV* were stamped at the bottom of it.

He carried the map by its wire across the hall, down the escalator, across the second-floor hall, and into the storeroom. Tapping on the light, he brought the map to the table and laid it carefully face-down.

With the corner of a fingernail he tore the taut paper backing along the bottom and sides of the frame, pulled it out from under the wire, and pressed it back so that it stayed. White cardboard lay in the frame, pinned down by ranks of short brads.

He searched in the cartons of smaller relics until he found a rusted pair of pincers with a yellow sticker around one handle. He used the pincers to pull the brads from the frame, then lifted out the cardboard and another piece of cardboard that lay beneath it.

The back of the map was brown-blotched but untorn, with no holes that would have justified the patching. A line of brown writing was faintly visible: *Wyndham, MU 7-2161*—some kind of early nameber.

He picked at the map's edges and lifted it from the glass, turned it over and raised it sagging above his head against the white light of the ceiling. Islands showed through all the patches: here a large one, "Madagascar"; here a cluster of small ones, "Azores." The patch in Stability Bay showed a line of four small ones, "Andaman Islands." He remembered none of the patch-covered islands from the maps at the MFA.

He put the map back down in the frame, face-up, and leaned his hands on the table and looked at it, grinned at its pre-U oddity, its eight blue almost-invisible rectangles. *Lilac!* he thought. *Wait till I tell you!*

With the head of the frame propped on piles of books and his flashlight standing under the glass, he traced on a sheet of paper the four small "Andaman Islands" and the shoreline of "Bay of Bengal." He copied down the names and locations of the other islands and traced the map's scale, which was in "miles" rather than kilometers.

One pair of medium-size islands, "Falkland Islands," was off the coast of Arg ("Argentina") opposite "Santa Cruz," which seemed to be ARG20400. Something teased his memory in that, but he couldn't think what.

He measured the Andaman Islands; the three that were closest together were about a hundred and twenty "miles" in overall length—somewhere around two hundred kilometers, if he remembered correctly; big enough for several cities! The shortest approach to them would be from the other side of Stability Bay, SEA77122, if he and Lilac (and King? Snowflake? Sparrow?) were to go there. *If* they were to go? Of course they would go, now that he had found the islands. They'd manage it somehow; they *had* to.

He turned the map face-down in the frame, put back the pieces of cardboard, and pushed the brads back into their holes with a handle-end of the pincers —wondering as he did so why ARG20400 and the "Falkland Islands" kept poking at his memory.

He slipped the frame's backing in under the wire—Sunday night he would bring tape and make a better job of it—and carried the map back up to the third floor. He hung it on its hook and made sure the loose backing didn't show from the sides.

ARG20400 . . . A new zinc mine being cut underneath it had been shown recently on TV; was that why it seemed significant? He'd certainly never been there . . .

He went down to the basement and got three tobacco leaves from behind the hot-water tank. He brought them up to the storeroom, got his smoking things from the carton he kept them in, and sat down at the table and began cutting the leaves.

Could there possibly be another reason why the islands were covered and unmapped? And who did the covering?

Enough. He was tired of thinking. He let his mind go—to the knife's shiny blade, to Hush and Sparrow cutting tobacco the first time he'd seen them. He had asked Hush where the seeds had come from, and she'd said that King had had them.

And he remembered where he had seen *ARG20400*—the nameber, not the city itself.

A screaming woman in torn coveralls was being led into Medicenter Main by red-cross-coveralled members on either side of her. They held her arms and seemed to be talking to her, but she kept on screaming—short sharp screams, each the same as the others, that screamed again from building walls and screamed again from farther in the night. The woman kept on screaming and the walls and the night kept screaming with her.

He waited until the woman and the members leading her had gone into the building, waited longer while the far-off screams lessened to silence, and then he slowly crossed the walkway and went in. He lurched against the admission scanner as if off balance, clicking his bracelet below the plate on metal, and went slowly and normally to an up-gliding escalator. He stepped onto it and rode with his hand on the rail. Somewhere in the building the woman still screamed, but then she stopped.

The second floor was lighted. A member passing in the hallway with a tray of glasses nodded to him. He nodded back.

The third and fourth floors were lighted too, but the escalator to the fifth floor wasn't moving and there was darkness above. He walked up the steps, to the fifth floor and the sixth.

He walked by flashlight down the sixth-floor hallway—quickly now, not slowly—past the doors he had gone through with the two doctors, the woman who had called him "young brother" and the scar-cheeked man who had watched him. He walked to the end of the hallway, shining his light on the door marked *600A* and *Chief, Chemotherapeutics Division*.

He went through the anteroom and into King's office. The large desk was neater than before: the scuffed telecomp, a pile of folders, the container of pens —and the two paperweights, the unusual square one and the ordinary round one. He picked up the round one—*ARG20400* was inscribed on it—and held its cool plated-metal weight on his palm for a moment. Then he put it down, next to King's young smiling snapshot at Uni's dome.

He went around behind the desk, opened the center drawer, and searched in it until he found a plastic-coated section roster. He scanned the half column of Jesuses and found Jesus HL09E6290. His classification was 080A; his residence, G35, room 1744.

He paused outside the door for a moment, suddenly realizing that Lilac might be there too, dozing next to King under his outstretched possessing arm. *Good!* he thought. *Let her hear it at first hand!* He opened the door, went in, and closed it softly behind him. He aimed his flashlight toward the bed and switched it on.

King was alone, his gray head encircled by his arms.

He was glad and sorry. More glad, though. He would tell her later, come to her triumphantly and tell her all he had found.

He tapped on the light, switched off the flashlight, and put it in his pocket. "King," he said.

The head and the pajamaed arms stayed unmoving.

"King," he said, and went and stood beside the bed. "Wake up, Jesus HL," he said.

King rolled onto his back and laid a hand over his eyes. Fingers chinked and an eye squinted between them.

"I want to speak to you," Chip said.

"What are you doing here?" King asked. "What time is it?"

Chip glanced at the clock. "Four-fifty," he said.

King sat up, palming at his eyes. "What the hate's going on?" he said. "What are you doing here?"

Chip got the desk chair and put it near the foot of the bed and sat down. The room was untidy, coveralls caught in the chute, tea stains on the floor.

King coughed into the side of a fist, and coughed again. He kept the fist at his mouth, looking red-eyed at Chip, his hair pressed to his scalp in patches.

Chip said, "I want to know what it's like on the Falkland Islands."

King lowered his hand. "On what islands?" he said.

"Falkland," Chip said. "Where you got the tobacco seeds. And the perfume you gave Lilac."

"I made the perfume," King said.

"And the tobacco seeds? Did you make them?"

King said, "Someone gave them to me."

"In ARG20400?"

After a moment King nodded.

"Where did *he* get them?"

"I don't know."

"You didn't ask?"

"No," King said, "I didn't. Why don't you get back where you're supposed to be? We can talk about this tomorrow night."

"I'm staying," Chip said. "I'm staying here until I hear the truth. I'm due for a treatment at 8:05. If I don't take it on time, everything's going to be finished—me, you, the group. You're not going to be king of anything."

"You brother-fighter," King said, "get out of here."

"I'm staying," Chip said.

"I've *told* you the truth."

"I don't believe it."

"Then go fight yourself," King said, and lay down and turned over onto his stomach.

Chip stayed as he was. He sat looking at King and waiting.

After a few minutes King turned over again and sat up. He threw aside the blanket, swung his legs around, and sat with his bare feet on the floor. He scratched with both hands at his pajamaed thighs. " 'Americanueva,' " he said, "not 'Falkland.' They come ashore and trade. Hairy-faced creatures in cloth and leather." He looked at Chip. "Diseased, disgusting savages," he said, "who speak in a way that's barely understandable."

"They exist, they've survived."

"That's *all* they've done. Their hands are like wood from working. They steal from one another and go hungry."

"But they haven't come back to the Family."

"They'd be better off if they did," King said. "They've still got religion going. And alcohol-drinking."

"How long do they live?" Chip asked.

King said nothing.

"Past sixty-two?" Chip asked.

King's eyes narrowed coldly. "What's so magnificent about living," he said, "that it has to be prolonged indefinitely? What's so fantastically beautiful about life here or life there that makes sixty-two not enough of it instead of too fighting much? Yes, they live past sixty-two. One of them claimed to be eighty, and looking at him, I believed it. But they die *younger* too, in their thirties, even in their twenties—from work and filth and defending their 'money.' "

"That's only one group of islands," Chip said. "There are seven others."

"They'll all be the same," King said. "They'll all be the same."

"How do you know?"

"How can they *not* be?" King asked. "Christ and Wei, if I'd thought a halfway-human life was possible I'd have said something!"

"You should have said something anyway," Chip said. "There are islands right here in Stability Bay. Leopard and Hush might have got to them and still be living."

"They'd be dead."

"Then you should have let them choose where they died," Chip said. "You're not Uni."

He got up and put the chair back by the desk. He looked at the phone screen, reached over the desk, and took the adviser's-nameber card from under the rim of it: *Anna SG38P2823.*

"You mean you don't know her nameber?" King said. "What do you do, meet in the dark? Or haven't you worked your way out to her extremities yet?"

Chip put the card into his pocket. "We don't meet at all," he said.

"Oh come on," King said, "I know what's been going on. What do you think I am, a dead body?"

"Nothing's been going on," Chip said. "She came to the museum once and I gave her the word lists for Français, that's all."

"I can just imagine," King said. "Get out of here, will you? I need my sleep."
He lay back on the bed, put his legs in under the blanket, and spread the
blanket up over his chest.

"Nothing's been going on," Chip said. "She feels that she owes you too
much."

With his eyes closed, King said, "But we'll soon take care of that, won't
we?"

Chip said nothing for a moment, and then he said, "You should have told
us. About Americanova."

"Americanueva," King said, and then said nothing more. He lay with his
eyes closed, his blanketed chest rising and falling rapidly.

Chip went to the door and tapped off the light. "I'll see you tomorrow
night," he said.

"I hope you get there," King said. "The two of you. To Americanueva. You
deserve it."

Chip opened the door and went out.

King's bitterness depressed him, but after he had been walking for fifteen
minutes or so he began to feel cheerful and optimistic, and elated with the
results of his night of extra clarity. His right-hand pocket was crisp with a map
of Stability Bay and the Andaman Islands, the names and locations of the other
incurable strongholds, and Lilac's red-printed nameber card. Christ, Marx,
Wood, and Wei, what would he be capable of with no treatments at all?

He took the card out and read it as he walked. *Anna SG38P2823.* He would
call her after the first chime and arrange to meet her—during the free hour
that evening. Anna SG. Not she, not an "Anna"; a Lilac she was, fragrant,
delicate, beautiful. (Who had picked the name, she or King? Incredible. The
hater thought they had been meeting and fucking. If only!) *Thirty-*eight P,
twenty-*eight* twenty-*three.* He walked to the swing of the nameber for a while,
then realized he was walking too briskly and slowed himself, pocketing the
card again.

He would be back in his building before the first chime, would shower,
change, call Lilac, eat (he was starving), then get his treatment at 8:05 and keep
his 8:15 dental appointment ("It feels much better today, sister. The throb-
bing's almost completely gone"). The treatment would dull him, fight it, but
not so much that he wouldn't be able to tell Lilac about the Andaman Islands
and start planning with her—and with Snowflake and Sparrow if they were
interested—how they would try to get there. Snowflake would probably choose
to stay. He hoped so; it would simplify things tremendously. Yes, Snowflake
would stay with King, laugh and smoke and fuck with him, and play that
mechanical paddle-ball game. And he and Lilac would go.

Anna SG, *thirty-*eight P, twenty-*eight* twenty-*three . . .*

He got to the building at 6:22. Two up-early members were coming down his hallway, one naked, one dressed. He smiled and said, "Good morning, sisters."

"Good morning," they said, smiling back.

He went into his room, tapped on the light, and Bob was on the bed, lifting himself up on his elbows and blinking at him. His telecomp lay open on the floor, its blue and amber lights gleaming.

Six

He closed the door behind him.

Bob swung his legs off the bed and sat up, looking at him anxiously. His coveralls were partway open. "Where've you been, Li?" he asked.

"In the lounge," Chip said. "I went back there after Photography Club—I'd left my pen there—and I suddenly got very tired. From being late on my treatment, I guess. I sat down to rest and"—he smiled—"all of a sudden it's morning."

Bob looked at him, still anxiously, and after a moment shook his head. "I checked the lounge," he said. "And Mary KK's room, and the gym, and the bottom of the pool."

"You must have missed me," Chip said. "I was in the corner behind—"

"I *checked* the *lounge*, Li," Bob said. He pressed closed his coveralls and shook his head despairingly.

Chip moved from the door, walked a slow away-from-Bob curve toward the bathroom. "I've got to ure," he said.

He went into the bathroom and opened his coveralls and urined, trying to find the extra mental clarity he had had before, trying to think of an explanation that would satisfy Bob or at worst seem like only a one-night aberration. Why had Bob come there anyway? How long had he been there?

"I called at eleven-thirty," Bob said, "and there was no answer. Where have you been between then and now?"

He closed his coveralls. "I was walking around," he said—loudly, to reach Bob in the room.

"Without touching scanners?" Bob said.

Christ and Wei.

"I must have forgot," he said, and turned on the water and rinsed his fingers. "It's this toothache," he said. "It's gotten worse. The whole side of my head aches." He wiped his fingers, looking in the mirror at Bob on the bed looking back at him. "It was keeping me awake," he said, "so I went out and walked around. I told you that story about the lounge because I know I should have gone right down to the—"

"It was keeping *me* awake too," Bob said, "that 'toothache' of yours. I saw you during TV and you looked tense and abnormal. So finally I pulled the nameber of the dental-appointment clerk. You were offered a Friday appointment but you said your treatment was on Saturday."

Chip put the towel down and turned and stood facing Bob in the doorway.

The first chime sounded, and "One Mighty Family" began to play.

Bob said, "It was all an act, wasn't it, Li—the slowdown last spring, the sleepiness and overtreatedness."

After a moment Chip nodded.

"Oh, brother," Bob said. "What have you been doing?"

Chip didn't say anything.

"Oh, brother," Bob said, and bent over and switched his telecomp off. He closed its cover and snapped the catches. "Are you going to forgive me?" he asked. He stood the telecomp on end and steadied the handle between the fingers of both hands, trying to get it to stay standing up. "I'll tell you something funny," he said. "I have a streak of vanity in me. I do. Correction, I did. I thought I was one of the two or three best advisers in the house. In the house, hate; in the *city*. Alert, observant, *sensitive* . . . 'Comes the rude awakening.' " He had the handle standing, and slapped it down and smiled drily at Chip. "So you're not the only sick one," he said, "if that's any consolation."

"I'm not sick, Bob," Chip said. "I'm healthier than I've been in my entire life."

Still smiling, Bob said, "That's kind of contrary to the evidence, isn't it?" He picked up the telecomp and stood up.

"You can't see the evidence," Chip said. "You've been dulled by your treatments."

Bob beckoned with his head and moved toward the door. "Come on," he said, "Let's go get you fixed up."

Chip stayed where he was. Bob opened the door and stopped, looking back.

Chip said, "I'm perfectly healthy."

Bob held out his hand sympathetically. "Come on, Li," he said.

After a moment Chip went to him. Bob took his arm and they went out into the hallway. Doors were open and members were about, talking quietly, walking. Four or five were gathered at the bulletin board, reading the day's notices.

"Bob," Chip said, "I want you to listen to what I'm going to say to you."

"Don't I always listen?" Bob said.

"I want you to try to open your mind," Chip said. "Because you're not a stupid member, you're bright, and you're good-hearted and you want to help me."

Mary KK came toward them from the escalators, holding a pack of coveralls with a bar of soap on top of it. She smiled and said, "Hi," and to Chip, "Where were you?"

"He was in the lounge," Bob said.

"In the middle of the night?" Mary said.

Chip nodded and Bob said, "Yes," and they went on to the escalators, Bob keeping his hand lightly on Chip's arm.

They rode down.

"I know you think your mind is open already," Chip said, "but will you try to open it even more, to listen and think for a few minutes as if I'm just as healthy as I say I am?"

"All right, Li, I will," Bob said.

"Bob," Chip said, "we're not free. None of us is. Not one member of the Family."

"How can I listen as if you're healthy," Bob said, "when you say something like that? Of course we're free. We're free of war and want and hunger, free of crime, violence, aggressiveness, sel—"

"Yes, yes, we're free *of* things," Chip said, "but we're not free to *do* things. Don't you see that, Bob? Being 'free of' really has nothing to do with being free at all."

Bob frowned. "Being free to do what?" he said.

They stepped off the escalator and started around toward the next one. "To choose our own classifications," Chip said, "to have children when we want, to go where we want and do what we want, to refuse treatments if we want . . ."

Bob said nothing.

They stepped onto the next escalator. "Treatments really do dull us, Bob," Chip said. "I know that from my own experience. There are things in them that 'make us humble, make us good'—like in the rhyme, you know? I've been undertreated for half a year now"—the second chime sounded—"and I'm more awake and alive than I've *ever* been. I think more clearly and feel more deeply. I fuck four or five times a week, would you believe that?"

"No," Bob said, looking at his telecomp riding on the handrail.

"It's true," Chip said. "You're more sure than ever that I'm sick now, aren't you. Love of Family, I'm not. There are others like me, thousands, maybe millions. There are islands all over the world, there may be cities on the mainland too"—they were walking around to the next escalator—"where people live in true freedom. I've got a list of the islands right here in my pocket. They're not on maps because Uni doesn't want us to know about them, because they're *defended* against the Family and the people there won't *submit* to being treated. Now, you want to help me, don't you? To *really* help me?"

They stepped onto the next escalator. Bob looked grievingly at him. "Christ and Wei," he said, "can you doubt it, brother?"

"All right, then," Chip said, "this is what I'd like you to do for me: when we get to the treatment room tell Uni that I'm okay, that I fell asleep in the lounge the way I told you. Don't input anything about my not touching scanners or the way I made up the toothache. Let me get just the treatment I would have got yesterday, all right?"

"And that would be helping you?" Bob said.

"Yes, it would," Chip said. "I know you don't think so, but I ask you as my brother and my friend to—to respect what I think and feel. I'll get away to one of these islands somehow and I won't harm the Family in any way. What the Family has given me, I've given back to it in the work I've done, and I didn't ask for it in the first place, and I had no choice about accepting it."

They walked around to the next escalator.

"All right," Bob said when they were riding down, "I listened to *you*, Li; now *you* listen to *me*." His hand above Chip's elbow tightened slightly. "You're very, very sick," he said, "and it's entirely my fault and I feel miserable about it. There are no islands that aren't on maps; and treatments don't dull us; and if we had the kind of 'freedom' you're thinking about we'd have disorder and overpopulation and want and crime and war. Yes, I'm going to help you, brother. I'm going to tell Uni everything, and you'll be cured and you'll thank me."

They walked around to the next escalator and stepped onto it. *Third floor —Medicenter,* the sign at the bottom said. A red-cross-coveralled member riding toward them on the up escalator smiled and said, "Good morning, Bob."

Bob nodded to him.

Chip said, "I don't *want* to be cured."

"That's proof that you need to be," Bob said. "Relax and trust me, Li. No, why the hate should you? Trust Uni, then; will you do that? Trust the members who programmed Uni."

After a moment Chip said, "All right, I will."

"I feel awful," Bob said, and Chip turned to him and struck away his hand. Bob looked at him, startled, and Chip put both hands at Bob's back and swept him forward. Turning with the movement, he grasped the handrail—hearing Bob tumble, his telecomp clatter—and climbed out onto the up-moving central incline. It wasn't moving once he was on it; he crept sideways, clinging with fingers and knees to metal ridges; crept sideways to the up-escalator handrail, caught it, and flung himself over and down into the sharp-staired trench of humming metal. He got quickly to his feet—"Stop him!" Bob shouted below —and ran up the upgoing steps taking two in each stride. The red-crossed member at the top, off the escalator, turned. "What are you—" and Chip took him by the shoulders—elderly wide-eyed member—and swung him aside and pushed him away.

He ran down the hallway. "Stop him!" someone shouted, and other members: "Catch that member!" "He's sick; stop him!"

Ahead was the dining hall, members on line turning to look. He shouted, "Stop that member!" running at them and pointing; "Stop him!" and ran past them. "Sick member in there!" he said, pushing past the ones at the doorway, past the scanner. "Needs help in there! Quickly!"

In the dining hall he looked, and ran to the side, through a swing-door to the behind-the-dispensers section. He slowed, walked quickly, trying to still his breathing, past members loading stacks of cakes between vertical tracks, members looking down at him while dumping tea powder into steel drums. A cart filled with boxes marked *Napkins;* he took the handle of it, swung it around, and pushed it before him, past two members standing eating, two more gathering cakes from a broken carton.

Ahead was a door marked *Exit,* the door to one of the corner stairways. He pushed the cart toward it, hearing raised voices behind him. He rammed the cart against the door, butted it open, and went with the cart out onto the landing; closed the door and brought the cart handle back against it. He backed down two steps and pulled the cart sideways to him, wedged it tight between the door and the stair-rail post with one black wheel turning in air.

He hurried down the stairs.

He had to get out, out of the building and onto the walkways and plazas. He would walk to the museum—it wouldn't be open yet—and hide in the storeroom or behind the hot-water tank until tomorrow night, when Lilac and the others would be there. He should have grabbed some cakes just now. Why hadn't he thought of it? Hate!

He left the stairway at the ground floor and walked quickly along the hallway, nodded at an approaching member. She looked at his legs and bit her lip worriedly. He looked down and stopped. His coveralls were torn at the knees and his right knee was bruised, with blood in small beads on the surface.

"Can I do anything?" the member asked.

"I'm on my way to the medicenter now," he said. "Thanks, sister." He went on. There was nothing he could do about it; he would have to take his chances. When he got outside, away from the building, he would tie a tissue around the knee and fix the coveralls as best he could. The knee began to sting, now that he knew about it. He walked faster.

He turned into the back of the lobby and paused, looked at the escalators planing down on either side of him and, up ahead, the four glass scanner-posted doors with the sunny walkway beyond them. Members were talking and going out, a few coming in. Everything looked ordinary; the murmur of voices was low, unalarmed.

He started toward the doors, walking normally, looking straight ahead. He would do his scanner trick—the knee would be an excuse for the stumbling if anyone noticed—and once he was out on— The music stopped, and "Excuse me," a woman's voice loudspeakered, "would everyone please stay exactly where he is for a moment? Would everyone please stop moving?"

He stopped, in the middle of the lobby.

Everyone stopped, looked around questioningly and waited. Only the members on the escalators kept moving, and then they stopped too and looked down at their feet. One member walked down steps. "Don't move!" several members called to her, and she stopped and blushed.

He stood motionless, looking at the huge stained-glass faces above the doors: bearded Christ and Marx, hairless Wood, smiling slit-eyed Wei. Something slipped down his shin: a drop of blood.

"Brothers, sisters," the woman's voice said, "an emergency has arisen. There's a member in the building who's sick, very sick. He's acted aggressively and run away from his adviser"—members drew breath—"and he needs every one of us to help find him and get him to the treatment room as quickly as possible."

"Yes!" a member behind Chip said, and another said, "What do we do?"

"He's believed to be somewhere below the fourth floor," the woman said; "a twenty-seven-year-old—" A second voice spoke to her, a man's voice, quick and unintelligible. A member about to step on the nearest escalator was looking at Chip's knees. Chip looked at the picture of Wood. "He'll probably try to leave the building," the woman said, "so the two members nearest each exit will move to it and block it, please. No one else move; only the two members nearest each exit."

The members near the doors looked at one another, and two moved to each door and put themselves uneasily side by side in line with the scanners. "It's awful!" someone said. The member who had been looking at Chip's knees was looking now at his face. Chip looked back at him, a man of forty or so; he looked away.

"The member we're looking for," a man's voice on the speaker said, "is a twenty-seven-year-old male, nameber Li RM35M4419. That's Li, RM, 35M, 4419. First we'll check among ourselves and then we'll search the floors we're on. Just a minute, just a minute, please. UniComp says the member is the only Li RM in the building, so we can forget the rest of his nameber. All we have to look for is Li RM. Li RM. Look at the bracelets of the members around you. We're looking for Li RM. Be sure that every member within your sight is checked by at least one other member. Members who are in their rooms will come out now into the hallways. Li RM. We're looking for Li RM."

Chip turned to a member near him, took his hand and looked at his bracelet. "Let me see yours," the member said. Chip raised his wrist and turned away, went toward another member. "I didn't see it," the member said. Chip took the other member's hand. His arm was touched by the first member, saying, "Brother, I didn't see."

He ran for the doors. He was caught and arm-pulled around—by the member who had been looking at him. He clenched his hand to a fist and hit the member in the face and he fell away.

Members screamed. "It's him!" they cried. "There he is!" "Help him!" "Stop him!"

He ran to a door and fist-hit one of the members there. His arm was grabbed by the other, saying in his ear, "Brother, brother!" His other arm was caught by other members; he was clutched around the chest from behind.

"We're looking for Li RM," the man on the speaker said. "He may act aggressively when we find him but we mustn't be afraid. He's depending on us for our help and our understanding."

"Let go of me!" he cried, trying to pull himself free of the arms tightly holding him.

"Help him!" members cried. "Get him to the treatment room!" "Help him!"

"Leave me alone!" he cried. "I don't *want* to be helped! Leave me *alone,* you brother-fighting haters!"

He was dragged up escalator steps by members panting and flinching, one of them with tears in his eyes. "Easy, easy," they said, "we're helping you. You'll be all right, we're helping you." He kicked, and his legs were caught and held.

"I don't *want* to be helped!" he cried. "I want to be left alone! I'm healthy! I'm healthy! I'm not sick!"

He was dragged past members who stood with hands over ears, with hands pressed to mouths below staring eyes.

"*You're* sick," he said to the member whose face he had hit. Blood was leaking from his nostrils, and his nose and cheek were swollen; Chip's arm was locked under his. "You're dulled and you're drugged," Chip said to him. "You're dead. You're a dead man. You're *dead!*"

"Shh, we love you, we're helping you," the member said.

"*Christ and Wei, let GO of me!*"

He was dragged up more steps.

"He's been found," the man on the speaker said. "Li RM has been found, members. He's being brought to the medicenter. Let me say that again: Li RM has been found, and is being brought to the medicenter. The emergency is over, brothers and sisters, and you can go on now with what you were doing. Thank you; thank you for your help and cooperation. Thank you on behalf of the Family, thank you on behalf of Li RM."

He was dragged along the medicenter hallway.

Music started in mid-melody.

"You're all dead," he said. "The whole Family's dead. Uni's alive, only Uni. But there are islands where *people* are living! Look at the map! Look at the map in the Pre-U Museum!"

He was dragged into the treatment room. Bob was there, pale and sweating, with a bleeding cut over his eyebrow; he was jabbing at the keys of his telecomp, held for him by a girl in a blue smock.

"Bob," he said, "Bob, do me a favor, will you? Look at the map in the Pre-U Museum. Look at the map from 1951."

He was dragged to a blue-lighted unit. He grabbed the edge of the opening, but his thumb was pried up and his hand forced in; his sleeve torn back and his arm shoved in all the way to the shoulder.

His cheek was soothed—by Bob, trembling. "You'll be all *right,* Li," he said. "Trust Uni." Three lines of blood ran from the cut into his eyebrow hairs.

His bracelet was caught by the scanner, his arm touched by the infusion disc. He clamped his eyes shut. *I will not be made dead!* he thought. *I will not be made dead! I'll remember the islands, I'll remember Lilac! I will not be made dead! I will not be made dead!* He opened his eyes, and Bob smiled at him. A strip of skin-colored tape was over his eyebrow. "They *said* three o'clock and they *meant* three o'clock," he said.

"What do you mean?" he asked. He was lying in a bed and Bob was sitting beside it.

"That's when the doctors said you'd wake up," Bob said. "Three o'clock. And that's what it is. Not 2:59, not 3:01, but three o'clock. These mems are so clever it scares me."

"Where am I?" he asked.

"In Medicenter Main."

And then he remembered—remembered the things he had thought and said, and worst of all, the things he had done. "Oh, Christ," he said. "Oh, Marx. Oh, Christ and Wei."

"Take it easy, Li," Bob said, touching his hand.

"Bob," he said, "oh, Christ and Wei, Bob, I—I pushed you down the—"

"Escalator," Bob said. "You certainly did, brother. That was the most surprised moment in my life. I'm fine though." He tapped the tape above his eyebrow. "All closed up and good as new, or will be in a day or two."

"I *hit* a member! With my hand!"

"He's fine too," Bob said. "Two of those are from him." He nodded across the bed, at red roses in a vase on a table. "And two from Mary KK, and two from the members in your section."

He looked at the roses, sent to him by the members he had hit and deceived and betrayed, and tears came into his eyes and he began to tremble.

"Hey, easy there, come on," Bob said.

But Christ and Wei, he was thinking only of himself! "Bob, listen," he said, turning to him, getting up on an elbow, back-handing at his eyes.

"Take it easy," Bob said.

"Bob, there are *others,*" he said, "others who're just as sick as I was! We've got to find them and help them!"

"We know."

"There's a member called 'Lilac,' Anna SG38P2823, and another one—"

"We know, we know," Bob said. "They've already been helped. They've all been helped."

"They have?"

Bob nodded. "You were questioned while you were out," he said. "It's Monday. Monday afternoon. They've already been found and helped—Anna SG; and the one you called 'Snowflake,' Anna PY; and Yin GU, 'Sparrow.' "

"And King," he said. "Jesus HL; he's right here in this building; he's—"

"No," Bob said, shaking his head. "No, we were too late. That one—that one is dead."

"He's dead?"

Bob nodded. "He hung himself," he said.

Chip stared at him.

"From his shower, with a strip of blanket," Bob said.

"Oh, Christ and Wei," Chip said, and lay back on the pillow. Sickness, sickness, sickness; and he had been part of it.

"The others are all fine though," Bob said, patting his hand. "And you'll be fine too. You're going to a rehabilitation center, brother. You're going to have yourself a week's vacation. Maybe even more."

"I feel so ashamed, Bob," he said, "so fighting ashamed of myself . . ."

"Come on," Bob said, "You wouldn't feel ashamed if you'd slipped and broken an ankle, would you? It's the same thing. *I'm* the one who should feel ashamed, if anyone should."

"I *lied* to you!"

"I let myself be lied to," Bob said. "Look, nobody's really responsible for anything. You'll see that soon." He reached down, brought up a take-along kit, and opened it on his lap. "This is yours," he said. "Tell me if I missed anything. Mouthpiece, clippers, snapshots, nameber books, picture of a horse, your—"

"That's sick," he said. "I don't want it. Chute it."

"The picture?"

"Yes."

Bob drew it from the kit and looked at it. "It's nicely done," he said. "It's not accurate, but it's—nice in a way."

"It's sick," he said. "It was done by a sick member. Chute it."

"Whatever you say," Bob said. He put the kit on the bed and got up and crossed the room; opened the chute and dropped the picture down.

"There are islands full of sick members," Chip said. "All over the world."

"I know," Bob said. "You told us."

"Why can't we help them?"

"That I *don't* know," Bob said. "But Uni does. I told you before, Li: trust Uni."

"I will," he said, "I will," and tears came into his eyes again.

A red-cross-coveralled member came into the room. "How are we feeling?" he asked.

Chip looked at him.

"He's pretty low," Bob said.

"That's to be expected," the member said. "Don't worry; we'll get him evened up." He went over and took Chip's wrist.

"Li, I have to go now," Bob said.

"All right," Chip said.

Bob went over and kissed his cheek. "In case you're not sent back here, good-by, brother," he said.

"Good-by, Bob," Chip said. "Thanks. Thanks for everything."

"Thank Uni," Bob said, and squeezed his hand and smiled. He nodded at the red-crossed member and went out.

The member took an infusion syringe from his pocket and snapped off its cap. "You'll be feeling perfectly normal in no time at all," he said.

Chip lay still and closed his eyes, wiped with one hand at tears while the member pushed up his other sleeve. "I was so sick," he said. "I was so sick."

"Shh, don't think about it," the member said, gently infusing him. "It's nothing to think about. You'll be fine in no time."

III
Getting
Away

One

Old cities were demolished; new cities were built. The new cities had taller buildings, broader plazas, larger parks, monorails whose cars flew faster though less frequently.

Two more starships were launched, toward Sirius B and 61 Cygni. The Mars colonies, repopulated and safeguarded now against the devastation of 152, were expanding daily; so too were the colonies on Venus and the Moon, the outposts on Titan and Mercury.

The free hour was extended by five minutes. Voice-input telecomps began to replace key-input ones, and totalcakes came in a pleasant second flavor. Life expectancy increased to 62.4.

Members worked and ate, watched TV and slept. They sang and went to museums and walked in amusement gardens.

On the two-hundredth anniversary of Wei's birth, in the parade in a new city, a huge portrait banner of smiling Wei was carried at one of its poles by a member of thirty or so who was ordinary in every respect except that his right eye was green instead of brown. Once long ago this member had been sick, but now he was well. He had his assignment and his room, his girlfriend and his adviser. He was relaxed and content.

A strange thing happened during the parade. As this member marched along, smiling, holding the banner pole, he began to hear a nameber saying itself over and over in his head: Anna SG, *thirty*-eight P, twenty-*eight* twenty *-three;* Anna SG, *thirty*-eight P, twenty-*eight* twenty-*three.* It kept repeating itself to him, in time with his marching. He wondered who the nameber belonged to, and why it should be repeating itself in his head that way.

Suddenly he remembered: it was from his sickness! It was the nameber of one of the other sick ones, the one called "Lovely"—no, "Lilac." Why, after so long, had her nameber come back to him? He stamped his feet down harder, trying not to hear it, and was glad when the signal to sing was given.

He told his adviser. "It's nothing to think about," she said. "You probably saw something that reminded you of her. Maybe you even saw *her*. There's nothing to be afraid of in remembering—unless, of course, it becomes bothersome. Let me know if it happens again."

But it didn't happen again. He was well, thank Uni.

One Christmas Day, when he had another assignment, was living in another city, he bicycled with his girlfriend and four other members to the outlying parkland. They brought cakes and cokes with them, and lunched on the ground near a grove of trees.

He had set his coke container on an almost-level stone and, reaching for it while talking, knocked it over. The other members refilled his container from theirs.

A few minutes later, while folding his cake wrapper, he noticed a flat leaf lying on the wet stone, drops of coke shining on its back, its stem curled upward like a handle. He took the stem and lifted the leaf, and the stone underneath it was dry in the leaf's oval shape. The rest of the stone was wet-black, but where the leaf had been it was dry-gray. Something about the moment seemed significant to him, and he sat silently, looking at the leaf in his one hand, the folded cake wrapper in his other, and the dry leaf shape on the stone. His girlfriend said something to him and he took himself away from the moment, put the leaf and the wrapper together and gave them to the member who had the litter bag.

The image of the dry leaf shape on the stone came into his mind several times that day, and on the next day too. Then he had his treatment and he forgot about it. In a few weeks, though, it came into his mind again. He wondered why. Had he lifted a leaf from a wet stone that way sometime before? If he had, he didn't remember it . . .

Every now and then, while he was walking in a park or, oddly enough, waiting on line for his treatment, the image of the dry leaf shape came into his mind and made him frown.

There was an earthquake. (His chair flung him off it; glass broke in the microscope and the loudest sound he had ever heard roared from the depths of the lab.) A seismovalve half the continent away had jammed and gone undetected, TV explained a few nights later. It hadn't happened before and it wouldn't happen again. Members must mourn, of course, but it was nothing to think about in the future.

Dozens of buildings had collapsed, hundreds of members had died. Every medicenter in the city was overloaded with the injured, and more than half the treatment units were damaged; treatments were delayed up to ten days.

A few days after he was to have had his, he thought of Lilac and how he had loved her differently and more—more *excitingly*—than he loved everyone else. He had wanted to tell her something. What was it? Oh yes, about the islands. The islands he had found hidden on the pre-U map. The islands of incurables . . .

His adviser called him. "Are you all right?" he asked.

"I don't think so, Karl," he said. "I need my treatment."

"Hold on a minute," his adviser said, and turned away and spoke softly to his telecomp. After a moment he turned back. "You can get it tonight at seven-thirty," he said, "but you'll have to go to the medicenter in T24."

He stood on a long line at seven-thirty, thinking about Lilac, trying to remember exactly what she looked like. When he got near the treatment units, the image of a dry leaf shape on a stone came into his mind.

Lilac called him (she was right there in the same building) and he went to her room, which was the storeroom in the Pre-U. Green jewels hung from her earlobes and glittered around her rose-brown throat; she was wearing a gown of gleaming green cloth that exposed her pink-tipped soft-cone breasts. "Bon soir, Chip," she said, smiling. "Comment vastu? Je m'ennuyais tellement de toi." He went to her and took her in his arms and kissed her—her lips were warm and soft, her mouth opening—and he awoke to darkness and disappointment; it was a dream, it had only been a dream.

But strangely, frighteningly, everything was in him: the smell of her perfume (parfum) and the taste of tobacco and the sound of Sparrow's songs, and desire for Lilac and anger at King and resentment of Uni and sorrow for the Family and happiness in feeling, in being alive and awake.

And in the morning he would have a treatment and it would all be gone. At eight o'clock. He tapped on the light, squinted at the clock: 4:54. In a little more than three hours . . .

He tapped the light off again and lay open-eyed in the dark. He didn't want to lose it. Sick or not, he wanted to keep his memories and the capacity to explore and enjoy them. He didn't want to think about the *islands*—no, never; that was *real* sickness—but he wanted to think about Lilac, and the meetings of the group in the relic-filled storeroom, and once in a while, maybe, to have another dream.

But the treatment would come in three hours and everything would be gone. There was nothing he could do—except hope for another earthquake, and what chance was there of that? The seismovalves had worked perfectly in the years since and they would go on working perfectly in the years ahead. And what short of an earthquake could postpone his treatment? Nothing. Nothing at all. Not with Uni knowing that he had lied for a postponement once before.

A dry leaf shape on stone came into his mind but he chased it away to think of Lilac, to see her as he had seen her in the dream, not to waste his three short hours of aliveness. He had forgotten how large her eyes were, how lovely her smile and her rose-brown skin, how moving her earnestness. He had forgotten so fighting much: the pleasure of smoking, the excitement of deciphering Français . . .

The dry leaf shape came back, and he thought about it, irritated, to find out why his mind hung on to it, to get rid of it once and for all. He thought back to the ridiculously meaningless moment; saw again the leaf, with the drops of coke shining on it; saw his fingers lifting it by its stem, and his other hand holding the folded foil cake wrapper, and the dry gray oval on the black coke-wet stone. He had spilled the coke, and the leaf had been lying there, and the stone underneath it had—

He sat up in bed and clasped his hand to his pajamaed right arm. "Christ and Wei," he said, frightened.

He got up before the first chime and dressed and made the bed.

He was the first one in the dining room; ate and drank, and went back to his room with a cake wrapper folded loosely in his pocket.

He opened the wrapper, put it on the desk, and smoothed it down flat with his hand. He folded the square of foil neatly in half, and the half into thirds. He pressed the packet flat and held it; it was thin despite its six layers. Too thin? He put it down again.

He went into the bathroom and, from the cabinet's first-aid kit, got cotton and the cartridge of tape. He brought them back to the desk.

He put a layer of cotton on the foil packet—a layer smaller than the packet itself—and began covering the cotton and the packet with long overlapping strips of skin-colored tape. He stuck the tape ends lightly to the desktop.

The door opened and he turned, hiding what he was doing and putting the tape cartridge into his pocket. It was Karl TK from next door. "Ready to eat?" he asked.

"I already have," he said.

"Oh," Karl said. "See you later."

"Right," he said, and smiled.

Karl closed the door.

He finished the taping and then peeled the tape ends from the desk and carried the bandage he had made into the bathroom. He laid it foil-side up on the edge of the sink and pushed up his sleeve.

He took the bandage and put the foil carefully against the inner surface of his arm, where the infusion disc would touch him. He clasped the bandage and pressed its tape border tightly to his skin.

A leaf. A shield. Would it work?

If it did, he would think only of Lilac, not of the islands. If he found himself thinking of the islands, he would tell his adviser.

He drew down his sleeve.

At eight o'clock he joined the line in the treatment room. He stood with his arms folded and his hand over the sleeve-covered bandage—to warm it in case the infusion disc was temperature-sensitive.

I'm sick, he thought. *I'll get all the diseases: cancer, smallpox, cholera, everything. Hair will grow on my face!*

He would do it just this once. At the first sign of anything wrong he would tell his adviser.

Maybe it wouldn't work.

His turn came. He pushed his sleeve to his elbow, put his hand wrist-deep into the unit's rubber-rimmed opening, and then pushed his sleeve to his shoulder and in the same moment slid his arm all the way in.

He felt the scanner finding his bracelet, and the infusion disc's slight pressure against the cotton-packed bandage . . . Nothing happened.

"You're done," a member said behind him.

The unit's blue light was on.

"Oh," he said, and pushed down his sleeve as he drew out his arm.

He had to go right to his assignment.

After lunch he went back to his room and, in the bathroom, pushed up his sleeve and pulled the bandage from his arm. The foil was unbroken, but so was skin after a treatment. He tore the foil packet from the tape.

The cotton was grayish and matted. He squeezed the bandage over the sink, and a trickle of waterlike liquid ran from it.

Awareness came, more of it each day. Memory came, in sharper, more anguishing detail.

Feeling came. Resentment of Uni grew into hatred; desire for Lilac grew into hopeless hunger.

Again he played the old deceptions; was normal at his assignment, normal with his adviser; normal with his girlfriend. But day by day the deceptions grew more irritating to maintain, more infuriating.

On his next treatment day he made another bandage of cake wrapper, cotton, and tape; and squeezed from it another trickle of waterlike liquid.

Black specks appeared on his chin and cheeks and upper lip—the beginnings of hair. He took apart his clippers, wired the cutter blade to one of the handles, and before the first chime each morning, rubbed soap on his face and shaved the specks away.

He dreamed every night. Sometimes the dreams brought orgasms.

More and more maddening it became, to pretend relaxation and content-
ment, humility, goodness. On Marxmas Day, at a beach, he trotted along the
shore and then ran, ran from the members trotting with him, ran from the
sunbathing, cake-eating Family. He ran till the beach narrowed into tumbled
stone, and ran on through surf and over slippery ancient abutments. Then he
stopped, and alone and naked between ocean and soaring cliffs, clenched his
hands into fists and hit at the cliffs; cried "Fight it!" at the clear blue sky and
wrenched and tore at the untearable chain of his bracelet.

It was 169, the fifth of May. Six and a half years he had lost. *Six and a half
years!* He was thirty-four. He was in USA90058.

And where was she? Still in Ind, or was she somewhere else? Was she on
Earth or on a starship?

And was she alive, as he was, or was she dead, like everyone else in the
Family?

Two

It was easier now, now that he had bruised his hands and shouted; easier to walk slowly with a contented smile, to watch TV and the screen of his microscope, to sit with his girlfriend at amphitheater concerts.

Thinking all the while of what to do . . .

"Any friction?" his adviser asked.

"Well, a little," he said.

"I thought you didn't look right. What is it?"

"Well, you know, I was pretty sick a few years ago—"

"I know."

"And now one of the members I was sick with, the one who *got* me sick, in fact, is right here in the building. Could I possibly be moved somewhere else?"

His adviser looked doubtfully at him. "I'm a little surprised," he said, "that UniComp's put the two of you together again."

"So am I," Chip said. "But she's here. I saw her in the dining hall last night and again this morning."

"Did you speak to her?"

"No."

"I'll look into it," his adviser said. "If she *is* here and it makes you uncomfortable, of course we'll get you moved. Or get *her* moved. What's her nameber?"

"I don't remember all of it," Chip said. "Anna ST38P."

His adviser called him early the next morning. "You were mistaken, Li," he said. "It wasn't that member you saw. And by the way, she's Anna SG, not ST."

"Are you sure she's not here?"

"Positive. She's in Afr."

"That's a relief," Chip said.

"And Li, instead of having your treatment Thursday, you're going to have it today."

"I am?"

"Yes. At one-thirty."

"All right," he said. "Thank you, Jesus."

"Thank Uni."

He had three cake wrappers folded and hidden in the back of his desk drawer. He took one out, went into the bathroom, and began making a bandage.

She was in Afr. It was nearer than Ind but still an ocean away. And the width of Usa besides.

His parents were there, in '71334; he would wait a few weeks and then claim a visit. It was a little under two years since he had seen them last; there was a fair chance that the claim would be granted. Once in Afr he could call her —pretend to have an injured arm, get a child to touch the plate of an outdoor phone for him—and find out her exact location. *Hello, Anna SG. I hope you're as well as I am. What city are you in?*

And then what? Walk there? Claim a car ride to someplace near, an installation involved with genetics in one way or another? Would Uni realize what he was up to?

But even if it all happened, even if he got to her, what would he do *then?* It was too much to hope that she too had lifted a leaf from a wet stone one day. No, fight it, she would be a normal member, as normal as he himself had been until a few months ago. And at his first abnormal word she would have him in a medicenter. Christ, Marx, Wood, and Wei, what could he *do?*

He could forget about her, that was one answer; strike out on his own, now, for the nearest free island. There would be women there, probably a lot of them, and some of them would probably have rose-brown skin and large less-slanted-than-normal eyes and soft-looking conical breasts. Was it worth risking his own aliveness on the slim chance of awakening hers?

Though *she* had awakened *his,* crouching before him with her hands on his knees . . .

Not at the risk of her own, though. Or at least not at as *great* a risk.

He went to the Pre-U Museum; went the old way, at night, without touching scanners. It was the same as the one in IND26110. Some of the exhibits were slightly different, standing in different places.

He found another pre-U map, this one made in 1937, with the same eight blue rectangles pasted to it. Its backing had been cut and crudely taped; someone else had been at it before him. The thought was exciting; someone else had found the islands, was maybe on the way to one at that very moment.

In another storeroom—this one with only a table and a few cartons and a curtained boothlike machine with rows of small levers—he again held a map to the light, again saw the hidden islands. He traced on paper the nearest one, "Cuba," off Usa's southeast tip. And in case he decided to risk seeing Lilac, he traced the shape of Afr and the two islands near it, "Madagascar" to the east and little "Majorca" to the north.

One of the cartons held books; he found one in Français, *Spinoza et ses contemporains.* Spinoza and his contemporaries. He looked through it and took it.

He put the reframed map in its place and browsed through the museum. He took a wrist-strap compass that still seemed to be working, and a bone-handled "razor" and the stone for sharpening it.

"We're going to be reassigned soon," his section head said at lunch one day. "GL4 is taking over our work."

"I hope I go to Afr," he said. "My parents are there."

It was a risky thing to say, slightly unmemberlike, but maybe the section head had an indirect influence on who went where.

His girlfriend was transferred and he went with her to the airport to see her off—and to see whether it was possible to get aboard a plane without Uni's permission. It didn't seem to be; the close single line of boarding members would allow no false touching of the scanner, and by the time the last member in the line was touching, a member in orange coveralls was at his side ready to stop the escalator and sink it in its pit. Getting off a plane presented the same difficulty: the last member out touched the scanner while two orange-coveralled members looked on; they reversed the escalator, touched, and went aboard with steel containers for the cake and drink dispensers. He might manage to get on a plane waiting in the hangar area—and hide in it, although he didn't recall any hiding place in planes—but how could he know where it would eventually go?

Flying was impossible, till Uni said he could fly.

He claimed the visit to his parents. It was denied.

New assignments were posted for his section. Two 663's were sent to Afr, but not he; he was sent to USA36104. During the flight he studied the plane. There was no hiding place. There was only the long seat-filled hull, the bathroom at the front, the cake and drink dispensers at the back, and the TV screens, with an actor playing Marx on all of them.

USA36104 was in the southeast, close to Usa's tip and Cuba beyond it. He could go bicycling one Sunday and keep bicycling; go from city to city, sleeping in the parkland between them and going into the cities at night for cakes and drinks; it was twelve hundred kilometers by the MFA map. At '33037 he could find a boat, or traders coming ashore like the ones in ARG20400 that King had spoken of.

Lilac, he thought, *what else can I do?*

He claimed the visit to Afr again, and again it was denied.

He began bicycling on Sundays and during the free hour, to ready his legs. He went to the '36104 Pre-U and found a better compass and a tooth-edged knife he could use for cutting branches in the parkland. He checked the map there; this one's backing was intact, unopened. He wrote on it, *Yes, there are islands where members are free. Fight Uni!*

Early one Sunday morning he set out for Cuba, with the compass and a map he had drawn in one of his pockets. In the bike's basket, *Wei's Living Wisdom* lay on a folded blanket along with a container of coke and a cake; within the blanket was his take-along kit, and in that were his razor and its sharpening stone, a bar of soap, his clippers, two cakes, the knife, a flashlight, cotton, a cartridge of tape, a snapshot of his parents and Papa Jan, and an extra set of coveralls. Under his right sleeve there was a bandage on his arm, though if he were taken for treatment it would almost certainly be found. He wore sun-glasses and smiled, pedaling southeast among other cyclists on the path toward '36081. Cars skimmed past in rhythmic sequence over the roadway that paralleled the path. Pebbles kicked by the cars' airjets pinged now and then against the metal divider.

He stopped every hour or so and rested for a few minutes. He ate half a cake and drank some of the coke. He thought about Cuba, and what he would take from '33037 to trade there. He thought about the women on Cuba. Probably they would be attracted by a new arrival. They would be completely untreated, passionate beyond imagining, as beautiful as Lilac or even more beautiful . . .

He rode for five hours, and then he turned around and rode back.

He forced his mind to his assignment. He was the staff 663 in a medicenter's pediatrics division. It was boring work, endless gene examinations with little variation, and it was the sort of assignment from which one was seldom transferred. He would be there for the rest of his life.

Every four or five weeks he claimed a visit to his parents in Afr.

In February of 170 the claim was granted.

He got off the plane at four in the morning Afr time and went into the waiting room, holding his right elbow and looking uncomfortable, his kit slung on his left shoulder. The member who had got off the plane behind him, and who had helped him up when he had fallen, put her bracelet to a phone for him. "Are you sure you're all right?" she asked.

"I'm fine," he said, smiling. "Thanks, and enjoy your visit." To the phone he said, "Anna SG38P2823." The member went away.

The screen flashed and patterned as the connection was made, and then it went dark and stayed dark. *She's been transferred,* he thought; *she's off the continent.* He waited for the phone to tell him. But she said, "Just a second, I can't—" and was there, blurry-close. She sat back down on the edge of her bed, rubbing her eyes, in pajamas. "Who is it?" she asked. Behind her a member turned over. It was Saturday night. Or was she married?

"It's Li RM," he said.

"Who?" she asked. She looked at him and leaned closer, blinking. She was more beautiful than he remembered; a little older-looking, beautiful. Were there ever such eyes?

"Li RM," he said, making himself be only courteous, memberlike. "Don't you remember? From IND26110, back in 162."

Her brow contracted uneasily for an instant. "Oh yes, of course," she said, and smiled. "Of course I remember. How are you, Li?"

"Very well," he said. "How are you?"

"Fine," she said, and stopped smiling.

"Married?"

"No," she said. "I'm glad you called, Li. I want to thank you. You know, for helping me."

"Thank Uni," he said.

"No, no," she said. "Thank you. Belatedly." She smiled again.

"I'm sorry to call at this hour," he said. "I'm passing through Afr on a transfer."

"That's all right," she said. "I'm glad you did."

"Where are you?" he asked.

"In '14509."

"That's where my sister lives."

"Really?" she said.

"Yes," he said. "Which building are you in?"

"P51."

"She's in A-something."

The member behind her sat up and she turned and said something to him. He smiled at Chip. She turned and said, "This is Li XE."

"Hello," Chip said, thinking *'14509, P51; '14509, P51.*

"Hello, brother," Li XE's lips said; his voice didn't reach the phone.

"Is something wrong with your arm?" Lilac asked.

He was still holding it. He let it go. "No," he said. "I fell getting off the plane."

"Oh, I'm sorry," she said. She glanced beyond him. "There's a member waiting," she said. "We'd better say good-by now."

"Yes," he said. "Good-by. It was nice seeing you. You haven't changed at all."

"Neither have you," she said. "Good-by, Li." She rose and reached forward and was gone.

He tapped off and gave way to the member behind him.

She was dead; a normal healthy member lying down now beside her boy-friend in '14509, P51. How could he risk talking to her of anything that wasn't as normal and healthy as she was? He should spend the day with his parents and fly back to Usa; go bicycling next Sunday and this time not turn back.

He walked around the waiting room. There was an outline map of Afr on one wall, with lights at the major cities and thin orange lines connecting them. Near the north was '14510, near where she was. Half the continent from '71330, where he was. An orange line connected the two lights.

He watched the flight-schedule signboard flashing and blinking, revising the *Sunday 18 Feb* schedule. A plane for '14510 was leaving at 8:20 in the evening, forty minutes before his own flight for USA33100.

He went to the glass that faced the field and watched members single-filing onto the escalator of the plane he had left. An orange-coveralled member came and waited by the scanner.

He turned back to the waiting room. It was nearly empty. Two members who had been on the plane with him, a woman holding a sleeping infant and a man carrying two kits, put their wrists and the infant's wrist to the scanner at the door to the carport—*yes,* it greened three times—and went out. An orange-coveralled member, on his knees by a water fountain, unscrewed a plate at its base; another pushed a floor polisher to the side of the waiting room, touched a scanner—*yes*—and pushed the polisher out through a swing-door.

He thought for a moment, watching the member working at the fountain, and then he crossed the waiting room, touched the carpet-door scanner—*yes* —and went out. A car for '71334 was waiting, three members in it. He touched the scanner—*yes*—and got into the car, apologizing to the members for having kept them waiting. The door closed and the car started. He sat with his kit in his lap, thinking.

When he got to his parents' apartment he went in quietly, shaved, and then woke them. They were pleased, even happy, to see him.

The three of them talked and ate breakfast and talked more. They claimed a call to Peace, in Eur, and it was granted; they talked with her and her Karl, her ten-year-old Bob and her eight-year-old Yin. Then, at his suggestion, they went to the Museum of the Family's Achievements.

After lunch he slept for three hours and then they railed to the Amusement Gardens. His father joined a volleyball game, and he and his mother sat on a bench and watched. "Are you sick again?" she asked him.

He looked at her. "No," he said. "Of course not. I'm fine."

She looked closely at him. She was fifty-seven now, gray-haired, her tan skin wrinkled. "You've been thinking about something," she said. "All day."

"I'm well," he said. "Please. You're my mother; believe me."

She looked into his eyes with concern.

"I'm well," he said.

After a moment she said, "All right, Chip."

Love for her suddenly filled him; love, and gratitude, and a boylike feeling of oneness with her. He clasped her shoulder and kissed her cheek. "I love you, Suzu," he said.

She laughed. "Christ and Wei," she said, "what a memory you have!"

"That's because I'm healthy," he said. "Remember that, will you? I'm healthy and happy. I want you to remember that."

"Why?"

"Because," he said.

He told them that his plane left at eight. "We'll say good-by at the carport," he said. "The airport will be too crowded."

His father wanted to come along anyway, but his mother said no, they would stay in '334; she was tired.

At seven-thirty he kissed them good-by—his father and then his mother, saying in her ear, "Remember"—and got on line for a car to the '71330 airport. The scanner, when he touched it, said *yes*.

The waiting room was even more crowded than he had hoped it would be. Members in white and yellow and pale blue walked and stood and sat and waited in line, some with kits and some without. A few members in orange moved among them.

He looked at the signboard; the 8:20 flight for '14510 would load from lane two. Members were in line there, and beyond the glass, a plane was swinging into place against a rising escalator. Its door opened and a member came out, another behind him.

Chip made his way through the crowd to the swing-door at the side of the room, false-touched its scanner, and pushed through; into a depot area where crates and cartons stood ranked under white light, like Uni's memory banks. He unslung his kit and jammed it between a carton and the wall.

He walked ahead normally. A cart of steel containers crossed his path, pushed by an orange-coveralled member who glanced at him and nodded.

He nodded back, kept walking, and watched the member push the cart out through a large open portal onto the floodlit field.

He went in the direction from which the member had come, into an area where members in orange were putting steel containers on the conveyor of a washing machine and filling other containers with coke and steaming tea from the taps of giant drums. He kept walking.

He false-touched a scanner and went into a room where coveralls, ordinary ones, hung on hooks, and two members were taking off orange ones. "Hello," he said.

"Hello," they both said.

He went to a closet door and slid it open; a floor polisher and bottles of green liquid were inside. "Where are the cuvs?" he asked.

"In there," one of the members said, nodding at another closet.

He went to it and opened it. Orange coveralls were on shelves; orange toeguards, pairs of heavy orange gloves.

"Where did you come from?" the member asked.

"RUS50937," he said, taking a pair of coveralls and a pair of toeguards. "We kept the cuvs in there."

"They're supposed to be in *there,*" the member said, closing white coveralls.

"I've been in Rus," the other member, a woman, said. "I had two assignments there; first four years and then three years."

He took his time putting on the toeguards, finishing as the two members chuted their orange coveralls and went out.

He pulled the orange coveralls on over his white ones and closed them all the way to his throat. They were heavier than ordinary coveralls and had extra pockets.

He looked in other closets, found a wrench and a good-sized piece of yellow paplon.

He went back to where he had left his kit, got it out, and wrapped the paplon around it. The swing-door bumped him. "Sorry," a member said, coming in. "Did I hurt you?"

"No," he said, holding the wrapped kit.

The orange-coveralled member went on.

He waited for a moment, watching him, and then he tucked the kit under his left arm and got the wrench from his pocket. He gripped it in his right hand, in a way that he hoped looked natural.

He followed after the member, then turned and went to the portal that opened onto the field.

The escalator leaning against the flank of the lane-two plane was empty. A cart, probably the one he had seen pushed out, stood at the foot of it, beside the scanner.

Another escalator was sinking into the ground, and the plane it had served was on its way toward the runways. There was an 8:10 flight to Chi, he recalled.

He crouched on one knee, put his kit and the wrench down on concrete, and pretended to have trouble with his toeguard. Everyone in the waiting room would be watching the plane for Chi when it lifted; that was when he would go onto the escalator. Orange legs rustled past him, a member walking toward the hangers. He took off his toeguard and put it back on, watching the plane pivot . . .

It raced forward. He gathered his kit and the wrench, stood up, and walked normally. The brightness of the floodlights unnerved him, but he told himself that no one was watching him, everyone was watching the plane. He walked to the escalator, false-touched the scanner—the cart beside it helped, justifying his awkwardness—and stepped onto the upgoing stairs. He clutched his paplon-wrapped kit and the damp-handled wrench as he rose quickly toward the open plane door. He stepped off the escalator and into the plane.

Two members in orange were busy at the dispensers. They looked at him and he nodded. They nodded back. He went down the aisle toward the bathroom.

He went into the bathroom, leaving the door open, and put his kit on the floor. He turned to a sink, worked its faucets, and tapped them with the wrench. He got down on his knees and tapped the drainpipe. He opened the jaws of the wrench and put them around the pipe.

He heard the escalator stop, and then start again. He leaned over and looked out the door. The members were gone.

He put down the wrench, got up, closed the door, and pulled open the orange coveralls. He took them off, folded them lengthwise, and rolled them into as compact a bundle as he could. Kneeling, he unwrapped his kit and opened it. He squeezed in the coveralls, and folded the yellow paplon and put that in too. He took the toeguards off his sandals, nested them together, and tucked them into one of the kit's corners. He put the wrench in, stretched the cover tight, and pressed it closed.

With the kit slung on his shoulder, he washed his hands and face with cold water. His heart was beating quickly but he felt good, excited, alive. He looked in the mirror at his one-green-eyed self. *Fight Uni!*

He heard the voices of members coming aboard the plane. He stayed at the sink, wiping his already-dry hands.

The door opened and a boy of ten or so came in.

"Hi," Chip said, wiping his hands. "Did you have a nice day?"

"Yes," the boy said.

Chip chuted the towel. "First time you've flown?"

"*No,*" the boy said, opening his coveralls. "I've done it lots of times." He sat down on one of the toilets.

"See you inside," Chip said, and went out.

The plane was about a third filled, with more members filing in. He took the nearest empty aisle seat, checked his kit to make sure it was securely closed, and stowed it below.

It would be the same at the other end. When everyone was leaving the plane he would go into the bathroom and put on the orange coveralls. He would be working at the sink when the members came aboard with the refill containers, and he would leave after they left. In the depot area, behind a crate or in a closet, he would get rid of the coveralls, the toeguards, and the wrench; and then he would false-touch out of the airport and walk to '14509. It was eight kilometers east of '510; he had checked on a map at the MFA that morning. With luck he would be there by midnight or half past.

"Isn't that odd," the member next to him said.

He turned to her.

She was looking toward the back of the plane. "There's no seat for that member," she said.

A member was walking slowly up the aisle, looking to one side and then the other. All the seats were taken. Members were looking about, trying to be of help to him.

"There *must* be one," Chip said, lifting himself in his seat and looking about. "Uni couldn't have made a mistake."

"There isn't," the member next to him said. "Every seat is filled."

Conversation rose in the plane. There was indeed no seat for the member. A woman took a child onto her lap and called to him.

The plane began moving and the TV screens went on, with a program about Afr's geography and resources.

He tried to pay attention to it, thinking there might be information in it that would be useful to him, but he couldn't. If he were found and treated now, he would never get alive again. This time Uni would make certain that he would see no meaning in even a thousand leaves on a thousand wet stones.

He got to '14509 at twenty past midnight. He was wide awake, still on Usa time, with afternoon energy.

First he went to the Pre-U, and then to the bike station on the plaza nearest building P51. He made two trips to the bike station, and one to P51's dining hall and its supply center.

At three o'clock he went into Lilac's room. He looked at her by flashlight while she slept—looked at her cheek, her neck, her dark hand on the pillow —and then he went to the desk and tapped on the lamp.

"Anna," he said, standing at the foot of the bed, "Anna, you have to get up now."

She mumbled something.

"You have to get up now, Anna," he said. "Come on, get up."

She raised herself with a hand at her eyes making little sounds of complaint. Sitting, she drew the hand away and peered at him; recognized him and frowned bewilderedly.

"I want you to come for a ride with me," he said. "A bike ride. You mustn't talk loud and you mustn't call for help." He reached into his pocket and took out a gun. He held it the way it seemed meant to be held, with his first finger across the trigger, the rest of his hand holding the handle, and the front of it pointed at her face. "I'll kill you if you don't do what I tell you," he said. "Don't shout now, Anna."

Three

She stared at the gun, and at him.

"The generator's weak'" he said, "but it made a hole a centimeter deep in the wall of the museum and it'll make a deeper one in you. So you'd better obey me. I'm sorry to frighten you, but eventually you'll understand why I'm doing it."

"This is terrible!" she said. "You're still sick!"

"Yes," he said, "and I've gotten worse. So do as I say or the Family will lose two valuable members; first you, and then me."

"How can you *do* this, Li?" she said. "Can't you see yourself—with a *weapon* in your hand, *threatening* me?"

"Get up and get dressed," he said.

"Please, let me call—"

"Get dressed," he said. "Quickly!"

"All right," she said, turning aside the blanket. "All right, I'll do exactly as you say." She got up and opened her pajamas.

He backed away, watching her, keeping the gun pointed at her.

She took off her pajamas, let them fall, and turned to the shelf for a set of coveralls. He watched her breasts and the rest of her body, which in subtle ways—a fullness of the buttocks, a roundness of the thighs—was different too from the normal. How beautiful she was!

She stepped into the coveralls and put her arms into the sleeves. "Li, I beg you," she said, looking at him, "let's go down to the medicenter and—"

"Don't talk," he said.

She closed the coveralls and put her feet into her sandals. "Why do you want to go *bicycling?*" she said. "It's the middle of the night."

"Pack your kit," he said.

"My take-along?"

"Yes," he said. "Put in another set of cuvs and your first-aid kit and your clippers. And anything that's important to you that you want to keep. Do you have a flashlight?"

"What are you planning to *do?*" she asked.

"Pack your kit," he said.

She packed her kit, and when she had closed it he took it and slung it on his shoulder. "We're going to go around behind the building," he said. "I've got two bikes there. We're going to walk side by side and I'll have the gun in my pocket. If we pass a member and you give any indication that anything's wrong, I'll kill you *and* the member, do you understand?"

"Yes," she said.

"Do whatever I tell you. If I say stop and fix your sandal, stop and fix your sandal. We're going to pass scanners without touching them. You've done that before; now you're going to do it again."

"We're not coming back here?" she said.

"No. We're going far away."

"Then there's a snapshot I'd like to take."

"Get it," he said. "I told you to take whatever you wanted to keep."

She went to the desk, opened the drawer, and rummaged in it. *A snapshot of King?* he wondered. No, King was part of her "sickness." Probably one of her family. "It's in here somewhere," she said, sounding nervous, not right.

He hurried to her and pushed her aside. *Li RM gun 2 bicy* was written on the bottom of the drawer. A pen was in her hand. "I'm trying to help you," she said.

He felt like hitting her but stopped himself; but stopping was wrong, she would know he wouldn't hurt her; he hit her face with his open hand, stingingly hard. "Don't try to trick me!" he said. "Don't you realize how sick I am? *You'll* be dead and maybe a dozen *other* members will be dead if you do something like this again!"

She stared wide-eyed at him, trembling, her hand at her cheek.

He was trembling too, knowing he had hurt her. He snatched the pen from her hand, made zigzags over what she had written, and covered it with papers and a nameber book. He threw the pen in the drawer and closed it, took her elbow and pushed her toward the door.

They went out of her room and down the hallway, walking side by side. He kept his hand in his pocket, holding the gun. "Stop shaking," he said. "I won't hurt you if you do what I tell you."

They rode down escalators. Two members came toward them, riding up. "You and them," he said. "And anyone else who comes along."

She said nothing.

He smiled at the members. They smiled back. She nodded at them.

"This is my second transfer this year," he said to her.

They rode down more escalators, and stepped onto the one leading to the lobby. Three members, two with telecomps, stood talking by the scanner at one of the doors. "No tricks now," he said.

They rode down, reflected at a distance in dark-outside glass. The members kept talking. One of them put his telecomp on the floor.

They stepped off the escalator. "Wait a minute, Anna," he said. She stopped and faced him. "I've got an eyelash in my eye," he said. "Do you have a tissue?"

She reached into her pocket and shook her head.

He found one under the gun and took it out and gave it to her. He stood facing the members and held his eye wide open, his other hand in his pocket again. She held the tissue to his eye. She was still trembling. "It's only an eyelash," he said. "Nothing to be nervous about."

Beyond her the member had picked up his telecomp and the three were shaking hands and kissing. The two with telecomps touched the scanner. *Yes,* it winked, *yes.* They went out. The third member came toward them, a man in his twenties.

Chip moved Lilac's hand away. "That's it," he said, blinking. "Thanks, sister."

"Can I be of help?" the member asked. "I'm a 101."

"No, thanks, it was just an eyelash," Chip said. Lilac moved. Chip looked at her. She put the tissue in her pocket.

The member, glancing at the kit, said, "Have a good trip."

"Thanks," Chip said. "Good night."

"Good night," the member said, smiling at them.

"Good night," Lilac said.

They went toward the doors and saw in them the reflection of the member stepping onto an upgoing escalator. "I'm going to lean close to the scanner," Chip said. "Touch the side of it, not the plate."

They went outside. "Please, Li," Lilac said, "for the sake of the Family, let's go back in and go up to the medicenter."

"Be quiet," he said.

They turned into the passageway between the building and the next one. The darkness grew deeper and he took out his flashlight.

"What are you going to do to me?" she asked.

"Nothing," he said, "unless you try to trick me again."

"Then what do you want me for?" she asked.

He didn't answer.

There was a scanner at the cross-passage behind the buildings. Lilac's hand went up; Chip said, "No!" They passed it without touching, and Lilac made a distressed sound and said under her breath, "Terrible!"

The bikes were leaning against the wall where he had left them. His blanket-wrapped kit was in the basket of one, with cakes and drink containers squeezed in with it. A blanket was draped over the basket of the other; he put Lilac's kit down into it and closed the blanket around it, tucking it snugly. "Get on," he said, holding the bike upright for her.

She got on and held the handlebars.

"We'll go straight along between the buildings to the East Road," he said. "Don't turn or stop or gear up unless I tell you to."

He got astride the other bike. He pushed the flashlight down into the side of the basket, with the light shining out through the mesh at the pavement ahead.

"All right, let's go," he said.

They pedaled side by side down the straight passage that was all darkness except for columns of lesser darkness between buildings, and far above a narrow strip of stars, and far ahead the pale blue spark of a single walkway light.

"Gear up a little," he said.

They rode faster.

"When are you due for your next treatment?" he asked.

She was silent, and then said, "Marx eighth."

Two weeks, he thought. Christ and Wei, why couldn't it have been tomorrow or the next day? Well, it could have been worse; it could have been *four* weeks.

"Will I be able to get it?" she asked.

There was no point in disturbing her more than he had already. "Maybe," he said. "We'll see."

He had intended to go a short distance every day, during the free hour when cyclists would attract no attention. They would go from parkland to parkland, passing one city or perhaps two, and make their way by small steps to '12082 on Afr's north coast, the city nearest Majorca.

That first day, though, in the parkland north of '14509, he changed his mind. Finding a hiding place was harder than he expected; not until long after sunrise—around eight o'clock, he guessed—were they settled under a rock-ledge canopy fronted by a thicket of saplings whose gaps he had filled with cut branches. Soon after, they heard a copter's hum; it passed and repassed above them while he pointed the gun at Lilac and she sat motionless, watching him, a half-eaten cake in her hands. At midday they heard branches cracking, leaves slashing, and a voice no more than twenty meters away. It spoke unintelligibly, in the slow flat way one addressed a telephone or a voice-input telecomp.

Either Lilac's desk-drawer message had been found or, more likely, Uni had put together his disappearance, her disappearance, and two missing bicycles.

So he changed his mind and decided that having been looked for and missed, they would stay where they were all week and ride on Sunday. They would make a sixty- or seventy-kilometer hop—not directly to the north but to the northeast—then settle and hide for another week. Four or five Sundays would bring them in a curving path to '12082, and each Sunday Lilac would be more herself and less Anna SG, more helpful or at least less anxious to see him "helped."

Now, though, she was Anna SG. He tied and gagged her with blanket strips and slept with the gun at his hand till the sun went down. In the middle of the night he tied and gagged her again, and carried away his bike. He came back in a few hours with cakes and drinks and two more blankets, towels and toilet paper, a "wristwatch" that had already stopped ticking, and two Français books. She was lying awake where he had left her, her eyes anxious and pitying. Held captive by a sick member, she suffered his abuses forgivingly. She was sorry for him.

But in daylight she looked at him with revulsion. He touched his cheek and felt two days' stubble. Smiling, slightly embarrassed, he said, "I haven't had a treatment in almost a year."

She lowered her head and put a hand over her eyes. "You've made yourself into an animal," she said.

"That's what we are, really," he said. "Christ, Marx, Wood, and Wei made us into something dead and unnatural."

She turned away when he began to shave, but she glanced over her shoulder, glanced again, and then turned and watched distastefully. "Don't you cut your skin?" she asked.

"I did in the beginning," he said, pressing taut his cheek and working the razor easily, watching it in the side of his flashlight propped on a stone. "I had to keep my hand at my face for days."

"Do you always use tea?" she asked.

He laughed. "No," he said. "It's a substitute for water. Tonight I'm going to go looking for a pond or a stream."

"How often do you—do that?" she asked.

"Every day," he said. "I missed yesterday. It's a nuisance, but it's only for a few more weeks. At least I hope so."

"What do you mean?" she said.

He said nothing, kept shaving.

She turned away.

He read one of the Français books, about the causes of a war that had lasted thirty years. Lilac slept, and then she sat on a blanket and looked at him and at the trees and at the sky.

"Do you want me to teach you this language?" he asked.

"What for?" she said.

"Once you wanted to learn it," he said. "Do you remember? I gave you lists of words."

"Yes," she said, "I remember. I learned them, but I've forgotten them. I'm well now; what would I want to learn it now for?"

He did calisthenics and made her do them too, so that they would be ready for Sunday's long ride. She followed his directions unprotestingly.

That night he found, not a stream, but a concrete-banked irrigation channel about two meters wide. He bathed in its slow-flowing water, then brought filled drink containers back to the hiding place and woke Lilac and untied her. He led her through the trees and stood and watched while she bathed. Her wet body glistened in the faint light of the quarter moon.

He helped her up onto the bank, handed her a towel, and stayed close to her while she dried herself. "Do you know why I'm doing this?" he asked her.

She looked at him.

"Because I love you," he said.

"Then let me go," she said.

He shook his head.

"Then how can you say you love me?"

"I do," he said.

She bent over and dried her legs. "Do you want me to get sick again?" she asked.

"Yes," he said.

"Then you *hate* me," she said, "you don't love me." She stood up straight.

He took her arm, cool and moist, smooth. "Lilac," he said.

"Anna."

He tried to kiss her lips but she turned her head and drew away. He kissed her cheek.

"Now point your gun at me and 'rape' me," she said.

"I won't do that," he said. He let go of her arm.

"I don't know why not," she said, getting into her coveralls. She closed them fumblingly. "Please, Li," she said, "let's go back to the city. I'm *sure* you can be cured, because if you were really sick, *incurably* sick, you *would* 'rape' me. You'd be much less kind than you are."

"Come on," he said, "let's get back to the place."

"Please, Li—" she said.

"*Chip*," he said. "*My* name is *Chip*. Come on." He jerked his head and they started through the trees.

Toward the end of the week she took his pen and the book he wasn't reading and drew pictures on the inside of the book's cover—near-likenesses of Christ and Wei, groups of buildings, her left hand, and a row of shaded crosses and sickles. He looked to make sure she wasn't writing messages that she would try to give to someone on Sunday.

Later he drew a building and showed it to her.

"What is it?" she asked.

"A building," he said.

"No it isn't."

"It is," he said. "They don't all have to be blank and rectangular."

"What are the ovals?"

"Windows."

"I've never seen a building like this one," she said. "Not even in the Pre-U. Where is it?"

"Nowhere," he said. "I made it up."

"Oh," she said. "Then it *isn't* a building, not really. How can you draw things that aren't real?"

"I'm sick, remember?" he said.

She gave the book back to him, not looking at his eyes. "Don't joke about it," she said.

He hoped —well, didn't *hope,* but thought it might possibly happen—that Saturday night, out of custom or desire or even only memberlike kindness, she would show a willingness for him to come close to her. She didn't, though. She was the same as she had been every other night, sitting silently in the dusk with her arms around her knees, watching the band of purpling sky between the shifting black treetops and the black rock ledge overhead.

"It's Saturday night," he said.

"I know," she said.

They were silent for a few moments, and then she said, "I'm not going to be able to have my treatment, am I?"

"No," he said.

"Then I might get pregnant," she said. "I'm not supposed to have children and neither are you."

He wanted to tell her that they were going someplace where Uni's decisions were meaningless, but it was too soon; she might become frightened and unmanageable. "Yes, I suppose you're right," he said.

When he had tied her and covered her, he kissed her cheek. She lay in the darkness and said nothing, and he got up from his knees and went to his own blankets.

Sunday's ride went well. Early in the day a group of young members stopped them, but it was only to ask their help in repairing a broken drive chain, and Lilac sat on the grass away from the group while Chip did the job. By sundown they were in the parkland north of '14266. They had gone about seventy-five kilometers.

Again it was hard to find a hiding place, but the one Chip finally found— the broken walls of a pre-U or early-U building, roofed with a sagging mass of vines and creepers—was larger and more comfortable than the one they had used the week before. That same night, despite the day's riding, he went into '266 and brought back a three-day supply of cakes and drinks.

Lilac grew irritable that week. "I want to clean my *teeth,*" she said, "and I want to take a shower. How long are we going to go on this way? Forever?

You may enjoy living like an animal but *I* don't; I'm a human being. And I can't sleep with my hands and feet tied."

"You slept all right last week," he said.

"Well I can't now!"

"Then lie quietly and let *me* sleep," he said.

When she looked at him it was with annoyance, not with pity. She made disapproving sounds when he shaved and when he read; answered curtly or not at all when he spoke. She balked at doing calisthenics, and he had to take out the gun and threaten her.

It was getting close to Marx eighth, her treatment day, he told himself, and this irritability, a natural resentment of captivity and discomfort, was a sign of the healthy Lilac who was buried in Anna SG. It ought to have pleased him, and when he thought about it, it did. But it was much harder to live with than the previous week's sympathy and memberlike docility.

She complained about insects and boredom. There was a rain night and she complained about the rain.

One night Chip woke and heard her moving. He shone his flashlight at her. She had untied her wrists and was untying her ankles. He retied her and struck her.

That Saturday night they didn't speak to each other.

On Sunday they rode again. Chip stayed close to her side and watched her carefully when members came toward them. He reminded her to smile, to nod, to answer greetings, to act as if nothing was wrong. She rode in grim silence, and he was afraid that despite the threat of the gun she might call out for help at any moment or stop and refuse to go on. "Not just you," he said; "everyone in sight. I'll kill them all, I swear I will." She kept riding. She smiled and nodded resentfully. Chip's gearshift jammed and they went only forty kilometers.

Toward the end of the third week her irritation subsided. She sat frowning, picking at blades of grass, looking at her fingertips, turning her bracelet around and around her wrist. She looked at Chip curiously, as if he were someone strange whom she hadn't seen before. She followed his instructions slowly, mechanically.

He worked on his bike, letting her awaken in her own time.

One evening in the fourth week she said, "Where are we going?"

He looked at her for a moment—they were eating the day's last cake—and said, "To an island called Majorca. In the Sea of Eternal Peace."

" 'Majorca'?" she said.

"It's an island of incurables," he said. "There are seven others all over the world. More than seven, really, because some of them are groups. I found them on a map in the Pre-U, back in Ind. They were covered over and they're not shown on MFA maps. I was going to tell you about them the day I was— 'cured.' "

She was silent, and then she said, "Did you tell King?"

It was the first time she had mentioned him. Should he tell her that King hadn't needed to be told, that he had known all along and withheld it from them? What for? King was dead; why diminish her memory of him? "Yes, I did," he said. "He was amazed, and very excited. I don't understand why he —did what he did. You know about it, don't you?"

"Yes, I know," she said. She took a small bite of cake and ate it, not looking at him. "How do they live on this island?" she asked.

"I have no idea," he said. "It might be very rough, very primitive. Better than this, though." He smiled. "Whatever it's like," he said, "it's a free life. It might be highly civilized. The first incurables must have been the most independent and resourceful members."

"I'm not sure that I want to go there," she said.

"Just think about it," he said. "In a few days you'll be sure. You're the one who had the idea that incurable colonies might exist, do you remember? You asked me to look for them."

She nodded. "I remember," she said.

Later in the week she took a new Français book that he had found and tried to read it. He sat beside her and translated it for her.

That Sunday, while they wre riding along, a member pedaled up on Chip's left and stayed even with them. "Hi," he said.

"Hi," Chip said.

"I thought all the old bikes had been phased out," he said.

"So did I," Chip said, "but these are what was there."

The member's bike had a thinner frame and a thumb-knob gear control. "Back in '935?" he asked.

"No, '939," Chip said.

"Oh," the member said. He looked at their baskets, filled with their blanket-wrapped kits.

"We'd better speed up, Li," Lilac said. "The others are out of sight."

"They'll wait for us," Chip said. "They have to; we have the cakes and blankets."

The member smiled.

"No, come on, let's go faster," Lilac said. "It's not fair to make them wait around."

"All right," Chip said, and to the member, "Have a good day."

"You too," he said.

They pedaled faster and pulled ahead.

"Good for you," Chip said. "He was just going to ask why we're carrying so much."

Lilac said nothing.

They went about eighty kilometers that day and reached the parkland northwest of '12471, within another day's ride of '082. They found a fairly good hiding place, a triangular cleft between high rock spurs overhung with trees. Chip cut branches to close off the front of it.

"You don't have to tie me anymore," Lilac said. "I won't run away and I won't try to attract anyone. You can put the gun in your kit."

"You want to go?" Chip said. "To Majorca?"

"Of course," she said. "I'm anxious to. It's what I've always wanted—when I've been myself, I mean."

"All right," he said. He put the gun in his kit and that night he didn't tie her.

Her casual matter-of-factness didn't seem right to him. Shouldn't she have shown more enthusiasm? Yes, and gratitude too; that was what he had expected, he admitted to himself: gratitude, expressions of love. He lay awake listening to her soft slow breathing. Was she really asleep or was she only pretending? Could she be tricking him in some unimaginable way? He shone his flashlight at her. Her eyes were closed, her lips parted, her arms together under the blanket as if she were still tied.

It was only Marx twentieth, he told himself. In another week or two she would show more feeling. He closed his eyes. When he woke she was picking stones and twigs from the ground. "Good morning," she said pleasantly.

They found a narrow trickle of stream nearby, and a green-fruited tree that he thought was an "olivier." The fruit was bitter and strange-tasting. They both preferred cakes.

She asked him how he had avoided his treatments, and he told her about the leaf and the wet stone and the bandages he had made. She was impressed. It was clever of him, she said.

They went into '12471 one night for cakes and drinks, towels, toilet paper, coveralls, new sandals; and to study, as well as they could by flashlight, the MFA map of the area.

"What will we do when we get to '082?" she asked the next morning.

"Hide by the shore," he said, "and watch every night for traders."

"Would they do that?" she asked. "Risk coming ashore?"

"Yes," he said, "I think they would, away from the city."

"But wouldn't they be more likely to go to Eur? It's nearer."

"We'll just have to hope they come to Afr too," he said. "And I want to get some things from the city for *us* to trade when we get *there*, things that they're likely to put a value on. We'll have to think about that."

"Is there any chance that we can find a boat?" she asked.

"I don't think so," he said. "There aren't any offshore islands, so there aren't likely to be any powerboats around. Of course, there are always amusement-garden rowboats, but I can't see us rowing two hundred and eighty kilometers; can you?"

"It's not impossible," she said.

"No," he said, "if worse comes to worst. But I'm counting on traders, or maybe even some kind of organized rescue operation. Majorca has to defend itself, you see, because Uni knows about it; it knows about all the islands. So the members there might keep a lookout for newcomers, to increase their population, increase their strength."

"I suppose they might," she said.

There was another rain night, and they sat together with a blanket around them in the inmost narrow corner of their place, tight between the high rock spurs. He kissed her and tried to work open the top of her coveralls, but she stopped his hand with hers. "I know it doesn't make sense," she said, "but I still have a little of that only-on-Saturday-night feeling. Please? Could we wait till then?"

"It *doesn't* make sense," he said.

"I know," she said, "but please? Could we wait?"

After a moment he said, "Sure, if you want to."

"I do, Chip," she said.

They read, and decided on the best things to take from '082 for trading. He checked over the bikes and she did calisthenics, did them longer and more purposefully than he did.

On Saturday night he came back from the stream and she stood holding the gun, pointing it at him, her eyes narrowed hatingly. "He called me before he did it," she said.

He said, "What are you—" and "King!" she cried. "He called me! You lying, hating—" She squeezed the gun's trigger. She squeezed it again, harder. She looked at the gun and looked at him.

"There's no generator," he said.

She looked at the gun and looked at him, drawing a deep breath through flaring nostrils.

"Why the hate do you—" he said, and she swept back the gun and threw it at him; he raised his hands and it hit him in the chest, making pain and no air in him.

"*Go* with you?" she said. "*Fuck* with you? After you killed him? Are you—are you *fou*, you green-eyed cochon, chien, batard!"

He held his chest, found breath. "Didn't kill him!" he said. "He killed *himself*, Lilac! Christ and—"

"Because you lied to him! Lied about us! Told him we'd been—"

"That was *his* idea; I *told* him it wasn't true! I told him and he wouldn't believe me!"

"You *admitted* it," she said. "He said he didn't care, we deserved each other, and then he tapped off and—"

"Lilac," he said, "I swear by my love of the Family, I *told him it wasn't true!*"

"*Then why did he kill himself?*"

"Because he knew!"

"Because you told him!" she said, and turned and grabbed up her bike—its basket was packed—and rammed it against the branches piled at the place's front.

He ran and caught the back of the bike, held it with both hands. "You stay here!" he said.

"Let go of it!" she said, turning.

He took the bike at its middle, wrenched it away from her, and flung it aside. He grabbed her arm. She hit at him but he held her. "He knew about the *islands!*" he said. "The *islands!* He'd *been* near one, traded with the members! That's how I know they come ashore!"

She stared at him. "What are you talking about?" she said.

"He'd had an assignment near one of the islands," he said. "The Falklands, off Arg. And he'd met the members and traded with them. He hadn't told us because he knew we would want to go, and *he didn't* want to! That's why he killed himself! He knew you were going to find out, from me, and he was ashamed of himself, and tired, and he wasn't going to be 'King' anymore."

"You're lying to me the way you lied to him," she said, and tore her arm free, her coveralls splitting at the shoulder.

"That's how he got the perfume and tobacco seeds," he said.

"I don't want to hear you," she said. "Or see you. I'm going by myself." She went to her bike, picked up her kit and the blanket trailing from it.

"Don't be stupid," he said.

She righted the bike, dumped the kit in the basket, and jammed the blanket in on top of it. He went to her and held the bike's seat and handlebar. "You're not going alone," he said.

"Oh yes I am," she said, her voice quavering. They held the bike between them. Her faced was blurred in the growing darkness.

"I'm not going to let you," he said.

"I'll do what *he* did before I go with *you.*"

"You listen to me, you—" he said. "I could have been on one of the islands half a year ago! I was on my way and I turned back, because I didn't want to leave you dead and brainless!" He put his hand on her chest and pushed her hard, sent her back flat against rock wall and slung the bike rolling and bumping away. He went to her and held her arms against the rock. "I came all the way from Usa," he said, "and I haven't enjoyed this animal life any more than you have. I don't give a fight whether you love me or hate me"— "I hate you," she said—"you're going to stay with me! The gun doesn't work but other things do, like rocks and hands. You won't have to kill yourself because—" Pain burst in his groin—her knee—and she was away from him and at the branches, a pale yellow shape, thrashing, pushing.

He went and caught her by the arm, swung her around, and threw her shrieking to the ground. "*Batard!*" she shrieked. "*You sick aggressive—*" and he dived onto her and clapped his hand over her mouth, clamped it down as tight as he could. Her teeth caught the skin of his palm and bit it, bit it harder. Her legs kicked and her fisted hands hit his head. He got a knee on her thigh, a foot on her other ankle; caught her wrist, let her other hand hit him, her teeth go on biting. "Someone might be here!" he said. "It's Saturday night! Do you want to get us *both* treated, you stupid garce?" She kept hitting him, biting his palm.

The hitting slowed and stopped; her teeth parted, let go. She lay panting, watching him. "Garce!" he said. She tried to move the leg under his foot, but he bore down harder against it. He kept holding her wrist and covering her mouth. His palm felt as if she had bitten flesh out of it.

Having her under him, having her subdued, with her legs held apart, suddenly excited him. He thought of tearing off her coveralls and "raping" her. Hadn't she said they should wait till Saturday night? And maybe it would stop all the cloth about King, and her hating him; stop the fighting—that was what they had been doing, *fighting*—and the Français hate-names.

She looked at him.

He let go of her wrist and took her coveralls where they were split at the shoulder. He tore them down across her chest and she began hitting him again and straining her legs and biting his palm.

He tore the coveralls away in stretching splitting pieces until her whole front was open, and then he felt her; felt her soft fluid breasts and her stomach's smoothness, her mound with a few close-lying hairs on it, the moist lips below. Her hands hit his head and clutched at his hair; her teeth bit his palm. He kept feeling her with his other hand—breasts, stomach, mound, lips; stroking, rubbing, fingering, growing more excited—and then he opened his coveralls. Her leg wrenched out from under his foot and kicked. She rolled, trying to throw him off her, but he pressed her back down, held her thigh, and threw his leg over hers. He mounted squarely atop her, his feet on her ankles locking her legs bent outward around his knees. He ducked his loins and thrust himself at her; caught one of her hands and fingers of the other. "Stop," he said, "stop," and kept thrusting. She bucked and squirmed, bit deeper into his palm. He found himself partway inside her; pushed, and was all the way in. "Stop," he said, "stop." He moved his length slowly; let go of her hands and found her breasts beneath him. He caressed their softness, the stiffening nipples. She bit his hand and squirmed. "Stop," he said, "stop it, Lilac." He moved himself slowly in her, then faster and harder.

He got up onto his knees and looked at her. She lay with one arm over her eyes and the other thrown back, her breasts rising and falling.

He stood up and found one of his blankets, shook it out and spread it over her up to her arms. "Are you all right?" he asked, crouching beside her.

She didn't say anything.

He found his flashlight and looked at his palm. Blood was running from an oval of bright wounds. "Christ and Wei," he said. He poured water over it, washed it with soap, and dried it. He looked for the first-aid kit and couldn't find it. "Did you take the first-aid kit?" he asked.

She didn't say anything.

Holding his hand up, he found her kit on the ground and opened it and got out the first-aid kit. He sat on a stone and put the kit in his lap and the flashlight on another stone alongside.

"Animal," she said.

"I don't bite," he said. "And I also don't try to kill. Christ and Wei, you thought the gun was working." He sprayed healer on his palm; a thin coat and then a thicker one.

"Cochon," she said.

"Oh come on," he sid, "don't start that again."

He unwrapped a bandage and heard her getting up, heard her coveralls rustling as she took them off. She came over nude and took the flashlight and went to her kit; took out soap, a towel, and coveralls, and went to the back of the place, where he had piled stones between the spurs, making steps leading out toward the stream.

He put the bandage on in the dark and then found her flashlight on the ground near her bike. He put the bike with his, gathered blankets and made the two usual sleeping places, put her kit by hers, and picked up the gun and the pieces of her coveralls. He put the gun in his kit.

The moon slid over one of the spurs behind leaves that were black and motionless.

She didn't come back and he began to worry that she had gone away on foot.

Finally, though, she came. She put the soap and towel into her kit and switched off the flashlight and got between her blankets.

"I got excited having you under me that way," he said. "I've always wanted you, and these last few weeks have been just about unbearable. You know I love you, don't you?"

"I'm going alone," she said.

"When we get to Majorca," he said, "*if* we get there, you can do what you want; but *until* we get there we're staying together. That's *it,* Lilac."

She didn't say anything.

He woke hearing strange sounds, squeals and pained whimpers. He sat up and shone the light on her; her hand was over her mouth, and tears were running down her temples from her closed eyes.

He hurried to her and crouched beside her, touching her head. "Oh Lilac, don't," he said. "Don't cry, Lilac, please don't." She was doing it, he thought, because he had hurt her, maybe internally.

She kept crying.

"Oh Lilac, I'm sorry!" he said. "I'm sorry, love! Oh Christ and Wei, I wish the gun *had* been working!"

She shook her head, holding her mouth.

"Isn't that why you're crying?" he said. "Because I hurt you? Then why? If you don't want to go with me, you don't really have to."

She shook her head again and kept crying.

He didn't know what to do. He stayed beside her, caressing her head and asking her why she was crying and telling her not to, and then he got his blankets, spread them alongside her, and lay down and turned her to him and held her. She kept crying, and he woke up and she was looking at him, lying on her side with her head propped on her hand. "It doesn't make sense for us to go separately," she said, "so we'll stay together."

He tried to recall what they had said before sleeping. As far as he could remember, nothing; she had been crying. "All right," he said, confused.

"I feel awful about the gun," she said. "How could I have done that? I was sure you had lied to King."

"I feel awful about what *I* did," he said.

"Don't," she said. "I don't blame you. It was perfectly natural. How's your hand?"

He took it out from under the blanket and flexed it; it hurt badly. "Not bad," he said.

She took it in her hand and looked at the bandage. "Did you spray it?" she asked.

"Yes," he said.

She looked at him, still holding his hand. Her eyes were large and brown and morning-bright. "Did you really start for one of the islands and turn back?" she asked.

He nodded.

She smiled. "You're tres fou," she said.

"No I'm not," he said.

"You are," she said, and looked at his hand again. She took it to her lips and kissed his fingertips one by one.

Four

They didn't get started until mid-morning, and then they rode quickly for a long while to make up for their laxness. It was an odd day, hazy and heavy-aired, the sky greenish gray and the sun a white disc that could be looked at with fully opened eyes. It was a freak of climate control; Lilac remembered a similar day in Chi when she was twelve or thirteen. ("Is that where you were born?" "No, I was born in Mex." "You were? I was too!") There were no shadows, and bikes coming toward them seemed to ride above the ground like cars. Members glanced at the sky apprehensively, and coming nearer, nodded without smiling.

When they were sitting on grass, sharing a container of coke, Chip said, "We'd better go slowly from now on. There are liable to be scanners in the path and we want to be able to pick the right moment for passing them."

"Scanners because of us?" she said.

"Not necessarily," he said. "Just because it's the city nearest to one of the islands. Wouldn't *you* set up extra safeguards if you were Uni?"

He wasn't as much afraid of scanners as he was that a medical team might be waiting ahead.

"What if there are members watching for us?" she said. "Advisers or doctors, with pictures of us."

"It's not very likely after all this time," he said. "We'll have to take our chances. I've got the gun, and the knife too." He touched his pocket.

After a moment she said, "Would you use it?"

"Yes," he said. "I think so."

"I hope we don't have to," she said.

"So do I."

"You'd better put your sunglasses on," she said.

"Today?" He looked at the sky.

"Because of your eye."

"Oh," he said. "Of course." He took his glasses out and put them on, looked at her and smiled. "There's not much that *you* can do," he said, "except exhale."

"What do you mean?" she said, then flushed and said, "They're not noticeable when I'm dressed."

"First thing I saw when I looked at you," he said. "First *things* I saw."

"I don't believe you," she said. "You're lying. You are. Aren't you?"

He laughed and poked her on the chin.

They rode slowly. There were no scanners in the path. No medical team stopped them.

All the bicycles in the area were new ones, but nobody remarked on their old ones.

By late afternoon they were in '12082. They rode to the west of the city, smelling the sea, watching the path ahead carefully.

They left their bikes in parkland and walked back, to a canteen where there were steps leading down to the beach. The sea was far below them, spreading away smooth and blue, away and away into greenish-gray haze.

"Those members didn't touch," a child said.

Lilac's hand tightened on Chip's. "Keep going," he said. They walked down concrete steps jutting from rough cliff face.

"Say, you there!" a member called, a man. "You two members!"

Chip squeezed Lilac's hand and they turned around. The member was standing behind the scanner at the top of the steps, holding the hand of a naked girl of five or six. She scratched her head with a red shovel, looking at them.

"Did you touch just now?" the member asked.

They looked at each other and at the member. "Of course we did," Chip said. "Yes, of course," Lilac said.

"It didn't say yes," the girl said.

"It did, sister," Chip said gravely. "If it hadn't we wouldn't have gone on, would we?" He looked at the member and let a smile show. The member bent and said something to the girl.

"No I *didn't,*" she said.

"Come on," Chip said to Lilac, and they turned and walked downward again.

"Little hater," Lilac said, and Chip said, "Just keep going."

They went all the way down and stopped at the bottom to take off their sandals. Chip, bending, looked up: the member and the girl were gone; other members were coming down.

The beach was half empty under the strange hazy sky. Members sat and lay on blankets, many of them in their coveralls. They were silent or talked softly, and the music of the speakers—"Sunday, Fun Day"—sounded loud and unnatural. A group of children jumped rope by the water's edge: "Christ, Marx, Wood, and Wei, led us to this perfect day; Marx, Wood, Wei, and Christ—"

They walked westward, holding hands and holding their sandals. The narrow beach grew narrower, emptier. Ahead a scanner stood flanked by cliff and sea. Chip said, "I've never seen one on a beach before."

"Neither have I," Lilac said.

They looked at each other.

"This is the way we'll go," he said. "Later."

She nodded and they walked closer to the scanner.

"I've got a fou impulse to touch it," he said. " 'Fight you, Uni; here I am.' "

"Don't you dare," she said.

"Don't worry," he said, "I won't."

They turned around and walked back to the center of the beach. They took their coveralls off, went into the water, and swam far out. Treading with their backs to the sea, they studied the shore beyond the scanner, the gray cliffs lessening away into greenish-gray haze. A bird flew from the cliffs, circled, and flew back. It disappeared, gone in a hairline cranny.

"There are probably caves where we can stay," Chip said.

A lifeguard whistled and waved at them. They swam back to the beach.

"It's five of five, members," the speakers said. "Litter and towels in the baskets, please. Be mindful of the members around you when you shake out your blankets."

They dressed, went back up the steps, and walked to the grove of trees where they had left their bikes. They carried them farther in and sat down to wait. Chip cleaned the compass and the flashlights and the knife, and Lilac packed the other things they had into a single bundle.

An hour or so after dark they went to the canteen and gathered a carton of cakes and drinks and went down to the beach again. They walked to the scanner and beyond it. The night was moonless and starless; the haze of the day was still above. In the water's lapping edge phosphorescent sparks glittered now and then; otherwise there was only darkness. Chip held the carton of cakes and drinks under his arm and shone his flashlight ahead of them every few moments. Lilac carried the blanket-bundle.

"Traders won't come ashore on a night like this," she said.

"Nobody else will be on the beach either," Chip said. "No sex-wild twelve-year-olds. It's a good thing."

But it wasn't he thought; it was a bad thing. What if the haze remained for days, for nights, blocking them at the very brink of freedom? Was it possible that Uni had *created* it, intentionally, for just that purpose? He smiled at himself. He was tres fou, exactly as Lilac had said.

They walked until they guessed themselves to be midway between '082 and the next city to the west, and then they put down the carton and the bundle and searched the cliff face for a usable cave. They found one within minutes; a low-roofed sand-floored burrow littered with cake wrappers and, intriguingly, two pieces—a green "Egypt," a pink "Ethiop"—torn from a pre-U map. They brought the carton and the bundle into the cave, spread their blankets, ate, and lay down together.

"Can you?" Lilac said. "After this morning and last night?"

"Without treatments," Chip said, "all things are possible."

"It's fantastic," Lilac said.

Later Chip said, "Even if we don't get any farther than this, even if we're caught and treated five minutes from now, it'll have been worth it. We've been ourselves, alive, for a few hours at least."

"I want all of my life, not just a little of it," Lilac said.

"You'll have it," Chip said. "I promise you." He kissed her lips, caressing her cheek in the darkness. "Will you stay with me?" he asked. "On Majorca?"

"Of course," she said. "Why shouldn't I?"

"You weren't going to," he said. "Remember? You weren't even going to come this far with me."

"Christ and Wei, that was *last night,*" she said, and kissed him. "Of course I'm going to stay," she said. "You woke me up and now you're stuck with me."

They lay holding each other and kissing each other.

"Chip!" she cried—in reality, not in his dream.

She wasn't beside him. He sat up and banged his head on stone, groped for the knife he had left stuck in the sand. "Chip! Look!"—as he found it and threw himself over onto knees and one hand. She was a dark shape crouched at the cave's blinding blue opening. He raised the knife, ready to slash whoever was coming.

"No, no," she said, laughing. "Come look! Come on! You won't believe it!"

Squinting at the brilliance of sky and sea, he crawled over to her. "Look," she said happily, pointing up the beach.

A boat sat on the sand about fifty meters away, a small three-rotor launch, old, with a white hull and a red skirting. It sat just clear of the water, tipped slightly forward. There were white splatters on the skirting and the windscreen, part of which seemed to be missing.

"Let's see if it's good!" Lilac said. With her hand on Chip's shoulder she started to rise from the cave; he dropped the knife, caught her arm, and pulled her back. "Wait a minute," he said.

"What for?" She looked at him.

He rubbed his head where he had bumped it, and frowned at the boat—so white and red and empty and convenient in the bright morning haze-free sun. "It's a trick of some kind," he said. "A trap. It's too convenient. We go to sleep and wake up and a boat's been delivered for us. You're right, I *don't* believe it."

"It wasn't 'delivered' for us," she said. "It's been here for weeks. Look at the bird stuff on it, and how deep in the sand the front of it is."

"Where did it come from?" he asked. "There are no islands nearby."

"Maybe traders brought it from Majorca and got caught on shore," she said. "Or maybe they left it behind on purpose, for members like us. You said there might be a rescue operation."

"And nobody's seen it and reported it in the time it's been here?"

"Uni hasn't let anyone onto this part of the beach."

"Let's wait," he said. "Let's just watch and wait a while."

Reluctantly she said, "All right."

"It's too convenient," he said.

"Why must everything be *in*convenient?"

They stayed in the cave. They ate and rebundled the blankets, always watching the boat. They took turns crawling to the back of the cave, and buried their wastes in sand.

Wave edges slipped under the back of the boat's skirting, then fell away toward low tide. Birds circled and landed on the windscreen and handrail, four that were sea gulls and two smaller brown ones.

"It's getting filthier every minute," Lilac said. "And what if it's *been* reported and today's the day it's going to be taken away?"

"Whisper, will you?" Chip said. "Christ and Wei, I wish I'd brought a telescope."

He tried to improvise one from the compass lens, a flashlight lens, and a rolled flap of the food carton, but he couldn't make it work.

"How long are we going to wait?" she asked.

"Till after dark," he said.

No one passed on the bench, and the only sounds were the waves' lapping and the wingbeats and cries of the birds.

He went to the boat alone, slowly and cautiously. It was older than it had looked from the cave; the hull's flaking white paint showed repair scars, and the skirting was dented and cracked. He walked around it without touching it, looking with his flashlight for signs—he didn't know what form they would take—of deception, of danger. He didn't see any; he saw only an old boat that had been inexplicably abandoned, its center seats gone, a third of its windscreen broken away, and all of it spattered with dried white birdwaste. He switched his light off and looked at the cliff—touched the boat's handrail and waited for an alarm. The cliff stayed dark and deserted in pale moonlight.

He stepped onto the skirting, climbed into the boat, and shone his light on its controls. They seemed simple enough: on-off switches for the propulsion rotors and the lift rotor, a speed-control knob calibrated to 100 KPH, a steering lever, a few gauges and indicators, and a switch marked *Controlled* and *Independent* that was set in the independent position. He found the battery housing on the floor between the front seats and unlatched its cover; the battery's fade-out date was April 171, a year away.

He shone his light at the rotor housings. Twigs were piled in one of them. He brushed them out, picked them all out, and shone the light on the rotor within; it was new, shiny. The other rotor was old, its blades nicked and one missing.

He sat down at the controls and found the switch that lighted them. A miniature clock said *5:11 Fri 27 Aug 169*. He switched on one propulsion rotor and then the other; they scraped but then hummed smoothly. He switched them off, looked at the gauges and indicators, and switched the control lights off.

The cliff was the same as before. No members had sprung from hiding. He turned to the sea behind him; it was empty and flat, silvered in a narrowing path that ended under the nearly full moon. No boats were flying toward him.

He sat in the boat for a few minutes, and then he climbed out of it and walked back to the cave.

Lilac was standing outside it. "Is it all right?" she asked.

"No, it's not," he said. "It wasn't left by traders because there's no message or anything in it. The clock stopped last year but it has a new rotor. I didn't try the lift rotor because of the sand, but even if it works, the skirting is cracked in two places and it may just wallow and get nowhere. On the other hand it may take us directly into '082—to a little seaside medicenter—even though it's supposed to be off telecontrol."

Lilac stood looking at him.

"We might as well try it though," he said. "If traders didn't leave it, they're not going to come ashore while it's sitting here. Maybe we're just two very lucky members." He gave the flashlight to her.

He got the carton and the blanket-bundle from the cave and held one under each arm. They started walking toward the boat. "What about the things to trade?" she said.

"We'll have *it*," he said. "A boat must be worth a hundred times more than cameras and first-aid kits." He looked toward the cliff. "All right, doctors!" he called. "You can come out now!"

"Shh, *don't!*" she said.

"We forgot the sandals," he said.

"They're in the carton."

He put the carton and the bundle into the boat and they scraped the birdwaste from the broken windscreen with pieces of shell. They lifted the front of the boat and hauled it around toward the sea, then lifted the back and hauled again.

They kept lifting and hauling at either end and finally they had the boat down in the surf, bobbing and veering clumsily. Chip held it while Lilac climbed aboard, and then he pushed it farther out and climbed in with her.

He sat down at the controls and switched on their lights. She sat in the seat beside him, watching. He glanced at her—she looked anxiously at him—and he switched on the propulsion rotors and then the lift rotor. The boat shook violently, flinging them from side to side. Loud clankings banged from beneath it. He caught the steering lever, held it, and turned the speed-control knob. The boat splashed forward and the shaking and clanging lessened. He turned the speed higher, to twenty, twenty-five. The clanking stopped and the shaking subsided to a steady vibration. The boat scuffed along on the water's surface.

"It's not lifting," he said.

"But it's moving," she said.

"For how long though? It's not built to hit the water this way and the skirting's cracked already." He turned the speed higher and the boat splashed through the crests of swells. He tried the steering lever; the boat responded. He steered north, got out his compass, and compared its reading with the direction indicator's. "Its' not taking us into '082," he said. "At least not yet."

She looked behind them, and up at the sky. "No one's coming," she said.

He turned the speed higher and got a little more lift, but the impact when they scraped the swells was greater. He turned the speed back down. The knob was at fifty-six. "I don't think we're doing more than forty," he said. "It'll be light when we get there, *if* we get there. It's just as well, I suppose; I won't get us onto the wrong island. I don't know how much this is throwing us off course."

Two other islands were near Majorca: EUR91766, forty kilometers to the northeast, the site of a copper-production complex; and EUR91603, eighty-five kilometers to the southwest, where there was an algae-processing complex and a climatonomy sub-center.

Lilac leaned close to Chip, avoiding the wind and spray from the broken part of the windscreen. Chip held the steering lever. He watched the direction indicator and the moonlit sea ahead and the stars that shone above the horizon.

The stars dissolved, the sky began to lighten, and there was no Majorca. There was only the sea, placid and endless all around them.

"If we're doing forty," Lilac said, "it should have taken seven hours. It's been more than that, hasn't it?"

"Maybe we haven't been doing forty," Chip said.

Or maybe he had compensated too much or too little for the eastward drift of the sea. Maybe they had passed Majorca and were heading toward Eur. Or maybe Majorca didn't exist—had been blanked from pre-U maps because pre-U members had "bombed" it to nothing and why should the Family be reminded again of folly and barbarism?

He kept the boat headed a hairline west of north, but slowed it down a little.

The sky grew lighter and still there was no island, no Majorca. They scanned the horizon silently, avoiding each other's eyes.

One final star glimmered above the water in the northeast. No, glimmered *on* the water. No—"There's a light over there," he said.

She looked where he pointed, held his arm.

The light moved in an arc from side to side, then up and down as if beckoning. It was a kilometer or so away.

"Christ and Wei," Chip said softly, and steered toward it.

"Be careful," Lilac said. "Maybe it's—"

He changed hands on the steering lever and got the knife from his pocket, laid it in his lap.

The light went out and a small boat was there. Someone sat waving in it, waving a pale thing that he put on his head—a hat—and then waving his empty hand and arm.

"One member," Lilac said.

"One *person,*" Chip said. He kept steering toward the boat—a rowboat, it looked like—with one hand on the lever and the other on the speed-control knob.

"Look at him!" Lilac said.

The waving man was small and white-bearded, with a ruddy face below his broad-brimmed yellow hat. He was wearing a blue-topped white-legged garment.

Chip slowed the boat, steered it near the rowboat, and switched all three rotors off.

The man—old past sixty-two and blue-eyed, fantastically blue-eyed—smiled with brown teeth and gaps where teeth were missing and said, "Running from the dummies, are you? Looking for liberty?" His boat bobbed in their side-waves. Poles and nets shifted in it—fish-catching equipment.

"Yes," Chip said. "Yes, we are! We're trying to find Majorca."

"Ma*jor*ca?" the man said. He laughed and scratched his beard. "My*or*ca," he said. "Not Ma*jor*ca, My*or*ca! But *Liberty* is what it's called now. It hasn't been called Myorca for—God knows, a hundred years, I guess! Liberty, it is."

"Are we near it?" Lilac asked, and Chip said, "We're friends. We haven't come to—interfere in any way, to try to 'cure' you or anything."

"We're incurables ourselves," Lilac said.

"You wouldn't be coming this way if you wasn't," the man said. "That's what I'm here for, to watch for folks like you and help them into port. Yes, you're near it. That's it over there." He pointed to the north.

And now on the horizon a dark green bar lay low and clear. Pink streaks glowed above its western half—mountains lit by the sun's first rays.

Chip and Lilac looked at it, and looked at each other, and looked again at Majorca-Myorca-Liberty.

"Hold fast," the man said, "and I'll tie onto your stern and come aboard."

They turned in their seats and faced each other. Chip took the knife from his lap, smiled, and tossed it to the floor. He took Lilac's hands.

They smiled at each other.

"I thought we'd gone past it," she said.

"So did I," he said. "Or that it didn't even exist anymore."

They smiled at each other, and leaned forward and kissed each other.

"Hey, give me a hand here, will you?" the man said, looking at them over the back of the boat, clinging with dirty-nailed fingers.

They got up quickly and went to him. Chip kneeled on the back seat and helped him over.

His clothes were made of cloth, his hat woven of flat strips of yellow fiber. He was half a head shorter than they and smelled strangely and strongly. Chip grasped his hard-skinned hand and shook it. "I'm Chip," he said, "and this is Lilac."

"Glad to meet you," the bearded blue-eyed old man said, smiling his ugly-toothed smile. "I'm Darren Costanza." He shook Lilac's hand.

"Darren Costanza?" Chip said.

"That's the name."

"It's beautiful!" Lilac said.

"You've got a good boat here," Darren Costanza said, looking about.

"It doesn't lift," Chip said, and Lilac said, "But it got us here. We were lucky to find it."

Darren Costanza smiled at them. "And your pockets are filled with cameras and things?" he said.

"No," Chip said, "we decided not to take anything. The tide was in and—"

"Oh, that was a mistake," Darren Costanza said. "Didn't you take *anything?*"

"A gun without a generator," Chip said, taking it from his pocket. "And a few books and a razor in the bundle there."

"Well, this is worth something," Darren Costanza said, taking the gun and looking at it, thumbing its handle.

"We'll have the boat to trade," Lilac said.

"You should have taken more," Darren Costanza said, turning from them and moving away. They glanced at each other and looked at him again, about to follow, but he turned, holding a different gun. He pointed it at them and put Chip's gun into his pocket. "This old thing shoots bullets," he said, backing farther away to the front seats. "Doesn't need a generator," he said. "Bang, bang. Into the water now, real quick. Go on. Into the water."

They looked at him.

"*Get in the water, you dumb steelies!*" he shouted. "You want a bullet in your head?" He moved something at the back of the gun and pointed it at Lilac.

Chip pushed her to the side of the boat. She clambered over the rail and onto the skirting—saying "What is he doing this for?"—and slipped down into the water. Chip jumped in after her.

"Away from the boat!" Darren Costanza shouted. "Clear away! Swim!"

They swam a few meters, their coveralls ballooning around them, then turned, treading water.

"What are you *doing* this for?" Lilac asked.

"Figure it out for yourself, steely!" Darren Costanza said, sitting at the boat's controls.

"We'll drown if you leave us!" Chip cried. "We can't swim that far!"

"Who told you to come here?" Darren Costanza said, and the boat rushed splashing away, the rowboat dragging from its back carving up fins of foam.

"You fighting brother-hater!" Chip shouted. The boat turned toward the eastern tip of the far-off island.

"He's taking it himself!" Lilac said. "*He's* going to trade it!"

"The sick selfish pre-U—" Chip said. "Christ, Marx, Wood, and Wei, I had the knife in my hand and I threw it on the floor! 'Waiting to help us into port'! He's a *pirate,* that's what he is, the fighting—"

"Stop! Don't!" Lilac said, and looked at him despairingly.

"Oh Christ and Wei," he said.

They pulled open their coveralls and squirmed themselves out of them. "Keep them!" Chip said. "They'll hold air if we tie the openings!"

"Another boat!" Lilac said.

A speck of white was speeding from west to east, midway between them and the island.

She waved her coveralls.

"Too far!" Chip said. "We've got to start swimming!"

They tied the sleeves of their coveralls around their necks and swam against the chilly water. The island was impossibly far away—twenty or more kilometers.

If they could take short rests against the inflated coveralls, Chip thought, they could get far enough in so that another boat might see them. But who would be on it? Members like Darren Costanza? Foul-smelling *pirates* and *murderers?* Had King been right? *"I hope you get there,"* King said, *lying in his bed with his eyes closed. "The two of you. You deserve it."* Fight that brother-hater!

The second boat had got near their pirated one, which was heading farther east as if to avoid it.

Chip swam steadily, glimpsing Lilac swimming beside him. Would they get enough rest to go on, to make it? Or would they drown, choke, slide languidly downward through darkening water . . . He drove the image from his mind; swam and kept swimming.

The second boat had stopped; their own was farther from it than before. But the second boat seemed bigger now, and bigger still.

He stopped and caught Lilac's kicking leg. She looked around, gasping, and he pointed.

The boat hadn't stopped; it had turned and was coming toward them.

They tugged at the coverall sleeves at their throats, loosed them and waved the light blue, the bright yellow.

The boat turned slightly away, then back, then away in the other direction. *"Here!"* they cried, *"Help! Here! Help"*—waving the coveralls, straining high in the water.

The boat turned back and away again, then sharply back. It stayed pointed at them, enlarging, and a horn sounded—loud, loud, loud, loud, loud.

Lilac sank against Chip, coughing water. He ducked his shoulder under her arm and supported her.

The boat came skimming to full-size white closeness—*I.A.* was painted large and green on its hull; it had one rotor—and splatted to a stop with a wave that washed over them. "Hang on!" a member cried, and something flew in the air and splashed beside them: a floating white ring with a rope. Chip grabbed it and the rope sprang taut, pulled by a member, young, yellow-haired. He drew them through the water. "I'm all right," Lilac said in Chip's arm. "I'm all right."

The side of the boat had rungs going up it. Chip pulled Lilac's coveralls from her hand, bent her fingers around a rung, and put her other hand to the rung above. She climbed. The member, leaning over and stretching, caught her hand and helped her. Chip guided her feet and climbed up after her.

They lay on their backs on warm firm floor under scratchy blankets, hand in hand, panting. Their heads were lifted in turn and a small metal container was pressed to their lips. The liquid in it smelled like Darren Costanza. It burned in their throats, but once it was down it warmed their stomachs surprisingly.

"Alcohol?" Chip said.

"Don't worry," the young yellow-haired man said, smiling down at them with normal teeth as he screwed the container onto a flask, "one sip won't rot your brain." He was about twenty-five, with a short beard that was yellow too, and normal eyes and skin. A brown belt at his hips held a gun in a brown pocket; he wore a white cloth shirt without sleeves and tan cloth trousers patched with blue that ended at his knees. Putting the flask on a seat, he unfastened the front of his belt. "I'll get your coveralls," he said. "Catch your breath." He put the gun-belt with the flask and climbed over the side of the boat. A splash sounded and the boat swayed.

"At least they're not all like that other one," Chip said.

"He has a gun," Lilac said.

"But he left it here," Chip said. "If he were—sick, he would have been afraid to."

They lay silently hand in hand under the scratchy blankets, breathing deeply, looking at the clear blue sky.

The boat tilted and the young man climbed back aboard with their dripping coveralls. His hair, which hadn't been clipped in a long time, clung to his head in wet rings. "Feeling better?" he asked, smiling at them.

"Yes," they both said.

He shook the coveralls over the side of the boat. "I'm sorry I wasn't here in time to keep that lunky away from you," he said. "Most immigrants come from Eur, so I generally stay to the north. What we need are *two* boats, not one. Or a longer-range spotter."

"Are you a—policeman?" Chip asked.

"*Me?*" The young man smiled. "No," he said, "I'm with Immigrants' Assistance. That's an agency we've been generously allowed to set up, to help new immigrants get oriented. And get ashore without being drowned." He hung the coveralls over the boat's railing and pulled apart their clinging folds.

Chip raised himself on his elbows. "Does this happen often?" he asked.

"Stealing immigrants' boats is a popular local pastime," the young man said. "There are others that are even more fun."

Chip sat up, and Lilac sat up beside him. The young man faced them, pink sunlight gleaming on his side.

"I'm sorry to disappoint you," he said, "but you haven't come to any paradise. Four fifths of the island's population is descended from the families who were here before the Unification or who came here right after; they're inbred, ignorant, mean, self-satisfied—and they despise immigrants. 'Steelies,' they call us. Because of the bracelets. Even after we take them off."

He took his gun-belt from the seat and put it around his hips. "*We* call *them* 'lunkies,' " he said, fastening the belt's buckle. "Only don't ever say it out loud or you'll find five or six of them stamping on your ribs. That's another of their pastimes."

He looked at them again. "The island is run by a General Costanza," he said, "with the—"

"That's who took the boat!" they said. "Darren Costanza!"

"I doubt it," the young man said, smiling. "The General doesn't get up this early. Your lunky must have been pulling your leg."

Chip said, "The *brother*-hater!"

"General Costanza," the young man said, "has the Church and the Army behind him. There's very little freedom even for lunkies, and for us there's virtually none. We have to live in specified areas, 'Steelytowns,' and we can't step outside them without a good reason. We have to show identity cards to every lunky cop, and the only jobs we can get are the lowest, most back-breaking ones." He took up the flask. "Do you want some more of this?" he asked. "It's called 'whiskey.' "

Chip and Lilac shook their heads.

The young man unscrewed the container and poured amber liquid into it. "Let's see, what have I left out?" he said. "We're not allowed to own land or weapons. I turn in my gun when I set foot on shore." He raised the container and looked at them. "Welcome to Liberty," he said, and drank.

They looked disheartenedly at each other, and at the young man.

"That's what they call it," he said. "Liberty."

"We thought they would welcome. newcomers," Chip said. "To help keep the Family away."

The young man, screwing the container back onto the flask, said, "Nobody comes here except two or three immigrants a month. The last time the Family tried to treat the lunkies was back when there were five computers. Since Uni went into operation not one attempt has been made."

"Why not?" Lilac asked.

The young man looked at them. "Nobody knows," he said. "There are different theories. The lunkies think that either 'God' is protecting them or the Family is afraid of the Army, a bunch of drunken incapable louts. Immigrants think—well, some of them think that the island is so depleted that treating everyone on it simply isn't worth Uni's while."

"And others think—" Chip said.

The young man turned away and put the flask on a shelf below the boat's controls. He sat down on the seat and turned to face them. "Others," he said, "and I'm one of them, think that Uni is *using* the island, *and* the lunkies, and *all* the hidden islands all over the world."

"*Using* them?" Chip said, and Lilac said, "How?"

"As prisons for *us*," the young man said.

They looked at him.

"Why is there always a boat on the beach?" he asked. "*Always,* in Eur and in Afr—an old boat that's still good enough to get here. And why are there those handy patched-up maps in museums? Wouldn't it be easier to make *fake ones* with the islands *really* omitted?"

They stared at him.

"What do you do," he said, looking at them intently, "when you're programming a computer to maintain a perfectly efficient, perfectly stable, perfectly cooperative society? How do you allow for biological freaks, 'incurables,' possible troublemakers?"

They said nothing, staring at him.

He leaned closer to them. "You leave a few 'un-unified' islands all around the world," he said. "You leave maps in museums and boats on beaches. The computer doesn't have to weed out your bad ones; *they do the weeding themselves.* They wiggle their way happily into the nearest isolation ward, and *lunkies* are waiting, with a General Costanza in charge, to take their boats, jam them into Steelytowns, and keep them helpless and harmless—in ways that high-minded disciples of Christ, Marx, Wood, and Wei would never *dream* of stooping to."

"It can't *be,*" Lilac said.

"A lot of us think it can," the young man said.

Chip said, "Uni *let us* come here?"

"No," Lilac said. "It's too—twisted."

The young man looked at her, looked at Chip.

Chip said, "I thought I was being so fighting clever!"

"So did I," the young man said, sitting back. "I know just how you feel."

"No, it can't be," Lilac said.

There was silence for a moment, and then the young man said, "I'll take you in now. I.A. will take off your bracelets and get you registered and lend you twenty-five bucks to get started." He smiled. "As bad as it is," he said, "it's better than being with the Family. Cloth is more comfortable than paplon —really—and even a rotten fig tastes better than totalcakes. You can have children, a drink, a cigarette—a couple of rooms if you work hard. Some steelies even get rich—entertainers, mostly. If you 'sir' the lunkies and stay in Steelytown, it's all right. No scanners, no advisers, and not one 'Life of Marx' in a whole year's TV."

Lilac smiled. Chip smiled too.

"Put the coveralls on," the young man said. "Lunkies are horrified by nakedness. It's 'ungodly.' " He turned to the boat's controls.

They put aside the blankets and got into their moist coveralls, then stood behind the young man as he drove the boat toward the island. It spread out green and gold in the radiance of the just-risen sun, crested with mountains and dotted with bits of white, yellow, pink, pale blue.

"It's beautiful," Lilac said determinedly.

Chip, with his arm about her shoulders, looked ahead with narrowed eyes and said nothing.

Five

They lived in a city called Pollensa, in half a room in a cracked and crumbling Steelytown building with intermittent power and brown water. They had a mattress and a table and a chair, and a box for their clothing that they used as a second chair. The people in the other half of the room, the Newmans— a man and woman in their forties with a nine-year-old daughter—let them use their stove and TV and a shelf in the "fridge" where they stored their food. It was the Newman's room; Chip and Lilac paid four dollars a week for their half of it.

They earned nine dollars and twenty cents a week between them. Chip worked in an iron mine, loading ore into carts with a crew of other immigrants alongside an automatic loader that stood motionless and dusty, unrepairable. Lilac worked in a clothing factory, attaching fasteners to shirts. There too a machine stood motionless, furred with lint.

Their nine dollars and twenty cents paid for the week's rent and food and railfare, a few cigarettes, and a newspaper called the *Liberty Immigrant.* They saved fifty cents toward clothing replacement and emergencies that might arise, and gave fifty cents to Immigrants' Assistance as partial repayment of the twenty-five-dollar loan they had been given on their arrival. They ate bread and fish and potatoes and figs. At first these foods gave them cramps and constipation, but they soon came to like them, to relish the different tastes and consistencies. They looked forward to meals, although the preparation and the cleaning up afterward became a bother.

Their bodies changed. Lilac's bled for a few days, which the Newmans assured them was natural in untreated women, and it grew more rounded and supple as her hair grew longer. Chip's body hardened and strengthened from his work in the mine. His beard grew out black and straight, and he trimmed it once a week with the Newmans' scissors.

They had been given names by a clerk at the Immigration Bureau. Chip was named Eiko Newmark, and Lilac, Grace Newbridge. Later, when they married—with no application to Uni, but with forms and a fee and vows to "God" —Lilac's name was changed to Grace Newmark. They still called themselves Chip and Lilac, however.

They got used to handling coins and dealing with shopkeepers, and to traveling on Pollensa's rundown overcrowded monorail. They learned how to sidestep natives and avoid offending them; they memorized the Vow of Loyalty and saluted Liberty's red-and-yellow flag. They knocked on doors before opening them, said *Wednesday* instead of Woodsday, *March* instead of Marx. They reminded themselves that *fight* and *hate* were acceptable words but *fuck* was a "dirty" one.

Hassan Newman drank a great deal of whiskey. Soon after coming home from his job—in the island's largest furniture factory—he would be playing loud games with Gigi, his daughter, and fumbling his way through the room's dividing curtain with a bottle clutched in his three-fingered saw-damaged hand. "Come on, you sad steelies," he would say, "Where the hate are your glasses? Come on, have a little cheer." Chip and Lilac drank with him a few times, but they found that whiskey made them confused and clumsy and they usually declined his offer. "Come on," he said one evening. "I know I'm the landlord, but I'm not exactly a lunky, am I? Or what is it? Do you think I'll expect you to receep—to re*cip* rocate? I know you like to watch the pennies."

"It's not that," Chip said.

"Then what is it?" Hassan asked. He swayed and steadied himself.

Chip didn't say anything for a moment, and then he said, "Well, what's the point in getting away from treatments if you're going to dull yourself with whiskey? You might as well be back in the Family."

"Oh," Hassan said. "Oh sure, I get you." He looked angrily at them, a broad, curly-bearded, bloodshot-eyed man. "Just wait," he said. "Wait till you've been here a little longer. Just wait till you've been here a little longer, that's all." He turned around and groped his way through the curtain, and they heard him muttering, and his wife, Ria, speaking placatingly.

Almost everyone in the building seemed to drink as much whiskey as Hassan did. Loud voices, happy or angry, sounded through the walls at all hours of the night. The elevator and the hallways smelled of whiskey, and of fish, and of sweet perfumes that people used against the whiskey and fish smells.

Most evenings, after they had finished whatever cleaning had to be done, Chip and Lilac either went up to the roof for some fresh air or sat at their table reading the *Immigrant* or books they had found on the monorail or borrowed from a small collection at Immigrants' Assistance. Sometimes they watched TV with the Newmans—plays about foolish misunderstandings in native families, with frequent stops for announcements about different makes of cigarettes and disinfectants. Occasionally there were speeches by General Costanza or the head of the Church, Pope Clement—disquieting speeches about shortages of food and space and resources, for which immigrants alone weren't to be blamed. Hassan, belligerent with whiskey, usually switched them off before they were over; Liberty TV, unlike the Family's, could be switched on and off at one's choosing.

One day in the mine, toward the end of the fifteen-minute lunch break, Chip went over to the automatic loader and began examining it, wondering whether it was in fact unrepairable or whether some part of it that couldn't be replaced might not be by-passed or substituted for in some way. The native in charge of the crew came over and asked him what he was doing. Chip told him, taking care to speak respectfully, but the native got angry. "You fucking steelies all think you're so God-damned smart!" he said, and put his hand on his gun handle. "Get over there where you belong and stay there!" he said. "Try to figure out a way to eat less food if you've got to have something to think about!"

All natives weren't quite that bad. The owner of their building took a liking to Chip and Lilac and promised to let them have a room for five dollars a week as soon as one became available. "You're not like some of these others," he said. "Drinking, walking around the hallways stark naked—I'd rather take a few cents less and have your kind."

Chip, looking at him, said, "There are reasons why immigrants drink, you know."

"I know, I know," the owner said. "I'm the first one to say it; it's terrible the way we treat you. But still and all, do *you* drink? Do *you* walk around stark naked?"

Lilac said, "Thank you, Mr. Corsham. We'll be grateful if you can get a room for us."

They caught "colds" and "the flu." Lilac lost her job at the clothing factory but found a better one in the kitchen of a native restaurant within walking distance of the house. Two policemen came to the room one evening, checking identity cards and looking for weapons. Hassan muttered something as he showed his card and they clubbed him to the floor. They stuck knives into the mattresses and broke some of the dishes.

Lilac didn't have her "period," her monthly few days of vaginal bleeding, and that meant she was pregnant.

One night on the roof Chip stood smoking and looking at the sky to the northeast, where there was a dull orange glow from the copper-production complex on EUR91766. Lilac, who had been taking washed clothes from a line where she had hung them to dry, came over to him and put her arm around him. She kissed his cheek and leaned against him. "It's not so bad," she said. "We've got twelve dollars saved, we'll have a room of our own any day now, and before you know it we'll have a baby."

"A steely," Chip said.

"No," Lilac said. "A baby."

"It stinks," Chips said. "It's rotten. It's inhuman."

"It's all there is," Lilac said. "We'd better get used to it."

Chip said nothing. He kept looking at the orange glow in the sky.

The *Liberty Immigrant* carried weekly articles about immigrant singers and athletes, and occasionally scientists, who earned forty or fifty dollars a week and lived in good apartments, who mixed with influential and enlightened natives, and who were hopeful about the chances of a more equitable relationship developing between the two groups. Chip read these articles with scorn —they were meant by the newspaper's native owners to lull and pacify immigrants, he felt—but Lilac accepted them at face value, as evidence that their own lot would ultimately improve.

One week in October, when they had been on Liberty for a little over six months, there was an article about an artist named Morgan Newgate, who had come from Eur eight years before and who lived in a four-room apartment in New Madrid. His paintings, one of which, a scene of the Crucifixion, had just been presented to Pope Clement, brought him as much as a hundred dollars each. He signed them with an *A,* the article explained, because his nickname was Ashi.

"Christ and Wei," Chip said.

Lilac said, "What is it?"

"I was at academy with this 'Morgan Newgate,'" Chip said, showing her the article. "We were good friends. His name was Karl. You remember that picture of the horse I had back in Ind?"

"No," she said, reading.

"Well, he drew it," Chip said. "He used to sign everything with an *A* in a circle." And yes, he thought, "Ashi" seemed like the name Karl had mentioned. Christ and Wei, so he had got away too!—had "got away," if you could call it that, to Liberty, to Uni's isolation ward. At least he was doing what he'd always wanted; for him Liberty really *was* liberty.

"You ought to call him," Lilac said, still reading.

"I will," Chip said.

But maybe he wouldn't. Was there any point, really, in calling "Morgan Newgate," who painted Crucifixions for the Pope and assured his fellow immigrants that conditions were getting better every day? But maybe Karl hadn't said that; maybe the *Immigrant* had lied.

"Don't just say it," Lilac said. "He could probably help you get a better job."

"Yes," Chip said, "he probably could."

She looked at him. "What's the matter?" she said. "Don't you want a better job?"

"I'll call him tomorrow, on the way to work," he said.

But he didn't. He swung his shovel into ore and lifted and heaved, swung and lifted and heaved. *Fight them all,* he thought: *the steelies who drink, the steelies who think things are getting better; the lunkies, the dummies; fight Uni.*

On the following Sunday morning Lilac went with him to a building two blocks from theirs where there was a working telephone in the lobby, and she waited while he paged through the tattered directory. *Morgan* and *Newgate* were names commonly given to immigrants, but few immigrants had phones; there was only one *Newgate, Morgan* listed, and that one in New Madrid.

Chip put three tokens into the phone and spoke the number. The screen was broken, but it didn't make any difference since Liberty phones no longer transmitted pictures anyway.

A woman answered, and when Chip asked if Morgan Newgate was there, said he was, and then nothing more. The silence lengthened, and Lilac, a few meters away beside a Sani-Spray poster, waited and then came close. "Isn't he there?" she asked in a whisper. "Hello?" a man's voice said.

"Is this Morgan Newgate?" Chip asked.

"Yes. Who's this?"

"It's Chip," Chip said. "Li RM, from the Academy of the Genetic Sciences."

There was silence, and then, "My God," the voice said, "Li! You got pads and charcoal for me!"

"Yes," Chip said. "And I told my adviser you were sick and needed help."

Karl laughed. "That's right, you did, you bastard!" he said. "This is great! When did you get over?"

"About six months ago," Chip said.

"Are you in New Madrid?"

"Pollensa."

"What are you doing?"

"Working in a mine," Chip said.

"Christ, that's a shut-off," Karl said, and after a moment, "It's hell here, isn't it?"

"Yes," Chip said, thinking *He even uses their words. Hell. My God. I'll bet he says prayers.*

"I wish these phones were working so I could get a look at you," Karl said.

Suddenly Chip was ashamed of his hostility. He told Karl about Lilac and about her pregnancy; Karl told him that he had been married in the Family but had come over alone. He wouldn't let Chip congratulate him on his success. "The things I sell are awful," he said. "Appealing little lunky children. But I manage to do my own work three days a week, so I can't complain.

Listen, Li—no, what is it, Chip? Chip, listen, we've got to get together. I've got a motorbike; I'll come down there one evening. No, wait," he said, "are you doing anything next Sunday, you and your wife?"

Lilac looked anxiously at Chip. He said, "I don't think so. I'm not sure."

"I'm having some friends over," Karl said. "You come too, all right? Around six o'clock."

With Lilac nodding at him, Chip said, "We'll try. We'll probably be able to make it."

"See that you do," Karl said. He gave Chip his address. "I'm glad you got over," he said. "It's better than *there* anyway, isn't it?"

"A little," Chip said.

"I'll expect you next Sunday," Karl said. "So long, brother."

"So long," Chip said, and tapped off.

Lilac said, "We're going, aren't we?"

"Do you have any idea what the railfare's going to be?" Chip said.

"Oh, Chip . . ."

"All right," he said. "All right, we'll go. But I'm not taking any favors from him. And you're not *asking* for any. You remember that."

Every evening that week Lilac worked on the best of their clothes, taking off the frayed sleeves of a green dress, remending a trouser leg so that the mend was less noticeable.

The building, at the very edge of New Madrid's Steelytown, was in no worse condition than many native buildings. Its lobby was swept, and smelled only slightly of whiskey and fish and perfume, and the elevator worked well.

A pushbutton was set in new plaster next to Karl's door: a bell to be rung. Chip pressed it. He stood stiffly, and Lilac held his arm.

"Who is it?" a man's voice asked.

"Chip Newmark," Chip said.

The door was unlocked and opened, and Karl—a thirty-five-year-old bearded Karl with the long-ago Karl's sharp-focused eyes—grinned and grabbed Chip's hand and said, "Li! I thought you weren't coming!"

"We ran into some good-natured lunkies," Chip said.

"Oh Christ," Karl said, and let them in.

He locked the door and Chip introduced Lilac. She said, "Hello, Mr. Newgate," and Karl, taking her held-out hand and looking at her face, said, "It's Ashi. Hello, Lilac."

"Hello, Ashi," she said.

To Chip, Karl said, "Did they hurt you?"

"No," Chip said. "Just 'recite the Vow' and that kind of cloth."

"Bastards," Karl said. "Come on, I'll give you a drink and you'll forget about it." He took their elbows and led them into a narrow passage walled with frame-to-frame paintings. "You look great, Chip," he said.

"So do you," Chip said. "Ashi."

They smiled at each other.

"Seventeen years, brother," Karl-Ashi said.

Men and women were sitting in a smoky brown-walled room, ten or twelve of them, talking and holding cigarettes and glasses. They stopped talking and turned expectantly.

"This is Chip and this is Lilac," Karl said to them. "Chip and I were at academy together; the Family's two worst genetics students."

The men and women smiled, and Karl began pointing to them in turn and saying their names. "Vito, Sunny, Ria, Lars . . ." Most of them were immigrants, bearded men and long-haired women with the Family's eyes and coloring. Two were natives: a pale erect beak-nosed woman of fifty or so, with a gold cross hanging against her black empty-looking dress ("Julia," Karl said, and she smiled with closed lips); and an overweight red-haired younger woman in a tight dress glazed with silvery beads. A few of the people could have been either immigrants or natives: a gray-eyed beardless man named Bob, a blond woman, a young blue-eyed man.

"Whiskey or wine?" Karl asked. "Lilac?"

"Wine, please," Lilac said.

They followed him to a small table set out with bottles and glasses, plates holding a slice or two of cheese and meat, and packets of cigarettes and matches. A souvenir paperweight sat on a pile of napkins. Chip picked it up and looked at it; it was from AUS21989. "Make you homesick?" Karl asked, pouring wine.

Chip showed it to Lilac and she smiled. "Not very," he said, and put it down.

"Chip?"

"Whiskey."

The red-haired native woman in the silvery dress came over, smiling and holding an empty glass in a ring-fingered hand. To Lilac she said, "You're absolutely beautiful. Really," and to Chip, "I think *all* you people are beautiful. The Family may not have any freedom but it's way ahead of us in physical appearance. I'd give anything to be lean and tan and slant-eyed." She talked on—about the Family's sensible attitude toward sex—and Chip found himself with a glass in his hand and Karl and Lilac talking to other people and the woman talking to him. Lines of black paint edged and extended her brown eyes. "You people are so much more *open* than we are," she said. "Sexually, I mean. You *enjoy* it more."

An immigrant woman came over and said, "Isn't Heinz coming, Marge?"

"He's in Palma," the woman said, turning. "A wing of the hotel collapsed."

"Would you excuse me, please?" Chip said, and sidestepped away. He went to the other end of the room, nodded at people sitting there, and drank some of his whiskey, looking at a painting on the wall—slabs of brown and red on a white background. The whiskey tasted better than Hassan's. It was less bitter and searing; lighter and more pleasant to drink. The painting with its brown and red slabs was only a flat design, interesting to look at for a moment but with nothing in it connected to life. Karl's (no, *Ashi's!*) *A*-in-a-circle was in one of its bottom corners. Chip wondered whether it was one of the bad paintings he sold or, since it was hanging there in his living room, part of his "own work" that he had spoken of with satisfaction. Wasn't he still doing the beautiful unbraceleted men and women he had drawn back at the Academy?

He drank some more of the whiskey and turned to the people sitting near him: three men and a woman, all immigrants. They were talking about furniture. He listened for a few minutes, drinking, and moved away.

Lilac was sitting next to the beak-nosed native woman—Julia. They were smoking and talking, or rather Julia was talking and Lilac was listening.

He went to the table and poured more whiskey into his glass. He lit a cigarette.

A man named Lars introduced himself. He ran a school for immigrant children there in New Madrid. He had been brought to Liberty as a child, and had been there for forty-two years.

Ashi came, holding Lilac by the hand. "Chip, come see my studio," he said.

He led them from the room into the passage walled with paintings. "Do you know who you were speaking to?" he asked Lilac.

"Julia?" she said.

"Julia *Costanza,*" he said. "She's the General's cousin. Despises him. She was one of the founders of Immigrants' Assistance."

His studio was large and brilliantly lighted. A half-finished painting of a native woman holding a kitten stood on an easel; on another easel stood a canvas painted with slabs of blue and green. Other paintings stood against the walls: slabs of brown and orange, blue and purple, purple and black, orange and red.

He explained what he was trying to do, pointing out balances, and opposing thrusts, and subtle shadings of color.

Chip looked away and drank his whiskey.

"Listen, you steelies!" he said, loudly enough so they all could hear him. "Stop talking about *furniture* for a minute and listen! You know what we've got to do? Fight Uni! I'm not being *rude,* I mean it literally. Fight Uni! Because it's Uni who's to blame—for everything! For lunkies, who're what they are because they don't have enough food, or space, or *connection with any outside world;* and for dummies, who're what they are because they're LPK'ed that way and tranquilized that way; and for *us,* who're what *we* are because Uni put us here to get rid of us! It's *Uni* who's to blame—it's frozen the world so there's no more change—and we've got to fight it! We've got to get up off our stupid beaten behinds and FIGHT IT!"

Ashi, smiling, slapped at his cheek. "Hey, brother," he said, "you've had a little too much, you know that? Hey, Chip, you hear me?"

Of course he'd had too much; of course, of course, of course. But it hadn't dulled him, it had freed him. It had opened up everything that had been closed inside him for months and months. Whiskey was *good!* Whiskey was *marvelous!*

He stopped Ashi's slapping hand and held it. "I'm okay, Ashi," he said. "I know what I'm talking about." To the others, sitting and swaying and smiling, he said, "We can't just give up and accept things, *adjust ourselves* to this prison! Ashi, you used to draw members without bracelets, and they were so beautiful! And now you're painting *color,* slabs of *color!*"

They were trying to get him to sit down, Ashi on one side of him and Lilac on the other, Lilac looking anxious and embarrassed. "You too, love," he said. "You're accepting, adjusting." He let them seat him, because standing hadn't been easy and sitting was better, more comfortable and sprawly. "We've got to fight, not adjust," he said. "Fight, fight, fight. We've got to fight," he said to the gray-eyed beardless man sitting next to him.

"By God, you're right!" the man said. "I'm with you all the way! Fight Uni! What'll we do? Go over in boats and take the Army along for good measure? But maybe the sea is monitored by satellite and doctors'll be waiting with clouds of LPK. I've got a better idea; we'll get a plane—I hear there's one on the island that actually flies—and we'll—"

"Don't tease him, Bob," someone said. "He just came over."

"That's obvious," the man said, getting up.

"There's a way to do it," Chip said. "There has to be. There's a way to do it." He thought about the sea and the island in the middle of it, but he couldn't think as clearly as he wanted. Lilac sat where the man had been and took his hand. "We've got to *fight,*" he said to her.

"I know, I know," she said, looking at him sadly.

Ashi came and put a warm cup to his lips. "It's coffee," he said. "Drink it."

It was very hot and strong; he swallowed a mouthful, then pushed the cup away. "The copper complex," he said. "On '91766. The copper must go ashore. There must be boats or barges; we could—"

"It's been done before," Ashi said.

Chip looked at him, thinking he was tricking him, making fun of him in some way, like the gray-eyed beardless man.

"Everything you're saying," Ashi said, "everything you're thinking—'fight Uni'—it's been said before and thought before. And tried before. A dozen times." He put the cup to Chip's lips. "Take some more," he said.

Chip pushed the cup away, staring at him, and shook his head. "It's not true," he said.

"It is, brother. Come on, take a—"

"It isn't!" he said.

"It is," a woman said across the room. "It's true."

Julia. It was Julia, General's-cousin-Julia, sitting erect and alone in her black dress with her little gold cross.

"Every five or six years," she said, "a group of people like you—sometimes only two or three, sometimes as many as ten—sets out to destroy UniComp. They go in boats, in submarines that they spend years building; they go on board the barges you just mentioned. They take guns, explosives, gas masks, gas bombs, gadgets; they have plans that they're sure will work. They never come back. I financed the last two parties and am supporting the families of men who were in them, so I speak with authority. I hope you're sober enough to understand, and to spare yourself useless anguish. Accepting and adjusting is all that's possible. Be grateful for what you have: a lovely wife, a child on the way, and a small amount of freedom that we hope in time will grow larger. I might add that in no circumstances whatsoever will I finance another such party. I am not as rich as certain people think I am."

Chip sat looking at her. She looked back at him with small black eyes above her pale beak of nose.

"They never come back, Chip," Ashi said.

Chip looked at him.

"Maybe they get to shore," Ashi said; "maybe they get to 'oo1. Maybe they even get into the dome. But that's as *far* as they get, because they're gone, every one of them. And Uni is still working."

Chip looked at Julia. She said, "Men and women exactly like you. As far back as I can remember."

He looked at Lilac, holding his hand. She squeezed it, looking compassionately at him.

He looked at Ashi, who held the cup of coffee toward him.

He blocked the cup and shook his head. "No, I don't want coffee," he said.

He sat motionless, with sudden sweat on his forehead, and then he leaned forward and began vomiting.

He was in bed, and Lilac was lying beside him sleeping. Hassan was snoring on the other side of the curtain. A sour taste was in his mouth, and he remembered vomiting. Christ and Wei! And on carpet—the first he'd seen in half a year!

Then he remembered what had been said to him by that woman, Julia, and by Karl—by Ashi.

He lay still for a while, and then he got up and tiptoed around the curtain and past the sleeping Newmans to the sink. He got a drink of water, and because he didn't want to go all the way down the hall, urined quietly in the sink and rinsed it out thoroughly.

He got back down beside Lilac and drew the blanket over him. He felt a little drunk again and his head hurt, but he lay on his back with his eyes closed, breathing lightly and slowly, and after a while he felt better.

He kept his eyes closed and thought about things.

After half an hour or so Hassan's alarm clock jangled. Lilac turned. He stroked her head and she sat up. "Are you all right?" she asked.

"Yes, sort of," he said.

The light went on and they winced. They heard Hassan grunting and getting up, yawning, farting. "Get up, Ria," he said. "Gigi? It's time to get up."

Chip stayed on his back with his hand on Lilac's cheek. "I'm sorry, darling," he said. "I'll call him today and apologize."

She took his hand and turned her lips to it. "You couldn't help it," she said. "He understood."

"I'm going to ask him to help me find a better job," Chip said.

Lilac looked at him questioningly.

"It's all out of me," he said. "Like the whiskey. All out. I'm going to be an industrious, optimistic steely. I'm going to accept and adjust. We're going to have a bigger apartment than Ashi some day."

"I don't want that," she said. "I would love to have two rooms, though."

"We will," he said. "In two years. Two rooms in two years; that's a promise."

She smiled at him.

He said, "I think we ought to think about moving to New Madrid where our rich friends are. That man Lars runs a school, did you know that? Maybe you could teach there. And the baby could go there when it's old enough."

"What could I teach?" she said.

"Something," he said. "I don't know." He lowered his hand and stroked her breasts. "How to have beautiful breasts, maybe," he said.

Smiling, she said, "We've got to get dressed."

"Let's skip breakfast," he said, drawing her down. He rolled onto her and they embraced and kissed.

"Lilac?" Ria called. "How was it?"

Lilac freed her mouth. "Tell you later!" she called.

While he was walking down the tunnel into the mine he remembered the tunnel into Uni, Papa Jan's tunnel down which the memory banks had been rolled.

He stopped still.

Down which the *real* memory banks had been rolled. And above them were the false ones, the pink and orange toys that were reached through the dome and the elevators, and which everyone thought was Uni itself; everyone including—it had to be!—all those men and women who had gone out to fight it in the past. But Uni, the real Uni, was on the levels below, and could be reached through the tunnel, through Papa Jan's tunnel from behind Mount Love.

It would still be there—closed at its mouth probably, maybe even sealed with a meter of concrete—but it would still be there; because nobody fills in all of a long tunnel, especially not an efficient computer. And there was space cut out below for more memory banks—Papa Jan had said so—so the tunnel would be needed again some day.

It was there, behind Mount Love.

A tunnel into Uni.

With the right maps and charts, someone who knew what he was doing could probably work out its exact location, or very nearly.

"You there! Get moving!" someone shouted.

He walked ahead quickly, thinking about it, thinking about it.

It was there. The tunnel.

Six

"If it's money, the answer is no," Julia Costanza said, walking briskly past clattering looms and immigrant women glancing at her. "If it's a job," she said, "I might be able to help you."

Chip, walking along beside her, said, "Ashi's already got me a job."

"Then it's money," she said.

"Information first," Chip said, "then maybe money." He pushed open a door.

"No," Julia said, going through. "Why don't you go to I.A.? That's what it's there for. What information? About what?" She glanced at him as they started up a spiral stairway that shifted with their weight.

Chip said, "Can we sit down somewhere for five minutes?"

"If I sit down," Julia said, "half this island will be naked tomorrow. That's probably acceptable to you, but it isn't to me. What information?"

He held in his resentment. Looking at her beak-nosed profile, he said, "Those two attacks on Uni you—"

"No," she said. She stopped and faced him, one hand holding the stairway's centerpost. "If it's about *that* I really won't listen," she said. "I knew it the minute you walked into that living room, the disapproving air you had. No. I'm not interested in any more plans and schemes. Go talk to somebody else." She went up the stairs.

He went quickly and caught up with her. "Were they planning to use a tunnel?" he asked. "Just tell me that; were they going in through a tunnel from behind Mount Love?"

She pushed open the door at the head of the stairway; he held it and went through after her, into a large loft where a few machine parts lay. Birds rose fluttering to holes in the peaked roof and flew out.

"They were going in with the other people," she said, walking straight through the loft toward a door at its far end. "The sightseers. At least that was the plan. They were going to go down in the elevators."

"And then?"

"There's no *point* in—"

"Just answer me, will you, please?" he said.

She glanced at him, angrily, and looked ahead. "There's supposed to be a large observation window," she said. "They were going to smash it and throw in explosives."

"Both groups?"

"Yes."

"They may have succeeded," he said.

She stopped with her hand on the door and looked at him, puzzled.

"That's not really Uni," he said. "It's a display for the sightseers. And maybe it's also meant as a false target for attackers. They could have blown it up and nothing would have happened—except that they would have been grabbed and treated."

She kept looking at him.

"The real thing is farther down," he said. "On three levels. I was in it once when I was ten or eleven years old."

She said, "Digging a tunnel is the most ri—"

"It's there already," he said. "It doesn't have to be dug."

She closed her mouth, looked at him, and turned quickly away and pushed open the door. It led to another loft, brightly lit, where a row of presses stood motionless with layers of cloth on their beds. Water was on the floor, and two men were trying to lift the end of a long pipe that had apparently fallen from the wall and lay across a stopped conveyor belt piled with cut cloth pieces. The wall end of the pipe was still anchored, and the men were trying to lift its other end and get it off the belt and back up against the wall. Another man, an immigrant, waited on a ladder to receive it.

"Help them," Julia said, and began gathering pieces of cloth from the wet floor.

"If that's how I spend my time, nothing's going to be changed," Chip said. "That's acceptable to you, but it isn't to me."

"Help them!" Julia said. "Go on! We'll talk later! You're not going to get anywhere by being cheeky!"

Chip helped the men get the pipe secured against the wall, and then he went out with Julia onto a railed landing on the side of the building. New Madrid stretched away below them, bright in the mid-morning sun. Beyond it lay a strip of blue-green sea dotted with fishing boats.

"Every day it's something else," Julia said, reaching into the pocket of her gray apron. She took out cigarettes, offered Chip one, and lit them with ordinary cheap matches.

They smoked, and Chip said, "The tunnel's there. It was used to bring in the memory banks."

"Some of the groups I wasn't involved with may have known about it," Julia said.

"Can you find out?"

She drew on her cigarette. In the sunlight she was older-looking, the skin of her face and neck netted with wrinkles. "Yes," she said. "I suppose so. How do *you* know about it?"

He told her. "I'm sure it's not filled in," he said. "It must be fifteen kilometers long. And besides, it's going to be used again. There's space cut out for more banks for when the Family gets bigger."

She looked questioningly at him. "I thought the colonies had their own computers," she said.

"They do," he said, not understanding. And then he understood. It was only in the colonies that the Family was growing; on Earth, with two children per couple and not every couple allowed to reproduce, the Family was getting smaller, not bigger. He had never connected that with what Papa Jan had said about the space for more memory banks. "Maybe they'll be needed for more telecontrolled equipment," he said.

"Or maybe," Julia said, "your grandfather wasn't a reliable source of information."

"He was the one who had the idea for the tunnel," Chip said. "It's there; I know it is. And it may be a way, the *only* way, that Uni can be gotten at. I'm going to try it, and I want your help, as much of it as you can give me."

"You want my *money*, you mean," she said.

"Yes," he said. "And your help. In finding the right people with the right skills. And in getting information that we'll need, and equipment. And in finding people who can teach us skills that we don't have. I want to take this very slowly and carefully. I want to come back."

She looked at him with her eyes narrowed against her cigarette smoke. "Well, you're not an absolute imbecile," she said. "What kind of job has Ashi found for you?"

"Washing dishes at the Casino."

"God in heaven!" she said. "Come here tomorrow morning at a quarter of eight."

"The Casino leaves my mornings free," he said.

"Come here!" she said. "You'll get the time you need."

"All right," he said, and smiled at her. "Thanks," he said.

She turned away and looked at her cigarette. She crushed it against the railing. "I'm not going to pay for it," she said. "Not all of it. I can't. You have no idea how expensive it's going to be. Explosives, for instance: last time they cost over two thousand dollars, and that was five years ago; God knows what they'll be today." She scowled at her cigarette stub and threw it away over the railing. "I'll pay what I can," she said, "and I'll introduce you to people who'll pay the rest if you flatter them enough."

"Thank you," Chip said. "I couldn't ask for more. Thank you."

"God in heaven, here I go again," Julia said. She turned to Chip. "Wait, you'll find out," she said: "the older you get the more you stay the same. I'm an only child who's used to having her way, that's my trouble. Come on, I've got work to do."

They went down stairs that led from the landing. "Really," Julia said. "I have all kinds of noble reasons for spending my time and money on people like you—a Christian urge to help the Family, love of justice, freedom, democracy —but the truth of the matter is, I'm an only child who's used to having her way. It *maddens* me, it absolutely *maddens* me, that I can't go anywhere I please on this planet! Or *off* it, for that matter! You have no idea how I *resent* that damned computer!"

Chip laughed. "I *do!*" he said. "That's just the way *I* feel."

"It's a monster straight out of hell," Julia said.

They walked around the building. "It's a monster, all right," Chip said, throwing away his cigarette. "At least the way it is now. One of the things I want to try to find out is whether, if we got the chance, we could change its programming instead of destroying it. If the *Family* were running *it,* instead of vice versa, it wouldn't be so bad. Do you really believe in heaven and hell?"

"Let's not get into religion," Julia said, "or you're going to find yourself washing dishes at the Casino. How much are they paying you?"

"Six-fifty a week."

"Really?"

"Yes."

"I'll give you the same," Julia said, "but if anyone around here asks, say you're getting five."

He waited until Julia had questioned a number of people without learning of any attack party that had known about the tunnel, and then, confirmed in his decision, he told his plans to Lilac.

"You *can't!*" she said. "Not after all those other people went!"

"They were aiming at the wrong target," he said.

She shook her head, held her brow, looked at him. "It's—I don't know what to *say,*" she said. "I thought you were—done with all this. I thought we were *settled.*" She threw her hands out at the room around them, their New Madrid room, with the walls they had painted, the bookshelf he had made, the bed, the refrigerator, Ashi's sketch of a laughing child.

Chip said, "Honey, I may be the only person on any of the islands who knows about the tunnel, about the real Uni. I *have* to make use of that. How can I *not* do it?"

"All right, *make* use of it," she said. "Plan, help *organize* a party—fine! I'll help you! But why do you have to *go? Other* people should do it, people without families."

"I'll be here when the baby's born," he said. "It's going to take longer than that to get everything ready. And then I'll only be gone for—maybe as little as a week."

She stared at him. "How can you *say* that?" she said. "How can you say you'll—you could be gone forever! You could be caught and treated!"

"We're going to learn how to fight," he said. "We're going to have guns and—"

"Others should go!" she said.

"How can I ask them, if I'm not going myself?"

"Ask them, that's all. Ask them."

"No," he said. "*I've* got to go too."

"You *want* to go, that's what it is," she said. "You don't *have* to go; you *want* to."

He was silent for a moment, and then he said, "All right, I want to. Yes. I can't think of not being there when Uni is beaten. I want to throw the explosive myself, or pull the switch myself, or do whatever it is that's finally done—myself."

"You're sick," she said. She picked up the sewing in her lap and found the needle and started to sew. "I mean it," she said. "You're sick on the subject of Uni. It didn't *put* us here; we're lucky to have *got* here. Ashi's right: it would have killed us the way it kills people at sixty-two; it wouldn't have wasted boats and islands. We got away from it; it's *already* been beaten; and you're sick to want to go back and beat it again."

"It put us here," Chip said, "because the programmers couldn't justify killing people who were still young."

"Cloth," Lilac said. "They justified killing old people, they'd have justified killing *infants.* We got away. And now you're going back."

"What about our parents?" he said. "*They're* going to be killed in a few more years. What about Snowflake and Sparrow—the whole Family, in fact?"

She sewed, jabbing the needle into green cloth—the sleeves from her green dress that she was making into a shirt for the baby. "Others should go," she said. "People without families."

Later, in bed, he said, "If anything *should* go wrong, Julia will take care of you. And the baby."

"That's a great comfort," she said. "Thanks. Thanks very much. Thank Julia too."

It stayed between them from that night on: resentment on her part and refusal to be moved by it on his.

IV
Fighting Back

One

He was busy, busier than he'd been in his entire life: planning, looking for people and equipment, traveling, learning, explaining, pleading, devising, deciding. And working at the factory too, where Julia, despite the time off she allowed him, made sure she got her six-fifty-a-week's worth out of him in machinery repair and production speed-up. And with Lilac's pregnancy advancing, he was doing more of the at-home chores too. He was more exhausted than he'd ever been, and more wide awake; more sick of everything one day and more sure of everything the next; more alive.

It, the plan, the project, was like a machine to be assembled, with all the parts to be found or made, and each dependent for its shape and size on all the others.

Before he could decide on the size of the party, he had to have a clearer idea of its ultimate aim; and before he could have that, he had to know more about Uni's functioning and where it could be most effectively attacked.

He spoke to Lars Newman, Ashi's friend who ran a school. Lars sent him to a man in Andrait, who sent him to a man in Manacor.

"I knew those banks were too small for the amount of insulation they seemed to have," the man in Manacor said. His name was Newbrook and he was near seventy; he had taught in a technological academy before he left the Family. He was minding a baby granddaughter, changing her diaper and annoyed about it. "Hold *still,* will you?" he said. "Well, assuming you can get in," he said to Chip, "the power source is what you've obviously got to go for. The reactor or, more likely, the rea*ctors.*"

"But they could be replaced fairly quickly, couldn't they?" Chip said. "I want to put Uni out of commission for a good long time, long enough for the Family to wake up and decide what it wants to do with it."

"Damn it, hold *still!*" Newbrook said. "The refrigerating plant, then."

"The refrigerating plant?" Chip said.

"That's right," Newbrook said. "The internal temperature of the banks has to be close to absolute zero; raise it a few degrees and the grids won't—there, *you see* what you've done?—the grids won't be superconductive anymore. You'll erase Uni's memory." He picked up the crying baby and held her against his shoulder, patting her back. "Shh, shh," he said.

"Erase it permanently?" Chip asked.

Newbrook nodded, patting the crying baby. "Even if the refrigeration's restored," he said, "all the data will have to be fed in again. It'll take years."

"That's exactly what I'm looking for," Chip said.

The refrigerating plant.

And the stand-by plant.

And the second stand-by plant, if there was one.

Three refrigeration plants to be put out of operation. Two men for each, he figured; one to place the explosives and one to keep members away.

Six men to stop Uni's refrigeration and then hold its entrances against the help it would summon with its thawing faltering brain. Could six men hold the elevators and the tunnel? (And had Papa Jan mentioned other shafts in the other cut-out space?) But six was the minimum, and the minimum was what he wanted, because if any one man was caught while they were on their way, he would tell the doctors everything and Uni would be expecting them at the tunnel. The fewer the men, the less the danger.

He and five others.

The yellow-haired young man who ran the I.A. patrol boat—Vito Newcome, but he called himself Dover—painted the boat's railing while he listened, and then, when Chip spoke about the tunnel and the real memory banks, listened without painting; crouched on his heels with the brush hanging in his hand and squinted up at Chip with flecks of white in his short beard and on his chest. "You're sure of it?" he asked.

"Positive," Chip said.

"It's about time somebody took another crack at that brother-fighter." Dover Newcome looked at his thumb, white-smeared, and wiped it on his trouser thigh.

Chip crouched beside him. "Do you want to be in on it?" he asked.

Dover looked at him and, after a moment, nodded. "Yes," he said. "I certainly do."

Ashi said no, which was what Chip had expected; he asked him only because not asking, he thought, would be a slight. "I just don't feel it's worth the risk," Ashi said. "I'll help you out in any way I can, though. Julia's already hit me for a contribution and I've promised a hundred dollars. I'll make it more than that if you need it."

"Fine," Chip said. "Thanks, Ashi. You *can* help. You can get into the Library, can't you? See if you can find any maps of the area around EUR-zip-one, U or pre-U. The larger the better; maps with topographical details."

When Julia heard that Dover Newcome was to be in the group, she objected. "We need him here, on the boat," she said.

"You won't once we're finished," Chip said.

"God in heaven," Julia said. "How do you get by with so little confidence?"

"It's easy," Chip said. "I have a friend who says prayers for me."

Julia looked coldly at him. "Don't take anyone else from I.A.," she said. "And don't take anyone from the factory. And don't take anyone with a family that *I* may wind up supporting!"

"How do you get by with so little faith?" Chip said.

He and Dover between them spoke to some thirty or forty immigrants without finding any others who wanted to take part in the attack. They copied names and addresses from the I.A. files, of men and women over twenty and under forty who had come to Liberty within the previous few years, and they called on seven or eight of them every week. Lars Newman's son wanted to be in the group, but he had been born on Liberty, and Chip wanted only people who had been raised in the Family, who were accustomed to scanners and walkways, to the slow pace and the contented smile.

He found a company in Pollensa that would make dynamite bombs with fast or slow mechanical fuses, provided they were ordered by a native with a permit. He found another company, in Calvia, that would make six gas masks, but they wouldn't guarantee them against LPK unless he gave them a sample for testing. Lilac, who was working in an immigrant clinic, found a doctor who knew the LPK formula, but none of the island's chemical companies could manufacture any; lithium was one of its chief constituents, and there hadn't been any lithium available for over thirty years.

He was running a weekly two-line advertisement in the *Immigrant,* offering to buy coveralls, sandals, and take-along kits. One day he got an answer from a woman in Andrait, and a few evenings later he went there to look at two kits and a pair of sandals. The kits were shabby and outdated, but the sandals were good. The woman and her husband asked why he wanted them. Their name was Newbridge and they were in their early thirties, living in a tiny wretched rat-infested cellar. Chip told them, and they asked to join the group —insisted on joining it, actually. They were perfectly normal-looking, which was a point in their favor, but there was a feverishness about them, a keyed-up tension, that bothered Chip a little.

He went to see them again a week later, with Dover, and that time they seemed more relaxed and possibly suitable. Their names were Jack and Ria. They had had two children, both of whom had died in their first few months. Jack was a sewer worker and Ria worked in a toy factory. They said they were healthy and seemed to be.

Chip decided to take them—provisionally, at least—and he told them the details of the plan as it was taking shape.

"We ought to blow up the whole fucking thing, not just the refrigerating plants," Jack said.

"One thing has to be very clear," Chip said. "I'm going to be in charge. Unless you're prepared to do exactly as I say every step of the way, you'd better forget the whole thing."

"No, you're absolutely right," Jack said. "There *has* to be one man in charge of an operation like this; it's the only way it can work."

"We can offer suggestions, can't we?" Ria said.

"The more the better," Chip said. "But the decisions are going to be mine, and you've got to be ready to go along with them."

Jack said, "I am," and Ria said, "So am I."

Locating the entrance of the tunnel turned out to be more difficult than Chip had anticipated. He collected three large-scale maps of central Eur and a highly detailed pre-U topographic one of "Switzerland" on which he carefully transcribed Uni's site, but everyone he consulted—former engineers and geologists, native mining engineers—said that more data was needed before the tunnel's course could be projected with any hope of accuracy. Ashi became interested in the problem and spent occasional hours in the Library copying references to "Geneva" and "Jura Mountains" out of old encyclopedias and works on geology.

On two consecutive moonlit nights Chip and Dover went out in the I.A. boat to a point west of EUR91766 and watched for the copper barges. These passed, they found, at precise intervals of four hours and twenty-five minutes. Each low flat dark shape moved steadily toward the northwest at thirty kilometers an hour, its rolling afterwaves lifting the boat and dropping it, lifting it and dropping it. Three hours later a barge would come from the opposite direction, riding higher on the water, empty.

Dover calculated that the Eur-bound barges, if they maintained their speed and direction, would reach EUR91772 in a little over six hours.

On the second night he brought the boat alongside a barge and slowed to match its speed while Chip climbed aboard. Chip rode on the barge for several minutes, sitting comfortably on its flat compacted load of copper ingots in wood cribs, and then he climbed back aboard the boat.

Lilac found another man for the group, an attendant at the clinic named Lars Newstone who called himself Buzz. He was thirty-six, Chip's age, and taller than normal; a quiet and capable-seeming man. He had been on the island for nine years and at the clinic for three, during which he had picked up a certain amount of medical knowledge. He was married but living apart from his wife. He wanted to join the group, he said, because he had always felt that "somebody ought to do something, or at least try. It's wrong," he said, "to let Uni—*have* the world without trying to get it back."

"He's fine, just the man we need," Chip said to Lilac after Buzz had left their room. "I wish I had two more of him instead of the Newbridges. Thank you."

Lilac said nothing, standing at the sink washing cups. Chip went to her, took her shoulders, and kissed her hair. She was in the seventh month of her pregnancy, big and uncomfortable.

At the end of March, Julia gave a dinner party at which Chip, who had by then been working four months on the plan, presented it to her guests—natives with money who could each be counted on, she had said, for a contribution of at least five hundred dollars. He gave them copies of a list he had prepared of all the costs that would be involved, and passed around his "Switzerland" map with the tunnel drawn in in its approximate position.

They weren't as receptive as he had thought they would be.

"Thirty-six hundred for explosives?" one asked.

"That's right, sir," Chip said. "If anyone knows where we can get them cheaper, I'll be glad to hear about it."

"What's this 'kit reinforcing'?"

"The kits we're going to carry; they're not made for heavy loads. They have to be taken apart and remade around metal frames."

"You people can't buy guns and bombs, can you?"

"I'll do the buying," Julia said, "and everything will stay on my property until the party leaves. I have the permits."

"When do you think you'll go?"

"I don't know yet," Chip said. "The gas masks are going to take three months from when they're ordered. And we still have one more man to find, and training to go through. I'm hoping for July or August."

"Are you sure this is where the tunnel actually is?"

"No, we're still working on that. That's just an approximation."

Five of the guests gave excuses and seven gave checks that added up to only twenty-six hundred dollars, less than a quarter of the eleven thousand that was needed.

"Lunky bastards," Julia said.

"It's a beginning, anyway," Chip said. "We can start ordering things. And take on Captain Gold."

"We'll do it again in a few weeks," Julia said. "What were you so nervous for? You've got to speak more forcefully!"

The baby was born, a boy, and they named him Jan. Both his eyes were brown.

On Sundays and Wednesday evenings, in an unused loft in Julia's factory, Chip, Dover, Buzz, Jack, and Ria studied various forms of fighting. Their teacher was an officer in the army, Captain Gold, a small smiling man who obviously disliked them and seemed to take pleasure in having them hit one another and throw one another to the thin mats spread on the floor. "Hit! Hit! Hit!" he would say, bobbing before them in his undershirt and army trousers. "Hit! Like this! *This* is hitting, not *this! This* is waving at someone! God almighty, you're hopeless, you steelies! Come on, Green-eye, *hit him!*"

Chip swung his fist at Jack and was in the air and on his back on a mat.

"Good, you!" Captain Gold said. "That looked a little human! Get up, Green-eye, you're not dead! What did I tell you about keeping low?"

Jack and Ria learned most quickly; Buzz, most slowly.

Julia gave another dinner, at which Chip spoke more forcefully, and they got thirty-two hundred dollars.

The baby was sick—had a fever and a stomach infection—but he got better and was fine-looking and happy, sucking hungrily at Lilac's breasts. Lilac was warmer than before, pleased with the baby and interested in hearing Chip tell about the money-raising and the gradual coming-into-being of the plan.

Chip found a sixth man, a worker on a farm near Santany, who had come over from Afr shortly before Chip and Lilac had. He was a little older than Chip would have liked, forty-three, but he was strong and quick-moving, and sure that Uni could be beaten. He had worked in chromatomicrography in the Family, and his name was Morgan Newmark, though he still called himself by his Family name, Karl.

Ashi said, "I think I could find the damned tunnel myself now," and handed Chip twenty pages of notes that he had copied from books in the Library. Chip brought them, along with the maps, to each of the people he had consulted before, and three of them were now willing to hazard a projection of the tunnel's likeliest course. They came up, not unexpectedly, with three different places for the tunnel's entrance. Two were within a kilometer of each other and one was six kilometers away. "This is enough if we can't do better," Chip said to Dover.

The company that was making the gas masks went out of business—without returning the eight-hundred-dollar advance Chip had given them—and another maker had to be found.

Chip talked again with Newbrook, the former technological academy teacher, about the type of refrigerating plants Uni would be likely to have. Julia gave another dinner and Ashi gave a party; three thousand dollars more was collected. Buzz had a run-in with a gang of natives and, though he surprised them by fighting effectively, came out of it with two cracked ribs and a fractured shinbone. Everyone began looking for another man in case he wasn't able to go.

Lilac woke Chip one night.

"What's wrong?" he said.

"Chip?" she said.

"Yes?" He could hear Jan breathing, asleep in his cradle.

"If you're right," she said, "and this island is a prison that Uni has put us on—"

"Yes?"

"And attacks have been made from here before—"

"Yes?" he said.

She was silent—he could see her lying on her back with her eyes open—and then she said, "Wouldn't Uni put *other* people here, 'healthy' members, to warn it of other attacks?"

He looked at her and said nothing.

"Maybe to—take part in them?" she said. "And get everyone 'helped' in Eur?"

"No," he said, and shook his head. "It's—no. They would have to get treatments, wouldn't they? To *stay* 'healthy'?"

"Yes," she said.

"You think there's a secret medicenter somewhere?" he asked, smiling.

"No," she said.

"No," he said. "I'm sure there aren't any—'espions' here. Before Uni would go to those lengths, it *would* simply kill incurables the way you and Ashi say it would."

"How do you *know?*" she said.

"Lilac, there *are* no espions," he said. "You're just looking for things to worry about. Go to sleep now. Go on. Jan's going to be up in a little while. Go on."

He kissed her and she turned over. After a while she seemed to be asleep.

He stayed awake.

It couldn't be. They would need treatments . . .

How many people had he told about the plan, the tunnel, the real memory banks? There was no counting. Hundreds! And each must have told others . . .

He'd even put the ad in the *Immigrant: Will buy kits, cuvs, sandals* . . .

Someone who was *in the group?* No. Dover?—impossible. Buzz?—no, never. Jack or Ria?—no. Karl? He didn't really know Karl that well yet— pleasant, talked a lot, drank a little more than he should have but not enough to worry about—no, Karl *couldn't* be anything but what he seemed, working on a farm out in the middle of nowhere . . .

Julia? He was out of his head. Christ and Wei! God in heaven!

Lilac was just worrying too much, that was all.

There couldn't be any espions, any people around who were secretly on Uni's side, because they would need treatments to stay that way.

He was going ahead with it no matter what.

He fell asleep.

The bombs came: bundles of thin brown cylinders taped around a central black one. They were stored in a shed behind the factory. Each had a small metal handle, blue or yellow, lying taped against its side. The blue handles were thirty-second fuses; the yellow, four-minute ones.

They tried one in a marble quarry at night; wedged it in a cleft and pulled its fuse handle, blue, with fifty meters of wire from behind a pile of cut blocks. The explosion when it came was thunderous, and where the cleft had been they found a hole the size of a doorway, running with rubble, churning with dust.

They hiked in the mountains—all except Buzz—wearing kits weighted with stones. Captain Gold showed them how to load a bullet-gun and focus an L-beam; how to draw, aim, and shoot—at planks propped against the factory's rear wall.

"Are you giving another dinner?" Chip asked Julia.

"In a week or two," she said.

But she didn't. She didn't mention money again, and neither did he.

He spent some time with Karl, and satisfied himself that he wasn't an "espion."

Buzz's leg healed almost completely, and he insisted he would be able to go.

The gas masks came, and the remaining guns, and the tools and the shoes and the razors; and the plastic sheeting, the remade kits, the watches, the coils of strong wire, the inflatable raft, the shovel, the compasses, the binoculars.

"Try to hit me," Captain Gold said, and Chip hit him and split his lip.

It took till November to get everything done, almost a year, and then Chip decided to wait and go at Christmas, to make the move to 'ooi on the holiday, when bike paths and walkways, carports and airports, would be at their busiest; when members would move a little less slowly than normal and even a "healthy" one might miss the plate of a scanner.

On the Sunday before they were to go, they brought everything from the shed into the loft and packed the kits and the secondary kits they would unpack when they landed. Julia was there, and Lars Newman's son John, who was going to bring back the I.A. boat, and Dover's girlfriend Nella—twenty-two and yellow-haired as he, excited by it all. Ashi looked in and so did Captain Gold. "You're nuts, you're all nuts," Captain Gold said, and Buzz said, "Scram, you lunky." When they were done, when all the kits were plastic-wrapped and tied, Chip asked everyone not in the group to go outside. He gathered the group in a circle on the mats.

"I've been thinking a lot about what happens if one of us gets caught," he said, "and this is what I've decided. If anyone, even *one,* gets caught—the rest of us will turn around and go back."

They looked at him. Buzz said, "After all this?"

"Yes," he said. "We won't have a chance, once anyone's treated and telling a doctor that we're going in through the tunnel. So we'll go back, quickly and quietly, and find one of the boats. In fact, I want to try to spot one when we land, before we start traveling."

"Christ and Wei!" Jack said. "Sure, if three or *four* get caught, but *one?*"

"That's the decision," Chip said. "It's the right one."

Ria said, "What if *you* get caught?"

"Then Buzz is in charge," Chip said, "and it's up to him. But meanwhile that's the way it's going to be: if anyone gets caught we all turn back."

Karl said, "So let's nobody get caught."

"Right," Chip said. He stood up. "That's all," he said. "Get plenty of sleep. Wednesday at seven."

"Woodsday," Dover said.

"Woodsday, Woodsday, Woodsday," Chip said. "Woodsday at seven."

. . .

He kissed Lilac as if he were going out to see someone about something and would be back in a few hours. "'By, love," he said.

She held him and kept her cheek against his and didn't say anything.

He kissed her again, took her arms from around him, and went to the cradle. Jan was busy reaching for an empty cigarette box hanging on a string. Chip kissed his cheek and said good-by to him.

Lilac came to him and he kissed her. They held each other and kissed, and then he went out, not looking back at her.

Ashi was waiting downstairs on his motorbike. He drove Chip to Pollensa and the pier.

They were all in the I.A. office by a quarter of seven, and while they were clipping one another's hair the truck came. John Newman and Ashi and a man from the factory loaded the kits and the raft onto the boat, and Julia unpacked sandwiches and coffee. The men clipped their beards and shaved their faces bare.

They put bracelets on and closed links that looked like ordinary ones. Chip's bracelet said Jesus AY31G6912.

He said good-by to Ashi, and kissed Julia. "Pack your kit and get ready to see the world," he said.

"Be careful," she said. "And try praying."

He got on the boat, sat on the deck in front of the kits with John Newman and the others—Buzz and Karl, Jack and Ria; strange-looking and Family-like with their clipped hair, their beardless similar faces.

Dover started the boat and steered it out of the harbor, then turned it toward the faint orange glow that came from '91766.

Two

In pallid pre-dawn light they slipped from the barge and pushed the kit-loaded raft away from it. Three of them pushed and three swam along beside, watching the black high-cliffed shore. They moved slowly, keeping about fifty meters out. Every ten minutes or so they changed places; the ones who had been swimming pushed, the ones who had been pushing swam.

When they were well below '91772 they turned and pushed the raft in. They beached it in a small sandy cove with towering rock walls, and unloaded the kits and unwrapped them. They opened the secondary kits and put on coveralls; pocketed guns, watches, compasses, maps; then dug a hole and packed into it the two emptied kits and all the plastic wrappings, the deflated raft, their Liberty clothing, and the shovel they had used for digging. They filled the hole and stamped it level, and with kits slung on their shoulders and sandals in their hands, began walking in single file down the narrow strip of beach. The sky lightened and their shadows appeared before them, sliding in and out over rocky cliff-base. Near the back of the line Karl started whistling "One Mighty Family." The others smiled, and Chip, at the front, joined it. Some of the others did too.

Soon they came to a boat—an old blue boat lying on its side, waiting for incurables who would think themselves lucky. Chip turned, and walking backward, said, "Here it is, if we need it," and Dover said, "We won't," and Jack, after Chip had turned and they had passed it, picked up a stone, turned, threw it at the boat, and missed.

They switched their kits from one shoulder to the other as they walked. In a little less than an hour they came to a scanner with its back to them. "Home again," Dover said, and Ria groaned, and Buzz said, "Hi, Uni, how are you?" —patting the scanner's top as he passed it. He was walking without limping; Chip had looked around a few times to check.

The strip of beach began to widen, and they came to a litter basket and more of them, and then lifeguard platforms, speakers and a clock—*6:54 Thu 25 Dec 171 Y.U.*—and a stairway zigzagging up the cliff with red and green bunting wound around some of its railing supports.

They put their kits down, and their sandals, and took their coveralls off and spread them out. They lay down on them and rested under the sun's growing warmth. Chip mentioned things that he thought they should say when they spoke to the Family—afterwards—and they talked about that and about the extent to which Uni's stopping would block TV and how long the restoring of it would take.

Karl and Dover fell asleep.

Chip lay with his eyes closed and thought about some of the problems the Family would face as it awakened, and different ways of dealing with them.

"Christ, Who Taught Us" began on the speakers at eight o'clock, and two red-capped lifeguards in sunglasses came walking down the zigzag stairs. One of them came to a platform near the group. "Merry Christmas," he said.

"Merry Christmas," they said to him.

"You can go in now if you want," he said, climbing up onto the platform.

Chip and Jack and Dover got up and went into the water. They swam around for a while, watching members come down the stairs, and then they went out and lay down again.

When there were thirty-five or forty members on the beach, at 8:22, the six got up and began putting on their coveralls and shouldering their kits.

Chip and Dover went up the stairs first. They smiled and said "Merry Christmas" to members coming down, and easily false-touched the scanner at the top. The only members nearby were at the canteen with their backs turned.

They waited by a water fountain, and Jack and Ria came up, and then Buzz and Karl.

They went to the bike racks, where twenty or twenty-five bikes were lined up in the nearest slots. They took the last six, put their kits in the baskets, mounted, and rode to the entrance of the bike path. They waited there, smiling and talking, until no cyclists and no cars were going by, and then they passed the scanner in a group, touching their bracelets to the side of it in case someone could see them from a distance.

They rode toward EUR91770 singly and in twos, spaced out widely along the path. Chip went first, with Dover behind him. He watched the cyclists who approached them and the occasional cars that rushed past. *We're going to do it,* he thought. *We're going to do it.*

.   .   .

They went into the airport separately and gathered near the flight-schedule signboard. Members pressed them close together; the red-and-green-streamered waiting room was densely crowded, and so voice-filled that Christmas music could only intermittently be heard. Beyond the glass, large planes turned and moved ponderously, took members on from three escalators at once, let lines of members off, rolled to and from the runways.

It was 9:35. The next flight to EUR00001 was at 11:48.

Chip said, "I don't like the idea of staying here so long. The barge either used extra power or came in late, and if the difference was conspicuous, Uni may have figured out what caused it."

"Let's go now," Ria said, "and get as close to '001 as we can and then bike again."

"We'll get there a lot sooner if we wait," Karl said. "This isn't such a bad hiding place."

"No," Chip said, looking at the signboard, "let's go—on the 10:06 to '00020. That's the soonest we can manage it, and it's only about fifty kilometers from '001. Come on, the door's over that way."

They made their way through the crowd to the swing-door at the side of the room and clustered around its scanner. The door opened and a member in orange came out. Excusing himself, he reached between Chip and Dover to touch the scanner—*yes*, it winked—and went on.

Chip slipped his watch from his pocket and checked it against a clock. "It's lane six," he said. "If there's more than one escalator, be on line for the one at the back of the plane; and make sure you're near the end of the line but with at least six members behind you. Dover?" He took Dover's elbow and they went through the door into the depot area. A member in orange standing there said, "You're not supposed to be in here."

"Uni okayed it," Chip said. "We're in airport design."

"Three-thirty-seven A," Dover said.

Chip said, "This wing is being enlarged next year."

"I see what you meant about the ceiling," Dover said, looking up at it.

"Yes," Chip said. "It could easily go up another meter."

"Meter and a half," Dover said.

"Unless we run into trouble with the ducts," Chip said.

The member left them and went out through the door.

"Yes, all the ducts," Dover said. "Big problem."

"Let me show you where they lead," Chip said. "It's interesting."

"It certainly is," Dover said.

They went into the area where members in orange were readying cake and drink containers, working more quickly than members usually did.

"Three-thirty-seven A?" Chip said.

"Why not?" Dover said, and pointed at the ceiling as they separated for a member pushing a cart. "You see the way the ducts run?" he said.

"We're going to have to change the whole setup," Chip said. "In here too."

They false-touched and went into the room where coveralls hung on hooks. No one was in it. Chip closed the door and pointed to the closet where the orange coveralls were kept.

They put orange coveralls on over their yellow ones, and toeguards on their sandals. They tore openings inside the pockets of the orange coveralls so that they could reach into the pockets of the inner ones.

A member in white came in. "Hello," he said. "Merry Christmas."

"Merry Christmas," they said.

"I was sent up from '765 to help out," he said. He was about thirty.

"Good, we can use it," Chip said.

The member, opening his coveralls, looked at Dover, who was closing his. "What have you got the other ones on underneath for?" he asked.

"It's warmer that way," Chip said, going to him.

He turned to Chip, puzzled. "Warmer?" he said. "What do you want to be warmer for?"

"I'm sorry, brother," Chip said, and hit him in the stomach. He bent forward, grunting, and Chip swung his fist up under his jaw. The member straightened and fell backward; Dover caught him under the arms and lowered him to the floor. He lay with his eyes closed, as if sleeping.

Chip, looking down at him, said, "Christ and Wei, it works."

They tore up a set of coveralls and tied the member's wrists and ankles and knotted a sleeve between his teeth; then lifted him and put him into the closet where the floor polisher was.

The clock's 9:51 became 9:52.

They wrapped their kits in orange coveralls and went out of the room and past the members working at the cake and drink containers. In the depot area they found a half-empty carton of towels and put the wrapped kits into it. Carrying the carton between them, they went out through the portal onto the field.

A plane was opposite lane six, a large one, with members leaving it on two escalators. Members in orange waited at each escalator with a container cart.

They went away from the plane, toward the left; crossed the field diagonally with the carton between them, skirting a slow-moving maintenance truck and approaching the hangars that lay in a flat-roofed wing extending toward the runways.

They went into a hangar. A smaller plane was there, with members in orange underneath it, lowering a square black housing from it. Chip and Dover carried the carton to the back of the hangar where there was a door in the side wall. Dover opened it, looked in, and nodded to Chip.

They went in and closed the door. They were in a supply room: racks of tools, rows of wood crates, black metal drums marked *Lub Oil SG*. "Couldn't be better," Chip said as they put the carton on the floor.

Dover went to the door and stood at its hinge side. He took out his gun and held it by its barrel.

Chip, crouching, unwrapped a kit, opened it, and took out a bomb, one with a yellow four-minute handle.

He separated two of the oil drums and put the bomb on the floor between them, with its taped-down handle facing up. He took his watch out and looked at it. Dover said, "How long?" and he said, "Three minutes."

He went back to the carton and, still holding the watch, closed the kit and rewrapped it and closed the carton's leaves.

"Is there anything we can use?" Dover asked, nodding at the tool racks.

Chip went to one and the door of the room opened and a member in orange came in. "Hello," Chip said, and took a tool from the rack and put the watch in his pocket. "Hello," the member said, coming to the other side of the rack. She glanced over it at Chip. "Who're you?" she asked.

"Li RP," he said. "I was sent up from '765 to help." He took another tool from the rack, a pair of calipers.

"It's not as bad as Wei's Birthday," the member said.

Another member came to the door. "We've got it, Peace," he said. "Li had it."

"I asked him and he said he didn't," the first member said.

"Well he did," the second member said, and went away.

The first member went after him. "He was the first one I asked," she said.

Chip stood and watched the door as it slowly closed. Dover, behind it, looked at him and closed it all the way, softly. Chip looked back at Dover, and then at his hand holding the tools. It was shaking. He put the tools down, let his breath out, and showed his hand to Dover, who smiled and said, "Very unmemberlike."

Chip drew a breath and got the watch from his pocket. "Less than a minute," he said, and went to the drums and crouched. He pulled the tape from the bomb's handle.

Dover put his gun into his pocket—poked it into the inner one—and stood with his hand on the doorknob.

Chip, looking at the watch and holding the fuse handle, said, "Ten seconds." He waited, waited, waited—and then pulled the handle up and stood as Dover opened the door. They picked up the carton and carried it from the room and pulled the door closed.

They walked with the carton through the hangar—"Easy, easy," Chip said—and across the field toward the plane opposite lane six. Members were filing onto the escalators, riding up.

"What's that?" a member in orange with a clipboard asked, walking along with them.

"We were told to bring it over there," Chip said.

"Karl?" another member said at the other side of the one with the clipboard. He stopped and turned, saying "Yes?" and Chip and Dover kept walking.

They brought the carton to the plane's rear escalator and put it down. Chip stayed opposite the scanner and looked at the escalator controls; Dover slipped through the line and stood at the scanner's back. Members passed between them, touching their bracelets to the green-winking scanner and stepping onto the escalator.

A member in orange came to Chip and said, "I'm on this escalator."

"Karl just told me to take it," Chip said. "I was sent up from '765 to help."

"What's wrong?" the member with the clipboard asked, coming over. "Why are there three of you here?"

"I thought I was on this escalator," the other member said. The air shuddered and a loud roar clapped from the hangars.

A black pillar, vast and growing, stood on the wing of hangars, and rolling orange fire was in the black. A black and orange rain fell on the roof and the field, and members in orange came running from the hangars, running and slowing and looking back up at the fiery pillar on the roof.

The member with the clipboard stared, and hurried forward. The other member hurried after him.

The members on line stood motionless, looking upward toward the hangars. Chip and Dover caught at their arms and drew them forward. "Don't stop," they said. "Keep moving, please. There's no danger. The plane is waiting. Touch and step on. Keep moving, please." They herded the members past the scanner and onto the escalator and one was Jack—"Beautiful," he said, gazing past Chip as he false-touched; and Ria, who looked as excited as she had the first time Chip had seen her; and Karl, looking awed and somber; and Buzz, smiling, Dover moved to the escalator after Buzz; Chip thrust a wrapped kit to him and turned to the other members on line, the last seven or eight, who stood looking toward the hangars. "Keep moving, please," he said. "The plane is waiting for you. Sister!"

"There is no cause for alarm," a woman's voice loudspeakered. "There has been an accident in the hangars but everything is under control."

Chip urged the members to the escalator. "Touch and step on," he said. "The plane's waiting."

"Departing members, please resume your places in line," the voice said. "Members who are boarding planes, continue to do so. There will be no interruption of service."

Chip false-touched and stepped onto the escalator behind the last member. Riding upward with his wrapped kit under his arm, he glanced toward the hangars: the pillar was black and smudging; there was no more fire. He looked ahead again, at pale blue coveralls. "All personnel except forty-sevens and forty-nines, resume your assigned duties," the woman's voice said. "All personnel except forty-sevens and forty-nines, resume your assigned duties. Everything is under control." Chip stepped into the plane and the door slid down behind him. "There will be no interruption of—" Members stood confusedly, looking at filled seats.

"There are extra passengers because of the holiday," Chip said. "Go forward and ask members with children to double up. It can't be helped."

The members moved down the aisle, looking from one side of the plane to the other.

The five were sitting in the last row, next to the dispensers. Dover took his wrapped kit from the aisle seat and Chip sat down. Dover said, "Not bad."

"We're not up yet," Chip said.

Voices filled the plane: members telling members about the explosion, spreading the news from row to row. The clock said *10:06* but the plane wasn't moving.

The *10:06* became *10:07*.

The six looked at one another, and looked forward, normally.

The plane moved; swung gently to the side and then pulled forward. It moved faster. The light dimmed and the TV screens flicked on.

They watched *Christ's Life* and a years-old *Family at Work*. They drank tea and coke but couldn't eat; there were no cakes on the plane, because of the hour, and though they had foil-wrapped rounds of cheese in their kits, they would have been seen eating them by the members who came to the dispensers. Chip and Dover sweated in their double coveralls. Karl kept dozing off, and Ria and Buzz on either side of him nudged him to keep him awake and watching.

The flight took forty minutes.

When the location sign said *EUR00020,* Chip and Dover got up from their seats and stood at the dispensers, pressing the buttons and letting tea and coke flow down the drains. The plane landed and rode and stopped, and members began filing off. After a few dozen had gone through the doorway nearby, Chip and Dover lifted the emptied containers from the dispensers, set them on the floor and raised their covers, and Buzz put a wrapped kit into each. Then Buzz, Karl, Ria, and Jack got up and the six went to the doorway. Chip, carrying a container against his chest, said, "Would you excuse us, please?" to an elderly member and went out. The others followed close behind him. Dover, carrying the other container, said to the member, "You'd better wait till I'm off the escalator," and the member nodded, looking confused.

At the bottom of the escalator Chip leaned his wrist toward the scanner and then stood opposite it, blocking it from the members in the waiting room. Buzz, Karl, Ria, and Jack passed in front of him, false-touching, and Dover leaned against the scanner and nodded to the member waiting above.

The four went toward the waiting room, and Chip and Dover crossed the field to the portal and went through it into the depot area. Setting down the containers, they took the kits out of them and slipped between two rows of crates. They found a cleared space near the wall and took off the orange coveralls and pulled the toeguards from their sandals.

They left the depot area through the swing-door, their kits slung on their shoulders. The others were waiting around the scanner. They went out of the airport by twos—it was almost as crowded as the one in '91770—and gathered again at the bike racks.

By noon they were north of '00018. They ate their rounds of cheese between the bike path and the River of Freedom, in a valley flanked by mountains that rose to awesome snow-streaked heights. While they ate they looked at their maps. By nightfall, they calculated, they could be in parkland a few kilometers from the tunnel's entrance.

A little after three o'clock, when they were nearing '00013, Chip noticed an approaching cyclist, a girl in her early teens, who was looking at the faces of the northbound cyclists—his own as she passed him—with an expression of concern, of memberlike wanting-to-help. A moment later he saw another approaching cyclist looking at faces in the same slightly anxious way, an elderly woman with flowers in her basket. He smiled at her as she passed, then looked ahead. There was nothing out of the ordinary in the path and the road beside it; a few hundred meters ahead both path and road turned to the right and disappeared behind a power station.

He rode onto grass, stopped, and looking back, signaled to the others as they came along.

They pushed their bikes farther onto the grass. They were on the last stretch of parkland before the city: a span of grass, then picnic tables and a rising slope of trees.

"We're never going to make it if we stop every half hour," Ria said.

They sat down on the grass.

"I think they're checking bracelets up ahead," Chip said. "Telecomps and red-crossed coveralls. I noticed two members coming this way who looked as if they were trying to spot the sick one. They had that how-can-I-help look."

"Hate," Buzz said.

Jack said, "Christ and Wei, Chip, if we're going to start worrying about members' *facial expressions,* we might as well just turn around and go home."

Chip looked at him and said, "A bracelet check isn't so unlikely, is it? Uni must know by now that the explosion at '91770 was no accident, and it might have figured out exactly why it happened. This is the shortest route from '020 to Uni—and we're coming to the first sharp turn in about twelve kilometers."

"All right, so they're checking bracelets," Jack said. "What the hate are we carrying guns for?"

"Yes!" Ria said.

Dover said, "If we shoot our way through we'll have the whole bike path after us."

"So we'll drop a bomb behind us," Jack said. "We've got to move fast, not sit on our asses as if we're in a chess game. These dummies are half dead anyway; what difference does it make if we kill a few of them? We're going to help all the rest, aren't we?"

"The guns and bombs are for when we need them," Chip said, "not for when we can avoid using them." He turned to Dover. "Take a walk in the woods there," he said. "See if you can get a look at what's past the turn."

"Right," Dover said. He got up and crossed the grass, picked something up and brought it to a litter basket, and went in among the trees. His yellow coveralls became bits of yellow that vanished up the slope.

They turned from watching him. Chip took out his map.

"Shit," Jack said.

Chip said nothing. He looked at the map.

Buzz rubbed his leg and took his hand from it abruptly.

Jack tore bits of grass from the ground. Ria, sitting close to him, watched him. "What's your suggestion," Jack said, "if they *are* checking bracelets?"

Chip looked up from the map and, after a moment, said, "We'll go back a little way and cut east and by-pass them."

Jack tore up more grass and then threw it down. "Come on," he said to Ria, and stood up. She sprang up beside him, bright-eyed.

"Where are you going?" Chip said.

"Where we planned to go," Jack said, looking down at him. "The parkland near the tunnel. We'll wait for you until it gets light."

"Sit down, you two," Karl said.

Chip said, "You'll go with all of us when I say we'll go. You agreed to that at the beginning."

"I've changed my mind," Jack said. "I don't like taking orders from *you* any more than I like taking them from Uni."

"You're going to ruin everything," Buzz said.

Ria said, "*You* are! Stopping, turning back, by-passing—if you're going to do a thing, *do* it."

"Sit down and wait till Dover gets back," Chip said.

Jack smiled. "You want to make me?" he said. "Right out here in front of the Family?" He nodded to Ria and they picked up their bikes and steadied the kits in the baskets.

Chip got up, putting the map in his pocket. "We can't break the group in two this way," he said. "Stop and think for a minute, will you, Jack? How will we know if—"

"You're the stopper-and-thinker," Jack said. "I'm the one who's going to walk down that tunnel." He turned and pushed his bike away. Ria pushed hers along with him. They went toward the path.

Chip took a step after them and stopped, his jaw tight, his hands fisted. He wanted to shout at them, to take his gun out and force them back—but there were cyclists passing, members on the grass nearby.

"There's nothing you can do, Chip," Karl said, and Buzz said, "The brother-fighters."

At the edge of the path Jack and Ria mounted their bikes. Jack waved. "So long!" he called. "See you in the lounge at TV!" Ria waved too and they pedaled away.

Buzz and Karl waved after them.

Chip snatched up his kit from his bike and slung it on his shoulder. He took another kit and tossed it in Buzz's lap. "Karl, you stay here," he said. "Buzz, come on with me."

He went into the woods and realized he had moved quickly, angrily, abnormally, but thought *Fight it!* He went up the slope in the direction Dover had taken. *God DAMN them!*

Buzz caught up with him. "Christ and Wei," he said, "don't *throw* the kits!"

"God *damn* them!" Chip said. "The first time I saw them I knew they were no good! But I shut my eyes because I was so fighting—God damn *me!*" he said. "It's *my* fault. Mine."

"Maybe there's no bracelet check and they'll be waiting in the parkland," Buzz said.

Yellow flickered among the trees ahead: Dover coming down. He stopped, then saw them and came on. "You're right," he said. "Doctors on the ground, doctors in the air—"

"Jack and Ria have gone on," Chip said.

Dover looked at him wide-eyed and said, "Didn't you stop them?"

"How?" Chip said. He caught Dover's arm and turned him around. "Show us the way," he said.

Dover led them quickly up the slope through the trees. "They'll never get through," he said. "There's a whole medicenter, and barriers to prevent the bikes from turning."

They came out of the trees onto an incline of rock, Buzz last and hurrying. Dover said, "Get down or we'll be seen."

They dropped to their stomachs and crawled up the incline to its rim. Beyond lay the city, '00013, its white slabs standing clean and bright in the sunlight, its interweaving rails glittering, its border of roadways flashing with cars. The river curved before it and continued to the north, blue and slender, with sightseeing boats drifting slowly and a long line of barges passing under bridges.

Below, they looked into a rock-walled half bowl whose floor was a semicircular plaza where the bike path branched; it came down from the north around the power station, and half of it turned, passed over the car-rushing road, and bridged to the city, while the other half went on across the plaza and followed the river's curving eastern bank with the road coming up to rejoin it. Before it branched, barriers channeled the oncoming cyclists into three lines, each of them passing before a group of red-cross-coveralled members standing beside a short unusual-looking scanner. Three members in antigrav gear hovered face-down in the air, one over each group. Two cars and a copter were in the nearer part of the plaza, and more members in red-crossed coveralls stood by the line of cyclists who were leaving the city, hurrying them along when they slowed to look at the ones who were touching the scanners.

"Christ, Marx, Wood, and Wei," Buzz said.

Chip, while he looked, pulled his kit open at his side. "They must be in the line somewhere," he said. He found his binoculars and put them to his eyes and focused them.

"They are," Dover said. "See the kits in the baskets?"

Chip swept the line and found Jack and Ria; they were pedaling slowly, side by side in wood-barriered lanes. Jack was looking ahead and his lips were moving. Ria nodded. They were steering with their left hands only; their right hands were in their pockets.

Chip passed the binoculars to Dover and turned to his kit. "We've got to help them get through," he said. "If they make it over the bridge they may be able to lose themselves in the city."

"They're going to shoot when they get to the scanners," Dover said.

Chip gave Buzz a blue-handled bomb and said, "Take off the tape and pull when I tell you. Try to get it near the copter; two birds with one net."

"Do it before they start shooting," Dover said.

Chip took the binoculars back from him and looked through them and found Jack and Ria again. He scanned the lines ahead of them; about fifteen bikes were between them and the groups at the scanners.

"Do they have bullets or L-beams?" Dover asked.

"Bullets," Chip said. "Don't worry, I'll time it right." He watched the lines of slow-moving bikes, gauging their speed.

"They'll probably shoot anyway," Buzz said. "Just for fun. Did you see that look in Ria's eyes?"

"Get ready," Chip said. He watched until Jack and Ria were five bikes from the scanners. "Pull," he said.

Buzz pulled the handle and threw the bomb underhanded to the side. It hit stone, tumbled downward, bounded off a projection, and landed near the side of the copter. "Get back," Chip said. He took another look through the binoculars, at Jack and Ria two bikes from the scanners looking tense but confident, and slipped back between Buzz and Dover. "They look as if they're going to a party," he said.

They waited, their cheeks on stone, and the explosion roared and the incline shuddered. Metal crashed and grated below. There was silence, and the bomb's bitter smell; and then voices, murmuring and rising louder. "Those two!" someone shouted.

They edged forward to the rim.

Two bikes were racing onto the bridge. All the others had stopped, their riders standing one-footed, facing toward the copter—tipped to its side below and smoking—and turning now toward the two bikes speeding and the red-cross-coveralled members running after them. The three members in the air veered and flew toward the bridge.

Chip raised the binoculars—to Ria's bent back and Jack's ahead of her. They pedaled rapidly in depthless flatness, seeming to get no farther away. A glittering mist appeared, partly obscuring them.

Above, a hovering member downpointed a cylinder gushing thick white gas.

"He's got them!" Dover said.

Ria stood astride her bike; Jack looked over his shoulder at her.

"Ria, not Jack," Chip said.

Jack stopped and turned with his gun aimed upward. It jerked, and jerked again.

The member in the air went limp (*crack* and *crack,* the shots sounded), the white-gushing cylinder falling from his hand.

Members fleeing the bridge bicycled in both directions, ran wide-eyed on the flanking walkways.

Ria sat by her bike. She turned her head, and her face was moist and glittering. She looked troubled. Red-crossed coveralls blurred over her.

Jack stared, holding his gun, and his mouth opened big and round, closed and opened again in glittering mist. ("Ria!" Chip heard, small and far away.) Jack raised his gun ("Ria!") and fired, fired, fired.

Another member in the air (*crack, crack, crack*) went limp and dropped his cylinder. Red spattered on the walkway below him, and more red.

Chip lowered the binoculars.

"Your *gas mask!*" Buzz said. He had binoculars too.

Dover was lying with his face in his arms.

Chip sat up and looked with only his eyes: at the narrow emptied bridge with a faraway cyclist in pale blue wobbling down the middle of it and a member in the air following him at a distance; at the two dead or dying members, turning slowly in the air, drifting; at the red-cross-coveralled members, walking now in a bridge-wide line, and one of them helping a member in yellow by a fallen bike, taking her about the shoulders and leading her back toward the plaza.

The cyclist stopped and looked back toward the red-cross-coveralled members, then turned and bent forward over the front of his bike. The member in the air flew quickly closer and pointed his arm; a thick white feather grew from it and brushed the cyclist.

Chip raised the binoculars.

Jack, gray-snouted in his gas mask, leaned to his left in glittering mist and put a bomb on the bridge. Then he pedaled, skidded, sideslipped, and fell. He raised himself on one arm with the bike lying between his legs. His kit spilled from the bike's basket, lay by the bomb.

"Oh Christ and Wei," Buzz said.

Chip took down the binoculars, looked at the bridge, and then wound the binoculars' neckstrap tightly around their middle.

"How many?" Dover asked, looking at him.

Chip said, "Three."

The explosion was bright, loud, and long. Chip watched Ria, walking from the bridge with the red-cross-coveralled member leading her. She didn't turn around.

Dover, up on his knees and looking, turned to Chip.

"His whole kit," Chip said. "He was sitting next to it." He put the binoculars into his kit and closed it. "We've got to get out of here," he said. "Put them away, Buzz. Come on."

He meant not to look, but before they left the incline he did.

The middle of the bridge was black and rubbled, and its sides were burst outward. A bicycle wheel lay outside the blackened area, and there were other smaller things toward which the red-cross-coveralled members slowly moved. Pieces of pale blue were on the bridge and floating on the river.

They went back to Karl and told him what had happened, and the four of them got on their bikes and rode south for a few kilometers and went into parkland. They found a stream and drank from it and washed.

"And now we turn back?" Dover said.

"No," Chip said, "not all of us."

They looked at him.

"I said that we would," he said, "because if anyone got caught, I wanted him to believe it, and say it when he was questioned. The way Ria's probably saying it right now." He took a cigarette that they were passing around— despite the risk of the smoke smell traveling—and drew on it and passed it to Buzz. "*One* of us is going to go back," he said. "At least I hope only one will go—to set off a bomb or two between here and the coast and take a boat, to make it look as if we've stuck to the plan. The rest of us will hide in parkland, work our way closer to '001, and go for the tunnel in two weeks or so."

"Good," Dover said, and Buzz said, "I never thought it made sense to give up so easily."

"Will three of us be enough?" Karl asked.

"We won't know till we try," Chip said. "Would six have been enough? Maybe it can be done by one, and maybe it can't be done by a dozen. But after coming this far, I fighting well mean to find out."

"I'm with you; I was just asking," Karl said. Buzz said, "I'm with you too," and Dover said, "So am I."

"Good," Chip said. "Three stand a better chance than one, that I *do* know. Karl, you're the one who goes back."

Karl looked at him. "Why me?" he asked.

"Because you're forty-three," Chip said. "I'm sorry, brother, but I can't think of any other basis for deciding."

"Chip," Buzz said, "I think I'd better tell you: my leg has been hurting me for the past few hours. I can make it back or I can go on, but—well, I thought you ought to know."

Karl gave Chip the cigarette. It was down to a couple of centimeters; he snuffed it into the ground. "All right, Buzz, you'd better be the one," he said. "Shave first. We'd all better shave, in case we run into anyone."

They shaved, and then Chip and Buzz worked out a route for Buzz to the nearest part of the coast, about three hundred kilometers away. He would set off a bomb at the airport at 'oooi5 and another when he was near the sea. He kept two extra in case he needed them and gave his others to Chip. "With luck you'll be on a boat by tomorrow night," Chip said. "Make sure there's nobody counting heads when you take it. Tell Julia, and Lilac too, that we'll be hiding for at least two weeks, maybe longer."

Buzz shook hands with all of them, wished them luck, and took his bike and left.

"We'll stay right here for a while and take turns getting some sleep," Chip said. "Tonight we'll go into the city for cakes and cuvs."

"Cakes," Karl said, and Dover said, "It's going to be a long two weeks."

"No it isn't," Chip said. "That was in case *he* gets caught. We're going to do it in four or five days."

"Christ and Wei," Karl said, smiling, "you're really being cagey."

Three

They stayed where they were for two days—slept and ate and shaved and practiced fighting, played children's word games, talked about democratic government and sex and the pygmies of the equatorial forests—and on the third day, Sunday, they bicycled north. Outside of '00013 they stopped and went up onto the incline overlooking the plaza and the bridge. The bridge was partly repaired and closed off by barriers. Lines of cyclists crossed the plaza in both directions; there were no doctors, no scanners, no copter, no cars. Where the copter had been, there was a rectangle of fresh pink paving.

Early in the afternoon they passed '001 and glimpsed at a distance Uni's white dome beside the Lake of Universal Brotherhood. They went into the parkland beyond the city.

The following evening, at dusk, with their bikes hidden in a branch-covered hollow and their kits on their shoulders, they passed a scanner at the parkland's farther border and went out onto the grassy slopes that approached Mount Love. They walked briskly, in shoes and green coveralls, with binoculars and gas masks hung about their necks. They held their guns, but as the darkness grew deeper and the slope more rocky and irregular, they pocketed them. Now and then they paused, and Chip put a hand-covered flashlight to his compass.

They came to the first of the three presumed locations of the tunnel's entrance, and separated and looked for it, using their flashlights guardedly. They didn't find it.

They started for the second location, a kilometer to the northeast. A half moon came over the shoulder of the mountain, wanly lighting it, and they searched its base carefully as they crossed the rock-slope before it.

The slope became smooth, but only in the strip where they were walking— and they realized that they were on a road, old and scrub-patched. Behind them it curved away toward the parkland; ahead it led into a fold in the mountain.

They looked at one another, and took out their guns. Leaving the road, they moved close to the side of the mountain and edged along slowly in single file —first Chip, then Dover, then Karl—holding their kits to keep them from bumping, holding their guns.

They came to the fold, and waited against the mountainside, listening.

No sound came from within.

They waited and listened, and then Chip looked back at the others and raised his gas mask and fastened it.

They did the same.

Chip stepped out into the opening of the fold, his gun before him. Dover and Karl stepped out beside him.

Within was a deep and level clearing; and opposite, at the base of sheer mountain wall, the black round flat-bottomed opening of a large tunnel.

It appeared to be completely unprotected.

They lowered their masks and looked at the opening through their binoculars. They looked at the mountain above it and, taking a few steps forward, looked at the fold's outcurving walls and the oval of sky that roofed it.

"Buzz must have done a good job," Karl said.

"Or a bad one and got caught," Dover said.

Chip swung his binoculars back to the opening. Its rim had a glassy sheen, and pale green scrub lay along its bottom. "It feels like the boats on the beaches," he said. "Sitting there wide open . . ."

"Do you think it leads back to Liberty?" Dover asked, and Karl laughed.

Chip said, "There could be fifty traps that we won't see until it's too late." He lowered his binoculars.

Karl said, "Maybe Ria didn't say anything."

"When you're questioned at a medicenter you say *everything*," Chip said. "But even if she didn't, wouldn't it at least be closed? That's what we've got the tools for."

Karl said, "It must still be in use."

Chip stared at the opening.

"We can always go back," Dover said.

"Sure, let's," Chip said.

They looked all around them, and raised their masks into place, and walked slowly across the clearing. No gas jetted, no alarms sounded, no members in antigrav gear appeared in the sky.

They walked to the opening of the tunnel and shone their flashlights into it. Light shimmered and sparked in high plastic-lined roundness, all the way to the place where the tunnel seemed to end, but no, was bending to its downward angle. Two steel tracks reached into it, wide and flat, with a couple of meters of unplasticked black rock between them.

They looked back at the clearing and up at the opening's rim. They stepped inside the tunnel, looked at one another, and lowered their masks and sniffed.

"Well," Chip said. "Ready to walk?"

Karl nodded, and Dover, smiling, said, "Let's go."

They stood for a moment, and then walked ahead on the smooth black rock between the tracks.

"Will the air be all right?" Karl asked.

"We've got the masks if it isn't," Chip said. He shone his flashlight on his watch. "It's a quarter of ten," he said. "We should be there around one."

"Uni'll be up," Dover said.

"Till we put it to sleep," Karl said.

The tunnel bent to a slight incline, and they stopped and looked—at plastic roundness glimmering away and away and away into blackest black.

"Christ and Wei," Karl said.

They started walking again, at a brisker pace, side by side between the tracks. "We should have brought the bikes," Dover said. "We could have coasted."

"Let's keep the talk to a minimum," Chip said. "And just one light at a time. Yours now, Karl."

They walked without talking, behind the light of Karl's flashlight. They took their binoculars off and put them in their kits.

Chip felt that Uni was listening to them, was recording the vibrations of their footsteps or the heat of their bodies. Would they be able to overcome the defenses it surely was readying, outfight its members, resist its gases? (Were the gas masks any good? Had Jack fallen because he had got his on too late, or would getting it on sooner have made no difference?)

Well, the time for questioning was over, he told himself. This was the time for going ahead. They would meet whatever was waiting for them and do their best to get to the refrigerating plants and blast them.

How many members would they have to hurt, to kill? Maybe none, he thought; maybe the threat of their guns would be enough to protect them. (Against helpful unselfish members seeing Uni in danger? No, never.)

Well, it had to be; there was no other way.

He turned his thoughts to Lilac—to Lilac and Jan and their room in New Madrid.

The tunnel grew cold but the air stayed good.

They walked on, into plastic roundness that glimmered away into blackest black with the tracks reaching into it. *We're here,* he thought. *Now. We're doing it.*

. . .

At the end of an hour they stopped to rest. They sat on the tracks and divided a cake among them and passed a container of tea around. Karl said, "I'd give my arm for some whiskey."

"I'll buy you a case when we get back," Chip said.

"You heard him," Karl said to Dover.

They sat for a few minutes and then they got up and started walking again. Dover walked on a track. "You look pretty confident," Chip said, flashing his light at him.

"I am," Dover said. "Aren't you?"

"Yes," Chip said, shining his light ahead again.

"I'd feel better if there were six of us," Karl said.

"So would I," Chip said.

It was funny about Dover: he had hidden his face in his arms when Jack had started shooting, Chip remembered, and now, when *they* would soon be shooting, perhaps killing, he seemed cheerful and carefree. But maybe it was a cover-up, to hide anxiety. Or maybe it was just being twenty-five or twenty-six, however old he was.

They walked, shifting their kits from one shoulder to the other.

"Are you sure this thing ends?" Karl said.

Chip flicked the light at his watch. "It's eleven-thirty," he said. "We should be past the halfway mark."

They kept walking into the plastic roundness. It grew a little less cold.

They stopped again at a quarter of twelve, but they found themselves restless and got up in a minute and went on.

Light glinted far away in the center of the blackness, and Chip pulled out his gun. "Wait," Dover said, touching his arm, "it's *my* light. Look!" He switched his flashlight off and on, off and on, and the glint in the blackness went and came back with it. "It's the end," he said. "Or something on the tracks."

They walked on, more quickly. Karl took his gun out too. The glint, moving slightly up and down, seemed to stay the same distance from them, small and faint.

"It's moving away from us," Karl said.

But then, abruptly, it grew brighter, was nearer.

They stopped and raised their masks, fastened them, and walked on.

Toward a disc of steel, a wall that sealed the tunnel to its rim.

They went close to it but didn't touch it. It would slide upward, they saw; bands of fine vertical scratches ran down it and its bottom was shaped to fit over the tracks.

They lowered their masks and Chip put his watch to Dover's light. "Twenty of one," he said. "We made good time."

"Or else it goes on on the other side," Karl said.

"You would think of that," Chip said, pocketing his gun and unslinging his kit. He put it down on the rock, got on one knee beside it, and pulled it open. "Come closer with the light, Dover," he said. "Don't touch it, Karl."

Karl, looking at the wall, said, "Do you think it's electrified?"

"Dover?" Chip said.

"Hold on," Dover said.

He had backed a few meters into the tunnel and was shining his light at them. The tip of his L-beam protruded into it. "Don't panic, you're not going to be hurt," he said. "Your guns don't work. Drop yours, Karl. Chip, let me see your hands, then put them on your head and stand up."

Chip stared above the light. There was a glistening line: Dover's clipped blond hair.

Karl said, "Is this a joke or what?"

"Drop it, Karl," Dover said. "Put down your kit too. Chip, let me see your hands."

Chip showed his empty hands and put them on his head and stood up. Karl's gun clattered on the rock, and his kit bumped. "What *is* this?" he said, and to Chip, "What's he *doing?*"

"He's an espion," Chip said.

"A what?"

Lilac had been right. An espion in the group. But *Dover?* It was impossible. It couldn't be.

"Hands on your head, Karl," Dover said. "Now turn around, both of you, and face the wall."

"You brother-fighter," Karl said.

They turned around and faced the steel wall with their hands on their heads.

"Dover," Chip said. "Christ and Wei—"

"You little bastard," Karl said.

"You're not going to be hurt," Dover said. The wall slid upward—and a long concrete-walled room extended before them, with the tracks going halfway into it and ending. A pair of steel doors were at the room's far end.

"Six steps forward and stop," Dover said. "Go on. Six steps."

They walked six steps forward and stopped.

Kit-strap fittings clinked behind them. "The gun is still on you," Dover said—from lower down; he was crouching. They glanced at each other. Karl's eyes questioned; Chip shook his head.

"All right," Dover said, his voice coming from his standing height again. "Straight ahead."

They walked through the concrete-walled room, and the steel doors at the end of it slid apart. White-tiled wall stood beyond.

"Through and to the right," Dover said.

They went through the doorway and turned to the right. A long white-tiled corridor stretched before them, ending at a single steel door with a scanner beside it. The right-hand wall of the corridor was solid tile; the left was broken by evenly spaced steel doors, ten or twelve of them, each with its scanner, about ten meters apart.

Chip and Karl walked side by side down the corridor with their hands on the heads. *Dover!* Chip thought. The first person he had gone to! And why not? So bitterly anti-Uni he had sounded, that day on the I.A. boat! It was Dover who had told him and Lilac that Liberty was a prison, that Uni had let them get to it! "Dover!" he said. "How the hate can you—"

"Just keep walking," Dover said.

"You're not dulled, you're not treated!"

"No."

"Then—*how? Why?*"

"You'll see in a minute," Dover said.

They neared the door at the end of the corridor and it slid abruptly open. Another corridor stretched beyond it: wider, less brightly lit, dark-walled, not tiled.

"Keep going," Dover said.

They went through the doorway and stopped, staring.

"Go ahead," Dover said.

They walked on.

What kind of corridor was this? The floor was carpeted, with a gold-colored carpet thicker and softer than any Chip had ever seen or walked on. The walls were lustrous polished wood, with numbered gold-knobbed doors *(12, 11)* on both sides. Paintings hung between the doors, beautiful paintings that were surely pre-U: a woman sitting with folded hands, smiling knowingly; a hillside city of windowed buildings under a strange black-clouded sky; a garden; a woman reclining; a man in armor. A pleasant odor spiced the air; tangy, dry, impossible to name.

"Where *are* we?" Karl asked.

"In Uni," Dover said.

Ahead of them double doors stood open; a red-draped room lay beyond.

"Keep going," Dover said.

They went through the doorway and into the red-draped room; it spread away on both sides, and members, people, were sitting and smiling and starting to laugh, were laughing and rising and some were applauding; young people, old people, were rising from chairs and sofas, laughing and applauding; applauding, applauding, *they all were applauding!;* and Chip's arm was pulled down—by Dover, laughing—and he looked at Karl, who looked at him, stupefied; and still they were applauding, men and women, fifty, sixty of them, alert- and alive-looking, in coveralls of silk not paplon, green-gold-blue-white-purple; a tall and beautiful woman, a black-skinned man, a woman who looked like Lilac, a man with white hair who must have been over ninety; applauding, applauding, laughing, applauding . . .

Chip turned, and Dover, grinning, said, "You're awake," and to Karl, "It's real, it's happening."

"*What* is?" Chip said. "What the hate *is* this? Who *are* they?"

Laughing, Dover said, "They're the *programmers,* Chip! And that's what *you're* going to be! Oh if you could only see your faces!"

Chip stared at Karl, and at Dover again. "Christ and Wei, what are you *talking* about?" he said. "The programmers are *dead!* Uni's—it goes on by *itself,* it doesn't have—"

Dover was looking past him, smiling. Silence had spread through the room. Chip turned around.

A man in a smiling mask that looked like Wei (Was this really happening?) was coming to him, moving springily in red silk high-collared coveralls. "Nothing goes on by itself," he said in a voice that was high-pitched but forceful, his smiling mask-lips moving like real ones. (But *was* it a mask—the yellow skin shrunken tight over the sharp cheekbones, the glinting slit-eyes, the wisps of white hair on the shining yellow head?) "You must be 'Chip' with the one green eye," the man said, smiling and holding out his hand. "You'll have to tell me what was wrong with the name 'Li' that inspired you to change it." Laughter lifted around them.

The outstretched hand was normal-colored and youthful. Chip took it (*I'm going mad,* he thought), and it gripped his hand strongly, squeezed his knucklebones to an instant's pain.

"And you're Karl," the man said, turning and holding out his hand again. "Now if *you* had changed your name I could understand it." Laughter rose louder. "Shake it," the man said, smiling. "Don't be afraid."

Karl, staring, shook the man's hand.

Chip said, "You're—"

"Wei," the man said, his slit-eyes twinkling. "From here up, that is." He touched his coveralls' high collar. "From here down," he said, "I'm several other members, principally Jesus RE who won the decathlon in 163." He smiled at them. "Didn't you ever bounce a ball when you were a child?" he asked. "Didn't you ever jump rope? 'Marx, Wood, Wei, and Christ; all but Wei were sacrificed.' It's still true, you see. 'Out of the mouths of babes.' Come, sit down, you must be tired. Why couldn't you use the elevators like everyone else? Dover, it's good to have you back. You've done very well, except for that awful business at the '013 bridge."

They sat in deep and comfortable red chairs, drank pale yellow tart-tasting wine from sparkling glasses, ate sweetly stewed cubes of meat and fish and who-knew-what brought on delicate white plates by young members who smiled at them admiringly—and as they sat and drank and ate, they talked with Wei.

With *Wei!*

How old was that tight-skinned yellow head, living and talking on its lithe red-coveralled body that reached easily for a cigarette, crossed its legs casually? The last anniversary of his birth had been what—the two-hundred-and-sixth, the two-hundred-and-seventh?

Wei died when he was sixty, twenty-five years after the Unification. Generations before the building of Uni, which was programmed by his "spiritual heirs." Who died, of course, at sixty-two. So the Family was taught.

And there he sat, drinking, eating, smoking. Men and women stood listening around the group of chairs; he seemed not to notice them. "The islands have been all those things," he said. "At first they were the strongholds of the original incurables; and then, as you put it, 'isolation wards' to which we let later incurables 'escape,' although we weren't so kind as to supply boats in those days." He smiled and drew on his cigarette. "Then, however," he said, "I found a better use for them, and now they serve as, forgive me, wildlife preserves, where natural leaders can emerge and prove themselves exactly as you have done. Now we supply boats and maps, rather obliquely, and 'shepherds' like Dover who accompany returning members and prevent as much violence as they can. And prevent, of course, the final intended violence, Uni's destruction—although the visitors' display is the usual target, so there's no real danger whatsoever."

Chip said, "I don't know where I am." Karl, spearing a cube of meat with a small gold fork, said, "Asleep in the parkland," and the men and women nearby laughed.

Wei, smiling, said, "Yes, it's a disconcerting discovery, I'm sure. The computer that you thought was the Family's changeless and uncontrolled master is in fact the Family's servant, controlled by members like yourselves—enterprising, thoughtful, and concerned. Its goals and procedures change continually, according to the decisions of a High Council and fourteen sub-councils. We enjoy luxuries, as you can see, but we have responsibilities that more than justify them. Tomorrow you'll begin to learn. Now, though"—he leaned forward and pressed his cigarette into an ashtray—"it's very late, thanks to your partiality to tunnels. You'll be shown to your rooms; I hope you find them worth the walk." He smiled and rose, and they rose with him. He shook Karl's hand—"Congratulations, Karl," he said—and Chip's. "And congratulations to you, Chip," he said. "We suspected a long time ago that sooner or later you would be coming. We're glad you haven't disappointed us. *I'm* glad, I mean; it's hard to avoid talking as if Uni has feelings too." He turned away and people crowded around them, shaking their hands and saying, "Congratulations, I never thought you'd make it before Unification Day, it's awful isn't it when you come in and everyone's sitting here congratulations you'll get used to things before you congratulations."

The room was large and pale blue, with a large pale-blue silken bed with many pillows, a large painting of floating water lilies, a table of covered dishes and decanters, dark green armchairs, and a bowl of white and yellow chrysanthemums on a long low cabinet.

"It's beautiful," Chip said. "Thank you."

The girl who had led him to it, an ordinary-looking member of sixteen or so in white paplon, said, "Sit down and I'll take off your—" She pointed at his feet.

"Shoes," he said, smiling. "No. Thanks, sister; I can do it myself."

"Daughter," she said.

"Daughter?"

"The programmers are our Fathers and Mothers," she said.

"Oh," he said. "All right. Thanks, daughter. You can go now."

She looked surprised and hurt. "I'm supposed to stay and take care of you," she said. "Both of us." She nodded toward a doorway beyond the bed. Light and the sound of running water came from it.

Chip went to it.

A pale-blue bathroom was there, large and gleaming; another young member in white paplon kneeled by a filling tub, stirring her hand in the water. She turned and smiled and said, "Hello, Father."

"Hello," Chip said. He stood with his hand on the jamb and looked back at the first girl—drawing the cover from the bed—and back again at the second girl. She smiled up at him, kneeling. He stood with his hands on the jamb. "Daughter," he said.

Four

He was sitting in bed—had finished his breakfast and was reaching for a cigarette—when a knock at the door sounded. One of the girls went to answer it and Dover came in, smiling and clean and brisk in yellow silk. "How you doing, brother?" he asked.

"Pretty well," Chip said, "pretty well." The other girl lit his cigarette, took the breakfast tray, and asked him if he wanted more coffee. "No, thanks," he said. "Do you want some coffee?"

"No, thanks," Dover said. He sat in one of the dark green chairs and leaned back, his elbows on the chair arms, his hands meshed across his middle, his legs outstretched. Smiling at Chip, he said, "Over the shock?"

"Hate, no," Chip said.

"It's a long-standing custom," Dover said. "You'll enjoy it when the next group comes in."

"It's cruel, really cruel," Chip said.

"Wait, you'll be laughing and applauding with everyone else."

"How often do groups turn up?"

"Sometimes not for years," Dover said, "sometimes a month apart. It averages out to one-point-something people a year."

"And you were in contact with Uni the whole time, you brother-fighter?"

Dover nodded and smiled. "A telecomp the size of a matchbox," he said. "In fact, that's what I kept it in."

"Bastard," Chip said.

The girl with the tray had taken it out, and the other girl changed the ashtray on the night table and took her coveralls from a chairback and went into the bathroom. She closed the door.

Dover looked after her, then looked at Chip quizzically. "Nice night?" he asked.

"Mm-hmm," Chip said. "I gather they're not treated."

"Not in all departments, that's for sure," Dover said. "I hope you're not sore at me for not dropping a hint somewhere along the way. The rules are ironclad: no help beyond what's asked of you, no suggestions, no nothing; stay on the sidelines as much as you can and try to prevent bloodshed. I shouldn't have even been doing that routine on the boat—about Liberty being a prison—but I'd been there for two years and nobody was even *thinking* of trying anything. You can see why I wanted to move things along."

"Yes, I certainly can," Chip said. He tipped ashes from his cigarette into the clean white tray.

"I'd just as soon you didn't say anything to Wei about it," Dover said. "You're having lunch with him at one o'clock."

"Karl too?"

"No, just you. I think he's got you pegged as High Council material. I'll come by at ten-of and take you to him. You'll find a razor inside there—a thing that looks like a flashlight. This afternoon we'll go to the medicenter and start de-whiskerizing."

"There's a medicenter?"

"There's everything," Dover said. "A medicenter, a library, a gym, a pool, a theater—there's even a garden that you'd swear was up on top. I'll show you around later."

Chip said, "And this is where we—stay?"

"All except us poor shepherds," Dover said. "I'll be going out to another island, but not for at least six months, thank Uni."

Chip put his cigarette out. He pressed it out thoroughly. "What if I don't want to stay?" he said.

"Don't *want to?*" Dover said.

"I've got a wife and a baby, remember?"

"Well, so do lots of the others," Dover said. "You've got a bigger obligation here, Chip; an obligation to the whole Family, *including* the members on the islands."

"Nice obligation," Chip said. "Silk coveralls and two girls at once."

"That was for last night only," Dover said. "Tonight you'll be lucky to get one." He sat up straight. "Look," he said, "I know there are—surface attractions here that make it all look—questionable. But the Family *needs* Uni. Think of the way things were on Liberty! And it needs untreated programmers to run Uni and—well, Wei'll explain things better than I can. And one day a week we wear paplon anyway. And eat cakes."

"A whole day?" Chip said. "Really?"

"All right, all right," Dover said, getting up. He went to a chair where Chip's green coveralls lay and picked them up and felt their pockets. "Is everything here?" he asked.

"Yes," Chip said. "Including some snapshots I'd like to have."

"Sorry, nothing you came in with," Dover said. "More rules." He took Chip's shoes from the floor and stood and looked at him. "Everyone's a little unsure at first," he said. "You'll be proud to stay once you've got the right slant on things. It's an obligation."

"I'll remember that," Chip said.

There was a knock at the door, and the girl who had taken the tray came in with blue silk coveralls and white sandals. She put them on the foot of the bed.

Dover, smiling, said, "If you want a paplon it can be arranged."

The girl looked at him.

"Hate, no," Chip said. "I guess I'm as worthy of silk as anyone else around here."

"You are," Dover said. "You are, Chip. I'll see you at ten of one, right?" He started to the door with the green coveralls over his arm and the shoes in his hand. The girl hurried ahead to open the door for him.

Chip said, "What happened to Buzz?"

Dover stopped and turned, regretful-looking. "He was caught in '015," he said.

"And treated?"

Dover nodded.

"More rules," Chip said.

Dover nodded again and turned and went out.

There were thin steaks cooked in a lightly spiced brown sauce, small browned onions, a sliced yellow vegetable that Chip hadn't seen on Liberty—"Squash," Wei said—and a clear red wine that was less enjoyable than the yellow of the night before. They ate with gold knives and forks, from plates with wide gold borders.

Wei, in gray silk, ate quickly, cutting his steak, forking it into his wrinkle-lipped mouth, and chewing only briefly before swallowing and raising his fork again. Now and then he paused, sipped wine and pressed his yellow napkin to his lips.

"These things existed," he said. "Would there have been any point in destroying them?"

The room was large and handsomely furnished in pre-U style: white, gold, orange, yellow. At a corner of it, two white-coveralled members waited by a wheeled serving table.

"Of course it seems wrong at first," Wei said, "but the ultimate decisions *have* to be made by untreated members, and untreated members can't and shouldn't live their lives on cakes and TV and *Marx Writing*." He smiled. "Not even on *Wei Addressing the Chemotherapists*," he said, and put steak into his mouth.

"Why can't the Family make its decisions itself?" Chip asked.

Wei chewed and swallowed. "Because it's incapable of doing so," he said. "That is, of doing so reasonably. Untreated it's—well, you had a sample on your island; it's mean and foolish and aggressive, motivated more often by selfishness than by anything else. Selfishness and fear." He put onions into his mouth.

"It achieved the Unification," Chip said.

"Mmm, yes," Wei said, "but after what a struggle! And what a fragile structure the Unification was until we buttressed it with treatments! No, the Family had to be helped to full humanity—by treatments today, by genetic engineering tomorrow—and decisions have to be made for it. Those who have the means and the intelligence have the duty as well. To shirk it would be treason against the species." He put steak into his mouth and raised his other hand and beckoned.

"And part of the duty," Chip said, "is to kill members at sixty-two?"

"Ah, *that*," Wei said, and smiled. "Always a principal question, sternly asked."

The two members came to them, one with a decanter of wine and the other with a gold tray that he held at Wei's side. "You're looking at only part of the picture," Wei said, taking a large fork and spoon and lifting a steak from the tray. He held it with sauce dripping from it. "What you're neglecting to look at," he said, "is the immeasurable number of members who would die far *earlier* than sixty-two if not for the peace and stability and well-being we give them. Think of the mass for a moment, not of individuals within the mass." He put the steak on his plate. "We add many more years to the Family's total life than we take away from it," he said. "Many, many more years." He spooned sauce onto the steak and took onions and squash. "Chip?" he said.

"No, thanks," Chip said. He cut a piece from the half steak before him. The member with the decanter refilled his glass.

"Incidentally," Wei said, cutting steak, "the actual time of dying is closer now to sixty-three than sixty-two. It will grow still higher as the population on Earth is gradually reduced." He put steak into his mouth.

The members withdrew.

Chip said, "Do you include the members who don't get born in your balance of years added and taken away?"

"No," Wei said, smiling. "We're not that unrealistic. If those members *were* born, there would be no stability, no well-being, and eventually no Family." He put squash into his mouth and chewed and swallowed. "I don't expect your feelings to change in one lunch," he said. "Look around, talk with everyone, browse in the library—particularly in the history and sociology banks. I hold informal discussions a few evenings a week—once a teacher, always a teacher —sit in on some of them, argue, discuss."

"I left a wife and a baby on Liberty," Chip said.

"From which I deduce," Wei said, smiling, "that they weren't of overriding importance to you."

Chip said, "I expected to be coming back."

"Arrangements can be made for their care if necessary," Wei said. "Dover told me you had already done so."

"Will I be allowed to go back?" Chip asked.

"You won't want to," Wei said. "You'll come to recognize that we're right and your responsibility lies here." He sipped wine and pressed his napkin to his lips. "If we're wrong on minor points and you sit on the High Council some day and correct us," he said. "Are you interested in architecture or city planning, by any chance?"

Chip looked at him and, after a moment, said, "I've thought once or twice about designing buildings."

"Uni thinks you should be on the Architectural Council at present," Wei said. "Look in on it. Meet Madhir, the head of it." He put onions into his mouth.

Chip said, "I really don't *know* anything . . ."

"You can learn if you're interested," Wei said, cutting steak. "There's plenty of time."

Chip looked at him. "Yes," he said. "Programmers seem to live past sixty-two. Even past sixty-three."

"Exceptional members have to be preserved as long as possible," Wei said. "For the Family's sake." He put steak into his mouth and chewed, looking at Chip with his slit-eyes. "Would you like to hear something incredible?" he said. "Your generation of programmers is almost certain to live indefinitely. Isn't that fantastic? We old ones are going to die sooner or later—the doctors say maybe not, but Uni says we will. You younger ones though, in all probability you *won't* die. Ever."

Chip put a piece of steak into his mouth and chewed it slowly.

Wei said, "I suppose it's an unsettling thought. It'll grow more attractive as you get older."

Chip swallowed what was in his mouth. He looked at Wei, glanced at his gray-silk chest, and looked at his face again. "That member," he said. "The decathlon winner. Did he die naturally or was he killed?"

"He was killed," Wei said. "With his permission, given freely, even eagerly."

"Of course," Chip said. "He was treated."

"An athlete?" Wei said. "They take very little. No, he was proud that he was going to become—allied to me. His only concern was whether I would keep him 'in condition'—a concern that I'm afraid was justified. You'll find that the children, the ordinary members here, vie with one another to give parts of themselves for transplant. If you wanted to replace that eye, for

instance, they'd be slipping into your room and begging you for the honor."
He put squash into his mouth.

Chip shifted in his seat. "My eye doesn't bother me," he said. "I like it."

"You shouldn't," Wei said. "If nothing could be done about it, then you
would be justified in accepting it. But an imperfection that can be remedied?
That we must *never* accept." He cut steak. " 'One goal, one goal only, for all
of us—perfection,' " he said. "We're not there yet, but some day we will be:
a Family improved genetically so that treatments no longer are needed; a corps
of ever-living programmers so that the islands too can be unified; perfection,
on Earth and moving 'outward, outward, outward to the stars.' " His fork,
with steak on it, stopped before his lips. He looked ahead of him and said, "I
dreamed of it when I was young: a universe of the gentle, the helpful, the
loving, the unselfish. I'll live to see it. I shall live to see it."

Dover led Chip and Karl through the complex that afternoon—showed them
the library, the gym, the pool, and the garden ("Christ and Wei." "Wait till
you see the sunsets and the stars"); the music room, the theater, the lounges;
the dining room and the kitchen ("I don't know, from somewhere," a member
said, watching other members taking bundles of lettuce and lemons from a
steel carrier. "Whatever we need comes in," she said, smiling. "Ask Uni").
There were four levels, passed through by small elevators and narrow escalators. The medicenter was on the bottom level. Doctors named Boroviev and
Rosen, young-moving men with shrunken faces as old-looking as Wei's, welcomed them and examined them and gave them infusions. "We can replace
that eye one-two-three, you know," Rosen said to Chip, and Chip said, "I
know. Thanks, but it doesn't bother me."

They swam in the pool. Dover went to swim with a tall and beautiful woman
Chip had noticed applauding the night before, and he and Karl sat on the edge
of the pool and watched them. "How do you feel?" Chip asked.

"I don't know," Karl said. "I'm pleased, of course, and Dover says it's all
necessary and it's our duty to help, but—I don't know. Even if they're running
Uni, it's Uni anyway, isn't it?"

"Yes," Chip said. "That's how I feel."

"There would have been a mess up above if we'd done what we planned,"
Karl said, "but it would have been straightened out eventually, more or less."
He shook his head. "I honestly don't know, Chip," he said. "Any system the
Family set up on its own would certainly be a lot less *efficient* than Uni is, than
these people are; you can't deny that."

"No, you can't," Chip said.

"Isn't it fantastic how long they live?" Karl said. "I still can't get over the
fact that—look at those breasts, will you? Christ and Wei."

A light-skinned round-breasted woman dived into the pool from the other
side.

Karl said, "Let's talk some more later on, all right?" He slipped down into the water.

"Sure, we've got plenty of time," Chip said.

Karl smiled at him and kicked off and swam arm-over-arm away.

The next morning Chip left his room and walked down a green-carpeted painting-hung corridor toward a steel door at the end of it. He hadn't gone very far when "Hi, brother," Dover said and came along and walked beside him. "Hi," Chip said. He looked ahead again and, walking, said, "Am I being guarded?"

"Only when you go in this direction," Dover said.

Chip said, "I couldn't do anything with my bare hands even if I wanted to."

"I know," Dover said. "The old man's cautious. Pre-U mind." He tapped his temple and smiled. "Only for a few days," he said.

They walked to the end of the corridor and the steel door slid open. White-tiled corridor stretched beyond it; a member in blue touched a scanner and went through a doorway.

They turned and started back. The door whispered behind them. "You'll get to see it," Dover said. "He'll probably give you the tour himself. Want to go to the gym?"

In the afternoon Chip looked in at the offices of the Architectural Council. A small and cheerful old man recognized him and welcomed him—Madhir, the Council's head. He looked to be over a hundred; his hands too—all of him apparently. He introduced Chip to other members of the Council: an old woman named Sylvie, a reddish-haired man of fifty or so whose name Chip didn't catch, and a short but pretty woman called Gri-gri. Chip had coffee with them and ate a piece of pastry with a cream filling. They showed him a set of plans they were discussing, layouts that Uni had made for the rebuilding of "G-3 cities." They talked about whether or not the layouts should be redone to different specifications, asked questions of a telecomp and disagreed on the significance of its answers. The old woman Sylvie gave a point-by-point explanation of why she felt the layouts were needlessly monotonous. Madhir asked Chip if he had an opinion; he said he didn't. The younger woman, Gri-gri, smiled at him invitingly.

There was a party in the main lounge that night—"Happy new year!" "Happy U year!"—and Karl shouted in Chip's ear, "I'll tell you one thing I don't like about this place! No whiskey! Isn't that a shut-off? If wine is okay, why not whiskey?" Dover was dancing with the woman who looked like Lilac (not really, not half as pretty), and there were people Chip had sat with at meals and met in the gym and the music room, people he had seen in one part of the complex or another, people he hadn't seen before; there were more than had been there the other night when he and Karl had come in—almost a hundred of them, with white-paploned members channeling trays among them. "Happy U year!" someone said to him, an elderly woman who had been at his lunch table, Hera or Hela. "It's almost 172!" she said. "Yes," he said, "half an hour." "Oh, there he is!" she said, and moved forward. Wei was in the doorway, in white, with people crowding around him. He shook their hands and kissed their cheeks, his shriveled yellow face grin-split and gleaming, his eyes lost in wrinkles. Chip moved back farther into the crowd and turned away. Gri-gri waved, jumping up to see him over people between them. He waved back at her and smiled and kept moving.

He spent the next day, Unification Day, in the gym and the library.

He went to a few of Wei's evening discussions. They were held in the garden, a pleasant place to be. The grass and the trees were real, and the stars and the moon were near reality, the moon changing phase but never position. Bird warblings sounded from time to time and a gentle breeze blew. Fifteen or twenty programmers were usually at the discussions, sitting on chairs and on the grass. Wei, in a chair, did most of the talking. He expanded on quotations from the *Living Wisdom* and deftly traced the particulars of questions to their encompassing generalities. Now and then he deferred to the head of the Educational Council, Gustafsen, or to Boroviev, the head of the Medical Council, or to another of the High Council members.

At first Chip sat at the edge of the group and only listened, but then he began to ask questions—why parts, at least, of treatments couldn't be put back on a voluntary basis; whether human perfection might not include a degree of selfishness and aggressiveness; whether selfishness, in fact, didn't play a considerable part in their own acceptance of alleged "duty" and "responsibility." Some of the programmers near him seemed affronted by his questions, but Wei answered them patiently and fully; seemed even to welcome them, heard his "Wei?" over the askings of the others. He moved a little closer in from the group's edge.

One night he sat up in bed and lit a cigarette and smoked in the dark.

The woman lying beside him stroked his back. "It's right, Chip," she said. "It's what's best for everyone."

"You read minds?" he said.

"Sometimes," she said. Her name was Deirdre and she was on the Colonial Council. She was thirty-eight, light-skinned, and not especially pretty, but sensible, shapely, and good company.

"I'm beginning to think it *is* what's best," Chip said, "and I don't know whether I'm being convinced by Wei's logic or by lobsters and Mozart and you. Not to mention the prospect of eternal life."

"That scares me," Deirdre said.

"Me too," Chip said.

She kept stroking his back. "It took me two months to cool down," she said.

"Is that how you thought of it?" he said. "Cooling down?"

"Yes," she said. "And growing up. Facing reality."

"So why does it feel like giving in?" Chip said.

"Lie down," Deirdre said.

He put out his cigarette, put the ashtray on the night table, and turned to her, lying down. They held each other and kissed. "Truly," she said. "It's best for everybody, in the long run. We'll improve things gradually, working in our own councils."

They kissed and caressed each other, and then they kicked down the sheet and she threw her leg over Chip's hip and his hardness slipped easily into her.

He was sitting in the library one morning when a hand took his shoulder. He looked around, startled, and Wei was there. He bent, pushing Chip aside, and put his face down to the viewer hood.

After a moment he said, "Well, you've gone to the right man." He kept his face at the hood another moment, and then stood up and let go of Chip's shoulder and smiled at him. "Read Liebman too," he said. "And Okida and Marcuse. I'll make a list of titles and give it to you in the garden this evening. Will you be there?"

Chip nodded.

His days fell into a routine: mornings at the library, afternoons at the Council. He studied construction methods and environment planning; examined factory flow charts and circulation patterns of residential buildings. Madhir and Sylvie showed him drawings of buildings under construction and buildings planned for the future, of cities as they existed and (plastic overlay) cities as they might some day be modified. He was the eighth member of the Council; of the other seven, three were inclined to challenge Uni's designs and change them, and four, including Madhir, were inclined to accept them without question. Formal meetings were held on Friday afternoons; at other times seldom more than four or five of the members were in the offices. Once only Chip and Gri-gri were there, and they wound up locked together on Madhir's sofa.

After Council, Chip used the gym and the pool. He ate with Deirdre and Dover and Dover's woman-of-the-day and whoever else joined them—sometimes Karl, on the Transportation Council and resigned to wine.

One day in February, Chip asked Dover if it was possible to get in touch with whoever had replaced him on Liberty and find out if Lilac and Jan were all right and whether Julia was providing for them as she had said she would.

"Sure," Dover said. "No problem at all."

"Would you do it then?" Chip said. "I'd appreciate it."

A few days later Dover found Chip in the library. "All's well," he said. "Lilac is staying home and buying food and paying rent, so Julia must be coming through."

"Thanks, Dover," Chip said. "I was worried."

"The man there'll keep an eye on her," Dover said. "If she needs anything, money can come in the mail."

"That's fine," Chip said. "Wei told me." He smiled. "Poor Julia," he said, "supporting all those families when it isn't really necessary. If she knew she'd have a fit."

Dover smiled. "She would," he said. "Of course, everyone who set out didn't get here, so in some cases it *is* necessary."

"That's right," Chip said. "I wasn't thinking."

"See you at lunch," Dover said.

"Right," Chip said. "Thanks."

Dover went, and Chip turned to the viewer and bent his face to the hood. He put his finger on the next-page button and, after a moment, pressed it.

He began to speak up at Council meetings and to ask fewer questions at Wei's discussions. A petition was circulated for the reduction of cake days to one a month; he hesitated but signed it. He went from Deirdre to Blackie to Nina and back to Deirdre; listened in the smaller lounges to sex gossip and jokes about High Council members; followed crazes for paper-airplane making and speaking in pre-U languages ("Français" was pronounced "Fransay," he learned).

One morning he woke up early and went to the gym. Wei was there, jumping astride and swinging dumbbells, shining with sweat, slab-muscled, slim-hipped; in a black supporter and something white tied around his neck. "Another early bird, good morning," he said, jumping his legs out and in, out and in, swinging the dumbbells out and together over his white-wisped head.

"Good morning," Chip said. He went to the side of the gym and took off his robe and hung it on a hook. Another robe, blue, hung a few hooks away.

"You weren't at the discussion last night," Wei said.

Chip turned. "There was a party," he said, toeing off his sandals. "Patya's birthday."

"It's all right," Wei said, jumping, swinging the dumbbells. "I just mentioned it."

Chip walked onto a mat and began trotting in place. The white thing around Wei's neck was a band of silk, tightly knotted.

Wei stopped jumping and tossed down the dumbbells and took a towel from one of the parallel bars. "Madhir's afraid you're going to be a radical," he said, smiling.

"He doesn't know the half of it," Chip said.

Wei watched him, still smiling, wiping the towel over his big-muscled shoulders and under his arms.

"Do you work out every morning?" Chip asked.

"No, only once or twice a week," Wei said. "I'm not athletic by nature." He rubbed the towel behind him.

Chip stopped trotting. "Wei, there's something I'd like to speak to you about," he said.

"Yes?" Wei said. "What is it?"

Chip took a step toward him. "When I first came here," he said, "and we had lunch together—"

"Yes?" Wei said.

Chip cleared his throat and said, "You said that if I wanted to I could have my eye replaced. Rosen said so too."

"Yes, of course," Wei said. "Do you want to have it done?"

Chip looked at him uncertainly. "I don't know, it seems like such—vanity," he said. "But I've always been aware of it—"

"It's not vanity to correct a flaw," Wei said. "It's negligence not to."

"Can't I get a lens put on?" Chip said. "A brown lens?"

"Yes, you can," Wei said, "if you want to cover it and not correct it."

Chip looked away and then back at him. "All right," he said, "I'd like to do it, have it done."

"Good," Wei said, and smiled. "I've had eye changes twice," he said. "There's blurriness for a few days, that's all. Go down to the medicenter this morning. I'll tell Rosen to do it himself, as soon as possible."

"Thank you," Chip said.

Wei put his towel around his white-banded neck, turned to the parallel bars, and lifted himself straight-armed onto them. "Keep quiet about it," he said, hand-walking between the bars, "or the children will start pestering you."

It was done, and he looked in his mirror and both his eyes were brown. He smiled and stepped back, and stepped close again. He looked at himself from one side and the other, smiling.

When he had dressed he looked again.

Deirdre, in the lounge, said, "It's a tremendous improvement! You look wonderful! Karl, Gri-gri, look at Chip's eye!"

Members helped them into heavy green coats, thickly quilted and hooded. They closed them and put on thick green gloves, and a member pulled open the door. The two of them, Wei and Chip, went in.

They walked together along an aisle between steel walls of memory banks, their breath clouding from their nostrils. Wei spoke of the banks' internal temperature and of the weight and number of them. They turned into a narrower aisle where the steel walls stretched ahead of them convergingly to a faraway crosswall.

"I was in here when I was a child," Chip said.

"Dover told me," Wei said.

"It frightened me then," Chip said. "But it has a kind of—majesty to it; the order and precision . . ."

Wei nodded, his eyes glinting. "Yes," he said. "I look for excuses to come in."

They turned into another cross-aisle, passed a pillar, and turned into another long narrow aisle between back-to-back rows of steel memory banks.

In coveralls again, they looked into a vast railed pit, round and deep, where steel and concrete housings lay, linked by blue arms and sending thicker blue arms branching upward to a low brightly glowing ceiling. ("I believe you had a special interest in the refrigerating plants," Wei said, smiling, and Chip looked uncomfortable.) A steel pillar stood beside the pit; beyond it lay a second railed and blue-armed pit, and another pillar, another pit. The room was enormous, cool and hushed. Transmitting and receiving equipment lined its two long walls, with red pinpoint lights gleaming; members in blue drew out and replaced two-handled vertical panels of speckled black and gold. Four red-dome reactors stood at one end of the room, and beyond them, behind glass, half a dozen programmers sat at a round console reading into microphones, turning pages.

"There you are," Wei said.

Chip looked around at it all. He shook his head and blew out breath. "Christ and Wei," he said.

Wei laughed happily.

They stayed awhile, walking about, looking, talking with some of the members, and then they left the room and walked through white-tiled corridors. A steel door slid open for them, and they went through and walked together down the carpeted corridor beyond.

Five

Early in September of 172, a party of seven men and women accompanied by a "shepherd" named Anna set out from the Andaman Islands in Stability Bay to attack and destroy Uni. Announcements of their progress were made in the programmers' dining room at each mealtime. Two members of the party "failed" in the airport at SEA77120 (head-shakings and sighs of disappointment), and two more the following day in a carport in EUR46209 (head-shakings and sighs of disappointment). On the evening of Thursday, September tenth, the three others—a young man and woman and an older man —came single-file into the main lounge with their hands on their heads, looking angry and frightened. A stocky woman behind them, grinning, pocketed a gun.

The three stared foolishly, and the programmers rose, laughing and applauding, Chip and Deirdre among them. Chip laughed loud, applauded hard. All the programmers laughed loud and applauded hard as the newcomers lowered their hands and turned to one another and to their laughing applauding shepherd.

Wei in gold-trimmed green went to them, smiling, and shook their hands. The programmers hushed one another. Wei touched his collar and said, "From here up, at any rate. From here down . . ." The programmers laughed and hushed one another. They moved closer, to hear, to congratulate.

After a few minutes the stocky woman slipped out of the crush and left the lounge. She turned to the right and went toward a narrow upgoing escalator. Chip came after her. "Congratulations," he said.

"Thanks," the woman said, glancing back at him and smiling tiredly. She was about forty, with dirt on her face and dark rings under her eyes. "When did you come in?" she asked.

"About eight months ago," Chip said.

"Who with?" The woman stepped onto the escalator.

Chip stepped on behind her. "Dover," he said.

"Oh," she said. "Is he still here?"

"No," Chip said. "He was sent out last month. Your people didn't come in empty-handed, did they?"

"I wish they had," the woman said. "My shoulder is killing me. I left the kits by the elevator. I'm going to get them now." She stepped off the escalator and walked back around it.

Chip went with her. "I'll give you a hand with them," he said.

"It's all right, I'll pick up one of the boys," the woman said, turning to the right.

"No, I don't mind doing it," Chip said.

They walked down a corridor past the glass wall of the pool. The woman looked in and said, "That's where I'm going to be in fifteen minutes."

"I'll join you," Chip said.

The woman glanced at him. "All right," she said.

Boroviev and a member came into the corridor toward them. "Anna! Hello!" Boroviev said, his eyes sparkling in his withered face. The member, a girl, smiled at Chip.

"Hello!" the woman said, shaking Boroviev's hand. "How are you?"

"Fine!" Boroviev said. "Oh, you look exhausted!"

"I am."

"But everything's all right?"

"Yes," the woman said. "They're downstairs. I'm on my way to get rid of the kits."

"Get some rest!" Boroviev said.

"I'm going to," the woman said, smiling. "Six months of it."

Boroviev smiled at Chip, and taking the member's hand, went past them and down the corridor. The woman and Chip went ahead toward the steel door at the corridor's end. They passed the archway to the garden, where someone was singing and playing a guitar.

"What kind of bombs did they have?" Chip asked.

"Crude plastic ones," the woman said. "Throw and boom. I'll be glad to get them into the can."

The steel door slid open; they went through and turned to the right. White-tiled corridor stretched before them with scanner-posted doors in the left-hand wall.

"Which council are you on?" the woman asked.

"Wait a second," Chip said, stopping and taking her arm.

She stopped and turned and he punched her in the stomach. Catching her face in his hand, he smashed her head back hard against the wall. He let it come forward, smashed it back again, and let go of her. She slid downward —a tile was cracked—and sank heavily to the floor and fell over sideways, one knee up, eyes closed.

Chip stepped to the nearest door and opened it. A two-toilet bathroom was inside. Holding the door with his foot, he reached over and took hold of the woman under her arms. A member came into the corridor and stared at him, a boy of about twenty.

"Help me," Chip said.

The boy came over, his face pale. "What happened?" he asked.

"Take her legs," Chip said. "She passed out."

They carried the woman into the bathroom and set her down on the floor. "Shouldn't we take her to the medicenter?" the boy asked.

"We will in a minute," Chip said. He got on one knee beside the woman, reached into the pocket of her yellow-paplon coveralls, and took out her gun. He aimed it at the boy. "Turn around and face the wall," he said. "Don't make a sound."

The boy stared wide-eyed at him, and turned around and faced the wall between the toilets.

Chip stood up, passed the gun between his hands, and holding it by its taped barrel, stepped astride the woman. He raised the gun and quickly swung its butt down hard on the boy's close-clipped head. The blow drove the boy to his knees. He fell forward against the wall and then sideways, his head stopping against wall and toilet pipe, red gleaming in his short black hair.

Chip looked away and at the gun. He passed it back to a shooting grip, thumbed its safety catch aside, and turned it toward the bathroom's back wall: a red thread, gone, shattered a tile and drilled dust from behind it. Chip put the gun into his pocket, and holding it, stepped over the woman and moved to the door.

He went into the corridor, pulled the door tightly closed, and walked quickly, holding the gun in his pocket. He came to the end of the corridor and followed its left turn.

A member coming toward him smiled and said, "Hello, Father."

Chip nodded, passing him. "Son," he said.

A door was ahead in the right-hand wall. He went to it, opened it, and went through. He closed the door behind him and stood in a dark hallway. He took out the gun.

Opposite, under a ceiling that barely glowed, were the pink, brown, and orange memory-banks-for-visitors, the gold cross and sickle, the clock on the wall—*9:33 Thu 10 Sep 172 Y.U.*

He went to the left, past the other displays, unlighted, dormant, increasingly visible in the light from an open door to the lobby.

He went to the open door.

On the floor in the center of the lobby lay three kits, a gun, and two knives. Another kit lay near the elevator doors.

Wei leaned back, smiling, and drew on his cigarette. "Believe me," he said, "that's how everybody feels at this point. But even the most stubbornly disapproving come to see that we're wise and we're right." He looked at the programmers standing around the group of chairs. "Isn't that so, Chip?" he said. "Tell them." He looked about, smiling.

"Chip went out," Deirdre said, and someone else said, "After Anna." Another programmer said, "Too bad, Deirdre," and Deirdre, turning, said, "He didn't go out after Anna, he went out; he'll be right back."

"A little tired, of course?" someone said.

Wei looked at his cigarette and leaned forward and pressed it out. "Everyone here will confirm what I'm saying," he said to the newcomers, and smiled. "Excuse me, will you?" he said. "I'll be back in a little while. Don't get up." He rose, and the programmers parted for him.

Straw filled half the kit, held in place by a wood divider; on the other side, wires, tools, papers, cakes, whatnot. He brushed straw away—from more dividers that formed square straw-filled compartments. He fingered in one and found only straw and hollowness; in another, though, there was something soft-surfaced but firm. He pulled away straw and lifted out a heavy whitish ball, a claylike handful with straw sticking to it. He put it on the floor and took out two more—another compartment was empty—and a fourth one. He ripped the wood framework from the kit, put it aside, and dumped out straw, tools, everything; put the four bombs close together in the kit, opened the other two kits and took out their bombs and put them in with the four—five from one kit, six from the other. Room for three more remained.

He got up and went for the fourth kit by the elevators. A sound in the hallway spun him around—he had left the gun by the bombs—but the doorway was empty-dark and the sound (whisper of silk?) was no more. If it had been at all. His own sound, it might have been, reflected back at him.

Watching the doorway, he backed to the kit, caught up its strap, and brought it quickly to the other kits; kneeled again and brought the gun close to his side. He opened the kit, pulled out straw, and lifted out three bombs and fitted them in with the others. Three rows of six. He covered them and pressed the kit closed, then put his arm through the strap and lodged it on his shoulder. He raised the kit carefully against his hip. The bombs in it shifted heavily.

The gun with the kits was an L-beam too, newer-looking than the one he had. He picked it up and opened it. A stone was in the generator's place. He put the gun down, took one of the knives—black-handled, pre-U, its blade worn thin but sharp—and slipped it into his right-hand pocket. Taking the working gun and holding the kit with his fingers under its bottom, he got up from his knees, stepped over an empty kit, and went quietly to the doorway.

Darkness and silence were outside it. He waited till he could see more clearly, then walked to the left. A giant telecomp clung to the display wall (it had been broken, hadn't it, when he had been there before?); he passed it and stopped. Someone lay near the wall ahead, motionless.

But no, it was a stretcher, two stretchers, with pillows and blankets. The blankets Papa Jan and he had wrapped around them. The very same two, conceivably.

He stood for a moment, remembering.

Then he went on. To the door. The door that Papa Jan had pushed him through. And the scanner beside it, the first he had ever passed without touching. How frightened he had been!

This time you don't have to push me, Papa Jan, he thought.

He opened the door a bit, looked in at the landing—brightly lit, empty—and went in.

And down the stairs into coolness. Quickly now, thinking of the boy and the woman upstairs, who might soon be coming to, crying an alarm.

He passed the door to the first level of memory banks.

And the second.

And came to the end of the stairs, the bottom-level door.

He put his right shoulder against it, held the gun ready, and turned the knob with his left hand.

He eased the door slowly open. Red lights gleamed in dimness, one of the walls of transmitting-receiving equipment. The low ceiling glowed faintly. He opened the door wider. A railed refrigerator pit lay ahead of him, blue arms upreaching; beyond it, a pillar, a pit, a pillar, a pit. The reactors were at the other end of the room, red domes doubled in the glass of the dimly lit programming room. Not a member in sight, closed doors, silence—except for a whining sound, low and steady. He opened the door wider, stepping into the room with it, and saw the second wall of equipment sparked with red lights.

He went farther into the room, caught the door edge behind him and let it pull itself away toward closing. He lowered the gun, thumbed the strap up off his shoulder, and let the kit down gently to the floor. His throat was clamped, his head torn back. A green-silk elbow was under his jaw, the arm crushing his neck, choking him. His gun-wrist was locked in a powerful hand and "You liar, liar," Wei whispered in his ear, "what a pleasure to kill you."

He pulled at the arm, punched it with his free left hand; it was marble, a statue's arm in silk. He tried to back his feet into a stance for throwing Wei off him, but Wei moved backward too, keeping him arched and helpless, dragging him beneath the turning glowing ceiling; and his hand was bent around and smashed, smashed, smashed against hard railing, and the gun was gone, clanging in the pit. He reached back and grabbed Wei's head, found his ear and wrenched at it. His throat was crushed tighter by the hard-muscled arm and the ceiling was pink and pulsing. He thrust his hand down into Wei's collar, squeezed his fingers under a band of cloth. He wound his hand in it, driving his knuckles as hard as he could into tough ridged flesh. His right hand was freed, his left seized and pulled at. With his right he caught the wrist at his neck, pulled the arm open. He gasped air down his throat.

He was flung away, thrown flat against red-lit equipment, the torn band wound around his hand. He grabbed two handles and pulled out a panel, turned and flung it at Wei coming at him. Wei struck it aside with an arm and kept coming, both hands raised to chop. Chip crouched, his left arm up. ("Keep *low*, Green-eye!" Captain Gold shouted.) Blows hit his arm; he punched at Wei's heart. Wei backed off, kicking at him. He got away from the wall, circled outward, stuffed his numbed hand down into his pocket and found the knife handle. Wei rushed at him and chopped at his neck and shoulders. With his left arm raised, he cut the knife up out of his pocket and stuck it into Wei's middle—partway in, then hard, all the way, hilt into silk. Blows kept hitting him. He pulled the knife out and backed away.

Wei stayed where he was. He looked at Chip, at the knife in his hand, looked down at himself. He touched his waist and looked at his fingers. He looked at Chip.

Chip circled, watching him, holding the knife.

Wei lunged. Chip knifed, slashed Wei's sleeve, but Wei caught his arm in both hands and drove him back against railing, kneeing at him. Chip caught Wei's neck and squeezed, squeezed as hard as he could inside the torn green-and-gold collar. He forced Wei off him, turned from the railing, and squeezed, kept squeezing while Wei held his knife-arm. He forced Wei back around the pit. Wei struck with one hand at his wrist, knocked it downward; he pulled his arm free and knifed at Wei's side. Wei dodged and spilled over the railing, fell into the pit and fell flat on his back on a cylindrical steel housing. He slid off it and sat leaning against blue pipe, looking up at Chip with his mouth open, gasping, a black-red stain in his lap.

Chip ran to the kit. He picked it up and walked back quickly down the side of the room, holding the kit on his arm. He put the knife in his pocket—it fell through but he let it—ripped the kit open and tucked its cover back under it. He turned and walked backward toward the end of the equipment wall, stopped and stood facing the pits and the pillars between them.

He backhanded sweat from his mouth and forehead, saw blood on his hand and wiped it on his side.

He took one of the bombs from the kit, held it back behind his shoulder, aimed, and threw it. It arched into the center pit. He put his hand on another bomb. A *thunk* sounded from the pit, but no explosion came. He took out the second bomb and threw it harder into the pit.

The sound it made was flatter and softer than the first bomb's.

The railed pit stayed as it was, blue arms reaching up from it.

Chip looked at it, and looked at the rows of white strawstuck bombs in the kit.

He took out another one and hurled it as hard as he could into the nearer pit.

A *thunk* again.

He waited, and went cautiously toward the pit; went closer, and saw the bomb on the cylindrical steel housing, a blob of white, a white clay breast.

A high-pitched gasping sound came sifting from the farthest pit. Wei. He was laughing.

These three were her *bombs, the shepherd's,* Chip thought. *Maybe she did something to them.* He went to the middle of the equipment wall and stood squarely facing the center pit. He hurled a bomb. It hit a blue arm and stuck to it, round and white.

Wei laughed and gasped. Scrapings, sounds of movement, came from the pit he was in.

Chip hurled more bombs. *One of them may work, one of them* will *work!* ("Throw and boom," she had said. "Glad to get them into the can." She wouldn't have lied to him. What had gone wrong with them?) He hurled bombs at the blue arms and the pillars, plastered the square steel pillars with flat white overlapping discs. He hurled all the "bombs," hurled the last one clean across the room; it splattered wide on the opposite equipment wall.

He stood with the empty kit in his hand.

Wei laughed loud.

He was sitting astride a pit railing, holding the gun in both hands, pointing it at Chip. Black-red smears ran down his clinging coverall legs; red leaked over his sandal straps. He laughed more. "What do you think?" he asked. "Too cold? Too damp? Too dry? Too old? Too what?" He took one hand from the gun, reached back behind him, and eased down off the railing. Lifting his leg over it, he winced and drew in breath hissingly. "Ooh Jesus Christ," he said, "you really hurt this body. Sss! You really did it damage." He stood and held the gun with both hands again, facing Chip. He smiled. "Idea," he said. "You give me yours, right? You hurt a body, you give me another one. Fair? And —neat, *economical!* What we have to do now is shoot you in the head, very carefully, and then between us we'll give the doctors a long night's work." He smiled more broadly. "I promise to keep you 'in condition,' Chip," he said, and walked forward with slow stiff steps, his elbows tight to his sides, the gun clasped before him chest-high, aimed at Chip's face.

Chip backed to the wall.

"I'll have to change my speech to newcomers," Wei said. " 'From here down I'm Chip, a programmer who almost fooled me with his talk and his new eye and his smiles in the mirror.' I don't think we'll have any more newcomers though; the risk has begun to outweigh the amusement."

Chip threw the kit at him and lunged, leaped at Wei and threw him backward to the floor. Wei cried out, and Chip, lying on him, wrestled for the gun in his hand. Red beams shot from it. Chip forced the gun to the floor. An explosion roared. He tore the gun from Wei's hand and got off him, got up to his feet and backed away and turned and looked.

Across the room, a cave, crumbling and smoking, hollowed the middle of the wall of equipment—where the bomb he had thrown had been splattered. Dust shimmered in the air and a wide arc of black fragments lay on the floor.

Chip looked at the gun and at Wei. Wei, on an elbow, looked across the room and up at Chip.

Chip backed away, toward the end of the room, toward its corner, looking at the white-plastered pillars, the white-hung blue arms over the center pit. He raised the gun.

"Chip!" Wei cried. "It's *yours!* It'll be *yours* some day! We *both* can live! Chip, listen to me," he said, leaning forward, "there's *joy* in having it, in controlling, in being the only one. That's the absolute truth, Chip. You'll see for yourself. There's *joy* in having it."

Chip fired the gun at the farther pillar. A red thread hit above the white discs; another hit directly on one. An explosion flashed and roared, thundered and smoked. It subsided and the pillar was bent slightly toward the other side of the room.

Wei moaned grievingly. A door beside Chip started to open; he pushed it closed and stood back against it. He fired the gun at the bombs on the blue arms. Explosion roared, flame erupted, and a louder explosion blasted from the pit, mashing him against the door, breaking glass, flinging Wei to the swaying wall of equipment, slamming doors that had opened at the other side of the room. Flames filled the pit, a huge shuddering cylinder of yellow-orange, railed around and drumming at the ceiling. Chip raised his arm against the heat of it.

Wei climbed to all fours and onto his feet. He swayed and started stumblingly forward. Chip shot a red thread to his chest, and another, and he turned away and stumbled toward the pit. Flames feathered his coveralls, and he dropped to his knees, fell forward on the floor. His hair caught fire, his coveralls burned.

Blows shook the door and cries came from behind it. The other doors opened and members came in. "Stay back!" Chip shouted, and aimed the gun at the nearer pillar and fired. Explosion roared, and the pillar was bent.

The fire in the pit lowered, and the bent pillars slowly turned, screeching.

Members came into the room. "Get back!" Chip shouted, and they retreated to the doors. He moved into the corner, watching the pillars, the ceiling. The door beside him opened. "Stay back!" he shouted, pressing against it.

The steel of the pillars split and rolled open; a chunk of concrete slid from the nearer one.

The blackened ceiling cracked, groaned, sagged, dropped fragments.

The pillars broke and the ceiling fell. Memory banks crashed into the pits; mammoth steel blocks smashed down on one another and slid thunderously, butted into the walls of equipment. Explosions roared in the nearest and farthest pits, lifting blocks and cushioning them in flames.

Chip raised his arm against the heat. He looked where Wei had been. A block was there, its edge above the cracked floor.

More groaning and cracking sounded—from the blackness above, framed by the ceiling's broken fire-lit borders. And more banks fell, pounded down on the ones below, crushing and bursting them. Memory banks filled the opening, sliding, rumbling.

And the room, despite the fires, cooled.

Chip lowered his arm and looked—at the dark shapes of fire-gleaming steel blocks piled through the broken border of ceiling. He looked and kept looking, and then he moved around the door and pushed his way out through the members staring in.

He walked with the gun at his side through members and programmers running toward him down white-tiled corridors, and through more programmers running down carpeted corridors hung with paintings. "What is it?" Karl shouted, stopping and grabbing his arm.

Chip looked at him and said, "Go see."

Karl let go of him, glanced at the gun and at his face, and turned and ran.

Chip turned and kept walking.

Six

He washed, sprayed the bruises on his hand and some cuts on his face, and put on paplon coveralls. Closing them, he looked around at the room. He had planned to take the bedcover, for Lilac to use for dressmaking, and a small painting or something for Julia; now, though, he didn't want to. He put cigarettes and the gun in his pockets. The door opened and he pulled the gun out again. Deirdre stared at him, looking frantic.

He put the gun back in his pocket.

She came in and closed the door behind her. "It *was* you," she said.

He nodded.

"Do you *realize* what you've *done?*"

"What you didn't do," he said. "What you came here to do and talked yourself out of."

"I came here to stop it so it could be reprogrammed," she said, "not to destroy it completely!"

"It was *being* reprogrammed, remember?" he said, "And if I'd stopped it and forced a *real* programming—I don't know how, but if I had—it would still have wound up the same way sooner or later. The same *Wei.* Or a new one—me. 'There's joy in having it': those were his last words. Everything else was rationalization. And self-deception."

She looked away, angrily, and back at him. "The whole place is going to cave in," she said.

"I don't feel any tremors," he said.

"Well everyone's going. The ventilation may stop. There's danger of radiation."

"I wasn't planning to stay," he said.

She opened the door and looked at him and went out.

He went out after her. Programmers hurried along the corridor in both directions, carrying paintings, pillowcase bundles, dictypes, lamps. ("Wei was in it! He's dead!" "Stay away from the kitchen, it's a madhouse!") He walked among them. The walls were bare except for large frames hanging empty. ("Sirri says it was Chip, not the new ones!" "—twenty-five years ago, 'Unify the islands, we've got *enough* programmers,' but he gave me a quote about *selfishness.*")

The escalators were working. He rode up to the top level and went around through the steel door, half open, to the bathroom where the boy and the woman were. They were gone.

He went down one level. Programmers and members holding paintings and bundles were pushing into the room that led to the tunnel. He went into the merging crowd. The door ahead was down but must have been partway up because everyone kept moving forward slowly. ("Quickly!" "Move, will you?" "Oh Christ and Wei!")

His arm was grabbed and Madhir glared at him, hugging a filled tablecloth to his chest. "Was it *you?*" he asked.

"Yes," Chip said.

Madhir glared, trembled, flushed. "Madman!" he shouted. "Maniac! *Maniac!*"

Chip pulled his arm free and turned and moved forward.

"Here he is!" Madhir shouted. "Chip! He's the one! He's the one who did it! Here he is! Here! *He's the one who did it!*"

Chip moved forward with the crowd, looking at the steel door ahead, holding the gun in his pocket. ("You *brother*-fighter, are you crazy?" "He's mad, he's mad!")

They walked up the tunnel, quickly at first, then slowly, an endless straggle of dark laden figures. Lamps shone here and there along the line, each lamp drawing with it a section of shining plastic roundness.

Chip saw Deirdre sitting at the side of the tunnel. She looked at him stonily. He kept walking, the gun at his side.

Outside the tunnel they sat and lay in the clearing, smoked and ate and talked in huddles, rummaged in their bundles, traded forks for cigarettes.

Chip saw stretchers on the ground, four or five of them, a member holding a lamp beside them, other members kneeling.

He put the gun in his pocket and went over. The boy and the woman lay on two of the stretchers, their heads bandaged, their eyes closed, their sheeted chests moving. Members were on two other stretchers, and Barlow, the head of the Nutritional Council, was on another, dead-looking, his eyes closed. Rosen kneeled beside him, taping something to his chest through cut-open coveralls.

"Are they all right?" Chip asked.

"The others are," Rosen said. "Barlow's had a heart attack." He looked up at Chip. "They're saying that Wei was in there," he said.

"He was," Chip said.

"You're sure?"

"Yes," Chip said. "He's dead."

"It's hard to believe," Rosen said. He shook his head and took a small something from a member's hand and screwed it onto what he had taped to Barlow's chest.

Chip watched for a moment, then went over to the entrance of the clearing and sat down against stone and lit a cigarette. He toed his sandals off and smoked, watching members and programmers come out of the tunnel and walk around and find places to sit. Karl came out with a painting and a bundle.

A member came toward him. Chip took the gun out of his pocket and held it in his lap.

"Are you Chip?" the member asked. He was the older of the two men who had come in that evening.

"Yes," Chip said.

The man sat down next to him. He was about fifty, very dark, with a jutting chin. "Some of them are talking about rushing you," he said.

"I figured they would be," Chip said. "I'm leaving in a second."

"My name's Luis," the man said.

"Hello," Chip said.

They shook hands.

"Where are you going?" Luis asked.

"Back to the island I came from," Chip said. "Liberty. Majorca. Myorca. You don't know how to fly a copter by any chance, do you?"

"No," Luis said, "but it shouldn't be too hard to figure out."

"It's the landing that worries me," Chip said.

"Land in the water."

"I wouldn't want to lose the copter, though. Assuming I can find one. You want a cigarette?"

"No, thanks," Luis said.

They sat silently for a moment. Chip drew on his cigarette and looked up. "Christ and Wei, real stars," he said. "They had fake ones down there."

"Really?" Luis said.

"Really."

Luis looked over at the programmers. He shook his head. "They're talking as if the Family's going to die in the morning," he said. "It isn't. It's going to be born."

"Born to a lot of trouble, though," Chip said. "It's started already. Planes have crashed . . ."

Luis looked at him and said, "Members haven't died who were supposed to die . . ."

After a moment Chip said, "Yes. Thanks for reminding me."

Luis said. "Sure, there's going to be trouble. But there are members in every city—the undertreated, the ones who write 'Fight Uni'—who'll keep things goign in the beginning. And in the end it's going to be better. Living people!"

"It's going to be more interesting, that's for sure," Chip said, putting his sandals on.

"You aren't going to stay on your island, are you?" Luis asked.

"I don't know," Chip said. "I haven't thought beyond getting there."

"You come back," Luis said. "The Family needs members like you."

"Does it?" Chip said. "I had an eye changed down there, and I'm not sure I only did it to fool Wei." He crushed his cigarette out and stood up. Programmers were looking around at him; he pointed the gun at them and they turned quickly away.

Luis stood up too. "I'm glad the bombs worked," he said, smiling. "I'm the one who made them."

"They worked beautifully," Chip said. "Throw and boom."

"Good," Luis said. "Listen, I don't know about any eye; you land on land and come back in a few weeks."

"I'll see," Chip said. "Good-by."

"Good-by, brother," Luis said.

Chip turned and went out of the clearing and started down rocky slope toward parkland.

He flew over roadways where occasional moving cars zigzagged slowly past series of stopped ones; along the River of Freedom, where barges bumped blindly against the banks; past cities where monorail cars clung motionless to the rail, copters hovering over some of them.

As he grew more sure of his handling of the copter he flew lower; looked into plazas where members milled and gathered; skimmed over factories with stopped feed-in and feed-out lines; over construction sites where nothing moved except a member or two; and over the river again, passing a group of members tying a barge to the shore, climbing onto it, looking up at him.

He followed the river to the sea and started across it, flying low. He thought of Lilac and Jan, Lilac turning startled from the sink (he *should* have taken the bedcover, why hadn't he?). But would they still be in the room? Could Lilac, thinking him caught and treated and never coming back, have—married someone else? No, never. (Why not? Almost nine months he'd been gone.) No, she wouldn't. She—

Drops of clear liquid hit the copter's plastic front and streaked back along its sides. Something was leaking from above, he thought, but then he saw that the sky had gone gray, gray on both sides and darker gray ahead, like the skies in some pre-U paintings. It was *rain* that was hitting the copter.

Rain! In the daytime! He flew with one hand, and with a fingertip of the other, followed on the inside of the plastic the paths of the streaking raindrops outside it.

Rain in the daytime! Christ and Wei, how strange! And how inconvenient!

But there was something pleasing about it too. Something natural.

He brought his hand back to its lever—*Let's not get overconfident, brother*—and smiling, flew ahead.

Completed in June, 1969,
in New York City,
and Dedicated to Adam Levin,
Jed Levin, and Nicholas Levin

The Stepford Wives

"Today the combat takes a different shape;
instead of wishing to put man in a prison,
woman endeavors to escape from one; she no longer seeks
to drag him into the realms of immanence
but to emerge, herself, into the light of transcendence.
Now the attitude of the males creates a new conflict:
it is with a bad grace that the man
lets her go."

—SIMONE DE BEAUVOIR
The Second Sex

One

The Welcome Wagon lady, sixty if she was a day but working at youth and vivacity (ginger hair, red lips, a sunshine-yellow dress), twinkled her eyes and teeth at Joanna and said, "You're really going to like it here! It's a nice town with nice people! You couldn't have made a better choice!" Her brown leather shoulderbag was enormous, old and scuffed; from it she dealt Joanna packets of powdered breakfast drink and soup mix, a toy-size box of non-polluting detergent, a booklet of discount slips good at twenty-two local shops, two cakes of soap, a folder of deodorant pads—

"Enough, enough," Joanna said, standing in the doorway with both hands full. "Hold. Halt. Thank you."

The Welcome Wagon lady put a vial of cologne on top of the other things, and then searched in her bag—"No, really," Joanna said—and brought out pink-framed eyeglasses and a small embroidered notebook. "I do the 'Notes on Newcomers,' " she said, smiling and putting on the glasses. "For the *Chronicle.*" She dug at the bag's bottom and came up with a pen, clicking its top with a red-nailed thumb.

Joanna told her where she and Walter had moved from; what Walter did and with which firm; Pete's and Kim's names and ages; what she had done before they were born; and which colleges she and Walter had gone to. She shifted impatiently as she spoke, standing there at the front door with both hands full and Pete and Kim out of earshot.

"Do you have any hobbies or special interests?"

She was about to say a time-saving no, but hesitated: a full answer, printed in the local paper, might serve as a signpost to women like herself, potential friends. The women she had met in the past few days, the ones in the nearby houses, were pleasant and helpful enough, but they seemed completely absorbed in their household duties. Maybe when she got to know them better she would find they had farther-reaching thoughts and concerns, yet it might be wise to put up that signpost. So, "Yes, several," she said. "I play tennis whenever I get the chance, and I'm a semi-professional photographer—"

"Oh?" the Welcome Wagon lady said, writing.

Joanna smiled. "That means an agency handles three of my pictures," she said. "And I'm interested in politics and in the Women's Liberation movement. Very much so in that. And so is my husband."

"*He* is?" The Welcome Wagon lady looked at her.

"Yes," Joanna said. "Lots of men are." She didn't go into the benefits-for-both-sexes explanation; instead she leaned her head back into the entrance hall and listened: a TV audience laughed in the family room, and Pete and Kim argued but below intervention level. She smiled at the Welcome Wagon lady. "He's interested in boating and football too," she said, "and he collects Early American legal documents." Walter's half of the signpost.

The Welcome Wagon lady wrote, and closed her notebook, clicked her pen. "That's just fine, Mrs. Eberhart," she said, smiling and taking her glasses off. "I know you're going to love it here," she said, "and I want to wish you a sincere and hearty 'Welcome to Stepford.' If there's any information I can give you about local shops and services, please feel free to call me; the number's right there on the front of the discount book."

"Thank you, I will," Joanna said. "And thanks for all this."

"Try them, they're good products!" the Welcome Wagon lady said. She turned away. "Good-by now!"

Joanna said good-by to her and watched her go down the curving walk toward her battered red Volkswagen. Dogs suddenly filled its windows, a black and brown excitement of spaniels, jumping and barking, paws pressing glass. Moving whiteness beyond the Volkswagen caught Joanna's eye: across the sapling-lined street, in one of the Claybrooks' upstairs windows, whiteness moved again, leaving one pane and filling the next; the window was being washed. Joanna smiled, in case Donna Claybrook was looking at her. The whiteness moved to a lower pane, and then to the pane beside it.

With a surprising roar the Volkswagen lunged from the curb, and Joanna backed into the entrance hall and hipped the door closed.

Pete and Kim were arguing louder. "B.M.! Diarrhea!" "Ow! Stop it!"

"Cut it out!" Joanna called, dumping the double handful of samples onto the kitchen table.

"She's kicking me!" Pete shouted, and Kim shouted, "I'm not! You diarrhea!"

"Now *stop* it," Joanna said, going to the port and looking through. Pete lay on the floor too close to the TV set, and Kim stood beside him, red-faced, keeping from kicking him. Both were still in their pajamas. "She kicked me twice," Pete said, and Kim shouted, "You changed the channel! He changed the channel!" "I did not!" "*I was watching Felix the Cat!*"

"Quiet!" Joanna commanded. "Absolute silence! Utter—complete—total—silence."

They looked at her, Kim with Walter's wide blue eyes, Pete with her own grave dark ones. "Race 'em to a flying finish!" the TV set cried. "No electricity!"

"A, you're too close to the set," Joanna said. "B, turn it off; and C, get dressed, both of you. That green stuff outside is grass, and the yellow stuff coming down on it is sunshine." Pete scrambled to his feet and powed the TV's control panel, blanking its screen to a dying dot of light. Kim began crying.

Joanna groaned and went around into the family room.

Crouching, she hugged Kim to her shoulder and rubbed her pajamaed back, kissed her silk-soft ringlets. "Ah, come on now," she said. "Don't you want to play with that nice Allison again? Maybe you'll see another chipmunk."

Pete came over and lifted a strand of her hair. She looked up at him and said, "Don't change *channels* on her."

"Oh, all right," he said, winding a finger in the dark strand.

"And don't *kick,*" she told Kim. She rubbed her back and tried to get kisses in at her squirming-away cheek.

It was Walter's turn to do the dishes, and Pete and Kim were playing quietly in Pete's room, so she took a quick cool shower and put on shorts and a shirt and her sneakers and brushed her hair. She peeked in on Pete and Kim as she tied her hair: they were sitting on the floor playing with Pete's space station.

She moved quietly away and went down the new-carpeted stairs. It was a good evening. The unpacking was done with, finally, and she was cool and clean, with a few free minutes—ten or fifteen if she was lucky—to maybe sit outside with Walter and look at their trees and their two-point-two acres.

She went around and down the hallway. The kitchen was spick-and-span, the washer pounding. Walter was at the sink, leaning to the window and looking out toward the Van Sant house. A Rorschach-blot of sweat stained his shirt: a rabbit with its ears bent outward. He turned around, and started and smiled. "How long have you been here?" he asked, dishtowel-wiping his hands.

"I just came in," she said.

"You look reborn."

"That's how I feel. They're playing like angels. You want to go outside?"

"Okay," he said, folding the towel. "Just for a few minutes though. I'm going over to talk with Ted." He slid the towel onto a rod of the rack. "That's why I was looking," he said. "They just finished eating."

"What are you going to talk with him about?"

They went out onto the patio.

"I was going to tell you," he said as they walked. "I've changed my mind; I'm joining that Men's Association."

She stopped and looked at him.

"Too many important things are centered there to just opt out of it," he said. "Local politicking, the charity drives and so on . . ."

She said, "How can you join an *outdated, old-fashioned*—"

"I spoke to some of the men on the train," he said. "Ted, and Vic Stavros, and a few others they introduced me to. They *agree* that the no-women-allowed business is archaic." He took her arm and they walked on. "But the only way to change it is from inside," he said. "So I'm going to help do it. I'm joining Saturday night. Ted's going to brief me on who's on what committees." He offered her his cigarettes. "Are you smoking or non- tonight?"

"Oh—*smoking*," she said, reaching for one.

They stood at the patio's far edge, in cool blue dusk twanging with crickets, and Walter held his lighter flame to Joanna's cigarette and to his own.

"Look at that sky," he said. "Worth every penny it cost us."

She looked—the sky was mauve and blue and dark blue; lovely—and then she looked at her cigarette. "Organizations can be changed from the outside," she said. "You get up petitions, you picket—"

"But it's easier from the inside," Walter said. "You'll see: if these men I spoke to are typical, it'll be the *Everybody's* Association before you know it. Co-ed poker. Sex on the pool table."

"If these men you spoke to were typical," she said, "it would be the Everybody's Association already. Oh, all right, go ahead and join; I'll think up slogans for placards. I'll have plenty of time when school starts."

He put his arm around her shoulders and said, "Hold off a little while. If it's not open to women in six months, I'll quit and we'll march together. Shoulder to shoulder. 'Sex, yes; sexism, no.' "

" 'Stepford is out of step,' " she said, reaching for the ashtray on the picnic table.

"Not bad."

"Wait till I really get going."

They finished their cigarettes and stood arm in arm, looking at their dark wide runway of lawn, and the tall trees, black against mauve sky, that ended it. Lights shone among the trunks of the trees: windows of houses on the next street over, Harvest Lane.

"Robert Ardrey is right," Joanna said. "I feel very territorial."

Walter looked around at the Van Sant house and then squinted at his watch. "I'm going to go in and wash up," he said, and kissed her cheek.

She turned and took his chin and kissed his lips. "I'm going to stay out a few minutes," she said. "Yell if they're acting up."

"Okay," he said. He went into the house by the living-room door.

She held her arms and rubbed them; the evening was growing cooler.

Closing her eyes, she threw her head back and breathed the smell of grass and trees and clean air: delicious. She opened her eyes, to a single speck of star in dark blue sky, a trillion miles above her. "Star light, star bright," she said. She didn't say the rest of it, but she thought it.

She wished—that they would be happy in Stepford. That Pete and Kim would do well in school, and that she and Walter would find good friends and fulfillment. That he wouldn't mind the commuting—though the whole idea of moving had been his in the first place. That the lives of all four of them would be enriched, rather than diminished, as she had feared, by leaving the city— the filthy, crowded, crime-ridden, but so-alive city.

Sound and movement turned her toward the Van Sant house.

Carol Van Sant, a dark silhouette against the radiance of her kitchen doorway, was pressing the lid down onto a garbage can. She bent to the ground, red hair glinting, and came up with something large and round, a stone; she put it on top of the lid.

"Hi!" Joanna called.

Carol straightened and stood facing her, tall and leggy and naked-seeming —but edged by the purple of a lighted-from-behind dress. "Who's there?" she called.

"Joanna Eberhart," Joanna said. "Did I scare you? I'm sorry if I did." She went toward the fence that divided her and Walter's property from the Van Sants'.

"Hi, Joanna," Carol said in her nasal New Englandy voice. "No, you didn't scay-er me. It's a nice night, isn't it?"

"Yes," Joanna said. "And I'm done with my unpacking, which makes it even nicer." She had to speak loud; Carol had stayed by her doorway, still too far away for comfortable conversation even though she herself was now at the flower bed edging the split-rail fence. "Kim had a great time with Allison this afternoon," she said. "They get along beautifully together."

"Kim's a sweet little girl," Carol said. "I'm glad Allison has such a nice new friend next door. Good night, Joanna." She turned to go in.

"Hey, wait a minute!" Joanna called.

Carol turned back. "Yes?" she said.

Joanna wished that the flower bed and fence weren't there, so she could move closer. Or, darn it, that Carol would come to *her* side of the fence. What was so top-priority-urgent in that fluorescent-lighted copper-pot-hanging kitchen? "Walter's coming over to talk with Ted," she said, speaking loud to Carol's naked-seeming silhouette. "When you've got the kids down, why don't you come over and have a cup of coffee with me?"

"Thanks, I'd like to," Carol said, "but I have to wax the family-room floor." *"Tonight?"*

"Night is the only time to do it, until school starts."

"Well, can't it wait? It's only three more days."

Carol shook her head. "No, I've put it off too long as it is," she said. "It's all over scuff-marks. And besides, Ted will be going to the Men's Association later on."

"Does he go every night?"

"Just about."

Dear God! "And you stay home and do housework?"

"There's always something or other that has to be done," Carol said. "You know how it is. I have to finish the kitchen now. Good night."

"Good night," Joanna said, and watched Carol go—profile of too-big bosom —into her kitchen and close the door. She reappeared almost instantly at the over-the-sink window, adjusting the water lever, taking hold of something and scrubbing it. Her red hair was neat and gleaming; her thin-nosed face looked thoughtful (and, damn it all, *intelligent*); her big purpled breasts bobbed with her scrubbing.

Joanna went back to the patio. No, she *didn't* know how it was, thank God. Not to be like that, a compulsive hausfrau. Who could blame Ted for taking advantage of such an asking-to-be-exploited patsy?

She could blame him, that's who.

Walter came out of the house in a light jacket. "I don't think I'll be more than an hour or so," he said.

"That Carol Van Sant is not to be believed," she said. "She can't come over for a cup of coffee because she has to *wax* the *family-room floor.* Ted goes to the Men's Association every night and *she* stays home doing *housework.*"

"Jesus," Walter said, shaking his head.

"Next to *her*," she said, "my mother is Kate Millett."

He laughed. "See you later," he said, and kissed her cheek and went away across the patio.

She took another look at her star, brighter now—*Get to work, you,* she thought to it—and went into the house.

The four of them went out together Saturday morning, seatbelted into their spotless new station wagon; Joanna and Walter in sunglasses, talking of stores and shopping, and Pete and Kim power-switching their windows down and up and down and up till Walter told them to stop it. The day was vivid and gem-edged, a signal of autumn. They drove to Stepford Center (white frame Colonial shopfronts, postcard pretty) for discount-slip hardware and phar-maceuticals; then south on Route Nine to a large new shopping mall—dis-count-slip shoes for Pete and Kim (what a wait!) and a no-discount jungle gym; then east on Eastbridge Road to a McDonald's (Big Macs, chocolate shakes); and a little farther east for antiques (an octagonal end table, no documents); and then north-south-east-west all over Stepford—Anvil Road, Cold Creek Road, Hunnicutt, Beavertail, Burgess Ridge—to show Pete and Kim (Joanna and Walter had seen it all house-hunting) their new school and the schools they would go to later on, the you'd-never-guess-what-it-is-from-the-outside non-polluting incinerator plant, and the picnic grounds where a community pool was under construction. Joanna sang "Good Morning Starshine" at Pete's request, and they all did "MacNamara's Band" with each one imitating a different instrument in the final part, and Kim threw up, but with enough warning for Walter to pull over and stop and get her unbuckled and out of the station wagon in time, thank God.

That quieted things down. They drove back through Stepford Center— slowly, because Pete said that *he* might throw up too. Walter pointed out the white frame library, and the Historical Society's two-hundred-year-old white frame cottage.

Kim, looking upward through her window, lifted a sucked-thin Life Saver from her tongue and said, "What's that big one?"

"That's the Men's Association house," Walter said.

Pete leaned to his seatbelt's limit and ducked and looked. "Is that where you're going tonight?" he asked.

"That's right," Walter said.

"How do you get to it?"

"There's a driveway farther up the hill."

They had come up behind a truck with a man in khakis standing in its open back, his arms stretched to its sides. He had brown hair and a long lean face and wore eyeglasses. "That's Gary Claybrook, isn't it?" Joanna said.

Walter pressed a fleeting horn-beep and waved his arm out the window. Their across-the-street neighbor bent to look at them, then smiled and waved and caught hold of the truck. Joanna smiled and waved. Kim yelled, "Hello, Mr. Claybrook!" and Pete yelled, "Where's Jeremy?"

"He can't hear you," Joanna said.

"I wish I could ride a truck that way!" Pete said, and Kim said, "Me too!"

The truck was creeping and grinding, fighting against the steep left-curving upgrade. Gary Claybrook smiled self-consciously at them. The truck was half filled with small cartons.

"What's he doing, moonlighting?" Joanna asked.

"Not if he makes as much as Ted says he does," Walter said.

"Oh?"

"What's moonlighting?" Pete asked.

The truck's brake lights flashed; it stopped, its left-turn signal winking.

Joanna explained what moonlighting was.

A car shot down the hill, and the truck began moving across the left lane. "Is that the driveway?" Pete asked, and Walter nodded and said, "Yep, that's it." Kim switched her window farther down, shouting, "Hello, Mr. Claybrook!" He waved as they drove past him.

Pete sprung his seatbelt buckle and jumped around onto his knees. "Can I go there sometime?" he asked, looking out the back.

"Mm-mmn, sorry," Walter said. "No kids allowed."

"Boy, they've got a great big fence!" Pete said. "Like in *Hogan's Heroes*!"

"To keep women out," Joanna said, looking ahead, a hand to the rim of her sunglasses.

Walter smiled.

"Really?" Pete asked. "Is that what it's for?"

"Pete took his belt off," Kim said.

"Pete—" Joanna said.

They drove up Norwood Road, then west on Winter Hill Drive.

As a matter of principle she wasn't going to do any housework. Not that there wasn't plenty to do, God knows, and some that she actually *wanted* to do, like getting the living-room bookshelves squared away—but not tonight, no sir. It could darn well wait. She wasn't Carol Van Sant and she wasn't Mary Ann Stavros—pushing a vacuum cleaner past a downstairs window when she went to lower Pete's shade.

No sir. Walter was at the Men's Association, fine; he *had* to go there to join, and he'd have to go there once or twice a week to get it changed. But she wasn't going to do housework while he was there (at least not this first time) any more than *he* was going to do it when *she* was out somewhere—which she was going to be on the next clear moonlit night: down in the Center getting some time exposures of those Colonial shopfronts. (The hardware store's irregular panes would wobble the moon's reflection, maybe interestingly.)

So once Pete and Kim were sound asleep she went down to the cellar and did some measuring and planning in the storage room that was going to be her darkroom, and then she went back up, checked Pete and Kim, and made herself a vodka and tonic and took it into the den. She put the radio on to some schmaltzy but nice Richard-Rodgersy stuff, moved Walter's contracts and things carefully from the center of the desk, and got out her magnifier and red pencil and the contact sheets of her quick-before-I-leave-the-city pictures. Most of them were a waste of film, as she'd suspected when taking them—she was never any good when she was rushing—but she found one that really excited her, a shot of a well-dressed young black man with an attaché case, glaring venomously at an empty cab that had just passed him. If his expression enlarged well, and if she darkened the background to bring up the blurred cab, it could be an arresting picture—one she was sure the agency would be willing to handle. There were plenty of markets for pictures dramatizing racial tensions.

She red-penciled an asterisk beside the print and went on looking for others that were good or at least part good but croppable. She remembered her vodka and tonic and sipped it.

At a quarter past eleven she was tired, so she put her things away in her side of the desk, put Walter's things back where they had been, turned the radio off, and brought her glass into the kitchen and rinsed it. She checked the doors, turned the lights off—except the one in the entrance hall—and went upstairs.

Kim's elephant was on the floor. She picked it up and tucked it under the blanket beside the pillow; then pulled the blanket up onto Kim's shoulders and fondled her ringlets very lightly.

Pete was on his back with his mouth open, exactly as he had been when she had checked before. She waited until she saw his chest move, then opened his door wider, switched the hall light off, and went into her and Walter's room.

She undressed, braided her hair, showered, rubbed in face cream, brushed her teeth, and got into bed.

Twenty of twelve. She turned the lamp off.

Lying on her back, she swung out her right leg and arm. She missed Walter beside her, but the expanse of cool-sheet smoothness was pleasant. How many times had she gone to bed alone since they were married? Not many: the nights he'd been out of town on Marburg-Donlevy business; the times she'd been in the hospital with Pete and Kim; the night of the power failure; when she'd gone home for Uncle Bert's funeral—maybe twenty or twenty-five times in all, in the ten years and a little more. It wasn't a bad feeling. By God, it made her feel like Joanna Ingalls again. Remember her?

She wondered if Walter was getting bombed. That was liquor on that truck that Gary Claybrook had been riding in (or had the cartons been too small for liquor?). But Walter had gone in Vic Stavros's car, so let him get bombed. Not that he really was likely to; he hardly ever did. What if Vic Stavros got bombed? The sharp curves on Norwood Road—

Oh nuts. Why worry?

The bed was shaking. She lay in the dark seeing the darker dark of the open bathroom door, and the glint of the dresser's handles, and the bed kept shaking her in a slow steady rhythm, each shake accompanied by a faint spring-squeak, again and again and again. It was Walter who was shaking! He had a fever! Or the d.t.'s? She spun around and leaned to him on one arm, staring, reaching to find his brow. His eye-whites looked at her and turned instantly away; all of him turned from her, and the tenting of the blanket at his groin was gone as she saw it, replaced by the shape of his hip. The bed became still.

He had been—masturbating?

She didn't know what to say.

She sat up.

"I thought you had the d.t.'s," she said. "Or a fever."

He lay still. "I didn't want to wake you," he said. "It's after two."

She sat there and caught her breath.

He stayed on his side, not saying anything.

She looked at the room, its windows and furniture dim in the glow from the night light in Pete and Kim's bathroom. She fixed her braid down straight and rubbed her hand on her midriff.

"You could have," she said. "Woke me. I wouldn't have minded."

He didn't say anything.

"Gee whiz, you don't have to do *that,*" she said.

"I just didn't want to wake you," he said. "You were sound asleep."

"Well, next time wake me."

He came over onto his back. No tent.

"Did you?" she asked.

"*No,*" he said.

"Oh," she said. "Well"—and smiled at him—"now I'm up." She lay down beside him, turning to him, and held her arm out over him; and he turned to her and they embraced and kissed. He tasted of Scotch. "I mean, consideration is fine," she said in his ear, "but Jesus."

It turned out to be one of their best times ever—for her, at least. "Wow," she said, coming back from the bathroom, "I'm still weak."

He smiled at her, sitting in bed and smoking.

She got in with him and settled herself comfortably under his arm, drawing his hand down onto her breast. "What did they do," she said, "show you dirty movies or something?"

He smiled. "No such luck," he said. He put his cigarette by her lips, and she took a puff of it. "They took eight-fifty from me in poker," he said, "and they chewed my ear off about the Zoning Board's evil intentions re Eastbridge Road."

"I was afraid you were getting bombed."

"Me? Two Scotches. They're not heavy drinkers. What did *you* do?"

She told him, and about her hopes for the picture of the black man. He told her about some of the men he had met: the pediatrician the Van Sants and the Claybrooks had recommended, the magazine illustrator who was Stepford's major celebrity, two other lawyers, a psychiatrist, the Police Chief, the manager of the Center Market.

"The psychiatrist should be in favor of letting women in," she said.

"He is," Walter said. "And so is Dr. Verry. I didn't sound out any of the others; I didn't want to come on as too much of an activist my first time there."

"When are you going again?" she asked—and was suddenly afraid (why?) that he would say *tomorrow.*

"I don't know," he said. "Listen, I'm not going to make it a way of life the way Ted and Vic do. I'll go in a week or so, I guess; I don't know. It's kind of provincial really."

She smiled and snuggled closer to him.

She was about a third of the way down the stairs, going by foot-feel, holding the damn laundry basket to her face because of the damn banister, when wouldn't you know it, the double-damn phone rang.

She couldn't put the basket down, it would fall, and there wasn't enough room to turn around with it and go back up; so she kept going slowly down, foot-feeling and thinking *Okay, okay* to the phone's answer-me-this-instant-ringing.

She made it to the bottom, put the basket down, and stalked to the den desk. "Hello," she said—the way she felt, with no put-on graciousness.

"Hi, is this Joanna Eberhart?" The voice was loud, happy, raspy; Peggy Clavenger-ish. But Peggy Clavenger had been with *París-Match* the last she'd heard, and wouldn't even know she was married, let alone where she was living.

"Yes," she said. "Who's this?"

"We haven't been formally introduced," the no-not-Peggy-Clavenger voice said, "but I'm going to do it right now. Bobbie, I'd like you to meet Joanna Eberhart. Joanna, I'd like you to meet Bobbie Markowe—that's *K O W E.* Bobbie has been living here in Ajax Country for five weeks now, and she'd like very much to know an 'avid shutterbug with a keen interest in politics and the Women's Lib movement.' That's you, Joanna, according to what it says here in the *Stepford Chronicle.* Or *Chronic Ill,* depending on your journalistic standards. Have they conveyed an accurate impression of you? Are you really not deeply concerned about whether pink soap pads are better than blue ones or vice versa? Given complete freedom of choice, would you just as soon *not* squeeze the Charmin? Hello? Are you still there, Joanna? Hello?"

"Hello," Joanna said. "Yes, I'm here. *And how* I'm here! Hello! Son of a gun, it pays to advertise!"

"What a pleasure to see a messy kitchen!" Bobbie said. "It doesn't quite come up to mine—you don't have the little peanut-butter hand-prints on the cabinets —but it's good, it's very good. Congratulations."

"I can show you some dull dingy bathrooms if you'd like," Joanna said.

"Thanks. I'll just take the coffee."

"Is instant okay?"

"You mean there's something else?"

She was short and heavy-bottomed, in a blue Snoopy sweatshirt and jeans and sandals. Her mouth was big, with unusually white teeth, and she had blue take-in-everything eyes and short dark tufty hair. And small hands and dirty toes. And a husband named Dave who was a stock analyst, and three sons, ten, eight, and six. And an Old English sheepdog and a corgi. She looked a bit younger than Joanna, thirty-two or -three. She drank two cups of coffee and ate a Ring Ding and told Joanna about the women of Fox Hollow Lane.

"I'm beginning to think there's a—nationwide contest I haven't heard about," she said, tonguing her chocolated fingertips. "A million dollars and —Paul Newman for the cleanest house by next Christmas. I *mean,* it's scrub, scrub, *scrub;* wax, wax, *wax*—"

"It's the same around here," Joanna said. "Even at night! And the men all—"

"The Men's Association!" Bobbie cried.

They talked about it—the antiquated sexist unfairness of it, the real *injustice*, in a town with no women's organization, not even a League of Women Voters. "Believe me, I've combed this place," Bobbie said. "There's the Garden Club, and a few old-biddy church groups—for which I'm not eligible anyway; 'Markowe' is upward-mobile for 'Markowitz'—and there's the very non-sexist Historical Society. Drop in and say hello to them. Corpses in lifelike positions."

Dave was in the Men's Association, and like Walter, thought it could be changed from within. But Bobbie knew better: "You'll see, we'll have to chain ourselves to the fence before we get any action. How *about* that fence? You'd think they were refining opium!"

They talked about the possibility of having a get-together with some of their neighbors, a rap session to wake them to the more active role they could play in the town's life; but they agreed that the women they had met seemed unlikely to welcome even so small a step toward liberation. They talked about the National Organization for Women, to which they both belonged, and about Joanna's photography.

"My God, these are *great!*" Bobbie said, looking at the four mounted enlargements Joanna had hung in the den. "They're *terrific!*"

Joanna thanked her.

" 'Avid shutterbug'! I thought that meant Polaroids of the kids! These are *marvelous!*"

"Now that Kim's in kindergarten I'm really going to get to work," Joanna said.

She walked Bobbie to her car.

"Damn it, *no,* " Bobbie said. "We ought to *try* at least. Let's talk to these hausfraus; there must be *some* of them who resent the situation a little. What do you say? Wouldn't it be great if we could get a group together—maybe even a NOW chapter eventually—and give that Men's Association a good shaking-up? Dave and Walter are kidding themselves; it's not going to change unless it's *forced* to change; fat-cat organizations never do. What do you say, Joanna? Let's ask around."

Joanna nodded. "We should," she said. "They can't all be as content as they seem."

She spoke to Carol Van Sant. "Gee, no, Joanna," Carol said. "That doesn't sound like the sort of thing that would interest me. Thanks for ay-isking me though." She was cleaning the plastic divider in Stacy and Allison's room, wiping a span of its accordion folds with firm downstrokes of a large yellow sponge.

"It would only be for a couple of hours," Joanna said. "In the evening, or if it's more convenient for everybody, sometime during school hours."

Carol, crouching to wipe the lower part of the span, said, "I'm sorry, but I just don't have much time for that sort of thing."

Joanna watched her for a moment. "Doesn't it bother you," she said, "that the central organization here in Stepford, the *only* organization that does anything significant as far as community projects are concerned, is off limits to women? Doesn't that seem a little archaic to you?"

" 'Ar-kay-ic'?" Carol said, squeezing her sponge in a bucket of sudsy water.

Joanna looked at her. "Out of date, old-fashioned," she said.

Carol squeezed the sponge out above the bucket. "No, it doesn't seem archaic to me," she said. She stood up straight and reached the sponge to the top of the next span of folds. "Ted's better equipped for that sort of thing than I am," she said, and began wiping the folds with firm downstrokes, each one neatly overlapping the one before. "And men need a place where they can relax and have a drink or two," she said.

"Don't women?"

"No, not as much." Carol shook her neat red-haired shampoo-commercial head, not turning from her wiping. "I'm sorry, Joanna," she said, "I just don't have time for a get-together."

"Okay," Joanna said. "If you change your mind, let me know."

"Would you mind if I don't walk you downstairs?"

"No, of course not."

She spoke to Barbara Chamalian, on the other side of the Van Sants. "Thanks, but I don't see how I could manage it," Barbara said. She was a square-jawed brown-haired woman, in a snug pink dress molding an exceptionally good figure. "Lloyd stays in town a lot," she said, "and the evenings he doesn't, he likes to go to the Men's Association. I'd hate to pay a sitter for just—"

"It could be during school hours," Joanna said.

"No," Barbara said, "I think you'd better count me out." She smiled, widely and attractively. "I'm glad we've met though," she said. "Would you like to come in and sit for a while? I'm ironing."

"No, thanks," Joanna said. "I want to speak to some of the other women."

She spoke to Marge McCormick ("I honestly don't think I'd be interested in that") and Kit Sundersen ("I'm afraid I haven't the time; I'm really sorry, Mrs. Eberhart") and Donna Claybrook ("That's a nice idea, but I'm so busy these days. Thanks for asking me though").

She met Mary Ann Stavros in an aisle in the Center Market. "No, I don't think I'd have time for anything like that. There's so much to do around the house. You know."

"But you go out *sometimes*, don't you?" Joanna said.

"Of course I do," Mary Ann said. "I'm out now, aren't I?"

"I mean *out*. For relaxation."

Mary Ann smiled and shook her head, swaying her sheaves of straight blond hair. "No, not often," she said. "I don't feel much need for relaxation.

See you." And she went away, pushing her grocery cart; and stopped, took a can from a shelf, looked at it, and fitted it down into her cart and went on.

Joanna looked after her, and into the cart of another woman going slowly past her. *My God,* she thought, *they even fill their carts neatly!* She looked into her own: a jumble of boxes and cans and jars. A guilty impulse to put it in order prodded her; but *I'm damned if I will!* she thought, and grabbed a box from the shelf—Ivory Snow—and tossed it in. Didn't even need the damn stuff!

She spoke to the mother of one of Kim's classmates in Dr. Verry's waiting room; and to Yvonne Weisgalt, on the other side of the Stavroses; and to Jill Burke, in the next house over. All of them turned her down; they either had too little time or too little interest to meet with other women and talk about their shared experiences.

Bobbie had even worse luck, considering that she spoke to almost twice as many women. "One taker," she told Joanna. "One eighty-five-year-old widow who dragged me through her door and kept me prisoner for a solid hour of close-up saliva spray. Any time we're ready to storm the Men's Association, Eda Mae Hamilton is ready and willing."

"We'd better keep in touch with her," Joanna said.

"Oh no, we're not done yet!"

They spent a morning calling on women together, on the theory (Bobbie's) that the two of them, speaking in planned ambiguities, might create the encouraging suggestion of a phalanx of women with room for one more. It didn't work.

"Jee-*zus!*" Bobbie said, ramming her car viciously up Short Ridge Hill. "Something *fishy* is going on here! We're in the Town That Time Forgot!"

One afternoon Joanna left Pete and Kim in the care of sixteen-year-old Melinda Stavros and took the train into the city, where she met Walter and their friends Shep and Sylvia Tackover at an Italian restaurant in the theater district. It was good to see Shep and Sylvia again; they were a bright, homely, energetic couple who had survived several bad blows, including the death by drowning of a four-year-old son. It was good to be in the city again too; Joanna relished the color and bustle of the busy restaurant.

She and Walter spoke enthusiastically about Stepford's beauty and quiet, and the advantages of living in a house rather than an apartment. She didn't say anything about how home-centered the Stepford women were, or about the absence of outside-the-home activities. It was vanity, she supposed; an unwillingness to make herself the object of commiseration, even Shep and Sylvia's. She told them about Bobbie and how amusing she was, and about Stepford's fine uncrowded schools. Walter didn't bring up the Men's Association and neither did she. Sylvia, who was with the city's Housing and Development Administration, would have had a fit.

But on the way to the theater Sylvia gave her a sharp appraising look and said, "A tough adjustment?"

"In ways," she said.

"You'll make it," Sylvia said, and smiled at her. "How's the photography? It must be great for you up there, coming to everything with a fresh eye."

"I haven't done a damn thing," she said. "Bobbie and I have been running around trying to drum up some Women's Lib activity. It's a bit of a backwater, to tell the truth."

"Running and drumming isn't your work," Sylvia said. "Photography is, or ought to be."

"I know," she said. "I've got a plumber coming in any day now to put in the darkroom sink."

"Walter looks chipper."

"He is. It's a good life really."

The play, a musical hit of the previous season, was disappointing. In the train going home, after they had hashed it over for a few minutes, Walter put on his glasses and got out some paper work, and Joanna skimmed *Time* and then sat looking out the window and smoking, watching the darkness and the occasional lights riding through it.

Sylvia was right; photography was her work. To hell with the Stepford women. Except Bobbie, of course.

Both cars were at the station, so they had to ride home separately. Joanna went first in the station wagon and Walter followed her in the Toyota. The Center was empty and stage-setty under its three streetlights—yes, she would take pictures there, *before* the darkroom was finished—and there were headlights and lighted windows up at the Men's Association house, and a car waiting to pull out of its driveway.

Melinda Stavros was yawning but smiling, and Pete and Kim were in their beds sound asleep.

In the family room there were empty milk glasses and plates on the lamp table, and crumpled balls of white paper on the sofa and the floor before it, and an empty ginger-ale bottle on the floor among the balls of paper.

At least they don't pass it on to their daughters, Joanna thought.

The third time Walter went to the Men's Association he called at about nine o'clock and told Joanna he was bringing home the New Projects Committee, to which he had been appointed the time before. Some construction work was being done at the house (she could hear the whine of machinery in the background) and they couldn't find a quiet place where they could sit and talk.

"Fine," she said. "I'm getting the rest of the junk out of the darkroom, so you can have the whole—"

"No, listen," he said, "stay upstairs with us and get into the conversation.

A couple of them are die-hard men-only's; it won't do them any harm to hear a woman make intelligent comments. I'm assuming you will."

"Thanks. Won't they object?"

"It's our house."

"Are you sure you're not looking for a waitress?"

He laughed. "Oh God, there's no fooling her," he said. "Okay, you got me. But an intelligent waitress, all right? Would you? It really might do some good."

"Okay," she said. "Give me fifteen minutes and I'll even be an intelligent *beautiful* waitress; how's that for cooperation?"

"Fantastic. Unbelievable."

There were five of them, and one, a cheery little red-faced man of about sixty, with toothpick-ends of waxed mustache, was Ike Mazzard, the magazine illustrator. Joanna, shaking his hand warmly, said, "I'm not sure I like you; you blighted my adolescence with those dream girls of yours!" And he, chuckling, said, "You must have matched up pretty well."

"Would you like to bet on that?" she said.

The other four were all late-thirties or early-forties. The tall black-haired one, laxly arrogant, was Dale Coba, the president of the association. He smiled at her with green eyes that disparaged her, and said, "Hello, Joanna, it's a pleasure." *One of the die-hard men-only's,* she thought; *women are to lay.* His hand was smooth, without pressure.

The others were Anselm or Axhelm, Sundersen, Roddenberry. "I met your wife," she said to Sundersen, who was pale and paunchy, nervous-seeming. "If you're the Sundersens across the way, that is."

"You did? We are, yes. We're the only ones in Stepford."

"I invited her to a get-together, but she couldn't make it."

"She's not very social." Sundersen's eyes looked elsewhere, not at her.

"I'm sorry, I missed your first name," she said.

"Herb," he said, looking elsewhere.

She saw them all into the living room and went into the kitchen for ice and soda, and brought them to Walter at the bar cabinet. "Intelligent? Beautiful?" she said, and he grinned at her. She went back into the kitchen and filled bowls with potato chips and peanuts.

There were no objections from the circle of men when, holding her glass, she said "May I?" and eased into the sofa-end Walter had saved for her. Ike Mazzard and Anselm-or-Axhelm rose, and the others made I'm-thinking-of-rising movements—except Dale Coba, who sat eating peanuts out of his fist, looking across the cocktail table at her with his disparaging green eyes.

They talked about the Christmas-Toys project and the Preserve-the-Landscape project. Roddenberry's name was Frank, and he had a pleasant pug-nosed blue-chinned face and a slight stutter; and Coba had a nickname—Diz, which hardly seemed to fit him. They talked about whether this year there shouldn't be Chanukah lights as well as a crèche in the Center, now that there were a fair number of Jews in town. They talked about ideas for new projects.

"May I say something?" she said.

"Sure," Frank Roddenberry and Herb Sundersen said. Coba was lying back in his chair looking at the ceiling (disparagingly, no doubt), his hands behind his head, his legs extended.

"Do you think there might be a chance of setting up some evening lectures for adults?" she asked. "Or parent-and-teenager forums? In one of the school auditoriums?"

"On what subject?" Frank Roddenberry asked.

"On any subject there's general interest in," she said. "The drug thing, which we're all concerned about but which the *Chronicle* seems to sweep under the rug; what rock music is all about—I don't know, *anything* that would get people out and listening and talking to each other."

"That's *interesting*," Claude Anselm-or-Axhelm said, leaning forward and crossing his legs, scratching at his temple. He was thin and blond; bright-eyed, restless.

"And maybe it would get the *women* out too," she said. "In case you don't know it, this town is a disaster area for baby-sitters."

Everyone laughed, and she felt good and at ease. She offered other possible forum topics, and Walter added a few, and so did Herb Sundersen. Other new-project ideas were brought up; she took part in the talk about them, and the men (except Coba, damn him) paid close attention to her—Ike Mazzard, Frank, Walter, Claude, even Herb looked right at her—and they nodded and agreed with her, or thoughtfully questioned her, and she felt very good indeed, meeting their questions with wit and good sense. *Move over, Gloria Steinem!*

She saw, to her surprise and embarrassment, that Ike Mazzard was sketching her. Sitting in his chair (next to still-watching-the-ceiling Dale Coba), he was pecking with a blue pen at a notebook on his dapper-striped knee, looking at her and looking at his pecking.

Ike Mazzard! Sketching *her*!

The men had fallen silent. They looked into their drinks, swirled their ice cubes.

"Hey," she said, shifting uncomfortably and smiling, "I'm no Ike Mazzard girl."

"Every girl's an Ike Mazzard girl," Mazzard said, and smiled at her and smiled at his pecking.

She looked to Walter; he smiled embarrassedly and shrugged.

She looked at Mazzard again, and—not moving her head—at the other men. They looked at her and smiled, edgily. "Well, *this* is a conversation killer," she said.

"Relax, you can move," Mazzard said. He turned a page and pecked again.

Frank said, "I don't think another b-baseball field is all that important."

She heard Kim cry "Mommy!" but Walter touched her arm, and putting his glass down, got up and excused himself past Claude.

The men talked about new projects again. She said a word or two, moving her head but aware all the time of Mazzard looking at her and pecking. Try being Gloria Steinem when Ike Mazzard is drawing you! It was a bit show-offy of him; she wasn't any once-in-a-lifetime-mustn't-be-missed, not even in the Pucci loungers. And what were the *men* so tense about? Their talking seemed forced and gap-ridden. Herb Sundersen was actually blushing.

She felt suddenly as if she were naked, as if Mazzard were drawing her in obscene poses.

She crossed her legs; wanted to cross her arms too but didn't. *Jesus, Joanna, he's a show-offy artist, that's all. You're dressed.*

Walter came back and leaned down to her. "Just a bad dream," he said; and straightening, to the men, "Anyone want a refill? Diz? Frank?"

"I'll take a small one," Mazzard said, looking at her, pecking.

"Bathroom down that way?" Herb asked, getting up.

The talking went on, more relaxed and casual now.

New projects.

Old projects.

Mazzard tucked his pen into his jacket, smiling.

She said "Whew!" and fanned herself.

Coba raised his head, keeping his hands behind it, and chin-against-chest, looked at the notebook on Mazzard's knee. Mazzard turned pages, looking at Coba, and Coba nodded and said, "You never cease to amaze me."

"Do I get to see?" she asked.

"Of course!" Mazzard said, and half rose, smiling, holding out the open notebook to her.

Walter looked too, and Frank leaned in to see.

Portraits of her; there were page after page of them, small and precise—and flattering, as Ike Mazzard's work had always been. Full faces, three-quarter views, profiles; smiling, not smiling, talking, frowning.

"These are *beautiful,*" Walter said, and Frank said, "Great, Ike!" Claude and Herb came around behind the sofa.

She leafed back through the pages. "They're—wonderful," she said. "I wish I could say they were absolutely accurate—"

"But they *are!*" Mazzard said.

"God bless you." She gave the notebook to him, and he put it on his knee and turned its pages, getting out his pen. He wrote on a page, and tore it out and offered it to her.

It was one of the three-quarter views, a non-smiling one, with the familiar no-capitals *ike mazzard* signature. She showed it to Walter; he said, "Thanks, Ike."

"My pleasure."

She smiled at Mazzard. "Thank you," she said. "I forgive you for blighting my adolescence." She smiled at all of them. "Does anyone want coffee?"

They all did, except Claude, who wanted tea.

She went into the kitchen and put the drawing on the place mats on top of the refrigerator. An Ike Mazzard drawing for *her*! Who'da thunk it, back home when she was eleven or twelve, reading Mom's *Journals* and *Companions*? It was foolish of her to have gotten so uptight about it. Mazzard had been nice to do it.

Smiling, she ran water into the coffee-maker, plugged it in, and put in the basket and spooned in coffee. She put the top on, pressed the plastic lid down onto the coffee can, and turned around. Coba leaned in the doorway watching her, his arms folded, his shoulder to the jamb.

Very cool in his jade turtleneck (matching his eyes, of course) and slate-gray corduroy suit.

He smiled at her and said, "I like to watch women doing little domestic chores."

"You came to the right town," she said. She tossed the spoon into the sink and took the coffee can to the refrigerator and put it in.

Coba stayed there, watching her.

She wished Walter would come. "You don't seem particularly dizzy," she said, getting out a saucepan for Claude's tea. "Why do they call you Diz?"

"I used to work at Disneyland," he said.

She laughed, going to the sink. "No, really," she said.

"That's really."

She turned around and looked at him.

"Don't you believe me?" he asked.

"No," she said.

"Why not?"

She thought, and knew.

"Why not?" he said. "Tell me."

To hell with him; she would. "You don't look like someone who enjoys making people happy."

Torpedoing forever, no doubt, the admission of women to the hallowed and sacrosanct Men's Association.

Coba looked at her—disparagingly. "How little you know," he said.

And smiled and got off the jamb, and turned and walked away.

"I'm not so keen on El Presidente," she said, undressing, and Walter said, "Neither am I. He's cold as ice. But he won't be in office forever."

"He'd better not be," she said, "or women'll never get in. When are elections?"

"Right after the first of the year."

"What does he do?"

"He's with Burnham-Massey, on Route Nine. So is Claude."

"Oh listen, what's his last name?"

"Claude's? Axhelm."

Kim began crying, and was burning hot; and they were up till after three, taking her temperature (a hundred and three at first), reading *Dr. Spock*, calling Dr. Verry, and giving her cool baths and alcohol rubs.

Bobbie found a live one. "At least she is compared to the rest of these clunks," her voice rasped from the phone. "Her name is Charmaine Wimperis, and if you squint a little she turns into Raquel Welch. They're up on Burgess Ridge in a two-hundred-thousand-dollar contemporary, and she's got a maid and a gardener and—now hear this—a tennis court."

"*Really?*"

"I thought that would get you out of the cellar. You're invited to play, and for lunch too. I'll pick you up around eleven-thirty."

"Today? I can't! Kim is still home."

"*Still?*"

"Could we make it Wednesday? Or Thursday, just to be safe."

"*Wednesday,*" Bobbie said. "I'll check with her and call you back."

Wham! Pow! Slam! Charmaine was good, *too* goddamn good; the ball came zinging straight and hard, first to one side of the court and then to the other; it kept her racing from side to side and then drove her all the way back—a just-inside-the-liner that she barely caught. She ran in after it, but Charmaine smashed it down into the left net corner—ungettable—and took the game and the set, six-three. After taking the first set six-two. "Oh God, I've had it!" Joanna said. "What a fiasco! *Oh boy!*"

"One more!" Charmaine called, backing to the serve line. "Come on, one more!"

"I can't! I'm not going to be able to walk tomorrow as it is!" She picked up the ball. "Come on, Bobbie, you play!"

Bobbie, sitting cross-legged on the grass outside the mesh fence, her face trayed on a sun reflector, said, "I haven't played since *camp,* for Chrisake."

"Just a game then!" Charmaine called. "One more game, Joanna!"

"All right, one more game!"

Charmaine won it.

"You killed me but it was great!" Joanna said as they walked off the court together. "Thank you!"

Charmaine, patting her high-boned cheeks carefully with an end of her towel, said, "You just have to get back in practice, that's all. You have a first-rate serve."

"Fat lot of good it did me."

"Will you play often? All I've got now are a couple of teen-age boys, both with permanent erections."

Bobbie said, "Send them to my place"—getting up from the ground.

They walked up the flagstone path toward the house.

"It's a terrific court," Joanna said, toweling her arm.

"Then *use* it," Charmaine said. "I used to play every day with Ginnie Fisher —do you know her?—but she flaked out on me. Don't *you*, will you? How about tomorrow?"

"Oh I couldn't!"

They sat on a terrace under a Cinzano umbrella, and the maid, a slight gray-haired woman named Nettie, brought them a pitcher of Bloody Mary's and a bowl of cucumber dip and crackers. "She's marvelous," Charmaine said. "A German Virgo; if I told her to lick my shoes she'd do it. What are you, Joanna?"

"An American Taurus."

"If you tell her to lick your shoes she spits in your eye," Bobbie said. "You don't really believe that stuff, do you?"

"I certainly do," Charmaine said, pouring Bloody Mary's. "You would too if you came to it with an open mind." (Joanna squinted at her: no, not Raquel Welch, but darn close.) "That's why Ginnie Fisher flaked out on me," she said. "She's a Gemini; they change all the time. Taureans are stable and dependable. Here's to tennis galore."

Joanna said, "This particular Taurean has a house and two kids and no German Virgo."

Charmaine had one child, a nine-year-old son named Merrill. Her husband Ed was a television producer. They had moved to Stepford in July. Yes, Ed was in the Men's Association, and no, Charmaine wasn't bothered by the sexist injustice. "Anything that gets him out of the house nights is fine with me," she said. "He's Aries and I'm Scorpio."

"Oh *well*," Bobbie said, and put a dip-loaded cracker into her mouth.

"It's a very bad combination," Charmaine said. "If I knew then what I know now."

"Bad in what way?" Joanna asked.

Which was a mistake. Charmaine told them at length about her and Ed's manifold incompatibilities—social, emotional, and above all, sexual. Nettie served them lobster Newburg and julienne potatoes—"Oi, my hips," Bobbie said, spooning lobster onto her plate—and Charmaine went on in candid detail. Ed was a sex fiend and a real weirdo. "He had this *rubber suit* made for me, at God knows what cost, in England. I ask you, *rubber*? 'Put it on one of your secretaries,' I said, 'you're not going to get *me* into it.' Zippers and padlocks all over. You can't lock up a Scorpio. Virgos, any time; their thing is to serve. But a Scorpio's thing is to go his own way."

"If *Ed* knew then what you know now," Joanna said.

"It wouldn't have made the least bit of difference," Charmaine said. "He's crazy about me. Typical Aries."

Nettie brought raspberry tarts and coffee. Bobbie groaned. Charmaine told them about other weirdos she had known. She had been a model and had known several.

She walked them to Bobbie's car. "Now look," she said to Joanna, "I know you're busy, but any time you have a free hour, *any* time, just come on over. You don't even have to call; I'm almost always here."

"Thanks, I will," Joanna said. "And thanks for today. It was great."

"*Any* time," Charmaine said. She leaned to the window. "And look, both of you," she said, "would you do me a favor? Would you read *Linda Goodman's Sun Signs*? Just read it and see how right she is. They've got it in the Center Pharmacy, in paper. Will you? Please?"

They gave in, smiling, and promised they would.

"*Ciao!*" she called, waving to them as they drove away.

"Well," Bobbie said, rounding the curve of the driveway, "she may not be ideal NOW material, but at least she's not in love with her vacuum cleaner."

"My God, she's beautiful," Joanna said.

"Isn't she? Even for these parts, where you've got to admit they *look* good even if they don't think good. Boy, what a marriage! How about that business with the suit? And I thought *Dave* had spooky ideas!"

"Dave?" Joanna said, looking at her.

Bobbie side-flashed a smile. "You're not going to get any true confessions out of *me,*" she said. "I'm a Leo, and our thing is changing the subject. You and Walter want to go to a movie Saturday night?"

They had bought the house from a couple named Pilgrim, who had lived in it for only two months and had moved to Canada. The Pilgrims had bought it from a Mrs. McGrath, who had bought it from the builder eleven years before. So most of the junk in the storage room had been left by Mrs. McGrath. Actually it wasn't fair to call it junk: there were two good Colonial side chairs that Walter was going to strip and refinish some day; there was a complete twenty-volume *Book of Knowledge,* now on the shelves in Pete's room; and there were boxes and small bundles of hardware and oddments that, though not finds, at least seemed likely to be of eventual use. Mrs. McGrath had been a thoughtful saver.

Joanna had transferred most of the not-really-junk to a far corner of the cellar before the plumber had installed the sink, and now she was moving the last of it—cans of paint and bundles of asbestos roof shingles—while Walter hammered at a plywood counter and Pete handed him nails. Kim had gone with the Van Sant girls and Carol to the library.

Joanna unrolled a packet of yellowed newspaper and found inside it an inch-wide paintbrush, its clean bristles slightly stiff but still pliable. She began rolling it back into the paper, a half page of the *Chronicle,* and the words WOMEN'S CLUB caught her eyes. HEARS AUTHOR. She turned the paper to the side and looked at it.

"For God's sake," she said.

Pete looked at her, and Walter, hammering, said, "What is it?"

She got the brush out of the paper and put it down, and held the half page open with both hands, reading.

Walter stopped hammering and turned and looked at her. "What is it?" he asked.

She read for another moment, and looked at him; and looked at the paper, and at him. "There was—a *women's* club here," she said. "Betty Friedan spoke to them. And *Kit Sundersen* was the president. Dale Coba's wife and Frank Roddenberry's wife were officers."

"Are you kidding?" he said.

She looked at the paper, and read: " 'Betty Friedan, the author of *The Feminine Mystique,* addressed members of the Stepford Women's Club Tuesday evening in the Fairview Lane home of Mrs. Herbert Sundersen, the club's president. Over fifty women applauded Mrs. Friedan as she cited the inequities and frustrations besetting the modern-day housewife . . .' " She looked at him.

"Can I do some?" Pete asked.

Walter handed the hammer to him. "When *was* that?" he asked her.

She looked at the paper. "It doesn't say, it's the bottom half," she said. "There's a picture of the officers. 'Mrs. Steven Margolies, Mrs. Dale Coba, author Betty Friedan, Mrs. Herbert Sundersen, Mrs. Frank Roddenberry, and Mrs. Duane T. Anderson.' " She opened the half page toward him, and he came to her and took a side of it. "If this doesn't beat everything," he said, looking at the picture and the article.

"I *spoke* to Kit Sundersen," she said. "She didn't say a *word* about it. She didn't have time for a get-together. Like all the others."

"This must have been six or seven years ago," he said, fingering the edge of the yellowed paper.

"Or more," she said. "*The Mystique* came out while I was still working. Andreas gave me his review copy, remember?"

He nodded, and turned to Pete, who was hammering vigorously at the counter top. "Hey, take it easy," he said, "you'll make half moons." He turned back to the paper. "Isn't this something?" he said. "It must have just petered out."

"With fifty members?" she said. "*Over* fifty? Applauding Friedan, not hissing her?"

"Well, it's not here now, is it?" he said, letting the paper go. "Unless they've got the world's worst publicity chairman. I'll ask Herb what happened next time I see him." He went back to Pete. "Say, that's good work," he said.

She looked at the paper and shook her head. "I can't believe it," she said. "Who were the women? They can't all have moved away."

"Come on now," Walter said, "you haven't spoken to every woman in town."

"Bobbie has, darn near," she said. She folded the paper, and folded it, and put it on the carton of her equipment. The paintbrush was there; she picked it up. "Need a paintbrush?" she said.

Walter turned and looked at her. "You don't expect me to *paint* these things, do you?" he asked.

"No, no," she said. "It was wrapped in the paper."

"Oh," he said, and turned to the counter.

She put the brush down, and crouched and gathered a few loose shingles. "How could she not have mentioned it?" she said. "She was the *president.*"

As soon as Bobbie and Dave got into the car, she told them.

"Are you sure it's not one of those newspapers they print in penny arcades?" Bobbie said. " 'Fred Smith Lays Elizabeth Taylor'?"

"It's the *Chronic Ill,*" Joanna said. "The bottom half of the front page. Here, if you can see."

She handed it back to them, and they unfolded it between them. Walter turned on the top light.

Dave said, "You could have made a lot of money by betting me and *then* showing me."

"Didn't think," she said.

" 'Over fifty women'!" Bobbie said. "Who the hell were they? What happened?"

"That's what *I* want to know," she said. "And why Kit Sundersen didn't mention it to me. I'm going to speak to her tomorrow."

They drove into Eastbridge and stood on line for the nine o'clock showing of an R-rated English movie. The couples in the line were cheerful and talkative, laughing in clusters of four and six, looking to the end of the line, waving at other couples. None of them looked familiar except an elderly couple Bobbie recognized from the Historical Society; and the seventeen-year-old McCormick boy and a date, holding hands solemnly, trying to look eighteen.

The movie, they agreed, was "bloody good," and after it they drove back to Bobbie and Dave's house, which was chaotic, the boys still up and the sheepdog galumphing all over. When Bobbie and Dave had got rid of the sitter and the boys and the sheepdog, they had coffee and cheesecake in the tornado-struck living room.

"I *knew* I wasn't uniquely irresistible," Joanna said, looking at an Ike Mazzard drawing of Bobbie tucked in the frame of the over-the-mantel picture.

"Every girl's an Ike Mazzard girl, didn't you know?" Bobbie said, tucking the drawing more securely into the frame's corner, making the picture more crooked than it already was. "Boy, I wish I looked *half* this good."

"You're fine the way you are," Dave said, standing behind them.

"Isn't he a doll?" Bobbie said to Joanna. She turned and kissed Dave's cheek. "It's *still* your Sunday to get up early," she said.

. . .

"Joanna Eberhart," Kit Sundersen said, and smiled. "How are you? Would you like to come in?"

"Yes, I would," Joanna said, "if you have a few minutes."

"Of course I do, come on in," Kit said. She was a pretty woman, black-haired and dimple-cheeked, and only slightly older-looking than in the *Chronicle's* unflattering photo. About thirty-three, Joanna guessed, going into the entrance hall. Its ivory vinyl floor looked as if one of those plastic shields in the commercials had just floated down onto it. Sounds of a baseball game came from the living room.

"Herb is inside with Gary Claybrook," Kit said, closing the front door. "Do you want to say hello to them?"

Joanna went to the living-room archway and looked in: Herb and Gary were sitting on a sofa watching a large color TV across the room. Gary was holding half a sandwich and chewing. A plate of sandwiches and two cans of beer stood on a cobbler's bench before them. The room was beige and brown and green; Colonial, immaculate. Joanna waited till a retreating ballplayer caught the ball, and said, "Hi."

Herb and Gary turned and smiled. "Hello, Joanna," they said, and Gary said, "How are you?" Herb said, "Is Walter here too?"

"Fine. No, he isn't," she said. "I just came over to talk with Kit. Good game?"

Herb looked away from her, and Gary said, "Very."

Kit, beside her and smelling of Walter's mother's perfume, whatever it was, said, "Come, let's go into the kitchen."

"Enjoy," she said to Herb and Gary. Gary, biting into his sandwich, eye-smiled through his glasses, and Herb looked at her and said, "Thanks, we will."

She followed Kit over the plastic-shield vinyl.

"Would you like a cup of coffee?" Kit asked.

"No, thanks." She followed Kit into the coffee-smelling kitchen. It was immaculate, of course—except for the open dryer, and the clothes and the laundry basket on the counter on top of it. The washer's round port was storming. The floor was more plastic shield.

"It's right on the stove," Kit said, "so it wouldn't be any trouble."

"Well, in that case . . ."

She sat at a round green table while Kit got a cup and saucer from a neatly filled cabinet, the cups all hook-hung, the plates filed in racks. "It's nice and quiet now," Kit said, closing the cabinet and going toward the stove. (Her figure, in a short sky-blue dress, was almost as terrific as Charmaine's.) "The kids are over at Gary and Donna's," she said. "I'm doing Marge McCormick's wash. She's got a bug of some kind and can barely move today."

"Oh, that's a shame," Joanna said.

Kit fingertipped the top of a percolator and poured coffee from it. "I'm sure she'll be good as new in a day or two," she said. "How do you take this, Joanna?"

"Milk, no sugar, please."

Kit carried the cup and saucer toward the refrigerator. "If it's about that get-together again," she said, "I'm afraid I'm still awfully busy."

"It isn't that," Joanna said. She watched Kit open the refrigerator. "I wanted to find out what happened to the Women's Club," she said.

Kit stood at the lighted refrigerator, her back to Joanna. "The Women's Club?" she said. "Oh my, that was years ago. It disbanded."

"Why?" Joanna asked.

Kit closed the refrigerator and opened a drawer beside it. "Some of the women moved away," she said—she closed the drawer and turned, putting a spoon on the saucer—"and the rest of us just lost interest in it. At least I did." She came toward the table, watching the cup. "It wasn't accomplishing anything useful," she said. "The meetings got boring after a while." She put the cup and saucer on the table and pushed them closer to Joanna. "Is that enough milk?" she asked.

"Yes, that's fine," Joanna said. "Thanks. How come you didn't tell me about it when I was here the other time?"

Kit smiled, her dimples deepening. "You didn't ask me," she said. "If you had I would have told you. It's no secret. Would you like a piece of cake, or some cookies?"

"No, thanks," Joanna said.

"I'm going to fold these things," Kit said, going from the table.

Joanna watched her close the dryer and take something white from the pile of clothes on it. She shook it out—a T-shirt. Joanna said, "What's wrong with *Bill* McCormick? Can't *he* run a washer? I thought he was one of our aerospace brains."

"He's taking care of Marge," Kit said, folding the T-shirt. "These things came out nice and white, didn't they?" She put the folded T-shirt into the laundry basket, smiling.

Like an actress in a commercial.

That's what she was, Joanna felt suddenly. That's what they *all* were, all the Stepford wives: actresses in commercials, pleased with detergents and floor wax, with cleansers, shampoos, and deodorants. Pretty actresses, big in the bosom but small in the talent, playing suburban housewives unconvincingly, too nicey-nice to be real.

"Kit," she said.

Kit looked at her.

"You must have been very young when you were president of the club," Joanna said. "Which means you're intelligent and have a certain amount of drive. Are you happy now? Tell me the truth. Do you feel you're living a full life?"

Kit looked at her, and nodded. "Yes, I'm happy," she said. "I feel I'm living a very full life. Herb's work is important, and he couldn't do it nearly as well if not for me. We're a unit, and between us we're raising a family, and doing optical research, and running a clean comfortable household, and doing community work."

"Through the Men's Association."

"Yes."

Joanna said, "Were the Women's Club meetings more boring than housework?"

Kit frowned. "No," she said, "but they weren't as useful as housework. You're not drinking your coffee. Is anything wrong with it?"

"No," Joanna said, "I was waiting for it to cool." She picked up the cup.

"Oh," Kit said, and smiled, and turned to the clothes and folded something.

Joanna watched her. Should she ask who the other women had been? No, they would be like Kit; and what difference would it make? She drank from the cup. The coffee was strong and rich-flavored, the best she'd tasted in a long time.

"How are your children?" Kit asked.

"Fine," she said.

She started to ask the brand of the coffee, but stopped herself and drank more of it.

Maybe the hardware store's panes would have wobbled the moon's reflection interestingly, but there was no way of telling, not with the panes where *they* were and the moon where *it* was. *C'est la vie.* She mooched around the Center for a while, getting the feel of the night-empty curve of street, the row of white shopfronts on one side, the rise to the hill on the other; the library, the Historical Society cottage. She wasted some film on streetlights and litter baskets—cliché time—but it was only black-and-white, so what the hell. A cat trotted down the path from the library, a silver-gray cat with a black moonshadow stuck to its paws; it crossed the street toward the market parking lot. No, thanks, we're not keen on cat pix.

She set up the tripod on the library lawn and took shots of the shopfronts, using the fifty-millimeter lens and making ten-, twelve-, and fourteen-second exposures. An odd medicinal smell soured the air—coming on the breeze at her back. It almost reminded her of something in her childhood, but fell short. A syrup she'd been given? A toy she had had?

She reloaded by moonlight, gathered the tripod, and backed across the street, scouting the library for a good angle. She found one and set up. The white clapboard siding was black-banded in the overhead moonlight; the windows showed bookshelved walls lighted faintly from within. She focused with extra-special care, and starting at eight seconds, took each-a-second-longer exposures up to eighteen. One of them, at least, would catch the inside bookshelved walls without overexposing the siding.

She went to the car for her sweater, and looked around as she went back to the camera. The Historical Society cottage? No, it was too tree-shadowed, and dull anyway. But the Men's Association house, up on the hill, had a surprisingly comic look to it: a square old nineteenth-century house, solid and symmetrical, tipsily parasolled by a glistening TV antenna. The four tall upstairs windows were vividly alight, their sashes raised. Figures moved inside.

She took the fifty-millimeter lens out of the camera and was putting in the one-thirty-five when headlight beams swept onto the street and grew brighter. She turned and a spotlight blinded her. Closing her eyes, she tightened the lens; then shielded her eyes and squinted.

The car stopped, and the spotlight swung away and died to an orange spark. She blinked a few times, still seeing the blinding radiance.

A police car. It stayed where it was, about thirty feet away from her on the other side of the street. A man's voice spoke softly inside it; spoke and kept speaking.

She waited.

The car moved forward, coming opposite her, and stopped. The young policeman with the unpolicemanlike brown mustache smiled at her and said, "Evening, ma'am." She had seen him several times, once in the stationery store buying packs of colored crepe paper, one each of every color they had.

"Hello," she said, smiling.

He was alone in the car; he must have been talking on his radio. About her? "I'm sorry I hit you with the spot that way," he said. "Is that your car there by the post office?"

"Yes," she said. "I didn't park it here because I was—"

"That's all right, I'm just checking." He squinted at the camera. "That's a good-looking camera," he said. "What kind is it?"

"A Pentax," she said.

"Pentax," he said. He looked at the camera, and at her. "And you can take pictures at night with it?"

"Time exposures," she said.

"Oh, sure," he said. "How long does it take, on a night like this?"

"Well, that depends," she said.

He wanted to know on what, and what kind of film she was using. And whether she was a professional photographer, and how much a Pentax cost, just roughly. And how it stacked up against other cameras.

She tried not to grow impatient; she should be glad she lived in a town where a policeman could stop and talk for a few minutes.

Finally he smiled and said, "Well, I guess I'd better let you go ahead with it. Good night."

"Good night," she said, smiling.

He drove off slowly. The silver-gray cat ran through his headlight beams. She watched the car for a moment, and then turned to the camera and checked the lens. Crouching to the viewfinder, she levered into a good framing of the Men's Association house and locked the tripod head. She focused, sharpening the finder's image of the high square tipsy-antennaed house. Two of its upstairs windows were dark now; and another was shade-pulled down to darkness, and then the last one.

She straightened and looked at the house itself, and turned to the police car's faraway taillights.

He had radioed a message about her, and then he had stalled her with his questions while the message was acted on, the shades pulled down.

Oh come on, girl, you're getting nutty! She looked at the house again. They wouldn't have a *radio* up there. And what would he have been afraid she'd photograph? An orgy in progress? Call girls from the city? (Or better yet, from right there in Stepford.) *ENLARGER REVEALS SHOCKING SECRET. Seemingly diligent housewives, conveniently holding still for lengthy time exposures, were caught Sunday night disporting at the Men's Association house by photographer Nancy Drew Eberhart of Fairview Lane . . .*

Smiling, she crouched to the viewfinder, bettered her framing and focus, and took three shots of the dark-windowed house—ten seconds, twelve, and fourteen.

She took shots of the post office, and of its bare flagpole silhouetted against moonlit clouds.

She was putting the tripod into the car when the police car came by and slowed. "Hope they all come out!" the young policeman called.

"Thanks!" she called back to him. "I enjoyed talking!" To make up for her city-bred suspiciousness.

"Good night!" the policeman called.

A senior partner in Walter's firm died of uremic poisoning, and the records of the trusts he had administered were found to be disquietingly inaccurate. Walter had to stay two nights and a weekend in the city, and on the nights following he seldom got home before eleven o'clock. Pete took a fall on the school bus and knocked out his two front teeth. Joanna's parents paid a short-notice three-day visit on their way to a Caribbean vacation. (They loved the house and Stepford, and Joanna's mother admired Carol Van Sant. "So serene and efficient! Take a leaf from *her* book, Joanna.")

The dishwasher broke down, and the pump; and Pete's eighth birthday came, calling for presents, a party, favors, a cake. Kim got a sore throat and was home for three days. Joanna's period was late but came, thank God and the Pill.

She managed to get in a little tennis, her game improving but still not as good as Charmaine's. She got the darkroom three-quarters set up and made trial enlargements of the black-man-and-taxi picture, and developed and printed the ones she had taken in the Center, two of which looked very good. She took shots of Pete and Kim and Scott Chamalian playing on the jungle gym.

She saw Bobbie almost every day; they shopped together, and sometimes Bobbie brought her two younger boys Adam and Kenny over after school. One day Joanna and Bobbie and Charmaine got dressed to the nines and had a two-cocktail lunch at a French restaurant in Eastbridge.

By the end of October, Walter was getting home for dinner again, the dead partner's peculations having been unraveled, made good, and patched over. Everything in the house was working, everyone was well. They carved a huge pumpkin for Halloween, and Pete went trick-or-treating as a front-toothless Batman, and Kim as Heckel or Jeckel (she was both, she insisted). Joanna gave out fifty bags of candy and had to fall back on fruit and cookies; next year she would know better.

On the first Saturday in November they gave a dinner party: Bobbie and Dave, Charmaine and her husband Ed; and from the city, Shep and Sylvia Tackover, and Don Ferrault—one of Walter's partners—and his wife Lucy. The local woman Joanna got to help serve and clean up was delighted to be working in Stepford for a change. "There used to be *so* much entertaining here!" she said. "I had a whole *round* of women that used to *fight* over me! And now I have to go to *Nor*wood, and *East*bridge, and New *Sharon*! And I *hate* night driving!" She was a plump quick-moving white-haired woman named Mary Migliardi. "It's that Men's Association," she said, jabbing tooth-picks into shrimp on a platter. "Entertaining's gone right out the window since *they* started up! The men go out and the women stay in! If my old man was alive he'd have to knock me on the head before I'd let him join!"

"But it's a very old organization, isn't it?" Joanna said, tossing salad at arm's length because of her dress.

"Are you kidding?" Mary said. "It's new! Six or seven years, that's all. Before, there was the Civic Association and the Elks and the Legion"—she toothpicked shrimp with machinelike rapidity—"but they all merged in with it once it got going. Except the Legion; they're still separate. Six or seven years, that's all. This isn't all you got for hors d'oeuvres, is it?"

"There's a cheese roll in the refrigerator," Joanna said.

Walter came in, looking very handsome in his plaid jacket, carrying the ice bucket. "We're in luck," he said, going to the refrigerator. "There's a good Creature Feature; Pete doesn't even want to come down. I put the Sony in his room." He opened the freezer section and took out a bag of ice cubes.

"Mary just told me the Men's Association is new," Joanna said.

"It's not *new*," Walter said, tearing at the top of the bag. A white dab of tissue clung to his jawbone, pinned by a dot of dried blood.

"Six or seven years," Mary said.

"Where we come from that's old."

Joanna said, "I thought it went back to the Puritans."

"What gave you that idea?" Walter asked, spilling ice cubes into the bucket.

She tossed the salad. "I don't know," she said. "The way it's set up, and that old house . . ."

"That was the Terhune place," Mary said, laying a stretch of plastic over the toothpicked platter. "They got it dirt-cheap. Auctioned for taxes and no one else bid."

The party was a disaster. Lucy Ferrault was allergic to something and never stopped sneezing; Sylvia was preoccupied; Bobbie, whom Joanna had counted on as a conversational star, had laryngitis. Charmaine was Miss Vamp, provocative and come-hithery in floor-length white silk cut clear to her navel; Dave and Shep were provoked and went thither. Walter (*damn* him!) talked law in the corner with Don Ferrault. Ed Wimperis—big, fleshy, well tailored, stewed—talked television, clamping Joanna's arm and explaining in slow careful words why cassettes were going to change everything. At the dinner table Sylvia got unpreoccupied and tore into suburban communities that enriched themselves with tax-yielding light industry while fortressing themselves with two- and four-acre zoning. Ed Wimperis knocked his wine over. Joanna tried to get light conversation going, and Bobbie pitched in valiantly, gasping an explanation of where the laryngitis had come from: she was doing tape-recordings for a friend of Dave's who "thinks 'e's a bleedin' 'Enry 'Iggins, 'e does." But Charmaine, who knew the man and had taped for him herself, cut her short with "Never make fun of what a Capricorn's doing; they *produce*," and went into an around-the-table sign analysis that demanded everyone's attention. The roast was overdone, and Walter had a bad time slicing it. The soufflé rose, but not quite as much as it should have—as Mary remarked while serving it. Lucy Ferrault sneezed.

"Never again," Joanna said as she switched the outside lights off; and Walter, yawning, said, "Soon enough for me."

"Listen, you," she said. "How could you stand there talking to Don while three women are sitting like stones on the sofa?"

Sylvia called to apologize—she had been passed up for a promotion she damn well knew she deserved—and Charmaine called to say they'd had a great time and to postpone a tentative Tuesday tennis date. "Ed's got a bee in his bonnet," she said. "He's taking a few days off, we're putting Merrill with the DaCostas —you don't know them, lucky you—and he and I are going to 'rediscover each other.' That means he chases me around the bed. And my period's not till next week, God damn it."

"Why not let him catch you?" Joanna said.

"Oh God," Charmaine said. "Look, I just don't enjoy having a big cock shoved into me, that's all. Never have and never will. And I'm not a lez either, because I tried it and *that's* no big deal. I'm just not interested in sex. I don't think any woman is, really, not even Pisces women. Are you?"

"Well I'm not a nympho," Joanna said, "but I'm interested in it, sure I am."

"*Really*, or do you just feel you're supposed to be?"

"Really."

"Well, to each his own," Charmaine said. "Let's make it Thursday, all right?

He's got a conference he can't get out of, thank God."

"Okay, Thursday, unless something comes up."

"Don't *let* anything."

"It's getting cold."

"We'll wear sweaters."

She went to a P.T.A. meeting. Pete's and Kim's teachers were there, Miss Turner and Miss Gair, pleasant middle-aged women eagerly responsive to her questions about teaching methods and how the busing program was working out. The meeting was poorly attended; aside from the group of teachers at the back of the auditorium, there were only nine women and about a dozen men. The president of the association was an attractive blond woman named Mrs. Hollingsworth, who conducted business with smiling unhurried efficiency.

She bought winter clothes for Pete and Kim, and two pairs of wool slacks for herself. She made terrific enlargements of "Off Duty" and "The Stepford Library," and took Pete and Kim to Dr. Coe, the dentist.

"Did we?" Charmaine asked, letting her into the house.

"Of course we did," she said. "I said it was okay if nothing came up."

Charmaine closed the door and smiled at her. She was wearing an apron over slacks and a blouse. "Gosh, I'm sorry, Joanna," she said. "I completely forgot."

"That's all right," she said, "go change."

"We can't play," Charmaine said. "For one thing, I've got too much work to do—"

"Work?"

"Housework."

Joanna looked at her.

"We've let Nettie go," Charmaine said. "It's absolutely unbelievable, the sloppy job she was getting away with. The place looks clean at first glance, but boy, look in the corners. I did the kitchen and the dining room yesterday, but I've still got all the other rooms. Ed shouldn't have to live with dirt."

Joanna, looking at her, said, "Okay, funny joke."

"I'm not joking," Charmaine said. "Ed's a pretty wonderful guy, and I've been lazy and selfish. I'm through playing tennis, and I'm through reading those astrology books. From now on I'm going to do right by Ed, and by Merrill too. I'm lucky to have such a wonderful husband and son."

Joanna looked at the pressed and covered racket in her hand, and at Charmaine. "That's great," she said, and smiled. "But I honestly can't believe you're giving up tennis."

"Go look," Charmaine said.

Joanna looked at her.

"Go look," Charmaine said.

Joanna turned and went into the living room and across it to the glass doors. She slid one open, hearing Charmaine behind her, and went out onto the terrace. She crossed the terrace and looked down the slope of flagstone-pathed lawn.

A truck piled with sections of mesh fencing stood on the tire-marked grass beside the tennis court. Two sides of the court's fence were gone, and the other two lay flat on the grass, a long side and a short one. Two men kneeled on the long side, working at it with long-handled cutters. They brought the handles up and together, and clicks of sound followed. A mountain of dark soil sat on the center of the court; the net and the posts were gone.

"Ed wants a putting green," Charmaine said, coming to Joanna's side.

"It's a *clay court!*" Joanna said, turning to her.

"It's the only level place we've got," Charmaine said.

"My God," Joanna said, looking at the men working the cutter handles. "That's crazy, Charmaine!"

"Ed plays golf, he doesn't play tennis," Charmaine said.

Joanna looked at her. "What did he *do* to you?" she said. "*Hypnotize* you?"

"Don't be silly," Charmaine said, smiling. "He's a wonderful guy and I'm a lucky woman who ought to be grateful to him. Do you want to stay awhile? I'll make you some coffee. I'm doing Merrill's room but we can talk while I'm working."

"All right," Joanna said, but shook her head and said, "No, no, I—" She backed from Charmaine, looking at her. "No, there are things *I* should be doing too." She turned and went quickly across the terrace.

"I'm sorry I forgot to call you," Charmaine said, following her into the living room.

"It's all right," Joanna said, going quickly, stopping, turning, holding her racket before her with both hands. "I'll see you in a few days, okay?"

"Yes," Charmaine said, smiling. "Please call me. And please give my regards to Walter."

Bobbie went to see for herself, and called about it. "She was moving the bedroom furniture. And they just moved in in July; how dirty can the place be?"

"It won't last," Joanna said. "It can't. People don't change that way."

"Don't they?" Bobbie said. "Around here?"

"What do you mean?"

"Shut up, Kenny! Give him that! Joanna, listen, I want to talk with you. Can you have lunch tomorrow?"

"Yes—"

"I'll pick you up around noon. I said *give* it to him! Okay? Noon, nothing fancy."

"Okay. Kim! You're getting water all over the—"

Walter wasn't particularly surprised to hear about the change in Charmaine. "Ed must have laid the law down to her," he said, turning a fork of spaghetti against his spoon. "I don't think he makes enough money for that kind of a setup. A maid must be at *least* a hundred a week these days."

"But her whole *attitude's* changed," Joanna said. "You'd think she'd be complaining."

"Do you know what Jeremy's allowance is?" Pete said.

"He's two years older than you are," Walter said.

"This is going to sound crazy, but I want you to listen to me without laughing, because either I'm right or I'm going off my rocker and need sympathy." Bobbie picked at the bun of her cheeseburger.

Joanna, watching her, swallowed cheeseburger and said, "All right, go ahead."

They were at the McDonald's on Eastbridge Road, eating in the car.

Bobbie took a small bite of her cheeseburger, and chewed and swallowed. "There was a thing in *Time* a few weeks ago," she said. "I looked for it but I must have thrown the issue out." She looked at Joanna. "They have a very low crime rate in El Paso, Texas," she said. "I *think* it was El Paso. Anyway, *somewhere* in Texas they have a very low crime rate, much lower than any-where *else* in Texas; and the reason is, there's a chemical in the ground that gets into the water, and it tranquilizes everybody and eases the tension. God's truth."

"I think I remember," Joanna said, nodding, holding her cheeseburger.

"Joanna," Bobbie said, "I think there's something *here.* In Stepford. It's possible, isn't it? All those fancy plants on Route Nine—electronics, comput-ers, aerospace junk, with Stepford Creek running right behind them—who knows *what* kind of crap they're dumping into the environment."

"What do you *mean?*" Joanna said.

"Just think for a minute," Bobbie said. She fisted her free hand and stuck out its pinky. "Charmaine's changed and become a hausfrau," she said. She stuck out her ring finger. "The woman you spoke to, the one who was president of the club; *she* changed, didn't she, from what she must have been before?"

Joanna nodded.

Bobbie's next finger flicked out. "The woman Charmaine played tennis with, before you; she changed too, Charmaine said so."

Joanna frowned. She took a French fry from the bag between them. "You think it's—because of a *chemical?*" she said.

Bobbie nodded. "Either leaking from one of those plants, or just *around,* like in El Paso or wherever." She took her coffee from the dashboard. "It *has* to be," she said. "It can't be a coincidence that Stepford women are all the way they are. And some of the ones we spoke to *must* have belonged to that club. A few years ago they were *applauding Betty Friedan,* and look at them now. *They've changed too."*

Joanna ate the French fry and took a bite of her cheeseburger. Bobbie took a bite of her cheeseburger and sipped her coffee.

"There's *something,"* Bobbie said. "In the ground, in the water, in the air —I don't know. It makes women interested in housekeeping and nothing else but. Who knows what chemicals can do? *Nobel-prize winners* don't even really know yet. Maybe it's some kind of hormone thing; that would explain the fantastic boobs. You've got to have noticed."

"I sure have," Joanna said. "I feel pre-adolescent every time I set foot in the market."

"*I* do, for God's sake," Bobbie said. She put her coffee on the dashboard and took French fries from the bag. "Well?" she said.

"I suppose it's—possible," Joanna said. "But it sounds so—fantastic." She took her coffee from the dashboard; it had made a patch of fog on the windshield.

"No more fantastic than El Paso," Bobbie said.

"More," Joanna said. "Because it affects only women. What does Dave think?"

"I haven't mentioned it to him yet. I thought I'd try it out on you first."

Joanna sipped her coffee. "Well, it's in the realm of *possibility,"* she said. "I *don't* think you're off your rocker. The thing to do, I guess, is write a very level-headed-sounding letter to the State—what, Department of Health? Environmental Commission? Whatever agency would have the authority to look into it. We could find out at the library."

Bobbie shook her head. "Mm-mmn," she said. "I *worked* for a government agency; forget it. *I* think the thing to do is move out. *Then* futz around with letters."

Joanna looked at her.

"I mean it," Bobbie said. "Anything that can make a hausfrau out of *Charmaine* isn't going to have any special trouble with *me. Or* with *you."*

"Oh come *on,"* Joanna said.

"There's something here, Joanna! I'm not kidding! This is Zombieville! And Charmaine moved in in July, *I* moved in in August, and *you* moved in in September!"

"All right, quiet down, I can hear."

Bobbie took a large-mouthed bite of her cheeseburger. Joanna sipped her coffee and frowned.

"Even if I'm wrong," Bobbie said with her mouth full, "even if there's no chemical doing anything"—she swallowed—"is this where you really want to live? We've each got one friend now, you after two months, me after three. Is *that* your idea of the ideal community? I went into Norwood to get my hair done for your party; I saw a *dozen* women who were rushed and sloppy and irritated and alive; I wanted to hug every one of them!"

"Find friends in Norwood," Joanna said, smiling. "You've got the car."

"You're so damn independent!" Bobbie took her coffee from the dashboard. "I'm asking Dave to move," she said. "We'll sell here and buy in Norwood or Eastbridge; all it'll mean is some headaches and bother and the moving costs—for which, if he insists, I'll hock the rock."

"Do you think he'll agree?"

"He damn well better had, or his life is going to get mighty miserable. I wanted to buy in Norwood all along; too many WASPs, he said. Well, I'd rather get stung by WASPs than poisoned by whatever's working around here. So you're going to be down to no friends at all in a little while—unless *you* speak to *Walter.*"

"About *moving?*"

Bobbie nodded. Looking at Joanna, she sipped her coffee.

Joanna shook her head. "I couldn't ask him to move again," she said.

"Why not? He wants you to be happy, doesn't he?"

"I'm not sure that I'm not. And I just finished the darkroom."

"Okay," Bobbie said, "stick around. Turn into your next-door neighbor."

"Bobbie, it *can't* be a chemical. I mean it *could,* but I honestly don't believe it. Honestly."

They talked about it while they finished eating, and then they drove up Eastbridge Road and turned onto Route Nine. They passed the shopping mall and the antique stores, and came to the industrial plants.

"Poisoner's Row," Bobbie said.

Joanna looked at the neat low modern buildings, set back from the road and separated each from the next by wide spans of green lawn: Ulitz Optics (where Herb Sundersen worked), and CompuTech (Vic Stavros, or was he with Instatron?), and Stevenson Biochemical, and Haig-Darling Computers, and Burnham-Massey-Microtech (Dale Coba—hiss!—and Claude Axhelm), and Instatron, and Reed & Saunders (Bill McCormick—how was Marge?), and Vesey Electronics, and AmeriChem-Willis.

"Nerve-gas research, I'll bet you five bucks."

"In a *populated area?*"

"Why not? With that gang in Washington?"

"Oh come *on,* Bobbie!"

Walter saw something was bothering her and asked her about it. She said, "You've got the Koblenz agreement to do," but he said, "I've got all weekend. Come on, what is it?"

So while she scraped the dishes and put them in the washer, she told him about Bobbie's wanting to move, and her "El Paso" theory.

"That sounds pretty far-fetched to me," he said.

"To me too," she said. "But women *do* seem to change around here, and what they change into is pretty damn dull. If Bobbie moves, and if Charmaine doesn't come back to her old self, which at least was—"

"Do *you* want to move?" he asked.

She looked uncertainly at him. His blue eyes, waiting for her answer, gave no clue to his feelings. "No," she said, "not when we're all settled in. It's a good house . . . And yes, I'm sure I'd be happier in Eastbridge or Norwood. I wish we'd looked in either one of them."

"*There's* an unequivocal answer," he said, smiling. " 'No and yes.' "

"About sixty-forty," she said.

He straightened from the counter he had been leaning against. "All right," he said, "if it gets to be zero-a hundred, we'll do it."

"You would?" she said.

"Sure," he said, "if you were really unhappy. I wouldn't want to do it during the school year—"

"No, no, of course not."

"But we could do it next summer. I don't think we'd lose anything, except the time and the moving and closing costs."

"That's what Bobbie said."

"So it's just a matter of making up your mind." He looked at his watch and went out of the kitchen.

"Walter?" she called, touching her hands to a towel.

"Yes?"

She went to where she could see him, standing in the hallway. "Thanks," she said, smiling. "I feel better."

"You're the one who has to be here all day, not me," he said, and smiled at her and went into the den.

She watched him go, then turned and glanced through the port to the family room. Pete and Kim sat on the floor watching TV—President Kennedy and President Johnson, surprisingly; no, figures of them. She watched for a moment, and went back to the sink and scraped the last few dishes.

Dave, too, was willing to move at the end of the school year. "He gave in so easily I thought I'd keel over," Bobbie said on the phone the next morning. "I just hope we *make* it till June."

"Drink bottled water," Joanna said.

"You think I'm not going to? I just sent Dave to get some."

Joanna laughed.

"Go ahead, laugh," Bobbie said. "For a few cents a day I'd rather be safe than sorry. And I'm writing to the Department of Health. The problem is, how do I do it without coming across like a little old lady without all her marbles? You want to help, and co-sign?"

"Sure," Joanna said. "Come on over later. Walter is drafting a trust agreement; maybe he'll lend us a few whereases."

. . .

She made autumn-leaf collages with Pete and Kim, and helped Walter put up the storm windows, and met him in the city for a partners-and-wives dinner —the usual falsely-friendly clothes-appraising bore. A check came from the agency: two hundred dollars for four uses of her best picture.

She met Marge McCormick in the market—yes, she'd had a bug but now she was fine, thanks—and Frank Roddenberry in the hardware store—"Hello, Joanna, how've you b-been?"—and the Welcome Wagon lady right outside. "A black family is moving in on Gwendolyn Lane. But I think it's *good,* don't you?"

"Yes, I do."

"All ready for winter?"

"I am now." Smiling, she showed the sack of birdseed she'd just bought.

"It's beautiful here!" the Welcome Wagon lady said. "You're the shutter-bug, aren't you? You should have a field day!"

She called Charmaine and invited her for lunch. "I can't, Joanna, I'm sorry," Charmaine said. "I've got so much to do around the house here. You know how it is."

Claude Axhelm came over one Saturday afternoon—to see her, not Walter. He had a briefcase with him.

"I've got this project I've been working on in my spare time," he said, walking around the kitchen while she fixed him a cup of tea. "Maybe you've heard about it. I've been getting people to tape-record lists of words and syllables for me. The men do it up at the house, and the women do it in their homes."

"Oh yes," she said.

"They tell me where they were born," he said, "and every place they've lived and for how long." He walked around, touching cabinet knobs. "I'm going to feed everything into a computer eventually, each tape with its geographical data. With enough samples I'll be able to feed in a tape *without* data"—he ran a fingertip along a counter edge, looking at her with his bright eyes—"maybe even a very *short* tape, a few words or a sentence—and the computer'll be able to give a geographical rundown on the person, where he was born and where he's lived. Sort of an electronic Henry Higgins. Not just a stunt though; I see it as being useful in police work."

She said, "My friend Bobbie Markowe—"

"Dave's wife, sure."

"—got laryngitis from taping for you."

"Because she rushed it," Claude said. "She did the whole thing in two evenings. You don't have to do it that fast. I leave the recorder; you can take as long as you like. Would you? It would be a big help to me."

Walter came in from the patio; he had been burning leaves out in back with Pete and Kim. He and Claude said hello to each other and shook hands. "I'm sorry," he said to Joanna, "I was supposed to tell you Claude was coming to speak to you. Do you think you'll be able to help him?"

She said, "I have so little free time—"

"Do it in odd minutes," Claude said. "I don't care if it takes a few *weeks.*"

"Well, if you don't mind leaving the recorder that long . . ."

"And you get a present in exchange," Claude said, unstrapping his briefcase on the table. "I leave an extra cartridge, you tape any little lullabies or things you like to sing to the kids, and I transcribe them onto a record. If you're out for an evening the sitter can play it."

"Oh, that'd be nice," she said, and Walter said, "You could do 'The Goodnight Song' and 'Good Morning Starshine.' "

"Anything you want," Claude said. "The more the merrier."

"I'd better get back outside," Walter said. "The fire's still burning. See you, Claude."

"Right," Claude said.

Joanna gave Claude his tea, and he showed her how to load and use the tape recorder, a handsome one in a black leather case. He gave her eight yellow-boxed cartridges and a black loose-leaf binder.

"My gosh, there's a lot," she said, leafing through curled and mended pages typed in triple columns.

"It goes quickly," Claude said. "You just say each word clearly in your regular voice and take a little stop before the next one. And see that the needle stays in the red. You want to practice?"

They had Thanksgiving dinner with Walter's brother Dan and his family. It was arranged by Walter and Dan's mother and was meant to be a reconciliation—the brothers had been on the outs for a year because of a dispute about their father's estate—but the dispute flared again, grown in bitterness as the disputed property had grown in value. Walter and Dan shouted, their mother shouted louder, and Joanna made difficult explanations to Pete and Kim in the car going home.

She took pictures of Bobbie's oldest boy Jonathan working with his microscope, and men in a cherry picker trimming trees on Norwood Road. She was trying to get up a portfolio of at least a dozen first-rate photos—to dazzle the agency into a contract.

The first snow fell on a night when Walter was at the Men's Association. She watched it from the den window: a scant powder of glittery white, swirling in the light of the walk lamppost. Nothing that would amount to anything. But more would come. Fun, good pictures—and the bother of boots and snowsuits.

Across the street, in the Claybrooks' living-room window, Donna Claybrook sat polishing what looked like an athletic trophy, buffing at it with steady mechanical movements. Joanna watched her and shook her head. *They never stop, these Stepford wives,* she thought.

It sounded like the first line of a poem.

They never stop, these Stepford wives. They something something *all their lives.* Work like robots. Yes, that would fit. *They work like robots all their lives.*

She smiled. Try sending *that* to the *Chronicle.*

She went to the desk and sat down and moved the pen she had left as a placemark on the typed page. She listened for a moment—to the silence from upstairs—and switched the recorder on. With a finger to the page, she leaned toward the microphone propped against the framed Ike Mazzard drawing of her. "Taker. Takes. Taking," she said. "Talcum. Talent. Talented. Talk. Talkative. Talked. Talker. Talking. Talks."

Two

She would only want to move, she decided, if she found an absolutely perfect house; one that, besides having the right number of right-size rooms, needed practically no redecoration and had an existing darkroom or something darn close to one. And it would have to cost no more than the fifty-two-five they had paid (and could still get, Walter was sure) for the Stepford house.

A tall order, and she wasn't going to waste too much time trying to fill it. But she went out looking with Bobbie one cold bright early-December morning.

Bobbie was looking *every* morning—in Norwood, Eastbridge, and New Sharon. As soon as she found something right—and she was far more flexible in her demands than Joanna—she was going to pressure Dave for an immediate move, despite the boys' having to change schools in the middle of the year. "Better a little disruption in their lives than a zombie-ized mother," she said. She really was drinking bottled water, and wasn't eating any locally grown produce. "You can buy bottled oxygen, you know," Joanna said.

"Screw you. I can see you now, comparing Ajax to your present cleanser."

The looking inclined Joanna to look more; the women they met—Eastbridge homeowners and a real-estate broker named Miss Kirgassa—were alert, lively, and quirky, confirming by contrast the blandness of Stepford women. And Eastbridge offered a wide range of community activities, for women and for men *and* women. There was even a NOW chapter in formation. "Why didn't you look here first?" Miss Kirgassa asked, rocketing her car down a zigzag road at terrifying speed.

"My husband had heard—" Joanna said, clutching the armrest, watching the road, tramping on wished-for brakes.

"It's *dead* there. We're much more with-it."

"We'd like to get back there to pack though," Bobbie said from in back.

Miss Kirgassa brayed a laugh. "I can drive these roads blindfolded," she said. "I want to show you two more places after this one."

On the way back to Stepford, Bobbie said, "That's for me. I'm going to be a broker, I just decided. You get out, you meet people, and you get to look in everyone's closets. And you can set your own hours. I mean it, I'm going to find out what the requirements are."

They got a letter from the Department of Health, two pages long. It assured them that their interest in environmental protection was shared by both their state and county governments. Industrial installations throughout the state were subject to stringent anti-pollutionary regulations such as the following. These were enforced not only by frequent inspection of the installations themselves, but also by regular examination of soil, water, and air samples. There was no indication whatsoever of harmful pollution in the Stepford area, nor of any naturally occurring chemical presence that might produce a tranquilizing or depressant effect. They could rest assured that their concern was groundless, but their letter was appreciated nonetheless.

"Bullshit," Bobbie said, and stayed with the bottled water. She brought a thermos of coffee with her whenever she came to Joanna's.

Walter was lying on his side, facing away from her, when she came out of the bathroom. She sat down on the bed, turned the lamp off, and got in under the blanket. She lay on her back and watched the ceiling take shape over her.

"Walter?" she said.

"Mm?"

"Was that any good?" she asked. "For you?"

"Sure it was," he said. "Wasn't it for you?"

"Yes," she said.

He didn't say anything.

"I've had the feeling that it hasn't been," she said. "Good for you. The last few times."

"No," he said. "It's been fine. Just like always."

She lay seeing the ceiling. She thought of Charmaine, who wouldn't let Ed catch her (or had she changed in *that* too?), and she remembered Bobbie's remark about Dave's odd ideas.

"Good night," Walter said.

"Is there anything," she asked, "that I—don't do that you'd like me to do? Or that I *do* do that you'd like me not to?"

He didn't say anything, and then he said, "Whatever *you* want to do, that's all." He turned over and looked at her, up on his elbow. "Really," he said, and smiled, "it's fine. Maybe I've been a little tired lately because of the commuting." He kissed her cheek. "Go to sleep," he said.

"Are you—having an affair with Esther?"

"Oh for God's sake," he said. "She's going with a *Black Panther.* I'm not having an affair with anybody."

"A Black Panther?"

"That's what Don's secretary told *him.* We don't even *talk* about sex; all I do is correct her spelling. Come on, let's get to sleep." He kissed her cheek and turned away from her.

She turned over onto her stomach and closed her eyes. She shifted and stirred, trying to settle herself comfortably.

They went to a movie in Norwood with Bobbie and Dave, and spent an evening with them in front of the fire, playing Monopoly kiddingly.

A heavy snow fell on a Saturday night, and Walter gave up his Sunday-afternoon football-watching, not very happily, to take Pete and Kim sledding on Winter Hill while she drove to New Sharon and shot a roll and a half of color in a bird sanctuary.

Pete got the lead in his class Christmas play; and Walter, on the way home one night, either lost his wallet or had his pocket picked.

She brought sixteen photos in to the agency. Bob Silverberg, the man she dealt with there, admired them gratifyingly but told her that the agency wasn't signing contracts with *anybody* at that time. He kept the photos, saying he would let her know in a day or two whether he felt any of them were marketable. She had lunch, disappointedly, with an old friend, Doris Lombardo, and did some Christmas shopping for Walter and her parents.

Ten of the pictures came back, including "Off Duty," which she decided at once she would enter in the next *Saturday Review* contest. Among the six the agency had kept and would handle was "Student," the one of Jonny Markowe at his microscope. She called Bobbie and told her. "I'll give him ten per cent of whatever it makes," she said.

"Does that mean we can stop giving him allowance?"

"You'd better not. My best one's made a little over a thousand so far, but the other two have only made about two hundred each."

"Well, that's not bad for a kid who looks like Peter Lorre," Bobbie said. "Him I mean, not you. Listen, I was going to call you. Can you take Adam for the weekend? Would you?"

"Sure," she said. "Pete and Kim would love it. Why?"

"Dave's had a brainstorm; we're going to have a weekend alone, just the two of us. Second-honeymoon time."

A sense of beforeness touched her; déjà vu. She brushed it away. "That's great," she said.

"We've got Jonny and Kenny booked in the neighborhood," Bobbie said, "but I thought Adam would have a better time at your place."

"Sure," Joanna said, "it'll make it easier to keep Pete and Kim out of each other's hair. What are you doing, going into the city?"

"No, just staying here. And getting snowed in, we hope. I'll bring him over tomorrow after school, okay? And pick him up late Sunday."

"Fine. How's the house-hunting?"

"Not so good. I saw a beauty in Norwood this morning, but they're not getting out till April first."

"So stick around."

"No, thanks. Want to get together?"

"I can't; I've *got* to do some cleaning. Really."

"You see? You're changing. That Stepford magic is starting to work."

A black woman in an orange scarf and a striped fake-fur coat stood waiting at the library desk, her fingertips resting on a stack of books. She glanced at Joanna and nodded with a near-smile; Joanna nodded and near-smiled back; and the black woman looked away—at the empty chair behind the desk, and the bookshelves behind the chair. She was tall and tan-skinned, with close-cropped black hair and large dark eyes—exotic-looking and attractive. About thirty.

Joanna, going to the desk, took her gloves off and got the postcard out of her pocket. She looked at Miss Austrian's namestand on the desk, and at the books under the long slim fingers of the black woman a few feet away. *A Severed Head* by Iris Murdoch, with *I Know Why the Caged Bird Sings* and *The Magus* underneath it. Joanna looked at the postcard; Skinner, *Beyond Freedom & Dignity* would be held for her until 12/11. She wanted to say something friendly and welcoming—the woman was surely the wife or daughter of the black family the Welcome Wagon lady had mentioned—but she didn't want to be white-liberal patronizing. Would she say something if the woman *weren't* black? Yes, in a situation like this she—"We could walk off with the whole place if we wanted to," the black woman said, and Joanna smiled at her and said, "We ought to; teach her to stay on the job." She nodded toward the desk.

The black woman smiled. "Is it always this empty?" she asked.

"I've never seen it *this* way before," Joanna said. "But I've only been here in the afternoon and on Saturdays."

"Are you new in Stepford?"

"Three months."

"Three *days* for me," the black woman said.

"I hope you like it."

"I think I will."

Joanna put her hand out. "I'm Joanna Eberhart," she said, smiling.

"Ruthanne Hendry," the black woman said, smiling and shaking Joanna's hand.

Joanna tipped her head and squinted. "I *know* that name," she said. "I've seen it someplace."

The woman smiled. "Do you have any small children?" she asked.

Joanna nodded, puzzled.

"I've done a children's book, *Penny Has a Plan,*" the woman said. "They've got it here; I checked the catalog first thing."

"Of *course,*" Joanna said. "Kim had it out about two weeks ago! And loved it! I did too; it's so good to find one where a girl actually *does* something besides make tea for her dolls."

"Subtle propaganda," Ruthanne Hendry said, smiling.

"You did the illustrations too," Joanna said. "They were terrific!"

"Thank you."

"Are you doing another one?"

Ruthanne Hendry nodded. "I've got one laid out," she said. "I'll be starting the real work as soon as we get settled."

"I'm sorry," Miss Austrian said, coming limping from the back of the room. "It's so quiet here in the morning that I"—she stopped and blinked, and came limping on—"work in the office. Have to get one of those bells people can tap on. Hello, Mrs. Eberhart." She smiled at Joanna, and at Ruthanne Hendry.

"Hello," Joanna said. "This is one of your authors. *Penny Has a Plan.* Ruthanne Hendry."

"Oh?" Miss Austrian sat down heavily in the chair and held its arms with plump pink hands. "That's a very popular book," she said. "We have two copies in circulation and they're both replacements."

"I *like* this library," Ruthanne Hendry said. "Can I join?"

"Do you live in Stepford?"

"Yes, I just moved here."

"Then you're welcome to join," Miss Austrian said. She opened a drawer, took out a white card, and put it down beside the stack of books.

At the Center luncheonette's counter, empty except for two telephone repairmen, Ruthanne stirred her coffee, and looking at Joanna, said, "Tell me something, on the level: was there much reaction to our buying here?"

"None at all that I heard of," Joanna said. "It's not a town where reactions can develop—to anything. There's no place where people really intersect, except the Men's Association."

"They're all right," Ruthanne said. "Royal is joining tomorrow night. But the *women* in the neighborhood—"

"Oh listen," Joanna said, "that doesn't have anything to do with *color,* believe me. They're like that with everybody. No time for a cup of coffee, right? Riveted on their housework?"

Ruthanne nodded. "I don't mind for myself," she said. "I'm very self-sufficient, otherwise I wouldn't have gone along with the move. But I—"

Joanna told her about the Stepford women, and how Bobbie was even planning to move away to avoid becoming like them.

Ruthanne smiled. "There's *nothing* that's going to make a hausfrau out of *me,"* she said. "If *they're* that way, fine. I was just concerned about it being about color because of the girls." She had two of them, four and six; and her husband Royal was chairman of the sociology department of one of the city universities. Joanna told her about Walter and Pete and Kim, and about her photography.

They exchanged phone numbers. "I turned into a hermit when I was working on *Penny,"* Ruthanne said, "but I'll call you sooner or later."

"I'll call *you,"* Joanna said. "If you're busy, just say so. I want you to meet Bobbie; I'm sure you'll like each other."

On the way to their cars—they had left them in front of the library—Joanna saw Dale Coba looking at her from a distance. He stood with a lamb in his arms, by a group of men setting up a crèche near the Historical Society cottage. She nodded at him, and he, holding the live-looking lamb, nodded and smiled.

She told Ruthanne who he was, and asked her if she knew that Ike Mazzard lived in Stepford.

"Who?"

"Ike Mazzard. The illustrator."

Ruthanne had never heard of him, which made Joanna feel very old. Or very white.

Having Adam for the weekend was a mixed blessing. On Saturday he and Pete and Kim played beautifully together, inside the house and out; but on Sunday, a freezing-cold overcast day when Walter laid claim to the family room for football-watching (fairly enough after last Sunday's sledding), Adam and Pete became, serially, soldiers in a blanket-over-the-dining-table fort, explorers in the cellar ("Stay out of that darkroom!"), and Star Trek people in Pete's room —all of them sharing, strangely enough, a single common enemy called Kim-She's-Dim. They were loudly and scornfully watchful, preparing defenses; and poor Kim *was* dim, wanting only to join them, not to crayon or help file negatives, not even—Joanna was desperate—to bake cookies. Adam and Pete ignored threats, Kim ignored blandishments, Walter ignored everything.

Joanna was glad when Bobbie and Dave came to pick Adam up.

But she was glad she had taken him when she saw how great they looked.

Bobbie had had her hair done and was absolutely beautiful—either due to make-up or love-making, probably both. And Dave looked jaunty and keyed up and happy. They brought bracing coldness into the entrance hall. "Hi, Joanna, how'd it go?" Dave said, rubbing leather-gloved hands; and Bobbie, wrapped in her raccoon coat, said, "I hope Adam wasn't any trouble."

"Not a speck," Joanna said. "You look marvelous, both of you!"

"We *feel* marvelous," Dave said, and Bobbie smiled and said, "It was a lovely weekend. Thank you for helping us manage it."

"Forget it," Joanna said. "I'm going to plunk Pete with *you* one of these weekends."

"We'll be glad to take him," Bobbie said, and Dave said, "Whenever you want, just say the word. *Adam? Time to go!*"

"He's up in Pete's room."

Dave cupped his gloved hands and shouted, *"Ad-am! We're here! Get your stuff!"*

"Take your coats off," Joanna said.

"Got to pick up Jon and Kenny," Dave said, and Bobbie said, "I'm sure you'd like some peace and quiet. It must have been hectic."

"Well, it hasn't been my most *restful* Sunday," Joanna said. "Yesterday was great though."

"Hi there!" Walter said, coming in from the kitchen with a glass in his hand.

Bobbie said, "Hello, Walter," and Dave said, "Hi, buddy!"

"How was the second honeymoon?" Walter asked.

"Better than the first," Dave said. "Just shorter, that's all." He grinned at Walter.

Joanna looked at Bobbie, expecting her to say something funny. Bobbie smiled at her and looked toward the stairs. "Hello, gumdrop," she said. "Did you have a nice weekend?"

"I don't want to go," Adam said, standing tilted to keep his shopping bag clear of the stair. Pete and Kim stood behind him. Kim said, "Can't he stay another night?"

"No, dear, there's school tomorrow," Bobbie said, and Dave said, "Come on, pal, we've got to collect the rest of the Mafia."

Adam came sulkily down the stairs, and Joanna went to the closet for his coat and boots. "Hey," Dave said, "I've got some information on that stock you asked me about." Walter said, "Oh, good," and he and Dave went into the living room.

Joanna gave Adam's coat to Bobbie, and Bobbie thanked her and held it open for Adam. He put his shopping bag down and winged back his arms to the coat sleeves.

Joanna, holding Adam's boots, said, "Do you want a bag for these?"

"No, don't bother," Bobbie said. She turned Adam around and helped him with his buttons.

"You smell nice," he said.

"Thanks, gumdrop."

He looked at the ceiling and at her. "I don't like you to *call* me that," he said. "I *used* to, but now I don't."

"I'm sorry," she said. "I won't do it again." She smiled at him and kissed him on the forehead.

Walter and Dave came out of the living room, and Adam picked up his shopping bag and said good-by to Pete and Kim. Joanna gave Adam's boots to Bobbie and touched cheeks with her. Bobbie's was still cool from outside, and she *did* smell nice. "Speak to you tomorrow," Joanna said.

"Sure," Bobbie said. They smiled at each other. Bobbie moved to Walter at the door and offered her cheek. He hesitated—Joanna wondered why—and pecked it.

Dave kissed Joanna, clapped Walter on the arm—"So long, buddy"—and steered Adam out after Bobbie.

"Can we go in the family room now?" Pete asked.

"It's all yours," Walter said.

Pete ran away and Kim ran after him.

Joanna and Walter stood at the cold glass of the storm door, looking out at Bobbie and Dave and Adam getting into their car.

"Fantastic," Walter said.

"Don't they look great?" Joanna said. "Bobbie didn't even look that good at the party. Why didn't you want to kiss her?"

Walter didn't say anything, and then he said, "Oh, I don't know, *cheek-*kissing. It's so damn show-business."

"I never noticed you objecting before."

"Then I've changed, I guess," he said.

She watched the car doors close, and its headlights flash on. "How about *us* having a weekend alone?" she said. "They'll take Pete, they said they would, and I'm sure the Van Sants would take Kim."

"That'd be great," he said. "Right after the holidays."

"Or maybe the Hendrys," she said. "*They've* got a six-year-old girl, and I'd like Kim to get to know a black family."

The car pulled away, red taillights shining, and Walter closed the door and locked it and thumbed down the switch of the outside lights. "Want a drink?" he asked.

"And how," Joanna said. "I need one after today."

Ugh, what a Monday: Pete's room to be reassembled and all the others straightened out, the beds to be changed, washing (and she'd let it pile up, of course), tomorrow's shopping list to make up, and three pairs of Pete's pants to be lengthened. That was what she was *doing;* never mind what *else* had to be done—the Christmas shopping, and the Christmas-card addressing, and making Pete's costume for the play (thanks for *that,* Miss Turner). Bobbie didn't call, thank goodness; this wasn't a day for kaffee-klatsching. *Is she right?* Joanna wondered. *Am I changing?* Hell, no; the housework *had* to be caught up with once in a while, otherwise the place would turn into—well, into *Bobbie's* place. Besides, a real Stepford wife would sail through it all very calmly and efficiently, not running the vacuum cleaner over its cord and then mashing her fingers getting the cord out from around the damn roller thing.

She gave Pete hell about not putting toys away when he was done playing with them, and he sulked for an hour and wouldn't talk to her. And Kim was coughing.

And Walter begged off his turn at K.P. and ran out to get into Herb Sundersen's full car. Busy time at the Men's Association; the Christmas-Toys project. (Who for? Were there needy children in Stepford? She'd seen no sign of any.)

She cut a sheet to start Pete's costume, a snowman, and played a game of Concentration with him and Kim (who only coughed once but keep the fingers crossed); and then she addressed Christmas cards down through the L's and went to bed at ten. She fell asleep with the Skinner book.

Tuesday was better. When she had cleaned up the breakfast mess and made the beds, she called Bobbie—no answer; she was house-hunting—and drove to the Center and did the week's main marketing. She went to the Center again after lunch, took pictures of the crèche, and got home just ahead of the school bus.

Walter did the dishes and *then* went to the Men's Association. The toys were for kids in the city, ghetto kids and kids in hospitals. Complain about *that,* Ms. Eberhart. Or would she still be Ms. Ingalls? Ms. Ingalls-Eberhart?

After she got Pete and Kim bathed and into bed she called Bobbie. It was odd that Bobbie hadn't called *her* in two full days. "Hello?" Bobbie said.

"Long time no speak."

"Who's this?"

"*Joanna.*"

"Oh, hello," Bobbie said. "How are you?"

"Fine. Are you? You sound sort of blah."

"No, I'm fine," Bobbie said.

"Any luck this morning?"

"What do you mean?"

"House-hunting."

"I went shopping this morning," Bobbie said.

"Why didn't you call me?"

"I went very early."

"I went around ten; we must have just missed each other."

Bobbie didn't say anything.

"Bobbie?"

"Yes?"

"Are you *sure* you're okay?"

"Positive. I'm in the middle of some ironing."

"At this hour?"

"Dave needs a shirt for tomorrow."

"Oh. Call me in the morning then; maybe we can have lunch. Unless you're going house-hunting."

"I'm not," Bobbie said.

"Call me then, okay?"

"Okay," Bobbie said. " 'By, Joanna."

"Good-by."

She hung up and sat looking at the phone and her hand on it. The thought struck her—ridiculously—that Bobbie had changed the way Charmaine had. No, not Bobbie; impossible. She must have had a fight with Dave, a major one that she wasn't ready to talk about yet. Or could she herself have offended Bobbie in some way without being aware of it? Had she said something Sunday about Adam's stay-over that Bobbie might have misinterpreted? But no, they'd parted as friendly as ever, touching cheeks and saying they'd speak to each other. (Yet even then, now that she thought about it, Bobbie had seemed different; she—hadn't said the sort of things she usually did, and she'd moved more slowly too.) Maybe she and Dave had been smoking pot over the weekend. They'd tried it a couple of times without much effect, Bobbie had said. Maybe this time . . .

She addressed a few Christmas cards.

She called Ruthanne Hendry, who was friendly and glad to hear from her. They talked about *The Magus,* which Ruthanne was enjoying as much as Joanna had, and Ruthanne told her about her new book, another Penny story. They agreed to have lunch together the following week. Joanna would speak to Bobbie, and the three of them would go to the French place in Eastbridge. Ruthanne would call her Monday morning.

She addressed Christmas cards, and read the Skinner book in bed until Walter came home. "I spoke to Bobbie tonight," she said. "She sounded— different, washed out."

"She's probably tired from all that running around she's been doing," Walter said, emptying his jacket pockets onto the bureau.

"She seemed different Sunday too," Joanna said. "She didn't say—"

"She had some make-up on, that's all," Walter said. "You're not going to start in with that chemical business, are you?"

She frowned, pressing the closed book to her blanketed knees. "Did Dave say anything about their trying pot again?" she asked.

"No," Walter said, "but maybe that's the answer."

They made love, but she was tense and couldn't really give herself, and it wasn't very good.

Bobbie didn't call. Around one o'clock Joanna drove over. The dogs barked at her as she got out of the station wagon. They were chained to an overhead line behind the house, the corgi up on his hind legs, pawing air and yipping, the sheepdog standing shaggy and stock-stoll, barking "Ruff, ruff, ruff, ruff, ruff." Bobbie's blue Chevy stood in the driveway.

Bobbie, in her immaculate living room—cushions all fluffed, woodwork gleaming, magazines fanned on the polished table behind the sofa—smiled at Joanna and said, "I'm sorry, I was so busy it slipped my mind. Have you had lunch? Come on into the kitchen. I'll fix you a sandwich. What would you like?"

She looked the way she had on Sunday—beautiful, her hair done, her face made-up. And she was wearing some kind of padded high-uplift bra under her green sweater, and a hip-whittling girdle under the brown pleated skirt.

In her immaculate kitchen she said, "Yes, I've changed. I realized I was being awfully sloppy and self-indulgent. It's no disgrace to be a good home-maker. I've decided to do my job conscientiously, the way Dave does his, and to be more careful about my appearance. Are you sure you don't want a sandwich?"

Joanna shook her head. "*Bobbie,*" she said, "I—Don't you see what's happened? Whatever's around here—it's got *you,* the way it got Charmaine!"

Bobbie smiled at her. "Nothing's got me," she said. "There's nothing around. That was a lot of nonsense. Stepford's a fine healthful place to live."

"You—don't want to move any more?"

"Oh no," Bobbie said. "That was nonsense too. I'm perfectly happy here. Can't I at least make you a cup of coffee?"

She called Walter at his office. "Oh good ahft*ernoon!*" Esther said. "So nice to speak to you! It must be a *super* day up there, or are you hyar in town?"

"No, I'm at home," she said. "May I speak to Walter, please?"

"I'm afraid he's in conference at the moment."

"It's important. Please tell him."

"Hold on a sec then."

She held on, sitting at the den desk, looking at the papers and envelopes she had taken from the center drawer, and at the calendar—*Tue. Dec. 14,* yester-day—and the Ike Mazzard drawing.

"He'll be right with you, Mrs. Eberhart," Esther said. "Nothing wrong with Peter or Kim, I hope."

"No, they're fine."

"Good. They must be having a—"

"Hello?" Walter said.

"Walter?"

"Hello. What is it?"

"Walter, I want you to listen to me and don't argue," she said. "Bobbie *has* changed. I was over there. The house looks like—It's *spotless,* Walter; it's *immaculate*! And she's got herself all—Listen, do you have the bankbooks? I've been looking for them and I can't find them. Walter?"

"Yes, I've got them," he said. "I've been buying some stock, on Dave's recommendations. What do you want them for?"

"To see what we've got," she said. "There was a house I saw in Eastbridge that—"

"Joanna."

"—was a little more than this one but—"

"Joanna, listen to me."

"I'm not going to stay here another—"

"Listen to me, damn it!"

She gripped the handset. "Go ahead," she said.

"I'll try to get home early," he said. "Don't do anything till I get there. You hear me? Don't make any commitments or anything. I think I can get away in about half an hour."

"I'm not going to stay here another day," she said.

"Just wait till I get there, will you?" he said. "We can't talk about this on the phone."

"Bring the bankbooks," she said.

"Don't do anything till I get there." The phone clicked dead.

She hung up.

She put the papers and envelopes back into the center drawer and closed it. Then she got the phone book from the shelf and looked up Miss Kirgassa's number in Eastbridge.

The house she was thinking of, the St. Martin house, was still on the market. "In fact I think they've come down a bit since you saw it."

"Would you do me a favor?" she said. "We may be interested; I'll know definitely tomorrow. Would you find out the rock-bottom price they'll take for an immediate sale, and let me know as soon as you can?"

"I'll get right back to you," Miss Kirgassa said. "Do you know if Mrs. Markowe has found something? We had an appointment this morning but she didn't show up."

"She changed her mind, she's not moving," she said. "But I am."

She called Buck Raymond, the broker they'd used in Stepford. "Just hypothetically," she said, "if we were to put the house on the market tomorrow, do you think we could sell it quickly?"

"No doubt about it," Buck said. "There's a steady demand here. I'm sure you could get what you paid, maybe even a little more. Aren't you happy in it?"

"No," she said.

"I'm sorry to hear that. Shall I start showing it? There's a couple here right now who are—"

"No, no, not yet," she said. "I'll let you know tomorrow."

"Now just hold on a minute," Walter said, making spread-handed calming gestures.

"No," she said, shaking her head. "No. Whatever it is takes four months to work, which means I've got one more month to go. Maybe less; we moved here September fourth."

"For God's sake, Joanna—"

"Charmaine moved here in July," she said. "She changed in November. Bobbie moved here in August and now it's December." She turned and walked away from him. The sink's faucet was leaking; she hit the handle back hard and the leaking stopped.

"You *had* the letter from the Department of Health," Walter said.

"Bullshit, to quote Bobbie." She turned and faced him. "There's *something*, there's *got* to be," she said. "Go take a look. Would you do that, please? She's got her bust shoved out to here, and her behind girdled down to practically nothing! The house is like a commercial. Like Carol's, and Donna's, and Kit Sundersen's!"

"She had to clean it sooner or later; it was a pigsty."

"She *changed*, Walter! She doesn't *talk* the same, she doesn't *think* the same —and I'm not going to wait around for it to happen to me!"

"We're not going to—"

Kim came in from the patio, her face red in its fur-edged hood.

"Stay out, Kim," Walter said.

"We want some supplies," Kim said. "We're going on a hike."

Joanna went to the cookie jar and opened it and got out cookies. "Here," she said, putting them into Kim's mittened hands. "Stay near the house, it's getting dark."

"Can we have Oreos?"

"We don't *have* Oreos. Go on."

Kim went out. Walter closed the door.

Joanna brushed crumbs from her hand. "It's a nicer house than this one," she said, "and we can have it for fifty-three-five. And we can get that for this one; Buck Raymond said so."

"We're not moving," Walter said.

"You *said* we would!"

"Next summer, not—"

"I won't be *me* next summer!"

"Joanna—"

"Don't you understand? It's going to happen to *me*, in *January*!"

"*Nothing's* going to happen to you!"

"That's what I told Bobbie! I kidded her about the bottled water!"

He came close to her. "There's nothing in the water, there's nothing in the air," he said. "They changed for exactly the reasons they told you: because they realized they'd been lazy and negligent. If Bobbie's taking an interest in her appearance, it's about time. It wouldn't hurt *you* to look in a mirror once in a while."

She looked at him, and he looked away, flushing, and looked back at her. "I mean it," he said. "You're a very pretty woman and you don't do a damn thing with yourself any more unless there's a party or something."

He turned away from her and went and stood at the stove. He twisted a knob one way and the other.

She looked at him.

He said, "I'll tell you what we'll do—"

"Do you *want* me to change?" she asked.

"Of course not, don't be silly." He turned around.

"Is *that* what you want?" she asked. "A cute little gussied-up hausfrau?"

"All I said was—"

"Is *that* why Stepford was the only place to move? Did somebody pass the message to you? 'Take her to Stepford, Wally old pal; there's something in the air there; she'll change in four months.' "

"There's nothing in the air," Walter said. "The message I got was good schools and low taxes. Now look, I'm trying to see this from your viewpoint and make some kind of fair judgment. You want to move because you're afraid you're going to 'change'; and I think you're being irrational and—a little hysterical, and that moving at this point would impose an undue hardship on all of us, especially Pete and Kim." He stopped and drew a breath. "All right, let's do this," he said. "You have a talk with Alan Hollingsworth, and if he says you're—"

"With who?"

"Alan Hollingsworth," he said. His eyes went from hers. "The psychiatrist. You know." His eyes came back. "If he says you're not going through some—"

"I don't need a psychiatrist," she said. "And if I did, I wouldn't want Alan Hollingsworth. I saw his wife at the P.T.A.; she's one of *them.* You *bet* he'd think I'm irrational."

"Then pick someone else," he said. "Anyone you want. If you're not going through some kind of—delusion or something, then we'll move, as soon as we possibly can. I'll look at that house tomorrow morning, and even put a deposit on it."

"I don't need a psychiatrist," she said. "I need to get out of Stepford."

"Now come on, Joanna," he said. "I think I'm being damn fair. You're asking us to undergo a major upheaval, and I think you owe it to all of us, including yourself—*especially* yourself—to make sure you're seeing things as clearly as you think you are."

She looked at him.

"Well?" he said.

She didn't say anything. She looked at him.

"Well?" he said. "Doesn't that sound reasonable?"

She said, "Bobbie changed when she was alone with Dave, and Charmaine changed when she was alone with Ed."

He looked away, shaking his head.

"Is that when it's going to happen to *me?*" she asked. "On *our* weekend alone?"

"It was *your idea,*" he said.

"Would *you* have suggested it if *I* hadn't?"

"Now you *see?*" he said. "Do you hear how you're talking? I want you to think about what I said. You can't disrupt all our lives on the spur of the moment this way. It's unreasonable to expect to." He turned around and went out of the kitchen.

She stood there, and put her hand to her forehead and closed her eyes. She stayed that way, and then lowered her hand, opened her eyes, and shook her head. She went to the refrigerator and opened it, and took out a covered bowl and a market-pack of meat.

He sat at the desk, writing on a yellow pad. A cigarette in the ashtray ribboned smoke up into the lamplight. He looked at her and took his glasses off.

"All right," she said. "I'll—speak to someone. But a woman."

"Good," he said. "That's a good idea."

"And you'll put a deposit on the house tomorrow?"

"Yes," he said. "Unless there's something radically wrong with it."

"There isn't," she said. "It's a good house and it's only six years old. With a good mortgage."

"Fine," he said.

She stood looking at him. "*Do* you want me to change?" she asked him.

"No," he said. "I'd just like you to put on a little lipstick once in a while. That's no big change. I'd like *me* to change a little too, like lose a few pounds for instance."

She pushed her hair back straight. "I'm going to work down in the darkroom for a while," she said. "Pete's still awake. Will you keep an ear open?"

"Sure," he said, and smiled at her.

She looked at him, and turned and went away.

She called the good old Department of Health, and they referred her to the county medical society, and *they* gave her the names and phone numbers of five women psychiatrists. The two nearest ones, in Eastbridge, were booked solid through mid-January; but the third, in Sheffield, north of Norwood, could see her on Saturday afternoon at two. Dr. Margaret Fancher; she sounded nice over the phone.

She finished the Christmas cards, and Pete's costume; bought toys and books for Pete and Kim, and a bottle of champagne for Bobbie and Dave. She had got a gold belt buckle for Walter in the city, and had planned to canvass the Route Nine antique stores for legal documents; instead she bought him a tan cardigan.

The first Christmas cards came in—from her parents and Walter's junior partners, from the McCormicks, the Chamalians, and the Van Sants. She lined them up on a living-room bookshelf.

A check came from the agency: a hundred and twenty-five dollars.

On Friday afternoon, despite two inches of snow and more falling, she put Pete and Kim into the station wagon and drove over to Bobbie's.

Bobbie welcomed them pleasantly; Adam and Kenny and the dogs welcomed them noisily. Bobbie made hot chocolate, and Joanna carried the tray into the family room. "Watch your step," Bobbie said, "I waxed the floor this morning."

"I noticed," Joanna said.

She sat in the kitchen watching Bobbie—beautiful, shapely Bobbie—cleaning the oven with paper towels and a spray can of cleaner. "What have you *done* to yourself, for God's sake?" she asked.

"I'm not eating the way I used to," Bobbie said. "And I'm getting more exercise."

"You must have lost ten pounds!"

"No, just two or three. I'm wearing a girdle."

"Bobbie, will you *please* tell me what *happened* last weekend?"

"Nothing happened. We stayed in."

"Did you smoke anything, take anything? Drugs, I mean."

"No. Don't be silly."

"Bobbie, you're not *you* any more! Can't you see that? You've become like the others!"

"Honestly, Joanna, that's nonsense," Bobbie said. "Of course I'm me. I simply realized that I was awfully sloppy and self-indulgent, and now I'm doing my job conscientiously, the way Dave does his."

"I know, I know," she said. "How does *he* feel about it?"

"He's very happy."

"I'll bet he is."

"This stuff really works. Do you use it?"

I'm not crazy, she thought. *I'm not crazy.*

Jonny and two other boys were making a snowman in front of the house next door. She left Pete and Kim in the station wagon and went over and said hello to him. "Oh, hi!" he said. "Do you have any money for me?"

"Not yet," she said, shielding her face against the downfall of thick flakes. "Jonny, I—I can't get over the way your mother's changed."

"Hasn't she?" he said, nodding, panting.

"I can't understand it," she said.

"Neither can I," he said. "She doesn't shout any more, she makes hot breakfasts . . ." He looked over at the house and frowned. Snowflakes clung to his face. "I hope it lasts," he said, "but I bet it doesn't."

Dr. Fancher was a small elfin-faced woman in her early fifties, with short swirls of graying brown hair, a sharp marionette nose, and smiling blue-gray eyes. She wore a dark blue dress, a gold pin engraved with the Chinese Yang-and-

Yin symbol, and a wedding ring. Her office was cheerful, with Chippendale furniture and Paul Klee prints, and striped curtains translucent against the brightness of sun and snow outside. There was a brown leather couch with a paper-covered headrest, but Joanna sat in the chair facing the mahogany desk, on which dozens of small white papers flag-edged the sides of a green blotter.

She said, "I'm here at my husband's suggestion. We moved to Stepford early in September, and I want to move away as soon as possible. We've put a deposit on a house in Eastbridge, but only because I insisted on it. He feels I'm—being irrational."

She told Dr. Fancher why she wanted to move: about Stepford women, and how Charmaine and then Bobbie had changed and become like them. "Have you been to Stepford?" she asked.

"Only once," Dr. Fancher said. "I heard that it was worth looking at, which it is. I've also heard that it's an insular, unsocial community."

"Which it is, believe me."

Dr. Fancher knew of the city in Texas with the low crime rate. "Lithium is what's doing it, apparently," she said. "There was a paper about it in one of the journals."

"Bobbie and I wrote to the Department of Health," Joanna said. "They said there was nothing in Stepford that could be affecting anyone. I suppose they thought we were crackpots. At the time, actually, I thought *Bobbie*—was being a little overanxious. I only helped with the letter because she asked me to . . ." She looked at her clasped hands and worked them against each other.

Dr. Fancher stayed silent.

"I've begun to suspect—" Joanna said. "Oh Jesus, 'suspect'; that sounds so —" She worked her hands together, looking at them.

Dr. Fancher said, "Begun to suspect what?"

She drew her hands apart and wiped them on her skirt. "I've begun to suspect that the men are behind it," she said. She looked at Dr. Fancher.

Dr. Fancher didn't smile or seem surprised. "Which men?" she asked.

Joanna looked at her hands. "My husband," she said. "Bobbie's husband, Charmaine's." She looked at Dr. Fancher. "All of them," she said.

She told her about the Men's Association.

"I was taking pictures in the Center one night a couple of months ago," she said. "That's where those Colonial shops are; the house overlooks them. The windows were open and there was—a smell in the air. Of medicine, or chemicals. And then the shades were pulled down, maybe because they knew I was out there; this policeman had seen me, he stopped and talked to me." She leaned forward. "There are a lot of sophisticated industrial plants on Route Nine," she said, "and a lot of the men who have high-level jobs in them live in Stepford and belong to the Men's Association. *Something* goes on there every night, and I don't think it's just fixing toys for needy children, and pool and poker. There's Ameri-Chem-Willis, and Stevenson Biochemical. They could be—concocting something that the Department of Health wouldn't know about, up there at the Men's Association . . ." She sat back in the chair, wiping her hands against her skirted thighs, not looking at Dr. Fancher.

Dr. Fancher asked her questions about her family background and her interest in photography; about the jobs she had held, and about Walter and Pete and Kim.

"Any move is traumatic to a degree," Dr. Fancher said, "and particularly the city-to-the-suburbs move for a woman who doesn't find her housewife's role totally fulfilling. It can feel pretty much like being sent to Siberia." She smiled at Joanna. "And the holiday season doesn't help matters any," she said. "It tends to magnify anxieties, for everyone. I've often thought that one year we should have a *real* holiday and skip the whole business."

Joanna made a smile.

Dr. Fancher leaned forward, and joining her hands, rested her elbows on the desk. "I can understand your not being happy in a town of highly home-oriented women," she said to Joanna. "*I* wouldn't be either; no woman with outside interests would. But I do wonder—and I imagine your husband does too—whether you would be happy in Eastbridge, or anywhere else at this particular time."

"I think I would be," Joanna said.

Dr. Fancher looked at her hands, pressing and flexing the wedding-ringed one with the other. She looked at Joanna. "Towns develop their character gradually," she said, "as people pick and choose among them. A few artists and writers came here to Sheffield a long time ago; others followed, and people who found them too Bohemian moved away. Now we're an artists-and-writers town; not exclusively, of course, but enough to make us different from Nor-wood and Kimball. I'm sure Stepford developed its character in the same way. That seems to me far more likely than the idea that the men there have banded together to chemically brainwash the women. And could they really do it? They could tranquilize them, yes; but these women don't sound tranquilized to me; they're hard-working and industrious within their own small range of interests. That would be quite a job for even the most advanced chemists."

Joanna said, "I know it sounds—" She rubbed her temple.

"It sounds," Dr. Fancher said, "like the idea of a woman who, like many women today, and with good reason, feels a deep resentment and suspicion of men. One who's pulled two ways by conflicting demands, perhaps more strongly than she's aware; the old conventions on the one hand, and the *new* conventions of the liberated woman on the other."

Joanna, shaking her head, said, "If only you could see what Stepford women are *like*. They're actresses in TV commercials, all of them. No, not even *that*. They're—they're like—" She sat forward. "There was a program four or five weeks ago," she said. "My children were watching it. These figures of all the Presidents, moving around, making different facial expressions. Abraham Lincoln stood up and delivered the Gettysburg Address; he was so lifelike you'd have—" She sat still.

Dr. Fancher waited, and nodded. "Rather than force an immediate move on your family," she said, "I think you should con—"

"Disneyland," Joanna said. "The program was from *Disneyland* . . . "

Dr. Fancher smiled. "I know," she said. "My grandchildren were there last summer. They told me they 'met' Lincoln."

Joanna turned from her, staring.

"I think you should consider trying therapy," Dr. Fancher said. "To identify and clarify your feelings. Then you can make the *right* move—maybe to Eastbridge, maybe back to the city; maybe you'll even find Stepford less oppressive."

Joanna turned to her.

"Will you think about it for a day or two and call me?" Dr. Fancher said. "I'm sure I can help you. It's certainly worth a few hours' exploration, isn't it?"

Joanna sat still, and nodded.

Dr. Fancher took a pen from its holder and wrote on a prescription pad.

Joanna looked at her. She stood up and took her handbag from the desk.

"These will help you in the meantime," Dr. Fancher said, writing. "They're a mild tranquilizer. You can take three a day." She tore off a slip and offered it to Joanna, smiling. "They *won't* make you fascinated with housework," she said.

Joanna took the slip.

Dr. Fancher stood up. "I'll be away Christmas week," she said, "but we could start the week of the third. Will you call me Monday or Tuesday and let me know what you've decided?"

Joanna nodded.

Dr. Fancher smiled, "It's *not* catastrophic," she said. "Really, I'm sure I can help you." She held out her hand.

Joanna shook it and went out.

The library was busy. Miss Austrian said they were down in the cellar. The door on the left, the bottom shelf. Put them back in their proper order. No smoking. Put out the lights.

She went down the steep narrow stairs, touching the wall with one hand. There was no banister.

The door on the left. She found the light switch inside. An eye-sting of fluorescence; the smell of old paper; the whine of a motor, climbing in pitch.

The room was small and low-ceilinged. Walls of shelved magazines surrounded a library table and four kitchen chairs, chrome and red plastic.

Big brown-bound volumes jutted from the bottom shelf all around the room, lying flat, piled six high.

She put her handbag on the table, and took her coat off and laid it over one of the chairs.

She started five years back, leafing backward through the half-a-year volume.

CIVIC AND MEN'S ASSOCIATIONS TO MERGE. The proposed union of the Stepford Civic Association and the Stepford Men's Association has been endorsed by the members of both organizations and will take place within weeks. Thomas C. Miller III and Dale Coba, the respective presidents . . .

She leafed back, through Little League ball games and heavy snowfalls, through thefts, collisions, school-bond disputes.

WOMEN'S CLUB SUSPENDS MEETINGS. The Stepford Women's Club is suspending its bi-weekly meetings because of declining membership, according to Mrs. Richard Ockrey, who assumed the club's presidency only two months ago on the resignation of former president Mrs. Alan Hollingsworth. "It's only a temporary suspension," Mrs. Ockrey said in her home on Fox Hollow Lane. "We're planning a full-scale membership drive and a resumption of meetings in the early spring . . ."

Do tell, Mrs. Ockrey.

She leafed back through ads for old movies and low-priced food, through fire at the Methodist Church and the opening of the incinerator plant.

MEN'S ASSOCIATION BUYS TERHUNE HOUSE. Dale Coba, president of the Stepford . . .

A zoning-law change, a burglary at CompuTech.

She dropped the next-earlier volume down onto the other one. Sitting, she opened the volume at its back.

LEAGUE OF WOMEN VOTERS MAY CLOSE.

So what's so surprising about that?

Unless the recent fall-off in membership is reversed, the Stepford League of Women Voters may be forced to close its doors. So warns the league's new president, Mrs. Theodore Van Sant of Fairview Lane . . .

Carol?

Back, back.

A drought was relieved, a drought grew worse.

MEN'S ASSOCIATION RE-ELECTS COBA. Dale Coba of Anvil Road was elected by acclamation to a second two-year term as president of the steadily expanding . . .

Back two years then.

She jumped three volumes.

A theft, a fire, a bazaar, a snowfall.

She flipped up the pages with one hand, turned them with the other; quickly, quickly.

MEN'S ASSOCIATION FORMED. A dozen Stepford men who repaired the disused barn on Switzer Lane and have been meeting in it for over a year, have formed the Stepford Men's Association and will welcome new members. Dale Coba of Anvil Road has been elected president of the association, Duane T. Anderson of Switzer Lane is vice-president, and Robert Sumner Jr. of Gwen-

dolyn Lane is secretary-treasurer. The purpose of the association, Mr. Coba says, is "strictly social—poker, man-talk, and the pooling of information on crafts and hobbies." The Coba family seems especially apt at getting things started; Mrs. Coba was among the founders of the Stepford Women's Club, although she recently withdrew from it, as did Mrs. Anderson and Mrs. Sumner. Other men in the Stepford Men's Association are Claude Axhelm, Peter J. Duwicki, Frank Ferretti, Steven Margolies, Ike Mazzard, Frank Roddenberry, James J. Scofield, Herbert Sundersen, and Martin I. Weiner. Men interested in further information should . . .

She jumped two more volumes, and now she turned pages in whole-issue clusters, finding each "Notes on Newcomers" in its page-two box.

. . . Mr. Ferretti is an engineer in the systems development laboratory of the CompuTech Corporation.

. . . Mr. Sumner, who holds many patents in dyes and plastics, recently joined the Ameri-Chem-Willis Corporation, where he is doing research in vinyl polymers.

"Notes on Newcomers," "Notes on Newcomers"; stopping only when she saw one of the names, skipping to the end of the article, telling herself she was right, she was right.

. . . Mr. Duwicki, known to his friends as Wick, is in the Instatron Corporation's microcircuitry department.

. . . Mr. Weiner is with the Sono-Trak division of the Instatron Corporation.

. . . Mr. Margolies is with Reed & Saunders, the makers of stabilizing devices whose new plant on Route Nine begins operation next week.

She put volumes back, took other volumes out, dropping them heavily on the table.

. . . Mr. Roddenberry is associate chief of the Compu-Tech Corporation's systems development laboratory.

. . . Mr. Sundersen designs optical sensors for Ulitz Optics, Inc.

And finally she found it.

She read the whole article.

New neighbors on Anvil Road are Mr. and Mrs. Dale Coba and their sons Dale Jr., four, and Darren, two. The Cobas have come here from Anaheim, California, where they lived for six years. "So far we like this part of the country," Mrs. Coba says. "I don't know how we'll feel when winter comes. We're not used to cold weather."

Mr. and Mrs. Coba attended U.C.L.A., and Mr. Coba did postgraduate work at the California Institute of Technology. For the past six years he worked in "audioanimatronics" at Disneyland, helping to create the moving and talking presidential figures featured in the August number of National Geographic. *His hobbies are hunting and piano-playing. Mrs. Coba, who majored in languages, is using her spare time to write a translation of the classic Norwegian novel* The Commander's Daughters.

Mr. Coba's work here will probably be less attention-getting than his work at

Disneyland; he has joined the research and development department of Burn-ham-Massey-Microtech.

She giggled.

Research and development! And *probably less attention-getting!*

She giggled and giggled.

Couldn't stop.

Didn't *want* to!

She laughed, standing up and looking at that "Notes on Newcomers" in its neat box of lines. *PROBABLY be less attention-getting!* Dear God in heaven!

She closed the big brown volume, laughing, and picked it up with a volume beneath it and swung them down to their place on the shelf.

"Mrs. Eberhart?" Miss Austrian upstairs. "It's five of six; we're closing."

Stop laughing, for God's sake. "I'm done!" she called. "I'm just putting them away!"

"Be sure you put them back in the right order."

"I will!" she called.

"And put the lights out."

"*Jawohl!*"

She put all the volumes away, in their right order more or less. "Oh God in heaven!" she said, giggling. "*Probably!*"

She took her coat and handbag, and switched the lights off, and went giggling up the stairs toward Miss Austrian peering at her. No wonder!

"Did you find what you were looking for?" Miss Austrian asked.

"Oh yes," she said, swallowing the giggles. "Thank you very much. You're a fount of knowledge, you and your library. Thank you. Good night."

"Good night," Miss Austrian said.

She went across to the pharmacy, because God knows she *needed* a tranquil-izer. The pharmacy was closing too; half dark, and nobody there but the Cornells. She gave the prescription to Mr. Cornell, and he read it and said, "Yes, you can have this now." He went into the back.

She looked at combs on a rack, smiling. Glass clinked behind her and she turned around.

Mrs. Cornell stood at the wall behind the side counter, outside the lighted part of the pharmacy. She wiped something with a cloth, wiped at the wall shelf, and put the something on it, clinking glass. She was tall and blond, long-legged, full-bosomed; as pretty as—oh, say an Ike Mazzard girl. She took something from the shelf and wiped it, and wiped at the shelf, and put the something on it, clinking glass; and took something from the shelf and—

"Hi there," Joanna said.

Mrs. Cornell turned her head. "Mrs. Eberhart," she said, and smiled. "Hello. How are you?"

"Just fine," Joanna said. "Jim-dandy. How are *you*?"

"Very well, thank you," Mrs. Cornell said. She wiped what she was holding, and wiped at the shelf, and put the something on it, clinking glass; and took something from the shelf and wiped it—

"You do that well," Joanna said.

"It's just dusting," Mrs. Cornell said, wiping at the shelf.

A typewriter peck-peck-pecked from in back. Joanna said, "Do you know the Gettysburg Address?"

"I'm afraid not," Mrs. Cornell said, wiping something.

"Oh come on," Joanna said. "Everybody does. 'Fourscore and seven years ago—' "

"I know that but I don't know the rest of it," Mrs. Cornell said. She put the something on the shelf, clinking glass, and took something from the shelf and wiped it.

"Oh, I see, not necessary," Joanna said. "Do you know 'This Little Piggy Went to Market'?"

"Of course," Mrs. Cornell said, wiping at the shelf.

"Charge?" Mr. Cornell asked. Joanna turned. He held out a small white-capped bottle.

"Yes," she said, taking it. "Do you have some water? I'd like to take one now."

He nodded and went in back.

Standing there with the bottle in her hand, she began to tremble. Glass clinked behind her. She pulled the cap from the bottle and pinched out the fluff of cotton. White tablets were inside; she tipped one into her palm, trembling, and pushed the cotton into the bottle and pressed the cap on. Glass clinked behind her.

Mr. Cornell came with a paper cup of water.

"Thank you," she said, taking it. She put the tablet on her tongue and drank and swallowed.

Mr. Cornell was writing on a pad. The top of his head was white scalp, like an under-a-rock *thing,* a slug, with a few strands of brown hair pasted across it. She drank the rest of the water, put the cup down, and put the bottle into her handbag. Glass clinked behind her.

Mr. Cornell turned the pad toward her and offered his pen, smiling. He was ugly; small-eyed, chinless.

She took the pen. "You have a lovely wife," she said, signing the pad. "Pretty, helpful, submissive to her lord and master; you're a lucky man." She held the pen out to him.

He took it, pink-faced. "I know," he said, looking downward.

"This town is full of lucky men," she said. "Good night."

"Good night," he said.

"Good night," Mrs. Cornell said. "Come again."

She went out into the Christmas-lighted street. A few cars passed by, their tires squishing.

The Men's Association windows were alight; and windows of houses farther up the hill. Red, green, and orange twinkled in some of them.

She breathed the night air deeply, and stomped boot-footed through a snowbank and crossed the street.

She walked down to the floodlit crèche and stood looking at it; at Mary and Joseph and the Infant, and the lambs and calves around them. Very lifelike it all was, though a mite Disneyish.

"Do *you* talk too?" she asked Mary and Joseph.

No answer; they just kept smiling.

She stood there—she wasn't trembling any more—and then she walked back toward the library.

She got into the car, started it, and turned on the lights; and cut across the street, backed, and drove past the crèche and up the hill.

The door opened as she came up the walk, and Walter said, "Where have you been?"

She kicked her boots against the doorstep. "The library," she said.

"Why didn't you *call*? I thought you had an accident, with the snow . . ."

"The roads are clear," she said, scuffing her boots on the mat.

"You should have called, for God's sake. It's after six."

She went in. He closed the door.

She put her handbag on the chair and began taking her gloves off.

"What's she like?" he asked.

"She's very nice," she said. "Sympathetic."

"What did she say?"

She put the gloves into her pockets and began unbuttoning her coat. "She thinks I need a little therapy," she said. "To sort out my feelings before we move. I'm 'pulled two ways by conflicting demands.' " She took the coat off.

"Well, that sounds like sensible advice," he said. "To me, anyway. How does it sound to you?"

She looked at the coat, holding it by the lining at its collar, and let it drop over the handbag and the chair. Her hands were cold; she rubbed them palm against palm, looking at them.

She looked at Walter. He was watching her attentively, his head cocked. Stubble sanded his cheeks and darkened his chin-cleft. His face was fuller than she had thought—he was gaining weight—and below his wonderfully blue eyes pouches of flesh had begun to form. How old was he now? Forty on his next birthday, March third.

"To me," she said, "it sounds like a mistake, a very big mistake." She lowered her hands and palmed her skirted sides. "I'm taking Pete and Kim into the city," she said. "To Shep and—"

"What for?"

"—Sylvia's or to a hotel. I'll call you in a day or two. Or have someone call you. Another lawyer."

He stared at her, and said, "What are you *talking* about?"

"I *know*," she said. "I've been reading old *Chronicles*. I know what Dale Coba *used* to do, and I know what he's doing *now*, he and those other— CompuTech Instatron geniuses."

He stared at her, and blinked. "I don't know what you're talking about," he said.

"Oh cut it out." She turned away and went down the hallway and into the kitchen, switching on the lights. The port to the family room showed darkness. She turned; Walter stood in the doorway. "I haven't the foggiest idea what you're talking about," he said.

She strode past him. "Stop lying," she said. "You've been lying to me ever since I took my first picture." She swung around and started up the stairs. "Pete!" she called. "Kim!"

"They're not here."

She looked at him over the banister as he came from the hallway. "When you didn't show up," he said, "I thought it would be a good idea to get them out for the night. In case anything was wrong."

She turned, looking down at him. "Where are they?" she asked.

"With friends," he said. "They're fine."

"*Which* friends?"

He came around to the foot of the stairs. "They're fine," he said.

She turned to face him, found the banister, held it. "Our weekend alone?" she said.

"I think you ought to lie down awhile," he said. He put a hand to the wall, his other hand to the banister. "You're not making sense, Joanna," he said. "Diz, of all people; where does *he* come into things? And what you just said about my lying to you."

"What did you do?" she said. "Put a rush on the order? Is that why everyone was so busy this week? Christmas toys; *that's* a hoot. What were *you* doing, trying it for size?"

"I honestly don't know what you're—"

"The dummy!" she said. She leaned toward him, holding the banister. "The robot! Oh very good; attorney surprised by a new allegation. You're wasting yourself in trusts and estates; you belong in a courtroom. What does it cost? Would you tell me? I'm dying to know. What's the going price for a stay-in-the-kitchen wife with big boobs and no demands? A fortune, I'll bet. Or do they do it dirt-cheap, out of that good old Men's Association spirit? And what happens to the real ones? The incinerator? Stepford Pond?"

He looked at her, standing with his hands to the wall and the banister. "Go upstairs and lie down," he said.

"I'm going out," she said.

He shook his head. "No," he said. "Not when you're talking like this. Go upstairs and rest."

She came down a step. "I'm not going to stay here to be—"

"You're not going out," he said. "Now go up and rest. When you've calmed down we'll—try to talk sensibly."

She looked at him standing there with his hands to the wall and the banister, looked at her coat on the chair—and turned and went quickly up the stairs. She went into the bedroom and closed the door; turned the key, switched on the lights.

She went to the dresser, pulled a drawer open, and got out a bulky white sweater; shook it unfolded and thrust her arms in and sleeved them. She pulled the turtleneck down over her head and gathered her hair and drew it free. The door was tried, tapped on.

"Joanna?"

"Scram," she said, pulling the sweater down around her. "I'm resting. You told me to rest."

"Let me in for a minute."

She stood watching the door, said nothing.

"Joanna, unlock the door."

"Later," she said. "I want to be alone for a while."

She stood without moving, watching the door.

"All right. Later."

She stood and listened—to silence—and turned to the dresser and eased the top drawer open. She searched in it and found a pair of white gloves. She wriggled a hand into one and the other, and pulled out a long striped scarf and looped it around her neck.

She went to the door and listened, and switched the lights off.

She went to the window and raised the shade. The walk light shone. The Claybrooks' living room was lighted but empty; their upstairs windows were dark.

She raised the window sash quietly. The storm window stood behind it.

She'd forgot about the damn storm window.

She pushed at its bottom. It was tight, wouldn't budge. She hit at it with the side of her gloved fist, and pushed again with both hands. It gave, swinging outward a few inches—and would swing no farther. Small metal arms at its sides reached open to their fullest. She would have to unclamp them from the window frame.

Light fanned out on the snow below.

He was in the den.

She stood straight and listened; a tiny-toothed chittering came from behind her, from the phone on the night table; came again and again, long, short, long.

He was dialing the den phone.

Calling Dale Coba to tell him she was there. Proceed with plans. All systems go.

She tiptoed slowly to the door, listened, and turned the key back and eased the door open, a hand held against it. Pete's Star Trek gun lay by the threshold of his room. Walter's voice burred faintly.

She tiptoed to the stairs and started slowly, quietly down, pressing close to the wall, looking down through the banister supports at the corner of the den doorway.

". . . not sure I can handle her myself . . ."

You're goddamn right you can't, counselor.

But the chair by the front door was empty, her coat and handbag (car keys, wallet) gone.

Still, this was better than going through the window.

She made it down to the hall. He talked, and was quiet. Look for the handbag?

He moved in the den and she ducked into the living room, stood at the wall, her back pressing tight.

His footsteps came into the hall, came near the doorway, stopped.

She held her breath.

A string of short hisses—his usual let's-see-now sound before tackling major projects; putting up storm windows, assembling a tricycle. (Killing a wife? Or did Coba the hunter perform that service?) She closed her eyes and tried not to think, afraid her thoughts would somehow beckon him.

His footsteps went up the stairs, slowly.

She opened her eyes and freed her breath bit by bit, waiting as he went higher.

She hurried quietly across the living room, around chairs, the lamp table; unlocked the door to the patio and opened it, unlocked the storm door and pushed it against a base of drifted snow.

She squeezed herself out and ran over snow, ran and ran with her heart pounding; ran toward dark tree trunks over snow that was sled-tracked, Pete-and-Kim-boot-marked; ran, ran, and clutched a trunk and swung around it and rushed-stumbled-groped through tree trunks, tree trunks. She rushed, stumbled, groped, keeping to the center of the long belt of trees that separated the houses on Fairview from the houses on Harvest.

She had to get to Ruthanne's. Ruthanne would lend her money and a coat, let her call an Eastbridge taxi or someone in the city—Shep, Doris, Andreas—someone with a car who would come pick her up.

Pete and Kim would be all right; she *had* to believe that. They'd be all right till she got to the city and spoke to people, spoke to a lawyer, got them back from Walter. They were probably being cared for beautifully by Bobbie or Carol or Mary Ann Stavros—by the things that were called by those names, that is.

And Ruthanne had to be *warned*. Maybe they could go together—though Ruthanne had time yet.

She came to the end of the belt of trees, made sure no cars were coming, and ran across Winter Hill Drive. Snow-pillowed spruce trees lined the far side of it; she hurried along behind them, her arms folded across her chest, her hands in their thin gloves burrowed in her armpits.

Gwendolyn Lane, where Ruthanne lived, was somewhere near Short Ridge Hill, out past Bobbie's; getting there would take almost an hour. More, probably, with the snow on the ground and the darkness. And she didn't dare hitchhike because any car could be Walter, and she wouldn't know till too late.

Not only Walter, she realized suddenly. They would *all* be out looking for her, cruising the roads with flashlights, spotlights. How could they let her get away and tell? *Every* man was a threat, every car a danger. She would have to make sure Ruthanne's husband wasn't there before she rang the bell; look through the windows.

Oh God, *could* she get away? None of the others had.

But maybe none of the others had tried. Bobbie hadn't, Charmaine hadn't. Maybe she was the first one to find out in time. If it *was* in time . . .

She left Winter Hill and hurried down Talcott Lane. Headlights flashed, and a car swung from a driveway ahead on the other side. She crouched beside a parked car and froze, and light swam under her and the car drove past. She stood and looked: the car was going slowly, and sure enough, a spotlight beam lanced from it and slid a wobble of light over housefronts and lawns of snow.

She hurried down Talcott, past silent houses with Christmas-lighted windows and Christmas-light-trimmed doors. Her feet and legs were cold, but she was all right. At the end of Talcott was Old Norwood Road, and from there she would take either Chimney Road or Hunnicutt.

A dog barked nearby, barked ragingly; but the barking dropped behind her as she hurried on.

A black arm of tree branch lay on the trodden snow. She set her boot across it and broke off half of it, and hurried on, holding the cold wet strength of branch in her thin-gloved hand.

A flashlight gleamed in Pine Tree Lane. She ran between two houses, ran over snow toward a snow-dome of bush; huddled behind it panting, holding the branch tightly in her aching-cold hand.

She looked out—at the backs of houses, their windows alight. From the rooftop of one a stream of red sparks lofted and danced, dying among the stars.

The flashlight came swaying from between two houses, and she drew back behind the bush. She rubbed a stockinged knee, warmed the other in the crook of her elbow.

Wan light swept toward her over snow, and spots of light slid away over her skirt and gloved hand.

She waited, waited longer, and looked out. A dark man-shape went toward the houses, following a patch of lighted snow.

She waited till the man had gone, and rose and hurried toward the next street over. Hickory Lane? Switzer? She wasn't sure which it was, but both of them led toward Short Ridge Road.

Her feet were numb, despite the boots' fleece lining.

A light shone blindingly and she turned and ran. A light ahead swung toward her and she ran to the side, up a cleared driveway, past the side of a garage, and down a long slope of snow. She slipped and fell, clambered to her feet still holding the branch—the lights were bobbing toward her—and ran over level snow. A light swung toward her. She turned, toward snow with no hiding place, and turned, and stood where she was, panting. "Get away!" she cried at the lights bobbing toward her, two on one side, one on the other. She raised the branch. "Get away!"

Flashlights bobbed toward her, and slowed and stopped, their radiance blinding. "Get away!" she cried, and shielded her eyes.

The light lessened. "Put them out. We're not going to hurt you, Mrs. Eberhart." "Don't be afraid. We're Walter's friends." The light went; she lowered her hand. "*Your* friends too. I'm Frank Roddenberry. You know me." "Take it easy, no one's going to hurt you."

Shapes darker than the darkness stood before her. "Stay away," she said, raising the branch higher.

"You don't need that."

"We're not going to hurt you."

"Then get away," she said.

"Everyone's out looking for you," Frank Roddenberry's voice said. "Walter's worried."

"I'll bet he is," she said.

They stood before her, four or five yards away; three men. "You shouldn't be running around like this, no coat on," one of them said.

"Get away," she said.

"P-put it down," Frank said. "No one's going to hurt you."

"Mrs. Eberhart, I was on the phone with Walter not five minutes ago." The man in the middle was speaking. "We know about this idea you've got. It's *wrong*, Mrs. Eberhart. Believe me, it's just not so."

"Nobody's making robots," Frank said.

"You must think we're a hell of a lot smarter than we really are," the man in the middle said. "Robots that can drive cars? And cook meals? And trim kids' hair?"

"And so real-looking that the kids wouldn't notice?" the third man said. He was short and wide.

"You must think we're a townful of geniuses," the man in the middle said. "Believe me, we're not."

"You're the men who put us on the moon," she said.

"*Who* is?" he said. "Not me. Frank, did you put anybody on the moon? Bernie?"

"Not me," Frank said.

The short man laughed. "Not me, Wynn," he said. "Not that I know of."

"I think you've got us mixed up with a couple of other fellows," the man in the middle said. "Leonardo da Vinci and Albert Einstein, maybe."

"My gosh," the short man said, "we don't want *robots* for wives. We want real women."

"Get away and let me go on," she said.

They stood there, darker than the darkness. "Joanna," Frank said, "if you were right and we could make robots that were so fantastic and lifelike, don't you think we'd cash in on it somehow?"

"That's right," the man in the middle said. "We could all be rich with that kind of know-how."

"Maybe you're going to," she said. "Maybe this is just the beginning."

"Oh my Lord," the man said, "you've got an answer for everything. *You* should have been the lawyer, not Walter."

Frank and the short man laughed.

"Come on, Joanna," Frank said, "p-put down that b-bat or whatever it is and—"

"Get away and let me go on!" she said.

"We can't do that," the man in the middle said. "You'll catch pneumonia. Or get hit by a car."

"I'm going to a friend's house," she said. "I'll be inside in a few minutes. I'd be inside *now* if you hadn't—oh Jesus . . ." She lowered the branch and rubbed her arm; and rubbed her eyes and her forehead, shivering.

"Will you let us *prove* to you that you're wrong?" the man in the middle said. "Then we'll take you *home,* and you can get some help if you need it."

She looked at his dark shape. "*Prove* to me?" she said.

"We'll take you to the house, the Men's Association house—"

"Oh no."

"Now just a second; just hear me out please. We'll take you to the house and you can check it over from stem to stern. I'm sure nobody'll object, under the circumstances. And you'll see there's—"

"I'm not setting foot in—"

"You'll see there's no robot factory there," he said. "There's a bar and a card room and a few other rooms, and that's it. There's a projector and some very X-rated movies; that's our big secret."

"And the slot machines," the short man said.

"Yes. We've got some slot machines."

"I wouldn't set foot in there without an armed guard," she said. "Of women soldiers."

"We'll clear everyone out," Frank said. "You'll have the p-place all to yourself."

"I won't go," she said.

"Mrs. Eberhart," the man in the middle said, "we're trying to be as gentle about this as we know how, but there's a limit to how long we're going to stand here parleying."

"Wait a minute," the short man said, "I've got an idea. Suppose one of these women you think is a robot—suppose she was to cut herself on the finger, and bleed. Would *that* convince you she was a real person? Or would you say we made robots with blood under the skin?"

"For God's sake, Bernie," the man in the middle said, and Frank said, "You can't—ask someone to cut herself just to—"

"Will you let her answer the question, please? Well, Mrs. Eberhart? Would that convince you? If she cut her finger and bled?"

"*Bernie* . . ."

"Just let her answer, damn it!"

Joanna stood staring, and nodded. "If she bled," she said, "I would—think she was—real . . ."

"We're not going to ask someone to cut herself. We're going to go to—"

"Bobbie would do it," she said. "If she's really Bobbie. She's my friend. Bobbie Markowe."

"On Fox Hollow Lane?" the short man asked.

"Yes," she said.

"You see?" he said. "It's two minutes from here. Just think for a second, will you? We won't have to go all the way in to the Center; we won't have to make Mrs. Eberhart go somewhere she doesn't want to . . ."

Nobody said anything.

"I guess it's—not a b-bad idea," Frank said. "We could speak to Mrs. Markowe . . ."

"She won't bleed," Joanna said.

"She will," the man in the middle said. "And when she does, you'll know you're wrong and you'll let us take you home to Walter, without any arguments."

"*If* she does," she said. "Yes."

"All right," he said. "Frank, you run on ahead and see if she's there and explain to her. I'm going to leave my flashlight on the ground here, Mrs. Eberhart. Bernie and I'll go a little ahead, and you pick it up and follow us, as far behind as makes you comfortable. But keep the light on us so we know you're still there. I'm leaving my coat too; put it on. I can hear your teeth chattering."

She was wrong, she knew it. She was wrong and frozen and wet and tired and hungry, and pulled eighteen ways by conflicting demands. Including to pee.

If they were killers, they'd have killed her *then*. The branch wouldn't have stopped them, three men facing one woman.

She lifted the branch and looked at it, walking slowly, her feet aching. She let the branch fall. Her glove was wet and dirty, her fingers frozen. She flexed them, and tucked her hand into her other armpit. She held the long heavy flashlight as steadily as she could.

The men walked with small steps ahead of her. The short man wore a brown coat and a red leather cap; the taller man, a green shirt and tan pants tucked into brown boots. He had reddish-blond hair.

His sheepskin coat lay warm on her shoulders. Its smell was strong and good —of animals, of life.

Bobbie would bleed. It was coincidence that Dale Coba had worked on robots at Disneyland, that Claude Axhelm thought he was Henry Higgins, that Ike Mazzard drew his flattering sketches. Coincidence, that she had spun into —into madness. Yes, madness. ("It's *not* catastrophic," Dr. Fancher said, smiling. "I'm sure I can help you.")

Bobbie would bleed, and she would go home and get warm.

Home to Walter?

When had it begun, her distrust of him, the feeling of nothingness between them? Whose fault was it?

His face had grown fuller; why hadn't she noticed it before today? Had she been too busy taking pictures, working in the darkroom?

She would call Dr. Fancher on Monday, would go and lie on the brown leather couch; would cry a little maybe, and try to become happy.

The men waited at the corner of Fox Hollow Lane.

She made herself walk faster.

Frank stood waiting in Bobbie's bright doorway. The men talked with him, and turned to her as she came slowly up the walk.

Frank smiled. "She says sure," he said. "If it'll make you feel b-better she'll be glad to do it."

She gave the flashlight to the green-shirted man. His face was broad and leathery, strong-looking. "We'll wait out here," he said, lifting the coat from her shoulders.

She said, "She doesn't have to . . ."

"No, go on," he said. "You'll only start wondering again later."

Frank came out onto the doorstep. "She's in the kitchen," he said.

She went into the house. Its warmth surrounded her. Rock music blared and thumped from upstairs.

She went down the hallway, flexing her aching hands.

Bobbie stood waiting in the kitchen, in red slacks and an apron with a big daisy on it. "Hi, Joanna," she said, and smiled. Beautiful bosomy Bobbie. But not a robot.

"Hi," she said. She held the doorjamb, and leaned to it and rested the side of her head against it.

"I'm sorry to hear you're in such a state," Bobbie said.

"Sorry to be in it," she said.

"I don't mind cutting my finger a little," Bobbie said, "if it'll ease your mind for you." She walked to a counter. Walked smoothly, steadily, gracefully. Opened a drawer.

"Bobbie . . ." Joanna said. She closed her eyes, and opened them. "Are you really Bobbie?" she asked.

"Of course I am," Bobbie said, a knife in her hand. She went to the sink. "Come here," she said. "You can't see from there."

The rock music blared louder. "What's going on upstairs?" Joanna asked.

"I don't know," Bobbie said. "Dave has the boys up there. Come here. You can't see."

The knife was large, its blade pointed. "You'll amputate your whole hand with that thing," Joanna said.

"I'll be careful," Bobbie said, smiling. "Come on." She beckoned, holding the large knife.

Joanna raised her head from the jamb, and took her hand from it. She went into the kitchen—so shining and immaculate, so un-Bobbie-like.

She stopped. *The music is in case I scream,* she thought. *She isn't going to cut her finger; she's going to—*

"Come on," Bobbie said, standing by the sink, beckoning, holding the point-bladed knife.

Not catastrophic, Dr. Fancher? Thinking they're robots not women? Thinking Bobbie would kill me? Are you sure you can help me?

"You don't have to do it," she said to Bobbie.

"It'll ease your mind," Bobbie said.

"I'm seeing a shrink after New Year's," she said. *"That'*ll ease my mind. At least I hope it will."

"Come on," Bobbie said. "The men are waiting."

Joanna went forward, toward Bobbie standing by the sink with the knife in her hand, so real-looking—skin, eyes, hair, hands, rising-falling aproned bosom—that she *couldn't* be a robot, she simply *couldn't* be, and that was all there was to it.

The men stood on the doorstep, blowing out steamy breath, their hands deep in their pockets. Frank hipped from side to side with the beat of the loud rock music.

Bernie said, "What's taking so long?"

Wynn and Frank shrugged.

The rock music blared.

Wynn said, "I'm going to call Walter and tell him we found her." He went into the house.

"Get Dave's car keys!" Frank called after him.

Three

The market parking lot was pretty well filled, but she found a good place up near the front; and that, plus the sun's warmth and the moist sweet smell of the air when she got out of the car, made her feel less bothered about having to be shopping. A *little* less bothered, anyway.

Miss Austrian came limping and caning toward her from the market's entrance, with a small paper bag in her hand and—she didn't believe it—a friendly smile on her Queen-of-Hearts white face. For her? "Good morning, Mrs. Hendry," Miss Austrian said.

What do you know, black is bearable. "Good morning," she said.

"March is certainly going out like a lamb, isn't it?"

"Yes," she said. "It seemed like it was going to be a two-headed lion."

Miss Austrian stopped and stood looking at her. "You haven't been in the library in months," she said. "I hope we haven't lost you to television."

"Oh no, not me," she said, smiling. "I've been working."

"On another book?"

"Yes."

"Good. Let me know when it's going to be published; we'll order a copy."

"I will," she said. "And I'll be in soon. I'm almost done with it."

"Have a good day," Miss Austrian said, smiling and caning away.

"Thanks. You too."

Well, there was *one* sale.

Maybe she'd been hypersensitive. Maybe Miss Austrian was cold to whites too until they'd been there a few months.

She went through the market's opening-by-themselves doors and found an empty cart. The aisles were the usual Saturday morning parade.

She went quickly, taking what she needed, maneuvering the cart in and out and around. "Excuse me. Excuse me, please." It still bugged her the way they shopped so languidly, gliding along as if they never sweated. How white could you get? Even filling their *carts* just so! She could shop the whole market in the time they did one aisle.

Joanna Eberhart came toward her, looking terrific in a tightly belted pale blue coat. She had a fine figure and was prettier than Ruthanne remembered, her dark hair gleaming in graceful drawn-back wings. She came along slowly, looking at the shelves.

"Hello, Joanna," Ruthanne said.

Joanna stopped and looked at her with thick-lashed brown eyes. "Ruthanne," she said, and smiled. "Hello. How are you?" Her bow lips were red, her complexion pale rose and perfect.

"I'm fine," Ruthanne said, smiling. "I don't have to ask how *you* are; you look marvelous."

"Thanks," Joanna said. "I've been taking better care of myself lately."

"It certainly shows," Ruthanne said.

"I'm sorry I haven't called you," Joanna said.

"Oh that's all right." Ruthanne hitched her cart over in front of Joanna's so people could get by them.

"I meant to," Joanna said, "but there's been so much to do around the house. You know how it is."

"That's all right," Ruthanne said. "I've been busy too. I'm almost done with my book. Just one more main drawing and a few small ones."

"Congratulations," Joanna said.

"Thanks," Ruthanne said. "What have *you* been up to? Have you taken any interesting pictures?"

"Oh no," Joanna said. "I don't do much photography any more."

"You don't?" Ruthanne said.

"No," Joanna said. "I wasn't especially talented, and I was wasting a lot of time I really have better uses for."

Ruthanne looked at her.

"I'll call you one of these days when I get caught up with things," Joanna said, smiling.

"What are you doing then, besides your housework?" Ruthanne asked her.

"Nothing, really," Joanna said. "Housework's enough for me. I used to feel I had to have other interests, but I'm more at ease with myself now. I'm much happier too, and so is my family. That's what counts, isn't it?"

"Yes, I guess so," Ruthanne said. She looked down at their carts, her own jumble-filled one against Joanna's neatly filled one. She hitched hers out of Joanna's way. "Maybe we can have that lunch," she said, looking at Joanna. "Now that I'm finishing the book."

"Maybe we can," Joanna said. "It was nice seeing you."

"Same here," Ruthanne said.

Joanna, smiling, walked away—and stopped, took a box from a shelf, looked at it, and fitted it down into her cart. She went away down the market aisle.

Ruthanne stood watching her, and turned and went on in the other direction.

She couldn't get to work. She paced and turned in the close-walled room; looked out the window at Chickie and Sara playing with the Cohane girls; leafed through the stack of finished drawings and found them not as amusing and skillful as she'd thought they were.

When she finally got going on Penny at the wheel of the *Bertha P. Moran,* it was practically five o'clock.

She went down to the den.

Royal sat reading *Men in Groups,* his feet in blue socks on the hassock. He looked up at her. "Done?" he asked. He had fixed the frame of his glasses with adhesive tape.

"Hell, no," she said. "I just got started."

"How come?"

"*I* don't know," she said. "*Something's* been bugging me. Listen, would you do me a favor? Now that it's moving I want to stay with it."

"Supper?" he said.

She nodded. "Would you take them to the pizza place? Or to McDonald's?"

He took his pipe from the table. "All right," he said.

"I want to get it done with," she said. "Otherwise I won't enjoy next weekend."

He laid the open book down across his lap and took his pipe-cleaning gadget from the table.

She turned to go, and looked back at him. "You sure you don't mind?" she asked.

He twisted the gadget back and forth in the pipe bowl. "Sure," he said. "Stay with it." He looked up at her and smiled. "I don't mind," he said.